Praise for the Seven Sisters series

'A great page-turner, full of drama and romance'
Daily Mail

'Riley is one of the strongest authors in this genre . . . excellent historical detail, heart-wrenching romance, and an engaging mystery'
Historical Novel Society

'Impressive research, historical detail, an amazing ability to evoke time and place, and sheer imaginative power to underpin a sumptuous, sweeping saga full of romance, passion, mystery, heartbreak and epic locations . . . An epic start to an epic series'
Lancashire Evening Post

'The locations are so evocative that you will feel instantly transported . . . A journey of epic proportions'
The Book Trail

Also by Lucinda Riley

Hothouse Flower
The Girl on the Cliff
The Light Behind the Window
The Midnight Rose
The Italian Girl
The Angel Tree
The Olive Tree
The Love Letter

The Seven Sisters Series

The Seven Sisters
The Shadow Sister
The Pearl Sister
The Moon Sister

The Storm Sister

LUCINDA RILEY

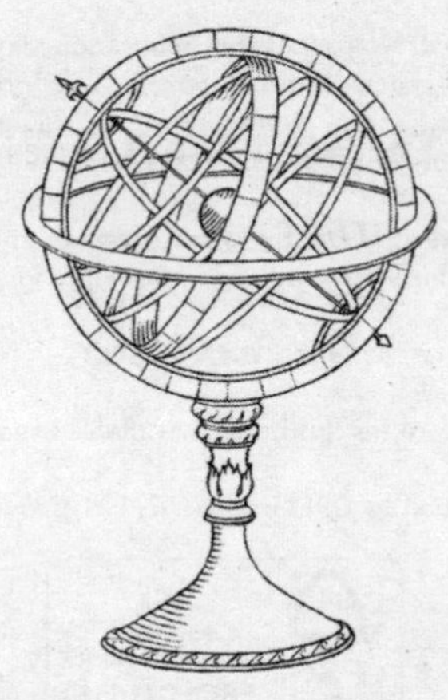

PAN BOOKS

First published 2015 by Macmillan

First published in paperback 2016 by Pan Books

This edition first published 2019 by Pan Books
an imprint of Pan Macmillan
The Smithson, 6 Briset Street, London EC1M 5NR

ISBN 978-1-5290-0346-8

7 9 8 6

A CIP catalogue record for this book is available from the British Library.

Printed and bound by CPI Group (UK) Ltd, Croydon, CRO 4YY

For Susan Moss, my 'soul' sister

Dear Reader,

Welcome to Ally's story. According to the legends of the Seven Sisters, she was the second daughter of Atlas and Pleione. During the Halcyon days, she watched over the Mediterranean Sea, keeping it safe for sailors. She was happily married to Ceyx, the King of Thessaly, and all was well until the day the couple angered Zeus. He sent a thunderstorm over the seas, causing Ceyx's boat to capsize and him to drown.

When I first had the idea of writing a series of books based on the Seven Sisters of the Pleiades, I had no idea where it would lead me. I was very attracted to the fact that each one of the mythological sisters was a unique and strong female. Some say they were the Seven Mothers who seeded our earth – there is no doubt that, in their stories, they were all highly fertile! And I wanted to celebrate the achievements of women, especially in the past, where so often their contribution to making our world the place it is today has been overshadowed by the more frequently documented achievements of men.

However, the definition of 'feminism' is equality, not domination, and the women I write about, both in the past and present, accept that they want and need love in their lives. Not necessarily in the traditional form of marriage and children, but the Seven Sisters series unashamedly celebrates the endless search for love and explores the devastating consequences when it is lost to us.

As I travel round the world, following in the footsteps of my factual and fictional female characters to research their stories, I am constantly humbled and awed by the tenacity and courage of the generations of women who came before me. Whether fighting the sexual and racial prejudices of times gone by, losing their loved ones to the devastation of war or disease, or making a new life on the other side of the world, these women paved the way for us to have the freedom of thought and deed that we enjoy today. And so often take for granted. I never forget that this freedom was won by thousands of generations of remarkable women, perhaps leading right back to the Seven Sisters themselves . . .

I hope you enjoy Ally's journey – although she was known as the leader, like her mythological counterpart Ally faces tragedy and loss, and must dig deep to find the courage to move forwards . . .

Lucinda

x

I would not creep along the coast but steer
Out in mid-sea, by guidance of the stars

George Eliot

Halvorsen Family Tree

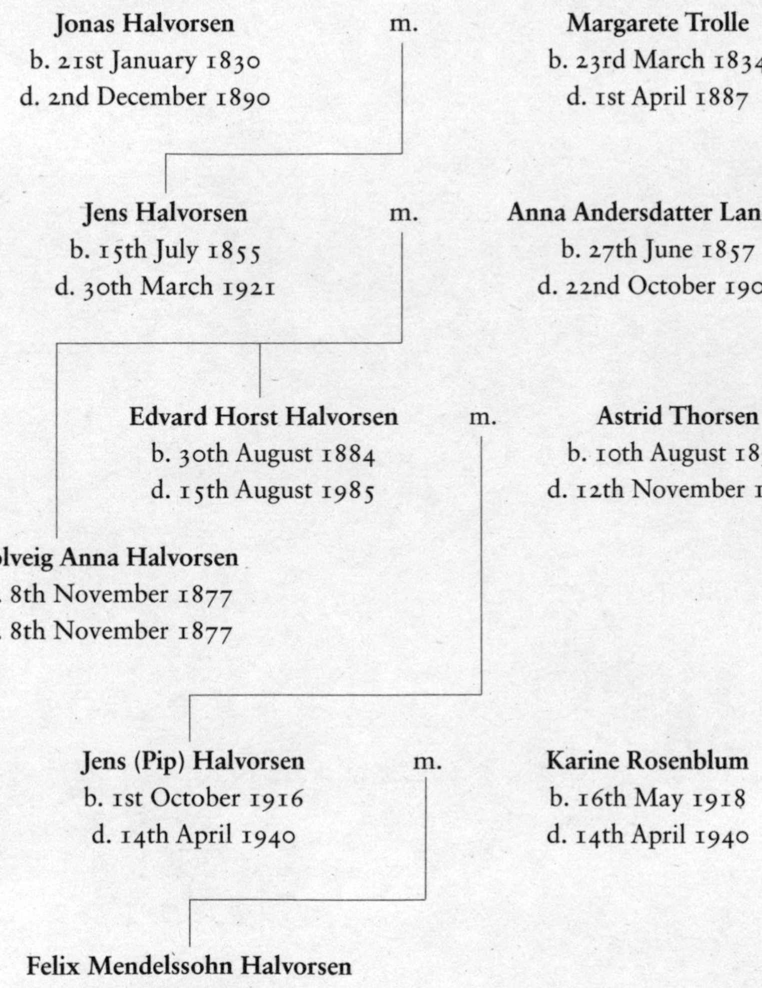

Jonas Halvorsen
b. 21st January 1830
d. 2nd December 1890
m.
Margarete Trolle
b. 23rd March 1834
d. 1st April 1887
Jens Halvorsen
b. 15th July 1855
d. 30th March 1921
m.
Anna Andersdatter Landvik
b. 27th June 1857
d. 22nd October 1907
Edvard Horst Halvorsen
b. 30th August 1884
d. 15th August 1985
m.
Astrid Thorsen
b. 10th August 1899
d. 12th November 1995
Solveig Anna Halvorsen
b. 8th November 1877
d. 8th November 1877
Jens (Pip) Halvorsen
b. 1st October 1916
d. 14th April 1940
m.
Karine Rosenblum
b. 16th May 1918
d. 14th April 1940
Felix Mendelssohn Halvorsen
b. 15th November 1938
Thom Felix Halvorsen
b. 1st June 1977

Cast of characters

Atlantis

Pa Salt – *the sisters' adoptive father (deceased)*
Marina (Ma) – *the sisters' guardian*
Claudia – *housekeeper at Atlantis*
Georg Hoffman – *Pa Salt's lawyer*
Christian – *the skipper*

The D'Aplièse Sisters

Maia
Ally (Alcyone)
Star (Asterope)
CeCe (Celaeno)
Tiggy (Taygete)
Electra
Merope (missing)

Ally

June 2007

"Morning Mood"

1

The Aegean Sea

I will always remember exactly where I was and what I was doing when I heard that my father had died.

I was lying naked in the sun on the deck of the *Neptune*, with Theo's hand resting protectively on my stomach. The deserted curve of golden beach on the island in front of us glimmered in the sun as it sat nestled in its rocky cove. The crystal-clear turquoise water was making a lazy attempt at forming waves as it hit the sands, foaming elegantly like the froth on a cappuccino.

Becalmed, I'd thought, *like me*.

We'd dropped anchor in the small bay off the tiny Greek island of Macheres at sunset the night before, then waded ashore to the cove carrying two cool boxes. One was filled with fresh red mullet and sardines that Theo had caught earlier that day, the other with wine and water. I'd set down my load on the sand, panting with effort, and Theo had kissed my nose tenderly.

'We are castaways on our very own desert island,' he'd announced, spreading his arms wide to gesture at the idyllic setting. 'Now, I'm off in search of firewood so we can cook our fish.'

I'd watched him as he turned from me and walked towards the rocks forming a crescent around the cove, heading for the tinder-dry sparse bushes that grew in the crevices. Given he was a world-class sailor, his slight frame belied his strength. Compared to the other men I crewed with in sailing competitions who seemed to be all rippling muscles and Tarzan-like chests, Theo was positively diminutive. One of the first things I'd noticed about him was his rather lopsided gait. He'd since told me how he'd broken his ankle falling out of a tree as a child and how it had never mended properly.

'I suppose it's another reason why I was always destined for a life on the water. When I'm sailing, no one can tell how ridiculous I look walking on land,' he'd chuckled.

We'd cooked our fish and later made love under the stars. The following morning was our last aboard together. And just before I'd decided I absolutely had to resume contact with the outside world by switching on my mobile, and then subsequently discovered my life had shattered into a million tiny pieces, I'd lain there next to him perfectly at peace. And, like a surreal dream, my mind had replayed the miracle of Theo and me, and how we'd come to be here in this beautiful place . . .

I'd first set eyes on him a year or so ago at the Heineken Regatta in St Maarten in the Caribbean. The winning crew was celebrating at the victory dinner and I was intrigued to discover that their skipper was Theo Falys-Kings. He was a celebrity in the sailing world, having steered more crews to victory in offshore races during the past five years than any other captain.

'He isn't what I imagined at all,' I commented under my breath to Rob Bellamy, an old crewmate with whom I'd sailed for the Swiss national team. 'He looks like a geek with those horn-rimmed glasses,' I added as I watched him stand up to move across to another table, 'and he has a very odd walk.'

'He's certainly not your average brawny sailor, admittedly,' agreed Rob. 'But Al, the guy is a total genius. He has a sixth sense when it comes to the water and there's no one I'd trust more as my skipper on stormy seas.'

I was introduced to Theo briefly by Rob later that evening and I noticed his hazel-flecked green eyes were thoughtful as he shook my hand.

'So, you're the famous Al D'Aplièse.'

Behind his British accent, his voice was warm and steady.

'Yes, to the latter part of that statement,' I said, embarrassed at the compliment, 'but I think it's *you* who's famous.' Doing my best not to let my gaze waver under his continued scrutiny, I saw his features soften as he let out a chuckle.

'What's so funny?' I demanded.

'To be frank, I wasn't expecting *you*.'

'What do you mean "*me*"?'

Theo's attention was diverted by a photographer wanting a team photo, so I never did get to hear what it was he meant.

After that, I began to notice him across the room at various social events for the regattas we took part in. He had an indefinable vibrancy about him and a soft, easy laugh that, despite his outwardly reserved demeanour, seemed to draw people to his side. If the event was formal, he was usually dressed in chinos and a crumpled linen jacket as a nod to protocol and the race sponsors, but his ancient deck shoes and unruly brown hair always made him look as if he'd just stepped off a boat.

On those first few occasions, it seemed as if we were dancing around each other. Our eyes met often, but Theo never attempted to continue our first conversation. It was only six weeks ago, when my crew had claimed victory in Antigua and we were celebrating at the Lord Nelson's Ball that marked the end of race week, when he tapped me on the shoulder.

'Well done, Al,' he said.

'Thanks,' I replied, feeling gratified that our crew had beaten his for a change.

'I'm hearing many good things about you this season, Al. Do you fancy coming to crew for me in the Cyclades Regatta in June?'

I'd already been offered a place on another crew, but had yet to accept. Theo saw my hesitation.

'You're already taken?'

'Provisionally, yes.'

'Well, here's my card. Have a think about it and let me know by the end of the week. I could really do with someone like you aboard.'

'Thanks.' I mentally pushed aside my hesitation. Who on earth turned down the chance to crew for the man currently known as 'The King of the Seas'? 'By the way,' I called out as he began to walk away from me, 'last time we talked, why did you say you weren't expecting "me"?'

He paused, his eyes sweeping briefly over me. 'I'd never met you in person; I'd just heard titbits of conversation about your sailing skills, that's all. And as I said, you aren't what I was expecting. Goodnight, Al.'

I mulled over our conversation as I walked back to my room in a little inn by St John's harbour, letting the night air wash over me and wondering why it was that Theo fascinated me so much. Street lights bathed the cheerful multi-coloured house fronts in a warm nocturnal glow, and from a distance, the lazy hum of people in the bars and cafés drifted towards me. I was oblivious to it all, exhilarated as I was by the race win – and by Theo Falys-King's offer.

As soon as I entered my room, I made a beeline for my laptop and wrote him an email to accept his offer. Before I sent it, I took a shower, then stopped to read it through again, blushing at how eager I sounded. Deciding to save it in my drafts folder and send it in a couple of days, I stretched out on my bed, flexing my arms to relieve the tension and soreness from the race that day.

'Well, Al,' I muttered to myself with a smile, '*that* will be an interesting regatta.'

I sent the email as planned and Theo contacted me immediately, saying how pleased he was I could join his crew. Then just two weeks ago, I found myself inexplicably nervous as I stepped aboard the race-rigged Hanse 540 yacht in Naxos harbour to begin training for the Cyclades Regatta.

The race was not overly demanding as competitive racing went, the entrants comprising a mix of serious sailors and weekend enthusiasts, all buoyed up by the prospect of eight days' fabulous sailing between some of the most beautiful islands in the world. And as one of the more experienced crews involved, I knew we were strongly fancied to win.

Theo's crews were always notoriously young. My friend

Rob Bellamy and me, both thirty, were the 'senior' members of the team in terms of age and experience. I'd heard that Theo preferred to recruit talent in the early stages of a sailor's career to prevent bad habits. The rest of the crew of six were in their early twenties: Guy, a burly Englishman; Tim, a laid-back Aussie; and Mick, a half-German, half-Greek sailor who knew the waters of the Aegean like the back of his hand.

Although I was eager to work with Theo, I hadn't stepped into it blindly; I'd done my best beforehand to gather information on the enigma that was 'The King of the Seas', by looking on the internet and talking to those who had crewed with him previously.

I'd heard that he was British and had studied at Oxford, which would account for his clipped accent, but on the internet, his profile said that he was an American citizen who had captained the Yale varsity sailing team to victory many times. One friend of mine had heard he came from a wealthy family, another that he lived on a boat.

'Perfectionist', 'Control freak', 'Hard to please', 'Workaholic', 'Misogynist' . . . These were other comments I had gathered, the latter coming from a fellow female sailor who claimed she'd been sidelined and mistreated on his crew, which did give me pause for thought. But the overwhelming sentiment was simple:

'Absolutely the best bloody skipper I have ever worked for.'

That first day aboard, I began to understand why Theo was afforded so much respect from his peers. I was used to shouty skippers, who screamed instructions and abuse at one and all, like bad-tempered chefs in a kitchen. Theo's understated approach was a revelation. He said very little as he put us through our paces, just surveyed us all from a distance. When the day was over, he gathered us together and pin-pointed our strengths and weaknesses in his calm, steady voice. I realised he'd missed nothing and his natural air of authority meant we hung on every word he said.

'And by the way, Guy, no more sneaking a cigarette during a practice under race conditions,' he added with a half-smile as he dismissed us all.

Guy blushed to the roots of his blond hair. 'That guy must have eyes in the back of his head,' he mumbled to me as we trooped off the boat to shower and change for dinner.

That first evening, I headed out from our pension with the rest of the crew, feeling happy I'd made the decision to join them in the race. We walked along Naxos harbour, the ancient stone castle lit up above the village and a jumble of twisting alleys winding down between the white-washed houses. The restaurants along the harbour front were teeming with sailors and tourists enjoying the fresh seafood and raising endless glasses of ouzo. We found a small family-run establishment in the back streets, with rickety wooden chairs and mismatching plates. The home-cooked food was just what we needed after a long day on the boat, the sea air giving us all a ravenous appetite.

My obvious hunger elicited stares from the men as I tucked into the moussaka and generous helpings of rice. 'What's the problem? Have you never seen a woman eat before?' I commented sarcastically, as I leant forward to grab another flatbread.

Theo contributed to the banter with the occasional dry observation, but left immediately after dinner, choosing not to participate in the post-supper bar crawl. I followed him shortly afterwards. Over my years as a professional sailor, I'd learnt that the boys' antics after dark were not something I wished to witness.

In the next couple of days, under Theo's thoughtful green gaze, we began to pull together and quickly became a smoothly efficient team, and my admiration for his methods grew apace. On our third evening on Naxos, feeling particularly tired from a gruelling day under the searing Aegean sun, I was the first to stand up from the dinner table.

'Right lads, I'm off.'

'Me too. Night boys. No hangovers aboard tomorrow, please,' Theo said, following me out of the restaurant. 'Can I join you?' he asked as he caught up with me in the street outside.

'Yes, of course you can,' I agreed, feeling suddenly tense that we were alone together for the first time.

We walked back to our pension along the narrow cobbled streets, the moonlight illuminating the little white houses with their blue-painted doors and shutters on either side. I did my best to make conversation, but Theo only contributed the odd 'yes' or 'no', and his taciturn responses began to irritate me.

As we reached the lobby of the pension, he suddenly turned to me. 'You really are an instinctive seaman, Al. You beat most of your crewmates into a cocked hat. Who taught you?'

'My father,' I said, surprised by the compliment. 'He took me out sailing on Lake Geneva from when I was very small.'

'Ah, Geneva. That explains the French accent.'

I readied myself for the typical 'say something sexy in French' type of comment that I usually got from men at this point, but it didn't come.

'Well, your father must be one hell of a sailor – he's done an excellent job on you.'

'Thanks,' I said, disarmed.

'How do you find being the only woman aboard? Although I'm sure it's not a one-off occurrence for you,' he added hastily.

'I don't think about it, to be honest.'

He looked at me perceptively through his horn-rimmed glasses. 'Really? Well, forgive me for saying so, but I think you do. I feel you sometimes try to overcompensate for it and that's when you make errors. I'd suggest you relax more and just be yourself. Anyway, goodnight.' He gave me a brief smile then mounted the white-tiled stairs to his room.

That night, as I lay in the narrow bed, the starched white sheets itched against my skin and my cheeks burnt at his criticism. Was it *my* fault that women were still a relative rarity – or, as some of my male crewmates would undoubtedly say, a novelty – aboard professional racing boats? And who did Theo Falys-Kings think he was?! Some kind of pop psychologist, going around analysing people who didn't need to be analysed?

I'd always thought I handled the woman-in-a-male-dominated-world thing well, and had been able to take friendly jibes and asides about my female status on the chin. I'd built myself a wall of inviolability in my career, and two different personas: 'Ally' at home, 'Al' at work. Yes, it was often hard and I'd learnt to hold my tongue, especially when the comments were of a pointedly sexist nature and alluded to my supposed 'blonde' behaviour. I'd always made a point of warding off such remarks by keeping my red-gold curls scraped back from my face and tied firmly in a ponytail, and by not wearing even a smidgen of make-up to accentuate my eyes or cover up my freckles. And I worked just as hard as any of the men on the boat – perhaps, I fumed inwardly, harder.

Then, still sleepless with indignation, I remembered my father telling me that much of the irritation people feel at personal observations was usually because there was a grain of truth in them. And as the night hours drew on, I had to concede that Theo was probably right. I wasn't being 'myself'.

The following evening, Theo joined me again as I walked back to the pension. For all his lack of physical stature, I found him hugely intimidating and I heard myself stumble over my words. As I struggled to explain my dual personas, he listened quietly before responding.

'Well, my father – whose opinion I don't normally rate to be fair,' he said, 'once stated that women would run the world if they only played to their strengths and stopped trying to be men. Maybe that's what you should try to do.'

'That's easy for a man to say, but has your father ever worked in a completely female-dominated environment? And would he "be himself" if he did?' I countered, irritated at being patronised.

'Good point,' Theo agreed. 'Well, at least it might help a little if I called you "Ally". It suits you far better than "Al". Would you mind?'

Before I had a chance to answer, he halted abruptly on the picturesque harbour front, where small fishing boats rocked gently between the larger yachts and motor cruisers as the soothing sounds of a calm sea lapped against their hulls. I watched him look up to the skies, his nostrils flaring visibly as he sniffed the air, checking to see what the dawn would bring weather-wise. It was something I had only ever seen old sailors do, and I chuckled suddenly at the projected image of Theo as an ancient, grizzled sea dog.

He turned to me with a puzzled smile. 'What's so funny?'

'Nothing. And if it makes you feel better, you're welcome to call me "Ally".'

'Thanks. Now, let's get back and grab some sleep. I have a hard day planned for us all tomorrow.'

Again that night, I was restless as I replayed our conversation in my mind. *Me*, who usually slept like a log, especially when I was training or competing.

And rather than Theo's advice helping me, over the next couple of days I made numerous silly mistakes, making me feel more like a rookie than the professional I was. I castigated myself harshly; but ironically, even though my crewmates teased me good-naturedly, never once was there a word of criticism from Theo.

On our fifth night, feeling horribly embarrassed and confused by my uncharacteristically sloppy performance level, I didn't even join the rest of the crew for dinner. Instead, I sat on the small terrace of the pension eating bread, feta cheese and olives provided by the kind owner. I drowned my sorrows in the rough red wine she poured me, and after a number of glasses, began to feel decidedly queasy and sorry for myself. I was just lurching unsteadily from the table, headed for bed, when Theo arrived on the terrace.

'Are you all right?' he asked, sliding his glasses up his nose to see me properly. I squinted back at him, but his outline had become inexplicably blurry.

'Yes,' I replied thickly, sitting back down hurriedly as everything I tried to focus on started to sway.

'Everyone was worried about you when you didn't turn up tonight. You're not sick, are you?'

'No.' I felt the burning sensation of bile rising in my throat. 'I'm fine.'

'You know, you can tell me if you are sick and I swear I won't count it against you. Can I sit down?'

I didn't answer. In fact, I found I couldn't as I struggled to control my nausea. He sat down in the plastic chair across the table from me anyway.

'So what's the problem?'

'Nothing,' I managed.

'Ally, you're an awful colour. Are you sure you're not ill?'

'I . . . Excuse me.'

With that, I staggered up and just made it to the edge of the terrace before I vomited over it onto the pavement below.

'Poor you.' I felt a pair of hands clasp me firmly around my waist. 'You're obviously not well at all. I'm going to help you to your room. What number is it?'

'I am . . . perfectly well,' I muttered stupidly, horrified beyond measure at what had just happened. And all in front of Theo Falys-Kings, who, for some reason, I was desperate to impress. All things considered, it could not have been worse.

'Come on.' He hoisted my limp arm over his shoulder and half-carried me past the disgusted gaze of the other guests.

Once in my room, I was sick a few more times, but at least it was into the toilet. Each time I emerged, Theo was waiting for me, ready to help me back to the bed.

'Really,' I groaned, 'I'll be fine in the morning, I promise.'

'You've been saying that in between rounds of vomit for the past two hours,' he said pragmatically, wiping the sticky sweat from my forehead with a cool, damp towel.

'Go to bed, Theo,' I murmured groggily. 'Really, I'm fine now. Just need to sleep.'

'In a while, I will.'

'Thanks for looking after me,' I whispered as my eyes began to shut.

'That's okay, Ally.'

And then, as I drifted in the half here, half there world of the few seconds before sleep, I smiled. 'I think I love you,' I heard myself say before I descended into oblivion.

I woke the next morning feeling shaky but better. As I climbed out of bed, I tripped over Theo, who had used a spare pillow and was curled up on the floor fast asleep. Shutting the bathroom door, I sank onto the edge of the bath and remembered the words I'd thought – or Christ, had I actually *spoken* them? – last night.

I think I love you.

Where on earth had that come from? Or had I dreamt I'd said it? After all, I'd been very unwell and might have been hallucinating. *God, I hope so*, I groaned to myself, my head in my hands. But . . . if I hadn't actually said it, why could I remember those words so vividly? They were ridiculously inaccurate, of course, but now Theo might think that I actually meant them. Which of course I didn't, surely?

Eventually, I emerged sheepishly from the bathroom and saw that Theo was about to leave. I couldn't meet his eye as he told me he was going to his own room to take a shower, and would come back to collect me in ten minutes to take me down for breakfast.

'Really, you go on your own, Theo. I don't want to risk it.'

'Ally, you have to eat something. If you can't keep food

down for an hour afterwards, I'm afraid you're banned from the boat until you can. You know the rules.'

'Okay,' I agreed miserably. As he left, I wished with all my heart that I could simply become invisible. Never in my life had I wanted to be somewhere else as much as I did at that moment.

Fifteen minutes later, we walked onto the terrace together. The other crew members looked up at us from the table with knowing smirks on their faces. I wanted to punch each and every one of them.

'Ally has a stomach bug,' Theo announced as we sat down. 'But by the looks of it, Rob, you missed out on some beauty sleep too.' The assembled crew members chuckled at Rob, who shrugged in embarrassment as Theo proceeded to talk calmly about the practice session he had planned.

I sat silently, appreciating that he'd moved the conversation on, but I knew what the others were all thinking. And the irony was, they were so, so wrong. I'd made a vow never to sleep with a crewmate, knowing how quickly women could get a reputation in the close-knit world of sailing. And now, it seemed I'd acquired one by default.

At least I was able to keep my breakfast down and was allowed aboard. From that moment on, I went out of my way to make it clear to everyone – especially to him – that I was not the slightest bit interested in Theo Falys-Kings. During the practices, I kept as far away from him as was possible on a small craft, and answered him in monosyllables. And in the evenings, after we finished dinner, I gritted my teeth and stayed on with the crew as he rose to leave and return to the pension.

Because, I told myself, I did not love him. And I did not

wish for anyone else to think I did either. However, as I set about convincing everyone around me, I realised there was no real conviction in my own mind. I found myself staring at him when I didn't think he was looking. I admired the calm, measured way he dealt with the crew and the perceptive comments he made that pulled us together and made us work better as a team. And how, despite his comparatively small stature, his body was firm and muscled beneath his clothes. I watched him as he proved himself time and again to be the fittest and strongest of all of us.

Every time my treacherous mind wandered in *that* direction, I did my best to reel it firmly back in. But I'd suddenly started noticing just how often Theo walked around without a shirt on. Granted, it was extremely hot during the day, but did he really have to be topless to look at the race maps . . . ?

'Do you need anything, Ally?' he asked me once, as he turned around to find me staring at him.

I don't even remember what I mumbled as I turned away, my face bright red with shame.

I was only relieved that he never mentioned what I may have said to him on the night I was so ill, and began to convince myself that I really must have dreamt it. But still, I knew something irrevocable had happened to me. Something that, for the first time in my life, I seemed to have no control over. As well as my usual clockwork sleeping pattern deserting me, my healthy appetite had disappeared too. When I did manage to doze off, I had vivid dreams about him, the kind that made me blush when I awoke and made my behaviour towards him even more awkward. As a teenager, I'd read love stories and dismissed them, preferring meaty thrillers. Yet, as I mentally listed my current symptoms, sadly, they all seemed to fit the same bill: I'd somehow managed to develop a massive crush on Theo Falys-Kings.

On the last night of training, Theo rose from the table after supper and told us we'd all done a spectacular job and that he had high hopes for winning the forthcoming regatta. After the toast, I was just about to depart for the pension when Theo's gaze fell on me.

'Ally, there's something I wanted to discuss with you. The regulations say we have to have a member of the crew who's in charge of first aid. It means nothing, just red tape and a case of signing a few forms. Would you mind?' He indicated a plastic file, then nodded to an empty table.

'I know absolutely nothing about first aid. And just because I'm a woman,' I added defiantly as we sat down at the table away from the others, 'doesn't mean I can nurse anyone better than the men. Why not ask Tim or one of the others to do it?'

'Ally, please shut up. It was just an excuse. Look.' Theo showed me the two sheets of blank paper he'd just taken out of his file. 'Right,' he said, handing me a pen, 'for the sake of form, particularly yours, we will now conduct a discussion about your responsibilities as the appointed crew member in charge of first aid. And at the same time, we will discuss the fact that on the night you were so ill, you told me that you thought you loved me. And the fact is, Ally, I think I might feel the same about you too.'

He paused and I looked at him in total disbelief to see if he was teasing me, but he was busy pretending to check the pages.

'What I'd like to suggest is that we find out what this means for both of us,' he continued. 'As from tomorrow, I'm taking my boat and disappearing for a long weekend. I'd like you to come with me.' Finally, he looked up at me. 'Will you?'

My mouth was opening and closing, probably in a very good impression of a goldfish, but I simply didn't know how to answer him.

'For goodness' sake, Ally, just say yes. Forgive the feeble analogy, but we're both in the same boat. We both know that there's something between us and has been ever since we first met a year ago. To be frank, from what I'd heard about you, I'd been expecting some muscly "he-she". And then you turned up, all blue eyes and gorgeous Titian hair, and completely disarmed me.'

'Oh,' I said, totally lost for words.

'So.' Theo cleared his throat and I realised that he was equally nervous. 'Let's go and do what we both love best: spend some time mucking about on the water and give whatever this "thing" is a chance to develop. If nothing else, you'll like the boat. It's very comfortable. And fast.'

'Will there . . . be anyone else on-board?' I asked him, eventually finding my voice.

'No.'

'So, you'll be skipper and I'll be your only crew?'

'Yes, but I promise I won't make you climb the rigging and sit in the crow's nest all night.' He smiled at me then, and his green eyes were full of warmth. 'Ally, just say you'll come.'

'Okay,' I agreed.

'Good. Now, perhaps you can sign on the dotted line to . . . er, seal the deal.' His finger indicated a spot on the blank sheet of paper.

I glanced at him and saw that he was still smiling at me. And finally, I offered him a smile back. I signed my name and passed the sheet of paper over to him. He studied it in a show of seriousness, then returned it to the plastic file. 'So, that's all sorted,' he said, raising his voice for the benefit of our fellow crew members, whose ears were no doubt on elastic. 'And I'll see you down at the harbour at noon to brief you on your duties.'

He gave me a wink and we walked sedately back to join the others, my measured pace belying the wonderful bubble of excitement I felt inside me.

2

It was fair to say that neither Theo nor I were sure what to expect as we set sail from Naxos on his Sunseeker, the *Neptune*, a sleek and powerful motor yacht that was a good twenty feet longer than the Hanse we were sailing in the race. I'd become used to sharing cramped quarters on boats with many others, and now that it was just the two of us, the amount of space between us felt conspicuous. The master cabin was a luxurious suite with a polished teak interior and when I saw the large double bed, I cringed as I remembered the circumstances of the last time we had slept in the same room.

'I picked her up very cheaply a couple of years ago when the owner went bankrupt,' he explained as he steered the craft out of Naxos harbour. 'At least it's put a roof over my head since then.'

'You actually live on this boat?' I said in surprise.

'I stay with my mum at her house in London during the longer breaks, but in the last year, I've been living on this in the rare moments I'm not sailing a boat to a race or competing. Although I've finally got to the stage of wanting a home of my own on dry land. In fact, I've just bought a place, although it needs an awful lot of work and God knows when I'll have the time to renovate it.'

I was already accustomed to the *Titan*, my father's ocean-going super yacht with its sophisticated computerised navigation, so the two of us shared the 'driving', as Theo liked to call it. But that first morning, I found it difficult to slip out of the usual protocol of being aboard with him. When Theo asked me to do something, I had to stop myself answering, 'Yes, skipper!'

There was a palpable air of tension between us – neither of us was sure how to cross over from the working relationship we'd had so far to a more intimate footing. Conversation was stilted, with me second-guessing everything I was saying in this strange situation and mostly resorting to idle small talk. Theo remained virtually silent and by the time we dropped anchor for lunch, I was starting to feel that the whole idea was a complete disaster.

I was grateful when he produced a bottle of chilled Provençal rosé to accompany our salad. I'd never been a big drinker, certainly not on the water, but somehow we managed to swiftly down the bottle between us. In order to prod Theo out of his awkward silence, I decided to talk to him about sailing. We went over our strategy for the Cyclades and discussed how different the racing would be in the upcoming Beijing Olympics. My final trials for a place in the Swiss squad were to take place at the end of the summer and Theo told me he'd be sailing for America.

'So you're American by birth? You sound British.'

'American father, English mother. I was at boarding school in Hampshire, then went to Oxford, then to Yale,' he clarified. 'I always was a bit of a swot.'

'What did you study?'

'Classics at Oxford, then a masters in psychology at Yale. I was lucky enough to be selected for the varsity sailing team and ended up captaining it. All very ivory-tower-type stuff. You?'

'I went to the Conservatoire de Musique de Genève and studied the flute. But that explains it.' I eyed him with a grin.

'What explains "what"?'

'The fact that you're so keen on analysing people. And half the reason you're such a successful skipper is because you're so good with your crew. Especially me,' I added, the alcohol making me brave. 'Your comments helped me, really, even if I didn't particularly like hearing them at the time.'

'Thanks.' He ducked his head shyly at the compliment. 'At Yale, they gave me free rein to combine my love of sailing with psychology and I developed a style of command that some might find unusual, but it works for me.'

'Were your parents supportive of your sailing?'

'My mother, yes, but my father . . . well, they split when I was eleven and an acrimonious divorce followed a couple of years later. Dad went back to live in the States after that. I'd stay with him there during the holidays when I was younger, but he was always at work or travelling and he employed nannies to look after me. He visited me when I was at Yale a few times to watch me compete, but I can't say I really know him very well. Only through what he did to my mum, and I accept that her antipathy towards him clouded my judgement. Anyway, I'd love to hear you play the flute, by the way,' he said, suddenly changing the subject and meeting my gaze properly, green eyes on blue. But the moment passed and he looked away again, shifting in his seat.

Frustrated that my attempts to draw him out seemed to be failing, I lapsed into an irritated silence too. After we'd carried the dirty plates down to the galley, I dived off the side of the boat and swam hard and fast to clear my wine-infused brain.

'Shall we go up onto the top deck and get some sun before we move on?' he asked me as I appeared back on-board.

'Okay,' I agreed, even though I could feel my pale freckled skin had already had more than enough sun. Normally when I was on the water, I covered myself in heavy-duty total sunblock, but as it was practically akin to painting myself white, it wasn't the most seductive look. I'd deliberately used a lighter sunscreen that morning, although I was beginning to think that the sunburn wouldn't be worth it.

Theo took two bottles of water from the ice box and we made our way to the comfortable sun deck on the prow of the yacht. We settled ourselves next to each other on the luxuriously padded cushioning and I glanced at him surreptitiously, my heart pounding uncontrollably at his half-naked nearness. I decided that if he didn't make a move soon, I'd have to do something very unladylike and simply pounce on him. I turned my head away from him to prevent further salacious thoughts from running through my mind.

'So, tell me about your sisters and this house that you live in on Lake Geneva. It sounds idyllic,' he said.

'It is . . . I . . .'

Given my brain was scrambled with desire and alcohol, the last thing I wanted to do was commence a long spiel about my complex family scenario. 'I'm feeling sleepy, can I tell you later?' I said, turning onto my front.

'Of course you can. Ally?'

I felt the light touch of his fingers on my back. 'Yes?' I turned back over and looked up at him, my throat tightening with breathless expectation.

'You're burning on your shoulders.'

'Oh. Right,' I snapped. 'Well, I'll go and sit downstairs in the shade, then.'

'Shall I come with you?'

I didn't answer, just shrugged as I stood up and clambered along the narrow part of the deck that led aft. Then his hand grabbed mine.

'Ally, what is it?'

'Nothing, why?'

'You seem very . . . tense.'

'Ha! So do you,' I retorted.

'Do I?'

'Yes,' I said as he followed me down the steps into the stern and I sat heavily on a bench in the shade.

'Sorry, Ally,' he sighed. 'I've never been very good at this bit.'

'What exactly is "this bit"?'

'Oh, you know. All the preamble, knowing how to play it. I mean, I respect you and like you, and I didn't want to make you feel as though I'd brought you aboard for a roll in the hay. You could well have thought that's all I wanted, since you're so sensitive anyway about being a female in a male world and—'

'For God's sake, Theo, I'm not!'

'Really, Ally?' Theo rolled his eyes in disbelief. 'To be honest, these days us guys are all scared we'll get slapped with a sexual harassment charge if we so much as gaze admiringly in the direction of a woman. It happened to me once with another female sailor who was on my crew.'

'Did it?' I feigned surprise.

'Yup. I think I said something like, "Hi Jo, so nice to have you aboard to liven all us boys up." I was doomed from that moment on.'

I stared at him. 'You *didn't* say that!'

'Oh, for God's sake, Ally, what I meant was that she would keep us all on our toes. Professionally, she had a fabulous reputation. And she took it the wrong way, for some reason.'

'I can't think why,' I commented acidly.

'Nor could I.'

'Theo, I was being facetious! I can see exactly why she took offence. You can't imagine the kinds of comments us women sailors get. No wonder she was sensitive about it.'

'Well, that's why I was extremely nervous about having you aboard in the first place. Especially as I found you so attractive.'

'I'm the polar opposite, remember?' I rounded on him. 'You criticised me for trying to be a man and not playing to my strengths!'

'Touché,' he said with a grin. 'And now here you are with me, alone, and I work with you and you might think—'

'Theo! This is getting ridiculous! I think it's you who's got the problem, not *me*!' I shot back at him, by now completely exasperated. 'You asked me onto your boat and I came of my own free will!'

'Yes, you did, but to be honest, Ally, this whole thing . . .' He paused and looked at me earnestly. 'You matter so much to me. And forgive me for behaving like an idiot, but it's been so long since I've done this . . . courting thing. And I don't want to get it wrong.'

My heart softened. 'Well, how about if you just try to stop analysing everything and relax a little? Then maybe I will too. Remember, I *want* to be here.'

'Okay, I'll try.'

'Good. Now,' I said, as I studied my sunburnt upper arms, 'as I really am starting to resemble an overripe tomato, I'm going to go downstairs to take a rest from the sun. And you're very welcome to join me if you want to.' I stood up and made my way to the stairs. 'And I promise I won't sue you for sexual harassment. In fact,' I added boldly, 'I might positively encourage some.'

I disappeared down the stairs, giggling at the blatancy of my invitation and wondering whether he'd respond to it. As I entered the cabin and lay down on the bed, I felt a sense of empowerment. Theo might be the boss at work, but I was determined to have parity in any personal relationship the two of us might have in the future.

Five minutes later, Theo appeared sheepishly at the door and apologised profusely for being 'ridiculous'. Eventually, I told him to shut up and come to bed.

Once *that* had happened, all was well between us. And in the following days, both of us realised it was something far deeper than physical attraction – that rare triumvirate of body, heart and mind. And finally, we immersed ourselves in the mutual joy of having found each other.

Our closeness grew at a faster pace than normal because we were already aware of each other's strengths and weaknesses, although it's fair to say we didn't talk much about the latter, simply glorifying in how wonderful we seemed to each other. We spent the hours making love, drinking wine and eating the fresh fish Theo caught from the back of the boat, with me lying lazily in his lap reading a book. Our physical hunger was coupled with an equally insatiable appetite to learn everything we could about each other. Alone together out on the peaceful sea, I felt we lived outside of time, needing nothing but each other.

On our second night, I lay under the stars in Theo's arms on the sun deck and told him about Pa Salt and my sisters. As everyone always did, Theo listened in fascination to the tale of my strange and magical childhood.

'So, let me get this straight: your father, nicknamed "Pa Salt" by your eldest sister, brought you and five other baby girls home from his travels around the world. Rather like other people would collect fridge magnets?'

'In a nutshell, yes. Although I like to believe I'm slightly more precious than a fridge magnet.'

'We'll see,' he said, nibbling my ear gently. 'Did he take care of all of you by himself?'

'No. We had Marina, who we've always called "Ma". Pa employed her as a nanny when he first adopted Maia, my oldest sister. She's practically our mother and we all adore her. She's from France originally, so that's one of the reasons we all grew up fluent in French, apart from it being one of the Swiss national languages. Pa was obsessed with us being bilingual, so he spoke to us in English.'

'He did a good job. I'd never have known it wasn't your first language, apart from your gorgeous French accent,' he said as he hugged me to him and pressed a kiss onto my hair. 'Did your father ever tell you why he adopted you all?'

'I asked Ma once, and she said that he was simply lonely

at Atlantis and had plenty of money to share. Us girls never really questioned why, we just accepted where we were, as all children do. We were a family; there never had to be a reason. We just . . . *are*.'

'It's like a fairy tale. The rich benefactor who adopts six orphans. Why all girls?'

'We've joked that maybe once he'd started naming us all after the Seven Sisters star cluster, adopting a boy would have spoilt the sequence,' I said with a chuckle. 'But to be honest, none of us have a clue.'

'So your proper name is "Alcyone", the second sister? That's a bit more of a mouthful than "Al",' he teased me.

'Yes, but nobody ever calls me that, except for Ma when she's cross with me,' I grimaced. 'And don't you dare start!'

'I love it, my little halcyon bird. I think it suits you. So why are there only six of you, when there should have been seven to fit with the mythology?'

'I've absolutely no idea. The last sister, who would have been called Merope if Pa had brought her home, never arrived,' I explained.

'That's rather sad.'

'Yes it is, although considering how much of a nightmare my sixth sister, Electra, was when she first came to Atlantis, I don't think any of us were looking forward to adding another screaming baby to our family.'

'"Electra"?' Theo recognised the name immediately. 'Not the famous supermodel?'

'They're one and the same, yes,' I replied warily.

Theo turned to me in amazement. I rarely, if ever, mentioned that Electra and I were related, as it engendered endless probing to find out who really lay behind one of the most photographed faces in the world.

'Well, well. And your other sisters?' he asked, pleasing me by asking nothing further about Electra.

'Maia is my big sister and the eldest. She's a translator – she took after Pa in her talent for languages. I've lost count of how many she speaks. And if you think Electra is beautiful, then you should see Maia. Whereas I'm all red hair and freckles, she has gorgeous tawny skin and dark hair and looks like an exotic Latin diva. Though in personality, she's very different. She's a virtual recluse, still living at home at Atlantis, saying she wants to be there to look after Pa Salt. All the rest of us think she's hiding . . . from what' – a sigh escaped me – 'I couldn't tell you. I'm sure something happened to her when she went away to university. She changed completely. Anyway, I absolutely adored her when I was a child and I still do now, even though I feel that she's cut me out over the past few years. To be fair, she's done that with everyone, but we used to be very close.'

'When you go within, you tend to go without, if you know what I mean,' Theo murmured.

'Very profound.' I nudged him with a smile. 'But yes, that's about the size of it.'

'And your next sister?'

'Is called Star and she's three years younger than me. My two middle sisters really come as a pair. CeCe, my fourth sister, was brought home by Pa only three months after Star, and they've been stuck together like glue ever since. They both had a somewhat nomadic existence after leaving university, working their way through Europe and the Far East, although apparently they're now intending to settle in London so CeCe can do an art foundation course. If you're going to ask me who Star actually *is* as a person, or what her talents and ambitions are, I really couldn't tell you, I'm afraid, because CeCe completely dominates her. She doesn't speak much and lets CeCe do the talking for both of them. CeCe's a very strong character, like Electra. As you can imagine, there's some tension between those two. Electra's as high-voltage as her name suggests, but very vulnerable underneath, I've always thought.'

'Your sisters would certainly make a fascinating psychological study, that's for sure,' Theo agreed. 'So, who comes next?'

'Tiggy, who is easy to describe as she's simply a sweetie. She graduated in biological sciences and worked in research at Servion Zoo for a while, before taking off to the highlands of Scotland to work in a deer sanctuary. She's very . . .' – I searched for the word – 'ethereal, with all her strange spiritual beliefs. She literally seems to float somewhere between heaven and earth. I'm afraid all of us have teased her mercilessly over the years when she's announced she's heard voices or seen an angel in the tree in the garden.'

'You don't believe in anything like that then?'

'I'd say my feet were firmly planted on the earth. Or at least, on water,' I corrected myself with a grin. 'I'm very practical by nature, and I suppose that's partly why my sisters have always looked to me as the "leader" of our little band. But that doesn't mean to say I don't have respect for what I don't know or understand. You?'

'Well, even though I've never seen an angel like your sister, I've always felt as though I was protected. Especially when I've been sailing. I've had a number of hairy moments aboard, and so far, touch wood, I've managed to come out of them unscathed. Perhaps Poseidon is rooting for me, to use a mythological analogy.'

'And long may that continue,' I muttered fervently.

'So, last but not least, tell me about this incredible father of yours.' Theo began to stroke my hair gently. 'What does he do for a living?'

'To be honest, again, none of us is exactly sure. Whatever it is, he's certainly been successful. His yacht, the *Titan*, is a Benetti,' I said, trying to put Pa's wealth into a language Theo could understand.

'Wow! That makes this look like a child's dinghy. Well, well, with your palaces on land and sea,' Theo teased me, 'I reckon you're a secret princess.'

'We've certainly lived well, yes, but Pa was determined to make sure we all earned our own money. There have never been *carte blanche* handouts to any of us as adults, unless it was, or is, for educational purposes.'

'Sensible man. So, are you close to him?'

'Oh, extremely. He's been . . . everything to me, and to all of us girls. I'm sure we all like to think we have a special relationship with him, but because the two of us shared a love of sailing, I spent a lot of time alone with him when I was growing up. And it's not just sailing he taught me. He's the kindest, wisest human being I've ever met.'

'So, you're a real Daddy's girl. Seems like I have a lot to live up to,' Theo remarked, his hand moving from my hair to caress my neck.

'Enough of me now, I want to know about you,' I said, distracted by his touch.

'Later, Ally, later . . . You should know the effect that

gorgeous French accent of yours has on me. I could listen to it all night.' Theo propped himself up on his elbow, leant over to kiss me full on the mouth and after that, we spoke no more.

3

The next morning, we'd just decided to sail to Mykonos for supplies when Theo called me down from the upper sun deck to join him on the bridge.

'Guess what?' he said, looking smug.

'What?'

'I was just chatting on the radio to Andy, a sailing friend of mine who's in the area on his catamaran, and he suggested we rendezvous in a bay off Delos for a drink later. He joked that there was a bloody great superyacht called the *Titan* currently moored right by him, so I wouldn't be able to miss him.'

'The *Titan*?!' I exclaimed. 'Are you sure?'

'Andy said it was a Benetti, and I doubt your father's boat has a doppelgänger. He also said there was another floating palace approaching him, and he was starting to feel claustrophobic, so he's moved off a couple of miles to the bay around the corner. So, shall we drop aboard for a cup of tea with your dad on the way to see Andy?' he asked me.

'I'm stunned,' I replied truthfully. 'Pa didn't tell me he was planning a trip down here, although I know that the Aegean is his favourite place to sail.'

'To be fair, Ally, he probably wasn't expecting you to be in such close proximity. You can double-check it's your father's boat through the binoculars when we get a little closer and then radio the skipper to let them know we're coming. It would be pretty embarrassing if it wasn't your father's yacht and we interrupted some Russian oligarch with a boat full of vodka and partying prostitutes. Actually, good point.' Theo turned towards me. 'Your father never rents out the *Titan*, does he?'

'Never,' I replied firmly.

'Right then, m'lady, take the binoculars and go back to relaxing up top, while your faithful captain takes the wheel. Give me a thumbs up through the window when you see the *Titan* and I'll put out a message on the radio saying we're approaching.'

As I climbed back up to the deck and sat tensely waiting for the *Titan* to appear on the horizon, I wondered how I would feel about the man I loved most in the world meeting the man I was growing to love more as each day passed. I thought back to whether Pa had ever met any of my previous boyfriends. Perhaps I'd introduced him once to someone I'd been having a fling with during my time at music school in Geneva, but that was as far as it had gone. To be blunt, so far there'd never been a 'significant other' who I'd felt I wanted to introduce to Pa or my family.

Until now . . .

Twenty minutes later, a familiar-shaped vessel came into view, and I trained my binoculars on it. And yes, it was definitely Pa's boat. I turned over and knocked on the glass window of the bridge behind me and gave Theo a thumbs up. He nodded and picked up the radio receiver.

Going below to the cabin, I tamed my wind-strewn hair into a neat ponytail and donned a T-shirt and some shorts, suddenly excited to be able to turn the tables on my father and surprise *him* for a change. Back up on the bridge, I asked Theo if Hans, my father's skipper, had radioed back yet.

'No. I just put out another message, but if we don't get a response, it looks like we'll just have to chance it and turn up unannounced. Interesting.' Theo picked up his binoculars and trained them on another boat close to the *Titan*. 'I know the owner of the other superyacht Andy mentioned. The boat's called the *Olympus*, and it belongs to the tycoon Kreeg Eszu. He owns Lightning Communications, a company that's sponsored a couple of the boats I've captained on, so I've met him a few times.'

'Really?' I was fascinated. Kreeg Eszu, in his own way, was as famous as Electra. 'What's he like?'

'Well, put it this way: I couldn't say I warmed to him. I sat next to him at dinner once and he talked about himself and his success all night. And his son, Zed, is even worse – a spoilt rich kid who thinks his father's money means he can get away with anything.' Theo's eyes filled with unusual anger.

My ears had pricked up. It wasn't the first time I'd heard Zed Eszu's name mentioned by someone close to me. 'He's that bad?'

'Yes, *that* bad,' he reiterated. 'A female friend of mine got involved with him and he treated her like dirt. Anyway . . .' Theo lifted the binoculars to his eyes again. 'I think we'd better have another go at radioing the *Titan*. It looks like she's on the move. Why don't you put out the message, Ally? If your father or his skipper is listening, they might recognise your voice.'

I did so, but there was no reply and I saw the boat continue to pick up speed and sail away from us.

'Shall we give chase?' Theo said as the *Titan* continued to head into the distance.

'I'll go and get my mobile and call Pa directly,' I said.

'And while you do, I'll ramp up the knots on this. They're almost certainly too far ahead, but I've never tried to catch a superyacht before and it might be fun,' he quipped.

Leaving Theo to play cat and mouse with Pa's boat, I went below to the cabin, hanging on to the door frame as he upped the speed. Searching through my rucksack for my mobile and trying to switch it on, I stared impatiently at the lifeless screen. It stared back at me like a neglected pet whom I'd forgotten to feed, and I knew that the battery had run out of charge. Rooting back through my rucksack to find the charger, and then again to find an American adapter suitable for the socket by the bed, I plugged it in and begged it to come back to life swiftly.

By the time I'd gone back up to the bridge, Theo had slowed our speed to a relatively normal pace.

'There's no way we're going to catch up with your father now, even at top speed. The *Titan* is going at full blast. Have you called him?'

'No, my mobile's charging at the moment.'

'Here, use mine.'

Theo handed his mobile to me, and I tapped in Pa Salt's number. It immediately went to voicemail and I left my father a message explaining the situation and asking him to call me back as soon as possible.

'Looks like your father's running away from you,' Theo teased me. 'Maybe he doesn't want to be seen just now.

Anyway, I'll radio Andy to find out his exact location and we'll go straight to meet him instead.'

My confusion must have shown on my face, because Theo took me in his arms and gave me a hug.

'Really, darling, I was only joking. Remember it's just an open radio line and the *Titan* may well have missed the messages. I've certainly been known to do that. You should have just called him on his mobile to begin with.'

'Yes.' I agreed. But as we sailed at a far more leisurely pace towards Delos to rendezvous with Theo's friend, I knew from my many hours of sailing with Pa that he insisted on the radio being on at all times, with Hans, his skipper, always alert for any messages for the *Titan*.

And in retrospect, I remember how unsettled I'd felt for the rest of the afternoon. Perhaps it had been a premonition of what was to come.

And so I awoke in Theo's arms the following morning in the beautiful deserted bay of Macheres, my heart heavy at the thought of heading back to Naxos later that afternoon. Theo had already talked about his plans to prepare for the race that would start in a few days and it seemed our halcyon time together was almost over, at least for now.

As I came to from my reverie, lying naked on the sun deck next to him, I had to force my mind to reboot outside the wonderful cocoon that was Theo and me. My phone was still charging from the day before and I made to get up and retrieve it.

'Where are you going?' Theo's hand held me fast.

'To get my phone. I really should listen to my messages.'

'Come straight back, won't you?'

I did and then he reached for me and ordered me to put the phone down for a little while longer. Suffice to say, it was another hour before I switched it on.

I knew there would probably be some messages from friends and family. But as I manoeuvred Theo's hand gently from my belly so as not to wake him, I noticed that I had an unusually large number of texts. And a number of voicemail alerts.

All the text messages were from my sisters.

Ally, please call as soon as you can. Love Maia.

Ally, CeCe here. We're all trying to get hold of you. Can you call Ma or one of us immediately?

Darling Ally, it's Tiggy. We don't know where you are, but we must speak to you.

And Electra's text sent shudders of terror through me: **Ally, oh my God! Isn't it awful? Can you believe it? Flying home from LA now.**

I stood up and walked to the prow of the yacht. It was obvious that something dreadful had happened. My hands trembled as I dialled my voicemail and waited to hear what it was that had prompted my sisters to contact me with such universal urgency.

And as I listened to the most recent message first, I knew.

'*Hi, this is CeCe again. Everyone else seems to be too scared to tell you, but we need you home urgently. Ally, I'm sorry to be the bearer of bad tidings, but Pa Salt has died. Sorry . . . sorry . . . Please call as soon as you can.*'

CeCe had probably thought she'd ended the call before

she had, as there was a sudden loud sob before the beep of the next message sounded.

I stared unseeingly into the distance, thinking of how I'd seen the *Titan* through the binoculars only yesterday. *There must be some mistake*, I comforted myself, but then I listened to the next voicemail from Marina, my mother in all but blood, asking me to contact her urgently too, and the same again from Maia, Tiggy and Electra . . .

'Oh my God, oh my God . . .'

I held on to the railing for support, my mobile slipping out of my hand and landing with a thump on the deck. I bent my head forwards as all the blood seemed to drain from me and I thought I might faint. Breathing heavily, I collapsed onto the deck and buried my head in my hands.

'It can't be true, it can't be true . . .' I moaned.

'Sweetheart, what on earth is it?' Theo, still naked, appeared beside me, crouching down and tipping my chin up to him. 'What's happened?'

I could only point at my dropped mobile.

'Bad news?' he asked as he picked it up, concern written across his face.

I nodded.

'Ally, you look like you've seen a ghost. Let's get you into the shade and find you a glass of water.'

With my mobile still in his hand, he half-lifted me from the deck and helped me down and onto a leather bench inside. I remember wondering randomly if I was always destined to be seen by him as helpless.

He hastily donned a pair of shorts and fetched me one of his T-shirts, gently helping my unresponsive body into it, then he armed me with a large brandy and a glass of water. My hands were shaking so much that I had to ask him to dial my voicemail so I could listen to the rest of my messages. I choked and spluttered as I swallowed the brandy, but it warmed my stomach and helped calm me.

'Here you go.' He handed me my mobile and I numbly re-listened to CeCe's message and all the rest, including three from Maia and one from Marina, then the unfamiliar voice of Georg Hoffman, who I vaguely remembered was Pa's lawyer. And a further five blank voicemails where the caller had obviously not known what to say and had rung off.

Theo's eyes never left my face as I placed my mobile on the seat next to me.

'Pa Salt is dead,' I whispered quietly, and stared into space for a long time after that.

'Oh God! How?'

'I don't know.'

'Are you absolutely sure?'

'Yes! CeCe was the only one brave enough to actually say the words. But I still don't understand how it's possible . . . it was only yesterday when we saw Pa's boat.'

'I'm afraid I can't offer an explanation for that, my darling. Here, the best thing you can do is ring home immediately,' he said, sliding my mobile back to me across the seat.

'I . . . *can't*.'

'I understand. Would you like me to do it? If you give me the number, I—'

'*NO!*' I shouted at him. 'No, I just need to get home. Now!' I stood up then, looking around me helplessly and then up to the skies, as if a helicopter might appear overhead and carry me to the place I so urgently needed to be.

'Listen, let me go on the internet and then make a few calls. Back in a bit.'

Theo disappeared up to the bridge as I sat, catatonic with shock.

My father . . . Pa Salt . . . dead?! I let out an outraged laugh at the ridiculousness of the idea. He was indestructible, omnipotent, *alive* . . .

'Please, no!' I shivered suddenly and felt my hands and feet tingling as though I was in the snowy Alps, rather than on a boat in the Aegean sun.

'Okay,' Theo said as he returned from the bridge. 'You'll miss the two forty flight from Naxos to Athens, so we're going to have to get there by boat. There's a flight from Athens to Geneva first thing tomorrow morning. I've booked you on it as there were only a few seats left.'

'So I can't get home today?'

'Ally, it's already one thirty, and it's a long way to Athens by boat, let alone flying to Geneva. I reckon if we do top speed most of the way, with a stop at Naxos for fuel, we can make it into the harbour by sunset tonight. Even I don't fancy taking this into a port as crowded as Piraeus in the dark.'

'Of course,' I replied dully, wondering how on earth I would cope with the endless in-between hours of the journey home.

'Right, I'll go and start her up,' Theo said. 'Want to come and sit with me?'

'In a while.'

Five minutes later, as I heard the rhythmic hydraulic clank of the anchor being raised and the soft hum of the engines purring into life, I stood up and walked to the stern, where I leant on the railings. I watched as we began to move away from the island, which I'd thought of last night as Nirvana but now would always be the place where I'd heard about my father's death. As the boat began to pick up speed, I felt nauseated with shock and guilt. For the past few days, I'd been totally and utterly selfish. I had thought only of *me*, and my happiness at finding Theo.

And while I had been making love, lying with Theo's arms around me, my father had been lying somewhere dying. How could I *ever* forgive myself for that?

Theo was as good as his word, and we arrived at Piraeus harbour in Athens at sunset. During the agonising journey, I lay across his lap on the bridge, as one of his hands gently stroked my hair and the other steered us safely across a choppy sea. Once in our berth, Theo went down to the galley and prepared some pasta, which he then spoon-fed me as if I was a child.

'Coming down to sleep?' he asked me and I could see he was exhausted from the concentration of the past few hours. 'We have to be up at four tomorrow to make your flight.'

I agreed, knowing he'd insist on staying up with me if I refused to go to bed. Steeling myself for a long, sleepless night, I let Theo lead me below, where he helped me into bed and wrapped his warm arms around me, cradling me to him.

'If it's any consolation, Ally, I love you. I don't just "think" I do any more, I *know*.'

I stared into the darkness and, having not shed a tear since the news, I found my eyes suddenly wet.

'And I promise I'm not just saying it to make you feel better. I'd have told you tonight anyway,' he added.

'I love you too,' I whispered.

'Really?'

'Yes.'

'Well, if you mean it, I'm more pleased than if I'd won this year's Fastnet Race. Now, try to sleep.'

And surprisingly, held fast by Theo and his admission of love, I did.

The following morning, as the taxi crawled through the Athens traffic, heavy even at sunrise, I saw Theo surreptitiously checking his watch. It was usually me in control of such things, monitoring the time for others, but at that moment, I was glad he was taking charge.

I checked in with forty minutes to spare, just as the desk was closing.

'Ally, darling, tell me, are you sure you're going to be okay?' Theo frowned. 'And are you positive you don't want me to come to Geneva with you?'

'Really, I'll be fine,' I said as I walked towards departures.

'Listen, if there's anything I can do, please let me know.'

We'd reached the end of the queue waiting to go through security as it wove snake-like between the barriers. I turned to Theo. 'Thank you, for everything. You've been amazing.'

'I really haven't, Ally, and listen' – he pulled me back towards him urgently – 'just remember I love you.'

'I will,' I whispered, managing a wan smile.

'And any time you don't feel brave, just call or text me.'

'I promise.'

'And by the way,' he said as he released me from his arms, 'I'll totally understand if you can't sail in the regatta, given the circumstances.'

'I'll let you know as soon as possible.'

'We'll lose without you.' He grinned suddenly. 'You're the best crewman I've got. Goodbye, my darling.'

'Bye.'

I joined the queue and was subsumed into the mass of trudging humanity. As I was about to dump my rucksack in a tray for X-ray, I turned back.

He was still there.

'I love you,' he mouthed. And with a kiss and a wave, he left.

As I waited in the departure lounge, and the surreal bubble of love that had encased me for the past few days burst abruptly, my stomach began to churn with dreadful trepidation at what I must face. I pulled out my mobile and called Christian, the young skipper of our family's speedboat, who would transport me from Geneva and along the lake to my childhood home. I left a message asking him to collect me at ten o'clock from the pontoon. I also asked him to say nothing to Ma or my sisters about my arrival, telling him I would contact them myself.

But as I boarded the plane and willed myself to make the call, I found that I couldn't do it. The dreadful prospect of another few hours alone, with the truth having been confirmed over the phone by one of my family, prohibited it. The plane began taxiing along the runway, and as we left the ground, flying up into the sunrise over Athens, I leant my hot cheek against the cool window as panic began to assail me.

To distract myself, I glanced unseeingly at the front page of an *International Herald Tribune* that I'd been handed by the cabin attendant. I was about to put it aside when a headline caught my eye.

'BILLIONAIRE TYCOON'S BODY WASHED UP ON GREEK ISLAND'

There was a photograph of a vaguely familiar face, with a caption beneath it.

'*Kreeg Eszu found dead on Aegean beach.*'

I stared at the headline in shock. Theo had told me it was *his* boat, the *Olympus*, which had been so close to Pa Salt's in the bay off Delos . . .

Letting the newspaper slip to the floor, I stared miserably out of the window. I didn't understand. I didn't understand anything anymore . . .

Nearly three hours later, as the plane began its descent into Geneva airport, my heart started beating so fast that I could barely catch my breath. I was going home, which normally engendered a feeling of happiness and excitement because the person I loved most in the world would be there to welcome me with open arms into our own magical world. But this time, I knew he would not be there to greet me. And never would be again.

4

'Would you like to drive, Mademoiselle Ally?' Christian indicated my usual seat in front of the wheel where I would sit and speed us across the still, calm waters of Lake Geneva.

'Not today, Christian,' I said and he nodded at me sombrely, his expression confirming that everything I knew already was true. He started the engine, and I slumped onto one of the seats at the back, my head hanging miserably, unable to look anywhere but down as I remembered how Pa Salt had sat me on his knee as a tiny child and let me steer for the first time. Now, just minutes away from not only having to face reality, but also having to acknowledge the fact that I'd failed to pick up my family's messages or respond to them, I wondered how any god could take me from the heights of joy to the abject despair I felt as we approached Atlantis.

From the lake, everything beyond the immaculate hedges that shielded the house from view looked as it always had. Surely, I prayed as Christian eased us into the jetty and I climbed out and moored the boat securely to the bollard, there'd been some mistake? Pa would be here to greet me any moment, he *had* to be here . . .

Within a few seconds, I saw CeCe and Star approaching

across the lawns. Then Tiggy appeared, and I heard her shout something through the open front door of the house as she hurried to catch up with her two older sisters. I began to run up the lawn to meet them, but my knees went weak with dread and I drew to a halt as I read their shared expressions.

Ally, I entreated myself, *you're the leader here, you have to pull yourself together . . .*

'Ally! Oh Ally, we're all so glad you're here!' Tiggy reached me first as I stood immobile on the grass, trying to appear calm. She threw her arms around me and hugged me tightly. 'We've been waiting for you to come for days!'

CeCe was the next to reach me, then Star – her shadow – who remained silent but joined Tiggy in our mutual embrace.

Eventually, I pulled away, noticing the tears in my sisters' eyes, and we walked up to Atlantis together in silence.

Seeing the house, I was struck by another pang of loss. Pa Salt had called this our private kingdom. Dating back to the eighteenth century, it even looked like a fairy-tale castle, with its four turrets and pink-painted exterior. Cocooned on its private peninsula and surrounded by magnificent gardens, I'd always felt safe here – but already it felt empty without Pa Salt.

As we arrived on the terrace, Maia, my eldest sister, emerged from the Pavilion that sat to the side of the main house. I could see her lovely features were marked by pain, but they lightened into relief as she saw me.

'Ally!' she breathed, as she rushed to greet me.

'Maia,' I said as she clasped her arms around me, 'isn't it absolutely awful?'

'Yes, just ghastly. But how did you hear? We've been trying to contact you for the last two days.'

'Shall we go inside?' I asked the assembled company. 'And then I'll explain.'

While my other sisters crowded around me as we walked into the house, Maia lagged behind. Even though she was the eldest and the one they looked to individually if they had an emotional problem, as a group, it was me who always took command. And I knew she was letting me do so now.

Ma was already waiting for us in the entrance hall and enveloped me in a warm, silent embrace. I let myself sink into the comfort of her arms and clutched her tightly to me. I was relieved when she suggested we all head into the kitchen – it had been a long journey and I was desperate for some coffee.

As Claudia, our housekeeper, prepared a large cafetière, Electra sidled into the room, her long, dark limbs managing to look effortlessly elegant in shorts and a T-shirt.

'Ally.' She greeted me quietly, and close up I could see how weary she looked, as if someone had burst her and drained the fire out of her incredible amber eyes. She gave me a brief hug and squeezed my shoulder.

I looked at each one of my sisters, thinking how rare it was these days that we were all gathered together. And as I thought of the reason, my heart jumped into my throat. Although I must eventually hear what had happened to Pa, I knew I had to tell them first where I'd been, what I'd seen there and why it had taken me so long to come home.

'Right.' I took a deep breath as I began. 'I'm going to tell you what happened, because to be honest, I'm still confused about it.' As we all sat down around the table, I noticed Ma standing to the side and gestured her to a chair. 'Ma, you should hear this too. Maybe you can help explain.'

As Ma sat down, I tried to gather my thoughts in order to explain the appearance of the *Titan* through my binoculars.

'So, there I was, down in the Aegean Sea, training for the Cyclades Regatta next week, when a sailing friend of mine asked me if I wanted to join him on his motor yacht for a long weekend. The weather was fantastic and it was great to actually relax on the water for a change.'

'Whose boat was it?' Electra asked, as I knew she would.

'I told you, just a friend,' I said evasively. As much as I wanted to share Theo with my sisters at some point, this was definitely not the moment for it. 'Anyway,' I continued, 'there we were a couple of afternoons ago, when my friend told me that another sailing mate of his had radioed him to say he'd spotted the *Titan* . . .'

Casting myself back to that moment, I took a sip of my coffee and then did my best to describe how our radio messages had gone unanswered and my sense of confusion as Pa Salt's boat had kept moving away from us. Everyone listened to my story with rapt attention and I saw a look of sadness pass between Ma and Maia. I then took a deep breath and told them that because of the dreadful mobile phone signal in the region, I hadn't received any of their messages until yesterday. I hated myself for lying but I couldn't bear to tell them I had simply switched it off. I also made no mention of the *Olympus* – the other yacht Theo and I had seen in the bay.

'So please,' I finally entreated them, 'can somebody tell me what on earth was going on? And why Pa Salt's boat was down in Greece when he was already . . . dead?'

We all turned to Maia. I knew she was weighing her

words before she spoke. 'Ally, Pa Salt had a heart attack three days ago. There was nothing anyone could do.'

Hearing how he'd died from my eldest sister made it so much more final. As I tried to stop the rising tears, she continued. 'His body was flown to the *Titan* and then sailed out to sea. He wanted to be laid to rest in the ocean; he didn't want to distress us.'

I stared at her as the dreadful realisation hit. 'Oh my God,' I whispered eventually. 'So the chances are that I happened upon his private funeral. No wonder the boat sped off as fast as it could away from me. I . . .'

Unable to pretend to be strong or calm any longer, I put my head in my hands and took deep breaths to control the panic I felt, as my sisters gathered around me to try and give me comfort. Not used to showing emotion in front of them, I heard myself apologising as I tried to regain my composure.

'It must be an awful shock for you to realise what was actually happening. We're all so sorry for you, Ally,' Tiggy said gently.

'Thank you,' I managed, and then muttered some platitudes about hearing Pa tell me once that he wanted to be buried at sea. It was such a ridiculous coincidence that I had come across the *Titan* on Pa Salt's final voyage; the thought made my head spin and I needed some air urgently. 'Listen,' I said as steadily as I could, 'would you all mind terribly if I had a little time alone?'

They all agreed I should and I left the kitchen with their warm words of support following after me.

Standing in the hallway, I looked around desperately, trying to navigate my body towards the comfort I craved, but knowing that whichever way I turned, he was gone and I would find none.

I stumbled out of the heavy oak front door, wanting nothing more than to be outside so I could release the feeling of panic that was pressing on my chest. My body automatically led me down to the jetty and I was relieved to see the Laser moored there. I climbed aboard, raised the sails and released the lines.

As I steered away from shore, I felt the wind was good, so I hoisted the spinnaker and blasted along the lake as fast as I could go. Eventually, having exhausted myself, I dropped anchor in an inlet shielded by a rocky peninsula.

I waited for my thoughts to flow, to try and make sense of what I'd just learnt. Currently, they were so jumbled that nothing much happened and I simply stared out over the water like an idiot thinking of absolutely nothing. And wishing I could grasp something that would allow me to understand. The tangled threads of my consciousness refused to loop into the devastating facts of what actually *was*. Being present at what had obviously been Pa Salt's funeral . . . why had *I* been there to see it? Was there a reason? Or was it just coincidence?

Gradually, as my heart rate began to slow and my brain eventually started to function again, the stark reality hit me. Pa Salt was gone, and there probably *was* no rhyme or reason. And if I, the eternal optimist, was going to get through this, I simply had to accept the facts for what they were. Yet all the normal touchstones I used when something dreadful happened seemed null and void, empty platitudes that were swept away on the tide of my grief and disbelief. I realised that whichever way my mind led me, the familiar paths of comfort had disappeared and nothing would *ever* make me feel better about my father leaving me without saying goodbye.

I sat there in the stern of the boat for a long time, knowing that another day was passing here on earth without him as part of it. And that somehow, I had to reconcile the dreadful guilt I felt for putting my own happiness first, when my sisters – and Pa – had so desperately needed me. I'd let them all down at the most important moment of all. I looked up to the heavens, tears streaming down my cheeks, and asked Pa Salt for his forgiveness.

I gulped down some water, then lay back in the stern to let the warm breeze dance over me. The gentle rocking of the craft soothed me as it always did, and I even dozed a little.

The moment is all we have, Ally. Never forget that, will you?

I came to, thinking that this had been one of Pa's favourite quotes. And even though I continued to blush in embarrassment at what I'd probably been doing with Theo when Pa drew his last breath – that stark juxtaposition of the processes of life beginning and ending – I told myself it wouldn't have mattered to him or the universe if I'd simply been having a cup of tea or been fast asleep. And I knew that, more than anyone, my father would have been very happy that I'd found someone like Theo.

As I set sail back to Atlantis, I felt a little calmer. There was still, however, one piece of information I had left out of the description I'd given my sisters of how I'd come across Pa's boat. I knew I needed to share it with someone to try and make sense of it.

As with all large groups of siblings, there were various

tribes within the whole; Maia and I were the eldest and it was to her that I decided to confide what I'd seen.

I moored the Laser to the jetty and made my way back up to the house, the weight on my chest at least feeling lighter than it had when I'd left. A breathless Marina caught up with me on the lawn and I greeted her with a forlorn smile.

'Ally, have you been out on the Laser?'

'Yes. I just needed some time to clear my head.'

'Well, you've just missed everyone. They've gone out on the lake.'

'Everyone?'

'Not Maia. She's shut herself away in the Pavilion to do some work.'

We shared a glance, and even though I could see how much Pa's death was weighing on Ma too, I loved her for always putting our worries and cares first. She was obviously very concerned about Maia, who I'd always had an inkling was her favourite.

'I was on my way to see her, so we'll keep each other company,' I said.

'In that case, can you tell her that Georg Hoffman, your father's lawyer, will be here shortly, but he wants a word with me first, for what reason I can't imagine. So she's to come up to the house in an hour's time. And you too, of course.'

'Will do,' I said.

Ma gave my hand a loving squeeze and set off back towards the main house.

When I reached the Pavilion I gave a gentle knock on the door but received no reply. Knowing that Maia always left it unlocked, I let myself in and called her name. Wandering into the sitting room, I saw my sister curled up asleep on the sofa, her perfect features relaxed, her glossy dark hair naturally arranged as though she was posing for a photo shoot. She sat up with an embarrassed start as I approached her.

'I'm sorry, Maia. You were asleep, weren't you?'

'I guess I was,' she said, blushing.

'Ma says that the other girls have gone out, so I thought I'd come and speak to you. Do you mind?'

'Not at all.'

She'd obviously been deeply asleep and to give her time to come to, I offered to make us both some tea. When we settled down with our steaming cups, I realised my hands were shaking and I needed something stronger than tea to tell her my story.

'There's some white wine in the fridge,' Maia said with an understanding smile, and went to fetch a glass of wine from the kitchen for me.

Having taken a gulp, I gathered my strength and told her about seeing Kreeg Eszu's boat near Pa's two days ago. To my surprise, she turned pale, and even though I had been rattled by the *Olympus* being so close, especially now I knew what had been happening on the *Titan*, Maia seemed far more shocked than I'd expected. I watched her attempt to recover herself, and then, as we chatted, try to make light of it and supply me with some solace.

'Ally, please, forget about the other boat being there – it's irrelevant. But the fact you were there to see the place where Pa chose to be buried is actually comforting. Perhaps, as Tiggy suggested, later in the summer we can all take a cruise together and lay a wreath on the water.'

'The worst thing is, I feel so guilty!' I said suddenly, unable to hold it in any longer.

'Why?'

'Because . . . those few days on the boat were so beautiful! I was so happy – happier than I've ever felt in my life. And the truth is, I didn't want anyone to contact me, so I turned off my mobile. And while it was off, Pa was dying! Just when he needed me, I wasn't there!'

'Ally, Ally . . .' Maia came to sit next to me, stroking my hair back from my face as she rocked me gently in her arms. 'None of us were there. And I honestly believe it's the way Pa wanted it to be. Please remember I live here, and even I had flown the nest when it happened. From what Ma has said, there really was nothing that could have been done. And we must all believe that.'

'Yes, I know. But it feels as though there are so many things I wanted to ask him, to tell him, and now he's gone.'

'I think we all feel that way. But at least we have each other.'

'Yes, we do. Thank you, Maia,' I replied. 'Isn't it amazing how our lives can turn on their heads in a matter of hours?'

'Yes, it is, and at some point,' she said with a smile, 'I'd like to know the reason for your happiness.'

I thought of Theo and enjoyed the comfort it provided. 'And at some point, I'll tell you, I promise. But not just yet. How are you, Maia?' I asked her, wanting to change the subject.

'I'm okay,' she shrugged. 'Still in shock like everyone.'

'Yes, of course you are, and telling our sisters can't have been easy. I'm sorry that I wasn't here to help you.'

'Well, at least the fact that you're here now means we can meet with Georg Hoffman and begin to move on.'

'Oh yes,' I said, checking my watch, 'I forgot to say that

Ma has asked us to be up at the house in an hour. He's due here any minute, but he wants to have a chat with her first apparently. So,' I sighed, 'can I please have another glass of wine while we wait?'

5

At seven o'clock, Maia and I walked up to the house to meet with Georg Hoffman. Our sisters had already been waiting a while on the terrace, enjoying the evening sun, but tense with impatience. Electra, as usual, was covering her nervousness by making sarcastic comments about Pa Salt's flair for drama and mystery, when Marina finally arrived with Georg. I saw he was tall, grey-haired and dressed immaculately in a dark grey suit – the epitome of a successful Swiss lawyer.

'Sorry to keep you so long, girls, there was something I had to organise,' the lawyer said. 'My condolences to you all.' He shook each of our hands in turn. 'May I sit down?'

Maia indicated the chair next to her and as Georg sat down, I sensed his tension as he twisted his expensive but discreet watch around his wrist. Marina excused herself and went into the house to leave us alone with him.

'Well, girls,' he began. 'I am so very sorry that the first time I meet you in person is under such tragic circumstances. But of course, I feel as though I know each of you very well through your father, and firstly I must tell you that he loved you all very much.' I watched as genuine emotion crossed his features. 'Not only that, but he was passionately proud of who you have all become. I spoke to him just before he . . . left us, and he wanted me to tell all of you this.'

He looked at each of us kindly in turn, before turning to the file in front of him. 'The first thing to do is to get the finances out of the way and reassure all of you that you will be provided for, at some level, for the rest of your lives. However, your father was adamant that you should not live like lazy princesses, so you will all receive an income which will be enough to keep the wolf from the door, but never allow you to live your lives in luxury. That part, as he stressed to me, is what you must all earn yourselves, just as he did. However, your father's estate is held in trust for all of you and he has given me the honour of managing it for him. It will be down to my discretion to give you further financial help if you come to me with a proposition or a problem.'

None of us said anything as we listened intently.

'This house is also part of the trust, and Claudia and Marina have both agreed that they are happy to stay on and take care of it. On the day of the last sister's death, the trust will be dissolved and Atlantis can be sold and the proceeds divided between any children you all may have. If there are none, then the money will go to a charity of your father's choice. Personally,' Georg commented, finally laying aside his lawyerly formality, 'I think what your father has done is most clever: making sure the house is here for the rest of your lives, so you know you have a safe place to return to. But of course, your father's ultimate wish is for all of you to fly away and forge your own destinies.'

All of us sisters exchanged glances, wondering what kind of changes this would bring about for us. For me, I supposed, my financial future at least would not be affected. I had always been independent and worked hard for everything I had. As for my destiny . . . I thought of Theo and what I hoped we would continue to share together.

'Now,' said Georg, snapping me out of my thoughts, 'there is one further thing that your father has left you, and I must ask you all to come with me. Please, this way.'

We followed Georg, uncertain of where he was taking us, as he led us around the side of the house and across the grounds until we eventually reached Pa Salt's hidden garden, tucked away behind a line of immaculately clipped yew hedges. We were greeted by a burst of colour from the lavender, lovage and marigolds that always attracted butterflies in the summer. Pa's favourite bench sat underneath a bower of white roses, and tonight they hung lazily down over where he should have been sitting. He had loved to watch us girls play on the little shingle beach that led from the garden to the lake when we were younger, me clumsily attempting to paddle the small green canoe he had given me for my sixth birthday.

'This is what I wish to show you,' said Georg, once again pulling me out of my reverie as he pointed to the centre of the terrace. A striking sculpture had appeared there, resting on a stone plinth about as high as my hip, and we all gathered round to have a closer look. A golden ball shot through by a thin metal arrow sat amidst a cluster of metal bands that wound intricately around it. As I noticed the outline of the continents and oceans delicately engraved on the encased golden ball, I realised it was a globe and that the arrowhead was pointing straight to where the North Star would be. A larger metal band looped around the globe's equator, engraved with the twelve astrological signs of the zodiac. It looked like some kind of ancient navigational tool, but what did Pa mean by it?

'It's an armillary sphere,' Georg stated, for the benefit of all of us. He then explained that armillary spheres had existed for thousands of years and that the ancient Greeks had originally used them to determine the positions of the stars, as well as the time of day.

Understanding its use now, I took in the sheer brilliance of the ancient design. We breathed words of admiration, but it was Electra who cut in impatiently. 'Yes, but what does it have to do with us?'

'It isn't part of my remit to explain that,' said Georg apologetically. 'Although, if you look closely, you'll see that all of your names appear on the bands I pointed out just now.'

And there they were, the script defined and elegant on the metal. 'Here's yours, Maia.' I pointed to it. 'It has numbers after it, which look to me like a set of coordinates,' I said, turning to my own and studying them. 'Yes, I'm sure that's what they are.'

There were further inscriptions beside the coordinates and it was Maia who realised that they were written in Greek, commenting that she would translate them later.

'Okay, so this is a very nice sculpture and it's sitting on the terrace.' CeCe's patience was wearing thin. 'But what does it actually mean?' she asked.

'Once again, that is not for me to say,' said Georg. 'Now, Marina is pouring some champagne on the main terrace, as per your father's instructions. He wanted all of you to toast his passing. And then after that, I will give you each an envelope from him, which I hope will explain far more than I am able to tell you.'

Mulling over the possible locations of the coordinates, I walked back to the terrace with the others. We were all muted, trying to take in what our legacy from our father meant. As Ma poured us each a flute of champagne, I wondered how much of this evening's activities she had already known about, but her face was impassive.

Georg raised his glass in a toast. 'Please join me in celebrating your father's remarkable life. I can only tell you that this was the funeral he wished for: all his girls gathered together at Atlantis, the home he was honoured to share with you for all these years.'

'To Pa Salt,' we said together, raising our glasses.

As we sipped our champagne in silent thought, I reflected on what we had seen and I desperately wanted some answers. 'So, when do we get these letters?' I asked.

'I'll go and get them now.' Georg stood up and left the table.

'Well, this has to be the most bizarre wake I've ever attended,' said CeCe.

'Can I have some more champagne?' I asked Ma, as questions flew around the table and Tiggy began to weep quietly.

'Well, I just wish he was here to explain in person,' Tiggy whispered.

'But he isn't, darling,' I said, rallying as I felt the atmosphere sinking into gloom and despondency. 'And somehow I feel this is fitting. He made it as easy as possible. And now we must take strength from each other.'

All my sisters nodded in sad agreement, even Electra, and I clasped Tiggy's hand as Georg returned and placed six large vellum envelopes on the table. I glanced at them and saw all our names written in Pa's distinctive handwriting on the front of them.

'These letters were lodged with me approximately six weeks ago,' said Georg. 'In the event of your father's death, I was instructed to hand one to each of you.'

'So, are we meant to open them now, or later, when we're alone?' I asked him.

'Your father made no stipulation on this point,' Georg replied. 'All he said was that you should open them whenever each of you is ready and feels comfortable to do so.'

As I looked at my sisters, I knew that we were probably all thinking that we'd prefer to read our letters in private.

'So, my job is now done,' Georg said with a nod. He gave us each his card, telling us he was there for us. 'But I'm sure that, knowing your father, he will have anticipated already what it is that you might all need. So, now it is time for me to leave you. Once again, girls, my condolences to you.'

I appreciated how difficult it must have been for him to pass on Pa's mysterious legacy to us and I was glad when Maia thanked him for us all.

'Goodbye. You know where I am if you need me.' With a sombre smile, and saying he'd let himself out, he left the terrace.

Ma rose from the table too. 'I think we could all do with something to eat. I'll tell Claudia to bring supper out here,' she said and disappeared inside the house.

The thought of eating had not crossed my mind all day. I was still focussed on the letters and the armillary sphere. 'Maia, do you think you could go back to the armillary sphere and translate the quotations on it?' I asked her.

'Of course,' she said, as Marina and Claudia returned with plates and cutlery. 'After supper, I will.'

Electra eyed the plates and stood up to leave. 'I hope you guys don't mind, but I'm not hungry.'

As Electra left, CeCe turned to Star. 'Are you hungry?'

Star was tightly clasping her envelope in her hand. 'I think we should eat something,' she murmured quietly.

It was the sensible thing to do, and when it arrived, the five of us attempted to force down the home-made pizza slices and salad. Then slowly, one by one, my sisters all left to be alone, until only Maia and I remained.

'Do you mind, Maia, if I go to bed too? I feel completely exhausted.'

'Of course not,' she answered. 'You were the last one to hear and you're still getting over the shock.'

'Yes, I think I am,' I agreed, standing up and kissing her gently on the cheek. 'Goodnight, darling Maia.'

'Goodnight.'

I felt guilty for leaving her at the table all alone, but just like the rest of my sisters, I needed some time to myself. And the letter I held was burning through my fingertips. Wondering where I could go to find solitude and peace, I decided that my childhood bedroom would give me the most comfort right now, so I climbed up the two flights of stairs.

All of our rooms were on the top floor of the house, and when Maia and I were little we had sometimes played at being princesses in a tower. My bedroom was bright and simply decorated, with its plain magnolia walls and blue and white checked curtains. Tiggy had once said it looked rather like an old-fashioned cabin on a boat. The round mirror was framed by a lifebelt with the words 'SS Ally' stencilled onto it – a Christmas present from Star and CeCe years ago.

As I sat down on my bed and looked at my envelope, I wondered whether my other sisters were opening theirs eagerly, or whether they were filled with trepidation at what they might contain. Mine had a slight bulge that shifted as I picked it up and held it. Out of all the sisters I'd always been the most eager to open Christmas or birthday presents, and as I studied the envelope, I felt the same with this. I tore it open and as I pulled out a thick sheet of paper, I jumped in surprise as something small and solid dropped out onto the duvet. With a start I realised it was a little brown frog.

After peering at it closely for a moment and then feeling foolish for thinking that it could possibly be a living creature, I picked up the little model. Its back was dappled with yellow and it had sweet, expressive eyes. I ran my fingers over its surface as it sat snugly in the palm of my hand, completely perplexed as to why Pa Salt had included it in my letter. As far as I could remember, frogs had never been of special importance to either of us. Perhaps it was one of Pa Salt's little jokes and the letter would explain it.

Picking it up, I unfolded the paper and began to read.

Atlantis
Lake Geneva
Switzerland

My dearest Ally,

As I start to write this letter, I can imagine you – my beautiful, vibrant second daughter – racing through the words eagerly to reach the end. And then having to read it slowly all over again.

Anyway, by now you will know I am no longer with you and I'm sure the shock will have been great for each and every one of you girls. I also know that, as the optimist among your sisters, the one whose positivity and zest for life has lit up mine, you will grieve for my loss, but then, as you always have done, pick yourself up and move on. Just as you should.

Perhaps, out of all my daughters, you are the child who is most like me. And I can only say how proud I've always been of you, and that I hope and pray that even though I'm no longer there to watch over you, you will continue to live your life as you have done so far. Fear is the most powerful enemy human beings face, and your lack of it is the greatest gift that God has bestowed on you. Don't lose it, even now in your grief, dearest Ally, will you?

The reason I'm writing to you, apart from to say an official goodbye, is that I decided some time ago that it was only right for me to leave all of you girls a clue as to your original heritage. When I say this, I don't mean that I wish you to drop everything immediately, but one never knows exactly what will happen in the future. And when you might need or wish to find out.

You will already have seen the armillary sphere and the coordinates engraved on it. These indicate a location which will help you to begin your journey. There is also a book on the shelf in my study by a man long dead named Jens Halvorsen. It will tell you many things, and perhaps help you decide if you wish to explore your origins further. And if you do, you're resourceful enough to find out how.

My darling girl, you were born with many gifts – almost too many, I've sometimes thought. And having too much of anything can be as difficult as having too little. I also fear that due to my delight in our shared passion for the sea, I may have blown you off course when there was another route just as easily available to you. You were such a talented musician and I adored listening to you play the flute. If I have, forgive me, but know that some of those days we spent out on the lake together remain the happiest I've ever spent. So from the bottom of my heart, thank you.

Enclosed with this letter is one of my most precious possessions. Even if you do not decide to discover your past, treasure it and perhaps one day, hand it down to your own children.

Dearest Ally, I am reassured that even after the blow you've taken as you read this, your tenacity and positivity will allow you to be whatever and with whomever you wish. Don't waste a second of your life, will you?

I'll be watching over you.

Your loving father,

Pa Salt x

Just as Pa had guessed, I had to read the letter twice, having raced through it the first time. And I knew I would read it a hundred times more in the days and years to come.

I lay back on my bed, the little frog in my hand, still none the wiser as to what relevance it held for me and thinking about what Pa had said in his letter. I then decided I wanted to talk to Theo about it, thinking he'd help me to make sense of it. Instinctively, I reached into my bag for my phone to see if he had messaged me, but then remembered I had left it in the kitchen to charge when I'd arrived home that morning.

I walked quietly along the landing, not wishing to disturb my sisters. I saw that Electra's door was ajar, and peered around it carefully in case she was asleep. Her back was towards me and she was sitting on the edge of her bed, taking a drink out of a bottle. At first, I thought it must be water, but as she took another slug, I realised it was vodka. I watched as she screwed the top back on, then pushed the bottle under her bed.

Withdrawing from the door before she saw me, I tiptoed along the landing and down the first flight of stairs, unsettled by what I'd just seen. Out of all of us, Electra was by far the most obsessed with her health, and it surprised me that she was drinking spirits at this time of night. But then, perhaps the usual rules didn't apply to any of us at this sad, difficult moment.

On instinct, I paused on the middle landing and headed towards Pa's first-floor suite of rooms, suddenly desperate to feel him close to me.

I tentatively pushed the door open and tears sprang to my eyes as I stared at the high single bed on which my father had apparently drawn his last breath. The room was so very different to the rest of the house – utilitarian and sparse, with its bare polished floorboards and the wooden-framed bed, a battered mahogany nightstand beside it. On top of it sat Pa's alarm clock. I remembered coming in here once when I was very young and being fascinated by it. Pa had let me press the switch up and down, up and down, to stop and start the alarm bell. I'd giggled in delight each time it rang.

'I must wind it every day or it stops ticking,' he'd told me, doing just that.

The alarm clock wasn't ticking now.

I walked across the room and sat down on the bed. The sheets were uncreased and pristine, but still the tips of my fingers reached out and stroked the starched white cotton of the pillow where his head had last rested.

I wondered where his old Omega Seamaster watch could be and what had happened to the rest of what undertakers would call his 'personal effects'. I could still picture the watch on his wrist, with its simple, elegant gold dial and the leather strap that had bad chafing on the fourth hole. I'd once bought him a replacement strap for Christmas and he'd promised he'd use it when the old one finally broke, but it never had.

My sisters and I often pondered the fact that Pa could have bought any timepiece he'd wanted or chosen designer labels to cover his body, yet it seemed to all of us that he'd worn the same set of clothes – when he wasn't sailing at least – ever since we could remember. His old tweed jacket had always been teamed with a perfectly laundered snowy-white shirt, discreet gold initialled cufflinks at the wrist, and dark trousers with militarily precise creases down the front. His feet had invariably been clad in brown brogues with gleaming toecaps. In fact, I thought, as I glanced around his bedroom and my eyes fell on the small mahogany wardrobe and chest of drawers – the only other pieces of furniture in the room – Pa's personal needs had always bordered on the frugal.

I looked at the framed photograph of him and us girls aboard the *Titan* that stood atop the chest of drawers. Even though he'd been in his seventies when the picture was taken, it was plain to see he had the physique of a much younger man. Tall and deeply tanned, his attractive weathered features were creased into a broad smile as he lounged against the railings of the yacht, surrounded by his daughters. And then my gaze strayed to the only picture hanging on the wall, which sat directly opposite the narrow bed.

I stood up and went to study it. It was a charcoal sketch of a very pretty young woman, who I guessed must be in her early twenties. As I looked more closely, I saw that her expression held sadness in it. The features were striking, but almost too large for her narrow, heart-shaped face. Her huge eyes were in proportion to her full lips, and I could see a dimple on each side of her mouth. She had an abundance of thick, curly hair that fell to beyond her shoulders. There was a signature at the bottom of it, but I couldn't make out the letters.

'Who are you?' I asked her. 'And who was my father . . . ?'

With a sigh, I returned to Pa's bed, lay down and curled myself up into a small ball. Tears dribbled out of my eyes, soaking the pillow that still smelt of his clean, lemony scent.

'I'm here, darling Pa,' I murmured, 'but where are you?'

6

I woke the next morning on Pa's bed, feeling groggy but cleansed. I didn't even remember falling asleep and I had no idea what time it was now. I rose from the bed and went to look out of the window. I decided that whatever Pa Salt's bedroom lacked in luxury, the vista from his window more than made up for. It was a glorious day, the sunlight glinting off the smooth surface of the lake, which seemed to stretch out to a misty infinity left and right. Looking straight ahead, I could see the lush green of the hillside that rose steeply from the shore on the other side of the lake. And for those few seconds, Atlantis felt magical again.

I went upstairs to my own room, took a shower and emerged thinking about Theo and how worried he must be that I hadn't contacted him yet to say I'd arrived. Dressing hastily, I grabbed my laptop and ran down the stairs to the kitchen to retrieve my mobile, which I'd been on my way to collect last night. There were several texts from Theo waiting for me, and my heart warmed as I read them.

Just checking in. Sending all my love.

Goodnight, darling Ally. My thoughts are with you.

Don't want to disturb you. Call or text when you can. Miss you. x

The texts were loving and undemanding – not even requesting an immediate reply. I smiled as I texted him back, remembering Pa's letter, telling me I could be anything or be with anybody I wanted.

And right now, I wanted to be with Theo.

Claudia was standing at the kitchen worktop, mixing some batter in a bowl. She offered me hot coffee as a greeting, which I accepted gratefully.

'Am I the first down?' I asked her.

'No, Star and CeCe have already left on the launch to go to Geneva.'

'Really?' I said as I took a sip of the rich, dark liquid. 'And the others aren't up yet?'

'If they are, I haven't seen them,' she said calmly, continuing to beat the batter with her strong, capable hands.

I took a fresh croissant from the breakfast feast laid out along the centre of the long table and bit into the buttery pastry. 'Isn't it wonderful that we can all stay here at Atlantis? I'd thought the house might have to be sold.'

'Yes, it's very good indeed. For everyone. Will you be wanting anything else?' Claudia asked me as she tipped the contents of the bowl into a baking tray and laid it beside the oven.

'No, thank you.'

She nodded at me, then divested herself of her apron and left the kitchen.

Throughout our childhood, Claudia had been as much of a fixture at Atlantis as Ma or Pa Salt. Her German accent made her sound severe, but we all knew what a soft heart she had underneath. I thought how little all of us knew about her background. But then, as children, or even as young adults, we had never thought to question the where, how and why. Claudia, like everything else in the charmed universe we had grown up in, just *was*.

I wondered then about the coordinates on the armillary sphere and how the secrets they held could completely unsettle everything we had known – or *didn't* know – about ourselves. It was a daunting thought, but Pa Salt had obviously left them for us for a reason and I had to trust his decision to do so. Now it was up to each of us individually to explore them further, or not, as we chose.

I picked up a pen and notepad from the sideboard, and left the kitchen by the back door, blinking in the morning light. It was refreshing to have the cool air on my skin. Not yet warmed by the sun, the grass was still fresh and dewy as it brushed the sides of my feet. The gardens lay in perfect tranquillity, with only the occasional trill of birdsong floating on the air and the gentle lapping of the water on the lake shore to disturb the silence.

I retraced my footsteps from last night around the side of the house towards Pa's special garden, admiring the many varieties of roses that had just opened their buds and were spreading their heavy scent into the morning air.

The golden ball in the centre of the armillary sphere glinted in the sunlight, which was already casting sharp shadows onto the navigational bands. I wiped the dew from the band with my name on it using my sleeve, and traced the Greek inscription with my finger, wondering what it said and how long ago Pa had planned this.

Getting to work, I carefully noted down the coordinates

for all of us, trying not to second-guess where any of them – especially mine – would lead. And then I noticed something. Counting the bands again, my fingers touched the seventh. It was inscribed with one word: 'Merope'.

'Our missing seventh sister,' I breathed, wondering why on earth Pa had thought to add her name to the sphere when it was too late for him now to ever bring her home. *So many mysteries*, I thought as I returned to the house. *And no one to answer my questions*.

Back in the kitchen, and with the coordinates in front of me, I fired up my laptop, eating another croissant as I waited in frustration for an internet signal that had obviously taken a holiday and left a novice temp to fill in for it. When it eventually decided to work, I investigated sites that used co-ordinates to pinpoint locations and settled on Google Earth. I considered which of us sisters I should begin with and decided I would go in age order, but leave myself until last. Typing in Maia's coordinates, wondering if they would be recognised, I watched the spinning globe zoom in and pinpoint an exact location.

'Wow,' I muttered under my breath in fascination, 'they actually work.'

It was a frustrating hour as the signal came and went, but by the time Claudia re-entered the kitchen to begin preparing lunch, I'd managed to write down the bare facts of every single set of coordinates, except my own.

I typed them in, holding my breath for an agonisingly long time as the computer worked its magic.

'Goodness!' I murmured as I read the details.

'Excuse me?' asked Claudia.

'Nothing,' I said quickly, scribbling the location down on the notepad next to me.

'You'll be wanting lunch, Ally?'

'Yes, that would be great, thank you,' I answered distractedly, mulling over the fact that the location the search had pinpointed for me was apparently an art museum. It didn't make any sense, but then, I wasn't sure any of my sisters' co-ordinates did either.

I looked up as Tiggy arrived in the kitchen, and gave me a sweet smile. 'Only you and me for lunch?'

'Seems like it, yes.'

'Well, that'll be lovely, won't it?' she said as she floated towards the table. For all her odd spiritual ideas, as I watched her sit down opposite me, I envied her inner peace. This stemmed from a total belief that there was more to life than life itself, as she was fond of saying. She seemed to carry the freshness of the Scottish Highlands in her clear skin and thick chestnut hair, and her calmness was reflected in her soft brown eyes.

'How are you, Ally?'

'I'm okay. How are you?'

'Coping, just. I can feel him around me, you know. As if' – she sighed, as she swept her hands through her glossy curls – 'he hasn't gone at all.'

'Sadly, he's *not* here, Tiggy.'

'Yes, but just because you can't see someone, does that mean they don't exist?'

'In my book, yes,' I replied briskly, not sure I was in the mood for Tiggy's esoteric comments. The only way I knew how to deal with Pa's loss was to accept it as soon as I could.

Claudia broke into our conversation by placing a Caesar

salad in front of us. 'There's enough for all of you, but if no one else arrives, they can have it for supper.'

'Thank you. By the way,' I said as I helped myself to the salad, 'I've written down all the coordinates and found out how to look them up on Google Earth. Do you want yours, Tiggy?'

'At some point, yes. But not now. I mean, does it matter?'

'I'm not sure, to be honest.'

'Because wherever I originally came from, it's Pa Salt and Ma who've looked after me and brought me up to be the person I am. Maybe I'll take them, then if I feel the need to look, I can. I sort of . . .' – Tiggy sighed, and I saw her uncertainty – 'don't want to believe I came from anywhere else. Pa Salt's my father and always will be.'

'I understand. So, just out of interest, where do you think Pa Salt is, Tiggy?' I asked her as we both began to eat.

'I don't know, Ally, but he's definitely not gone, that's for sure.'

'Is that in your world, or mine?'

'Is there a difference? Well, to me there isn't anyway,' she qualified before I could answer. 'We're just energy, all of us. And every single thing around us is too.'

'Well, that's one way of looking at it, I suppose,' I replied, hearing the cynical edge to my voice. 'I know these beliefs work for you, Tiggy. But right now, with Pa only just laid to rest, it doesn't do it for me.'

'No, I understand, Ally. But the circle of life goes on, and it isn't just us humans, it's all of nature too. A rose blooms to its full beauty, then it dies, and another on the same plant blooms in its place. And Ally' – she glanced at me and gave a small smile – 'I have a feeling that despite this terrible news, something good is happening to you at the moment.'

'Really?' I eyed her suspiciously.

'Yes.' She reached a hand over to mine. 'Just enjoy it while you can, won't you? Nothing is forever, as you know.'

'I do,' I said, feeling suddenly defensive and vulnerable at her accurate comment. I changed the subject. 'So how are you?'

'I'm well, yes . . .' Tiggy seemed to be trying to reassure herself as much as me. 'I am.'

'Still enjoying mothering your deer at the sanctuary?'

'I absolutely adore my job. It suits me perfectly, although I never get a moment to myself, as we're so short-staffed. Talking of which, I really have to get back as soon as possible. I've checked out flights and I'm leaving this afternoon. Electra's coming to the airport with me too.'

'So soon?'

'Yes, but what can we do here? I'm sure Pa would prefer us all to be getting on with our lives and not moping around feeling sorry for ourselves.'

'Yes, you're right,' I agreed. And for the first time, I thought beyond this terrible hiatus and towards the future. 'I'm meant to be crewing in the Cyclades Regatta in a few days' time.'

'Then do it, Ally, really,' she urged me.

'Maybe I will,' I murmured.

'Right, I've got to go and pack and then say goodbye to Maia. Out of all of us, this probably affects her the most. She's devastated.'

'I know. Here, take your coordinates.' I handed her the sheet of paper on which I'd written them.

'Thanks.'

I watched as Tiggy stood up and then paused at the kitchen door, staring at me sympathetically. 'And always remember that I'm only a phone call away if you need me in the next few weeks.'

'Thanks, Tiggy. The same goes for you.'

Having helped Claudia clear away the plates, I wandered back upstairs to my room, wondering whether I too should leave Atlantis. Tiggy was right: there was nothing left to do here. And the thought of being back on the water – not to mention in Theo's arms – propelled me back downstairs with my laptop to check if there were any seats on a flight to Athens in the next twenty-four hours. Entering the kitchen, I saw Ma, who was standing with her back to me at the window, obviously deep in thought. She heard me enter and turned with a smile, but not before I'd glimpsed the fleeting sadness in her eyes.

'Hello, *chérie*. How are you today?'

'Contemplating whether to fly back to Athens and take part in the Cyclades race as I'd originally planned. But I'm worried about leaving you and the other girls here. Especially Maia.'

'I think it's an excellent idea to go and race, *chérie*. And just what your father would have told you to do, I'm sure. Don't worry about Maia. I'm here for her.'

'I know you are,' I said, thinking how, even if she wasn't our real mother, it was impossible to think of any other parent loving and supporting us all more.

I stood up and went towards her, enveloping her in my arms and hugging her tightly. 'And remember, we're all here for you too.'

I went upstairs to find Electra and hand her the coordinates before she left. Knocking on her bedroom door, she opened it but didn't invite me in.

'Hi, Ally. I'm in a rush, packing.'

'I just brought you your coordinates from the armillary sphere. Here.'

'I don't think I want them. Honestly, Ally, what was it with our father? It's like he's playing some kind of game with us from beyond the grave,' she said darkly.

'He only wanted to let us know where we came from, Electra, just in case we needed the information.'

'Then why didn't he just do as most other normal human beings would? Like, write the facts down on paper, instead of subjecting us to some weird genealogical treasure hunt? Christ, the man always was a control freak.'

'Electra, please! He probably didn't want to reveal everything immediately, in case we'd prefer *not* to know. So he just left us enough information to find out if we wanted to.'

'Well, I don't,' she said flatly.

'Why are you so angry with him?' I asked her gently.

'I'm not, I . . .' Her amber eyes flashed in pain and confusion. 'Okay. I am. I . . .' She shrugged and shook her head. 'I can't explain.'

'Well, take this anyway.' I offered her the envelope, knowing from experience not to probe any further. 'You don't have to do anything with them.'

'Thanks, Ally. Sorry.'

'Don't worry. Are you sure you're all right, Electra?'

'I . . . yeah, I'm all right. Now I've got to pack. See you later.'

The door closed in my face and I walked away knowing full well she was lying.

That afternoon, Maia, Star, CeCe and I made our way down to the jetty to see Electra and Tiggy off. Maia handed them their translated quotations as well.

'I think Star and I might be on our way later too,' commented CeCe as we walked up to the house.

'Really? Couldn't we stay a little longer?' asked Star plaintively. And as always, I noted the physical contrast between them: Star, tall and thin to the point of emaciation with her white-blonde hair and pale-as-snow skin, and CeCe, dark-skinned and stocky.

'What's the point? Pa's gone, we've seen the lawyer and we need to get to London as soon as possible to find somewhere to live.'

'You're right,' said Star.

'What will you do with yourself in London while CeCe's at art school?' I asked.

'I'm not quite sure yet,' said Star, glancing at CeCe.

'You're thinking of taking a cordon bleu course, aren't you, Star?' CeCe answered for her. 'She's an amazing cook, you know.'

Maia and I shared a concerned look, as CeCe took Star off with the intention of checking flights to Heathrow that evening.

'Don't say it,' Maia sighed when they had gone. 'I know.'

We walked towards the terrace, discussing our concerns about Star and CeCe's relationship. They had always been inseparable to the extreme. I only hoped that with CeCe concentrating on her art course, they might disentangle themselves a little.

I noticed how pale Maia looked and realised that she hadn't eaten lunch. Telling her to sit down on the terrace, I went into the kitchen to find Claudia and asked her to prepare some food. Claudia gave me an understanding look and began to assemble sandwiches as I returned outside to Maia.

'Maia, I don't want to pry, but did you open your letter last night?' I asked carefully.

'Yes, I did. Well, this morning actually.'

'And it's obviously upset you.'

'Initially yes, but I'm okay now Ally, really,' she said. 'How about you?'

Her tone had become abrupt and I knew it meant that I should back off. 'Yes, I opened mine,' I said. 'And it was beautiful and it made me cry, but it also uplifted me. By the way, I've spent the morning looking the coordinates up on the internet. I now know exactly where all of us originally came from. And there are a few surprises in there, I can tell you,' I added, as Claudia brought out a plate of sandwiches and placed it on the table before swiftly withdrawing.

'You know exactly where we were born? Where *I* was born?' she asked tentatively.

'Yes, or at least where Pa found us,' I clarified. 'Do you want to know, Maia? I can tell you, or I can leave it to you to look up yourself.'

'I . . . I'm not sure.'

'All I can say is, Pa certainly got around,' I joked lamely.

'So you know where you're from?' she asked.

'Yes, though it doesn't make sense just yet.'

'What about the others? Did you tell them you know where they were born?'

'No, but I've explained to them how to look up the co-ordinates on Google Earth. Shall I explain to you too? Or just tell you where Pa found you?' I suggested.

'At the moment, I'm simply not sure,' she said, casting her beautiful eyes downwards.

'Well, as I said, it's very easy to look it up yourself.'

'Then I'll probably do that when I'm ready,' she said.

I offered to write down the instructions for the coordinates for her, but doubted whether she would ever have the courage to look them up. 'Did you have a chance to translate any of the quotes that were engraved in Greek on the armillary sphere?' I asked her.

'Yes, I have them all.'

'Well, I'd really like to know what Pa chose for me. Would you tell me, please?'

'I can't remember exactly, but I can go back to the Pavilion and write it down for you,' said Maia.

'So it seems that between us, you and I can provide the rest of the sisters with the information they need if they want to explore their past.'

'We can, but perhaps it's too soon for any of us to think whether we'll go back and follow the clues Pa has given us.'

'Maybe so,' I sighed, thinking of Theo and the weeks ahead. 'Besides, I have the Cyclades race starting and I'm going to have to leave here as soon as possible to join the crew. To be honest, Maia, after what I saw a couple of days ago, getting back on the water is going to be hard.'

'I can imagine. But you'll be fine, I'm sure,' she reassured me.

'I hope so. It's honestly the first time I've had cold feet since I began racing competitively.'

Saying this out loud to my big sister was a relief. Currently, whenever I thought of the Cyclades, the only image that sprang to mind was of Pa lying in his coffin at the bottom of the sea.

'You've put everything into your sailing for years, Ally, so you mustn't let it faze you. Do it for Pa. He wouldn't have wanted you to lose your confidence,' Maia encouraged me.

'You're right. Anyway, will you be okay here by yourself?'

'Of course I will. Please don't worry about me. I have Ma, and my work. I'll be fine.'

As I helped Maia finish off the sandwiches, I made her promise we would keep in touch and asked if she'd like to come sailing with me later in the summer, even though I knew she probably wouldn't.

CeCe appeared on the terrace. 'We've managed to get two seats on a flight to Heathrow. Christian is taking us to the airport in an hour.'

'Then I might see if I can get a flight to Athens and come with you. Don't forget to write out the quotation for me, will you, Maia?' I said as I left to go in search of my laptop.

Having found a last-minute evening flight to Athens, I packed hurriedly. Checking round my bedroom to make sure I had everything, my eyes alighted on my flute, sitting snugly inside its protective case on my shelf. It had remained unopened for a long time. On a whim, thinking about Pa's mention of it in his letter, I pulled it down and decided to take it with me. Theo had said he'd like to hear me play, and perhaps, after a practice, I would. Then I went downstairs to find Ma to say goodbye.

She hugged me tightly, setting two warm kisses on my cheeks. 'Please take care, *chérie*, and come back to see me when you can.'

'I will, Ma. Promise,' I said. Then Maia and I walked down to the jetty together.

'Good luck in the race,' she said, and handed me my envelope containing the translated quotation Pa had chosen for me.

Giving her a last embrace, I climbed aboard the launch, where CeCe and Star were already waiting for me. We all waved to Maia as Christian pulled away from the jetty. Setting off across the lake, I thought of how Pa Salt had always told me that one should never look back. Yet I knew I would, time and time again, at what *had* been, and was no longer.

I walked away from CeCe and Star to the stern of the boat, still clutching the envelope, feeling it was fitting to read Pa's quotation while I was on Lake Geneva, where he and I had sailed together so many times. I opened the envelope and eased out the piece of paper inside it.

In moments of weakness, you will find your greatest strength.

As Atlantis receded into the distance, the house disappearing behind the trees, I begged Pa's words to flow through me and help me find the courage I needed to carry on.

7

Theo had texted me to say he'd meet me at Athens airport. As I appeared out of arrivals, he walked towards me looking anxious, then took me in his arms.

'Sweetheart, I've been so worried about you. How are you? You must be shattered, you poor thing. And you've lost weight,' he added as he felt my ribs.

'I'm okay,' I told him firmly, breathing in his wonderful, reassuring smell. He took my rucksack and we went out into the dark, stifling heat of an Athens evening in July.

We climbed into a taxi, with its sticky plastic seats and smell of stale tobacco, apparently heading for a hotel in the harbour at Faliro, where the Cyclades race would start.

'I'm serious when I say that if you're not up to this, really, we can manage without you,' Theo said as we motored along the city streets.

'I don't know whether to take that as a compliment or an insult,' I retorted.

'Definitely a compliment, given that you're an integral part of the crew. But because it's you and I love you, I don't want you to feel any pressure.'

I love you. Every time he said those words with such naturalness, I felt a small thrill. And now he was here, next to me, holding my hand and still saying it. And I loved him too for his honesty, his openness and his refusal to play games. As he'd said to me once during those wonderful few days on the *Neptune* before I'd heard about Pa Salt's death, if I broke his heart, he'd just have to find another one instead.

'Really, I know it's what Pa would want me to do. Get back onto a boat and into my life and not sit around moping. And, of course, win.'

'Ally.' He squeezed my hand. 'We'll do it for him. I promise.'

When I went aboard the Hanse the following morning with the other members of the crew to begin our last few days of training, they also seemed infused with a real urge to triumph. And I was touched that every one of them tried to make my life as easy as possible. The Cyclades was nothing like as arduous as other offshore races I'd crewed on: eight days overall, but with a twenty-four-hour stopover and a rest day at each island we'd sail to.

Theo had noticed I'd brought along my flute. 'Why don't you bring it on-board? You can serenade us all to spur us on,' he'd suggested.

As we sped through the water in the glorious sunset on our first day of racing, I lifted the instrument to my lips and smiled at Theo before launching into an improvised woodwind version of *Fantasia on a Theme by Thomas Tallis*, a piece made famous by the epic seafaring movie *Master and Commander.* Theo grinned back at me from the helm, silently acknowledging the joke as we sailed into Milos harbour. The boys all applauded me graciously and I felt as if I'd paid my own small tribute to Pa Salt.

We won the first leg of the race outright, then came third in the second leg and second in the third. Which put us joint first with a Greek crew. The penultimate night of the race found us in the port of Finikas on Syros, a small and idyllic Greek island, the residents of which had laid on a celebration in the harbour for all the crews. After supper, Theo gathered us all together.

'Gentlemen – and lady – I understand you'll think I'm a killjoy, but your skipper is commanding all of you to have an early night. While the competition' – he nodded in the direction of the Greek crew, already half-drunk and clasping each other by the shoulder, dancing a Zorba routine to a bouzouki accompaniment – 'are making merry, we will get our beauty sleep and awake refreshed in the morning ready to kill. Okay?'

There was the odd groan, but everyone dutifully returned to the boat and went to their respective cabins.

Given the proximity in which we were living with the rest of the crew, Theo and I had developed a night-time routine so that we could snatch a few moments together without arousing suspicion. As the only female, I had my own stuffy cubbyhole in the prow of the boat, while Theo slept on the bench in the galley-cum-sitting area.

I would wait until I'd heard the others use the tiny locker room containing a sink and a loo. Then, when all was quiet, I'd creep upstairs into the darkness, where a warm hand would be waiting to pull me towards him. We'd have a nervous five-minute cuddle, like teenagers scared to be caught together by their parents. Then, in order to establish an alibi in case anyone should hear me creeping about, I would tiptoe back down to the galley and open the cooler box, grab a bottle of water, then walk back to my cabin and shut the door noisily. We were convinced we'd performed the charade so well that no one on the crew had the faintest idea of what was happening between us. As he pulled me to him on the last night before the finish, I felt extra passion in his goodnight kisses.

'Jesus, I hope you're prepared to spend at least twenty-four hours in bed with me to make up for all the frustration I've suffered in the past few days,' he groaned.

'Aye, aye, captain. Whatever you say. But it's hardly fair to order the rest of the crew to bed early and the skipper to then disobey his own orders,' I whispered into his ear as I removed a roving hand from my left breast.

'You're right, as always. So go, my Juliet, remove thyself from my sight, or forsooth, I shall be unable to restrain my lust for thee.'

Giggling, I kissed him one last time and extracted myself from his embrace.

'I love you, sweetheart. Sleep well.'

'And I love you,' I mouthed in return.

Theo's disciplinary tactics once again paid off. It had been tense being neck and neck with the Greek team for the final leg of the race, but as Theo commented triumphantly when we passed the gun in Vouliagmeni harbour on Saturday a good five minutes before they did, it must have been the ouzo that got them in the end. At the closing ceremony, the rest of the crew placed the victory crown made from laurel leaves on my head, the cameras flashed and champagne was sprayed over everyone. As I was handed a bottle to swig out of, I raised it into the air and silently told Pa Salt that this was for him. And sent up a fervent 'I miss you' to the heavens.

After the celebration dinner, Theo took my hand at the table and hauled me to my feet.

'First of all, a toast to Ally. Given the circumstances, I think we can all agree that she was incredible.'

The boys cheered and I found tears pricking my eyes at their genuine warmth.

'And secondly, I'd like you all to consider joining my crew in the Fastnet Race in August. I'm sailing the *Tigress* on its maiden voyage. Some of you may have heard of it – it's a brand-new boat which has only just been launched. And having seen it, I'm sure it can definitely sail us to another victory. What do you say?'

'The *Tigress*?' said Rob excitedly. 'I'm in!'

The rest of the boys joined him in eager agreement.

'Am I included?' I asked him quietly.

'Ally, of course you are.'

And with that, Theo turned to me, put his arms around me and kissed me hard on the lips.

This engendered another round of cheering as I pulled away from him, blushing to the roots of my hair.

'And that's the last thing I was going to announce. It seems Ally and I are an item. So if anyone has a problem with that, just let me know, okay?'

I watched the boys all raise their eyebrows in boredom.

'Old news,' Rob sighed.

'Yeah, what's the big deal?' said Guy.

We both looked at the crew in astonishment.

'You knew?' said Theo.

'Apologies, skipper, but we've all lived cheek by jowl for the past few days and, since no one else has yet had the pleasure of touching Al's backside without getting a thump for it, or been awarded a goodnight kiss and cuddle, it didn't take a genius to work it out,' said Rob. 'We've all known for ages. Sorry.'

'Oh,' was all Theo could manage, as he squeezed me tighter.

'Get a room!' shouted Guy, while the rest of the crew made various lewd comments.

Theo kissed me again and I wanted to fall through the floor in embarrassment as I realised that love really could be blind.

So, we did 'get a room' – a hotel room in fact, in Vouliagmeni. Theo was true to his word, keeping us both more than occupied for twenty-four hours. Lying in bed, we talked about plans for the Fastnet Race and beyond.

'So, are you free to join me on the *Tigress*?'

'I am now, yes. I'd normally be joining Pa Salt and some of my sisters for our annual holiday on the *Titan* in August . . .' I swallowed hard and continued quickly. 'Then in September, if I get through the final trials, I'll hopefully start training with the Swiss team for the Beijing Olympics.'

'I'll be there too with the Americans.'

'I'm sure you'll be quite the competition and I can't have you winning,' I teased him.

'Well, thank you, fair lady. I hope I'll rise to the challenge.' Theo gave me a mock bow. 'So, what about the next few days? I'm taking what I'd like to think is a well-earned holiday at my family's summer home. It's only a few hours' sailing from here. Then, of course, I'm off to the Isle of Wight to prepare for the Fastnet. Would you come with me?'

'For the holiday or the Fastnet?'

'Both. Although, being serious for a second, I know you're an experienced sailor, but the Fastnet is something else. I crewed on the last one two years ago and we nearly lost one of our crew as we were going round the Rock. Matt was literally blown off the boat. It's dangerous and' – Theo breathed in deeply – 'to be honest, I'm now starting to wonder if it's a good idea for me to have suggested you join the crew.'

'Why? Because I'm a girl?'

'For God's sake, Ally, get over yourself! Of course it's not that. It's because I love you and I couldn't live with myself if something happened to you. Anyway, let's think about it over the next few days, shall we? Preferably with a drink on a terrace overlooking the sea. Tomorrow morning, I've got to hand the Hanse back over to the owner down at the harbour, which is where I've moored the *Neptune*, so we could head straight off. What do you reckon?'

'Actually, I was thinking I should go home,' I said. 'Be with Ma, and Maia.'

'I totally understand if you feel you should. Although being selfish, I'd love it if you could come with me. It sounds as though this next year will be crazy for both of us.'

'I really want to come, but I'll need to call Ma first and make sure everything's okay, then take it from there.'

'Why don't you do that while I take a shower?' Theo dropped a kiss on the top of my head, before hopping out of bed and heading for the bathroom.

When I called her, Ma assured me that everything at Atlantis was fine, and there was absolutely no need for me to return. 'You take a holiday, *chérie*. Maia has decided to go away for a while, so she's not here anyway.'

'Has she? I'm amazed,' I commented. 'But are you sure you aren't lonely by yourself? I promise that this time my mobile will be on at all times if you need me.'

'I am fine and I won't, *chérie*,' she replied stoically. 'Sadly, the worst has happened already.'

I ended the call and felt suddenly low, as I did every time I allowed myself to remember Pa was no longer here. But Ma was right. The worst *had* happened. And I wished for once that I belonged to a religion with set rules to cope with the bleak aftermath of death. Even if I'd considered such rules archaic in the past, I now saw they were a ritual designed to help human beings through their darkest moments of loss.

The following morning, Theo and I checked out of the hotel and walked down to the harbour.

After a celebratory drink on-board with the owner of the Hanse – who was delighted with the win and was already talking to Theo about future regattas – we walked along the harbour and climbed aboard the *Neptune*. Before setting sail, Theo charted our course on the navigation system. He refused point-blank to tell me where we were heading, and as he helmed the boat out of Vouliagmeni harbour and once more onto the open sea, I busied myself restocking the fridge and the cooler box with beer, water and wine.

As we cruised through the calm aquamarine waters, no matter how hard I tried to concentrate on the beauty of the seascape, the dichotomy of emotion I'd experienced on my last voyage aboard the *Neptune* came flooding back. I found myself thinking that there were similarities between Pa Salt and my lover: they both enjoyed mystery, and most definitely liked to be in control.

Just as I was contemplating whether I'd fallen in love with a father figure, I felt the *Neptune* slow down and heard the anchor being dropped. When Theo appeared on deck next to me, I decided I wouldn't share my recent thoughts with him. With his love for analysis, I knew I'd never hear the last of it.

Over beers and a feta salad with fresh olives that I'd bought from a stall in the harbour, I explained to Theo properly about the armillary sphere with its quotations and engraved coordinates. And the letter Pa Salt had written to me.

'Well, it certainly sounds like he was well prepared. It must have taken some planning.'

'Oh yes, he was that sort of person. Everything was always organised perfectly.'

'Sounds like my kind of man,' Theo said, mirroring my earlier thoughts. 'I've written my will and issued instructions for my funeral too.'

'Don't say that,' I said with a shudder.

'Sorry, Ally, but all sailors are in a dangerous game and one just never knows.'

'Anyway, I'm sure Pa would have liked you a lot.' I looked at my watch to swiftly change the subject. 'Should we be leaving to go to wherever it is we're headed?'

'Soon, yes. I want to time our arrival perfectly.' Theo smiled secretively. 'Swim?'

Three hours later, when I saw the setting sun flood the sky above a tiny island with a deep orange glow, reflecting off the white-washed houses dotted along the coastline, I understood why he'd wanted to wait.

'See? Isn't it just perfect?' breathed Theo, who had one hand on the wheel and one arm around me as he steered us into the little harbour.

'Yes,' I agreed, as I studied the way the sunset's rays had seeped into the clouds, rather like an egg yolk gently releasing its contents after it had been burst. 'Pa always said that Greek sunsets were the most beautiful in the world.'

'Then that's another thing we would have agreed on.' Theo kissed my neck tenderly.

Given my earlier thoughts, I decided I'd definitely steer clear of Pa Salt's likes and dislikes for the duration of our holiday.

'Will you tell me where we are now?' I asked as we drew into the port and a swarthy youth hurried to grasp the rope I threw in order to secure the boat.

'Does it matter? You'll find out in due course. For now, let's simply call it "Somewhere".'

Expecting we'd have to haul our rucksacks up the steep hillside, I was surprised when Theo told me to leave them where they were. Having locked the cabin securely, we disembarked and Theo paid the youth a few euros for his efforts. Then he took my hand and led me along the harbour front to a row of mopeds. He fumbled in his pocket for a key and then fiddled with a padlock, which released the twisted mass of heavy metal chains wound around one of the bikes.

'The Greeks are lovely people, but the economy is fairly desperate just now, so it's better to take precautions. I never want to arrive here and find both wheels are missing. Climb aboard,' he offered and I did so reticently, my heart sinking.

I hated mopeds. During my gap year, I'd done as Pa Salt had suggested and set off to see the world with two friends,

Marielle and Hélène. We'd started in the Far East and visited Thailand, Cambodia and Vietnam. Making our way back to Europe, where I had secured myself a summer waitressing job on the island of Kythnos, we had travelled through Turkey on hired mopeds. On our way down from Bodrum airport to Kalkan, Marielle had misjudged a treacherous hairpin bend and crashed.

Finding her seemingly lifeless body in the scrub on the hillside, then standing in the middle of the road waiting desperately for any vehicle to pass and help us, was something I'd never forgotten.

The road had remained deserted, and eventually I'd grasped my mobile and called the only person I could think of who would know what to do. I explained to Pa Salt what had happened, and where, and he told me not to worry, that help was on its way. An agonising half an hour later, a helicopter had landed with a pilot and a paramedic. They airlifted the three of us to a hospital in Dalaman. Marielle survived with a shattered pelvis and three broken ribs, but the knock to her head still caused her serious migraines to this day.

Sitting on the back of Theo's moped that evening, having never been near one since Marielle's accident, my stomach somersaulted with dread.

'All set?' he asked.

'As I'll ever be,' I muttered, wrapping my arms like a vice around his waist. As we set off up the narrow lanes of 'Somewhere', I decided that if Theo was one of those harum-scarum male drivers who wanted to impress me, I would demand he stop and then I'd jump off. And even though he wasn't, I still closed my eyes as we left the port behind us and set off along a steep and dusty road. Eventually, after we'd been climbing for what to me seemed like an eternity, but was in reality probably less than fifteen minutes, I felt him brake and the bike lean to one side as he put a foot on terra firma and stopped the engine.

'Right, this is it.'

'Good.'

I opened my eyes feeling shaky with relief and concentrated on climbing off.

'Isn't it beautiful?' Theo eulogised. 'I mean, the views climbing up here are spectacular, but I think this has to be the best.'

As I'd had my eyes tightly shut all the way here, I didn't know anything about the views. He took my hand and led me across some rough, dry grass, and I saw ancient olive trees peppering the sloping land below us, which fell sharply into the sea beyond. I nodded to indicate that yes, it was.

'Where are we going?' I asked him as he continued to lead me on through the olive grove. I couldn't see a single dwelling in front of us. Only an ancient barn, probably meant for the goats.

'There.' He pointed to the barn and turned to me. 'Home sweet home. Isn't it amazing?'

'It's . . . I . . .'

'Ally, you're awfully pale. Are you feeling okay?'

'Yes,' I assured him as we finally arrived at the barn and I wondered which one of us had lost the plot. If this really was his 'home', then even if I had to walk every kilometre back down in the dark, I would. I wasn't spending the night here for anything.

'I know it looks like a shack at the moment, but I've recently bought it and I wanted you to be the first to see it, especially at sunset. I know it needs a lot of work, and of course the planning regulations here are fairly strict,' he continued as he heaved open the splintering wooden door and we entered the building. Through the roof, in the twilight, I could see the first stars beginning to appear in the enormous hole above me. The interior smelt strongly of goat, which made my already churning stomach turn over again.

'What do you think?' he asked me.

'I think that, as you say, it has a beautiful view.' As I stood listening to Theo explaining how he'd employed an architect, and his plans for the kitchen just here and a huge sitting room there and a terrace beyond overlooking the sea, I shook my head helplessly and stumbled outside, unable to stand the smell of goat any longer. Running over the rough, dried earth outside, I managed to get round the corner of the barn before I doubled over and dry-retched.

'Ally, what is it? Are you ill again?'

Theo was quickly by my side, his arms supporting me as I shook my head miserably.

'No, really, I'm fine. I just . . . I just . . .'

And then I sat down in the grass and bawled my eyes out like a little girl. I told him about the moped accident and how I was missing my father so very badly and how sorry I was that he was seeing me upset again.

'Ally, it's you who needs to forgive me. This is my fault. Of course you're exhausted from the race and the trauma of your father's death. You do such a great impression of being tough that I, the man who likes to pride himself on being the ultimate reader of people, have failed you. Now, I'm going to phone a friend, and get him to come up here by car and collect us immediately.'

Too tired to argue, I sat on the grass and watched Theo stand up and make a call on his mobile. The sun was now being subsumed by the sea beneath us, and as I calmed down, I decided that Theo was right. The view was indeed stunning.

Ten minutes later, with Theo following behind on the moped, I was being driven sedately down the hill in an extraordinarily old Volvo by an equally old man who Theo briefly introduced as Kreon. Halfway down, the car turned right and proceeded along another dusty, bumpy road, seeming to lead to nowhere again. But this time, when we reached the end of the track, I saw the welcoming lights of a beautiful house perched right on the edge of a cliff.

'Make yourself at home, sweetheart,' said Theo as he led me into a spacious entrance hall and a middle-aged, dark-eyed woman appeared and embraced him warmly, murmuring endearments in Greek. 'Irene here is our housekeeper,' he explained. 'She'll show you to your room and run you a bath. I'm going down to the port with Kreon to get our stuff from the boat.'

The bath turned out to sit on a terrace, which was carved – like the rest of the house – into the jagged rocks that plunged steeply down the cliff and into the foaming sea. Having luxuriated in a frothing pool of scented water, I climbed out and padded into the gorgeous airy bedroom. Then I went to explore and found myself in a stylishly furnished sitting room, which led onto a huge main terrace with a spectacular view and an infinity pool that an Olympic competitor would not have sniffed at. I concluded that this house was a little like Atlantis, but suspended in the air.

Soon after, wrapped in a soft cotton robe that I'd found on the bed, I sat down in one of the comfortably upholstered chairs on the terrace. Irene appeared with a bottle of white wine in a cooler and two glasses.

'Thank you.'

I sipped my drink as I gazed out into the star-studded darkness, appreciating the luxury of the surroundings after several days of sailing. I also knew now that when I took Theo home to Atlantis, he would be completely at ease there. So many times in the past, when I'd taken a friend from boarding school home to stay, or for a sailing trip on the *Titan*, I'd seen how their gregarious personalities were quashed under their awe of how we lived. And then they would leave, and when I'd next see them, I'd feel what I now guessed was animosity emanating from them, and the friendship would never be quite the same again.

Thankfully, there'd be none of those problems with Theo. His family obviously lived as well as mine did. I chuckled at the thought that both of us spent at least three-quarters of our lives lying on hard bunks in airless cabins, feeling lucky if the one cramped shower cubicle produced even a trickle of water – be it hot or cold.

I felt a hand on my shoulder and then a kiss on my cheek.

'Hello, my love. Are you feeling better?'

'Yes, much, thanks. Nothing quite like a hot bath after a few days of racing.'

'No, there isn't,' Theo agreed as he poured himself a glass of wine from the bottle and sat down opposite me. 'I'm about to do the same. And once again, Ally, please forgive me. I know I can be very single-minded when I'm on a mission. I just really wanted to show you my new house.'

'Really, it's fine. I'm sure that when it's finished it will be wonderful.'

'Not as wonderful as this one, obviously, but at least it will be mine. And sometimes,' he said with a shrug, 'that's all that matters, isn't it?'

'To be honest, I've never thought about having a home of my own. I'm away competing so much that getting a place seems rather pointless when I can simply go back to Atlantis. And we sailors earn so little that I couldn't afford much at all.'

'Hence me buying a goat barn,' Theo agreed. 'But equally, I suppose there's no point in denying that both of us have always had a safety net to catch us if we fall. Personally, I'd prefer to starve than go cap in hand to my father for money. Privilege comes with a price, don't you think?'

'Maybe, yes, but I doubt anyone would feel sorry for either of us.'

'I'm not suggesting we deserve sympathy, Ally, but despite this materialistic modern world believing the opposite, I don't think money can solve every problem. Take my father, for example. He invented a chip to go inside computers that made him a multi-millionaire by the age of thirty-five, the same age as I am now. Throughout my childhood, he loved telling me how he'd had to struggle when he was younger and how I should realise how lucky I was. Of course, his experience wasn't – and isn't – mine, because I was brought up *with* money. It's almost like a full circle: my father had nothing and was inspired to make what he could of his life, whereas I've ostensibly had everything, yet he's made me feel guilty for having it. So I've spent my life trying to get by without his help, being permanently broke and feeling I've never lived up to his expectations. Was it similar for you?' he asked me.

'No, although we were definitely taught the value of

money. Pa Salt always said that we were born to be ourselves, and could only strive to be the best we could possibly be. I always felt he was very proud of me, especially when it came to the sailing. I suppose it helped because it was a joint passion. Although he did say something quite strange in the letter he left me. He inferred that I hadn't continued with my music career because I'd wanted to please him by becoming a professional sailor.'

'And is that true?'

'Not really. I loved both, but the opportunities for sailing were presented to me and I took them. Life happens like that, doesn't it?'

'Yup,' Theo agreed. 'Interestingly, I'm a complete mix of my parents. My father's flair for the technical, and my mother's love for sailing.'

'Well, as I'm adopted, I have absolutely no idea what's in my genes. My upbringing was all about nurture, not nature.'

'Then wouldn't it be fascinating for you to find out if your genes have played a part in your life so far? Maybe one day you should use your father's clues and find out where you came from. It would be an amazing anthropological study.'

'I'm sure it would,' I said, stifling a yawn, 'but I'm too tired to think about it. And you smell of goat. It's high time you went for your bath.'

'You're right. On my way, I'll tell Irene to put supper on the table and I'll be back down in ten.' Theo kissed me on the nose and left the terrace.

8

Having calmed down from the initial passionate rush that had characterised the beginning of our relationship, during the lazy few days on 'Somewhere', Theo and I took time to get to know each other properly. I found myself confiding things in him that I'd never told another human being. Tiny, unimportant details to anyone else, but which meant so much to me. Theo's attention never wavered as he listened, his green eyes upon me with that intense gaze of his. Somehow he managed to make me feel more cherished than I'd ever felt in my life. He was especially interested in Pa Salt and my sisters – 'the luxury orphanage', as he'd termed our existence at Atlantis.

One sultry morning, when the air was so still that both Theo and I had remarked that a thunderstorm must be imminent, he came to join me on the daybed which sat in the shade on the terrace.

'Where have you been?' I asked him as he sat down.

'Sadly, I've been having a very dull conference call with our Fastnet sponsor, the team manager and the owner of the *Tigress*. And while they discussed semantics, I was doodling.'

'Were you?'

'Yes. Did you ever try making anagrams out of your name or writing it backwards when you were younger? I did, and it spelt something ridiculous,' he said with a smile. '"Oeht".'

'Of course I did and it's equally silly. Mine is "Ylla".'

'Did you ever make anagrams of your surname?'

'No,' I said, wondering where this was leading.

'Okay. Well, I love playing around with words and just now, when I was bored stupid during the conference call, I was fiddling with yours.'

'And?'

'Okay, so I know I'm anal and love a mystery, but I also know a little about Greek mythology, having studied classics at Oxford and lived here every summer since I was a child,' Theo explained. 'Can I show you what I found?'

'If you insist,' I said as he handed me a piece of paper with a few words scribbled on it.

'You see what D'Aplièse spells?'

'Pleiades.' I spoke the word he'd written below my surname, which apparently Theo had conjured out of 'D'Aplièse'.

'Yes. And you recognise that word?'

'It certainly sounds familiar,' I granted him grudgingly.

'Ally, it's the Greek name of the star cluster which contains the Seven Sisters.'

'So? What are you saying?' I looked at him, feeling irrationally defensive.

'Just that it's a pretty big coincidence that you and your sisters are all called after the seven, or should I say six' – Theo checked himself – 'famous stars, and that your surname is an anagram of "Pleiades". Was that your father's surname too?'

I could feel heat burning in my cheeks as I searched my memory to see if I could remember anyone ever calling Pa

'Mr D'Aplièse'. Our household staff and those on the *Titan* called him 'sir', apart from Marina, who'd refer to him as 'Pa Salt', as us girls did, or 'your father'. I tried to think if I'd ever seen a surname written on any mail that arrived for him, but I could only remember official-looking envelopes and deliveries which would be addressed in the name of one of Pa's many companies.

'Probably,' I replied eventually.

'Sorry, Ally.' Theo had read my discomfort. 'I was just trying to find out if he simply invented a surname for all you girls, or whether it was his name too. Anyway, darling, lots of people change their name by deed poll. It's very cute actually. You are "Alcyone Pleiades". And as for the nickname "Pa Salt", I—'

'Enough, Theo!'

'Sorry, it's just fascinating to me. I'm convinced there was far more to your father than met the eye.'

I excused myself then and went inside the house, feeling uncomfortable that Theo had seen something so intimate about my family – even though it was just letters he'd played with – that me and my sisters had never noticed before. Or if they *had*, it had never been openly discussed between us.

When I returned to the terrace, Theo followed my lead and said no more about it. Over lunch he told me more about his own parents and their acrimonious divorce. He'd been shuttled constantly between his mother in England, and America for holidays with his father. Being Theo, he related the whole story almost in the third person – analytically, as though it was little to do with him – but I could feel his underlying tension and subconscious anger. It sounded to me as if Theo had never given his father a chance, out of loyalty to his mother. However, I didn't feel confident enough just yet to say so, but felt in time that I would.

In bed that night, still unsettled by the revelation of my surname, I couldn't sleep. If our surname was an anagram made up by Pa because of his obsession with the stars and the mythology of The Seven Sisters, then who were we?

And more importantly, who had *he* been?

The awful truth was, I knew now that I could never find out.

The following day, I borrowed Theo's laptop and looked up The Seven Sisters of the Pleiades. Even though Pa had talked to all of us about the stars, and Maia in particular had spent a lot of time with him in his domed observatory perched atop Atlantis, I had never taken much of an interest. Any information Pa had passed on to me was of the technical variety when we were out sailing together. He'd done his best to show me how to use the stars to navigate on the sea and had told me that The Seven Sisters had famously been used by sailors to guide them for thousands of years. Eventually, I closed the computer down, thinking that whatever the reasons behind Pa's naming of us all, it was simply another mystery that would never be revealed. And pursuing it would only unsettle me further.

I put all this to Theo over lunch, and he agreed with me.

'I apologise, Ally, really. I should never have mentioned it. What's important is the present, and the future. And whoever your father was, all I care about is that he did something right by scooping you up as a baby. And although there's more I've discovered that I'm itching to tell you . . .' He eyed me speculatively.

'Theo!'

'Okay, okay,' he agreed. 'I understand it's not for now.'

It wasn't, although later that afternoon – and perhaps just as Theo had intended – I took out Pa's letter from the back of my diary where I'd secreted it and reread it. Maybe, I thought, one day I should go and follow the trail he had left for me. And at the very least, find the book he'd mentioned, that was sitting on a shelf in his study at Atlantis . . .

As we neared the end of our time together, I felt as though Theo had become part of me. When I repeated this phrase to myself, I could hardly believe it was me saying it. And yet, even though it was a romantic notion, I really did feel as though he was my twin soul. With him, I felt complete.

And I only realised how scary this newfound status might be when, in his normal calm way, he discussed the logistics of leaving 'Somewhere' – which I now knew to be the island of Anafi – and heading back to reality.

'Firstly, I have to go and visit my mum in London. Then I'll pick up the *Tigress* from Southampton and sail her over to the Isle of Wight. At least that will give me a chance to get the feel of her. What about you, darling?'

'I should go home for a bit too,' I said. 'Ma does a very good job of sounding okay, but without Maia there, or Pa, I feel I should be with her.'

'So, I've been looking up flights. Why don't we sail to Athens together on the *Neptune* at the weekend, then you take a flight to Geneva? I looked online and there's availability on a lunchtime flight, which leaves around the same time as mine to London.'

'Great. Thanks,' I replied brusquely, suddenly feeling horribly vulnerable – scared of being without him and of what our future would bring. Or even if there would *be* one after 'Somewhere'.

'Ally, what's the matter?'

'Nothing. I've had a lot of sun today and I should go and get an early night.' I stood up and made to leave the terrace, but he caught my hand before I could.

'We haven't finished the rest of the conversation, so please sit down.' Planting me back firmly in the chair, he kissed me on the lips. 'Obviously, we need to discuss plans for way beyond our flight home. For example, the Fastnet. I've been thinking about it a lot since we've been here, and I want to make a suggestion.'

'Go ahead,' I said, sounding contrary even to myself. These weren't the kind of 'plans' I was interested in hearing about just now.

'I want you to come and train with the crew. However, if I feel weather conditions are too dangerous to have you aboard for the actual race, or if you begin the race but I tell you at some point that you're going ashore, you have to swear you'll obey my orders.'

With effort, I nodded. 'Aye, aye, skipper.'

'Don't be facetious, Ally. I'm serious. I've told you before that I couldn't live with myself if anything happened to you.'

'Isn't it my decision to make?'

'No. As your skipper, let alone your lover, it's mine.'

'So *I'm* not allowed to stop *you* if I think it's too dangerous to sail?'

'Of course not!' Theo shook his head in frustration. 'It's me who will make the decision. For better, for worse.'

'What if it's "for worse" and I know it is?'

'Then you'll tell me, and I'll hear your warning, but ultimately, I'll decide.'

'So why can't I? It's not fair, I—'

'Ally, this is getting ridiculous. We're going round in circles, and besides, I'm sure none of this will happen. All I'm trying to say to you is that you have to listen to me, okay?'

'Okay,' I agreed sullenly. This was the nearest the two of us had come to an argument and with so little time left in this perfect place, I was loathe to let the situation deteriorate further.

'And more importantly' – I saw Theo's eyes soften as he reached out a hand towards me and stroked my face with his fingers – 'let's not forget there's a whole future beyond the Fastnet. Really, this has been the best few weeks of my life, despite all the trauma. Darling Ally, you know it's not my style to descend into romantic verbosity, but it would be great to work out a way that we could always be together. What do you think?'

'Sounds good to me,' I mumbled, unable to switch from 'extremely irritated' to 'let's spend our life together' within the space of a few seconds. I almost glanced over to the papers Theo had with him to see if 'Discuss future with Ally' was noted on the schedule.

'And old-fashioned as it seems, I know I won't ever find another you. So given that neither of us are spring chickens and we've both been round the block, I'm just telling you that

I *am* sure. And I'd be over the moon to marry you tomorrow. You?'

I looked at him, trying to take in what he was saying and failing. 'Is this a Theo-style proposal?' I snapped.

'I suppose it is, yes. Well?'

'I hear what you're saying.'

'And . . . ?'

'Well, to be blunt, Theo, this is hardly a scene out of *Romeo and Juliet*.'

'No. It isn't. I'm no good at the big moments, as you've seen. I just want to get them out of the way and get on with . . . *living*, I suppose. And I really would like to live with you . . . I mean, marry you,' he corrected himself.

'We don't have to get married.'

'No, but that's where my traditional upbringing kicks in, I suppose. I want to be with you for the rest of my life, and therefore, I must formally propose. I'd like for you to be Mrs Falys-Kings and to be able to say "my wife and I" to people.'

'I may not want your surname. Lots of women don't take their husband's name these days,' I countered.

'True, true,' he agreed calmly, 'but it's so much cleaner, don't you think? Sharing one name? Just for bank accounts, and it also saves explanations during telephone calls with electricians and plumbers and—'

'Theo?'

'Yes?'

'For God's sake, just shut up! However infuriatingly practical you can be sometimes, before you analyse me out of a positive response, I'd marry you tomorrow, too.'

'Would you really?'

'Yes, of course I would.' I then noticed what I thought was

the beginning of tears forming in his eyes. And the part of me that was so like him realised that even the most outwardly self-assured humans were rendered vulnerable when it came to believing that the person they loved loved them back. And wanted them and needed them just as desperately. I moved closer to him and hugged him tightly.

'Well, isn't that wonderful?' He smiled, surreptitiously wiping his eyes.

'Considering how rubbish that proposal was, yes.'

'Good. Well . . . even though it's again rather old-fashioned and you can blame it on my upbringing, I'd quite like it if we could go shopping tomorrow and choose something that marks the fact you're promised to me.'

'You mean, we become "betrothed"?' I teased him. 'Even though you do sound as though you've walked straight out of an Austen novel, I'd be delighted.'

'Thank you.' Then he looked up towards the stars, shook his head, and looked at me. 'Isn't this a miracle?'

'Which bit of it?'

'All of it. I mean, I've spent thirty-five years feeling alone on the planet, and then you arrive out of the blue. And suddenly I understand it.'

'Understand what?'

He shook his head, and gave a small shrug. 'Love'.

We did as Theo had asked and the next morning he took me to the island's capital, Chora, which, in reality, was little more than a sleepy white-washed village perched on a hill overlooking the southern coast of the island. We wandered around the quaint narrow streets, where we found a couple of tiny shops selling hand-made jewellery alongside a mishmash of food supplies and household goods, and a small street market with a few trinket stalls. Jewellery in general had never been my thing, and after half an hour of trying on various rings, I could see that Theo was getting frustrated.

'Surely there must be something that you want?' he urged me, as we stopped at the last market stall.

In fact, my eye had settled on something.

'Would you mind if it wasn't actually a ring?'

'Right now, I don't care if it's a nipple piercing, as long as I've got something you're happy with and we can get some lunch. I'm starving.'

'Okay, then I'd like that.'

I pointed to an 'evil eye': a traditional Greek pendant of a stylised blue glass eye dangling on a delicate silver chain.

The stall-keeper unhooked it from the display and held it out to us on his palm so we could take a closer look, indicating the handwritten price tag. Theo took off his sunglasses and picked up the pendant between his thumb and forefinger to study it. 'Ally, it's very sweet, but at fifteen euros, it's hardly a diamond ring.'

'I like it. Sailors wear them to ward off stormy seas. And after all, my name means I am the protectress of sailors.'

'I know, though I'm really not sure an evil eye is an appropriate engagement token.'

'Well, I love it, and before we both drive ourselves mad and give up, can it be this, please?'

'As long as you promise to protect me.'

'Of course I do,' I said, wrapping my arms around his waist.

'Okay. Although I warn you, just for the sake of form, I might have to present you with something that's more . . . traditional in the future.'

A few minutes later, we walked away from the market with the tiny talisman strung around my neck.

'In retrospect,' he said as we strolled back through the quiet streets to find a beer and some lunch, 'I think chaining you around the neck is far more appropriate than by a mere finger, although we will have to get you a proper ring eventually. However, I'm not sure I can run to Tiffany or Cartier, I'm afraid.'

'Now who's showing their roots?' I teased him as we sat down at a table in the shade outside a taverna. 'And just for the record, I hate designer labels.'

'You're right. Forgive me for showing my ingrained Connecticut country-club past. Anyway,' he said, grabbing a plastic menu, 'what do you fancy for lunch?'

The following day, having reluctantly parted with Theo at Athens airport, I sat on the plane feeling lost without him. I kept turning involuntarily to my surprised neighbour to tell Theo something I'd just thought of, only to remember he wasn't there. I admitted to myself that I felt completely bereft without him.

I hadn't told Ma I was coming home, thinking it would be nice to just turn up and surprise her. And as the aircraft carried me towards Geneva, and I steeled myself for arriving to an Atlantis that had lost its heart, my emotions swerved between the joy of what I had found and the dreadfulness of what I'd lost and was returning to. And this time my sisters wouldn't be there to fill the gaping hole Pa Salt had left behind.

When I arrived at Atlantis, for the first time ever, no one came down to meet me at the jetty, which depressed me further. Claudia was not at her usual station in the kitchen either, but there was a freshly baked lemon sponge cake on the countertop, which just happened to be my favourite. Cutting a generous slice, I left the kitchen and climbed the stairs to my room. I slung my rucksack onto the floor and sat down on the bed, studying the magnificent view of the lake over the trees and listening to the unnerving silence.

I stood up again and wandered over to the shelves to pull down the ship in a bottle Pa Salt had given me for my seventh birthday. I stared at the intricate wood and canvas model inside the glass and smiled as I remembered how I'd pestered Pa to tell me how it could have got inside the thin bottleneck.

'It's magic, Ally,' he'd whispered secretively. 'And we must all believe in that.'

Retrieving my diary from my rucksack and desperate to feel him close again, I drew out the letter he'd written me. Checking the details, I decided I would go downstairs to his study and look for the book he'd suggested I read.

I stood in the doorway of his study, letting the familiar smell of citrus, fresh air and safety fill my nostrils.

'Ally! Forgive me for not being here when you arrived. I didn't know you were coming, but what a wonderful surprise!'

'Ma!' I turned around to embrace her. 'How are you? I had a few days off and I wanted to make sure you were all right.'

'Yes, yes . . .' she said rather hurriedly. 'And how are you, *chérie*?'

I felt her keen, intelligent eyes appraise me. 'You know me, Ma, I'm never sick.'

'And we both know I wasn't asking after your health, Ally,' Ma replied gently.

'I've been busy, so I think that has helped. We won the regatta, by the way,' I offered lamely, not ready to tell Ma about Theo and the possible happiness I'd found just yet. Being here at Atlantis with Pa gone made it feel inappropriate.

'Maia is here too. She went to Geneva earlier, just after the . . . friend she brought with her from Brazil left. She'll be back soon, and will be happy to see you, I'm sure.'

'And I her. She sent me an email a few days ago and she sounded really happy. I can't wait to hear more about her trip.'

'Now, how about a cup of tea? Come into the kitchen and you can tell me all about the regatta.'

'Okay.' I followed Ma dutifully out of Pa's study. Perhaps it was just that I had turned up at home without calling first, but I sensed she was tense, her usual serenity temporarily deserting her. We chatted about Maia and the Cyclades race and twenty minutes later, we heard the launch approaching. I went to greet Maia on the jetty.

'Surprise!' I said, throwing my arms open to her.

'Ally!' Maia looked amazed. 'What are you doing here?'

'Strangely enough, this is my home too,' I said with a grin as we walked up to the house together arm in arm.

'I know, but I wasn't expecting you.'

We decided to sit on the terrace, and I went to fetch a jug

of Claudia's home-made lemonade. I studied Maia as I listened to her talk of her recent trip to Brazil, and thought she looked more alive than I'd seen her for years. Her skin glowed, and her eyes sparkled. Discovering her past through Pa Salt's posthumous clues certainly seemed to have helped to heal her.

'And Ally, there's something else I want to tell you. That perhaps I should have told you a long time ago . . .'

Then she told me what it was that had happened at university to make her hide away ever since. Tears came to my eyes as I listened to the story, and I reached out my hand to comfort her.

'Maia, how dreadful that you had to go through that all alone. Why on earth didn't you tell me? I'm your sister! I always thought we were close. I would have been there for you, I really would.'

'I know, Ally, but you were only just sixteen at the time. And, besides, I was ashamed.'

I asked then who this dreadful person was who had caused my sister so much pain.

'Oh, no one you'd know. He was someone I met at university called Zed.'

'Zed Eszu?'

'Yes. You may have heard his name on the news. His father was the tycoon who committed suicide.'

'And whose boat I saw close to Pa's that terrible day when I heard he'd died, if you remember,' I said with a shudder.

'Ironically, it was Zed who inadvertently forced me onto the plane to Rio when I was originally deciding whether to go or not. After fourteen years of silence, he left me a voicemail message out of the blue, saying he had to come to Switzerland and asking if we could meet up.'

I looked at her oddly. 'He wanted to meet *you*?'

'Yes. He said he'd heard about Pa's death and suggested that perhaps we could cry on each other's shoulders. If anything was going to send me scurrying away from Switzerland, that was it.'

I asked her if Zed knew what had happened to her all those years ago.

'No.' Maia shook her head firmly. 'And if he did, I doubt he'd care.'

'I think you were definitely best rid of him,' I said darkly.

'You know him, then?'

'Not personally, no. But I have a . . . friend that does. Anyway,' I said, recovering before Maia could question me further, 'it sounds as though getting on that plane was the best thing you've ever done. Now, you still haven't told me much about this gorgeous Brazilian you had in tow. I think Ma rather fell for him. When I arrived she could talk of nothing else. He's a writer, apparently?'

We chatted briefly about him, and then Maia asked about me. Deciding this was *her* moment to talk of having found someone after all these years, I refrained from telling her about Theo and talked about the Fastnet and the upcoming Olympic trials instead.

'Ally! That's fantastic! Do let me know how you get on, won't you?' she begged me.

'Of course I will.'

At that moment Marina appeared on the terrace.

'Maia, *chérie*, I didn't know you were home until I saw

Claudia just now. Christian gave me this earlier; I'm afraid I forgot to give it to you.'

Marina handed Maia an envelope and her eyes lit up as she recognised the handwriting. 'Thank you, Ma.'

'Will you two girls be wanting supper?' Ma asked us.

'If there's any going, absolutely. Maia?' I looked at her. 'Will you join me? It's not often we get the chance for a catch-up these days.'

'Yes, of course,' she said, standing up. 'But if you don't mind, I'm going back to the Pavilion for a while.'

Ma and I looked knowingly at Maia and the letter clasped in her hands.

'See you later, *chérie*,' said Marina.

As I followed Ma back into the house, I felt extremely unsettled by what Maia had just told me. In one sense, it was good that we had cleared the air and that I now understood why Maia had become so distant after university and thrown herself into what had amounted to self-imposed exile. But the fact she'd told me it was Zed Eszu who had been the cause of her pain was a different matter altogether . . .

With six girls in the family, and each one of us so very different, the amount of gossip about boyfriends and love affairs had varied depending on the character of the particular sister. Up until now, Maia had been totally closed about her private life and Star and CeCe had each other and rarely talked to the rest of us. Which left Electra and Tiggy, who had *both* confided in me over the years . . .

I went upstairs to my room, pacing restlessly and pondering the morals of knowing something that potentially affected other people that I loved, and whether one should share such information or keep quiet. However, having just had Maia open up to me for the first time in years, I decided it was *her* decision whether or not to tell our other siblings the story. What good would it do to have me interfere?

Having decided that, I checked my mobile, and smiled spontaneously as I saw a text from Theo.

My darling Ally. I miss you. Trite but true.

I replied immediately.

Me too (even triter).

As I took a shower before going down to join Maia for dinner, I longed to tell her of my own wonderful newfound love, but I reminded myself again that, after all these years, this must be her moment and mine could wait for another time.

Over supper, Maia announced that she was returning to Brazil the following day.

'We only have one life, don't we, Ma?' she said as she sat there glowing with happiness, and I thought she'd never looked more beautiful.

'Yes, we do,' said Ma. 'And if the past few weeks have taught us anything, it's that.'

'No more hiding,' Maia said as she raised her glass. 'Even if it doesn't work out, at least I will have tried.'

'No more hiding,' I toasted her with a smile.

9

Marina and I waved and blew kisses as we watched Maia leave Atlantis.

'I'm so happy for her,' said Ma, surreptitiously wiping her eyes as we turned and walked back to the house, where we chatted about Maia's difficult past and apparently rosy future over a cup of tea. It was obvious from what Ma said that she shared similar feelings about Zed Eszu too. I finished my tea and then I told her I needed to go and check my emails.

'Is it okay if I use Pa's study?' I asked, knowing it had the best internet signal in the house.

'Of course it is. Remember, this is yours and your sisters' house now,' Ma said with a sad smile.

Bringing my laptop down from my bedroom, I opened the door to my father's study, which looked as it always had, its oak-panelled walls complementing the comfortable antique furniture. I sat down tentatively in Pa Salt's leather-seated captain's chair, placing my laptop on the walnut desk in front of me. As it went through the process of opening, I swivelled the chair round to gaze blankly at the cornucopia of objects Pa had kept on his shelves. There was no particular theme to them and I'd always assumed they were just items that had taken his fancy on his varied travels. My eyes then sought out the floor-to-ceiling bookshelf that lined one wall, wondering where the book he'd mentioned in his letter might be. As I noted Dante nestling alongside Dickens and Shakespeare alongside Sartre, I realised the books were organised in alphabetical order, and were as eclectic and varied in taste as Pa himself had been.

The temperamental laptop then decided to tell me it wanted to shut down, having just opened up, so while I waited for it to reboot, I stood up and went over to Pa's CD player. All of us had tried to move him on to an iPod, but even though he had a raft of sophisticated computers and electronic communication equipment in his study, he'd said he was too old to change, and preferred to physically 'see' the music he wanted to play. Switching the CD player on, fascinated to discover what Pa Salt had been listening to last, the room was suddenly filled with the beautiful opening bars of Grieg's 'Morning Mood' from the *Peer Gynt* Suite.

I was rooted to the spot, as a wave of memories assailed me. It had been Pa's favourite orchestral piece, and he'd often asked me to play the opening bars for him on my flute. It had become the theme tune of my childhood and it reminded me of all the glorious sunrises we'd shared when he'd taken me out on the lake and patiently taught me to sail.

I missed him so very much.

And I also missed someone else.

As the music swelled from the hidden speakers, filling the room with glorious sound, on instinct, I picked up the receiver of the phone on Pa's desk to make a call.

Holding the receiver to my ear as I made to dial the

number, I realised someone else in the house was already on the line.

The shock of hearing the familiar, resonant tones of the voice that had comforted me from childhood forced me to interrupt the conversation.

'Hello?!' I said, hurriedly reaching over and turning the CD player down to make absolutely sure it was him.

But the voice at the other end had become a monotonous bleeping, and I knew he had gone.

I sat, gulping in breaths, then stood up, went into the hall and shouted for Ma. My cries also brought Claudia running from the kitchen. By now, I was sobbing hysterically and as Ma appeared at the top of the stairs, I went towards her.

'Ally, *chérie*, what on earth is the matter?'

'I . . . I just heard him, Ma! I heard him!'

'Who, *chérie*?'

'Pa Salt! He was speaking on the line when I picked up the study phone to dial a number. Oh my God! He's not dead, he isn't dead!'

'Ally.' I saw Ma shoot Claudia a sharp glance as she put an arm around me and led me into the drawing room. 'Please, *chérie*, try and calm down.'

'How can I?! I knew instinctively that he wasn't dead, Ma, which means he's somewhere still alive. And someone in this house was talking to him . . .' I looked at her accusingly.

'Ally, really, I understand what you think you heard, but there is a simple explanation for it.'

'And what on earth could that be?'

'The telephone rang a few minutes ago. I heard it but was too far away to pick it up, so it clicked into voicemail. What I'm sure you heard was your father's voicemail message.'

'But I was sitting right in front of the handset and I didn't hear the telephone ring before I picked it up!'

'But you were playing music very loudly, Ally. I could certainly hear it all the way upstairs in my room. Perhaps the ring was drowned out.'

'You're sure that you weren't on the telephone to him? Or maybe Claudia was?' I asked her desperately.

'Ally, however much you need me to tell you something different, I'm afraid that I can't. Do you want to use your mobile and dial the house number? If you leave it for four rings, you'll hear your father's voice message. Try it, please,' she entreated me.

I shrugged, now feeling embarrassed that I had accused Ma and Claudia of lying to me.

'No, of course I believe you,' I said. 'I just . . . *wanted* it to be him. To think that this whole terrible situation had all been a mistake.'

'It's what we all wish, Ally, but your father's gone, and nothing any of us can do will bring him back.'

'Yes, I know. I'm sorry.'

'Don't apologise, *chérie*. If there's anything I can do . . .'

'No,' I said as I stood up. 'I'll go and make my phone call.'

Marina smiled at me with sympathy in her eyes as I walked back into Pa Salt's study, where I sat down once more at the desk and studied the phone. Picking up the receiver, I dialled Theo's number and his mobile phone went to voicemail. Wanting to speak to the real thing and not a machine, I replaced the receiver abruptly without leaving a message.

Then I remembered that I still needed to look for the book that Pa Salt had wanted me to read. Standing up and scanning the titles of the 'H' section in the bookshelves, I found it within a few seconds and pulled it off the shelf.

Grieg, Solveig og Jeg
En biografi av Anna og Jens Halvorsen
Jens Halvorsen

Not understanding any more than that this was some form of biography, I took it back to the desk and sat down.

The book was obviously old, the pages inside it yellowing and frail. I saw the date of publication was 1907 – exactly one hundred years ago. Being a musician, I immediately knew to what Mr Halvorsen was almost certainly referring. Solveig was the sad heroine in Ibsen's poem and featured in the world-famous music written to accompany the stage play by the composer Edvard Grieg. Turning a further page, I saw there was also a foreword in which I recognised the words 'Grieg' and 'Peer Gynt'. But sadly, that was all I could read, as the rest of the words were in what I presumed was Norwegian – the native language of both Grieg and Ibsen – and therefore indecipherable.

With a sigh of disappointment, I leafed through the pages and found some black-and-white plates depicting a tiny woman in theatrical costume, dressed as a country peasant. Below the plate, it read, '*Anna Landvik som Solveig, September 1876*'. I studied the photographs intently, and realised that whoever Anna Landvik was, she'd been very young when the photograph had been taken. Underneath the heavy stage make-up, the girl looked barely older than a child. I leafed through the other plates and saw her as she grew older, and then did a double take as I stared at the familiar features of Edvard Grieg himself. Anna Landvik was standing by a grand piano and Grieg was behind it, applauding her.

There were other plates too, of a handsome young man – the biographer of the book – sitting formally in a photograph next to Anna Landvik, who was holding a young child in her arms. Frustrated by the fact that the book could reveal little more to me due to the language barrier, I felt my curiosity pique. I needed to get it translated, and thought that Maia, being a translator herself, would probably know of someone who could help.

Given my musicality, the thought that my ancestors might have had a connection with one of the great composers – and one who was a particular favourite of mine and Pa's – was deeply moving. Was this why he had loved the *Peer Gynt* Suite so much? Maybe he'd played it to me because he knew of my connection to it.

Once again, I mourned his passing and the questions that would always remain unanswered.

'*Chérie,* are you all right?'

Stirred out of my thoughts, I looked up to see Ma standing in the doorway. 'I'm fine.'

'You were reading?'

'Yes,' I said, putting a protective hand over the book.

'Well, lunch is ready on the terrace.'

'Thank you, Ma.'

Over a goat's cheese salad and a glass of chilled white wine, I again apologised to Ma for my hysterical outburst earlier.

'Really, there's no need,' comforted Ma. 'So, we both know about Maia, but you have said very little about yourself. Tell me, how you are, Ally? I feel there is something good that has happened. You too look different.'

'Actually . . . the thing is, Ma, I've met someone as well.'

'I thought you had,' she said with a smile.

'Which is why I didn't receive everyone's voice messages. I was with him when Pa died and I'd switched my phone off,' I blurted out suddenly, needing to get the truth off my chest. 'I'm so, so sorry. I feel so guilty, Ma.'

'Well, you shouldn't. Who was to know what would happen?'

'The truth is,' I sighed, 'I feel I'm on an emotional rollercoaster – I don't think I've ever been happier or sadder, all at the same time. It's very strange. I feel guilty about being happy.'

'I doubt very much that your father would want you to feel like that, *chérie*. So, who is this man who has stolen your heart?'

I then told her everything. And even just speaking Theo's name made me feel better.

'Is he "the one", Ally? I've certainly never heard you talk of any man like this before.'

'I think he might be, yes. In fact, he's . . . well, he's proposed.'

'Goodness!' Ma looked at me in surprise. 'And have you accepted?'

'I have, yes, although we won't get married for ages, I'm sure. But he gave me this.' I tugged the silver chain from beneath my collar and showed her the evil eye pendant. 'I know it's ridiculously fast, but it just feels so right. For both of us. And you know me, Ma, I've never been one to get carried away romantically, so this has all come as a bit of a shock.'

'I do know you, Ally, and that's why I realise that this must be serious.'

'He reminds me of Pa, as a matter of fact. I wish he could have met Theo,' I sighed, taking a mouthful of the salad. 'Changing the subject, do you think Pa genuinely wanted us all to go and find out where we came from?'

'I think he wished to provide you with the necessary information, in case you ever wanted to. Of course, it is up to you to decide.'

'Well, it certainly seems to have helped Maia. While she was finding out about her past, she found her future at the same time.'

'Yes, she did,' said Ma.

'But I think I may have already found mine, without needing to delve into my history. Perhaps I'll investigate one day, but not now. I just want to try to enjoy the present and see where it leads.'

'And so you should. I hope that you'll bring Theo here soon so that I can meet him.'

'I will, Ma,' I said as I smiled at the thought of such an occasion. 'I promise.'

After several days of Claudia's home-cooking, regular sleep and the glorious July weather, I felt refreshed and calm. I'd taken the Laser out onto the lake every afternoon and enjoyed leisurely sailing sessions. And as the sun beat down, I'd lain on the boat letting my feelings for Theo suffuse me. I felt closer both to him and to Pa when I was out on the water. Slowly, I realised I was coming to terms with losing Pa and beginning to accept it. And although I'd told Marina I wasn't going to investigate my past for now, I'd already emailed Maia to ask if she knew a Norwegian translator. She'd said she didn't, but would make some enquiries. A couple of days later, she had emailed me back with the contact details for a Magdalena Jensen. I'd called and spoken to Magdalena, and she'd said she would be happy to begin translating the book for me. After taking photocopies of the cover and of the photographs just in case the book got lost, I'd carefully packaged it up and sent it to her by FedEx.

As I packed my rucksack in readiness to travel over to the Isle of Wight, just off the coast of England, to begin training, a tingle of trepidation ran up my spine at what was to come. The Fastnet Race was a serious undertaking and Theo would be in command of a hand-picked and highly experienced crew of twenty. I myself had never attempted anything so challenging. I would need to be on my mettle and prepared to watch and learn. In retrospect, it was a huge honour that Theo had even asked me.

'Ready to go?' said Ma as I appeared in the hall with my rucksack and my flute, which Theo had asked me to bring along again. He seemed to genuinely love hearing me play.

'I am.'

She drew me to her and embraced me, and I felt enveloped in all the comfort and security she represented.

'You will take care in the race, won't you, *chérie*?' she asked as we left the house to walk down to the jetty.

'Please don't worry, Ma. I have the best captain there is, I promise. Theo will keep me safe.'

'Then just make sure you listen to him, won't you, Ally? I know how strong-minded you can be.'

'Of course I will,' I said with a wry smile, thinking how well she knew me.

'Keep in touch, Ally,' she called, watching me steer the launch out from the jetty as Christian threw the lines and himself aboard.

'I will, Ma.'

And as the launch accelerated along the lake, I felt that I was truly sailing towards my future.

10

'Hello, Ally.'

I stared at Theo in surprise, while the melting pot of humanity that was London Heathrow airport surged past me. 'What are you doing here?'

'And what kind of a question is that? Anyone would think you weren't pleased to see me,' he grumbled playfully, before pulling me into his arms in the centre of the arrivals channel and kissing me.

'Of course I'm pleased!' I giggled as we came up for air, thinking how he always managed to confound my expectations. 'I thought you were busy on the *Tigress*. Come on,' I added, disentangling myself from him, 'we're causing a human traffic jam here.'

He led me out of the terminal to the taxi rank. 'Hop in,' he said as he issued the driver with instructions.

'Surely we're not taking a taxi all the way down to the ferry for the Isle of Wight?' I queried as we set off. 'It's miles away.'

'No, of course we're not, Ally. But given that once we get there, we'll be training full on, I thought it might be a nice idea for us to have a night together before I become

"Skipper" again and you're just "Al".' With that, he wrapped me against him. 'Missed you, sweetheart,' he whispered.

'Me too,' I said, seeing the taxi driver smirking at us in his rear-view mirror.

To my utter surprise and delight, the taxi pulled up in front of Claridge's hotel, where Theo checked us in to a room. We proceeded to spend a glorious afternoon and evening making up for lost time. Before I switched off the light that night, I looked at him sleeping beside me, drinking him in. And knew I belonged wherever he was.

'Right, before we get on the train to Southampton, we have to pay a duty call,' Theo said as we ate breakfast in bed the next morning.

'Do we? To whom?'

'My mother. I'm sure I've told you she lives here in London and she's dying to meet you. So I'm afraid you'll have to get that perfect backside of yours out of bed while I take a shower.'

I got up and rifled through my belongings, fretting about the fact that I was – to all intents and purposes – about to meet my future mother-in-law. I didn't have anything smarter than the jeans, sweatshirts and trainers I'd packed for the rare evenings when I wasn't on the boat and dressed from head to toe in Gore-Tex – the weatherproof but deeply unsexy sister of Lycra.

I walked into the bathroom to hunt through my washbag for my token mascara and lipstick, but realised I must have left them at Atlantis. 'I don't even have any make-up with me,' I wailed to Theo through the shower door.

'Ally, I love you unadorned,' he said as he emerged from the steamy cubicle. 'You know how I loathe women who wear a lot of make-up. Now, can you hurry up and get into the shower? We need to leave pronto.'

Forty minutes later, after driving through a maze of streets that Theo told me were in an area of London called Chelsea, the taxi drew up outside a pretty white townhouse. Three marble steps led to the front door, on either side of which stood stone pots overflowing with sweet-smelling gardenias.

'Here we are,' he said as he bounded up the steps, took a key out of his pocket and unlocked the door. 'Mum?' he called as we entered the hallway and I followed him along a narrow corridor into an airy kitchen, dominated by a rustic oak table and a huge Welsh dresser crammed with brightly-coloured pottery.

'Out here, darling!' chimed a female voice through the open French windows.

We walked out onto a stone terrace, where a slim woman with dark blonde hair pulled back into a short ponytail was pruning roses in the small but abundantly stocked walled garden.

'Mum was brought up in the English countryside and tries to recreate it in the centre of London,' Theo murmured fondly as the woman looked up and acknowledged us both with a delighted smile.

'Hello, darling. Hello, Ally.'

As she walked towards me, the same intense gaze of her son fell upon me from her cornflower-blue eyes. I thought she was extraordinarily pretty, with the doll-like features and pale skin of the typical English rose.

'I've heard so much about you, I feel I know you already,' she said as she kissed me warmly on both cheeks.

'Hi, Mum,' Theo said as he hugged her. 'You're looking well.'

'Am I? I was counting the grey hairs in the mirror only this morning.' She gave a mock sigh. 'Sadly, age comes to us all. Now, what can I get you both to drink?'

'Coffee?' asked Theo as he looked at me enquiringly.

'Perfect,' I agreed. 'By the way, what's your mother's name?' I whispered to Theo as we followed her back into the house. 'I don't think I'm quite at the stage where I can address her as "Mum".'

'God, sorry! Her name is Celia.' Theo reached for my hand and squeezed it. 'Okay?'

'Yes, absolutely.'

Over coffee, Celia asked me about myself and then when I told her about Pa Salt's death, she comforted me with warmth and sympathy. 'I don't think any child recovers fully from the loss of a parent, especially a daughter who loses her father. I know I was devastated when I lost mine. The most you can hope for is acceptance. And it's still very early days for you, Ally. I hope my son isn't working you too hard,' she added, eyeing Theo.

'He really isn't, Celia. And to be honest, hanging around moping makes everything much worse. I find it's better to keep busy.'

'Well, I'll certainly be very glad when this Fastnet Race is over. And maybe when you have children of your own, you'll understand that my heart's in my mouth for the entirety of every race Theo enters.'

'Honestly, Mum. I've competed in it twice before and I know what I'm doing,' Theo protested.

'And he really is a magnificent skipper, Celia. His crew would do anything for him,' I added.

'I'm sure, and of course I'm extremely proud of him, but I do sometimes wish he'd chosen to be an accountant or a stockbroker, or at least something that wasn't quite so fraught with danger.'

'Come on, Mum, you're not normally so anxious. As we've discussed over and over again, I could get run over by a bus tomorrow. And besides, it's you who taught me to sail in the first place.' He nudged her affectionately.

'Forgive me, I'll shut up. As I said earlier, it must be old age setting in and all the maudlin thoughts that go with it. Talking of which, have you seen or heard from your father recently?' Celia asked him and I heard the slight edge to her voice.

Theo paused for a second before replying. 'Yes. He sent me an email saying he was at his house in the Caribbean.'

'Alone?' Celia raised an elegantly arched eyebrow.

'No idea. And neither do I care,' said Theo firmly, immediately changing the subject by asking his mother if she was going abroad during August.

I listened quietly as the two of them discussed her imminent plans for a week in the South of France and then a few days in Italy towards the end of the month. It was obvious from the easy way they spoke together that they completely adored each other.

After an hour or so, Theo drained his second cup of coffee and looked reluctantly at his watch. 'I'm afraid we have to be off, Mum.'

'Really? Won't you stay for a spot of lunch? I can knock together a little salad for us, it's really no trouble.'

'I'm afraid not. We've got a full crew meeting aboard the *Tigress* at five and it'd be rather poor form if the captain were late. So we're aiming to catch the twelve thirty train from Waterloo.' He stood up. 'I'll just nip to the bathroom and I'll see you both out in the hall.'

'It's been so good to meet you, Ally,' Celia said after Theo left the kitchen. 'When he told me that you were "the one", I was understandably nervous. He's my only child and is everything to me. But I can see now that you're perfectly matched.'

'Thank you for saying that. We're very happy,' I said with a smile.

As we rose from the table and made our way to the hall, she reached out her hand and placed it on my arm. 'Take care of him, won't you? He's never seemed to understand danger.'

'I'll do my best, Celia.'

'I—'

She was about to say more, when Theo reappeared beside us.

'Bye, Mum. I'll call you, but don't worry if you don't hear from me during race week.'

'I'll try not to,' Celia replied with a catch in her voice. 'And I'll be there to cheer you on at the finish line in Plymouth.'

I moved away towards the front door, not wishing to intrude on their goodbye, but I couldn't help noticing how Celia hugged him as if she couldn't bear to let him go. Eventually, Theo gently extricated himself, and she waved us off with a forced smile as we left the house.

On the train journey down to Southampton, Theo seemed distracted and unusually quiet.

'Are you all right?' I asked him as he gazed pensively out of the window.

'I'm just worried about Mum, that's all. She didn't seem herself today. She's never normally so gloomy; usually sends me off with a bright smile and a quick hug.'

'She obviously adores you.'

'And I her. She's made me everything I am, and has always championed my sailing. Maybe she *is* just getting old,' he concluded with a shrug. 'And of course, I doubt she'll ever get over my father and their divorce.'

'Does she still love him, do you think?'

'Almost certainly, although that doesn't necessarily mean that she *likes* him. How could she? When she found out about his string of affairs, she was beyond devastated. Poor Mum was so humiliated that even though it broke her heart, she asked him to leave.'

'God, how awful.'

'Yes, it is. Of course, Dad still adores her deep down too. They're both miserable apart, but I suppose there's always a thin line between love and hate. Maybe it's like living with an alcoholic: at some point, you have to make the decision between losing the person you love and your own sanity. And no one can save us from ourselves, however much they love us, can they?'

'No, they can't.'

Theo grasped my hand suddenly. 'Never let the same happen to us, will you, Ally?'

'Never,' I replied fervently.

The next ten days were – as always before a race – frenetic, tense and exhausting, made more so by the Fastnet's reputation as one of the toughest and most technically demanding races in the world. Regulations stated that 50 per cent of the crew must have completed 300 miles of offshore racing together within the past twelve months. On the first evening, as Theo gathered all twenty crew members together on the *Tigress*, I realised I was far less experienced than most of them. While Theo was well known for nurturing young talent and had included the crew from the Cyclades regatta, he was obviously taking no chances and had hand-picked the rest from amongst the crème de la crème of the international sailing fraternity.

The route was exacting and dangerous, taking in the south coast of England before crossing the Celtic Sea to Fastnet Rock on the coast of Ireland and then sailing back to finish in Plymouth. Strong westerly and south westerly winds, treacherous currents and notoriously unpredictable weather systems had put paid to many a boat's chances in previous races. And as we were all too aware, there'd been a number of fatalities over the years. No crew that entered approached the Fastnet lightly, least of all one like ours whose aim was to win.

We rose with the dawn each day and spent hours on the water, repeating the necessary manoeuvres over and over, testing the capabilities of both the crew and the superb state-of-the-art boat to their limits. During some training sessions, even though I could see that Theo was becoming frustrated when a member was not playing the 'team game' as he called it, he never once lost his cool. Over dinner each evening, strategy and tactics for every part of the race were discussed and refined endlessly, with Theo having the final say.

As well as actual sailing practice, we had several in-depth safety briefings and drills using the sophisticated safety equipment aboard and we were all issued with an EPIRB, a personal transmitter, to attach to our life vests. Even when we weren't under sail, the crew worked tirelessly on the boat, meticulously going over every last detail under Theo's watchful eye, from checking the kit inventory, to testing the pumps and winches, to rigging and checking the full sail wardrobe. Theo, amongst his many other duties as captain, allocated the bunks and a watch rotation system.

Thanks to his inspired leadership, *esprit de corps* was riding high by the time we received our final pep talk from him the night before the start of the race on 12th August. And each and every member of the crew stood up and cheered him.

We were now fully prepared. The only fly in the ointment was the appalling weather forecast for the next few days.

'I have to go to the Royal Ocean Racing Club now for the skippers' briefing, sweetheart,' Theo said to me with a quick peck on the cheek as the rest of the crew began to disperse. 'You go back to our hotel and take a long, hot bath. It's the last one you're going to get for a while.'

I did so, trying my best to enjoy the luxury of piping-hot water, but when I later looked out of the window, I saw the way the wind had picked up and was roaring in over the harbour, violently buffeting the two hundred and seventy one boats gathered in it and around the island. My stomach suddenly lurched. It was the last thing we needed and Theo's face was sombre when he joined me later in our hotel room.

'What news?' I asked him.

'All bad, I'm afraid. As we already knew, the forecast is dire, and they're even thinking they might have to put off the start of the race tomorrow. There's a severe weather warning out for gale-force winds. To be honest, Ally, it couldn't be worse.'

He sat down looking totally deflated and I went over to him and massaged his shoulders.

'Theo, you have to remember that it's only a race.'

'I know, but to win this would be the pinnacle of my career so far. I'm thirty-five, Ally, and I can't keep doing this forever. Damn it!' he said as he thumped the arm of the chair with his fist. 'Why this year?'

'Well, let's see what tomorrow brings. Weather forecasts are often wrong.'

'But the reality isn't,' he sighed, indicating the darkening skies outside. 'Anyway, you're right, there's nothing I can do. They're going to telephone all the skippers tomorrow morning at eight o'clock to let us know whether they'll delay the start. So it's my turn for a hot bath and an early night.'

'I'll go and run you one.'

'Thanks. And Ally?'

'Yes?' I turned as I walked towards the bathroom.

Theo smiled at me. 'I love you.'

As he'd feared, the race was delayed for the first time in its eighty-three-year history. The crew sat glumly together over lunch at the Royal London Yacht Club, each one of us watching the skies through the window and hoping for a miracle. Another decision would be made first thing in the morning, so after lunch, Theo and I traipsed despondently back to our hotel on the harbour.

'It will clear up eventually, Theo, it always does.'

'Ally, I've been on every possible internet site, not to mention contacting the meteorological centre personally, and it looks like there's a depression that's set in for the next few days. Even if we do manage to start the race, it's going to be unbelievably tough to make it to the finish. Anyway' – he looked at me and grinned suddenly – 'at least there's time for another hot bath.'

We ate dinner in the hotel restaurant together that Sunday evening, both of us feeling tense and unsettled. Theo even allowed himself a glass of wine, something he'd never normally do the night before a race, and we returned to our room a little calmer than when we'd left. He made love to me that night with particular urgency and passion; afterwards, he collapsed onto the pillows and pulled me into his arms.

Just as we were drifting off to sleep, I heard him say, 'Ally?'

'Yes?'

'If all goes well tomorrow, we'll be off. But it's going to be rough. I'm just reminding you now of the promise you made to me on "Somewhere". If I tell you I want you off the boat, you'll obey my orders as a skipper.'

'Theo, I—'

'Seriously, Ally, I can't put you aboard tomorrow unless I'm confident you'll do as you're told.'

'Then yes,' I replied with a shrug. 'You're my captain. I have to do as I'm told.'

'And before you say it again, it's not because you're a

woman, or that I doubt your proficiency in any way. It's because I love you.'

'I know.'

'Good. Sleep well, my love.'

The news came through early the next morning that the Fastnet Race would begin – a full twenty-five hours after the planned start. Having contacted the crew, Theo left for the boat immediately and I could see he was already focused and re-energised.

An hour later, I joined him with the rest of the crew aboard the *Tigress*. Even in the harbour, the boats were rocking perilously from side to side as the wind and waves battered them.

'Christ, and to think I could be skippering a luxury chartered yacht around the Caribbean right now,' muttered Rob, as we heard the gunfire to signal the start and waited tensely for our turn to leave the harbour. As we did so, Theo mustered us all on deck for a '*bon voyage*' photo.

Even the most seasoned sailors among us looked slightly green as we finally left the protection of the harbour. The extreme seas, swirled into a foaming frenzy by the wind, soaked each and every one of us in seconds.

Throughout the turbulent eight hours that followed, as the wind continued to gather pace, Theo remained calm, his balance rarely faltering as he helmed the boat through the wild water, issuing an almost constant stream of orders to keep us on course and maintain our speed. The sails were reefed and unreefed a dozen times as we negotiated the fiercely unpredictable conditions, including forty-knot squalls that seemed to blow up out of nowhere. And all the time, the slanting rain pounded down on us relentlessly.

Two of us had been assigned to galley duties that first day. We tried heating soup, but even using the gimballed stove which was designed to hold the pots level, the pitching of the boat was so violent that the contents still sloshed everywhere, scalding us on more than one occasion, so we resorted to microwaving some of the precooked ration packs. The crew came down in shifts, shivering in their race gear and too exhausted to remove it for the short time they were eating. But their looks of gratitude reminded me that in a race, the domestic tasks were equally as important as what went on above deck.

Theo was in the last shift to eat and as he wolfed his food down, he told me there were a number of vessels that had already decided to take shelter in various ports along the south coast of England.

'It's going to be a lot worse when we leave the Channel and we're out in the Celtic Sea. Especially in the dark,' he said as he looked at his watch. It was almost eight o'clock in the evening and the light was beginning to fade.

'What does everyone else think?' I asked him.

'They're all for going on. And I think the boat can take it—'

At that moment, we were both thrown off the benches as the *Tigress* gave a huge lurch to starboard and I yelped as the edge of the table dug sharply into my stomach. Theo – the man who I'd genuinely believed could walk on water – was now picking himself up from the floor.

'Okay, that's it,' he said as he saw me double over in pain. 'As you said, it's only a race. We're going into port.'

And before I could say anything, he was climbing the stairs to the deck two at a time.

An hour later, Theo helmed us into Weymouth harbour. All of us were soaked to the skin despite our high-tech weather-proof clothing, and completely exhausted. Once we'd anchored, taken down the sails and checked all the equipment for damage, Theo called us into the main cabin. We sat slumped wherever there was room in our orange race gear, looking like half-dead lobsters caught in a fisherman's net.

'It's too dangerous to carry on tonight, and I won't put any of your lives at risk. However, the good news is that nearly all the other boats in contention have already taken shelter, so we might still have an outside chance. Ally and Mick are going to cook some pasta for later and in the meantime, you can all take a shower in the order on the rota. As soon as the sun rises, we're off again. Someone put the kettle on so we can make some tea to warm up. We're going to need all our wits about us come the morning.'

Mick and I staggered to our feet and headed towards the galley. As we loaded a large pan with pasta and warmed the ready-made sauce, Mick made us cups of tea and I sipped mine gratefully, imagining the warmth flowing all the way into my cold toes.

'It could do with a splash of something stronger,' Mick said with a grin. 'You can understand why the sailors of old lived on rum, can't you?'

'Hey, Al, you're next for the shower,' called Rob.

'Don't worry, I'm fine to miss my turn and go later.'

'Good man,' he said appreciatively. 'I'll pretend to be you.'

Never had my dubious culinary skills been more appreciated than they were that night. Soon after we'd eaten and washed up the plastic bowls, everyone started dispersing to sleep while they could. As the boat wasn't designed for so many crew to sleep at the same time, people were arranging themselves on the benches or rolling themselves up in their lightweight sleeping bags on the floor.

I went to take my shower, wondering whether the freezing cold water, which was all that was left at the end of the queue, made me feel better or worse. I emerged to find Theo waiting for me outside.

'Ally, I need to talk to you.' He took me by the hand and pulled me through the now dimmed cabin full of inert bodies and into the tiny space crammed with navigation equipment that he called his 'office'. He made me sit down and took my hands in his.

'Ally, do you believe I love you?'

'Yes, of course.'

'And do you believe I think that you're an incredible sailor?'

'I'm not sure.' I gave him a quizzical half-smile. 'Why?'

'Because I'm not taking you any further in the race. There's a dinghy coming to collect you in a few minutes. You're booked in to a bed and breakfast on the harbour. Sorry,' he said. 'I just can't.'

'Can't what?'

'Risk it. The forecast is appalling, and I've already spoken to several other skippers who are talking of retiring. I think the *Tigress* can go on, but I simply can't have you on her. Do you understand?'

'No. I don't. Why me? Why not the others?' I protested.

'Please, darling, you know why. And' – he paused before he continued – 'if you want to know the truth, it makes it far harder for me to concentrate and get on with the job at hand while you're aboard.'

I stared at him in shock and bewilderment. 'I . . . Please let me stay, Theo,' I begged him.

'Not this time, no. We have many more races to run together, sweetheart. And a lot won't involve water. Let's not jeopardise those.'

'But why is it okay for you to continue when you're so worried about me doing the same? If other boats are thinking of retiring, then why won't you?' My anger was beginning to smoulder as his devastating announcement sank into my brain.

'Because this race has always been my destiny, Ally. I simply can't let everyone down. Right, you'd better pack up your kit. Your ride will be here any minute.'

'But what about *me* letting everyone down? What about me letting *you* down?' I said, wanting to shout at him but aware of the sleeping crew nearby. 'I'm meant to be your protectress!'

'You'll certainly be letting me down if you continue to argue with me,' he said sharply. 'Collect your things. Now. That's an order from your captain. Please obey it.'

'Yes, skipper,' I replied petulantly, knowing I must accept defeat. But as I went to retrieve my rucksack, I was furious with Theo for all sorts of confused reasons. Climbing up onto the deck, I saw the lights of the dinghy approaching across the harbour and went aft to let the ladder down.

Fully intending to leave without saying another word to Theo, I caught the painter that was thrown by the dinghy's skipper and secured it to one of the deck cleats as he drew alongside. I'd just mounted the ladder to climb down, when a torch flashed on my face from above.

'You're staying at The Warwick Guesthouse,' came Theo's voice.

'Right,' I said flatly, throwing my rucksack into the listing dinghy and taking another step down, before a hand grasped my arm and he pulled me back towards him.

'Ally, for God's sake, I love you. I love you . . .' he murmured as he folded me into his arms, my toes teetering on the top rung of the ladder. 'Never forget that, will you?'

Despite my anger, my heart melted. 'Never,' I said, taking the torch from his hand and shining it into his face, imprinting his features onto my memory. 'Keep safe, my darling,' I whispered, as Theo reluctantly let me go in preparation to release the painter, and I climbed down the steps and jumped into the waiting craft.

That night, exhausted as I was from the most arduous day's sailing I'd ever endured, I couldn't sleep. On top of which, having searched through my rucksack, I realised that in my hurry to leave the boat, I'd left my mobile on-board. Now I could have no direct contact with Theo and I kicked myself for my stupidity. As I paced around my room, I veered between indignation at being unceremoniously dumped ashore, and raw fear as I peered out at the rolling clouds and torrential rain in the harbour below me, and heard the continual clang of wind-blown rigging. I knew how much this race meant to Theo, but I worried that his wish to win could cloud his professional judgement. And suddenly I saw the sea for what it was: a roaring, uncontrollable beast that could reduce human beings to flotsam with its magnificent strength.

As a murky dawn began to emerge, I spotted the *Tigress* on the move once more, heading out of Weymouth harbour and into the open sea.

My fingers clasped my engagement necklace tightly, and I knew there was no more I could do. 'Goodbye, my love,' I whispered and watched the *Tigress* until it was a tiny dot tossed on the cruel waves of the open sea.

I spent the next few hours feeling completely cut off. Eventually, I realised it was pointless staying alone and miserable in Weymouth, so I packed my rucksack and set off by train and ferry back to Cowes. At least I would be near the Fastnet Control Centre and I could find out first-hand how things were going, rather than having to rely on the internet. All the boats had GPS trackers aboard, but I knew they were notoriously unreliable in rough weather.

Three and a half hours later, I checked into the same hotel Theo and I had stayed at during the practice and walked along to the Royal Yacht Squadron to see what I could find out. My heart sank as I recognised a number of crews who had begun the race with us gathered miserably in huddles around the tables.

Spotting Pascal Lemaire, a Frenchman I'd crewed with a few years ago, I went over to speak to him.

'Hi, Al,' he said in surprise. 'I didn't know the *Tigress* had retired.'

'She hasn't, or at least as far as I know. My skipper ordered me ashore yesterday. He thought it was too dangerous.'

'He's right, it is. Dozens of boats are either officially out of the race, or are waiting in port until the weather calms down. Our skipper made the decision to withdraw. It was hell out there for the smaller boats like ours. I've rarely seen weather like it. Your guys should be okay on a hundred-footer, though. That boat your boyfriend is sailing is as good as it gets,' he reassured me as he saw the anguished look in my eyes. 'Want a drink? There's a lot of us in here drowning our sorrows tonight.'

I accepted the offer, and joined the group as they inevitably began comparing the weather to that during the 1979 Fastnet Race, when one hundred and twelve boats had been knocked down by the waves and eighteen people, including three rescuers, had lost their lives. But after half an hour, distracted and nervous about the *Tigress* and Theo, I made my excuses and donned my fleece before walking down the rain-swept road to the Fastnet Control Centre, based at the Royal Ocean Racing Club a short distance away. I immediately asked if there was any information on the *Tigress*.

'Yes, she's a few miles past Bishop Rock at the moment and making good progress,' the operator said as he checked his screen. 'She's currently lying fourth. Mind you, at this rate, with the number of retirements being announced, she might win it by default,' he added with a sigh.

Comforted at least that as far as anyone could tell, all was well and Theo was safe, I walked back to the Royal Yacht Squadron and grabbed a sandwich as I watched more exhausted, bedraggled crews arrive. The wind had gathered pace again, I heard them saying, but I was too distracted to be able to engage in their conversations, so I wended my way back to the hotel and eventually managed to snatch a fitful couple of hours' sleep. In the end, I gave up and at five the next morning, as a grey dawn struggled to break, I was back at the Control Centre. As I walked in, a hush fell over the room.

'Any news?'

I watched the operators exchange anxious glances.

'What's happened?' I asked, my heart suddenly in my mouth. 'Is the *Tigress* all right?'

Again, the exchange of glances.

'We received a distress call at about three thirty this morning. Man overboard, apparently. A coastguard search and rescue helicopter was scrambled. We're still waiting for news.'

'Do they know who? What happened?'

'Sorry, love, we don't have any details at the moment. Why don't you go and get yourself a cup of tea and we'll let you know as soon as we hear anything.'

I nodded, trying to control the hysteria that was building inside me. The *Tigress* was a state-of-the-art craft, with a superb communications system. I knew they were lying to me about not knowing the details. And if they were, it could only mean one thing.

My heart was beating so fast, I thought I might pass out, and I headed for the sanctuary of the ladies, collapsing onto the toilet seat and gulping in breaths as panic overwhelmed me. Maybe I was wrong, maybe they simply couldn't divulge the details until they'd clarified exactly what had happened. But in the depths of my soul, I already knew.

11

A helicopter brought Theo's body back to the mainland. Kindly, the race director offered me a car to take me across to Southampton on the ferry later and then, if I wanted, to the hospital where his body would lie in the morgue.

'You and Theo's mother are down on his entry form as his next of kin. I'm sorry to say it, but one of you will probably have to . . . well . . . fill in the appropriate paperwork. Should I contact Mrs Falys-Kings or will you?'

'I . . . don't know,' I replied numbly.

'Perhaps I should do it. I'm very concerned that she might hear it on the radio or television. Sadly, this is going to be big news all over the world. I'm so very sorry, Ally. I won't give you the usual platitudes about Theo doing something he loved. I am simply devastated for you, for his crew and for sailing.'

I didn't reply. There were no words.

'Right then,' he said, obviously not knowing what else to do with me as I sat there catatonic in his office. 'Would you like me to take you back to your hotel so perhaps you can get some rest?'

I shrugged hopelessly, realising he meant well, but doubting I'd ever be able to 'rest' again. 'It's fine, thanks, I'll walk.'

'Anything I can do, Ally, please get in touch. You have my mobile number, so let me know if you want that car. The rest of the crew are currently sailing the *Tigress* back to Cowes. I'm sure they'll want to speak to you at some point, tell you exactly what happened, if you're up to it. And in the meantime, I'll make the phone call to Theo's mother.'

I trudged mindlessly back towards my hotel along the harbour front, stopping for a moment to stare out over the cruel grey sea. And as I stood there, I screamed obscenities at it, howling like a banshee, demanding to know why it had taken my father and now Theo away from me.

And at that moment, I swore to myself that I would never set foot on a boat again.

The next few hours were a void. I sat in my room, unable to think or feel or process anything.

All I knew was that now, there was nothing left.

Nothing.

The telephone rang by my bed and I stood up robotically to answer it. Reception told me there were some friends of mine waiting to see me downstairs. 'A Mr Rob Bellamy and three others,' the woman confirmed.

Through my numbness, I knew that, however painful it would be to face the crew, I had to go and hear how Theo had died. I told the receptionist to tell them I'd meet them in the hotel lounge.

When I entered the room, Rob, Chris, Mick and Guy were waiting for me. They too were in shock, could hardly look at me as they mumbled their condolences.

'We did everything we could . . .'

'So brave to dive in after Rob . . .'

'Nobody's fault, a tragic accident . . .'

I nodded and managed brief replies to their sympathetic words, giving my best impression of a functional human being. Finally, Mick, Chris and Guy got up to leave. But Rob said he'd stay.

'Thanks, boys,' I said, giving them a pathetic wave as they left.

'Al, if you'll excuse me, I need a drink.' Rob signalled to the waitress lolling by her service station in the corner. 'And before I tell you exactly what happened, so do you.'

Eventually, armed with a brandy each, Rob took a deep breath and I saw there were tears in his eyes.

'Please, Rob, just tell me,' I urged him.

'Okay. We were hove to, not underway, because the weather was so dire. I was up there on the foredeck doing my watch shift when Theo came to relieve me. Just as I'd unfastened my harness from the jackstay, a huge wave hit me and I was hurled off the boat and into the sea. Apparently I was knocked out, so I would have drowned for sure, but Theo raised the alarm, threw in the danbuoy and then leapt over the side himself. I was still out cold, but the rest of the boys were all on deck by this time and they told me that Theo somehow managed to swim to me, tow me to the danbuoy and prop me up inside it, but then another huge wave dragged him away from me and under the water. They completely lost sight of him after that, it was so dark and so rough, and you know as well as I do it's impossible to spot someone in the water in those conditions. If only he'd managed to stay clinging onto the buoy' – Rob stifled a sob – 'then he might have made it. The crew radioed for a rescue helicopter and they found me and winched me aboard, thanks to the light attached to the danbuoy. But Theo . . . well, they eventually located his . . . his . . . body an hour later by tracking the signal from his EPIRB. Christ, Al, I'm so bloody sorry. I can never forgive myself for this.'

For the first time since I'd heard, I felt some kind of real emotion flooding back into my veins. I put my hand on his. 'Rob, we all know the perils of sailing, and Theo knew them better than anyone else.'

'I know all that, Al, but if I hadn't unclipped my harness at that moment . . . shit!' he said as he put a hand to his brow to cover his eyes. 'You two were meant to be together . . . and it's my fault that now you won't be. You must hate me!'

Rob sobbed uncontrollably then and all I could do was pat his shoulder mechanically. The worst thing was, part of me *did* hate him, because he'd survived and Theo hadn't.

'It wasn't your fault. He did what any captain would have done, Rob. And I wouldn't have expected any less of him. Some things just . . .' I bit my lip to stop my own tears as I ran out of placations.

'Forgive me, Ally, it shouldn't be me sitting here blubbing.' Rob guiltily wiped his eyes. 'I just needed to confess how I felt.'

'Thank you. And I really appreciate you telling me the whole story. It can't have been easy for you, either.'

We sat in silence for a while before Rob made to stand up. 'Anything I can do, please call. And talking of which' – Rob dug into his jeans pocket – 'I found this in the galley. Is it yours?'

'Yes. Thanks.' I took my mobile from him.

'Theo saved my life,' he whispered. 'He's a bloody hero. I'm . . . sorry.'

I watched a despairing Rob leave the lounge, and sat there

thinking that now I'd seen the crew, there was nothing to keep me here. I was sure too that Celia would want to identify her son's body. As I stood up, desperate to leave this place that had formed the backdrop to my personal annihilation, I wondered where I should go. Home to Geneva, I supposed. But there too, I realised, a gaping hole of loss awaited me.

There was no sanctuary.

Entering my room, I began to pack mindlessly.

This time, I left my mobile off for the polar opposite reason to when I'd been on the boat with Theo. I was too devastated to speak to my family and tell them. Besides, none of my sisters knew about our relationship. I'd blithely assumed there would be plenty of time for them to meet Theo in the future. And given that he and I had known each other for such a short time, how could I explain to them what he'd meant to me? That even though we'd only been physically united for a few short weeks, I felt as though our souls had been together for a lifetime?

When Pa Salt had died, I supposed that at least it had been the natural order in the circle of life. And I'd had Theo there to comfort me, to offer me the hope of a new beginning. As I thought this, it dawned on me how much I'd relied on him to fill the yawning space that Pa had left behind. But now, he'd gone too. As had any dreams for the future. In a few bleak hours, not only Theo but my lifelong passion for sailing had been brutally snatched away from me.

Just as I was about to leave the room with my rucksack, the telephone on the bedside table rang.

'Hello?' I answered cautiously.

'Ally, it's Celia. The race director said you were staying at the New Holmwood Hotel.'

'I . . . hello.'

'How are you feeling?' she asked.

'Terrible,' I muttered, not having the strength to put on a brave face any longer. But understanding that at least with her, there was no need to. 'You?'

'The same. I've just come back from the hospital.'

There was silence from both of us, as we each digested the dreadful finality that her words represented. I could almost *feel* Celia fighting back the tears before speaking.

'I was wondering, Ally, where are you going now?'

'I'm not sure. I . . . don't know.'

'Then how about you come over on the ferry to Southampton? We can travel up to London together and you could come and stay with me for a few days. The rabid media attention this whole thing is starting to receive is a nightmare. We could put up the barricades and lie low at my house for a while. What do you think?'

'I think' – I gulped as tears spilled over my eyelids in grateful relief – 'that I'd love to.'

'You have my number, so let me know what time you'll be at Southampton railway station and I'll meet you there.'

'I will, Celia. And thank you.'

I have often thought since that if it hadn't been for Celia calling me at that darkest moment, I may well have thrown myself into the churning sea after Theo as the ferry had taken me across to Southampton.

When we met at the station, and I saw her sheet-white face, half hidden behind a pair of enormous black sunglasses, I ran into her open arms, exactly as I would have into Ma's. We stood there together for a long time, two relative strangers, yet bonded completely by our pain, each of us with the only other person we knew who could understand.

When we arrived at Waterloo, we took a cab to the pretty white house in Chelsea and Celia made us an omelette, both of us realising that we hadn't eaten a thing since the news. She also poured us each a large glass of wine and we sat out on the terrace in the warm, calm August evening.

'Ally, I need to tell you something. You may consider it absurd, but the thing is' – a huge shudder racked Celia's delicate frame – 'when you two were last here, I *knew*. When I kissed him goodbye, I felt it was forever.'

'Yes, Theo sensed your fear, Celia. He wasn't himself on the train back to Southampton after we'd seen you.'

'Was it my foresight he was feeling, or his own? Do you remember, he went to use the bathroom and said he would meet us in the hall just before you left? Well, after I'd shut the front door behind you both, I walked back towards the kitchen and found this propped up on the hall table, addressed to me.'

She pushed forward a large envelope and I saw the word '*Mum*' written in Theo's stylish looping hand on the front.

'I opened it,' Celia continued, 'and found a brand-new copy of his will inside, plus a letter to me. And also one to you, Ally.'

'I . . .' My hand went to my mouth. 'Oh God.'

'I've read mine, but yours is here, still unopened of course. Perhaps you can't bear to read it just yet, but I must give it to you, just as he asked me to do in my letter.'

She drew a smaller envelope from the larger one and handed it to me. I grasped it with shaking hands. 'But Celia, if he had a premonition, then why didn't he abort the race like so many other skippers did?'

'I think we both know why, Ally. As a sailor yourself, you realise that every time you board a boat at the start of a race, you're facing danger. As Theo said that day to both of us, he could easily have been run over by a bus,' she said, giving a sad shrug. 'Perhaps he simply felt it was his destiny to—'

'Die at the age of thirty-five?! Surely not? If he felt that, then how could he have loved me? He asked me to marry him! We had our entire lives in front of us. No.' I shook my head vehemently. 'I can't accept that.'

'Of course you can't, and you must forgive me for mentioning it, but I find it comforting in an odd way. Death is so confusing. None of us ever truly accepts the mortality of those we love. And yet, other than birth, it is the one definite thing that will happen to each and every one of us.'

I looked down at the unopened letter sitting in my hands. 'Maybe you're right, Celia,' I sighed in resignation. 'Yet why would he have left a new will or a note to both of us if he *hadn't* had some kind of premonition?'

'To be fair, you know Theo: always organised and efficient, even in death.'

This made us both smile, despite ourselves.

'Yes. Just like my father. Well, I suppose I should read his letter.'

'In your own time. And now, if you'll excuse me, Ally dear, I'm going to go up and have a long soak in the tub.'

Celia left me then, and I knew it was more to give me time alone than because she actually wanted a bath.

Taking a slug of wine, I put the glass down and, with trembling fingers, opened the envelope. It didn't escape me that this was the second letter from beyond the grave I had been given to read in the space of a few weeks.

From me, of no particular fixed abode
(In fact, I'm on a train from Southampton coming up to meet you at Heathrow)

My darling,

This is, I accept, a faintly ridiculous notion I've recently got into my head. But as you already know and my mother will reiterate, I'm nothing if not organised. She's had a copy of my will ever since I first began competing in races. Not that I have much to leave to anybody, but I think it's easier for those left behind if one makes everything clear.

And of course, now you've arrived in my life and become the centre of my universe and the person I hope to spend the rest of my life with, things have changed. Just because everything is 'unofficial' at present, until I put the ring on your finger to add to the chain you already wear around your neck, it seems vital to make sure everyone knows, at least financially, what our intentions are, in case anything happens to me.

I'm sure you will be overwhelmed and thrilled (hah!) when I tell you that I'm leaving you my goat barn on 'Somewhere'. I could see the night you first saw it how much you loved it (not) but the land it's on, with the planning permission, is worth something at least. ('Something on Somewhere' – a possible name for the house, do you think?) And I also want you to have the Neptune, *my current home on the sea. To be honest, those are my only material possessions of any value. Apart from my moped, but I think you'd be rightly insulted if I left you that. Oh, and I shouldn't forget the meagre trust fund I have from my generous father – that will at least pay for any further dodgy red wine you care to drink on 'Somewhere' in the future.*

Sorry, we're on a bumpy bit of track just now so forgive the appalling handwriting – I'm sure that I will be snatching this letter back from Mum the minute we come home from this race to at least type it up. But if by the faintest chance I don't, because I've copped it, I can rest easy that all is as I would wish it to be.

Now Ally – I might get emotional here – I want to tell you how much I love you and what you've meant to me in the short time we've known each other, which is everything. Literally, you've rocked my boat (hope you appreciate the seafaring analogy) and I can't wait to spend the rest of my life holding you as you vomit, discussing the origins of your weird surname and finding out each and every tiny thing about you as we grow old and toothless together.

And if by any chance you do get to read this, look up at the stars, and know I am looking down on you. And probably having a beer with your Pa as I hear all about your bad childhood habits.

My Ally – Alcyone – you have no idea what joy you've brought me.

Be HAPPY! That is your gift.
Theo xxx

I sat there in the fading evening, laughing and crying at the same time. The letter was so innately Theo that my heart broke all over again.

Celia and I met the following morning at breakfast. Last night, she'd shown me to my room but had not asked me a single thing about what the letter had contained and I was grateful for that. She told me that she had to go out to register Theo's death and arrange for his body to be brought back to London, and that we should decide together on a date for the funeral.

'Ally, there's also something else Theo said in his note to me. He asked if you would play your flute at his funeral.'

'Really?'

I looked at her, amazed by Theo's level of forward-thinking.

'Yes,' she sighed. 'He'd already issued instructions for the service years ago. A celebratory memorial-cum-funeral service, followed by a cremation – which by the way, he insisted no one was to attend. And then for his ashes to be scattered in Lymington harbour, where he first learnt to sail with me. Do you feel up to it?'

'I . . . don't know.'

'Well, he told me you played the flute beautifully. As you might guess, the music he chose isn't conventional, just as he wasn't. He wanted you to play "Jack's the Lad" from *Fantasia on British Sea Songs*. I'm sure you've heard it on the Last Night of the Proms?'

'Yes, I know it. I don't think there's a seafarer alive who

wouldn't at least know the melody – it's basically the tune of the old "Sailor's Hornpipe".'

I ran over some of the notes in my head, notes I'd played many years ago, but still knew intimately. Everything about the request was so Theo: it encapsulated his love for sailing and his innate joy in being alive.

'Yes, I think I'd love to play it.'

Then, for the first time since his death, I burst into tears.

During those next few dreadful days, we battened down the hatches as the media camped outside the door. We lived like recluses, only venturing out to buy food and both of us a black dress for the funeral. And as we went through the ghastly tasks that made me respect Pa Salt far more for his self-orchestrated burial, my respect for Celia also grew. Even though it was obvious Theo had been everything to her, she was never greedy with her grief.

'I don't suppose he ever mentioned it to you, Ally, but Theo always loved Holy Trinity Church on Sloane Street, not far from here. He went to a prep school a stone's throw away, and that was his local church. I remember watching him sing the solo in "Away in a Manger" at a carol service there when he was eight or so,' she said with a fond smile. 'What do you think about holding his funeral service there?'

The fact she was including my opinion in her decisions touched me beyond belief, even if my comments were irrelevant. She'd had a lifetime of knowing Theo – her only son – and yet she had the grace and empathy to see and understand what I felt for him. And what he had felt for me.

'Whatever you think is best, Celia, really.'

'Is there anyone you want to invite to the funeral?'

'Apart from who you've invited already, like the crew and the general sailing fraternity, no one knew us as a couple,' I replied honestly. 'So, I don't think they'd understand.'

But *she* did. And often, when we both found ourselves in the kitchen at three o'clock in the morning, when the pain was at its starkest, we'd sit at the table and talk endlessly about Theo, trying to find the comfort we craved. Small memories, of which Celia had a vast thirty-five-year reserve, whereas mine spanned only a matter of weeks. Through her, I came to know Theo better, and never tired of seeing a childhood picture, or reading a misspelt letter he'd written from boarding school.

However much I knew this was not reality, I was comforted that Celia and I were keeping him alive with every word we spoke. And that was the most important thing of all.

12

'Ready?' Celia asked me as our car arrived in front of Holy Trinity Church. I nodded, and with a quick squeeze of hands in mutual solidarity, we climbed out past the clicking cameras and walked inside. The church was cavernous and the sight of it packed to bursting with standing room only at the back almost reduced me to the tears I'd sworn I would not shed.

Theo was already waiting for me on the altar as I walked down the aisle towards his coffin with Celia. I swallowed hard at this dreadful parody of the wedding we might have celebrated, had he lived.

Taking our seats in the front pew, the service began. Theo had chosen a mixture of music for his memorial service. After the vicar's address, it was my turn. I joined the small orchestra of violins, a cello, two clarinets and an oboe that Celia had managed to gather together at the front of the church. Sending up a silent prayer, I placed the lip plate of the flute to my mouth and began to play. And as the rest of the orchestra joined me, and the tempo became faster, I saw the congregation begin to smile, and then, one by one, rise. Until they were all on their feet, performing the traditional bended-knee movement of the 'Sailor's Hornpipe' jig, every one of them with their arms crossed and held out in front of them. Our little orchestra upped the pace, playing as if our lives depended on it as the congregation bobbed faster and faster up and down in time to the music.

As we finished, a roar went up from them, and the cheers and clapping began. There was an encore, as of course there always was whenever the piece was played. I took myself and my flute back to the front pew and sat down beside Celia. She squeezed my hand tightly.

'Thank you, my darling Ally, thank you so very much.'

Then Rob walked to the front of the church, ascended the steps in front of Theo's coffin and adjusted the microphone.

'Theo's mother, Celia, has asked me to say a few words. As you all know, Theo lost his life saving mine. I can never thank him now for what he did for me that night, but I know his sacrifice has brought terrible suffering to Celia and to Ally, the woman he loved. Theo, from everyone who has ever crewed with you, we send our love, respect and thanks. You were simply the best. And Ally' – he looked directly at me – 'this is what he asked to be played for you.'

Again, I felt Celia's hand on mine, as one of the choir stood up and gave a beautiful rendition of 'Somewhere', from *West Side Story*. I tried to smile at the secret joke that Theo had meant for me, but the poignancy of the words moved me beyond measure. As it finished, eight of Theo's crew members from the Fastnet Race, including Rob, gently hoisted the coffin onto their broad shoulders and began to file out of the church. Celia led me with her, the first in the procession of mourners who fell in behind the coffin.

As we made our way out, I saw some familiar faces sitting in the church. Star and CeCe were among the crowd, smiling at me with love and sympathy as I passed them. Celia and I stood outside on Sloane Street, watching as Theo's coffin was placed in the hearse that would take his body on its solitary journey to the crematorium. As it drew away and we both said a silent final goodbye, I turned to her and asked how my sisters had known.

'Theo asked me in his letter to contact Marina if anything happened to him, so that she and your sisters would be aware. He thought you might need them.'

The congregation gradually trickled out of the front of the church and milled around on the pavement, greeting each other quietly. Several people made a beeline for me, mostly sailing friends, all offering their condolences and expressing surprise at my hitherto hidden musical talent. I glanced around me and saw a tall man wearing a suit and dark glasses standing apart from the crowd. Something about him looked so desolate that I excused myself from the pack and went over to him.

'Hello,' I said. 'I'm Ally, Theo's girlfriend. I've been told to tell everyone that they're welcome to come back to Celia's house for something to eat and drink. It's only five minutes' walk from here.'

He turned to me, his glasses shielding any expression in his eyes. 'Yes, I know where it is. I used to live there.'

And then I realised this man was Theo's father. 'I'm very pleased to meet you.'

'I'm sure you can probably understand that, however much I'd like to come back, unfortunately I won't be welcome.'

I didn't know how to answer him, just looked at my feet, embarrassed. It was obvious he was grief-stricken and whatever had happened in the past between him and his wife, he had lost a son too.

'That's a shame,' I managed.

'You must be the girl Theo told me he was going to marry. He sent me an email just a few weeks ago,' he continued in his soft American drawl, so different to Theo's clipped English tones. 'I'm going to leave now, but here, Ally, take my card. I'm in town for the next few days and it would be great to talk to you about my son. Despite what I'm sure you've heard about me, I loved him very much. I guess you're bright enough to know there's always another side to every story.'

'Yes,' I replied, remembering Pa Salt once telling me exactly the same thing.

'You'd better get back, but it's been great to meet you. Bye for now, Ally,' he said as he turned and walked slowly away from me. I felt despair leaking from his every pore.

Turning back to the rest of the crowd, I saw CeCe and Star waiting respectfully for me to finish my conversation. I walked towards them and they both threw their arms around me.

'My God, Ally,' said CeCe. 'We've all been leaving you messages on your mobile since we heard! We're so, so sorry, aren't we, Star?'

'Yes.' Star nodded and I realised she was close to tears herself. 'It was such a beautiful service, Ally.'

'Thank you.'

'And wonderful to hear you playing the flute. You haven't lost your touch,' CeCe added.

I saw Celia waving to me and indicating the large black car waiting at the kerb.

'Listen, I have to go with Theo's mum, but will you come back to the house?'

'I'm afraid we can't,' CeCe said. 'But listen, our apartment's only over the bridge in Battersea, so when you're feeling a bit better, just give us a bell and pop round, yes?'

'We'd really love to see you, Ally,' said Star, giving me another hug. 'All the girls send their love to you. Take care of yourself, won't you?'

'I'll try. And thanks again for coming. I can't tell you how much I appreciate it.'

As I climbed into the car, I watched the two of them walk down the road together, and felt hugely touched by their presence.

'Your sisters are so sweet. What a wonderful thing it is to have siblings. Like Theo, I'm an only child,' Celia commented as the car moved away from the kerb.

'Are you okay?' I asked her.

'No, but it was the most wonderful, uplifting service. And I can't tell you what it meant to me to hear you play.' She paused for a few seconds then sighed heavily. 'I noticed you talking to Theo's father, Peter, just now.'

'Yes.'

'He must have been hiding at the back of the church. I didn't see him when I came in. If I had, I'd have asked him to come and sit up front with us.'

'Would you?'

'Of course! We may not be the best of friends anymore, but I'm sure he's as equally devastated as I am. I presume he said he wouldn't come back to the house?'

'Yes, although he did say he was in town for a few days and would like to see me.'

'Oh dear. It's so dreadfully sad that we couldn't even be reunited for our own son's funeral. Anyway,' she said as the car pulled up in front of the house, 'I'm so grateful for your support. I couldn't have got through this without you, Ally. Now, let's go and greet our guests and celebrate our boy's life.'

A couple of days later, I woke up in the comfortable, rather dated guest room in Celia's house. Flower-sprigged Colefax and Fowler curtains hung at the windows, matching the counterpane of the large wooden bed I was lying in and coordinating with the now faded striped wallpaper. I glanced at the clock and saw that it was almost half past ten. Since the memorial service, I'd finally begun to sleep again, but almost unnaturally heavily and I would wake in the morning as if I had a hangover, or had taken one of the sleeping pills that Celia had offered me but I'd refused. I lay in the dim light feeling just as exhausted as when I'd gone to bed – even though I'd slept solidly for over ten hours – and contemplated the fact that I really couldn't continue to hide away here with Celia, comforted as we were by our endless talk of Theo. Celia was off to Italy tomorrow and even though she'd kindly said I was welcome to join her, I knew I must move on.

The question was, where I would go from here?

I'd already decided that I'd contact the Swiss national sailing team coach to tell him I wouldn't be joining him and the crew for the Olympic trials. Even though Celia had told me repeatedly that I mustn't allow what had happened to ruin my future and diminish my passion, every time I thought about getting back on the water, a shiver ran through me. Perhaps one day it would pass, but not in time to begin what I knew would be months of arduous training for the most important sporting event on the planet. There would be too many people at the training camp who'd known Theo, and even though talking to his mother had provided a wonderful outlet, I felt incredibly vulnerable when anyone else mentioned him.

But now that I was without Theo and also no longer sailing, the days in front of me were suddenly empty, an endless void I had no idea how to fill.

Perhaps, I mused, I was the new 'Maia' of the family, destined to return to Atlantis and grieve in solitary splendour as she once had. I was fully aware that Maia had taken wing and flown off to her new life in Rio, which meant I could easily go home and install myself in her nest at the Pavilion.

What I had come to understand from the past few weeks was that I had lived a gilded life before, and if I was to judge myself and my faults, I would have to acknowledge that I had always looked down on anyone weaker than myself. I hadn't understood why they couldn't get up, dust themselves down from whatever trauma they had borne and move on. Brutally, I'd begun to realise that until one had experienced loss and deep pain oneself, it was impossible to truly empathise with others in the same predicament.

Trying desperately to remain positive, I told myself that at least what had happened to me would perhaps make me a better person. And inspired by this thought, I eventually pulled out my mobile. I was ashamed to admit that I hadn't turned it on since Theo's death, over two weeks ago now. Seeing the battery was dead again, I plugged it in to charge. I went to take a shower and as I did so, heard the insistent 'pings' of the backlog of voicemails and texts arriving as the mobile came back to life.

Drying myself and getting dressed, I mentally prepared myself before picking up my phone and scrolling through the endless text messages from Ma and my sisters, and the countless others who had heard about Theo. **Ally, I wish I could be there with you, I can't imagine how you must be feeling, but I'm sending you all my love,** Maia had written. **Ally, I've tried to call you, but you're not picking up. Ma's told me and I'm devastated for you. I'm here for you, Ally, night and day, if you need me. Tiggy x.**

Then I moved on to the voicemails. Doubtless most of them, like the texts, would be from people offering condolences. But as I dialled in to retrieve them, my stomach did a flip when I heard the oldest message left ten days ago. It was a bad connection and his words sounded muffled, but I knew it was Theo.

> **'Hi, my love. I'm calling on the satellite phone while I've got the chance. We're sitting out somewhere in the Celtic Sea. The weather is bloody awful and even my famous sea legs have deserted me. I know you're cross I kicked you off the boat, but before I try and get a couple of hours' kip, I just want you to know it's got absolutely nothing to do with your sailing abilities. And to be honest, I wish you were aboard now, as you're worth ten of the men here. You know it has everything to do with the fact that I love you, my darling Ally. And I just hope you'll still be speaking to me when I get back! Goodnight, sweetheart. I love you, again. Bye.'**

I abandoned all thought of listening to other waiting messages and simply replayed Theo's again, and again, soaking in every word. I knew from the time it was left that he must have called only an hour or so before he went onto the deck to see Rob being hurled off it. And went to his death to save him. I wasn't sure how you saved a message forever, but I knew I had to find out.

'I love you too,' I whispered. And any last vestiges of anger that I'd held inside me about him ordering me off the boat that day dissipated into the air.

Over breakfast, Celia told me she was heading out to do some last-minute shopping for Italy.

'Have you decided where you're going next, Ally? You know you'd be more than welcome to stay here while I'm away. Or come with me. I'm sure you could get a last-minute flight to Pisa.'

'Thanks, it's so very kind of you, but I think I'll probably go home,' I said, worrying that I might be becoming a burden to Celia.

'Whatever you decide. Just let me know.'

After she'd left the house, I went upstairs and decided I was strong enough to give CeCe and Star a call. I dialled CeCe's number first, as she was the one that arranged everything for both of them, but it went to voicemail and so I called Star instead.

'Ally?'

'Hello, Star. How are you?'

'Oh, I'm well. But more importantly, how are you?'

'I'm okay. I was thinking I might pop round and see you tomorrow.'

'Well, I'll be by myself. CeCe's off to take photographs of Battersea Power Station. She wants to use it as inspiration for one of her art projects before it's turned into a new development.'

'Can I just come and see you then?'

'That would be lovely.'

'Good. When's the best time?'

'I'm here all day, Ally. Why don't you come for lunch?'

'Okay, I'll come over around one. See you tomorrow, Star.'

As I ended the call, I sat on my bed and realised that tomorrow's lunch would be the first time I'd ever spent more than a few minutes with my younger sister without CeCe present too.

I took my laptop out of my rucksack, thinking I should check my emails. I set it up on the dressing table, and plugged it in. There were further messages of condolence and the usual spam, including a girl supposedly called 'Tamara' offering me comfort now the nights were drawing in. Then I saw another name I didn't immediately recognise: Magdalena Jensen. After a few moments, I remembered she was the translator who was working on the book from Pa Salt's library for me and thanked God I hadn't pressed 'delete'.

From: Magdalenajensen1@trans.no
To: Allygeneva@gmail.com
Subject: 'Grieg, Solveig og Jeg / Grieg, Solveig and I
20th August 2007

Dear Ms D'Aplièse,

I am thoroughly enjoying translating Grieg, Solveig og Jeg. It's a fascinating read, and not a story I have come across before here in Norway. I thought you might be interested to start reading through the manuscript, so I have attached the pages I have done so far, up to page 200. I should have the remainder with you in the next ten days.

With kind regards,

Magdalena

Opening the attachment that contained the translation, I read the first page. And then the second, and by the third, I'd moved the laptop and plugged it in by the bed so that I could make myself comfortable while I continued . . .

Anna

Telemark, Norway

August 1875

13

Anna Andersdatter Landvik paused as she waited for Rosa, the oldest cow in the herd, to make her way down the steep slope. As usual, Rosa had been left behind by the others who had all moved on to fresh pastures.

'Sing to her, Anna, and she'll come,' her father always told her. 'She'll come for you.'

Anna sang a few notes of '*Per Spelmann*', Rosa's favourite song, and the tune flowed out of her, ringing bell-like down the valley. Knowing that it would take Rosa a while to lumber towards her, Anna sat down on the rough grass, folding her slender body into her favourite thinking position, with her knees tucked up to her chin and her arms wrapped around them. She breathed in the still warm evening air and admired the view, humming along to the buzzing of the insects in the field. The sun was beginning to sink towards the mountains on the other side of the valley, making the water of the lake below shimmer like molten rose-gold. Soon it would disappear completely and night would fall quickly.

In the last two weeks, as she'd counted the cows down from the mountainside, dusk had fallen noticeably earlier each day. After months of it being light until almost midnight,

Anna knew that tonight, her mother would have lit the oil lamps by the time she got back to the cabin. And that her father and younger brother would have arrived to help them close up the summer dairy and move the livestock back down the valley in preparation for winter. This event heralded the end of the Nordic summer and was the advent of what, for Anna, felt like interminable months of near perpetual darkness. The vivid green of the mountainside would soon be wearing a coat of thick white snow and she and her mother would leave the wooden dwelling where they spent the warmer months and return to their family farm just outside the small village of Heddal.

As Rosa came towards her, stopping occasionally to snuffle at some grass, Anna sang a few more lines of the song to encourage her. Her father, Anders, didn't think Rosa would see another summer. No one seemed to know exactly how old the animal was, but she was certainly not much younger than Anna's own eighteen years. The thought of Rosa no longer being there to greet her, with what she liked to think of as a look of recognition in her soft amber eyes, caused tears to well in her own eyes. The additional thought of the long, dark months ahead sent the brimming drops spilling down Anna's cheeks.

At least, she reflected, wiping them away hastily, she would get to see Gerdy and Viva, her cat and dog, when they returned to their farmhouse in Heddal. There was nothing Anna liked better than curling up in front of the warm stove, eating sweet *gomme* on bread, with Gerdy purring on her lap and Viva waiting to lick up the crumbs. Although she knew her mother wouldn't let her get away with just sitting around dreaming all winter.

'You'll have your own home to look after one day, *kjære*, and I won't be there to feed you and your husband!' her mother, Berit, told her regularly.

From churning butter, to darning clothes, feeding the chickens, or rolling out *lefse*, the flatbreads her father devoured by the dozen, Anna had little interest in her domestic duties and certainly had no thought of feeding an imaginary husband just yet. As hard as she had tried – and if she was completely honest with herself, she knew she didn't try hard enough – the results of her endeavours in the kitchen were often inedible or verging on disastrous.

'You've been making *gomme* for years, yet still it tastes no better,' her mother had remarked only last week, plopping down a bowl of sugar and a jug of fresh milk onto the kitchen table. 'It's high time you learnt to do it properly.'

But whatever Anna did, her *gomme* always turned out scrambled and burnt on the bottom. 'Traitor,' she had whispered to Viva, as even the ever-hungry farm dog had turned up her nose at it.

Although she had left school four years ago, Anna still missed the third week of every month when Frøken Jacobsen, the teacher who divided her time between the villages of Telemark county, had arrived with new things for them to learn. She had much preferred it to the strict lessons of Pastor Erslev, when they had to recite bible passages by rote and were tested in front of the whole class. Anna had hated it and had always felt hot at sensing everyone's eyes on her as she'd stumbled over unfamiliar words.

The pastor's wife, Fru Erslev, was much kinder and had more patience with her when she was learning hymns for the church choir. And often these days, she was given the solo part. Singing was so much easier than reading, Anna thought. When she sang, she simply closed her eyes, opened her mouth and a sound that seemed to please everyone came out of it.

Sometimes, she'd dream of performing in front of a congregation in a big church in Christiania. When she was singing, it was the one time she felt of any worth. But in reality – as her mother always reminded her – beyond singing the cows home and one day lulling her babies to sleep, she felt her talent was of little use. All her contemporaries from the choir were now either engaged to be married, or married, or suffering the consequences of what happened once they were. Which seemed to be that they felt sick and became fat, and eventually produced a red-faced, squawking baby and had to stop singing.

At the wedding of her elder brother, Nils, she had endured nudges and hints from the extended family about her own future nuptials, but as no suitor had so far volunteered for the position with Anna, this winter it would only be herself left behind with the *gammeljomfruene*, as her younger brother, Knut, called the unmarried older women of the village.

'God willing, you will find a husband who can ignore the food on his plate and instead gaze into those pretty blue eyes of yours,' her father, Anders, often teased her.

She knew that the question which lay in her family members' minds was whether Lars Trulssen – who had regularly partaken of her burnt offerings – would be that brave man. He and his ailing father lived on the neighbouring farm in Heddal. Her own two brothers had made Lars – an only child and motherless from the age of six – the unofficial third and he was often found at the Landvik family supper table in the evenings. She remembered how they had all played together in the long winters on the days when it snowed. Her rough and boisterous brothers had enjoyed burying each other in the snow, the distinctive red-gold Landvik hair marking them out in the white landscape. While, much to their dismay, the far more gentle Lars had always gone inside to read a book.

As the eldest son, Nils would, in the normal course of things, have remained with his new wife at the Landvik homestead after their marriage. But the recent death of his wife's parents had meant that she had inherited their farm in a village a few hours from Heddal and Nils had moved there to take over the running of it. It was left to Knut to spend all his time out on the Landvik farm helping their father.

So Anna often found herself sitting alone with Lars, who still came to visit regularly. He would sometimes tell her about the current book he was reading, and she would strain to hear his quiet voice as he told her fascinating stories of other worlds that seemed so much more exciting than Heddal.

'I've just finished *Peer Gynt*,' he told her one evening. 'The book was sent to me by my uncle in Christiania and I think you'd enjoy it. I believe it's Ibsen's best so far.'

Anna had looked down, not wanting to admit that she had no idea who Ibsen was, but Lars hadn't judged her and had told her all about Norway's greatest living playwright, who apparently came from Skien, a town very close to Heddal, and who was making Norwegian literature and culture known to the world. Lars said he'd read everything Ibsen had written. In fact, it seemed to Anna that Lars had read most books *anyone* had written, and had even confided in her his dreams of someday becoming a writer himself.

'But that isn't likely to happen here,' he had told her, his blue eyes nervously meeting hers. 'Norway is so small and many of us are ill-educated. But I hear that in America, if you work hard enough, you can be anything you want to be . . .'

Anna knew that Lars had even taught himself to read and write English in preparation for such an event. He wrote poems in the language and said he'd be sending them off soon to a publisher. Whenever he began talking about America, Anna felt a pang because she knew that he could never afford such a thing. His father was crippled with arthritis, his hands permanently frozen into semi-fists, so Lars now ran the farm single-handedly, still living in the dilapidated farmhouse.

When Lars was absent from the supper table, Anna's father often lamented how the Trulssen family land had been left untended properly for years, their pigs running riot and churning the soil so it became depleted and barren. 'No better than a bog, with all of this rain we've had recently,' her father would say. 'But that boy lives in the world of his books, not the real world of fields and farms.'

One evening last winter, as she'd been attempting to decipher the words to a new hymn that Fru Erslev had given her to learn, Lars had looked up from his book and watched her from the other side of the kitchen table.

'Want some help?' he'd asked her.

Blushing as she'd realised she had been sounding out the same words over and over in an effort to get them right, she'd debated whether she wanted him closer as he always smelt so terribly of pig. She'd eventually nodded shyly and he'd moved to sit next to her. Together, they had gone over each word until she felt she could read the hymn all the way through without a pause.

'Thank you for helping me,' she had said.

'My pleasure,' he'd replied with a blush. 'If you like, Anna,

I could help you to improve your reading and writing. As long as you promise to sing for me sometimes.'

Knowing her reading and writing had suffered through four years of neglect since she had left school, Anna had agreed. And after that, on many nights during the last winter, they had sat at the kitchen table, their heads together, Anna completely foregoing her embroidery, much to her mother's disgruntlement. They had quickly moved on from hymns to books that Lars had brought with him from home, wrapped in wax paper in order to keep the incessant snow and rain off the precious pages. And after they had worked, the books were closed and Anna would sing for him.

Although her parents had at first been concerned that she was becoming too bookish, they enjoyed listening to Anna read to them in the evenings.

'I'd have escaped from those trolls much faster,' she'd announced to them after reading *The Three Princesses of Whiteland* one night at the fireside.

'But one of the trolls had six heads,' Knut had pointed out.

'Six heads just slow you down,' she'd said with a grin.

She'd practised her writing too and Lars had chuckled when he'd seen how tightly she gripped the pencil, her knuckles white with tension.

'It's not going to run away from you,' he'd said, adjusting her hand around the pencil, carefully placing each finger in the right position.

One night, he'd shrugged on his wolf-skin coat to ward off the bitter cold and opened the door. As he'd done so, snowflakes the size of butterflies had blown through it. One landed on Anna's nose and Lars shyly reached out to wipe it away before it could melt. His big hand had felt rough on her skin and he'd quickly stuck it back in his coat pocket.

'Good night,' he'd murmured, before venturing out into the winter darkness, the flakes of snow melting on the floor as the door closed behind him.

Anna stood up as Rosa finally reached her. As she stroked the cow's velvety ears and then kissed the white star in the centre of her forehead, she couldn't help noticing the grey hairs around Rosa's soft pink mouth.

'Please be here next summer,' she murmured softly to her.

Having satisfied herself that Rosa was making her way slowly in the direction of the rest of the herd, grazing peacefully on the dusky slope below, Anna set off towards the cabin. As she walked, she decided that she was just not ready for change; all she wanted was to come back here every summer and sit in the fields with Rosa. Her family might think she was naive, but Anna knew exactly what was planned for her. And she remembered vividly the strange way Lars had behaved when he'd said goodbye to her for the summer.

He had given her the *Peer Gynt* poem by Ibsen to read, gently clasping one of her hands in his as she held the book in front of her. And she had frozen. His touch had signified a new kind of intimacy, very unlike the brother-and-sister relationship she had always thought they had. As her eyes had wandered to his face, she'd seen a different expression in his intense blue eyes and suddenly, he'd felt like a stranger. She had gone to bed that night, shuddering at the look he'd given her, for she knew exactly what it contained.

It seemed that her parents had already known of Lars' intentions.

'We could always buy the Trulssen land as Anna's dowry,' she had overheard her father saying to her mother late one night.

'Surely, we can find someone from a better family for Anna,' Berit had replied in a hushed voice. 'The Haakonssens still have an unmarried son, down in Bø.'

'I'd like to have her settled close by,' Anders had replied firmly. 'Buying the Trulssen land would mean no income at all for perhaps three years whilst the soil recovers, but if it does, then it would double our crop yield. I think Lars is the best that we can hope for, given Anna's . . . shortcomings.'

The comment had stung and Anna had grown ever more resentful as her parents had begun to openly discuss possible wedding plans for her and Lars. She wondered if they would ever simply ask her if *she* wanted to marry Lars. But they didn't, so Anna refrained from telling them that even though she liked him, she certainly wasn't convinced that she could love him.

Although she'd occasionally imagined what it would be like to kiss a man, she wasn't at all sure she'd like it in reality. And as for the other unknown thing – the act she knew had to happen in order to have children – well, that was something she could only guess at. Occasionally at night she'd hear a strange creaking and moaning from her parents' bedroom, but when she'd asked Knut about it, he'd only sniggered furtively and said it was how they had all arrived on the earth. If it was anything like when the bull was brought to a cow . . . Anna winced at the very idea, remembering how the bellowing creature had to be encouraged to clamber on top of its female conquest, with the farmhand helping to get the 'thing' inside her so she'd calf a few months later.

She only wished she could ask her mother if it was a similar process with humans, but could never pluck up the courage to do so.

What made it worse was that this summer she had struggled through *Peer Gynt*, and even now, having endlessly mulled the story over, she could not think for the life of her why the poor peasant girl at the centre of it – Solveig was her name – had wasted her whole life waiting for a dreadful, philandering man like Peer. And then, when he *did* return, taking him back and resting his lying, cheating head on her knee.

'I would have used it as a ball for Viva to play with,' she muttered as she neared their homestead. And the one thing she had categorically decided this summer was that she could never, *ever* marry a man she didn't love.

Reaching the end of the path, she saw the sturdy wood cabin up ahead, unchanged for generations. The turfed roof stood out as a bright, healthy green square amongst the darker foliage of the spruce trees in the forest that surrounded it. Anna took a scoop of water from the barrel that stood beside the front door and washed her hands to rid them of the smell of cow before stepping inside the cheerful sitting-room-cum-kitchen, where, as she'd predicted, the oil lamps were already lit and burning brightly.

The room housed a large table covered with a checked cloth, a carved pine dresser, an old wood-fired oven and a huge open fireplace, over which she and her mother heated the iron pot that was filled with porridge for breakfast and supper and meat and vegetables for the midday meal. To the rear of the cabin were the sleeping quarters: her parents' bedroom, Knut's bedroom, and the tiny bedroom where she herself slept.

Taking one of the lamps from the table, she crossed the well-worn wooden floor and pushed open the door to her room. The space was only just wide enough for her to squeeze through, since the bedstead butted right up to the door. Setting the lamp down on the nightstand, she removed her bonnet so that her hair fell in a curly Titian mane past her shoulders.

Picking up her faded looking glass, Anna sat down on the bed and checked her face, wiping away a smudge of dirt from her forehead to make herself presentable before supper. She studied her reflection in the cracked surface for a moment. She did not consider herself particularly comely. Her nose seemed far too small in comparison to her big blue eyes and full, curved lips. The only good thing about the winter coming, she reflected, was that the freckles which liberally peppered the bridge of her nose and her cheeks in the summer would subside and go into hibernation with her until next spring.

Sighing, she put the looking glass down, then manoeuvred herself out of the door and checked the clock on the kitchen wall. It was seven o'clock, and she was surprised that no one seemed to be at home, especially as she knew that her father and Knut were expected.

'Hello?' she called out, but there was no reply. Stepping outside into the fast-falling dusk, Anna walked round to the back of the cabin where a solid pine table sat on the rough earth. To her surprise, she saw her parents and Knut sitting with a stranger, whose face was illuminated by the glow of the oil lamp.

'Where on earth have you been, child?' asked her mother, rising from her seat.

'Checking the cows were down from the mountain, as you asked me to do.'

'You left hours ago,' chided Berit.

'I had to search for Rosa; the others had left her miles away on her own.'

'Well, at least you're back now.' Berit sounded relieved. 'This gentleman has travelled here with your father and brother to meet you.'

Anna glanced at the gentleman, wondering why on earth he'd do such a thing. No one had ever come 'to meet her' anywhere in her entire life. As she looked at him more closely, she saw that he was not from the country. He was dressed in a dark tailored jacket with wide lapels and a silk cravat at the neck, as well as flannel trousers that, although mud-spattered at the hem, were the kind worn by smart people from the big cities. He had a large moustache that turned up at each end, rather like the horns on top of a goat's head, and Anna guessed from the lines on his face that he was in his middle fifties. As she studied him, she could see that he was apprais-ing her too. Then he smiled at her, and the smile was full of approval.

'Come, Anna, and meet Herr Bayer.' Her father beckoned to her as he filled the gentleman's tin mug with home-made beer from the large jug on the table.

Anna walked tentatively towards the man, who immedi-ately stood up and held out his hand. She offered hers in return, and instead of shaking it, he clasped it in both of his.

'Frøken Landvik, I am privileged to make your acquaint-ance.'

'Are you?' she said, taken aback by the enthusiasm of his greeting.

'Anna, don't be rude!' admonished her mother.

'No, please,' the gentleman replied. 'I'm sure Anna didn't mean it to sound so. She is simply surprised to see me. I'm sure it's not every day your daughter arrives home at her hill-side retreat to find a stranger waiting for her. Now, Anna, if you will sit down, I will explain why I am here.'

Her parents and Knut looked on expectantly as she did so.

'Firstly, allow me to introduce myself. My name is Franz Bayer and I am a professor of Norwegian history at the University of Christiania. I am also a pianist and a music teacher. I and my like-minded friends spend most summers in Telemark county researching the national culture that you good people preserve so well in these parts, and seeking out young musical talent to represent it in the capital city of Christiania. When I arrived in the village of Heddal, I went as I always do in the first instance to the church, and there I met Fru Erslev, the wife of the pastor. She told me that she runs the choir and when I asked her if she had any exceptional voices amongst her ranks, she told me of yours. Naturally, I presumed you would be in the local vicinity. Then she informed me that you spent your summers up here, almost a day's travel away by horse and cart, but that fortuitously your father might be able to provide me with transport, which he did.' Herr Bayer dipped a bow to Anders. 'My dear young lady, I confess to having had a certain reticence when Fru Erslev told me of your location. However, she convinced me that the journey would be worthwhile. She tells me that you have the voice of an angel. And so' – he spread his arms and smiled broadly –

'here I am. And your dear parents have been most hospitable whilst we waited for your return.'

As Anna struggled to absorb Herr Bayer's words, she realised that her mouth was hanging slack with surprise and she quickly closed her lips together. She didn't want a sophisticated city dweller like him to assume that she was some half-witted country peasant.

'I am honoured that you have made the journey just to see me,' she said, dropping the most graceful curtsey she could manage.

'Well, if your choir mistress is right – and your parents too believe you have talent – then the honour is entirely mine,' Herr Bayer said gallantly. 'And of course, now you are here, I am delighted to say you have the opportunity to prove them all correct. I would dearly like you to sing for me, Anna.'

'Of course she will,' said Anders as Anna stood there, silent and uncertain. 'Anna?'

'But I only know folk songs and hymns, Herr Bayer.'

'Either will suffice, I can assure you,' he encouraged.

'Sing "*Per Spelmann*",' suggested her mother.

'That will do to start with,' Herr Bayer responded with a nod.

'But I have only sung it to the cows before.'

'Then imagine that I am your favourite cow, and you are calling me home,' Herr Bayer replied with a twinkle of amusement in his eyes.

'Very well, sir. I will try my best.'

Anna closed her eyes and tried to imagine herself back on the hillside, calling Rosa, just as she had done that very evening. Taking a deep breath, she began to sing. The words came to her without thinking as she sang the story of the poor fiddler who traded in his cow to get his violin back. And once the last clear note had disappeared into the night air, she opened her eyes.

She looked at Herr Bayer uncertainly, waiting for a verbal reaction. There was silence for a few moments as he studied her intently.

'Now perhaps a hymn – do you know "*Herre Gud, dit dyre Navn og Ære*"?' he said eventually.

Anna nodded and once again opened her mouth to sing. This time when she had finished, she saw Herr Bayer take out a large kerchief and dab his eyes.

'Young lady,' he said, his voice husky with emotion. 'That was sublime. And worth every hour of the backache I will suffer tonight from the journey up here.'

'Of course you must stay with us,' interjected Berit. 'You can take our son Knut's bedroom and he can sleep in the kitchen.'

'My dear lady, I am most grateful. I will indeed take you up on your offer, as we have much to discuss. Forgive my presumption, but is there a chance you can offer this weary traveller some bread? I have not eaten a thing since breakfast.'

'Please, sir, forgive me,' said Berit, horrified that in all the excitement she had completely forgotten about food. 'Of course, Anna and I will prepare something now.'

'And in the meantime, Herr Landvik and I will discuss how Anna's voice can be brought to the wider attention of the Norwegian public.'

Eyes wide, Anna dutifully followed her mother into the kitchen.

'What must he think of us? That we are so inhospitable – or poor – that we do not have food on our table for a guest!' Berit berated herself, as she set out a platter containing bread, butter and slices of cured pork. 'He is sure to return to Christiania and tell all his friends that the stories they have heard about our uncivilised ways are true.'

'Mor, Herr Bayer seems like a kind gentleman and I'm sure he will do nothing of the sort. If all is done for now, I must fetch more logs for the fire.'

'Well, hurry up about it, you need to lay the table.'

'Yes, Mor,' Anna said, as she walked outside, carrying a large wicker basket under her arm. After loading the basket with logs, she stood for a few moments looking at the twinkling lights that shone intermittently on the hillside towards the lake, indicating the sporadic presence of other human habitations. Her heart was still beating fast from the surprise of what had just occurred.

She had no clear idea of what it meant for her, although she *had* heard tales of other talented singers and musicians who had been whisked off to the city from villages all over Telemark county by professors such as Herr Bayer. She tried to think whether, if he *did* ask her to go with him, she'd actually want to. But as her experience beyond the dairy was confined to Heddal or the occasional trip to Skien, she couldn't even begin to contemplate what such a move might involve.

Hearing her mother calling her name, Anna turned and walked back to the cabin.

The following morning, in the few drowsy seconds between sleep and wakefulness, Anna stirred in her bed, knowing that yesterday something incredible had happened. Finally remembering what it was, she got up and began the cumbersome process of dressing in the bloomers, vest, cream blouse, black skirt and colourfully embroidered waistcoat that were her daily attire. After placing her cotton bonnet on her head and stuffing her hair inside it, she donned her boots.

Last night, after they'd eaten, she'd sung two more songs and another hymn, before being sent off to bed by her mother. The talk up until then had not been about Anna, but about the unusually warm weather and her father's predicted crop yield for the next year. But she had heard the hushed voices of her parents and Herr Bayer through the thin wooden walls and had known that it was her future they were discussing. At one point she had even dared to open her door a crack so she could eavesdrop.

'I worry of course that if Anna is to leave us for the city, my wife will be left to manage the household chores alone,' she'd heard her father saying.

'She may not be a natural when it comes to cooking and cleaning, but she is a hard worker and she also tends to the animals,' Berit had added.

'Well, I am sure we can come to an arrangement,' Herr Bayer had replied soothingly. 'I am of course prepared to recompense you for the loss of Anna's labour.'

Anna had held her breath in disbelief as a figure was mentioned. Unable to hear any more, she had closed the door as quietly as she could. 'So I am to be bought and sold like a cow at the market!' she'd muttered furiously to herself, outraged that money would even enter into her parents' decision. Yet she had also felt a tiny jitter of excitement. It had been a long time after that before sleep had overcome her.

Over a breakfast of porridge that morning, Anna sat silently as her family discussed Herr Bayer, who was still sleeping off the exertions of his journey. It seemed that the enthusiasm of last night had worn off and her family had begun to question the wisdom of allowing their only daughter to go off to the city with a stranger.

'All we have to go on is his word,' Knut said, sounding sour because he'd had to give up his bed to Herr Bayer. 'How do we know Anna will be safe with him?'

'Well, if Fru Erslev has sent him up here with her approval, then he must at least be a respected God-fearing man,' said Berit, preparing a more lavish bowl of porridge for their visitor, with a scoop of lingonberry preserve on top.

'I feel it would be best if I went to speak to the pastor and his wife when we return home to Heddal next week,' Anders said, and Berit nodded her approval.

'Then he must give us time to think, and visit us again to discuss it,' said Berit.

Anna didn't dare speak, knowing her future hung in the balance and feeling unsure as to which way she wanted the scales to tip. She slipped away before her mother could assign her more tasks, wanting to spend the day with the cows and think in peace and quiet. Humming to herself as she walked, she wondered why Herr Bayer was so interested in her when there were surely lots of better singers in Christiania. She had only a few days left on the mountains before going back down to Heddal for the winter, and she was suddenly overwhelmed by the realisation that she might not come back here at all next summer. Giving Rosa a hug and a kiss, Anna shut her eyes and sang again to stave off her tears.

Back home in Heddal a week later, Anders went to speak to Pastor Erslev and his wife, and was reassured about the professor's character and credentials. It seemed that Herr Bayer had taken other young girls under his wing and trained them into professional singers. One of whom, as Fru Erslev had rhapsodised, had even sung in the chorus at the Christiania Theatre.

When Herr Bayer visited them shortly afterwards, Berit had fussed around the kitchen and prepared the finest joint of pork she had for the midday meal. After they had eaten, Anna was sent outside to continue her usual tasks of feeding the chickens and filling the water troughs. She had hovered several times near the kitchen window, desperate to hear what those inside were saying, but could catch nothing. Finally, Knut came to fetch her.

As she took off her coat, she saw that her parents were sitting companionably with Herr Bayer, drinking her father's home-made beer. He greeted her with a jovial smile as she sat down at the table with Knut.

'So, Anna, your parents have agreed that you will come and live with me in Christiania for one year. I will be your mentor as well as your teacher and I have promised them that I will act faithfully *in loco parentis*. What do you say to that, eh?'

Anna stared at him and didn't answer, not wishing to sound ignorant, since she had absolutely no idea what 'mentor' or '*in loco parentis*' meant.

'Herr Bayer means that you will live with him in his apartment in Christiania and he will teach you to sing properly, introduce you to influential people, and ensure you are cared for as if you were his own daughter,' explained Berit, putting a comforting hand on Anna's knee.

Seeing the bewildered expression on Anna's face, Herr Bayer hastily sought to reassure her further. 'As I have told your parents, the living arrangements will of course be of the utmost propriety. My housekeeper, Frøken Olsdatter, also resides in my apartment and will be constantly on hand to chaperone you and take care of your needs. I have also presented your parents with letters of introduction from my university and the music fraternity in Christiania. So there is nothing for you to fear, my dear young lady, I can assure you.'

'I see.' Anna concentrated on the mug of coffee her mother had passed to her and sipped it steadily.

'Is this a plan that would please you, Anna?' asked Herr Bayer.

'I . . . think so.'

'Herr Bayer is also prepared to cover all expenses for you,' encouraged her father. 'It is a wonderful opportunity, Anna. He believes you have great talent.'

'I do indeed,' confirmed Herr Bayer. 'You have one of the purest voices I've ever heard. And you will also be educated, not just in music. You will learn other languages and I will provide tutors to improve your reading and writing—'

'Excuse me, Herr Bayer,' Anna couldn't help butting in, 'but I am already proficient in both.'

'Then that is a help and will mean we can get down to the business of training your voice faster than I'd expected. So, Anna, will you say yes?'

Anna desperately wanted to ask *why*: why did he want to pay her parents to spend his time nurturing both her and her voice, let alone have her to stay with him in his apartment?

But as no one else seemed to question it, she didn't feel it was her place to do so either.

'But Christiania is such a long way away and a year is such a long time . . .' Anna's voice trailed off as the enormity of what was being suggested suddenly hit her. Everything she knew – *had* known – up until now would no longer be. She was a simple girl from a farm in Heddal, and even though she'd considered her life and future to be dull, the leap she was being asked to make with only a few seconds' consideration suddenly felt too much for her.

'Well . . .'

Four pairs of eyes fell upon her.

'I . . .'

'Yes?' asked her parents and Herr Bayer in unison.

'When I've gone, please promise me that if Rosa dies, you won't eat her.'

And with that, Anna Landvik promptly burst into tears.

14

After Herr Bayer's departure, the Landvik home erupted into a hive of activity. Her mother began sewing Anna a valise in which she would carry her few possessions to Christiania. Her two best skirts and blouses, plus her undergarments, were washed and mended with the utmost care, for, as Berit said, no daughter of hers would look like a common peasant amongst those high-nosed city folk. Fru Erslev, the pastor's wife, gave her a new prayer book with crisp white pages, reminding her to say grace every night and not to be seduced by the 'heathen' ways of the city. It had been arranged that Pastor Erslev was to meet her at Drammen and escort her on the train to Christiania, as he had an ecclesiastical meeting he was travelling there to attend.

As for Anna herself, she found she barely had a spare moment to sit down and think through her decision. Whenever she felt niggling doubts creep in, she did her best to push them aside. Her mother had told her that Lars was coming to see her tomorrow and she felt her heart knocking painfully against her chest as she recalled her parents' whispered discussions about their marriage. It seemed that whatever lay in her future, whether it was here in Heddal or in Christiania, other people were making the decisions for her.

'Lars has arrived,' said Berit the next morning, as though she thought that Anna herself had not been listening anxiously for the sound of his boots stamping off the mud from the September rain. 'I will open the door. Why don't you receive him in the parlour?'

Anna nodded, knowing that the parlour was the 'serious' room. It housed the settle, their one piece of upholstered furniture, as well as a glass-fronted cabinet containing a mix of plates and small ornaments that her mother thought good enough to put on display. It had also housed the coffins of three of her grandparents when they had departed this world. As she walked along the narrow corridor towards it, Anna reflected that during her lifetime, the room had very rarely accommodated anyone that actually breathed. And as she opened the door, a puff of stale and closeted air escaped.

The conversation she was about to have presumably warranted these sober surroundings and she stood wondering exactly where she should place herself for when Lars entered. Hearing the heavy footsteps along the passage, Anna quickly moved to sit down on the settle, the cushions atop it almost as hard as the planks of pine that supported them.

There was a knock on the door and Anna had a sudden urge to giggle. Never before had anyone requested her permission to enter a room that wasn't her bedroom.

'Yes?' she replied.

The door opened and her mother's round face appeared. 'Lars is here.'

Anna watched as he entered the room. He had made an effort to brush down his thick blond hair and was wearing his best cream shirt and black breeches that he usually only wore to church, plus a waistcoat she hadn't seen before – midnight blue in colour, which Anna thought went well with his eyes. She supposed he was really quite handsome, but then, she also thought that about Knut, her own brother. And she certainly wouldn't want to marry *him*.

The two of them hadn't seen each other since Lars had handed her *Peer Gynt*, and she swallowed nervously as she remembered his hand holding hers. She stood up to greet him. 'Hello, Lars.'

'Would you like some coffee, Lars?' Berit asked him from the doorway.

'N-no, thank you, Fru Landvik.'

'Well then,' her mother said after a pause, 'I'll leave you alone to talk.'

'Would you like to sit down?' Anna asked Lars once Berit had left.

'Yes,' he said and did so.

Anna perched awkwardly at the other end of the settle, her hands knotting in her lap.

'Anna' – Lars cleared his throat – 'do you know why I'm here?'

'Because you're always here?' she offered, and he gave a soft laugh at her response, breaking the tension a little.

'Yes, I suppose I am. How has your summer been?'

'Like every summer before it and none the worse for that.'

'But surely this summer has been a special one for you?' he persisted.

'You mean because of Herr Bayer? The man from Christiania?'

'Yes, Fru Erslev has been telling everyone. She's very proud of you . . . and so am I,' he added. 'I think you are probably the most famous person in the whole of Telemark county. Apart from Herr Ibsen, of course. So you will go?'

'Well, Far and Mor think it's a wonderful opportunity for me. They tell me I'm honoured to have a man such as Herr Bayer willing to help me.'

'Indeed, they are right. But I'd like to know if *you* want to go?'

Anna pondered this.

'I think I must,' she said. 'It would be very rude to refuse, don't you agree? Especially as he travelled for a whole day up the hills to hear me sing.'

'Yes, I suppose it would.' Lars looked beyond her to the wall fashioned out of heavy pine logs and stared at the picture of Lake Skisjøen that hung there. There was a long silence, which Anna didn't know whether to break or not. Finally, Lars turned his attention back to her.

'Anna.'

'Yes, Lars?'

He took a deep breath and she noticed that he gripped the side of the armrest of the settle to stop his hand from shaking. 'Before you left for the summer, I talked with your father about the possibility of asking for your hand in . . . marriage. We agreed I would sell him my family's land and that we would farm it together. Did you know of any of this?'

'I've overheard my parents talking about it,' she confessed.

'Before Herr Bayer came, what was your opinion of the plan?'

'You mean about Far buying the land?'

'No' – Lars allowed himself an ironic smile – 'I meant about marrying me.'

'Well, to be truthful, I didn't think that you did want to marry me. You've never mentioned it.'

Lars looked at her in surprise. 'Anna, surely you must have had some idea of my feelings for you? For most of last winter, I was here night after night helping you with your letters.'

'But Lars, you've *always* been here, ever since I was small. You're . . . like my brother.'

A flash of pain crossed his face. 'The point is, Anna, I love you.'

She looked at Lars in amazement. She had assumed that he would see any proposed union as a matter of convenience, especially as she was hardly a catch, what with her limited domestic abilities. After all, from what she'd seen in her short life, most marriages seemed to be based on this premise. But now Lars had told her that he loved her . . . which was something different all together.

'That is most kind of you, Lars. To love me, I mean.'

'It is not "kind" Anna, it is . . .' He broke off, looking lost and confused. In the long silence, Anna contemplated how quiet their supper conversation would be if they did marry. Lars would likely concentrate on his food, and that really wouldn't be a good thing.

'I wish to know, Anna, if Herr Bayer had not asked you to go with him to Christiania, whether you would have accepted a proposal of marriage?'

As she thought of all he had done to help her last winter

and how fond of him she was, she knew there was only one answer she could give.

'I would have said yes.'

'Thank you,' he said, relief obvious in his expression. 'So, your father and I have agreed that, given the circumstances, the contracts for the purchase of my family's land will be drawn up immediately. Then I will wait for you for a year whilst you go to Christiania. Once you return, I will formally propose to you.'

At this, Anna began to panic. Lars had misunderstood. If he had asked her if she *loved* him like he said he loved her, she would have replied that she didn't.

'Anna, do you agree?'

Silence hung over the parlour as Anna tried to gather her thoughts.

'I hope that you can learn to love me as I do you,' he said quietly. 'And perhaps one day, we will travel to America together and begin a new life there. Now, this is for you, as a seal on our unofficial promise to each other. More useful than a ring, at least for now, I think.' He reached into his waistcoat pocket and pulled out a long, thin wooden box and gave it to her.

'I . . . thank you.' Brushing her fingers over the polished wood, Anna opened it. Nestled inside lay the most beautiful writing pen she had ever seen, and she knew it must have cost him dearly. The pen holder was carved out of a light pine, elegantly curved to fit perfectly into her hand, and the nib ended in a delicate point. She held it just as Lars had taught her to. Even if she didn't love him or want to marry him, his gift touched her heart and made her eyes brim with tears.

'Lars, it is the finest thing I have ever owned.'

'I will wait for you, Anna,' he said. 'And perhaps you can use the ink pen to write me letters describing your new life in Christiania?'

'Of course.'

'And you agree we will become formally betrothed next year when you are returned from Christiania?'

Feeling the full force of his love and looking down at her beautiful ink pen, Anna felt she could only say one thing.

'Yes.'

His face broke into a wide smile. 'Then I am content. Now, we will go and announce to your parents that we have reached an agreement.' Lars stood up, and took her hand in his. He bent his head towards it and kissed it. 'My Anna. Let us hope that God treats us both kindly.'

Two days later, all disturbing thoughts of Lars and what would happen in a year's time were wiped from Anna's mind as she rose early to embark on the long journey to Christiana. Feeling sick with nerves, she could barely force down the special pancakes that her mother had made her for breakfast. As Anders announced it was time to be on their way, Anna stood up, her legs feeling like goat's cheese beneath her. Glancing around the cosy kitchen one last time, she felt a sudden desperate urge to unpack her valise and call the whole thing off.

'It's all right, *kjære*,' Berit said, stroking Anna's long curls to calm her as they embraced, 'you'll be back to visit before you know it. Just don't forget to say your prayers every night, attend church on Sunday and brush your hair properly.'

'Mor, stop your fussing or she'll never get there,' said Knut dryly, taking his sister in his arms. 'And don't forget to have lots of fun,' he whispered in her ear, before thumbing the tears from her cheeks.

Her father drove her in their horse and cart to the town of Drammen – almost a day's journey away – from where she would take a train to the city with Pastor Erslev. They stayed overnight in a modest guesthouse that also had stabling for the horse, so that they could be up bright and early to get to the railway station in plenty of time for Anna's train.

Pastor Erslev was waiting on the platform, which was crowded with fellow travellers. When the train finally chugged in, she felt overwhelmed by the hissing plumes of steam and the noise of the screeching brakes as the passengers hurried to climb on-board. Anders helped her with the capacious valise as they followed the pastor towards the train.

'Far, I'm so scared,' she whispered.

'My Anna, if you find yourself unhappy, you can simply come home,' he replied gently, reaching out a hand to stroke her cheek. 'Now, let's get you settled on-board.'

They mounted the steps of the train then made their way through the carriage to find seats for the two travellers. After Anders had hoisted her valise onto the metal rack above her head, the guard blew his whistle and her father bent down swiftly to kiss Anna goodbye. 'Make sure you write to Lars regularly so we can all hear how you are getting on and remember what an honour has been bestowed upon you. Show those city folk that their country brethren know how to behave.'

'I will, Far, I promise.'

'Good girl. We will see you at Christmas. The Lord bless you, and keep you safe. Goodbye.'

'Rest assured I will deliver her into Herr Bayer's safekeeping,' Pastor Erslev said as he shook hands with Anders.

Anna did her best not to cry as her father left the train, coming alongside to wave her off through the window. But the train moved forward with a jolt and her father's face soon disappeared into the clouds of steam.

As Pastor Erslev opened his prayer book, Anna amused herself by looking round the carriage at the other occupants and felt suddenly conspicuous in her traditional dress. The rest of the men and women wore smart town clothes, making Anna feel exactly like the peasant she was. Reaching inside the pockets of her skirt, she pulled out the letter that Lars had given her yesterday when they'd said their farewells. He'd made her promise not to read it until she was on her way. Exaggerating the movement, just to show the other residents of the carriage that she might be a country girl but that she could *read*, Anna opened the seal.

The words in front of her, scripted in Lars' neat writing, presented her with a challenge, but she doggedly persevered.

Stalsberg Våningshuset
Tindevegen
Heddal

18th September 1875

Kjære Anna,

I wished to tell you I am proud of you. Take every opportunity you can to improve your voice and your knowledge of the wider world outside Heddal. Do not be fearful of it, and remember that underneath the fine clothes and the different ways of those you will meet, they are only human beings like you and I.

Meanwhile, I shall await you here, and long for the day you return. Please write to me to tell me you are safe in Christiania. We will all remain fascinated to hear any detail of your new life there.

For now, know I am your loving, and ever faithful,

Lars.

Anna folded the letter carefully and replaced it in her pocket. She found it difficult to equate the physical being of Lars, who was so awkward and quiet, with the flowing eloquence of the words he had written in the letter. As the train chugged towards Christiania and she watched Pastor Erslev dozing in the seat opposite her, a small drip of moisture hanging perilously from the end of his nose and never quite falling, Anna quashed the surge of panic she felt every time she thought of her forthcoming marriage. However, a year was a very long time in which many things might happen. People could be struck by lightning, or catch a bad chest cold and die. *She* might die, she thought, as the train lurched to the right suddenly. And with that thought, Anna closed her eyes and tried to take some rest.

'Good day, Pastor Erslev! And my dear Frøken Landvik, allow me to welcome you to Christiania. May I ask the favour of calling you Anna, given that we will be living in such close quarters?' Herr Bayer asked her as he took her valise and helped her down from the train.

'Yes, of course, sir,' Anna replied shyly.

'How was your journey, Pastor Erslev?' Herr Bayer asked the elderly priest as he limped along the bustling platform beside them.

'It was comfortable, thank you. Now, my duty is done and I can see Pastor Eriksonn waiting for me,' he said as he gave a wave to a small bald man dressed in identical robes to himself. 'So I will say goodbye, Anna.'

'Goodbye, Pastor Erslev.'

Anna watched the last link to all she had ever known disappear through the gates of the station and out onto a busy road where a number of horse-drawn carriages were waiting.

'Here, we too will hire one of these to speed us home. Normally I take the tram, but I fear it may be too much for you after your long journey.'

Having issued instructions to the driver, Herr Bayer helped Anna inside. As she sat down on the bench, upholstered in a soft red fabric and far more comfortable than her family's special settle at home, she felt thrilled to be travelling in such opulent style.

'It is only a short ride to my apartment,' Herr Bayer commented. 'And my housekeeper has prepared us some supper. You must be hungry after your journey.'

Anna secretly hoped that the journey in the carriage would take a very long time. She pushed aside the little brocade curtains and peered out of the window in wonder as they rode into the centre of the city. Rather than the rough narrow tracks that criss-crossed the town of Skien, here the thoroughfares were wide, tree-lined and very busy. They passed a horse-drawn tram, its passengers dressed smartly, the mens' heads crowned with shiny top hats and the womens' with extravagant creations adorned with flowers and ribbons. Anna tried to imagine herself wearing the same and suppressed a giggle.

'Of course there is much to discuss,' Herr Bayer went on, 'but we have plenty of time until . . .'

'Until what, sir?' Anna asked.

'Oh, until you are ready to greet a wider public, my dear young lady. Now, here we are.' He opened the window and called out to the driver to pull the carriage over. As he helped Anna step out and then collected her valise, she looked up at the tall stone building whose many floors with glinting windows seemed to stretch high up to the heavens above her.

'Sadly, we are yet to have one of those newfangled lift machines installed, so we must take the stairs,' he instructed her as they entered through the grand double doors and stood in the echoing marble-floored entrance hall. 'When I reach the apartment,' Herr Bayer commented as they began to ascend the curved staircase with its gleaming brass handrail, 'at least I feel as though I have earned my supper!'

Anna only counted three short flights of stairs, which felt far easier to climb than a mountain slope in the rain, before Herr Bayer led her along a wide corridor and unlocked a door.

'Frøken Olsdatter, we are back and Anna is here!' he called out as he led her along a passageway and into a huge drawing room, its walls covered in rich ruby-red wallpaper and containing a set of the biggest glass windows she'd ever seen.

'Where has that woman got to?' complained Herr Bayer.

'Excuse me one moment, Anna my dear, whilst I go and find her. Please, sit down and make yourself comfortable.'

Anna was too tense to be still, so instead she took the opportunity to study the room. Beside one of the windows stood a grand piano, and underneath another a huge mahogany desk overflowed with piles of sheet music. The centre of the room was dominated by a large and far grander version of her family's settle. Facing it were two elegant chairs covered in matching pink and brown striped material, and in between stood a low table made of handsome dark wood, piled high with books and a collection of snuff boxes. The walls were adorned with oil paintings of countryside landscapes, not unlike the vistas that surrounded her home in Heddal. There were also a number of framed certificates and letters. One of them caught her eye, and she walked forwards to look more closely.

Det kongelige Frederiks Universitet tildeler
Prof. Dr Franz Bjørn Bayer
æresprofessorat i historie
16th July 1847

Below the words was a red seal and a signature. Anna wondered how many years it must have taken at school for her mentor to achieve that.

'My goodness, it is getting dark in here already and it's barely past five o'clock!' said Herr Bayer as he swept back into the room, accompanied by a tall, slim woman whom Anna thought was perhaps of a similar age to her mother. She was wearing a dark wool dress with a high neck and a long full skirt, which although elegantly cut, was plain and unadorned, apart from a bunch of keys dangling from a fine chain around the waist. The woman's light brown hair was arranged in a neat bun at the nape of her neck.

'Anna, this is Frøken Olsdatter, my housekeeper.'

'I am pleased to make your acquaintance, Frøken Olsdatter,' Anna said, giving a curtsey, as she had always been taught to do as a show of respect to her elders.

'And I you, Anna,' said the woman, a half-smile in her warm brown eyes as she watched her rise from the curtsey. 'I am here to serve and take care of *you*,' she emphasised, 'so you must let me know if there is anything you need or if something is not satisfactory.'

'I . . .' Anna was confused. Surely this lady in her fine gown wasn't a servant? 'Thank you.'

'Light the lamps, will you, Frøken Olsdatter?' Herr Bayer instructed the woman. 'Anna, are you chilly? You must tell me if you are and we will light the stove also.'

It took Anna a minute or two to respond, as she was transfixed by the sight of Frøken Olsdatter using a length of cord to lower the chandelier that hung from the ceiling, then twist a brass knob in the centre before holding a lit wax taper to it. Delicate flames sprang to life along the ornately fashioned arms of the chandelier, filling the room with a soft golden glow as it was hoisted back into place above them. Anna then glanced at the stove Herr Bayer was referring to. It was fashioned out of some form of ceramic and was cream in colour. Its broad chimney reached right up to the high, delicately latticed ceiling and its carved mantelpiece was edged with gilt. Compared to her parents' ugly black iron contraption, that was not a stove, Anna thought, it was a work of art.

'Thank you, Herr Bayer, but I am perfectly warm.'

'Frøken Olsdatter, please take Anna's cloak and put it in her room along with her valise,' Herr Bayer requested.

Anna untied the ribbon from about her neck and the housekeeper removed the cloak from her shoulders. 'The big city must be rather overwhelming for you,' she said quietly as she folded the cloak over her arm. 'It certainly was for me when I first arrived here from Ålesund.'

In those few words, Anna knew immediately that Frøken Olsdatter had once been a country girl too. And that she understood.

'So, my dear young lady, we will sit down and take some tea. As soon as you have a moment to bring it, Frøken Olsdatter.'

'Very good, Herr Bayer.' The housekeeper nodded, picked up Anna's valise and left the room.

He indicated a chair where Anna should sit and sat down opposite her on the settle. 'We have much to talk about. And as there is no time like the present, I will begin to tell you of your new life here in Christiania. You say you can read and write proficiently, which will save us a great deal of time. Can you also read music?'

'No, I cannot,' Anna confessed.

She watched as Herr Bayer drew a leather-bound notebook towards him and picked up a lacquered ink pen that made the one Lars had given her look as if it was a rough piece of driftwood. He dipped the pen into an inkwell placed on the low table and began to write.

'And I take it you have no knowledge of other languages?'

'No, I do not.'

Again, he wrote in his notebook. 'Have you ever been to a

concert – by which I mean a musical performance – at a theatre or concert hall?'

'No, sir, never, only at the church.'

'Then we must rectify that as soon as possible. Do you know what an opera is?'

'I believe so. It's where the people on the stage sing the story rather than speak it.'

'Very good. And how is your counting?'

'I can count up to one hundred,' Anna said proudly.

Herr Bayer stifled a smile. 'And that is all you need in music, Anna. As a singer, one must know how to count the beats. Can you play an instrument?'

'My father has a *hardanger* fiddle and I learnt the basics of how to play that.'

'Well then, it seems you are already a very accomplished young lady,' he said with satisfaction as the housekeeper came in with a tray. 'Now we will take tea, and after that, if Frøken Olsdatter would be so kind, she will show you to your room. Then at seven o'clock, we will have supper together in the dining room.'

Anna's attention was drawn to the strangely shaped pot from which the housekeeper was pouring what looked like very weak coffee.

'It's Darjeeling tea,' said Herr Bayer.

Not wishing to appear ignorant, Anna took the delicate china cup to her lips, mimicking Herr Bayer. The taste was pleasant but rather nondescript compared with the strong coffee her mother made at home.

'In your room you will also find some plain clothes that I had Frøken Olsdatter run up for you. Of course, I could only guess at your size and, looking at you now, you are even more petite than I remembered so the clothes may well need adjusting,' Herr Bayer added. 'As you might already have surmised, traditional Norwegian dress is seldom worn in Christiania, other than on festival days.'

'I am sure that whatever Frøken Olsdatter has made for me will do me very well, sir,' Anna replied politely.

'My dear young lady, I admit I am mightily impressed with your composure so far. Having had the company of other young singers up from the country, I understand what a change of circumstances this is for you. Sadly, many of them run home like mice to their nests. I have a feeling that you will not be following them. Now, Anna, Frøken Olsdatter will take you to your room to settle in, whilst I tackle some of my interminable paperwork from the university. We shall meet again at seven for dinner.'

'As you wish, sir.'

Anna rose and saw that Frøken Olsdatter was already waiting for her at the door. She dropped Herr Bayer a curtsey and left the room, following Frøken Olsdatter further along the corridor until the housekeeper halted in front of a door and opened it.

'This is to be your room, Anna. I hope you will find it comfortable. The skirts and blouses I have made for you are hanging in the wardrobe. Try them on later and we will see if they need altering.'

'Thank you,' said Anna, her gaze falling on the enormous bed with its embroidered counterpane, which was twice the size of the one her parents shared at home. She saw that a new linen nightgown was already laid out at the bottom of it.

'I have unpacked some of your belongings and will help you see to the rest later. There's water in the jug on the nightstand if you are thirsty and the bathroom is at the end of the corridor.'

'Bathroom' was not a word that Anna was familiar with and she looked at Frøken Olsdatter uncertainly.

'The room which contains the water closet and the bathtub. Herr Bayer's late wife was American and insisted on such modern conveniences.' The housekeeper gave a slight raise of her eyebrows, whether of approval or the opposite, Anna couldn't guess. 'We will see you in the dining room at seven,' she said and promptly left the room.

Anna walked over to the wardrobe, opened it and let out a sigh of wonder at her new clothes. There were four fine cotton blouses fastened at the neck with small pearl buttons and two woollen skirts. But most thrillingly, there was also a formal bustled gown fashioned from a lustrous and shiny green fabric that she surmised must be silk. Closing the wardrobe with a shiver of pleasure, Anna then followed Frøken Olsdatter's directions and made her way down the corridor to the bathroom.

Of all the sights she had seen already that day, what met her eyes as she opened the door was the most miraculous of all. In one corner was a large wooden bench that held an enamel seat with a hole in the centre of it and had an iron ring pull on a chain above it. As she pulled it gingerly, water rushed in automatically and Anna realised it was an indoor privy. There was also a deep, shiny white bathtub in the middle of the tiled floor, which made the tin bath her family occasionally used in Heddal look like something only a goat would be washed in.

Marvelling over how these things could be possible, Anna returned to her room. The clock told her she had barely more than half an hour before she was expected for dinner with Herr Bayer. As she went to the wardrobe to select one of her new outfits to wear for the occasion, she noticed that Frøken Olsdatter had laid out writing paper and Anna's own pen on the small polished table under the window. She promised herself that she would write to Lars and her parents as soon as she had the chance, to tell them of everything she had already seen. Then she set about making herself presentable for her very first evening in Christiania.

15

Apartment 4
10 St Olav's Gate
Christiania

24th September 1875

Kjære Lars, Mor, Far and Knut,

Please forgive all the spelling mistakes and bad grammar, but I hope you can see that my penmanship has improved! I have been here now for five days and I feel I must share my wonder at city life.

The first thing – and I hope you do not feel I am being improper by mentioning it – is that there is an inside facility with a chain that you pull for disposal afterwards! There is also a bathtub which is filled for me with hot water twice a week! I worry that Frøken Olsdatter, who is the housekeeper here, and Herr Bayer think I have some disease which means I must spend hours in the full tub.

There is also gas-lamp lighting, and a stove in the drawing room that looks like a very grand church altar and which gives out so much heat that I often feel I will faint. Frøken Olsdatter organises the household routine and prepares and serves our food, and we also have a daily maid who comes each morning to clean the apartment and wash and iron the clothes, so I confess I hardly lift a finger compared to my duties at home.

We live three floors up, on a street called St Olav's Gate, which has a very pretty view of a park where the local people walk on Sundays. At least I can see green from my window and a few trees that are fast losing their leaves as winter approaches, but they do remind me of home so much. (It is unusual here to find more than a small patch of earth that is not crowded by roads or houses.)

As for my studies, I am learning to play the piano. Herr Bayer is very patient, but I think I am very stupid. My small fingers do not seem to spread across the notes in the way he wishes them to.

I should tell you what my day consists of, and then you can understand better. I am woken at eight by Frøken Olsdatter knocking on my door with a breakfast tray. At that moment, I confess I feel like a princess. I drink tea, which I'm slowly getting used to the taste of, and eat the fresh white bread which Herr Bayer tells me is the very thing in England and France. Next to it is a pot of preserved fruit that is spread onto the bread. After breakfast, I dress in the clothes that Frøken Olsdatter has made for me, which feel so modern compared to what I wore at home, and by nine o'clock I present myself in the drawing room to begin my music lesson with Herr Bayer. For an hour or so, he teaches me the notes on the piano and after that we study sheet music. I have to learn how the notes on the page go with the keys on the piano, and slowly, due to Herr Bayer's excellent teaching, I am starting to understand. After my lesson, Herr Bayer leaves to go to the university where he is a professor, or sometimes to meet friends for lunch.

And then comes the part of my day I enjoy most – the midday meal. The day after I arrived, Frøken Olsdatter served me lunch alone in the dining room, which has a very large table that makes me feel even more alone. (The top of it is so highly polished it shines like a mirror and I can see my reflection in it.) After the meal, I picked up my plate and glass and took them into the kitchen. Frøken Olsdatter looked shocked and said it was her job to collect the dirty tableware. But then out of the corner of my eye, I noticed something else that I had never seen before – a large black iron cooking range. Frøken Olsdatter showed me how she could place pots upon it and light gas burners beneath them to cook the food, rather than doing so over an open fire. It is very different from our kitchen at the farm, but it reminded me so much of home that I begged her, on the days when Herr Bayer was not at home for lunch, to allow me to eat with her. And that is what we have done every day since. We talk like friends and she is very kind and understands how strange this new life is for me. In the afternoons, I am meant to rest for an hour in my room, with a book that will 'expand the mind'. At present I am reading (or trying to read) a

Norwegian translation of plays by an English writer called William Shakespeare. I am sure you will have heard of him, but he is long dead and the first play I read was about a Scottish prince called Macbeth and was very sad. Everyone seemed to die!

I come out of my room once Herr Bayer returns from the university. We drink tea again and he talks to me of his day. Next week, he wishes to take me to the Christiania Theatre. We are seeing a ballet, performed by some Russians, which he tells me is a dance set to music where nobody speaks or sings (and that the men don't even wear proper trousers, but hose, like girls!). After tea, I return to my room, then change into the evening gown that Frøken Olsdatter has made me. I wish you could see it – it is so very beautiful and like nothing I have ever worn before. At dinner, we drink red wine that Herr Bayer has had sent over from France and eat an awful lot of fish in a white sauce which he tells me is very common here in Christiania. After dinner, Herr Bayer lights a cigar, which is tobacco wrapped in dried tobacco leaf, and takes a brandy. At this point, I retire to my room, usually very tired, to find a glass of hot cow's milk beside my bed.

On Sunday, Frøken Olsdatter accompanied me to church. Herr Bayer says he will come too in future, but he was busy this time. The church is the size of a cathedral and there were hundreds of people in it. So you can see my experiences are very different to the life I used to live in Heddal. Just now, I feel a little as though I am living in a dream. That nothing is real, and home seems a long way away.

I had thought that I had been brought by Herr Bayer to Christiania to sing. The truth is that all I have done so far is sing something called scales on a piano, which means repeating the notes in order, up and down and up again, with no words.

My address is at the top of the letter and I would be most grateful if you reply to this. I am sorry about all the ink blots. It is the first and longest letter I have ever written and it has taken me many hours. I am of course using the pen that you gave me, Lars, and I have put it on my desk so I can see it always.

Please tell Mor and Far and my brothers that I miss them and I hope you can read this to them. I cannot write another as it took me so long, and neither are they good at their letters.

I hope you are well and that your pigs are too.

Anna

Anna reread the letter painstakingly. It was the last of perhaps twelve drafts penned over the past five days, the rest of which she'd started, then discarded. She was aware that some of the words she'd used she had spelt as she spoke them and feared that they were incorrect. However, she reasoned, Lars would prefer an imperfect missive to none at all. She was bursting to tell her family about the transformation her life was currently undergoing. Having carefully folded the letter, she stood up and caught her reflection in the looking glass. She studied her face for a moment.

Am I still me? she asked it. Receiving no reply, she made her way to the bathroom.

Later that evening, climbing into bed, she listened to the voices and laughter drifting along the corridor. Herr Bayer was entertaining some guests, so tonight there had been no dinner with him at the polished dining table, rather a tray presented to her by Frøken Olsdatter, whose Christian name she now knew to be Lise.

'My dear young lady, allow me to explain,' Herr Bayer had said earlier, after he'd announced that she would not be present at dinner. 'You are making great progress, very fast. In fact, far faster than any other music student I have had the honour to mentor. But if I introduced you to my guests, they would surely entreat you to sing for them, after all I've told them of your potential. And we cannot show you off until you are fully formed, at which point we will bring you out of hiding in a blaze of glory.'

Even though Anna was getting used to Herr Bayer's elaborate use of language, she pondered what 'fully formed' actually meant. Was she to grow another hand? That would certainly help in her piano lessons. Or perhaps some extra toes, which would help her less than adequate posture. This flaw had been pointed out to her today by a theatre director, who had arrived at the apartment that afternoon. He'd told her that he was employed by Herr Bayer to teach her about something he called 'stage presence', for when she appeared at a theatre. Which seemed to have a lot to do with holding her head high and clenching her toes together inside her boots to make sure that when she reached the desired position, she stood stock-still.

'Then you wait, until they finish applauding. A small bow, like so' – the man had demonstrated by dipping his chin to his chest with his left arm taken across to his right shoulder – 'to show appreciation for their applause, and then you begin.'

For the following hour, the man had asked her to walk in and out of the drawing room, practising the same moves over and over again. It had been extremely tedious and very dispiriting, given that up to now, even if she could not cook or sew, she had at least felt she could walk proficiently.

Anna turned on her side in the enormous bed, feeling the downy softness of the pillow beneath her cheek, and wondered if she could ever become what Herr Bayer wished her to be.

As she'd told Lars in her letter, she thought she'd been brought here for her singing talent. And yet Herr Bayer had not asked her to sing a single song since she'd arrived. She understood that there were many things she had to learn and she could not have a more kind or patient mentor. Yet Anna sometimes felt as though she was losing her old self, ill-educated and unworldly as that was. She already felt stranded between two worlds: a girl who less than a week ago had never seen gaslight or an inside privy, yet had become used to a servant waiting on her, drinking red wine with supper and fish . . .

'Oh Lord!' she groaned out loud at the thought of the endless fish.

Perhaps Herr Bayer thought she was so stupid that she didn't have a clue about his intentions. But she had realised very quickly that not only had he brought her to Christiania to train her voice, but also to turn her into a lady who could be presented as such. She was being taught tricks, just like the animals at the fair that sometimes passed through Heddal. She thought about that first night Herr Bayer had arrived at her family's hillside cabin, when he'd spent a long time extolling the glories of Norway's regional culture. So she couldn't quite understand why he felt it so necessary to change her.

'I am not an experiment,' she whispered to herself firmly as finally she drifted off to sleep.

One frosty October morning, Anna arrived as usual in the drawing room for her lesson with Herr Bayer.

'My dear Anna, did you sleep well?'

'Very well indeed, thank you, Herr Bayer.'

'Good, good. Well, I am pleased to say that today, I feel you are ready for us to move on. So, we will begin to sing, yes?'

'Yes, Herr Bayer,' she replied guiltily, all too aware of her negative thoughts a few nights ago.

'Are you feeling well, Anna? You look quite pale.'

'I am well.'

'Good. Then we will waste no more time. I wish you to sing "*Per Spelmann*" to me as you did the first evening we met. I will follow you on the piano.'

Anna was still so bemused at this unexpected turn of events that she stood and stared at Herr Bayer silently.

'You are not ready?'

'I'm sorry. Yes, I am.'

'Good. Then you will sing.'

For the following forty-five minutes, Anna repeated the song she had known from the cradle endless times. At various points, Herr Bayer would stop her and tell her to use a little more of what he called '*vibrato*' on a specific note, or to hold a certain pause for longer, or to count the beats . . . She did her best to follow his instruction, but having first learnt it fourteen years ago and sung it the same way ever since, it was very hard indeed.

At eleven o'clock promptly, the front doorbell rang. She heard the sound of low voices in the corridor and Frøken Olsdatter entered the drawing room followed by a distinguished-looking dark-haired gentleman with a hawk-like nose and a receding hairline. Herr Bayer stood up from the piano and went to greet him.

'Herr Hennum, I am grateful for your time. This is Frøken Anna Landvik, the girl I have told you about.'

The gentleman turned to her and bowed. 'Frøken Landvik, Herr Bayer has sung himself in praise of your voice.'

'And now you will hear it!' Herr Bayer returned to the piano. 'Anna, sing as you sang to me that first night up in the hills.'

Anna looked at him, confused. If he wanted her to sing as she had originally, then why had he spent an hour trying to teach her differently? But it was too late to ask him, for he was already playing the opening bars, so she simply began to sing and gave her voice its freedom.

When she'd finished, she looked at Herr Bayer expectantly, not knowing whether she had sung well or indifferently. She'd remembered bits of what he'd told her, but not all of it, and everything felt muddled in her head.

'What do you think, Johan?' asked Herr Bayer standing up from the piano.

'Anna is exactly as you have described. And therefore perfect. Obviously raw, but then perhaps that is as it should be.'

'I was not expecting this to arise so soon. As I mentioned, Anna arrived in Christiania less than a month ago and I have only just begun to train her voice,' Herr Bayer responded.

As Anna listened to the two men discussing her and her abilities, she certainly felt as 'raw' as an uncooked piece of pork about to be thrown into her mother's pot.

'I am yet to receive the final score, but as soon as I do, I will bring it to you and then we will have Anna come to the theatre and sing for Herr Josephson. Now, I must take my leave. Frøken Landvik.' Johan Hennum bowed to her again. 'It was my pleasure to hear you sing, and doubtless I and many others will be given the opportunity again in the very near future. Good day to you both.'

Herr Hennum swept from the door, his cloak billowing behind him as he did so.

'Well done, Anna!' Herr Bayer came towards her, took her face in his hands and gave her a kiss on both cheeks.

'Please, sir, can you tell me who that man is?'

'It is of no matter now. All that does matter is that we have much work to do to prepare you.'

'Prepare me for what?'

But Herr Bayer was not listening to her; he was glancing at the clock. 'I am due to give a lecture in half an hour and must leave at once. Frøken Olsdatter,' he shouted, 'bring me my cloak immediately!' Walking past her to the door, he smiled once more. 'Rest now, Anna, and when I return we will begin to work.'

Even though over the next two weeks Anna tried to find out who Herr Hennum was and what it was they were working towards, Herr Bayer was maddeningly unforthcoming. What she didn't understand was why he suddenly wished her to sing through every folk song she'd ever learnt, rather than, as he'd mentioned to her parents, teaching her to sing the operas. *What use is that kind of music here in the city?* she thought miserably as she walked to the window one lunchtime when Herr Bayer had left the apartment to attend a meeting. She traced the pattern of the raindrops on the outside of the window and suddenly felt an urge to be outdoors. In the past month, she had hardly set foot outside the apartment, apart from going to church on a Sunday, and was beginning to feel like a caged animal. Perhaps Herr Bayer simply forgot that she had grown up and lived her entire life in open spaces. She yearned for some fresh air, the open pasture of her parents' farm, space to walk and to run free . . .

'Here, I am nothing more than an animal to be trained,' she stated to the empty room just before Frøken Olsdatter came in to tell her that luncheon was ready. Anna followed her into the kitchen.

'What is it, *kjære?* You look like a herring that's just been caught on a hook,' Frøken Olsdatter commented as they both sat down and Anna sipped her fish broth.

'Nothing,' said Anna, not wishing the housekeeper to question her current mood. She would only think her spoilt and difficult. After all, her place in their household was far superior in terms of position and comfort. Yet still, she felt Frøken Olsdatter's keen, intelligent eyes upon her.

'Tomorrow, Anna, I must go to the market in the square

to shop for meat and vegetables. Would you like to accompany me?'

'Oh yes! There is nothing I would like more,' she replied, touched that the woman had sensed exactly what was wrong.

'Then I shall take you, and perhaps we could spare the time to go for a stroll around the park beforehand. Herr Bayer is at the university tomorrow between the hours of nine and twelve, and then he will be out for lunch, so we have plenty of time. It will be our little secret, yes?'

'Yes.' Anna nodded in relief. 'Thank you.'

After that, the trips to the market were conducted twice weekly. Apart from Sundays when she went to church, these were the days she looked forward to most.

At the end of November, Anna realised that she had been in Christiania for over two months. On the makeshift calendar she had drawn for herself, she was marking off the days until she could return home to Heddal for Christmas. However, there had at least been snow in Christiania, which had cheered her somewhat. The women who walked in the park across the street now wore fur cloaks and hats and held their hands in fur muffs, which Anna decided were a very stupid fashion because if one wanted to itch one's nose, one might get frostbite of the fingers whilst one did so.

Inside the apartment, little had altered in her daily routine, although Herr Bayer had handed her a copy of Herr Ibsen's *Peer Gynt* last week and told her to read it.

'Oh, but I already have,' she'd been delighted to answer.

'Then that is all to the good. It will help you as you read it again.'

The first night, she had put the book to one side, thinking what a waste of time it was to do as Herr Bayer had asked when she already knew what happened at the end. But the next morning, he questioned her closely on the first five pages of the poem and, hardly able to remember anything, she had lied weakly and said that last night she'd had a bad headache and had gone to sleep early. So she read it again, and in fact was pleased with herself as she realised how much her reading skills had improved since the summer. There were now few words she could not decipher, and if any posed a problem, Herr Bayer was more than happy to assist her. But quite what this poem could possibly have to do with her future here in Christiania, Anna had absolutely no idea.

'My kjære Anna, last night I finally received the music I have been waiting for from Herr Hennum! And we will set to work with it this minute.'

Although she had no idea what the music might be, Anna could see her mentor was buzzing with excitement as he took his seat at the piano.

'To think that we have a copy of this in our own hands! Come, Anna, stand by me and I will play it for you.'

Anna did as she was asked, and stared at the music with interest. '"Solveig's Song",' she murmured, reading the title of the music written at the top.

'Yes, Anna. And you will be the first ever to sing it! What do you say to that, eh?'

Anna had learnt that this oft-repeated phrase of Herr Bayer's meant she must always answer in the affirmative.

'That I am very happy.'

'Good, good. It was hoped that Herr Grieg himself would

be travelling to Christiania to help the orchestra and the singers with his new composition, but sadly, both his parents have died recently, and he is still in mourning. Subsequently, he feels unable to make the journey from Bergen.'

'Herr Grieg wrote this?' she gasped.

'He did indeed. Herr Ibsen asked him to write the music to accompany his forthcoming stage production of *Peer Gynt*, which will be premiered at the Christiania Theatre in February. My dear young lady, both Herr Hennum – the man you met some weeks ago who is the revered conductor of our orchestra here – and I believe it is you who should sing Solveig.'

'*Me?*'

'Yes, Anna, *you*.'

'But . . . I have never stood upon a stage in my life! Let alone the most famous stage in Norway!'

'And that, my dear girl, is the beauty of it. Herr Josephson, the director of the theatre and of this production, has already cast an actress of renown in the part of Solveig. The trouble is, as Herr Hennum put it recently, she may be a great actress, but when she opens her mouth to sing, she sounds like a scalded cat. So, we need a voice of purity, someone who will stand offstage and sing as Madame Hansson mimes the words to this song and one other. Do you see, my dear?'

Anna *did* see, and couldn't help feeling a pang of disappointment that she *wouldn't* be seen. And that the actress with the scalded-cat voice would pretend that Anna's singing was her own. However, the fact that the conductor from the famous Christiania Theatre thought so much of her voice as to lend it to Madame Hansson was a huge compliment. And she did not wish to seem ungrateful.

'It is indeed a wonderful opportunity that has been presented to us,' Herr Bayer continued. 'Of course, nothing is definite yet. We must have you perform in front of Herr Josephson, the director of the play, to see if he believes your voice conveys the true spirit of Solveig. There must be such emotion, such feeling in your rendition of the songs that no one in the audience is without a tear in their eye. In fact, Herr Hennum told me that your voice will be the last thing the audience hears before the curtain drops. Herr Josephson has agreed to see us on the afternoon of the twenty-third of December, just before he departs for Christmas. He will make his decision then.'

'But I am leaving for Heddal on the twenty-first!' protested Anna, unable to stop herself. 'And if I must wait here until the afternoon of the twenty-third, I will not be able to return home in time for Christmas. The journey takes almost two days. I . . . can Herr Josephson not see us another time?'

'Anna, you must understand that Herr Josephson is a very busy man, and the fact he has granted us even a moment in his presence is an honour in itself. I fully understand it will not be your pleasure to stay here with me over the festive season, but equally, this may be the best opportunity you ever have to alter the entire course of your future. There will be many Christmases ahead of you with your family, but only one chance to secure the singing role of Solveig, in a piece in which Norway's most prominent dramatist and composer have combined their skills for the first time!' Herr Bayer shook his head in a rare moment of frustration. 'Anna, you must try to see what this could mean for you. And if you can't, then I suggest that you return home immediately and sing to your cows, rather than to a first-night audience at the Christiania

Theatre, in a premiere that will surely go down in history. Now, will you try to sing this, or will you not?'

Feeling as small and ignorant as he'd intended her to, Anna nodded slowly. 'Yes, Herr Bayer, of course.'

That night, however, Anna cried herself to sleep. Even if she was 'making history' as Herr Bayer had said, the thought of not being with her family at Christmas was simply too much for her to bear.

16

Christiania
16th January 1876

'Jens! Are you still alive?!' Jens Halvorsen was woken abruptly as his mother's voice came ringing through his bedroom door. 'Dora has told me she thinks you may have died in your sleep, for she has had no response from you all morning!'

Sighing, Jens climbed off his bed and studied his dishevelled – and still fully clothed – reflection in the looking glass. 'I will be down for breakfast in ten minutes,' he replied through the door.

'It is luncheon, Jens. You missed breakfast altogether!'

'I will be there.' Jens peered in close as he did every morning to check if his mane of wavy mahogany hair had collected any grey hairs. At only twenty years of age, Jens knew this was something he shouldn't worry about. But given that his father's hair had apparently turned white overnight at twenty-five – probably due to the shock of marrying his mother that same year – Jens woke with trepidation every morning.

Ten minutes later, dressed in a fresh set of clothes,

he appeared in the dining room as promised and kissed Margarete, his mother, on the cheek before taking his place at the table. Dora, their young housemaid, began to serve lunch.

'I do apologise, Mor. I had a terrible headache that kept me in bed this morning. I still feel quite bilious.'

Immediately, his mother's expression of irritation changed to one of sympathy. She reached across the table to touch his forehead. 'Indeed, you are a little warm. Perhaps you have a fever? My poor boy, can you face luncheon, or would you rather Dora bring you a tray in bed?'

'I am sure I can manage, although you must excuse me if I don't eat much.'

In truth, Jens was starving. Last night, he'd met up with some friends at a bar, and they'd ended up at a bordello down by the docks, which had provided a very satisfying finale to the evening. He'd drunk far too much aquavit and only vaguely remembered the carriage bringing him home, and how sick he had been in the ditch by the house. And subsequently, due to the freezing snow that lay tightly packed on its branches, his many failed attempts to climb the tree that abutted his bedroom window, which Dora always left open for him if he was out late.

Therefore, he reasoned with himself, his story wasn't exactly a lie. He *had* felt quite dreadful this morning, and had slept through Dora's timid attempts to wake him. He knew the maid was in love with him, which was why she colluded in his pretences whenever he needed her to.

'It was a shame that you were out last night, Jens. I had my good friend Herr Hennum, the conductor of the Christiania orchestra, here for supper.' Margarete interrupted his thoughts. His mother was a loyal patron of the arts, using his father's 'beer money', as the two of them privately called it, to fund her passion.

'And was it an enjoyable evening?'

'Yes, it was indeed. As I'm sure I've already told you, Herr Grieg has written a wonderful musical score to accompany Herr Ibsen's marvellous *Peer Gynt* poem.'

'Yes, Mor, you have told me.'

'The premiere will be held in February, but sadly, Herr Hennum tells me that the current orchestra is not up to Herr Grieg's expectations, or in fact his own. The music compositions are apparently complex, and must be played by a confident and proficient orchestra. Herr Hennum is looking for talented musicians who can play more than one instrument. I've told him of your skills on the piano, the violin and the flute and he has requested that you go to the theatre and play for him.'

Jens took a mouthful of the catfish brought in especially from the west coast of Norway. 'Mor, I am currently at university studying chemistry, to fit me out to take over the family brewery. You know very well Far would not allow me to leave to play in an orchestra. In fact, he would be furious.'

'Perhaps if it was a fait accompli, he may relent,' she said quietly.

'You are asking me to lie?' Jens felt suddenly as sick as he'd pretended to be earlier.

'I am saying that when you reach the age of twenty-one, you will be a man, and may make your own choices, whatever others may think of them. You would receive a wage from the orchestra, albeit not a large one, which would give you some modicum of financial independence.'

'It is six months to my birthday, Mor. For now, I am still dependent on my father and under his control.'

'Jens, please. Herr Hennum will hear you play at the theatre at one thirty tomorrow. I beg you, at least meet him. You never know what may come of it.'

'I am unwell,' he said as he stood up abruptly. 'Forgive me, Mor, but I'm returning to my bedroom to lie down.'

Margarete watched her son march across the room, open the door, then slam it behind him. She put her fingers to her forehead, feeling her own temples throbbing. She understood what had engendered Jens' departure and sighed guiltily.

Since her son had been little more than a toddler, she had sat him on her knee and taught him the keys of the piano. One of her most pleasant and abiding memories from his childhood had been watching his fat little fingers fly across the ivories. It had been her greatest wish for her only child to inherit her own musical talent, one she had not used to its full potential, due to her marriage to Jens' father.

Jonas Halvorsen, her husband, was not an artistic soul, and was interested only in the amount of kroner on the ledgers of the Halvorsen Brewing Company. From the start of their marriage, he had seen his wife's passion for music as something to be discouraged, and even more vehemently, that of his only son. Still, when Jonas was out at his office, Margarete had persevered with developing Jens' talent, and by the time he was six, he was effortlessly playing sonatas that would challenge a student three times his age.

When Jens was ten, defying her husband's disapproval, she had organised a recital at their house and invited the great and the good of the Christiania music establishment to attend. Every one of them who had listened to her little boy play had been enthralled and had predicted great things for his future.

'He must go to the Leipzig Conservatory when he is old enough and expand his knowledge and his skills, for you know that the opportunities here in Christiania are limited,' Johan Hennum, the newly installed conductor of the Christiania orchestra, had commented. 'With the right training, he has great potential.'

Margarete had said as much to her husband, who had responded with a cruel chuckle. 'My dear wife, I understand how much you long for our son to become a famous musician, but as you well know, Jens will join the family business when he's twenty-one. My forebears and I have not spent over one hundred and fifty years building it for it to be sold on my deathbed to one of my competitors. If Jens wishes to tinker with his instruments as he grows up, then of course I am happy for him to do so. But it is no future career for a son of mine.'

Margarete, however, was not to be deterred. For the next few years, she had continued to teach Jens to play the violin and the flute as well as the piano, knowing that to join any orchestra, a musician must be accomplished on more than one instrument. She'd tutored him in German and Italian, both of which she felt would help him tackle complex orchestral and operatic works.

Jens' father had continued to resolutely ignore the beautiful sounds which emanated from the music room and echoed throughout the house. The only time that Margarete could force him to listen was when Jens played the *hardanger* fiddle. She would sometimes encourage him to play to his father after dinner, and would watch as Jonas's features – aided by several glasses of good French wine – relaxed into a dreamy smile as he hummed along to a familiar folk song.

Yet despite her husband's indifference to Jens' talent, and his insistence that it could never become a career, Margarete continued to believe that a way forward could be found when Jens was older. But then, the little boy who had worked so diligently at his music lessons began to grow up, and Jonas had taken him into his own hands. Instead of the two hours a day of music practice, Jens trailed behind his father at the brewery as he oversaw production or the preparation of the accounts.

The situation had crystallised three years ago, when Jonas had insisted his son go to university to study chemistry which would, he said, fit him out for the brewery, even though Margarete had gone down on her knees to beg her husband to allow Jens to go and study at the Leipzig Conservatory.

'He has no passion for chemistry or business and such a talent for music!' Margarete had entreated him.

Jonas had looked at her coolly. 'I have indulged you up until now, but Jens is no longer a child and must realise where his responsibilities lie. He will be the fifth generation of Halvorsens to run our brewery. You have been deluding yourself if you thought your musical aspirations for our son would ever come to anything. Term starts in October. The matter is closed.'

'Please don't cry, Mor,' Jens had said to her after he'd heard the news from his devastated mother. 'I never expected anything else.'

Just as Margarete had known would happen, in being forced to give up music for a subject in which he had no aptitude or interest, Jens had done little studying at university. And even more dangerously, his natural high spirits and devil-may-care attitude had begun leading him astray.

As a light sleeper who woke at the slightest noise, she knew her son was often out until the small hours. Jens had a large circle of friends, who were all attracted by his *joie de vivre* and easy charm. Margarete knew he was generous to a fault, so much so that he would often come to her halfway through the month saying he'd used up the allowance from his father on gifts or loans for this friend or that, and could she possibly see her way to tiding him over?

She often smelt stale alcohol on his breath, and had considered the possibility that excessive drinking also played a part in the emptying of his pockets. She suspected too that there were women involved in his nocturnal exploits. Only last week she had seen a stain of lip paint upon his collar. But this at least she could understand: all young men – and even older ones – had their needs, as Margarete knew to her cost. It was just masculine nature.

In her mind, the problem was very simple: with the prospect of a future he did not want, and without his beloved music, Jens was unfulfilled and turning to drink and women to drown his sorrows. Margarete rose from the table, praying that Jens would go to meet Herr Hennum tomorrow. In her opinion, it was all that could save him.

Meanwhile, Jens lay on his bed upstairs thinking much the same thoughts as his mother. Long ago, he'd realised that a music career could never be a reality. In a few months' time, he would leave university and take his place in his father's brewery.

The thought appalled him.

He wasn't sure who he pitied most out of his parents: his father, a slave to his bank account and the endless machinations of his successful brewery, or his mother, who had brought a much-needed pedigree to the union, but was anxious and dissatisfied with life. Jens could see clearly that their marriage was little more than a deal that had been struck for mutual gain. The problem for him was that as their only offspring, he was forever being used as a pawn in their emotional chess game. Long ago, he'd learnt that he couldn't win. And these days, neither did he particularly care to try.

Although today, his mother had been right. He *was* almost of age. What if it *was* possible to reinvent the dream he'd once worked so hard for as a boy?

Hearing his mother leave the house after lunch, Jens slipped downstairs and, on a whim, entered the music room where his mother still took her occasional music pupils.

He sat down on the stool in front of the beautiful grand piano, his body automatically adopting the correct posture. Lifting the smooth wooden fallboard, he allowed his fingers to trail up and down over the keys, realising it must be over two years since he'd last played. He began with Beethoven's *Pathétique* sonata, which had always been a favourite of his, remembering his mother's patient tutoring and how easily it had come to him. 'You must put your entire body into your playing,' she had once said, 'as well as your heart and soul. These things are the mark of a true musician.'

Jens lost track of time as he played. And as the music swelled in the room, he forgot the struggle of the chemistry lectures he loathed and the future he dreaded, and allowed himself to disappear into the glorious music, just as he used to.

As the last note reverberated around the room, Jens found there were tears in his eyes, simply from the joy of playing. And he made up his mind to meet Herr Hennum tomorrow.

At one thirty the following day, Jens sat down on another piano stool in the deserted orchestra pit of the Christiania Theatre.

'So, Herr Halvorsen, I last heard you play ten years ago. Your mother tells me you have become an exceptional musician since,' said Johan Hennum, the esteemed conductor of the orchestra.

'My mother is somewhat biased, sir.'

'She also says that you have had no formal training at a music conservatory.'

'Unfortunately, no, sir. I have been at university for the past two and a half years studying chemistry.' Jens could already sense that the conductor believed he was wasting his time. He had probably agreed to see him as a favour to his mother in return for the generous funding she provided for the arts. 'But I should add that my mother has tutored me in music for many years. She is, as you know, a most respected teacher.'

'She is indeed. So, which do you regard as your main instrument out of the four your mother tells me you can play?'

'Certainly, I enjoy playing the piano the most, but I feel I am able to acquit myself equally well on the violin, the flute or the *hardanger* fiddle.'

'There is no part for the piano in Herr Grieg's orchestration for *Peer Gynt*. However, we are looking for a second violinist and another flautist. Here.' Hennum handed him some sheet music. 'See what you make of the flute part and I'll be back shortly to hear you play.' The conductor nodded at him and disappeared through a door beneath the stage.

Jens glanced through the music: 'Prelude to Act IV: "Morning Mood"'. Taking his flute from its case, he fastened it together. The theatre was almost as cold as the sub-zero temperature outside and he rubbed his numb fingers together vigorously in an attempt to get the blood circulating. Then he put the instrument to his lips and tried the first six notes . . .

'Right, Herr Halvorsen, shall we see how you've got on?' said Johan Hennum briskly as he returned to the orchestra pit five minutes later.

Jens felt a need to impress this man, to prove himself capable of the task at hand. Thanking God for his ability to sight-read – a skill that had always helped to convince his mother that he'd practised far more than he actually did – he began to play. Within seconds he found himself completely immersed in the haunting music, which was unlike anything he had ever heard before. As he finished the piece, he lowered the flute from his lips and looked at Hennum.

'For a first try, that really wasn't bad. Not bad at all. Now take this,' he said, handing Jens another sheet of music. 'It's the part for the first violin. See what you can do with it.'

Jens took his violin from its case and tuned it. Then he studied the music for a few minutes and practised the notes quietly before beginning to play.

'Very good, Herr Halvorsen. Your mother's description of your talent was not misplaced. And I admit to being surprised. You are certainly an excellent sight-reader, which will be essential in the weeks to come, as I put the rather disparate members of my orchestra together. I will have no time to spare for mollycoddling. And let me assure you, playing in an orchestra is very different to being a soloist. It will take you time to grasp the ways of it, and I should warn you that I tolerate no slack behaviour from my musicians. Normally, I'd be reticent to take on a novice, but needs must. I'd like you to start within a week. What do you say?'

Jens stared at him, astonished that this man seemed to be offering him a position. He'd been absolutely sure that his lack of experience would elicit a negative response. Then again, it was no secret that the Christiania orchestra was a ragbag mixture of musicians, given that there was no proper music school here and little talent to choose from. His mother had told him that a boy aged just ten had once played in it.

'I think that I would be honoured to take a place in your orchestra for such an important premiere,' he found himself answering.

'Then I am happy to have you, Herr Halvorsen. You have the makings of a fine musician. However, the wages are somewhat meagre – not that I believe that is a problem for you – and the hours of rehearsal in the next few weeks will be long and arduous. And as you may have noticed, the surroundings are less than comfortable. I suggest that you wrap up warmly.'

'Yes sir, I will.'

'You mentioned to me that you are currently studying at the university. I presume you are happy to put your employment with the orchestra before your lectures?'

'Yes,' Jens replied, knowing what his father would have to say on the matter, but deciding that since it was his mother who had got him into this in the first place, it was up to her to quash any objections at home. This was his route to freedom and he was taking it.

'Please tell your mother I am grateful to her for sending you to me.'

'I will, sir.'

'So, rehearsals begin next week. I will see you bright and early on Monday morning at nine o'clock. And now I must go in search of a decent bassoonist, which for the life of me I cannot find in this godforsaken city of ours. Good day to you, Herr Halvorsen, and please see yourself out.'

Jens watched the conductor leave the orchestra pit, feeling bemused by the sudden *volte-face* his life had just taken. He turned and looked into the gloom of the auditorium. He'd been here many times with his mother to watch concerts and operas, but as he sat down abruptly on the piano stool, he felt suddenly overwhelmed. Recently, he knew he'd been drifting, simply taking each day as it came, dreading graduation and his future as a brewer.

Just now, as he'd played Herr Grieg's exquisite new composition, he'd felt a spark of his old exhilaration. When he was younger, he used to lie in bed thinking up tunes in his head, then trying them out on the piano the next morning.

He'd never written them down, but it was composing his own music that really inspired him.

Now, in the dim light of the orchestra pit, Jens put his frozen fingers to the keys of the grand piano and cast his mind back to the melodies he'd composed as a boy. There was one in particular, not dissimilar in structure to Grieg's newest composition, reminiscent of folk songs from the past. Jens began to play it from memory to the empty auditorium.

17

Stalsberg Våningshuset
Tindevegen
Heddal

14th February 1876

Kjære Anna,

Thank you for your last letter. As always, your descriptions of life in Christiania are informative as well as amusing. They never fail to bring a smile to my face. And rest assured your penmanship and spelling improves each time. Here in Heddal, all is the same as it has ever been. Christmas was as always, but worse for the fact you were not here to celebrate it with us. As you know, it is the coldest and darkest part of the year, where it is not only the animals who hibernate, but us humans too. The snows have lasted longer and been deeper than usual and I have discovered there is a leak in our farmhouse roof, which will require me to replace the turf before the spring thaw or we will have an indoor lake on which we can skate. My father tells me it has not been replaced in his lifetime, so at least I feel it has served us well. Knut has promised to help me in the spring, for which I am grateful.

He himself has recently been courting a young lady from a village outside Skien. Her name is Sigrid and she is sweet and pretty, if a little quiet. The good news is that your parents approve of her. And wedding bells will chime from Heddal church this summer. I pray that you will be able to return home for the event.

It is hard to believe that you are part of the stage premiere of my favourite Ibsen poem, with the music written especially by Herr Grieg himself. Have you set eyes on Herr Ibsen at the theatre yet? Surely he will appear to check the piece is as he wishes it to be, although I believe he currently resides in Italy. You may not have time to write again before the opening night as it is only ten days away, and I imagine you are kept very busy with rehearsals. If you don't, then may I wish you and your beautiful voice the best of fortune.

Yours with admiration,

Lars

P.S. I enclose one of my poems, which I recently sent, along with others, to a publisher called Scribner in New York City, America. I have translated it back into Norwegian for you.

Anna read the poem, titled 'Ode on a Silver Birch'. As she had no idea what an 'ode' was, she skimmed through it briefly, not recognising many of the big words, then put it by the side of her plate to continue her breakfast. She wished her life was as exciting as Lars imagined it to be. So far, she had only been twice to the Christiania Theatre: once to perform for Herr Josephson just before Christmas, when it had been agreed that she should indeed sing the role of Solveig, and then again last week, when the actors had attempted their first run-through onstage so Anna could watch from the wings in order to understand the play.

Having laboured under the misconception that such a grand place as a theatre would be heated, Anna had spent the day sitting on a stool in the draughty wings, freezing half to death. They'd only managed to get through the first three acts before there had been a crisis. Henrik Klausen, the actor playing Peer, had tripped over the length of blue fabric under which ten little boys knelt and moved their bodies to give the impression of Peer crossing a stormy sea. He'd sprained his ankle severely and as there was no play without the lead character, rehearsals had been suspended.

Subsequently, Anna had caught a dreadful chill and had been in bed for the past four days, with Herr Bayer clucking like an old mother hen over her croaky voice.

'And with only a week to go!' he'd groaned to her. 'The timing really could not be any worse. You must take as much honey as you can bear, young lady. Let us hope it can help repair your vocal cords in time.'

Earlier this morning, she had tentatively sung a few scales after the obligatory dose of honey – she felt she might sprout wings and that yellow and brown stripes would appear on her body after the amount she had swallowed – and Herr Bayer had looked relieved.

'Thank the Lord, your voice is returning. Madame Thora

Hansson, the actress playing Solveig, will be arriving shortly so that the two of you can work together on the timing for her to mime to your singing. It is a great honour that she has agreed to come here to the apartment, as you are currently indisposed. As you know, she is one of the most famous actresses in Norway, and reputed to be Herr Ibsen's favourite,' Herr Bayer had added.

At half past ten, Thora Hansson swept into the apartment in her beautiful fur-lined velvet cloak. She entered the drawing room in a haze of strong French perfume, where Anna was waiting nervously for her.

'*Kjære*, excuse me if I do not approach you, for even though Herr Bayer tells me you are no longer infectious, I cannot afford to catch your ailment.'

'Of course, Madame Hansson,' Anna said demurely as she dipped a curtsey to her.

'At least I will not be using my voice this morning,' she smiled. 'For it is you who will be providing the heavenly sound. I will merely open and close my mouth and put my efforts into the visual portrayal of Herr Grieg's beautiful songs.'

'Yes, Madame.'

As Herr Bayer entered and began fussing around Madame Hansson, Anna studied the actress. At the theatre, she'd only glimpsed her from a distance and had presumed she was quite old. Yet close up, she could see that Madame Hansson was actually young, perhaps only a few years older than herself. She was very beautiful, with fine features and a head of thick dark brown hair. Anna struggled to believe that even in traditional costume, this sophisticated young woman could convince an audience she was a simple peasant girl from the hills.

A peasant girl like herself . . .

'Right, shall we begin? Anna, *poco a poco*,' Herr Bayer advised. 'We do not want to strain your voice during its recovery. So, if you are ready, Madame Hansson, we will start with "Solveig's Song" then move on to "The Cradle Song".'

For the rest of the morning, the two women practised what was in essence a duet, albeit with one of the singers mute. At various points, Anna could sense the actress's frustration if she opened her mouth at the wrong time and Anna's voice came in a beat later. Madame Hansson suggested that Anna leave the room so that Herr Bayer could get a feeling for whether the audience could truly believe it was her singing. Standing in the draughty corridor, with her head thumping and her throat now sore again from singing, Anna had begun to loathe the songs. She had to adhere exactly to the same length of notes and pauses so that Madame Hansson knew exactly when to open and close her own mouth. Part of what she normally enjoyed about singing was interpreting a song differently to her listeners each time, be they people, or just cows. Which in retrospect, seemed far preferable to singing, as she was at present, to a door.

Eventually, Herr Bayer clapped his hands. 'Perfect! I think we have it. Well done, Madame Hansson. Please, Anna, come back in.'

Anna did so, and Madame Hansson turned to her and smiled.

'I think it will work admirably. Just promise me that you will sing identically each night, won't you, my dear?'

'Of course, Madame Hansson.'

'Anna, you look quite pale. I think the morning's exertions have worn you out. I will tell Frøken Olsdatter that you will take a short rest and she will bring you luncheon in your room and some more honey to soothe your voice.'

'Yes, Herr Bayer,' she said obediently.

'Thank you, Anna, and no doubt we will see each other at the theatre in the next few days.' Madame Hansson smiled sweetly at her and Anna bobbed another curtsey before retiring to her bedroom.

Apartment 4,
10 St Olav's Gate
Christiania

23rd February 1876

Kjære Lars, Mor, Far and Knut,

I write in haste for today is the dress rehearsal and tomorrow is the opening night of Peer Gynt. I dearly wish that you could all be there for the occasion, but I do understand that the cost makes a visit impossible.

I am excited but a little nervous as well. Herr Bayer has shown me that all the newspapers are filled with stories about tomorrow, and there have even been rumours that the King and Queen will be in attendance in the Royal Box. (I personally doubt this – they live in Sweden, which even for the royal family would be a long way to travel just to see a play, but that is how the gossip goes here.) Inside the theatre the atmosphere is tense. Herr Josephson, the director, believes it will be a disaster as we are yet to run through the whole play without having to stop for hours while some technical problem is sorted out.

And Herr Hennum, the conductor, whom I like very much and who has always seemed calm before, shouts endlessly at his orchestra for not counting the beats.

Would you believe that I am yet to sing 'The Cradle Song' in the theatre itself because we still have not managed to get to the end of the play? Herr Hennum has assured me that it will definitely happen today.

Meanwile, I spend my time with the children who have been employed to play small characters, such as trolls and the like. When I was first directed to their dressing room, I felt insulted, because the other ladies of the chorus are in another. Perhaps they do not realise how old I am? But now I am glad of it because the children make me laugh and we play card games together to pass the time.

I can write no more now for I must leave for the theatre, but I should inform you, to what I know will be your great sadness, Lars, that Herr Ibsen has not yet appeared.

I send my love from Christiania to you all.

Anna

As she left the apartment to go to the theatre, Anna placed the letter on the silver salver in the hall.

The dress rehearsal had been running for almost four hours and Jens was tired, cold and irritable, as were the rest of the orchestra. The tension in the pit had risen to a crescendo over the past few days. More than once, Herr Hennum had shouted at him to pay attention, which Jens felt was unfair, given that Simen, the elderly first violinist who sat next to him, seemed to be permanently dozing. He imagined that he must be the only member of the orchestra below the age of fifty. However, the musicians were a friendly bunch, and he enjoyed their droll camaraderie.

So far, he'd managed to turn up on time every day, albeit with the occasional bad hangover. But as that seemed to be the case for the rest of the orchestra as well, Jens felt he fitted in perfectly. And of course, there were the lovely ladies of the chorus to admire on the stage during one of the interminable pauses while Herr Josephson arranged the actors to his liking.

After he had been offered his position in the orchestra, his mother's unbridled delight had almost brought him to tears.

'But what will we say to Far?' he'd asked her. 'You know that I must miss my lectures at the university in order to attend rehearsals.'

'I think it best that, for now, he is unaware of your sudden . . . change of direction. We will let him believe you are still attending the university. He will be none the wiser in the short term, I'm sure.'

In other words, Jens had surmised, his mother was too scared to tell him.

It hardly mattered now, he thought, as he tuned his violin, because if his resolve not to join the brewery was strong before, now it was unbreakable. Despite the long hours, the cold, and Hennum's often scathing comments, Jens knew for certain that the joy he'd once had in his music had returned to him. Herr Grieg's score contained a wealth of evocative passages, from the lively 'In the Hall of the Mountain King' to

'Anitra's Dance', during which Jens only had to close his eyes to mentally conjure up the exoticism of Morocco as he played the notes on his violin.

Yet still, his favourite passage was 'Morning Mood' at the beginning of Act IV. It formed the musical backdrop to the part of the play when Peer wakes at dawn in Africa, suffering from a hangover and knowing he's lost everything. Then Peer's thoughts turn to Norway, his homeland, and the sun rising over the Norwegian fjords. Jens never tired of playing it.

At present, both he and the other flautist, who was perhaps three times his age, were taking turns to play the haunting notes of the first four bars. As Hennum appeared in the pit and tapped his baton to gain their attention, Jens realised *he* wanted to be the one who played them on the opening night more than anything he'd ever wanted in his life.

'So, we commence Act IV,' the conductor announced, the break between acts having taken over an hour so far. 'Bjarte Frafjord, you will play first flute this morning. Five minutes, please,' Hennum added, as he went off to consult with Herr Josephson, the director, before they began.

A wave of disappointment swept over Jens. If Bjarte was playing the first flute part at the dress rehearsal, then the chances were that Hennum would want him to play it tomorrow on opening night too.

A few minutes later, Henrik Klausen, who was playing the title role of Peer Gynt, arrived to take his place hanging over the edge of the orchestra pit, from where he would pretend to vomit on the musicians, as his character recovered from the hangover he was supposed to be suffering.

'How are you all tonight, boys?' Henrik called down affably to the musicians below him.

There was a general murmuring as Hennum reappeared and took up his baton. 'Herr Josephson has promised me that we can run through Act IV with minimal interruption, so that we can finally get to Act V. Everybody ready?'

Hennum raised his baton and the sound of Bjarte's flute drifted up from the pit. *He really isn't as good as me*, Jens thought sulkily as he tucked his violin under his chin and prepared to play.

An hour later, apart from one minor hitch that seemed to have been quickly sorted out, they were nearing the end of Act IV. Jens glanced up at Madame Hansson, who was playing the part of Solveig. Even in her peasant costume, Jens could see she was extremely attractive and hoped he'd get a chance to make her acquaintance at the after-show party tomorrow evening.

He hastily refocused himself as Herr Hennum lifted his baton once more and the violinists launched into the first poignant bars of 'Solveig's Song'. Jens listened as Madame Hansson began to sing. It was a voice so pure, so perfect and evocative, that Jens found himself mentally disappearing off to the hillside hut in which Solveig and her sorrow resided. He'd had no idea that Madame Hansson could sing like this. It was one of the most glorious female voices he'd ever heard. It seemed to symbolise fresh air, youth, yet also the pain of lost hopes and dreams . . .

So enraptured was he that he earned a hard stare from Hennum when he came in a beat too late. When they finally reached the end of the play and the achingly sad notes of 'The Cradle Song' – sung by Solveig as the returned and chastened Peer rests his weary head in her lap – reverberated around the auditorium, Jens felt the hairs on the back of his neck rise at the sheer perfection of Madame Hansson's rendition. As the curtain fell a few minutes later, there was spontaneous applause from the assortment of theatre staff who had gathered to watch and listen.

'Did you hear that?' Jens said to Simen, who was already packing his violin away, ready to move swiftly out of the pit and across the road to the Engebret Café before last orders. 'I didn't know Madame Hansson had such a beautiful voice.'

'The Lord bless you, Jens! What we just heard is indeed a beautiful voice, as you say, but it does not belong to Madame Hansson. Couldn't you see that she was miming? The woman can't sing a note, so they had to bring in the voice of another to give the impression that she can. I'm sure Herr Josephson will be pleased that his illusion has succeeded.' Simen chuckled and patted Jens on his shoulder as he left the pit.

'Who is she?' he called to Simen's departing back as he disappeared under the stage.

'I think that's rather the point,' came the reply over Simen's shoulder. 'She is a ghost voice and no one has any idea.'

The owner of the voice that had so moved Jens Halvorsen was currently sitting in a carriage being driven home to Herr Bayer's apartment. Feeling conspicuous in the national costume that he'd said she should wear for her 'performances' so that she looked like the other ladies of the chorus who were clad in the same, she was glad to be alone for the journey home. It had been another long, exhausting day and she was grateful when Frøken Olsdatter opened the door to her and took her cloak.

'You must be very tired, Anna *kjære*. But tell me, how do you think you sang?' she asked as she gently ushered her charge towards her bedroom.

'I really don't know. When the curtain came down, I did as Herr Bayer told me: went to the stage door and got straight into the carriage. And here I am,' she sighed as she let Frøken Olsdatter help her undress and get into bed.

'Herr Bayer says you are allowed to sleep in tomorrow morning. He wants you and your voice to be fresh for the opening night. Now, your hot milk and honey is there on the nightstand.'

'Thank you.' Anna picked up the glass gratefully.

'Goodnight, Anna.'

'Goodnight, Frøken Olsdatter, and thank you.'

Johan Hennum appeared in the pit and clapped his orchestra to attention. 'So, everyone is ready?'

The conductor looked down at his orchestra fondly, and Jens mused how different the atmosphere in the theatre was compared to this time yesterday. Not only was the orchestra in full evening dress rather than their usual motley collection of street clothes, but the first-night audience, buzzing with expectation, had entered and taken their seats in the auditorium. The women unwrapped their furs to reveal an array of stunning gowns adorned with sumptuous jewellery, which sparkled in the soft glow of the ornate chandelier hanging from the centre of the ceiling.

'Gentlemen,' Hennum continued, 'tonight we are all honoured to be taking our place in history. Even though Herr Grieg cannot be present, we intend to make him proud. And to give his wonderful music the rendition it deserves. I'm sure that one day you will all tell your grandchildren you were part of this. And Herr Halvorsen, tonight you will play the first flute part in 'Morning Mood'. Right, if we are all ready . . .'

The conductor stood up on his plinth to indicate to the audience that the performance was about to begin. There was a sudden hushed silence, as if the entire auditorium was holding its breath. And in that moment, Jens sent up a prayer of gratitude that his most fervent wish had been granted.

No one waiting backstage during the performance knew quite what the audience was thinking. Anna walked slowly to the wings to perform her first song, accompanied by Rude, one of the young boys who performed in the crowd scenes.

'You can hear a pin drop out there, Frøken Anna. I've watched the audience from a hidden spot in the wings, and I think they like it.'

Anna took her position at the side of the stage, hidden by the flats of scenery, but placed so that she could still see Madame Hansson, and she felt suddenly frozen with fear. Even if she couldn't be seen and her name had only been put in the programme under the long list of 'Chorus', she knew that somewhere out there, Herr Bayer was listening. As was every important person in Christiania.

She felt Rude's small hand squeeze hers. 'Don't worry, Frøken Anna, we all think you sing beautifully.'

He left her alone then, and Anna stood watching Madame Hansson and listening carefully for her cue. As the orchestra played the first bars of 'Solveig's Song', Anna took a deep breath. And thinking of Rosa and her family back in Heddal, she let her voice soar.

Forty minutes later, as the final curtain fell, Anna was standing in the wings once more, having just sung 'The Cradle Song'. There was a stunned silence from the audience as the rest of the cast assembled onstage for the curtain call. Anna had not been asked to take a bow, so she remained where she was. Then, as the curtain rose again to reveal the cast, she was almost deafened by the sudden tumultuous applause. People were stamping their feet and shouting for an encore.

'Sing "Solveig's Song" again, Madame Hansson!' she heard someone shout, a request which the actress graciously refused with a shake of her head and an elegant wave of her hand. Finally, after Herr Josephson had appeared onstage to pass on apologies from both Ibsen and Grieg for their absences, and the last bow had been taken, the curtain came down for good and the cast began filing off the stage. Everyone ignored Anna as they walked past her, full of adrenaline and chattering excitedly about what seemed to have been a resounding success after so many weeks of work.

Anna went back to her dressing room to collect her cloak and said goodnight to the children, whose proud mothers were helping them change out of their costumes. Herr Bayer had said the carriage would be waiting for her outside and she must leave directly after the performance. As she made her way down the corridor towards the exit, she bumped into

Herr Josephson as he emerged from Madame Hansson's dressing room.

'Anna, you sang quite beautifully. I doubt there was a dry eye in the house. Well done.'

'Thank you, Herr Josephson.'

'Safe journey home,' he added with a nod and a small bow before turning away from her to knock on Henrik Klausen's dressing room door.

Anna walked to the stage door and reluctantly left the theatre.

'So, who is the girl who sings "Solveig's Song"?' asked Jens, scanning the crowd in the foyer. 'Is she here?'

'I wouldn't know, I've never seen her,' commented Isaac the cellist, who was already the worse for wear. 'She has the voice of an angel, but may look like a hag for all we know.'

Determined to find out, Jens cornered the conductor.

'Well done, my boy,' Hennum said as he clapped him on the shoulder, clearly in a euphoric mood after the success of the evening. 'I'm glad my faith in you was not misplaced. You could go a long way, with some practice and experience.'

'Thank you, sir. Pray tell me, who is the mystery girl who sang the words of Solveig so beautifully tonight? Is she here?'

'You mean Anna? She's our real-life Solveig from the hills. I'd doubt she has stayed behind for the party, though. She's Franz Bayer's ward and protégée; very young and not used to the city. He keeps a tight rein on her, so my guess is that your Cinderella has scurried home before the clock strikes midnight.'

'It is a shame, as I wished to tell her how her voice moved me. Also,' Jens continued, seizing the opportunity, 'I am a great admirer of Madame Hansson. Is it possible that you can introduce me so I can compliment her on her performance tonight?'

'Of course,' Herr Hennum agreed. 'I'm sure she'd be delighted to make your acquaintance. Follow me.'

18

The next morning, 'Cinderella' was sitting opposite Herr Bayer in the drawing room. They were drinking coffee as he looked through the review of last night's performance in *Dagbladet*, reading out any titbits he thought she might enjoy.

'*Madame Hansson proves a delight as the long-suffering peasant girl Solveig, and her pure, sweet voice was extremely pleasing to the ear.*'

'There.' He looked up at her. 'What do you think of that, eh?'

If it was *her* name written in the newspapers this morning, Anna thought, and *her* voice whose virtues they were extolling, she would indeed think a lot of it. But as this wasn't the case, she didn't think much of it at all.

'I am glad that they like the play and my voice,' she managed.

'Of course, it is the musical score by Herr Grieg the critics found particularly inspiring. His interpretation of Herr Ibsen's wonderful poem was simply sublime. So, Anna, as there is no performance today, you will take a well-deserved rest. My dear young lady, you should be most proud of yourself. You could not have sung more beautifully. Sadly, this is not a day of rest for me and I must be off to the university.' He stood up and walked towards the door. 'When I return tonight, we will celebrate our success over dinner. Good day to you.'

Once Herr Bayer had left, Anna finished her now lukewarm coffee, feeling deflated and strangely irritated. It was as if everything for the past few months had been leading up to last night. And now that it was over, nothing had changed. She wasn't sure what she'd expected to change, but she couldn't help feeling that something *should* have done.

Had Herr Bayer known about the need for a 'ghost' singer when he had found her in the mountains last summer, Anna wondered? And was that the reason why he had brought her to the city? She was fully aware that everyone at the theatre wished her to be invisible so that her voice could be attributed to Madame Hansson.

Picking up one of the newspapers, she stabbed her finger at the mention of the actress's 'pure' voice.

'It's *my* voice!' she cried. '*Mine . . .*'

Perhaps from the sheer build-up of pressure that had been released last night, like a cork popped from a bottle of Herr Bayer's French champagne, she threw herself onto the sofa and wept.

'Whatever is wrong Anna, *kjære*?'

Anna looked up, her face wet with tears, and saw that Frøken Olsdatter had entered the room unannounced.

'Nothing,' she muttered, hastily drying her eyes.

'Perhaps you are exhausted and overwhelmed by last night. And still recovering from your chill.'

'No, no . . . I am perfectly well, thank you,' Anna said firmly.

'Perhaps you are missing your family?'

'Yes, yes, I am. And the fresh air of the country. I . . . think I want to go back home to Heddal,' she whispered.

'There, there my dear. I understand. It is always the same for those of us who come from the country to the city. And the life you lead is a lonely one.'

'Do you miss your family?' Anna asked her.

'Not any longer, because I have grown used to it, but to begin with, I was very unhappy. My first employer was a mean-spirited woman who treated me and the other maids worse than her dogs. Twice I ran away, but I was found and brought back. Then I met Herr Bayer when he came to dinner at my mistress's house. Perhaps he sensed my misery, or maybe he genuinely required a housekeeper, but whatever the reason, he offered me a position that very evening. My employer didn't make a fuss. I think she was glad to be rid of me. And so Herr Bayer brought me here. For all his eccentricity, Anna, you should rest assured that he is a good and kind man.'

'I know,' said Anna, feeling even more guilty that she'd been feeling sorry for herself, when Frøken Olsdatter's life had been so much more difficult than her own.

'If it helps put your mind at rest, I can tell you I have seen a number of Herr Bayer's protégées walk through the front door during my years in his service. But I have never seen him as excited as he is by your talent. He told me himself last night that everyone had been in raptures about your singing.'

'But almost nobody knows it's *me*,' Anna said in a small voice.

'Not at present, no, but you must believe that one day they will. You are very young, *kjære*, and are lucky to have been part of such an auspicious production. The most important people in Christiania have heard you sing. Be patient, and trust in the Lord to guide your fate. Now, I am late for the market. Will you come with me to get some air?'

'Yes, I would love to,' Anna replied, rising to her feet. 'And thank you for being so kind.'

Not more than two miles away, Jens Halvorsen was also seriously discomfited and pacing his bedroom as he listened to the sound of raised voices coming from the morning room below. The deception that he and his mother had played on his father for the past few weeks had come to an abrupt end over breakfast this morning when his father had read the rapturous review of *Peer Gynt* in the newspaper. The reviewer had very kindly thought to mention that '*"Morning Mood" at the beginning of Act IV is, I believe, one of the highlights of Herr Grieg's musical score, with the enchanting and memorable opening bars played sublimely on the flute by Jens Halvorsen.*'

His father's expression had resembled a copper kettle forgotten on the stove and left to boil over.

'Why am I only hearing of this now?!' he had exploded.

'Because I felt it was unimportant for you to know,' Margarete had answered, and Jens knew she was steeling herself for a dreadful scene.

'You think this is "unimportant"?! I, a father who believes his son is studying hard at the university, discovers through a *newspaper* that he is moonlighting as a member of the Christiania orchestra! It is no less than an outrage!'

'He has missed little of his studies, I promise, Jonas.'

'Then please explain why the eminent critic goes on to describe how "*Herr Johan Hennum, conductor of the Christiania orchestra, has spent many months gathering together, and then rehearsing with, his musicians in order to do justice to Herr Grieg's complex orchestration.*" Do you seriously expect me to believe that our son, who is actually named in this very newspaper, merely learnt this music on a whim overnight? Good God!' Jonas shook his head vehemently. 'The pair of you must think that I'm an idiot from the hills. It would serve you both to refrain from treating me as such any longer.'

Margarete had then turned to Jens. 'I know you have some studying to do. I suggest you go and continue with it.'

'Yes, Mor.' With a mixture of guilt for leaving his mother to deal with his father's wrath and relief that he didn't have to face it himself, Jens had nodded at both of them and done as he'd been told.

Now as he paced his room, listening to his father still roaring at his mother, Jens decided that perhaps the newspaper incident was serendipitous: his father was bound to have learnt of his extra-curricular activities eventually. Part of him was sad that Jonas couldn't celebrate the fact that his son had been singled out for such praise, but he understood. Musicians in Christiania had no social status and a limited income. There was nothing for his father to admire in his pursuit of it as a career. Let alone in the thought of his son not taking his rightful place at the head of the Halvorsen Brewing Company.

Besides, Jens felt far too happy to let his father bring him down. He'd found his future in the orchestra and finally felt fulfilled. With the camaraderie of the other musicians, their humour and consummate drinking skills as they gathered at the Engebret Café after the performance each night, it was a world in which Jens felt totally comfortable. Not to mention the noticeably relaxed attitude of the young ladies in the play . . .

Last night, Herr Hennum had done as Jens had asked and introduced him to Madame Hansson. When the first-night celebrations were at an end, he'd noticed her eyes upon him and had subsequently offered to see her home safely to her apartment. It had been a pleasant interlude indeed – Thora was both experienced and eager and Jens had not left her bed until an icy dawn had broken. Tomorrow, he'd have to finesse the situation with Hilde Omvik, a pretty chorus girl who he had been seeing. It wouldn't do at all for Madame Hansson to hear gossip about his behaviour around the theatre. And after all, Hilde was due to be married in a week's time . . .

There was a knock on his door and he answered it immediately.

'Jens, I have done all I can, but your father would like to see you. Now.' His mother looked pale, her features strained.

'Thank you, Mor.'

'We will talk further when he has left for the brewery.'

She patted him on the shoulder, and Jens made his way downstairs to be informed by Dora that his father was waiting for him in the drawing room.

He sighed, knowing that anything serious which took place in the Halvorsen household happened in the drawing room. It was as cold and austere as his father. He opened the door and walked in. As usual, there was no fire in the grate, and a stark white light reflected from the snow heaped up outside streamed in through the large windows.

His father was standing by one of the windows and turned as Jens entered the room. 'Sit down.' He indicated a chair. Jens did so, trying to arrange his own face to display a suitable mix of apology and defiance.

'Firstly,' Jonas began, seating himself opposite his son in a large leather wing-backed chair, 'I want to tell you that I don't blame you. This is all your mother's fault for encouraging you in this ridiculous notion. However, Jens, you are of age in July and will become an adult who must make his own decisions. And you must decide to no longer be held in your mother's thrall.'

'Yes, sir.'

'The situation is as it has always been,' Jonas continued. 'You will join me at the brewery when you have finished your studies this summer. We will work together and one day, the company will be yours. You will be the fifth generation of Halvorsens to run the business that my great-great-grandfather began. Your mother insists that your studies have remained undisturbed by your performances in the orchestra, although personally I doubt that. What do you say, young man?'

'My mother is correct. I have missed very few lectures,' Jens lied smoothly.

'Even though I wish I could do it, I am aware it would do our family reputation no good at all to pull you out of the orchestra pit now, having made the commitment to Herr Hennum. So, it seems it is a fait accompli. Your mother and I have agreed that you must be allowed to continue until the run of *Peer Gynt* ends next month. During that time, I hope you will fully accept where your future lies.'

'Yes, sir.' Jens watched as his father paused and cracked his knuckles, a habit that irritated him beyond measure.

'So, there we are. Once this . . . novelty is over, I warn you, it will be the last time I will tolerate such behaviour. Unless you wish to continue a career as a professional musician, in which case I'd have no choice but to cut you off without an øre and have you leave this house immediately. The Halvorsen men have not worked for over one hundred and fifty years to watch our sole heir fritter away their legacy playing the fiddle.'

Jens was determined not to give his father the pleasure of seeing the shock register on his face. 'Yes, sir, I understand.'

'So then, I will be off to the brewery. I'm already over an hour late, and I must always set an example to my employees, as you must too when you join me. Good day to you, Jens.'

His father nodded at him and left, leaving Jens alone to think over his future. Feeling he couldn't face his mother, or, in fact, anybody at all, he collected his skates from the hallway, put on his fur jacket, hat and gloves and left the house to blow off some steam.

Apartment 4
10 St Olav's Gate
Christiania

10th March 1876

Kjære Lars, Mor, Far and Knut,

Thank you for your last letter and for saying that my spelling is better. I don't think it is, but I am trying hard. It is two weeks now since Peer Gynt *opened on the stage (although I didn't stand on it) at the Christiania Theatre. Herr Bayer tells me the whole city is talking about it and the 'house', as everyone calls the auditorium, is sold out for the whole time. They are talking of putting on more performances now because of the demand.*

Life goes on as normal here, apart from the fact that Herr Bayer is having me learn some Italian arias, which I find very difficult. Once a week, I have a professional opera singer called Günther come in to teach me. He is German and his accent makes it hard to understand a word he says. Also, he smells of unwashed clothes and he takes snuff all the time, which often dribbles out of his nose and lands in a puddle on his top lip. He is very old and thin, and I feel quite sorry for him.

When the run of Peer Gynt *comes to an end, I am not sure what I will do, other than what I always do every day here, which is learn to sing better and stay inside and eat fish. The theatre's season starts after Easter and there is talk of doing* Peer Gynt *again in the future. You will be pleased to hear that Herr Ibsen is rumoured to be coming from Italy to see the performance. I will let you know if he does.*

Please thank Mor for the new vests she knitted me. They are useful in this long winter. I look forward to warmer weather and I hope I can come home soon.

Anna

Anna folded the letter and sealed it with a sigh. She supposed her family was waiting avidly to hear gossip from the theatre, but she had none to offer. Closeted in the apartment day after day and hurried from the theatre at night, she was running out of new things to write.

She walked to the window and glanced up at the sky, seeing that it was still light at four o'clock in the afternoon. Spring was finally on its way, and after that would come summer . . . Anna put her forehead against the cool pane that separated her from fresh air. The thought of spending the warmer months shut away in here instead of up in the mountains with Rosa was almost too much to bear.

Rude arrived promptly in the orchestra pit for his nightly mission.

'Hello, Rude, how are you tonight?' Jens asked him.

'I am well, sir. Do you have a note or a message for me to deliver?'

'Indeed I do. Here.' He bent down so he could whisper in the boy's ear. 'Deliver this to Madame Hansson.' Jens pressed a coin and a letter into his small and eager hand.

'Thank you, sir. I will, sir.'

'Very good,' Jens said as Rude made to leave. 'Oh, by the way, who was that young lady I saw you leaving the stage door with last night as I passed by? Have you a girlfriend?' he teased his messenger.

'She may be the same height as me, but she's eighteen, sir. And far too old for me at the age of twelve,' Rude replied seriously. 'It was Anna Landvik. She's in the play.'

'Really?' I didn't recognise her, but then it was dark and I only caught a glimpse of her long red hair.'

'That is to say, sir, she is *in* the production, but you won't have seen her on the stage.' With a deliberately dramatic glance around, Rude beckoned Jens closer so he could whisper in his ear. 'She's Solveig's voice.'

'Ah, I see.' Jens nodded in mock seriousness. The fact that Madame Hansson's singing was not her own had become the worst-kept secret in the building. But they all had to keep up the pretence to the outside world.

'The lady is very pretty, is she not, sir?'

'Her hair is certainly. For that is all I saw from the back.'

'Personally, I feel sorry for her. Nobody is allowed to know it is she who sings so well. They have even put her with us in the children's dressing room. Well,' Rude said as the bell rang to indicate the performance would start in five minutes, 'I will deliver this safely for you.'

Jens pressed another coin into the boy's palm. 'Delay Frøken Landvik for me by the stage door tonight, so that I can take a proper look at our mystery singer.'

'I think I can manage that, sir,' agreed Rude, who then scurried off like a town rat, well satisfied with tonight's payment.

'On the prowl again, are we, Peer?' Simen, the first violinist, was not as deaf as he seemed and had obviously overheard parts of the conversation. It had become a joke in the orchestra pit that Jens' antics with the female members of the company closely resembled those of the play's eponymous hero.

'Hardly,' muttered Jens as Hennum appeared in the pit. His nickname had been amusing at first, but was now wearing extremely thin. 'You know I am devoted to Madame Hansson.'

'Then perhaps I'd had too much port, but I'm sure I saw you walking from Engebret last night with Jorid Skrovset on your arm.'

'I'm sure it was the port.' Jens took up his flute as Hennum indicated they were ready to begin.

After the performance that evening, Jens walked through the stage door and hovered near it, waiting for Rude to appear with the mystery girl. Usually, he'd go to Engebret while he waited for Thora to entertain her admirers in her dressing room and change. She would step into her carriage alone, then pick him up a few yards further down the road, wishing for no one to see them together.

Jens knew that it was his lowly status as a musician that made her refuse to let him squire her about town. He was starting to feel little better than a common whore who serviced a physical need, but was not good enough to be seen in public. Which was quite ridiculous, given he came from one of the most respected families in Christiania and was the current heir to the Halvorsen brewery empire. Thora constantly told him how she'd dined with the great and good of Europe, how Ibsen adored her and how he called her his muse. Jens had put up with her airs and graces so far because, in the privacy of her bedroom, she quite made up for the humiliation he had to suffer. But now Jens had had enough.

Finally, he saw two figures emerging from the stage door. They stopped for a moment on the threshold, briefly illuminated by the gaslight from the corridor behind as Rude pointed something out to the young woman. Peering surreptitiously from under his cap, Jens stared at her.

She was a delicate slip of a girl, with lovely blue eyes, a tiny nose and lips as pink as rosebuds set within a small heart-shaped face, her glorious Titian hair falling in waves about her shoulders. Not normally one to eulogise, Jens felt suddenly close to tears at the sight of her. She was a sheer breath of pure mountain air and made other women seem like primped and painted wooden dolls.

He stood, as if in a trance, hearing her say a soft 'goodnight' to Rude, then float past him before stepping straight into a waiting carriage.

'Did you see her, sir?'

As Anna's carriage pulled away, Rude's sharp eyes had immediately spotted Jens lurking in the shadows. 'I did my best, but I couldn't keep her any longer. My mother's waiting for me in the dressing room. I said I had to deliver a message to the stage door-keeper.'

'Yes. Does she always leave straight after the performance?'

'Every night, sir.'

'Then I must make a plan to meet with her.'

'I wish you luck with that, but I really must go.' Rude continued to hover, and eventually Jens dug in his pocket and handed him a further coin. 'Thank you. Goodnight, sir.'

Jens walked across the road to Engebret, ordering himself an aquavit as he sat on a stool at the bar staring into space.

'Are you unwell, my boy? You look quite pale. Another drink?' Einar, the cymbal player, asked him as he joined him at the bar. Jens admired Einar for his uncanny ability to leave the orchestra pit mid-performance counting the beats as he made his way across to Engebret. He'd then drink a beer whilst still continuing to count them, and return to his place in the pit just before he was required to crash his cymbals together again. The entire orchestra waited for the night when

Einar would miss his cue, but apparently, after ten years, he never had.

'Yes to both questions,' Jens said, tipping his glass towards his lips and swallowing the contents in one gulp. Having been furnished with a further aquavit, he wondered if he was indeed sickening for some malady, for he had felt strangely unsettled by the sight of Anna Landvik. He decided that, for tonight at least, Madame Hansson could return to her apartment alone.

19

'Frøken Anna, I have a letter for you.'

Anna looked up from her playing cards at Rude, who gave her a cheeky grin, then surreptitiously passed her a folded note. They were in the children's dressing room surrounded by the bustle of preparations for that evening's performance.

She was about to open the letter when Rude hissed at her. 'Not here. I was told that you must read it in private.'

'By whom?' Anna was confused.

Rude looked appropriately mysterious and shook his head. 'It is not my place to say. I am just the messenger.'

'Why would anyone want to write me a letter?'

'You'll have to read it to find out.'

Anna frowned at him as sternly as she could manage. 'Tell me,' she demanded.

'I won't.'

'Then I shall not continue playing our game of bezique.'

'No matter, I have to put my costume on anyway.' The young boy shrugged, stood up and left the table.

Part of her wanted to laugh at Rude's antics: he was a little monkey, always on the lookout to deliver a message or to lend a hand in return for a coin or some chocolate. She thought he would make a very successful conman, or possibly a spy, when he was older, for he was the fount of all gossip in the theatre. She realised that he knew exactly who had sent this mysterious missive and had probably read its contents, judging by the grubby fingerprints around the broken seal. She secreted the letter in her skirt pocket, deciding to read it when she was alone in bed tonight, then stood up and went to make herself ready for the evening's performance.

Christiania Theatre

15th March 1876

My dear Frøken Landvik,

Forgive this impertinent message and the means by which it is sent, given that we have never made each other's acquaintance in person. The truth is that since I first heard you sing on the night of the dress rehearsal, I have been entranced by your voice. And every night since, I have listened to you in rapture. Perhaps it would be possible to meet at the stage door tomorrow before the performance begins – say at a quarter past seven – so that we may be formally introduced?

I beg you to come.

Yours, with all sincerity,

An admirer

As she read the letter again, then secreted it in the drawer by her bed, Anna surmised it must be written by a man, as it would be most peculiar for a woman to write such a thing. Turning down the oil lamp and settling herself for sleep, she concluded that it was most likely some elderly gentleman, similar to Herr Bayer . . . which, Anna sighed, presented a deeply unexciting scenario.

'Are you meeting him tonight?' said Rude, his face a picture of innocence.

'Who?'

'You *know* who.'

'No, I don't. And besides, how would *you* even know that I've been invited to meet anyone, hmm?' Anna enjoyed the dismay on his face as he realised he'd inadvertently given himself away. 'I swear to you now that I will never again play a single card game with you, either for money or sweets, if you do not tell me the author's name.'

'Frøken Anna, I cannot. Forgive me.' Rude hung his head and shook it. 'It is more than my life's worth. I swore to the sender I would not.'

'Well, if you are unable to name this person, perhaps you can at least answer some questions with a "yes" or a "no"?'

'I can,' he agreed.

'Was it a gentleman who wrote the note?'

'Yes.'

'And is he under fifty?'

'Yes.'

'Under forty?'

'Yes.'

'Under thirty?'

'Frøken Anna, I cannot be sure of his age, but I think so.'

Well, at least that was something, she thought. 'Is he a regular member of the audience?'

'No . . . well, actually' – Rude scratched his head – 'yes, in a way. At least, he hears you sing every night.'

'So he is a member of the company?'

'Yes, but in a different way.'

'Is he a musician, Rude?'

'Frøken Anna, I feel compromised.' Rude gave a dramatic sigh of despair. 'I cannot say more.'

'Very well. I understand,' Anna said, satisfied with her successful interrogation. She glanced at the old and unreliable clock hanging on the wall and asked one of the mothers, who was embroidering quietly in the corner, what she thought the time was.

'I believe it is nearly seven, Frøken Landvik. I was just out in the corridor and Herr Josephson arrived. He's always so punctual,' she added.

'Thank you.' Anna looked at the clock on the wall again, relieved that it was more or less accurate tonight. Should she go? After all, if this man really was under thirty, it may be that he wanted to meet her for inappropriate reasons, rather than out of mere admiration for her voice. Despite herself, Anna blushed. The very idea that it might be inappropriate – and that it *might* be a relatively young man – excited her far more than it should.

The seconds on the clock ticked by as she agonised. At thirteen minutes past seven, she decided she was going. At fourteen minutes past, that she wasn't . . .

And at seven fifteen precisely, she found herself walking

down the corridor to the stage door, only to find the area deserted.

Halbert, the doorman, opened the window of his booth to ask what it was she needed. She shook her head and turned to walk back to the dressing room. A blast of cold air hit her as the stage door opened behind her and a second later, a hand was laid gently on her shoulder.

'Frøken Landvik?'

'Yes.'

'Forgive me. I was a few seconds late.'

Anna turned and found herself staring into the deep-set hazel eyes of the voice's owner. Her stomach gave a strange lurch, as it did before she had to sing. While Halbert sat in his box and regarded them both as if they were idiots, they simply stared at each other.

The young man in front of Anna looked to be about her own age and his face was truly handsome, crowned with a head of mahogany hair which curled above his collar. He was not tall, but his broad shoulders gave him a commanding air of masculinity. Anna felt suddenly as if all of her – physical, mental and emotional – was draining out and into this other unknown human being. It was the strangest sensation and it caused her to sway slightly.

'Are you quite well, Frøken Landvik? You look like you've seen a ghost.'

'Yes, I am perfectly well, thank you. I felt a little faint, that is all.'

The bell rang, giving the company and the orchestra their usual ten-minute warning before curtain up. 'Please,' he whispered under his breath, seeing a rapt Halbert still peering over his spectacles at them, 'we don't have much time. Let us speak in private outside, where at least you can take some air.' Jens put a supportive arm around her, noticing how her head tucked perfectly into his shoulder as he did so, then opened the stage door and gently guided her outside. She was so tiny, so perfect, so feminine and he felt immediately protective as she briefly leant on him as though it was the most natural thing in the world.

Anna stood beside him on the pavement, the young man's arm still around her, and took a few deep breaths of the crisp night air. 'Why was it you wanted to see me?' she asked him as she recovered her composure and realised how inappropriate it was to be in such close physical proximity to a man. And a strange man, at that. Yet if she was honest, he didn't feel like a stranger at all . . .

'To be frank, I'm not at all sure. At first it was your voice that fascinated me, but then I paid Rude to make sure he kept you lingering outside the stage door so that I could secretly lay eyes on you . . . Frøken Landvik, I must go now, or Herr Hennum will most likely disembowel me, but when can I see you again?'

'I don't know.'

'Tonight, after the performance?'

'No, Herr Bayer sends a carriage to wait for me and I leave the theatre immediately.'

'During the day?'

'No.' She put a hand to her face, her cheeks suddenly burning despite the chill of the evening. 'I cannot think. Besides . . .'

'What?'

'This is most unseemly. If Herr Bayer knew of our meeting, he would—'

The five-minute bell rang.

'I beg you, meet me at six o'clock here tomorrow,' Jens entreated her. 'Tell Herr Bayer you have been called early for a rehearsal.'

'I . . . I must bid you goodnight.' Anna turned away and started walking back towards the stage door. Opening it, she began to walk through but just as it was about to close behind her, he saw her tiny fingers grasp the edge of the door and pull it back open.

'May I at least know your name, sir?'

'Forgive me. My name is Jens. Jens Halvorsen.'

Anna wandered back to her dressing room in a daze and sat down to recover her composure. When she had, she decided that she must learn everything she could about Jens Halvorsen before committing herself to any further meetings.

That night, during the performance, she asked everyone she trusted, and even those she didn't, what they knew of him.

So far, she'd learnt that he played the violin and the flute in the orchestra and, very disappointingly, that his reputation with women was infamous at the theatre. So much so that the orchestra had apparently given him the nickname 'Peer', after the character's lothario-like ways. One of the chorus girls confirmed he had been seen with both Hilde Omvik and Jorid Skrovset. And worst of all, he was rumoured to be Madame Hansson's secret lover.

By the time she stood on the side of the stage to sing 'The Cradle Song', she was so distracted that she held on for longer than usual to a note, which caused Madame Hansson to close her mouth two beats too soon. She did not dare to look down into the orchestra pit in case she set eyes on him.

'I will not think about him,' Anna told herself determinedly as she extinguished the light from the oil lamp beside her bed that night. 'He is clearly a dreadful, heartless man,' she added, wishing the tales of his antics didn't thrill her. 'And besides, I am promised to be married.'

However, the next day, it took every ounce of willpower she had not to order the carriage early and tell Herr Bayer she had an extra rehearsal. Arriving at the theatre at her usual time of six forty-five, Anna saw that the pavement outside the stage door was empty. She berated herself harshly for the wave of disappointment that washed over her.

Walking into the dressing room, she was greeted by the usual gaggle of mothers busily embroidering in the corner, and the children who ran to her to see if she had brought them anything new to play with. Only one child hung back, and as she hugged the rest, she caught Rude's unusually mournful eyes over the heads of the others. Beginners were called, and with a final sorry glance in her direction, Rude left the dressing room to take his place onstage for the opening. In the interval, he cornered her.

'My friend tells me you failed to meet with him tonight. He was very sad. He sent you another letter.' He held out a sealed note.

Anna waved it away. 'Please tell him I am not interested.'

'Why?'

'I am not, Rude, and that is that.'

'But Frøken Anna,' he persisted, 'tonight I saw the misery in his eyes after you had failed to meet him.'

'Rude, you are a very talented young man, both as an actor and at extracting coins from adults. However, there are some things you don't yet understand . . .' Anna opened the door and left the dressing room, but he followed her doggedly.

'Like what?'

'Adult things,' she replied impatiently as she continued walking towards the wings. She wasn't needed to sing yet, but she wanted to escape from the boy's relentless inquisition.

'But I *do* know about adult things, Frøken Anna. I understand what gossip you must have heard since you learnt who your admirer was.'

'So if you know all about him, why would you continue to entreat me to meet him?' She rounded on him, stopping Rude in his tracks. 'His reputation is quite dreadful! And besides, I already have a young man, and one day' – Anna turned away again and continued walking towards the wings – 'we will be married.'

'Then I am very happy for you, but the gentleman in question has noble intentions towards you, I promise.'

'Oh, for goodness' sake, child! Let me be!'

'I will, but you should meet him, Frøken Anna. Business is business, as I'm sure you can understand, but what I've just told you now is for free. Here, at least take his letter.'

Before she could protest further, he pressed the piece of paper into Anna's hand, then scurried off down the corridor. She stood behind one of the scenery flats, well hidden from view, listening as the orchestra tuned up for the second act. Glancing down into the pit, she saw Jens Halvorsen take his place and unpack his flute from its case. As she peered forward cautiously, he looked up and, for a fleeting moment, their eyes met. The emotion in his expression was one of such disappointment, it unnerved her. Darting back behind the flats, Anna retraced her footsteps to the dressing room in a daze, passing Madame Hansson as she did so. The familiar cloud of French perfume pervaded the corridor as the actress swept along it. The woman barely acknowledged her and as Anna remembered the gossip she had heard about her secret lover, she hardened her heart. Jens Halvorsen was nothing but a cad, a charming ladies' man who would no doubt lead her to ruin. Entering the dressing room, she promised to play a game of cards with the children during the next interval, knowing she must keep herself occupied.

That night, upon her arrival at the apartment, she went immediately to the deserted drawing room. And with huge self-control, drew out the letter from her skirt pocket and threw it unopened into the flames of the stove.

Rude continued to bring her a new letter from Jens Halvorsen each night for the following two weeks, but Anna burnt them all the moment she arrived home. And tonight, her resolve had been strengthened further after she and everyone else along the backstage corridor had heard a loud wail echo through it, accompanied by the sound of glass being broken. The cast were all aware that these noises originated from Madame Hansson's dressing room.

'What was all that about?' she asked Rude.

'I can't tell you,' he replied stubbornly, folding his arms.

'Of course you can, you tell me everything else. I'll pay you,' she offered.

'Not even for money would I tell you. It would only give you the wrong impression.'

'Of what?'

Rude shook his head and walked away. Subsequently, as the gossip began to circulate freely during the performance, one of the chorus girls told her that Madame Hansson had discovered that Jens Halvorsen had been seen with Jorid, another girl in the chorus, a fortnight ago. As she'd already heard the story, it didn't come as a surprise to Anna, but it seemed that Madame Hansson was the only one in the building who hadn't known.

Arriving at the theatre for the first performance of the following week, Anna saw a huge bouquet of red roses resting on the counter of the booth beside the stage door. Walking past them on her way to the dressing room, she heard Halbert, the doorman, call out to her.

'Frøken Landvik?'

'Yes?'

'These flowers are for you.'

'*Me?*'

'Yes, you. Take them, please, they are cluttering up my booth.'

Blushing as red as the roses, she turned and retraced her footsteps back towards him.

'Well, Frøken Landvik, it seems you have an admirer. I wonder who that could be?' Halbert raised a disapproving eyebrow as Anna collected the enormous bouquet, unable to meet his gaze.

'Well!' she said to herself as she walked along the passage and headed straight for the freezing and smelly latrines that were shared by the women in the company. 'The cheek of it!

Especially with Madame Hansson and Jorid Skrovset both in the building. He's playing with me,' she muttered to herself angrily as she slammed the door and locked herself in. 'Now Madame Hansson's discovered his behaviour, he thinks he can turn the simple peasant girl's head with a few blooms.'

She read the small card that was attached to the flowers.

I am not as you imagine me to be. I beg you to give me a chance.

'Ha!' Anna tore the card into the tiniest pieces and sluiced them away down the latrine. There would be endless enquiries about the flowers in the dressing room and she wished to rid herself of any evidence of their provenance.

'Goodness, Anna!' said one of the mothers, as she entered the dressing room. 'Now, aren't they just beautiful?'

'Who are they from?' asked another.

The entire room went silent as they waited for her reply.

'Well, of course' – Anna swallowed after a pause – 'they are from Lars, my young man in Heddal.'

A chorus of oohs and ahhs echoed around the room.

'Is it a special occasion? It must be, to spend so much money on those?' said another mother.

'It's . . . my birthday,' Anna lied desperately.

At that, there was a chorus of 'Your birthday?' and 'Why didn't you tell us!'

For the rest of the evening, Anna went through the motions of being congratulated, hugged and given hurriedly put together tokens of everyone's affection, all the while ignoring the knowing smile on Rude's face.

'Now, Anna, as you know, the run of *Peer Gynt* is about to come to an end. I will be organising a summer soirée here at the apartment in June, to which I will invite the great and the good of Christiania to come and hear you sing. Finally, we will set to work and begin to launch your career. And the beauty is that the "ghost voice" will at last be able to reveal itself!'

'I see. Thank you, Herr Bayer.'

'Anna.' He paused with a frown as he studied her expression. 'You seem uncertain.'

'I am just tired. But I am very grateful for your attention.'

'I understand that the last few months have been somewhat difficult for you, Anna, but rest assured, many musical acquaintances of mine are privately aware to whom Solveig's beautiful voice really belongs. Now, take a rest, Anna, you really do look quite pale.'

'Yes, Herr Bayer.'

As Franz Bayer watched Anna leave the room, he understood her frustration, but what else could he have done? Her anonymity had been a part of the deal agreed with Ludvig Josephson and Johan Hennum. But now that was almost over and the arrangement had served its purpose. The lure of meeting the owner of the mysterious voice who had sung Solveig so exquisitely would be enough to bring all the influential members of Christiania's musical community here to his apartment for the soirée. He had big plans for young Anna Landvik.

20

Jens was feeling particularly low as he awoke at home a week after the run of *Peer Gynt* had come to an end. And although Hennum had promised him a permanent place in the orchestra for the visiting opera and ballet companies that required one, there was no more work to be had for a month until the new season started. On top of this, having attended a maximum of half a dozen lectures since the start of *Peer Gynt*, Jens was completely unprepared for his final examinations at the university. He knew without a doubt that he'd fail his degree.

Last week, before the penultimate performance, he had plucked up the courage to show Hennum the compositions he'd spent hours writing down when he should have been studying. After he'd played them, the conductor had pronounced them 'derivative', but good for a beginner.

'May I suggest, young man, that you go away and study at music school. You have talent as a composer, but you must learn how to "hear" the tune you have written as it will be played by each instrument. For example, does this piece' – Hennum indicated the music – 'open with a full orchestra? Or maybe . . .' He played the first four bars on the piano, which even to Jens' biased ears sounded like an homage to Herr

Grieg's 'Morning Mood'. 'Or perhaps a flute?' Herr Hennum gave him an ironic smile and Jens had the grace to blush.

'I see, sir, yes.'

'Then, when we come to the second passage, would this be played by the violins? Or perhaps a cello or a viola?' Hennum handed the sheet music back to Jens and patted him on the shoulder. 'My advice to you, if you are serious about wishing to follow in the footsteps of Herr Grieg and his eminent composer friends, is that you go and learn how to do this properly, both in your head and on paper.'

'But I can't do it here, for there is no one in Christiania to teach me,' Jens said.

'No. Therefore you must go abroad, as all our great Scandinavian musicians and composers have done. Perhaps to Leipzig, just as Herr Grieg did.'

Jens had walked away, cursing his naivety. And knowing that, if his father carried out his threat to cut him off if he chose to follow a musical path, there would be no money forthcoming to fund any attendance at a music school. He'd also begun to realise that his natural musical talent had seen him through so far, but now, this was no longer enough. He had to learn the proper techniques if he wished to become a composer. He had to *work* at it.

As Jens entered the stage door, he castigated himself for the healthy allowance he'd frittered away over the past three years. If he hadn't spent it on women and alcohol, he could have saved it for his future. Now, he thought miserably, it was almost certainly too late. He'd blown his chances and had no one to blame but himself.

Despite his determination not to fall back into his old ways once *Peer Gynt* was over, Jens had a splitting headache. Last night, in desperation, he'd taken himself off to Engebret to drown his sorrows with any musician he knew who happened to be there.

The house was silent, which told him it was mid-morning and his father had already left for the brewery, while his mother had no doubt departed to take coffee with one of her acquaintances. Ringing the bell for Dora – he needed coffee urgently – he waited for her to arrive. Which she did, after a pointed interval. Following her knock, he bade her enter and she came in sullenly and set the tray down on his bed with an unnecessary clatter.

'What time is it?' Jens asked.

'A half hour after eleven, sir. Is there anything else?'

He looked at her, knowing she was sulking because he'd given her so little attention recently. Debating whether he should expend the effort on placating her, just to make his life in the household easier, he sipped his coffee, thought of Anna, and decided he could not.

'No thank you, Dora.'

Averting his eyes from her stricken face, he picked up the newspaper from the tray and pretended to read it until the maid had left the room. When she had gone, Jens put it down and sighed heavily. He was thoroughly ashamed of himself for getting drunk the night before, but he'd felt so low and directionless that he'd simply wanted to forget. And Anna Landvik hadn't helped his mood either.

'What is wrong with you?' Simen had asked him last night. 'Women trouble, no doubt?'

'It's the girl who sang Solveig. I can't stop thinking about her. Simen, I truly believe I'm in love for the first time.'

At this, Simen had thrown back his head and laughed. 'Jens, can you not see the truth?'

'No! Why is this funny?'

'She is the only girl who has refused you! And that is why you believe you are "in love" with her! Yes, perhaps you are entranced by the idyll of her pure country ways, but surely you can see that in reality she would be completely unsuitable for an educated city boy like yourself?'

'You are wrong! Whether she is an aristocrat or a peasant, I would love her. Her voice, it is . . . the most exquisite sound I have ever heard. And she has the face of an angel too.'

Simen had glanced down at Jens' empty glass. 'And that is the aquavit talking. Trust me, my friend, you are merely suffering from your first experience of rejection, not love.'

As Jens sipped his lukewarm coffee, he wondered whether Simen had had a point. Yet, the memory of her face, and her heavenly voice, still haunted his dreams. And at present, with all the other dilemmas he was facing, he wished to God that he'd never set eyes on Anna Landvik. Or heard her sing.

'The soirée will be held on the fifteenth of June, the date of Herr Grieg's birthday,' Herr Bayer said to Anna when they met in the drawing room a few days after the last night of *Peer Gynt*. 'I will send him an invitation to meet his very first "Solveig", but I believe he is abroad. We will arrange a programme that encompasses some of his folk songs and, of course, those from *Peer Gynt*. Then "Violetta's Aria", from *La*

Traviata, then a hymn – perhaps "*Leid, Milde Ljos*". I wish for everyone to hear your wonderful range.'

'Will I still be able to return home to Heddal for my brother's wedding?' Anna asked him, thinking that if she did not breathe some fresh country air soon, she might well suffocate.

'Of course, my dear. You can leave for Heddal soon after the soirée and spend the summer there. Now, we begin in earnest tomorrow. We have one month to make you and your voice perfect.'

To prepare her for this task, Herr Bayer had lined up a number of tutors he thought appropriate to provide expert guidance on the songs she would sing. Günther returned to concentrate on the operatic arias, a choirmaster from the cathedral arrived with his bitten nails and shiny balding head to share his expertise on the hymn and Herr Bayer himself spent an hour a day coaching her on her vocal technique. A dressmaker arrived to take measurements and provide her with a wardrobe of beautiful clothes fit for a budding young star. And best of all, to Anna's delight, Herr Bayer began to take her out of the apartment to concerts and recitals.

On one such evening, before a visit to the Christiania Theatre for the first night of Rossini's *Il Barbiere di Siviglia* by a visiting Italian opera company, Anna walked into the drawing room in one of her exquisite new evening gowns, fashioned from midnight-blue silk.

'My dear young lady,' said Herr Bayer, rising as Anna entered and clapping his hands together, 'you look positively radiant tonight. That colour becomes you very well. Now, allow me to enhance it a little further.'

He presented her with a leather box, inside which lay a

sapphire necklace and matching drop earrings. The gleaming, multi-faceted stones were suspended by intricate gold filigree work, the mark of a master craftsman. Anna stared at the jewellery, hardly knowing what to say.

'Herr Bayer . . .'

'They were my wife's. And I would like you to wear them this evening. May I help fasten the necklace for you?'

Anna could hardly refuse, as he was already taking the necklace out of its box. She could feel the touch of his fingers on her neck as he fastened it.

'They suit you well,' he declared in satisfaction, standing close enough so she could smell his stale breath. 'Now, let us sally forth and present ourselves at the Christiania Theatre.'

Throughout the following month, Anna did her best to concentrate on her musical studies and enjoy her sojourns in Christiania. She wrote to Lars regularly and said her prayers fervently at night. However, thoughts of Jens Halvorsen the Bad, as she had named him, hoping it might help teach her treacherous heart a lesson, continued to arrive like clockwork in her head. Anna only wished she could speak to a friend about the affliction. Surely there must be a medicine to stop it?

'Dear Lord,' she sighed one night, rising from her prayers, 'I believe I am very, very sick.'

As the fifteenth of June approached, Anna could see that Herr Bayer was in a state of high excitement.

'Now, my dear,' he announced on the day of the soirée, 'I have engaged a violin player and a cellist to accompany you.

With myself on the piano, of course. They will both be here this morning to practise with us. Then this afternoon, you will take a rest in preparation for your big night.'

At eleven o'clock the doorbell rang, and Anna, who was waiting in the drawing room, heard Frøken Olsdatter open the door to greet the musicians. She stood up as they walked into the room with Herr Bayer.

'May I present Herr Isaksen, the cellist, and Herr Halvorsen, the violinist,' he announced. 'They both came highly recommended by my friend Herr Hennum.'

Anna experienced another wave of dizziness as Jens Halvorsen the Bad strode across the room to greet her.

'Frøken Landvik, I am indeed honoured to be part of your soirée tonight.'

'Thank you,' she managed, seeing the amusement dancing in his eyes. As her heart continued to bang against her ribcage, she herself found nothing remotely funny about the situation.

'So, we will start with the Verdi,' Herr Bayer suggested as the two musicians gathered close to him at the piano. 'Anna, are you paying attention?'

'Yes, Herr Bayer.'

'Then we begin.'

Anna knew she did not give of her best during the rehearsal and could sense Herr Bayer's irritation as she forgot all she had been taught and even became breathless at the end of the vibrato notes. *And it was all Jens Halvorsen the Bad's doing*, she thought furiously.

'That will have to suffice for now, gentlemen. Let us hope we are all more in harmony tonight. You are to be here punctually at six thirty for the start of the soirée at seven.'

Jens and his companion nodded politely, then bowed briefly to Anna. As he left the room, Jens' hazel eyes shot a meaningful parting glance in her direction.

'Anna, what is wrong with you?' Herr Bayer asked her. 'Surely it cannot be the accompaniment putting you off. You became perfectly used to singing with a full orchestra during *Peer Gynt*.'

'Forgive me, Herr Bayer, I have a slight headache.'

'And I think you are having a very understandable attack of nerves, my dear young lady.' His face softened and he patted her on the shoulder. 'You will eat a light lunch, then take a rest. And before the performance this evening, we will drink a small glass of wine together to calm your nerves. I have no doubt that tonight will be a huge success, and by tomorrow you will be the toast of Christiania.'

At five o'clock that evening, Frøken Olsdatter arrived in Anna's bedroom with a cup of water and the ubiquitous honey.

'I've filled a bath for you, my dear. While you take that, I'll lay out your clothes for tonight. Herr Bayer would like you to wear your midnight-blue gown and his wife's sapphires. He also suggests you wear your hair up. I will help you to dress it when you return.'

'Thank you.'

Anna lay in the bathtub with a flannel over her face trying to still her heartbeat, which had not stopped banging since she'd set eyes on Jens Halvorsen earlier today. Just the very sight of him had caused an extreme physical reaction in her knees, her throat and her heart. 'Lord, please give me strength and courage tonight,' she prayed as she dried herself. 'And forgive me if I wish that he could have a bilious attack about now and be too sick to come back and play.'

After she had dressed and her hair had been arranged by Frøken Olsdatter, Anna walked along the corridor to the drawing room. Thirty gilt and red-velvet chairs had been arranged in semi-circular rows facing the piano in the bay window of the room. Jens Halvorsen and the cellist were already chatting to Herr Bayer, whose face lit up as he saw her.

'You look quite perfect, my dear young lady,' he said approvingly, handing her a glass of wine. 'Now, let us all toast to this evening before the hubbub begins.'

As she took a sip, she could feel Jens' eyes rest briefly upon her décolletage; whether he was staring at the sparkling jewels or the expanse of bare white flesh beneath them, she didn't know, but she felt herself blushing.

'To you, Anna,' Herr Bayer toasted her.

'Yes, to Frøken Landvik,' said Jens, raising his glass to her.

'Now, you will go and sit in the kitchen with Frøken Olsdatter until I come for you.'

'Yes, Herr Bayer.'

'Good luck, my love,' Jens whispered under his breath as Anna walked to the door and left the room.

Whether it was the wine, or Jens Halvorsen the Bad accompanying her so empathetically on his fiddle that night, when the last note rang out in the hushed room, even Anna knew she had given of her best.

After an enthusiastic round of applause, the guests, who included Johan Hennum, crowded around her, congratulating her and suggesting public performances at the Freemasons' Hall and the Assembly Rooms. Herr Bayer stood beside her, beaming down at her proprietorially, as Jens hovered in the background. When Herr Bayer eventually left her side, Jens took his chance to speak to her.

'Frøken Landvik, permit me to add my congratulations on your performance tonight.'

'Thank you, Herr Halvorsen.'

'And please, Anna, I beg you,' he added in an undertone, 'I have been a man in torment since I last saw you. I cannot stop thinking about you, dreaming of you . . . don't you see that fate has conspired again to bring us together?'

The sound of her Christian name on his tongue was so intimate that Anna gazed blankly over his shoulder, knowing that if she met his eyes, she would be lost. For his words mirrored her own feelings exactly.

'Please may we meet? Anywhere, anytime . . . I—'

'Herr Halvorsen,' Anna said, finding her voice, 'I am returning home to Heddal very shortly for my brother's wedding.'

'Then permit me to see you when you return to Christiania. Anna, I . . .' Then, as he saw Herr Bayer approaching them, Jens bowed formally to her. 'This evening has been a pleasure, Frøken Landvik.' He lifted his eyes to hers and she saw a brief flicker of desperation in them.

'Wasn't she wonderful?' Herr Bayer slapped Jens on the shoulder. 'Those smooth rises into the middle and upper range and her magnificent vibrato . . . It is the best I've heard her perform!'

'Indeed, Frøken Landvik sang beautifully tonight. And now, I must take my leave,' said Jens. He looked at Herr Bayer expectantly.

'Of course, of course. Excuse me, my dear Anna, but I must settle my account with our young fiddle player.'

When she eventually retired to her room an hour later, Anna felt light-headed and giddy. Perhaps it was the euphoria of the evening's performance, or maybe the second glass of wine she'd unwisely accepted, but as Frøken Olsdatter helped her undress, she knew deep down it was because of Jens Halvorsen. It was intoxicating to think that he was still enamoured with her. As, she admitted reluctantly, she was with him . . .

Stalsberg Våningshuset
Tindevegen
Heddal

30th June 1876

Kjære Anna,

I write with sad news. My father passed away on Tuesday last. Thankfully, it was peaceful. And perhaps for the best, for, as you know, he suffered much pain. The funeral will have taken place before you receive this letter, but I felt I must inform you of it.

Your father says to tell you that the barley crop looks well and his worst fears were unfounded. Anna, when you return for your brother's wedding, we will have much to discuss for the future. Despite the sad news, I am happy I will set eyes on you again soon.

Until then,
Kjærlig hilsen,
Lars

Having read the letter, Anna lay back on her pillows feeling as though she was no better a person than Jens Halvorsen the Bad. Every moment since she'd seen him again at the soirée, she'd thought of nothing else. And even when Herr Bayer had told her delightedly of the further recitals that he'd arranged for her, she could not rouse herself to display the expected excitement.

He had asked last night for her presence in the drawing room today at eleven. Duly dressed, she walked disconsolately along the corridor. Entering the room, she could see her mentor was already in a state of high excitement.

'Anna! Do come in and hear our wonderful news. This morning, I met with Johan Hennum and Ludvig Josephson. You may remember that Herr Hennum attended your soirée and he told me that due to the popularity of *Peer Gynt*, they wish to include the play in their autumn season. They have suggested that you reprise your role as Solveig.'

Anna looked at him with a mixture of astonishment and despair. 'You mean stand on the side of the stage again and sing the songs whilst Madame Hansson pretends my voice is hers?'

'Anna, really! Do you even think that I would suggest that as a possibility? No, my dear young lady, they wish you to play the role in its entirety. Madame Hansson is currently unavailable, and having just been revealed as the talented owner of the ghost voice in Christiania's musical circles, they are keen to have you perform. To make the situation even better, Herr Grieg has announced he will finally come to Christiania to see the production. Both Johan and Ludvig feel your rendition of his songs cannot be improved upon. So, they wish you to attend an audition this coming Thursday, where they will decide if you have sufficient talent as an actress. Do you recollect any of the lines Solveig speaks in the play?'

'Yes, Herr Bayer. On many occasions I have mouthed them alongside Madame Hansson,' Anna replied, a small tingle of excitement creeping up her spine. Could it really be that they would want her as the star? And would Jens Halvorsen the Not So Bad Any Longer be playing in the orchestra . . . ?

'Excellent! Then today, we will forget your scales and the new aria I had planned for you to learn, and I will read all the other parts from *Peer Gynt* whilst you run through Solveig's lines.' He picked up a copy of the play from his desk and opened it. 'Please feel free to sit down. As you know, it is a long piece, but we will do the best we can. Ready?' he asked her.

'Yes, Herr Bayer,' said Anna as she recalled the words as best she could.

'Well, well!' Herr Bayer said an hour later as he looked at her in admiration. 'It seems that we not only have a voice, but a talent for portraying a character too.' He took her hand in his and kissed it. 'My dear young lady, may I say that you continue to astound me.'

'Thank you.'

'Have no fear for the audition, Anna. Perform exactly as you have today and the part is yours. Now, come, we will take luncheon together.'

On Thursday afternoon at two promptly, Anna met Herr Josephson on the stage at the theatre, and they sat down together to read through the script. She heard a slight tremor in her voice during the first few lines, but as she continued to read, she grew more confident. She read through both the scene where Solveig first meets Peer at a wedding, and then the final scene, when he returns to her after his travels around the world and Solveig forgives him.

'Excellent, Frøken Landvik!' Herr Josephson said with approval, as Anna looked up at him. 'I really don't feel I need to hear any more. I must admit I was not in favour of this idea when Herr Hennum suggested it to me, but you acquitted yourself very well indeed for a first read-through. We will have work to do to improve the strength of your voice and the expression in it, but I think I can agree that you should take the role of Solveig in the forthcoming season.'

'Anna! Isn't that wonderful news?' Herr Bayer, who had been sitting in the auditorium watching and listening intently, made his way up onto the stage.

'Rehearsals will begin in August for the September opening. I hope you have no plans to leave for the country at that time?' Herr Josephson asked her.

'Rest assured, Anna will be here,' replied Herr Bayer for her. 'Now, we come to the question of money. We must agree Frøken Landvik's fee for taking such a prominent role.'

Ten minutes later, they were back in the carriage and Herr Bayer suggested they go to the Grand Hotel for high tea and to celebrate Anna's further triumph.

'And on top of all the other advantages, there is every chance that Herr Grieg will come in the autumn to see you perform. Just think of that, my dear young lady! If he takes a shine to you, there may be the chance for travel overseas to other theatres or concert halls . . .'

Anna's thoughts floated away as she imagined Jens Halvorsen down in the orchestra pit, looking up at her as she spoke Solveig's words of love.

'So, I will write to your dear parents telling them of our wonderful news and begging them to allow me and Christiania to enjoy the pleasure of your company for a few more months whilst you perform in *Peer Gynt*. You will return home to attend your brother's wedding in July and be back here for August,' said Herr Bayer over dinner that evening. 'I too will be leaving Christiania as usual to stay in my family's summer house on Drøbak with my sister and my poor ailing mama.'

'So there will be no time for me to travel to the mountains?' Anna could hear the petulance in her voice, but she wanted to see with her own eyes if Rosa was still alive.

'Anna, there will be many more summers singing the cows home, but never again one preparing to take the leading role in a production of *Peer Gynt* at the Christiania Theatre. I shall also return, of course, when you begin rehearsals.'

'I'm sure that Frøken Olsdatter can take care of me if you are unable to return. I wouldn't like to impose my needs on you,' Anna answered politely.

'Don't even think of it, my dear young lady. These days, it seems your needs *are* mine.'

Anna found it a relief to retire to her room that evening. Herr Bayer's natural ebullience was, she knew, an endearing positive quality, but to live with it day in and day out became somewhat wearing. At least Lars was quiet, she thought, as she knelt to say her prayers, knowing she would see him very soon and forcing herself to recall his good qualities. But even as she spoke to Jesus about Lars, her thoughts flew from him to Jens Halvorsen.

'Please Lord, forgive my heart, for I do believe I have fallen in love with the wrong man. Help me love the one I am supposed to. And also,' she added before she stood up, trying to find something to say that was unselfish, 'can Rosa just be alive for one more summer?'

21

As Anna left for Heddal a week later, Jens carried a bundle of his most precious possessions into the centre of Christiania. He felt drained and exhausted from the nightmare of the past few hours.

In the dining room over breakfast that morning, Jens had sat as straight and proud as he could, his bread and preserves untouched in front of him. Taking a deep breath, he had spoken what he needed to say out loud.

'I have done my best to live up to your expectations, Far, but my future simply does not lie in the brewery business. I wish to become a full-time musician and one day, I hope, a composer. I am sorry, but I cannot change who I am.'

Jonas continued salting his eggs and then took a mouthful before he replied.

'So be it. You have made your decision. As I told you when this was first discussed, there will be no further funds and nothing for you in my will. From this moment on, you are no longer my son. I simply cannot bear to witness what you are throwing away and how you are betraying me. Therefore, as we agreed, I expect you to have left the house by the time I return from the office this evening.'

Even though Jens had been bracing himself for his father's response, it still came as a shock. He looked across the table to his mother's horrified face.

'But Jonas, *kjære*, it is your son's twenty-first birthday in a few days' time, and as you know, we have arranged a dinner for him. Surely you can allow him a few days' grace to celebrate with his parents and friends?'

'I hardly feel that any of us will be celebrating, given the circumstances. And if you believe I will soften my resolve in time, then you are sadly mistaken.' Jonas folded his newspaper twice as he always did. 'Now, I must leave for the brewery. Good day to you both.'

The worst part of the entire episode was watching his mother break down in tears the moment the front door slammed shut behind his father. He comforted her as best he could.

'I have let Far down. Perhaps I should change my mind and—'

'No, no . . . You *must* follow your passion. I only wish that I had when I was your age. Forgive me, Jens, *kjære*, but perhaps I was living in a fool's paradise. I believed that, when it came to it, your father would change his mind.'

'Well, I didn't, and therefore I was prepared for it. So, I must now do as he wishes and leave the house. Forgive me, Mor, I need to pack.'

'Perhaps I was wrong to encourage you.' Margarete wrung her hands. 'And to work against his plans for you when I should have accepted that he would win.'

'But he hasn't won, Mor. I do this of my own free will. And I can only say how grateful I am to you for giving me the gift of music. My future would be more miserable without it.'

An hour later, Jens arrived downstairs in the entrance hall, with two suitcases stuffed full of all the possessions he could carry.

His mother's tear-stained face met him at the drawing room door.

'Oh, my son,' she wept on his shoulder. 'Maybe in time, your father will regret what he has done today and ask you to come home.'

'I think we both know that he will not.'

'Where will you go?'

'I have friends in the orchestra, and I'm sure one of them will put a roof over my head temporarily. I'm more concerned about you, Mor. I feel I shouldn't leave you alone with him.'

'Don't worry about me, *kjære*. Just promise me you will write and let me know where you will be?'

'Of course,' he agreed.

Then his mother thrust a small package into his hands.

'I sold the diamond necklace and earrings your father gave me for my fortieth birthday, just in case he carried out his threat. The proceeds are in here. I've also enclosed my mother's gold wedding band which you can sell too if necessary.'

'Mor—'

'Hush now, they were mine and if he asks where they have gone, I will tell him the truth. It is enough to pay for a year's tuition and bed and board in Leipzig. Jens, swear to me you will not squander this money as you have done so often in the past.'

'Mor.' Jens found himself choked with emotion. 'I promise I will not.' And before he broke down completely, he folded her in his arms and tenderly kissed her goodbye.

'One day, I hope I can sit in the Christiania Theatre and watch you conduct the music you have written,' she said with a sad smile.

'That is a promise, Mor, and I will do whatever it takes to fulfil it.'

Then he left his home for the last time, feeling dazed but exhilarated by his decision and realising that, despite reassuring his mother, he hadn't really made a plan of where he would go if the worst *did* happen. Well, it *had*, and Jens headed straight to Engebret, hoping he might see a musician there he knew who could give him a bed for the night. Simen had kindly obliged, written down his address and said he'd see him there later on.

After a few beers to knock the edges off the enormity of what he'd just done, Jens found himself walking towards a part of the city he'd never been to before. And feeling highly conspicuous in his finely tailored clothes. His arms were aching from carrying his two heavy cases, and he made his way as quickly as possible, avoiding eye contact with all passers-by.

He had never been this far outside the city boundary and, unlike in the centre of Christiania, wooden houses had obviously not yet been banned as a fire risk. The buildings grew more dilapidated the further on he walked. Eventually, he stopped in front of an old timber-framed house and double-checked the address Simen had given him at Engebret. Knocking on the door, he heard a grunting and the sound of someone spitting within. The door opened and there was Simen, half-drunk as usual, smiling at him.

'Come in, come in, my boy, and welcome to my humble abode. It isn't much, but it's home.' Entering the house, the stuffy little front room smelt of rotting food and the tobacco that Simen smoked in his pipe. Jens saw that every inch of space was filled with musical instruments. Two cellos, a viola, a piano, numerous fiddles . . .

'Thank you for this, Simen. I am very grateful to you for taking me in.'

Simen waved aside his gratitude. 'Please, it is nothing. Any young man who gives up everything for his love of music deserves as much help as I can give him. I am proud of you, Jens, truly. Now follow me upstairs and we'll get you settled.'

'Quite a collection you have here,' said Jens as he picked his way carefully through the clutter of instruments and climbed up a set of narrow wooden stairs.

'I simply can't resist buying them. One of the cellos is almost a hundred years old,' Simen explained, while the stairs creaked in protest as Jens heaved his cases up them.

They arrived in a room containing a few battered chairs and a dusty table, covered in the detritus of a few days' worth of food and drink.

'There's a pallet somewhere which I can offer you to sleep on. Not what you're used to, I'm sure, but better than nothing. Now, my friend, some aquavit to celebrate your independence?' Simen picked up a bottle and a cloudy glass from the table. Sniffing the glass, he shook out a few remaining drops onto the floor.

'Thank you.'

Jens accepted the dirty glass. If this was to be his new life, he must embrace it wholeheartedly. He got very drunk that night, and woke up with a dreadful hangover, his bones aching from sleeping on the hard pallet. And realised that there would be no Dora arriving with coffee to soothe him.

Remembering in panic the package of money from his mother, Jens reached for his jacket to feel the pocket where he had stuffed it as he'd left the house. Finding it still safe, he opened it and saw the ring and that the amount of cash was indeed enough to provide him with a year's tuition in Leipzig. Or a comfortable bed in a hotel for the next few nights . . .

No. Jens checked himself. He had promised his mother and he would not let her down by squandering the money.

Anna boarded the train that would take her on the first stage of her journey home. It was dark when she arrived at Drammen station, and as she got down from the carriage, she saw her father waiting for her on the platform.

'Far! Oh, Far! I'm so happy to see you.' And much to Anders' surprise, she threw her arms around him in an uncharacteristic public display of emotion.

'There, there, Anna. I'm sure you must be weary after your journey. Come, let us make our way to our lodging house. Tonight you can sleep to your heart's content, then tomorrow we will travel home to Heddal.'

The next morning, refreshed after her night's sleep, Anna climbed up onto the cart and Anders tapped the horse to walk on. 'In the daylight, you seem different somehow. I think you have grown into a woman, daughter. You are beautiful.'

'Really, Far, I'm sure I'm not.'

'Everyone is looking forward to your arrival. Your mother is preparing a special evening meal for you tonight and Lars will be joining us. We received Herr Bayer's letter telling us of your success at the Christiania Theatre. He tells us that Solveig is no less than the leading role.'

'Yes, it is. But do you mind if I stay on in Christiania for longer, Far?'

'It would hardly be fair to complain after all Herr Bayer has done for you,' replied Anders placidly. 'He says you will become famous for it, that your voice is already the talk of the city. We are proud of you.'

'I think he exaggerates, Far,' Anna said with a blush.

'I doubt he does. Of course, Anna, you must speak with Lars. He is unhappy that your betrothal and marriage are once again delayed, but we hope he cares for you enough to understand.'

At the mention of Lars, Anna felt her stomach contract. Determined not to allow this to spoil her first day home, she did her best to push such thoughts to the back of her mind.

As they rode out of Drammen and into the open countryside, the day was bright and Anna closed her eyes, realising all she could hear was the clip-clopping of the pony's hooves and the birds singing in the trees. She breathed in the fresh, pure air like a caged animal suddenly released into the wild and decided that she might never return to Christiania again.

Anders told her that Rosa the cow had made it through another winter, which renewed Anna's faith that her prayers had been answered. Then he talked of the plans for Knut's wedding and of the frenzy of baking and cooking her mother was currently engaged in.

'Sigrid is a sweet girl and I think she will make a good wife for Knut,' Anders commented. 'Most importantly, your mother likes her too, which is helpful, as the happy couple will be living under our roof. Once you and Lars are wed, you will move to his farmhouse and we will think about building another homestead next year.'

When they arrived at the farm in the late afternoon, everyone came out to greet her. Even the old cat, Gerdy, ran out as fast as she could on her three legs, and Viva the dog followed boisterously after her, leaping up at Anna in joy.

Her mother gave her a long hug. 'I have been waiting all day to see you. How was your journey? Good Lord, you look thin! Your hair has grown too long and I'd say it needs a good trim . . .'

Anna listened to her mother chatter incessantly as they made their way to the farmhouse. The comforting smell of wood smoke, her mother's talcum powder and damp dog assailed her nostrils as she was led through to the kitchen.

'Put Anna's valise in her room,' Berit called to Knut, as she put the kettle on the range to make coffee. 'I hope you won't mind, Anna, but we have moved you into Knut's bedroom. It was too small to hold the double bed that Knut and Sigrid will be sharing after they are wed. Your father has taken away the bunks, and I think it is cosy with just one single. You will meet your new sister tomorrow when she comes for dinner. Oh, Anna, I am sure you will love her. She is so kind and her needlework is exquisite. She can also cook, which will be a great help to me, as my rheumatism has plagued me constantly this winter.'

For the following hour, Anna listened to her mother waxing lyrical about Sigrid. A little cross that she had been unceremoniously turfed out of her bedroom without so much as a 'by your leave', she did her best not to feel displaced by this apparent beacon of domestic perfection. After she had drunk her coffee, Anna took her leave to go and unpack before dinner.

Entering her new room, she saw that all her possessions had been stacked in the baskets her mother normally used to take the chickens to market. Sitting down on her brother's hard mattress, she wondered what had happened to her own childhood bed and decided that the way things seemed to be here, her father had probably chopped it up and used it as firewood for the stove. Feeling thoroughly disgruntled, Anna began to unpack her valise.

She unfolded the cushion cover she had spent hours embroidering as a wedding gift, since hearing of Knut's betrothal to Sigrid. As she'd sat night after night, pricking her fingers or pulling out the threads of a wrong stitch, she had despaired at her lack of skill. She flattened it out on the bed and stared at the frayed holes in the hessian fabric where she'd had to make stitch changes. Even if her cushion was consigned to the dog basket by her paragon of a new sister-in-law, Anna knew that at least every stitch had been sewn with love.

With her head held high, she left her room to join the family for her 'welcome home' dinner.

Lars arrived just as she was helping her mother serve the food. Holding a tureen of potatoes, Anna glanced at him as he walked into the kitchen and greeted Knut and her parents. Immediately, and irritatingly, Anna couldn't stop herself from comparing him to Jens Halvorsen the Bad. Physically, they were opposites, and whereas Jens was always the centre of attention, Lars only wanted to shy away from it.

'Anna, for goodness' sake, put those potatoes down, and say hello to Lars,' her mother chided her.

Anna set the dish of potatoes on the table and wiped her hands on her apron as she moved towards him.

'Hello, Anna,' he said softly. 'How are you?'

'I am well, thank you.'

'Was your journey here comfortable?'

'Very, thank you.' She could feel his embarrassment rising as he stared at her, struggling over what he should say next.

'You look . . . healthy,' he managed.

'Really?' Berit butted in. 'I think she looks far too skinny. It's all that fish they eat in the city. No fat on it.'

'Anna's always been slight – it's the way God intended her to be.' Lars gave her a small smile of support.

'I am sorry about your father's passing.'

'Thank you for your sympathy.'

'Shall we sit down, Berit? It's been a long journey there and back and your husband is hungry,' said Anders.

As they ate, Anna answered endless questions about her life in Christiania. Then the conversation turned to Knut's wedding and the attendant arrangements.

'You must be exhausted from your travelling, Anna,' said Lars.

'I am tired, yes,' she agreed.

'Then off to bed with you,' said Berit. 'There will be so much to do in the next few days, and no time for sleeping.'

Anna stood up. 'Goodnight, then.'

Lars' eyes never left her as she crossed the kitchen to go to her room. Halfway through getting undressed, she suddenly remembered that there was no bathroom in her parents' farmhouse. She put her clothes back on and went outside to use the facilities. Finally lying down, Anna struggled to get comfortable. The horsehair pillow felt like rock compared to the soft goose down she slept on at Herr Bayer's apartment, the bed felt narrow and the mattress lumpy. She mused on how much she had begun to take for granted without realising it. In Christiania, she had no domestic tasks to perform and a servant to wait on her hand and foot.

Anna, she chastised herself, *I do believe you are becoming spoilt*. And with that thought, she promptly fell asleep.

The week leading up to the wedding passed in a blur of cooking, cleaning, fetching and carrying as everyone busied themselves with last-minute preparations.

Despite wishing to dislike her brother's bride on principle for all the domestic things she could do so well, Anna found Sigrid to be all her mother had said she was. She was certainly not a beauty, but had a calm nature that counterbalanced Berit's hysteria as the big day drew ever closer. Sigrid, for her part, was in awe of Anna for living such a grand life in Christiania, treating her with great respect and bowing to her opinions without a murmur.

Anna's elder brother, Nils, arrived a day before the wedding, his wife and two children in tow. Anna hadn't seen them in more than a year and was delighted to become acquainted with her small nephews.

Amidst the joy of having the whole family reunited, however, one thing was playing on her mind: it seemed everyone assumed that when she returned from Christiania after the run of *Peer Gynt*, she would be moving to the run-down Trulssen homestead as Lars' wife. And sharing not only a room, but a *bed* with him.

The very idea made Anna feel quite ill and added to her sleeplessness at night.

On the morning of the wedding, Anna helped Sigrid into her bridal attire. This consisted of a deep red skirt and a white lawn blouse overlaid by a black bolero decorated with heavy pieces of gold-coloured metal. She studied the exquisite embroidery on the cream apron that fastened over the front of the skirt.

'The roses are so intricately stitched. I could never do that, Sigrid. You are so clever.'

'Anna, you simply don't have time with your busy life in the city. My trousseau took me many months of winter evenings to sew,' Sigrid replied. 'And besides, I can't sing as you do. You will sing at the wedding feast tonight, won't you?'

'If you wish me to, yes. And perhaps it's best we say that is my wedding present to you and Knut. I have sewn you something, but it is quite terrible,' she admitted.

'No matter, sister, I know it will have been fashioned out of love and that is all that matters. Now, can you hand me the crown and help me secure it?'

Anna took the heavy gold-plated wedding crown from its box. Held by the church for the past eighty years, every bride from the village had been married wearing it. She placed it on top of Sigrid's blonde hair. 'There, now you are truly a bride,' she said, as Sigrid stared at herself in the looking glass.

Berit popped her head around the door. 'Time to go, *kjære*. And may I say you look quite beautiful.'

Sigrid put her hand on Anna's. 'Thank you for your help, sister. It will be your turn next when you marry Lars.'

As she followed Sigrid to the waiting cart, strewn with

fresh flowers from the meadows, Anna shuddered involuntarily at the thought.

At the church, she watched her brother as he stood in front of the altar with Sigrid and Pastor Erslev. It was strange to think that Knut was now the head of a family, and would soon have his own redheaded children. She stole a glance at Lars, who was listening intently and, for once, was not looking at her.

After the ceremony, over a hundred people followed the bride and groom's cart back to the Landvik house. For weeks, Berit had been sending prayers up to the Lord to provide clear skies, as there was not enough room for everyone inside the farmhouse. Her prayers had been answered and the wooden tables laid out in the adjacent meadow were soon laden with food, much of it contributed by the guests themselves. Dishes of salted and spiced pork, tender beef roasted slowly on a spit and, of course, herring, kept stomachs filled and helped to soak up the home-made beer and aquavit which flowed freely throughout the celebrations.

Much later, as dusk began to fall, lanterns were lit and hung on wooden posts to create a makeshift square and the dancing began. The musicians launched into the upbeat tune of the *hallingkast*, and everyone cheered and cleared a circle in the centre. A young woman walked into the middle and held a hat up high on a stick in front of her and began challenging the men to come out and kick it off. Anna's brothers nudged each other and were the first in the circle to dance and jump around the girl, encouraged by the whooping and cheering crowd.

Breathless with laughter, Anna turned around to see Lars sitting morosely at a table by himself.

'Anna, will you do as you promised and sing for us?' Sigrid appeared by her side.

'Yes' – a panting Knut joined her in her plea – 'you must.'

'Sing "Solveig's Song"!' shouted someone from the crowd.

There was a chorus of approval at this suggestion. Anna walked into the centre of the dance square, composed herself and began to sing. As she did so, her thoughts returned unbidden to Christiania, to the young musician who had been so entranced by her voice that he'd continued to pursue her . . .

'*And we shall meet again, love, and never parted be. And never parted be . . .*'

There were tears in her eyes as the last note died away. Her audience was silent, then someone started to clap and the rest of the party followed until the whole meadow rang with cheers.

'Sing something else, Anna!'

'Yes! One of *our* songs.'

For the next half an hour, accompanied by her father on the fiddle, she had no further time to dwell on her own feelings as she went through the repertoire of folk songs that all the audience knew by heart. Then it was time for the bride and groom to depart for the night. With much good-natured jeering and wolf-whistling, Knut and Sigrid disappeared inside the house and the party began to disperse.

As she helped with the clearing up, Anna felt drained and unsettled. She moved like an automaton, ferrying plates and dishes to the barrel full of water that had been drawn from the well earlier for the purpose.

'You look tired, Anna.'

Feeling a hand touch her lightly on her shoulder, she

turned and saw Lars standing behind her. 'I am perfectly well,' she said, managing a weak smile.

'Did you enjoy the wedding?'

'Yes, everything was beautiful. Sigrid and Knut will be very happy together.'

As she turned back to concentrate on her task, she felt his hand slide off her shoulder. Out of the corner of her eye, she could see him with his head bent down, his hands in his pockets.

'Anna, I've missed you,' he said so quietly, she barely heard him. 'Do you . . . Have you missed me at all?'

She froze, the soapy plate sliding through her fingers. 'Of course, I've missed everyone here, but I've been so busy in Christiania.'

'With all your new friends, I suppose,' he said flatly.

'Yes, such as Frøken Olsdatter and the children at the theatre,' she answered quickly, continuing to wash the plate but secretly wishing he would go.

Lars hovered uncertainly for a few seconds and she could feel his eyes upon her. 'It has been a long day for everyone,' he said finally. 'I must take my leave . . . But first, Anna, I must ask you a question as I know you must return to Christiania tomorrow. And I wish you to answer it honestly. For both our sakes.'

Anna could hear the serious undercurrent in his voice. Her stomach flipped over. 'Of course, Lars.'

'Do you . . . do you still wish to marry me? Given what has changed and will continue to change for you, I swear I will understand if you do not.'

'I . . .' she bent her head over the plates, screwed her eyes closed and wished this moment could go away. 'I think so.'

'And yet I think you do not. Anna, please, it is better for both of us to know where we stand. I can only wait longer for you if there is hope. I cannot help but feel you have been uncomfortable about our proposed union from the start.'

'But what about Mor and Far and the land you have sold to them?'

Lars let out a heavy sigh. 'Anna, you have just told me everything I needed to know. I will take my leave now, but I will write to tell you how we must organise things. You need say nothing to your parents. I will take care of it all.' He reached down and drew one of her hands out of the water. Raising it to his lips, he kissed it. 'Goodbye, Anna, and God bless you.'

She watched him walk away into the darkness, realising that her betrothal to Lars Trulssen seemed to have ended before it had even begun.

Ally

August 2007

"Solveig's Song"

22

It was past lunchtime when I looked up from my laptop screen and the striped wallpaper beyond danced blurrily before slowly coming back into focus. Even though I had absolutely no idea how I fitted into a story that had taken place over one hundred and thirty years ago, what I'd read so far had fascinated me. At the Conservatoire in Geneva, I'd learnt about the lives of many composers and studied their masterpieces, but this book brought the era so vividly to life. And I was fascinated by the fact that Jens Halvorsen had been the flautist who had played those first iconic four bars at the premiere of one of my favourite pieces of music.

I thought of Pa's letter to me then, and wondered whether he had simply wanted me to read the story of how *Peer Gynt* came to be in order to encourage a rebirth of my love for music. As if he'd known I might need it . . .

And yes, playing at Theo's memorial service *had* comforted me. Even the time it had taken practising the piece had been a few welcome hours of release from thinking about him. And since then, I'd taken my flute out and played for pleasure. Or, more accurately, to salve the pain.

The question was whether this connection went deeper

and a blood tie existed between Anna and Jens, and me. Stretching like a fragile silk thread across one hundred and thirty years . . .

Could Pa Salt have known either Jens or Anna when he was much younger? I pondered. As Pa had been in his eighties when he'd died, I supposed there was a possibility, depending on when Jens and Anna had died themselves. Which, irritatingly, were facts I did not currently have at my disposal.

My ruminations were interrupted by the piercing trill of the house telephone. Knowing that Celia's ancient answering machine was broken and that the phone would therefore ring incessantly, I left the bedroom and ran downstairs to the hall to answer it.

'Hello?'

'Uh, hi, is Celia at home?'

'Not at present, no,' I answered, recognising the male voice with its American accent. 'This is Ally. Can I take a message?'

'Well, hello there, Ally. It's Peter here, Theo's dad. How're you doing?'

'I'm okay,' I answered automatically. 'Celia should be back around supper time tonight.'

'Too late for me, unfortunately. I was just calling to let her know I'm leaving this evening to fly back to the States. Felt I should speak to her before I did.'

'Well, I'll tell her you called, Peter.'

'Thanks.' There was a pause on the line. 'Ally, are you busy right now?'

'No, not really.'

'Then can we meet before I leave for the airport? I'm staying at the Dorchester; I could buy you afternoon tea. It's only a fifteen-minute cab ride from Celia's house.'

'I . . .'

'Please?'

'Okay,' I agreed reluctantly.

'Shall we say three in the Promenade? I have to leave for Heathrow at four.'

'See you then, Peter,' I said as I put the receiver down and wondered what on earth I had with me to wear to take tea at the Dorchester hotel.

When I walked into the hotel an hour later, I felt strangely guilty, as if I was betraying Celia. But Pa Salt had always brought me up never to judge anyone on hearsay. And Peter was Theo's father, so I had to give him a chance.

'Hi there, young lady,' he called, waving to me from a table in the opulent marble-pillared room that led off the lobby. He rose to greet me as I walked over and he shook my hand with a warm, firm grip. 'Please, sit down. I wasn't sure what you'd want, so as we're tight for time, I took the liberty of ordering the full works.'

He gestured to the low table, which held china platters of precision-cut finger sandwiches and a tiered cake stand filled with delicate French pastries and scones, accompanied by little bowls of jam and clotted cream. 'There's gallons of tea too, of course. Wow, the English love their tea!'

'Thank you,' I said, not feeling remotely hungry as I took a seat on the banquette opposite him. An immaculate white-gloved waiter immediately stepped forward to pour me a cup of tea, and as he did so, I studied Theo's father properly. He had dark eyes, pale skin that was hardly lined with age – given that he was probably in his early sixties – and a muscular frame beneath his casual but expensively tailored navy-blue blazer. I could see that he dyed his hair from the unnaturally matt-brown colour and I'd just decided Theo didn't resemble his father at all when Peter smiled at me. The lopsided set of his mouth was so like his son's, it made me catch my breath.

'So, Ally, how's it all going?' he asked me as the waiter glided away. 'Are you coping?'

'I have good moments and bad, I suppose. How about you?'

'If you want the truth, Ally, I'm not coping well at all. This has really knocked me sideways. I keep remembering Theo as a baby and what a cute little kid he was. It's just not the right order of things to have a child die before you, you know?'

'I do,' I sympathised, curious about this man who had been so negatively described by Celia and Theo. I could see he was trying to hold it together, but I felt his pain. It shone out of him, like a palpable presence.

'How's Celia dealing with it?' he asked.

'The same as all of us – with terrible difficulty. She's been wonderfully kind to me.'

'Maybe it's been therapeutic to have someone else to care for. I wish I did.'

'I should tell you,' I said as I took a smoked salmon sandwich and nibbled at it, 'that Celia told me she would have invited you to come and sit with her at the front of the church if she'd known you were there.'

'Really?' Peter's expression brightened a little. 'That's real good to know, Ally. Maybe I should have let her know I was coming, but I knew how grief-stricken she'd be and I didn't want to upset her further. You might already have guessed that I'm not exactly top of her Christmas card list.'

'Perhaps she finds it hard to forgive you for . . . you know . . . what you did to her.'

'Well now, young lady, as I said to you that day after the memorial service, there's always another side to a story, but we won't go there just now. And yes, I take an extra-large share of the blame, by the way. Between you and me, I still love Celia,' Peter sighed. 'I love her so goddam much, it's a physical pain. I know I let her down and did bad stuff, but we were married young, and in retrospect, I should have sowed my wild oats before and not during the marriage. Celia . . . well,' Peter said with a shrug, 'she was a real "lady" in that way, if you get my drift. We were simply opposites in that department. Anyway, I've sure learnt my lesson.'

'Yes,' I said, not wanting to pursue that line of explanation any further. 'Actually, I think she still loves you too.'

'Really?' Peter raised a suspicious eyebrow. 'Now that sure wasn't what I was expecting to hear from you.'

'No, probably not, but it's just in her eyes when she talks about you, even when she's saying something negative. Your son said to me once that there was a very thin line between love and hate.'

'Trust him to point it out – that's the kind of savvy, emotionally intelligent young man he was. I wish I had half of his understanding of human nature,' Peter sighed. 'He certainly didn't get it from me.'

I realised that I'd probably waded in far too deep, but as I was already up to my neck, I decided I might as well go with it. 'You know, I think Theo would have loved the thought of his parents meeting and maybe reconciling the past. If that was the only good thing to come out of this tragedy, at least it would be something.'

Peter stared at me as I sipped my tea. 'I think I can totally understand why my boy loved you so much. You're special, Ally. Although, however good your intentions are, I don't believe in miracles any more.'

'I do. Yes, I do,' I repeated. 'Even if Theo and I only had a few weeks together, he changed my life. It *is* a miracle that we met and fitted together so perfectly, and I know that even with all the pain, he's made me a better person.' It was my turn to tear up, and Peter reached across the table and patted my hand.

'Well, Ally, I sure do admire you. Trying to find the positive out of a negative. A long time ago, that's how I used to be.'

'Surely you can be like that again?'

'I think it all got knocked out of me during the divorce. Anyway, tell me about your plans for the future. Did my son leave you provided for?'

'Yes, he did. He actually changed his will before the race. I have his Sunseeker and an old barn on Anafi, near your lovely house. To be honest, even though I loved Theo to bits, I'm not sure I can see myself going to "Somewhere", as we called Anafi, and fighting the Greek authorities to build the house of his dreams.'

'He left you that crazy goat barn?' Peter threw back his head and laughed. 'Just for the record, I offered to buy Theo his own place on numerous occasions, but he always flat out refused.'

'Pride,' I said with a shrug.

'Or stupidity,' Peter countered. 'My boy was a sportsman

pursuing his passion. I understood he needed help financially, but he'd never take it. I'll bet you haven't bought your own home either, Ally. How can any young person earning even an average wage do that these days?'

'No, I haven't, although I do have the goat barn now,' I said with a smile.

'Well now, firstly I want to tell you that any time you want to go to my house on the island, you're more than welcome. Celia knows she can use it anytime too, but she refuses to go. Apparently it's to do with something I said to her when we were there together way back when. Don't ask what, because I can't remember. And let me tell you, Ally, if you ever need help with the local planning authorities, I'm your man. I've invested so much money in that island, I should be made mayor! Do you have the deeds of ownership yet?'

'Not yet, but apparently, once the estate's gone through probate, they'll be sent to me.'

'Well, anything you need, young lady, you just consider me there for you. It's the least I can do: to take care of the girl my boy loved.'

'Thanks.' We both sat in silence for a while, missing him.

'So,' Peter said eventually, 'you still haven't told me what your future plans are.'

'That's because I'm not sure of them.'

'Theo said you were a damn fine sailor, about to train in the Swiss Olympic squad.'

'I've pulled out. Don't ask me to explain, please Peter, but I simply can't do it.'

'No explanations necessary. And if you'll excuse me for the obvious metaphor, it seems you have another string to your bow. You're a fine musician, Ally. I was very moved by your flute playing at the memorial service.'

'That's very kind of you to say, Peter. But really, I was so rusty. I haven't played properly for years.'

'Well, it sure didn't sound like it to me. If I had a skill like yours, I'd treasure it. Does it run in the family?'

'I'm not sure. Maybe. My father died only a few weeks ago—'

'Ally!' Peter looked aghast. 'My God! How have you coped, losing both men in your life?'

'To be honest, I don't know.' I gulped, feeling a rush of emotion. I was okay as long as no one offered me sympathy. 'Anyway, the point is that I was adopted, along with my five sisters. And my father's parting gift to me was to give me clues to my past. And from what little I know so far, it may turn out that music *is* in my genes.'

'I see.' He looked at me, his dark eyes full of empathy. 'Are you going to find out more?'

'I'm not sure just yet. I certainly wasn't intending to when Theo was around. I was looking forward to the future.'

'Of course you were. You got anything at all planned for the next few weeks?'

'No, nothing.'

'Well then, there's your answer: go follow the clues you've been given. I sure would. And I think Theo would want you to. Now' – he looked at his watch – 'I'm sad I have to leave you, but I'm going to miss my flight if I don't. The bill's paid, so please stay here and finish up if you want. And I'll say it again: if you ever need anything, Ally, you just let me know.'

He rose and so did I. And then spontaneously, he enveloped me in his arms and gave me a tight hug. 'Ally, I wish we had more time to talk, but I'm glad to know you all the same. Today has been the only positive thing to take out of what's happened, and I thank you for that. And remember, someone once told me that life only throws at you what it feels you can deal with. And you are one seriously amazing young woman.' He handed me a card. 'Keep in touch.'

'I will,' I promised.

He gave me a sad wave and walked briskly from the table.

I sat back down, looking at the sumptuous spread in front of me and half-heartedly reached for a scone, unable to bear the thought of the food going to waste. I too wished we'd had longer to talk. Whatever Celia had said to me about her ex-husband, and whatever he might have done to her, I liked him. For all his reputed wealth and bad behaviour, there was something intrinsically vulnerable about him.

When I arrived home, I found Celia in her bedroom, packing a suitcase.

'Did you have a nice afternoon?' she asked me.

'Yes, thank you. I met Peter for afternoon tea. He rang here to speak to you after you left this morning and got me instead.'

'Well, I am surprised he called. Normally when he's in the UK, he doesn't.'

'Normally, he hasn't lost a son. He sends his love, anyway.'

'Good. Now then, Ally,' she said over-brightly, 'as you know, I'm off at the crack of dawn tomorrow. You're welcome to stay here for as long as you want to; you'll just need to put the burglar alarm on and post the keys through the front door when you decide to leave. Are you absolutely sure you don't want to come with me? It's beautiful in Tuscany at this time of the year. And Cora is not only my oldest friend, but also Theo's godmother.'

'Thank you so much for asking, but I think it's time to go out and find myself a life.'

'Well, just remember it's early days. I divorced Peter twenty years ago, and I still don't seem to have found myself one.' She shrugged sadly. 'Anyway, stay here for as long as you want.'

'Thank you. By the way, I went shopping on the way home and I'd like to cook tonight to say thank you. It's nothing fancy, just pasta, but it'll hopefully put you in the mood for Italy.'

'How sweet of you, Ally dear. That will be lovely.'

We sat out on the terrace for our last supper together. I had little appetite, and as I did my best to eat a few forkfuls, I noted that the drooping heads of Celia's roses were draining of colour, the edges of the petals brown and crisp. Even the air smelt different: heavier, with an earthy hint of the autumn to come. While we ate, we both slipped into our own thoughts, as we realised we were losing our bubble of mutual comfort and had to face the world again.

'I just wanted to say thank you for being here, Ally. I really don't know what I'd have done without you,' Celia said as we carried our empty plates into the kitchen.

'Or me without you,' I said, as Celia started to wash up and I picked up a tea towel to dry.

'I also want you to know that any time you're in London, you're to think of this house as your home, Ally.'

'Thank you.'

'I hate to mention it, but I'll be collecting Theo's ashes

when I get back from Italy. We'll need to make a date to go to Lymington and scatter them together.'

'Yes,' I gulped, 'of course.'

'I'm going to miss you, Ally. I really feel you're the daughter I never had. Now,' she added gruffly, 'I'd better get to bed. My taxi's arriving at four thirty and I'm certainly not expecting you to be up to see me off. So I'll say goodbye. But keep in touch, won't you?'

'Of course I will.'

I slept restlessly that night, the blank pages of my imminent future haunting my dreams. Up until now, I'd always known exactly where I was going and what I was doing. The sense of emptiness and lethargy I currently felt was new to me.

'Maybe this is what depression feels like,' I muttered as I hauled myself out of bed the next morning and, feeling slightly nauseous, forced myself to take a shower. As I towelled my hair dry, I typed 'Jens Halvorsen' into a search engine. Irritatingly, the few mentions of him were written in Norwegian, so I went to the site of an online book retailer, idly browsing for any books in English or French that might contain a mention of him.

And then I found it.

Grieg's Apprentice

Author: Thom Halvorsen

Release date (US edition) 30th August 2007

I scrolled down to find the brief synopsis.

'Thom Halvorsen, renowned violinist with the Bergen Philharmonic Orchestra, has written a biography of his

great-great-grandfather, Jens Halvorsen. It charts the life of a talented composer and musician who worked closely with Edvard Grieg. With the aid of fascinating family memoirs, we see Grieg afresh through the eyes of one who knew him intimately.'

I ordered the book immediately, although I saw that they were quoting a minimum of two weeks for delivery from the States. Then I had a brainwave, and, pulling Peter's card from my wallet, I wrote him an email, thanking him for afternoon tea. Then explained I needed to get hold of a book that was only available in America and could he possibly hunt it down for me? I didn't feel too guilty asking him; I was sure he had endless minions at his beck and call who could go in search of it.

Then I typed in *Peer Gynt*, and scrolling down through the various references, I came across the Ibsen Museum in Oslo – or Christiania, as Anna and Jens had known it – and its curator, Erik Edvardsen. He was apparently a world-renowned expert on Henrik Ibsen and perhaps he'd be willing to help me if I emailed him.

I was itching to continue my research and also to read what I had left of the book translation, but I reluctantly closed my laptop when I realised I was due in Battersea to see Star for lunch in half an hour.

I hailed a cab outside the house, and as we crossed the River Thames over an ornate and pretty pink bridge, I decided I was falling a little in love with London. There was something intrinsically elegant about it – stately almost – with none of the frenetic energy of New York or the blandness of

Geneva. Like everything in England, it seemed to have full confidence in its own history and uniqueness.

The cab stopped in front of what had obviously once been a warehouse. Sitting on the riverside, it and its neighbours would have provided easy access for the barges to bring in their loads of tea, silks and spices in days gone by. I paid the driver and rang the bell beside the number Star had given me. The door opened with an electronic buzz and her voice told me to take the lift to the third floor. I did so, and found Star waiting for me at the front door.

'Hello, darling, how are you?' she asked as we embraced each other.

'Oh, coping,' I lied as she led me into a cavernous white living space with floor-to-ceiling windows overlooking the Thames.

'Wow!' I said as I walked over to admire the view. 'This place is fantastic!'

'CeCe chose it,' said Star with a shrug. 'It's got room for her to work, and the light is good too.'

I looked around, noting the open-plan layout, the minimalist furniture dotted around on the blond-wood floorboards and the sleek spiral staircase that presumably led up to the bedrooms. It wasn't what I would have personally chosen as it was anything but cosy, but it was certainly impressive.

'Can I get you a drink?' Star asked. 'We have wine of all colours, and, of course, beer.'

'Whatever you're having, Star,' I said, following her over to the kitchen area, which was kitted out in ultra-modern stainless steel and frosted glass. She opened one door of the huge double refrigerator and seemed to hesitate.

'White wine?' I suggested.

'Yes, good idea.'

I observed my younger sister as she took down two glasses from a cabinet and opened the wine, thinking again how Star never seemed to express an opinion of her own or make a decision. Maia and I had discussed endlessly whether it was Star's natural personality to defer to others, or the result of CeCe's dominant role in their relationship.

'That smells good,' I said, pointing to a pot bubbling away on the industrial-sized hob. I could also see something cooking in the glass-fronted oven.

'I'm using you as a guinea pig, Ally. I'm trying out a new recipe and it's almost ready.'

'Great. Cheers, as they say here in England.'

'Yes, cheers.'

We both took a sip of our wine, but I put mine down on the countertop, as for some reason it had immediately turned acidic in my stomach. As I watched her stirring the contents of the pot, I reflected how very young Star looked, with her mist of white-blonde hair falling to her shoulders, and her long fringe that often fell into her enormous pale blue eyes, shielding them and their expressions like a protective curtain. I found it difficult to remember that Star was a grown woman of twenty-seven.

'So, how are you settling down in London Town?' I asked her.

'Well, I think. I like it here.'

'And how's the cookery course going?'

'I've finished that. It was fine.'

'So do you think you might pursue a career in cooking?' I ploughed on, hoping to elicit a more elaborate response.

'I don't think it's for me.'

'I see. Any idea what you might do next?'

'I don't know.'

Silence reigned then, as it often did in conversations with Star. Eventually she continued. 'So how are you really, Ally? It's all so awful for you, coming so soon after Pa's death.'

'I'm not sure how I am, to be honest. It's changed everything. My future was all mapped out and now suddenly it's gone. I've told the manager of the Swiss national squad I won't be taking part in the Olympic trials. I really couldn't face that just now. People have told me I'm wrong, and I feel guilty for not having the strength to continue, but it just doesn't seem right. What do you think?'

Star brushed back her fringe from her eyes and regarded me warily. 'I think that you must do exactly as you feel, Ally. But sometimes that's very difficult, isn't it?'

'Yes, it is. I don't want to let anyone down.'

'Exactly.' Star gave a small sigh as she turned her gaze towards the floor-length windows, then back to the hob as she began to serve the contents of the pot onto two plates. 'Shall we eat outside?'

'Why not?'

I turned my attention towards the river and to the terrace that ran the length of the windows and wondered rather meanly what on earth this place had cost to rent. It was hardly the typical apartment of a penniless art student and her apparently directionless sister. CeCe had obviously managed to cajole Georg Hoffman into releasing some funds the morning she and Star had visited him in Geneva.

We ferried the food out to the table, which stood against the backdrop of a myriad of sweet-smelling plants overflowing from giant pots along the edge of the terrace. 'These are beautiful. What is that?' I pointed to one, containing a riotous mass of orange, white and pink flowers.

'It's *Sparaxis tricolor*. More commonly called "wand-flower", but I don't think it really likes the breeze from the river. It really belongs in a sheltered corner of an English country garden.'

'Did you plant them?' I asked as I took a mouthful of the noodle seafood dish Star had prepared for the main course.

'Yes. I like plants. I always have. I used to help Pa Salt in his garden at Atlantis.'

'Did you? I had no idea. My goodness, this is delicious, Star,' I complimented her, even though I really wasn't hungry. 'I'm discovering all sorts of hidden talents you have today. My cooking is basic at best and I can't even grow cress in a pot, let alone all this.' I gesticulated to the abundance surrounding us on the terrace.

Again, there was a pregnant pause, but I refrained from filling the silence.

'Recently, I've been thinking about what talent actually is. I mean, are things that come easily to you a gift?' Star said tentatively. 'For example, did you really have to try to play the flute so beautifully?'

'No, I suppose I didn't. Not initially, anyway. But then, to get better, I had to practise endlessly. I don't think simply having a talent for something can compensate for sheer hard work. I mean, look at the great composers: it's not enough to hear the tunes in your head; you have to learn how to put them down in writing and how to orchestrate a piece. That takes years of practice and learning your craft. I'm sure there are millions of us who have a natural ability at something, but unless we harness that ability and dedicate ourselves to it, we can never reach our full potential.'

Star nodded slowly. 'Have you finished, Ally?' she asked, looking across the table at my barely touched plate.

'I have. Sorry, Star. It was gorgeous, really, but I'm afraid I haven't had much of an appetite recently.'

After that, we chatted about our sisters and what they'd been up to. Star told me about CeCe and how her 'installations' were keeping her busy. I commented on Maia's surprise move to Rio, and how wonderful it was for her that at last she'd found happiness.

'This has really cheered me up. And it's so great to see you, Star,' I said with a smile.

'And you. Where will you go now, do you think?'

'As a matter of fact, I might go to Norway and investigate what Pa Salt's coordinates indicate is my original place of birth.'

I'm sure I looked far more surprised at what I'd just said than Star did, as the thought entered my brain for the first time and began to take hold.

'Good,' Star said. 'I think you should.'

'Do you?'

'Why not? Pa's clues might change your life. They changed Maia's. And' – Star paused – 'perhaps mine too.'

'Really?'

'Yes.'

Another silence took hold and I knew it wasn't worth pursuing Star for further details of her revelation. 'Now, I really think I should be going. Thank you so much for lunch.' I stood up, suddenly feeling weary and needing to return to my sanctuary. 'Is it easy to get a taxi from here?' I said as she accompanied me to the front door.

'Yes, turn left and you're on the main road. Goodbye, Ally,' she said as she reached to kiss me on both cheeks. 'Let me know if you go to Norway.'

Back at Celia's silent house, I went up to my bedroom and opened the case that contained my flute. I stared at it intently, as if it could answer all the questions burning in my mind. The most pressing being where I would go from here. I knew I could almost certainly go and bury myself on 'Somewhere'. One telephone call to Peter and his beautiful house on Anafi would be mine for as long as I needed it. I could spend the next year concentrating on renovating Theo's precious goat barn – thoughts of *Mamma Mia*, the Abba musical, sprang to mind, and I chuckled and shook my head. However appealing the cocoon of 'Somewhere' appeared, I knew it would not move me forward. It would simply let me live in the world of Theo and I, which had been but wasn't any more.

Equally, would Atlantis be good for me? Was there anything left for me there now? But anything I might subsequently discover in Norway was firmly in my past too and I was someone who looked to the future. Yet perhaps with the 'now' being on hold, I had to reverse in order to move forward. I decided that my choice was stark: return to Atlantis or fly to Norway. Perhaps a few days of private contemplation in a new country – away from everything and everybody – would be a good thing. No one there would know my story and investigating the past would at least give me something to focus on. Even if it came to nothing.

I began to look up flights to Oslo, finding one that left that evening and had availability. I realised I'd have to leave almost immediately to get to Heathrow on time. I stared into space trying to make a decision.

'Come on, Ally.' I spoke to myself harshly, as my finger hovered over the button to confirm the seat. 'What have you got to lose?'

Nothing.

And besides, I was ready to know.

23

As the plane soared northward that late August evening, I skimmed through the information I had about the Ibsen Museum and the National Theatre in Oslo. Tomorrow morning, I decided, I'd visit both and see if anyone there could shed further light on the information I'd gleaned from Jens Halvorsen's book.

As I left the plane at Oslo airport, I felt an unexpected lightness in my step and something that almost resembled excitement. After clearing customs, I went straight to the information desk and asked the young woman behind the counter if she could suggest a hotel that was located close to the Ibsen Museum. She mentioned the Grand Hotel, called them and told me they only had availability at the more expensive end of the rooms.

'Fine,' I said. 'I'll take what they have.' The woman handed me a slip of paper that confirmed my booking, then ordered me a taxi and directed me outside to wait for it.

As we drove into the centre of Oslo, the darkness made it difficult to get my bearings or gain much of an impression of the city. On arrival at the imposing lamp-lit stone entrance to the Grand Hotel, I was immediately ushered inside and, with the formalities completed, shown to my room, which turned out to be named 'The Ibsen Suite'.

'Will this be sufficient for you, madam?' the bellboy asked me in English as he handed me the key.

I looked around the beautiful sitting room, with a chandelier dangling elegantly from the ceiling and various photographs of Henrik Ibsen adorning the striped silk walls, and smiled at the coincidence.

'It's wonderful, thank you very much.'

Once I'd tipped the bellboy and he'd left, I wandered around the suite in awe, thinking I could very easily move into it full-time. After taking a shower, I emerged from the bathroom to the sound of church bells ushering in the arrival of midnight and felt glad I was here. Sliding between the crisp linen sheets, I fell into a deep sleep.

I rose early the next morning, and went out onto the tiny balcony to view the city in the light of a fresh new day. Below me was a tree-lined square, flanked by a mixture of gorgeous old stone buildings and a few more modern ones. Casting my gaze upwards in the distance, I could see a pink castle perched on a hill.

I wandered back inside and realised I hadn't eaten since yesterday lunchtime. I ordered breakfast to be delivered to the room, then sat on the bed in my robe, feeling like a princess in my newfound palace. I studied the map the receptionist had given me last night and saw that the Ibsen Museum was only a short walk away.

After breakfast, I dressed and took the lift downstairs, armed with my map. As I crossed the square in front of the hotel, I suddenly smelt the all too familiar aroma of the sea, and I remembered that Oslo was built on a fjord. I also noticed the large number of fair-skinned redheads who passed me. In Switzerland, I'd been teased during my schooldays about my pale complexion, freckles and red-gold curls. At the time, it had hurt, as those things always did, and I remembered asking Ma if I could dye my hair.

'No, *chérie*, your hair is your crowning glory. One day all those nasty girls will be jealous of it,' had been her reply.

Well, I thought as I continued to walk, *I certainly won't stick out here.*

I came to a halt outside an impressive pale-brick building, the entrance to which was colonnaded with grey stone pillars.

'NATIONALTHEATER'

I read the engraved inscription above the elegant façade and noticed that just below it, the names of Ibsen and two other men I'd never heard of were engraved on stone plaques. Had this been the very building where *Peer Gynt* had been premiered, I wondered? To my disappointment, the theatre was shut at present, so I continued walking along the busy wide street until I arrived at the front door of the Ibsen Museum. Stepping inside, I found myself in a small bookshop, and on the wall to my left was a display board printed with the dates of the major events in Ibsen's gilded career. My heart beat a little faster as I read the date: '*24th February 1876 – premiere of* Peer Gynt *at the Christiania Theatre.*'

'*God morgen! Kan eg hjelpe deg?*' the girl behind the counter asked.

'Do you speak English?' was my first question.

'Of course,' she said with a smile. 'Can I help you?'

'Well, yes, or at least I hope so.' Taking the photocopy of

the book cover out of my bag, I placed it on the desk in front of her. 'My name's Ally D'Aplièse and I'm doing some research on a composer called Jens Halvorsen and a singer called Anna Landvik. They were both in the original premiere of *Peer Gynt* at the Christiania Theatre. I wondered if anyone here could tell me a little more about them.'

'I can't, as I'm just a student on the till,' she confessed, 'but I'll go upstairs and see if Erik, the director of the museum, is in.'

'Thank you.'

As she disappeared through a door at the back of the desk, I wandered around the shop and picked up an English translation of *Peer Gynt*. At the very least, I thought, I should read it.

'Yes, Erik's here, and he will come down to see you shortly,' confirmed the girl as she reappeared. I thanked her and paid for the book.

A few minutes later, an elegant white-haired man appeared.

'Hello, Miss D'Aplièse. I'm Erik Edvardsen,' he said, offering his hand in greeting. 'Ingrid says you're interested in Jens Halvorsen and Anna Landvik?'

'Yes,' I said, shaking his hand before showing him the photocopy of the book cover.

He took it and gazed at it with a nod. 'I believe we have a copy upstairs in the library. Would you like to follow me?'

He showed me through a door that led to an austere entrance hall. Compared to the modern decor of the bookshop, it was like taking a step back in time. He opened the old-fashioned gate to the lift, closed it behind us and pressed a button. As we rattled upwards, he indicated a particular floor as we passed it. 'That is the apartment in which Ibsen himself lived for the last eleven years of his life. We consider ourselves privileged to have custody of it. So,' he said as we emerged from the lift into an airy room, the walls of which were lined floor to ceiling with books, 'are you an historian?'

'Goodness, no,' I replied. 'The book was a legacy to me from my father, who died a few weeks ago. In fact, maybe I should say it's more of a clue, because I'm still not sure what it has to do with me. I'm currently having the whole text translated from Norwegian to English, and I've only read the first instalment. All I really know so far is that Jens was a musician who played the opening bars of "Morning Mood" at the premiere of *Peer Gynt*. And that Anna was the ghost voice for Solveig's songs.'

'To be honest, I'm not sure how much I can help you, because my subject is obviously Ibsen, rather than Grieg. You really need to see an expert on Grieg himself and the ideal person to help you is the curator of the Grieg Museum up in Bergen. However,' he said, as he scanned the bookshelves, 'there is one thing I can show you. Ah, there it is.' He pulled a large old book from the shelves. 'This was written by Rudolf Rasmussen – known as "Rude" – who was one of the children in the original production of *Peer Gynt*.'

'Yes! I've read about him in the book. He was a go-between delivering messages to Jens and Anna when they first fell in love at the theatre.'

'Really?' Erik said as he leafed through the pages. 'Here, these are pictures from that very first night, with all the cast members in costume.'

He handed the book to me, and I stared incredulously into the faces of the very people I'd just been reading about. There was Henrik Klausen as Peer Gynt and Thora Hansson as Solveig. I tried to imagine her looking like a glamorous star out of Solveig's peasant clothes. Other photographs showed the entire cast, although I knew Anna would not be in any of them.

'I can photocopy the pictures if you wish,' Erik suggested, 'and then you can study them at your leisure.'

'That would be wonderful, thank you.'

As Erik walked over to the photocopier that stood in a corner, my eyes fell on a print of an old theatre. 'I walked past the National Theatre today, and could just imagine how it was when *Peer Gynt* opened,' I commented to break the silence.

'Actually, *Peer Gyn*t didn't open at the National Theatre. It was premiered at the Christiania Theatre.'

'Oh. I'd presumed it was the same building that had simply changed its name?'

'Sadly, the old Christiania Theatre is long gone. It was in Bankplassen, fifteen minutes or so away from here. It's now a museum.'

I stared at Erik's back as my mouth fell open in amazement. 'Do you by any chance mean the Museum of Contemporary Art?'

'I do. The Christiania Theatre was closed in 1899 and anything musical moved to the newly built National Theatre. Here,' he said, handing me the photocopied sheets.

'Well, I'm sure I've taken up far too much of your time, but thank you very much for seeing me.'

'Before you leave, let me give you the email address of the curator at the Grieg museum. Tell him I sent you. I'm sure he'll be able to help you far more than I have.'

'Herr Edvardsen, I promise you, you've helped me very much indeed,' I assured him as he scribbled down the email address then handed it to me.

'Of course, even I bow to the fact that the fame of Grieg's music for *Peer Gynt* has far outstripped that of the poem itself,' he said with a smile as he led me towards the lift. 'It's become iconic across the world. Goodbye, Miss D'Aplièse. I'd love to know if you manage to solve the mystery. And I'm always here if you need any further help.'

'Thank you.'

As I left the museum, I almost skipped back to the Grand Hotel. The coordinates from the armillary sphere finally made sense. And as I entered the Grand Café, which occupied the front corner of the hotel, I gazed at the original mural of Ibsen on the wall and knew for certain that somehow, Jens and Anna were part of my story.

Over lunch, I emailed the curator of the Grieg museum, as Erik had suggested. Then out of curiosity, I took a taxi to the site of the old Christiania Theatre. The Museum of Contemporary Art stood in a square behind a fountain that played in the centre of it. Modern art really wasn't my thing, though I knew CeCe would love it, and I decided not to go in. Then I saw the Engebret Café across the square, walked towards it and pushed open the door.

Glancing around, I saw rustic wooden tables and chairs, which were just as I'd imagined from Jens' description in the book. A distinctive smell – of stale alcohol, dust and the very faint odour of damp – pervaded the air. I closed my eyes and pictured Jens and his orchestral cohorts in here well over a century ago, spending long hours drowning their sorrows in aquavit. I ordered a coffee at the bar and drank the hot, bitter liquid, feeling frustrated that I couldn't read any more of the story until the translator had sent me the rest of the book.

I left Engebret and, pulling out my map, decided to wander slowly back to the hotel, imagining Anna and Jens walking these very streets. The city had obviously grown since their day, but while parts of it were ultra-modern, many lovely old buildings remained. As I arrived back at the Grand Hotel, I decided that Oslo had an innate charm. There was something comforting about its compactness, and I felt very at home here.

Back in my room, I checked my emails and found that the curator of the Grieg museum had already responded:

Dear Miss D'Aplièse,

Yes, I am aware of Jens and Anna Halvorsen. Edvard Grieg was something of a mentor to both of them, as you may already know. I am here at Troldhaugen, just outside Bergen, from nine until four every day, and would be happy to meet you and help you with your research.

Yours sincerely,
Erling Dahl Jr

Having no idea where Bergen actually was, I googled a map of Norway and saw that it was up on the coast to the north-west of Oslo, clearly a plane journey away. I hadn't realised before just how vast the country actually was. There was another huge chunk of it continuing past Bergen, leading up towards the Arctic. I decided to book a flight for the following morning and emailed Mr Dahl back to say I'd be in Bergen by midday tomorrow.

It was just past six o'clock and still light outside. I imagined the long winters here when the sun disappeared after lunchtime and the snow fell heavily, blanketing everything it touched. And I mused on how my sisters had often commented that I seemed impervious to the cold, constantly opening windows to let in fresh air. I'd always thought I was simply used to it due to my sailing. But as I remembered Maia's ability to take any level of heat and turn a sultry brown within the space of a few minutes, compared to my tendency to turn beetroot, perhaps winter was part of my heritage, as sunny climes were part of Maia's?

My thoughts turned unbidden to Theo, as they always did when the night drew in. I knew he would have loved to accompany me on this journey, probably analysing my reactions to the situation every step of the way. As I climbed into the bed, which tonight felt far too big just for me, I wondered whether there would be anyone in my future who could possibly take his place. And I doubted there ever would be. Before I became maudlin, I set my alarm for seven o'clock the next morning, closed my eyes and tried to sleep.

24

The bird's-eye view of Norway from the plane was simply glorious. Below me were dark green forests lining the sides of deep blue fjords, and shining white snow-capped mountains, forever frozen, even at the start of September. On arrival at Bergen airport, I jumped into a taxi and instructed the driver to take me straight to Troldhaugen, once Grieg's home and now a museum. The view of the countryside from the busy dual carriageway was a blur of endless trees, but eventually we turned off the main road and drove up a narrow country lane.

The taxi drew up outside an enchanting pale-yellow clap-board villa and I paid the driver and climbed out, hoisting my rucksack over my shoulder. I stood for a few moments gazing up at its exterior, taking in the large picture windows with their green-painted frames, and the latticework balcony that jutted from the upper floor. A tower rose from one corner and the Norwegian flag flapped in the breeze from a tall pole.

I saw the villa was perched on a hillside overlooking a lake and was surrounded by grassy slopes and tall, majestic spruce trees. Marvelling at the tranquil beauty of the location, I walked inside a modern building that declared itself to be the entrance to the museum and introduced myself to the girl sitting behind the counter of the gift shop. As I asked her to tell the curator I was here, I looked down into the glass display case under the counter and caught my breath.

'*Mon Dieu!*' I murmured, the shock of what was staring up at me spinning me back to my mother tongue. There in the case was a row of small brown frogs identical to the one in Pa Salt's envelope.

'Erling, the curator, will be along in a moment,' said the girl, replacing the receiver of the phone.

'Thank you. Can I ask you why you're selling these frogs in the gift shop?'

'Grieg kept the original version with him at all times as a good luck talisman,' the girl explained. 'It sat in his pocket everywhere he went and he would kiss it goodnight before he slept.'

'Hello, Miss D'Aplièse. I'm Erling Dahl. How was your flight here?' An attractive silver-haired man had appeared beside me.

'Oh, it was fine, thank you,' I said, trying to gather my senses after the frog revelation. 'And please, call me Ally.'

'Okay, Ally. May I ask if you're hungry? Rather than sitting in my cramped office, we could go next door to the café, grab a sandwich and talk there. You can leave your luggage with Else.' He indicated the girl behind the counter.

'That sounds perfect,' I agreed, handing over my rucksack with a nod of thanks, then following him through a set of doors. The room we entered had walls made almost entirely of glass, allowing a breathtaking view of the lake through the trees. I took in the glistening expanse of water, dotted with tiny pine-fringed islands, before it receded to the distant shore on the misty horizon.

'Lake Nordås is magnificent, is it not?' said Erling. 'Sometimes we forget how lucky we are to work in such a place.'

'It's amazing,' I breathed. 'You are indeed lucky.'

When we had ordered coffees and open sandwiches, Erling asked me how he could help. Once again, I pulled out the photocopies I'd taken of Pa Salt's book and explained what I wanted to know.

He took the sheets and studied them. 'I've never read this book, although I know the bones of what it contains. I've recently helped Thom Halvorsen, Jens and Anna's great-great-grandson, with research for a new biography.'

'Yes. I have it on order from the States. You actually know Thom Halvorsen?'

'Of course. He lives only a few minutes' walk from here and the musical world in Bergen is small. He plays violin in the Philharmonic Orchestra and has recently been promoted to assistant conductor.'

'Then would it be possible to meet him?' I asked as our sandwiches arrived.

'I'm sure it would, yes, but presently he's on tour in the States with the orchestra. They return in the next few days. So how far have you got in your research?'

'I haven't finished reading the original biography yet as I'm still waiting for the rest of the translation. I've reached the point where Jens has been asked to leave his family home and Anna Landvik has been offered the role of Solveig.'

'I see.' Erling smiled at me, then checked his watch. 'Sadly, I don't have the time to tell you anything further now as we have our lunchtime concert here in half an hour. But perhaps it's best if you read the rest of Jens' original words anyway, and we can talk when you have.'

'Where is the concert?'

'In our purpose-built hall, which we call Troldsalen. We have guest pianists here performing Grieg's music throughout the summer months. Today the performance is the Piano Concerto in A Minor.'

'Really? Then would you mind if I came along to listen?'

'Not at all,' he said, standing up. 'Why don't you finish your sandwich, then make your way across to the concert hall, while I go and make sure all is well with our pianist?'

'I'd love to, thank you, Erling.'

After forcing down the rest of the sandwich, I followed the signs through the thickly wooded hillside to the building that nestled cosily within the pine trees. Once inside, I made my way down the steps of the steeply-raked auditorium and saw it was already two thirds full. The small stage, in the centre of which sat a magnificent Steinway grand piano, was framed by more huge glass windows, forming a stunning backdrop of fir trees and the lake beyond.

Shortly after I'd settled myself in a seat, Erling appeared on the stage with a slim, dark-haired young man who, even at a distance, was singularly striking in appearance. Erling addressed the audience, speaking in Norwegian first and then in English for the benefit of the many tourists present.

'I am honoured to present to you the pianist Willem Caspari. This young man has already made his mark performing across the globe, most recently playing at the Proms at the Royal Albert Hall in London. We are grateful that he has agreed to grace our small corner of the world with his presence.'

The audience gave a round of applause and Willem nodded impassively before sitting down at the piano, waiting for the auditorium to fall silent. As he began to play the opening bars, I closed my eyes, the music transporting me back to my days at the Conservatoire in Geneva, when I would attend concerts weekly and often perform in them myself. Classical music had once been such a passion for me, and yet I realised to my shame it must be at least ten years since I'd attended even the most modest of recitals. I felt my tension abate as I listened to Willem play, watching his skilled hands dancing lightly across the keys. And I promised myself that from now on, I would remedy the situation.

After the concert had finished, Erling sought me out and took me down to the stage to introduce me to Willem Caspari. His face had a dramatic angular bone structure, his white skin drawn tightly across high cheekbones, framing a pair of turquoise eyes and full, blood-red lips. Everything about him was immaculate, from his neat dark hair to his polished black shoes, and he rather reminded me of a handsome vampire.

'Thank you so much for that,' I said to Willem. 'It was absolutely beautiful.'

'My pleasure, Miss D'Aplièse,' he replied, discreetly wiping his hands with a snowy white handkerchief before shaking mine. He studied me intently as he did so. 'You know, I'm pretty sure we've met before.'

'Have we?' I said, embarrassed that I couldn't place him.

'Yes. I was a pupil at the Conservatoire in Geneva. I believe you had just started there when I was in my final year. Apart from having an excellent memory for faces, I remember your surname, because it struck me as unusual at the time. You're a flautist, aren't you?'

'Yes,' I said in surprise, 'or at least I was.'

'Really, Ally? That's something you didn't mention to me earlier,' said Erling.

'Well, it was a long time ago now.'

'You don't play anymore?' asked Willem, at the same time fastidiously straightening his lapels in what was obviously a subconscious ritual rather than an attempt to impress.

'Not really, no.'

'If I remember rightly, I came to a recital of yours once. You played "Sonata for Flute and Piano?"'

'Yes, I did. You really do have an incredible memory.'

'For things I want to remember, yes. It has its good and bad points, I can assure you.'

'How interesting, given that the musician Ally is currently researching was a flautist himself,' interjected Erling.

'And who is it that you're researching, if you don't mind me asking?' Willem queried, his luminous eyes fixed on mine.

'A Norwegian composer called Jens Halvorsen and his wife, Anna, who was a singer.'

'I'm afraid I don't know of them.'

'They were both very well known here in Norway, especially Anna,' said Erling. 'Now, depending on your plans, perhaps you'd like to take a look around Grieg's house and maybe visit the hut on the hillside where he composed his music?'

'Yes, thank you, I will.'

'Would you mind if I came with you?' asked Willem, still studying me with his head cocked to one side. 'I only arrived in Bergen last night and I haven't yet had the chance to look around myself.'

'Not at all,' I said, deciding it would be preferable to be walking alongside him rather than standing here being subjected to his seemingly dispassionate yet highly focussed scrutiny.

'Then I'll leave you both to it,' said Erling hastily. 'Pop into the office and say goodbye when you leave. And thank you for a breathtaking performance today, Willem.'

Willem and I followed Erling out of the hall and then together we wandered up the steps through the trees towards the house. We entered the villa itself and went into the wood-floored drawing room, which contained an old Steinway grand piano set next to a wall. The rest of the room was filled with an eclectic mix of rustic country furniture and more elegant pieces in walnut and mahogany. Portraits and landscape paintings jostled for attention on the mellow, pine-clad walls.

'It still feels like a real home in here,' I commented to Willem.

'Yes, it does,' he agreed.

Framed pictures of Grieg and his wife Nina were dotted all around the room, and one in particular, of the two of them standing beside the piano, drew my eye. Nina was smiling gently and Grieg's expression was impenetrable beneath his thick eyebrows and heavy moustache.

'They're both so tiny compared to the piano,' I said, 'like two little dolls!'

'They were barely five feet tall, apparently. And did you know that Grieg had a collapsed lung? He used a small pillow inside his jacket to fill it out for photographs, which is why his hand is always across his chest, holding it in place.'

'How fascinating,' I murmured, as we wandered round the room, examining the various exhibits.

'So, how come you gave up music?' Willem asked abruptly, repeating a conversational pattern I was beginning to recognise: it was as though he'd mentally ticked a box that said 'Item Processed', before moving on to the next topic on the list.

'I became a professional sailor.'

'And played the hornpipe instead?' He gave a short chuckle at his own joke. 'Do you miss playing?'

'To be honest, I haven't had time to in the past few years. Sailing has been my life.'

'And I can't imagine a life without music,' Willem said as he indicated Grieg's piano. 'This instrument is my passion and my pain, the driving force in my life. I actually have nightmares about getting arthritis in my fingers. Without my music, I'd have nothing, you see.'

'Then perhaps you have a stronger belief in your own ability than I did. I felt that I plateaued while I was at the Conservatoire. However much I practised, I didn't feel I was improving.'

'I've felt that every day for years, Ally. I think it goes with the territory. I must believe I *do* improve or I'd kill myself. Now, shall we take a look at the hut where the great man composed some of his masterpieces?'

The cabin was a short walk from the villa. Peering through the glass panes of the front door, I saw a modest upright piano standing against one wall, with a rocking chair placed next to it and a desk positioned directly in front of the large window facing the lake. And there, sitting on the desk, was another little frog, identical to mine. I chose not to share the thought with Willem.

'What a view,' he sighed. 'It's enough to inspire anyone.'

'But very isolated, don't you think?'

'I wouldn't mind. I'd be quite happy alone. I'm very self-sufficient,' he said with a shrug.

'So am I, but I still think it would eventually drive me mad.' I smiled at him. 'Let's walk back up, shall we?'

'Yes.' Willem checked his watch. 'There's a journalist coming to interview me at my hotel at four o'clock. The receptionist here said she'd call me a taxi. Where are you staying? Perhaps I could give you a lift back into town?'

'As a matter of fact, I haven't booked anywhere to stay yet,' I said as we walked back up the hillside. 'I'm sure I'll find somewhere through the tourist information centre in town.'

'You could check out my hotel. It's extremely clean and on the old harbour front, with a glorious view across the fjord. I'm very impressed by your relaxed outlook on accommodation,' he added as we walked back to the main reception area. 'When I'm travelling, I have to book weeks in advance and know exactly where I'm staying or I go into severe meltdown.'

'Maybe it's all the years of sailing that have given me a more *laissez-faire* attitude. I can sleep anywhere.'

'And maybe it's because I'm more anal than most people that I can't. My obsession with organisation drives everyone who knows me mad.'

I collected my rucksack from Else, the girl on the till, then waited by the entrance while Willem organised a taxi. As I watched him discreetly, I thought how his inner tension revealed itself physically in the way he carried himself: like a soldier, every sinew taut, hands clenching and unclenching as Else spoke to the taxi company.

Driven . . . was the word that sprang to my mind.

'So, where do you live when you're not sailing or running around looking for long-dead musicians and their wives?' he asked me when the taxi arrived and we climbed in.

'In Geneva, at my family home.'

'So you don't have a permanent place of your own?'

'No, I've never really needed one. I'm always away.'

'That's another way in which we're different. My apartment in Zurich is my haven. Mind you, I do have to stop myself from asking people to take their shoes off or pressing an anti-bacterial wipe into their hands when they come to see me.'

My mind flashed back to the way he'd surreptitiously cleaned his hands after playing the piano earlier.

'I know I'm odd,' he continued affably, 'so there's no need to be embarrassed about thinking it.'

'Most of the musicians I've ever met are eccentric. I'm tempted to think it's just part and parcel of being artistic.'

'Or possibly "autistic", as my shrink tells me. Maybe there's a fine line between the two. My mother says I need a significant other to sort me out, but I can't imagine anyone putting up with my foibles. Do you have a partner?'

'I . . . I did, but he died a few weeks ago,' I said, staring out of the car window.

'I am so sorry, Ally, my condolences.'

'Thank you.'

'I don't know what to say.'

'Don't worry, nobody does,' I comforted him.

'Is that why you're here in Norway?'

'Yes, I suppose it is.'

The taxi began to drive slowly along one side of the lovely harbour. It was flanked by wood-fronted buildings, painted in alternating shades of white, claret, ochre and yellow, with distinctive V-shaped red-tiled roofs. All the colours blurred suddenly in front of my eyes as I felt tears pricking them.

'Well' – Willem cleared his throat after an extended pause – 'I don't usually talk about this, but as a matter of fact, I have some hands-on experience with what you're going through. My partner died five years ago, just after Christmas. It's not a good memory.'

'Then I'm sorry too.' I patted his clenched fist, and it was his turn to look the other way.

'In my case, it was a blessed release. Jack was very, very ill by the end. You?'

'A sailing accident. One minute Theo was there, the next he wasn't.'

'To be honest, I don't know which is worse. I had time to come to terms with it, but I still had to watch someone I loved suffer. I'm still not over it, I suppose. Anyway, I don't mean to depress you any more than you probably are, I'm sorry.'

'Don't be. It's comforting in an odd sort of way to know other people who have been there,' I replied as the taxi drew to a halt outside a tall brick building.

'Here's my hotel. Why don't you come in and ask if they've got any rooms? I doubt you can do much better.'

'Certainly, view-wise I couldn't,' I agreed. As I stepped out of the taxi, I saw that the Havnekontoret hotel was only a few metres away from the edge of the quay, against which a beautiful old double-masted schooner was moored. 'Theo would have liked this,' I muttered, glad now I could say that and know he'd understand instantly.

'Yes. Here, let me take your luggage for you.'

I asked the taxi driver to wait for a few minutes as I followed Willem into the hotel and enquired about availability at the desk. Once a room was secured, I went back outside and told the taxi driver he could go.

'Well, I'm glad that's organised for you.' Willem was hovering tensely in the reception area. 'Apparently my journalist has arrived. I loathe them but there we are. I'll see you later.'

'Sure,' I said as he walked off in the direction of a woman who was waiting for him in the lobby.

After handing over my credit card, and getting the password for the Wi-Fi, I took the lift upstairs to my room. It was in the eaves of the building with a stunning vista of the harbour. Night was closing in already, so I changed out of my jeans into sweatpants and a hoody and switched on my laptop. As I waited for it to connect, I thought about Willem and how, despite all his strangeness, I'd liked him. Checking through my emails, I saw there was another from Magdalena Jensen, the translator.

From: Magdalenajensen1@trans.no
To: Allygeneva@gmail.com
Subject: Grieg, Solveig og Jeg / Grieg, Solveig and I
1st September 2007

Dear Ally,

Attached is the rest of the translation. I'll send the original copy of the book back to the address in Geneva. Hope you enjoy reading it. It's an interesting story.

With kind regards, Magdalena

Clicking on 'Open attachment', I watched impatiently as the next tranche of pages downloaded. And then I began to read again . . .

Anna

Christiania, Norway

August 1876

25

'Anna, *kjære*, what a delight it is to have you back with us,' Frøken Olsdatter said as she ushered Anna into the apartment and took her cloak. 'With Herr Bayer away in Drøbak, life here has been far too quiet. How was your time in the country?'

'It was lovely, thank you, although not long enough,' Anna said as she followed Frøken Olsdatter into the drawing room.

'Tea?'

'I'd love some,' Anna replied.

'Then I shall bring it in to you.'

As Frøken Olsdatter left the room, Anna thought how glad she was to be back in Christiania with the housekeeper's kind attentions. *And even if I have become spoilt, I do not care*, she said to herself as she breathed a sigh of relief that she would sleep on a comfortable mattress and wake to breakfast on a tray tomorrow morning. Never mind the thought of a hot bath . . .

Frøken Olsdatter broke into her thoughts as she came back with a tray of tea. 'Well, I have some news for you,' she said as she poured the liquid into two china cups and handed one to Anna. 'Herr Bayer is unable to return to Christiania at present. His poor mother is very sick and he cannot leave her. He thinks the end will come soon and, of course, he wishes to be there with her. So, you have been left in my care until he returns.'

'I am very sorry to hear that his dear mother is so ill,' Anna replied, even though she wasn't at all sorry Herr Bayer's arrival was delayed.

'Rehearsals are during the day, so I will chaperone you on the tram there and back. After you have finished your tea, you must go and inspect your new wardrobe. The winter clothes Herr Bayer ordered from the dressmaker have been delivered. They are very splendid indeed, I think. There is also a letter for you which I have put in your room.'

Ten minutes later, Anna opened her wardrobe door to find it filled with an array of beautiful hand-made garments. There were blouses fashioned from the softest silk and muslin, skirts made from fine wool, and two exquisite gowns: one the colour of topaz and the other a dusky rose-pink. There were also two new corsets, several pairs of bloomers and stockings as fine as spiders' webs.

The thought of Herr Bayer ordering such intimate items for her made her shudder, but she put it to the back of her mind, telling herself it must have been Frøken Olsdatter who had arranged the making of those. Sitting on a high shelf were two pairs of heeled shoes, one pair in the same dusky-pink silk of the dress with a little silver buckle, and the other pair a soft ivory colour with white embroidery. Trying the pink pair on, her eyes fell on a hatbox, which she carefully lifted down. She gasped as she took off the lid. The hat matched her pink dress and sported the most elaborate arrangement of feathers and ribbons she had ever seen. Anna thought back to her first arrival at Christiania railway station and how she had marvelled over the ladies' hats. This one, she thought as she set it carefully on her head, rivalled them all. As she practised walking around the room in her new shoes and head attire, she felt taller and older somehow, and thought incredulously how much she had changed since her arrival here.

Then, sitting down with the hat still perched on her head, Anna took the letter Frøken Olsdatter had left for her. With a sigh, she saw it was from Lars and opened it tentatively, dreading its contents.

Stalsberg Våningshuset
Tindevegen
Heddal

22nd July 1876

My dearest Anna,

I promised I would write to explain in detail the short conversation we had on the night of your brother's wedding.

In the past few months, it has become obvious to me that your life in Christiania has altered your hopes and visions for the future. Please, my dear Anna, do not feel guilty about this. It is only natural they should change. You have a great talent, and more to the point, that talent is being harnessed by important people who can nurture it and give it to the world.

Even if your parents believe that little has changed, I understand that an awful lot has. Appearing as Solveig at the Christiania Theatre this autumn is an opportunity that is bound to alter you further. However hard I find it, I must accept that to marry me may no longer appeal to you. If it ever did to begin with, which I doubt.

I understand that your morals and your good heart would never have allowed you to vocalise your true feelings. Apart from hurting me, you would not have risked disappointing your parents. Therefore, as we discussed, I will tell them that I have decided I cannot wait for you any longer. Already your father has bought my land and that financial arrangement suits me well. Just as you are not domestic, I am not a farmer, and now my father is dead there is little to keep me here.

And it seems there is another alternative.

Anna, I must tell you that I have heard from Scribner, the publisher in New York City to whom I told you I had sent my poems. They wish to print them and have offered me a small advance to do so. As you know, my dream has always been to travel to America. With the money from your father for the land, I have just enough to book my passage. You can imagine that the idea excites me and to have my poems published there is an immense honour. It would have been my dearest wish to make you my wife and take you with me, so we could make a new life together there. However, the timing is inappropriate for you. And Anna, to be truthful, even if it wasn't, I understand you could not love me as I have loved you.

I bear you no grudge and wish you well. In a

strange way, the Lord has offered us both freedom to pursue our paths, even if they cannot be intertwined. Although we are now not to be married, I hope I can remain your friend.

I sail for America in six weeks' time.

Lars

Anna laid the letter down on the bed next to her. And sat, deep in thought, feeling both moved and unsettled at the same time.

America . . . She chastised herself for having believed it was a pipe dream of Lars' and for not having taken him seriously. Now here he was, with his poems about to be published there, and the possibility of one day even following in the footsteps of Herr Ibsen himself.

For the first time, Anna stopped seeing Lars as a victim, a sad dog to be petted. Through his land being sold to her father as a dowry, as he had said in his letters, he too had a chance to escape Heddal and follow his dream, just like her.

This, at least, was comforting.

Would she have travelled to America with him had he asked her?

'No.'

The answer fell from her lips unbidden. She fell back on the bed and her new silk hat tipped forward over her eyes.

Apartment 4
10 St Olav's Gate
Christiania

4th August 1876

Dear Lars,

Thank you for your letter. I am very happy for your good fortune. I hope you will write to me from America. And please accept my gratitude for all you have done for me. Your help with my reading and writing made my life here in Christiania possible.

Send my love to Mor and Far. I hope they do not shout at you when you tell them the wedding will not take place, and it is generous of you to take the blame.

I hope you find a much better wife than me in America. I too wish to remain your friend.

I hope you are not sick on the sea.

Anna

As Anna applied the seal to the letter, the impact of what he had said hit her. Now that Lars was only her friend and was going to America, she decided she would miss him.

Should I have married him? she asked herself, standing up and wandering to the window to peer out on the street below. *He was so good and kind. And he will probably make his fortune there, while I may well die an old maid . . .*

Later, as Anna walked along the corridor to place the letter on the silver salver to be posted, she felt the last tenuous thread that bound her to her old life finally snap.

Rehearsals for *Peer Gynt* began three days later. The rest of the cast – many of them from the original production – were sweet and helpful to Anna, but whereas learning a song and then singing it caused her no problems at all, being an actress turned out to be more complicated than she had thought. Sometimes she'd move to the right place on the stage, but then forget to say her line as she did so; other times she'd remember both the former, but then fail to express the appropriate emotion on her face. Herr Josephson, the director, was very patient with her, but Anna felt it was a bit like having to rub her tummy and pat her head whilst dancing a polka all at the same time.

After rehearsals on the fourth day, she wondered despondently if she would ever get it right. On her way out of the theatre, she gave a little cry of shock when a hand grabbed her arm as she walked towards the stage door.

'Frøken Landvik, I heard you were back in Christiania. How was your time in the country?'

There was Jens Halvorsen the Bad. Anna's heart thumped at being so close to him, and although he loosened his grip on her arm, he left his hand resting there. She could feel the warmth of it through her sleeve, and she swallowed hard. Turning towards him, she was shocked to see the change in him. His normally shining curly hair hung lank about his face and his fine clothes were creased and filthy. He looked like he hadn't had a good bath in weeks, and her nose confirmed it.

'I . . . My chaperone is outside,' she whispered. 'Please leave me be.'

'I will, but not until I tell you that I have missed you desperately. Surely I have proved my love and loyalty to you by now? Please, I am begging you to say you will meet me.'

'No, I will not,' she replied.

'Well, there's nothing to stop me finding you here at the theatre, is there, Frøken Landvik?' he called to her as she hurried through the stage door and it shut with a bang behind her.

Every day for the following week, Jens waited for Anna to leave the theatre after rehearsals.

'Herr Halvorsen, this really is becoming most irritating,' she'd whisper under her breath to him, as Halbert, the doorman, took up his usual seat in the front row of their courtship.

'Excellent! Then maybe you will relent and at least let me take you to tea.'

'My chaperone will be happy to join us. Please inform her of your request,' she would tell him as she swept past him, trying to suppress a smile. In reality, the daily meetings were what she looked forward to most and she had begun to relax a little, knowing the two of them were playing a tantalising game of cat and mouse. Given the fact Lars was no longer 'waiting for her' – never mind that she had also spent the long summer dreaming of Jens – despite her best efforts, Anna's resolve began to crack.

On the following Monday after a long weekend cooped up at the apartment, Frøken Olsdatter announced that she had to cross the city on Herr Bayer's business. She had deemed Anna responsible enough to take the tram home alone and as Anna left the stage, she knew the moment had come to surrender.

Jens was waiting for her as usual in the corridor by the stage door.

'When will you say yes, Frøken Landvik?' he asked her

pitifully as she walked past him. 'I must admit, even given my endurance, your rejection is slowly wearing my resolve away.'

'Today?' she said, turning to him abruptly.

'I . . . well then . . . right.'

Anna relished his shock with satisfaction.

'We shall go to the Engebret Café across the square,' he said. 'It is a minute's walk away.'

Anna had heard about Engebret, and thought it sounded a very thrilling place indeed. 'But what if someone sees us? They would think it inappropriate if I am unchaperoned.'

'Hardly,' Jens chuckled. 'Engebret is mostly frequented by bohemians and drunken musicians who would not turn a hair if you stripped naked and danced on a table! No one will even notice us, I promise. Come, Frøken Landvik, we're wasting time.'

'Very well then.' A frisson of excitement passed through her.

They left the theatre in silence and walked across the square to the café, where Anna indicated a table in the darkest, quietest corner. Jens ordered tea for both of them.

'Tell me, Anna, how was your summer?'

'Far better than yours by the sight of you. You look . . . unwell.'

'Well, thank you for phrasing it so politely.' Jens gave a chuckle at her bluntness. 'I am not sick, simply poor these days and in need of a good bath and a change of clothes. Simen, who also plays in the orchestra, says I've become a true musician. He has been very kind to me by providing a roof over my head when I was forced to leave my home.'

'Goodness! Why?'

'My father disapproved of my musical aspirations. He

wished me to follow in his footsteps and run his brewery like my ancestors before me.'

Anna stared at him with new admiration. Surely, she thought, it must have required a great strength of character to put aside his family and homely comforts for the sake of his art?

'Anyway,' Jens continued, 'now that the season is beginning at the theatre and I am finally earning money, I'm moving to more suitable accommodation. Otto, the oboe player, told me yesterday that he will rent me a room in his apartment. His wife died recently, and as she was quite wealthy, I'm hoping to find myself in more salubrious surroundings. The apartment is only a five-minute walk from yours, Anna. We will almost be neighbours. You can come and take tea with me there.'

'I'm happy to hear that you'll be more comfortable,' she said shyly.

'And as I find myself down in the gutter, your star rises apace! Perhaps you will become the rich benefactress every musician needs,' he teased her as their tea arrived. 'Look at you in your fine clothes, and your smart Paris hat. Quite the picture of a wealthy young lady these days.'

'It may be that my star falls as swiftly as it seems to have risen. I think I am a terrible actress, and will probably lose my job very soon,' Anna confessed suddenly, glad to say it to someone.

'And I am equally sure that is not true. When the orchestra gathered for its first call yesterday, I heard Herr Josephson telling Hennum that you were "coming along nicely".'

'You don't understand, Herr Halvorsen. I've never worried about standing in front of an audience and singing, but saying words and playing a character is a very different thing. I think I may even have stage fright,' Anna said, fiddling distractedly with the handle of her tea cup. 'I cannot begin to imagine how I will ever find the courage to step out in front of an audience on the first night.'

'Anna . . . May I call you Anna and you call me Jens? I feel we must be well enough acquainted by now to allow this.'

'I suppose you may, yes. When we are in private, at least.'

'Thank you. Well, to continue, Anna, I'm sure you will look so beautiful and sing so enchantingly that no one will notice what you say.'

'That is kind . . . Jens, but I cannot sleep at night. I do not wish to let anybody down.'

'And I am sure you will not. Now tell me, how is your suitor back home?'

'He is bound for America. Without me,' she said carefully, averting her eyes. 'We are no longer promised to each other.'

'My condolences, but I confess that you have made me a happy man. I have thought of you constantly since we last met. You are the only thing that has kept me going through this difficult summer. And I find myself completely in love with you.'

Anna stared at him for a few moments before answering. 'How can this be? You hardly know me. We have never had longer than a few minutes of conversation. Surely you must love a person for their character? And to do that, you must know them well.'

'I know far more about you than you think. For example, I can see you are modest from the way you blushed when the audience rose to applaud you after your triumph at the soirée.

I know you have few airs about your appearance by the lack of paint on your face. I also understand that you are virtuous and loyal, with high morals, which has made my task of wooing you that much harder. And this also brings me to believe that you are as stubborn as a mule once you have decided something. For in my experience, it is a rare woman who wouldn't at least take a quick look at a suitor's letters before throwing them onto the fire – even if she *did* feel his ardent pursuit of her was inappropriate.'

Anna did her best not to show her amazement at his perception. 'Well,' she said, swallowing hard, 'there are many things you *don't* know. Such as the fact my mother despairs of my domestic abilities. I am a terrible cook and cannot sew. My father says I can only care for animals, not humans.'

'Then we shall live on love and buy a cat,' Jens responded with a grin.

'Forgive me, but I really must catch my tram and return home,' Anna said, rising and taking coins from her purse to place them on the table. 'Please let me pay for the tea. Goodbye . . . Jens.'

'Anna.' He caught her hand as she turned to leave. 'When will I see you again?'

'As you know very well, I am at the theatre every day between ten and four.'

'Then I'll be there at four tomorrow,' he called to her as he watched her hurry to the door. When she'd left, Jens looked down at the coins on the table and saw that it was enough to pay for the tea and to buy him a bowl of soup and a glass of aquavit.

Once safely on the tram, Anna closed her eyes and smiled dreamily. Being with Jens Halvorsen alone had been quite wonderful. Whether it was his new circumstances, or simply his perseverance in pursuing her, he no longer seemed like the proud, strutting cockerel she had once thought him.

'Oh Lord,' she prayed that night, 'please forgive me if I say I believe that Jens Halvorsen the Bad is no longer quite so bad. That he has been tested and has changed his ways. I have done my best not to yield to temptation as you know, but . . .' – Anna bit her lip – 'I think I might now. Amen.'

In the run-up to opening night, Anna and Jens met every day after rehearsals. Worried about tittle-tattle at the theatre, Anna suggested he wait for her inside Engebret. The café was at its quietest in the late afternoons, and slowly Anna began to relax and become less concerned about keeping up appearances. One day, when Jens had reached for her hand under the table, she had allowed him to take it. That had set a precedent, and they now sat together most days with their fingers surreptitiously entwined. It made the pouring of the tea and the milk somewhat difficult with only one hand available, but it was worth every second.

Jens was looking far more like his old self. He'd moved into Otto's apartment and, as he had graphically described to her, had benefited from a thorough delousing. There was a maid at the apartment who had also washed all his clothes, and Anna was relieved that he smelt far fresher.

But beyond all that, it was the memory of the touch of his skin on hers – an outwardly innocent touch, yet one that promised so much more – which consumed Anna's thoughts night and day. She finally understood how Solveig had felt and why she had sacrificed so much for her Peer.

Often, they sat together in silence, their tea ignored, just drinking each other in. Even though Anna told herself to be wary, she knew she had finally surrendered to him. And was being drawn further and further under his spell.

26

Three days before *Peer Gynt* opened the new season at the Christiania Theatre, the arduous process of bringing orchestra and cast together began once more. This time, Anna wasn't sharing a room backstage with Rude and the other children. She was in Madame Hansson's old dressing room, with a whole wall of mirrors and a chaise longue covered in velvet to rest on if she felt weary.

'Very nice, this is, isn't it, Anna?' Rude had commented as he'd taken a look around it. 'I'd say that some of us have gone up in the world in the past few months. Do you mind if I come in here sometimes and keep you company? Or are you too grand for me now?'

Anna had taken his chubby cheeks in her hands and chuckled. 'I may not have time for our card games, but you are welcome to come and visit me any time you wish.'

On the opening night, she walked into the dressing room to find it filled with flowers and good luck messages. There was even one from her parents and Knut, with a letter enclosed, which would doubtless refer to her broken engagement to Lars. She put that aside to read later. As Ingeborg, the make-up artist, painted her face, she read the other cards, appreciating the kind words people had written. And there was one in particular, accompanied by a single red rose, which sent a thrill through her as she read it.

I will be there, watching your ascent to the stars tonight. And I will feel every heartbeat that you do.
Sing, my beautiful bird. Sing!
J.

As Anna heard the call for 'Beginners', she sent up a prayer. 'Please, Lord, do not let me disgrace myself or my family name tonight. Amen.' Then she stood up to walk to the wings.

There were moments of that night which Anna knew would be indelibly printed on her memory. Like the dreadful one when she'd walked onto the stage in the second act and her mind had turned completely blank. She'd looked down into the orchestra pit in desperation and had seen Jens mouthing the lines to her. She hoped she'd recovered in time for the audience not to notice, but it had unnerved her for the rest of the performance. It was only during 'The Cradle Song' at the very end, as Peer's head lay upon her knees and they were alone on the stage, that she had felt confident again and let her voice and emotions rise up.

After the last note had died away, there had been many curtain calls and bouquets were handed to her and Marie, who played Peer's mother, Åse. She left the stage as the curtain finally dropped and burst into noisy sobs on Herr Josephson's shoulder.

'My dear, please, don't cry,' he soothed her.

'But I was terrible tonight! I know I was!'

'Not at all, Anna. Don't you see that all your natural uncertainty actually enhanced Solveig's vulnerability? And by the end . . . well, the audience was spellbound. The part could have been written for you, and I am sure that had they seen you, Herr Ibsen and Herr Grieg would have been satisfied. You also sang like a dream, as you always do. Now' – he put a finger to her cheek and wiped away a tear – 'go and celebrate your achievement.'

Anna's dressing room was crowded with well-wishers by the time she reached it, all wanting to be present at the crowning of a new and very much home-grown princess, and Anna did her best to say the right things to all of them. Then Herr Hennum entered and shooed everyone out of the room.

'It was a joy to conduct the orchestra tonight, and to watch you making your stage debut, Anna. And no, you were not perfect as an actress, but that is something you can learn as your confidence grows, which it will, I promise. Please, try to enjoy the adulation of Christiania, because you truly deserve it. Herr Josephson will be here to escort you to the first-night party in the foyer in fifteen minutes.' Then he bowed and left her in peace.

As she was changing, a short knock heralded the arrival of Rude. 'Sorry, Frøken Anna, but I've been asked to deliver a message to you.' He handed it to her with a cheeky grin. 'You look very beautiful tonight, may I say. And can you ask my mother if I can come to the party? She may let me if the request comes from you.'

'You know I can't, Rude, but now that you're here, can you fasten my dress for me?'

As Anna entered the foyer with Herr Josephson, she was greeted with a round of applause. Jens watched her from a distance and thought he had never loved her more, and he had told her as much in his note to her afterwards, delivered by Rude. He noticed how she smiled and made small talk, and thought how far his bird had flown since he'd first heard her sing.

Then his heart sank as he saw a familiar figure approach her, his oversized handlebar moustache almost bristling with joy as everyone stood back to let him pass.

'Anna! My dear young lady, even my mother's illness could not prevent me from being here to watch you on this glorious night. You were superb, *kjære*, truly superb.'

Jens noticed a slight slackening of Anna's features, then watched as she recovered herself and greeted Herr Bayer warmly. Jens left then, feeling depressed that, with the appearance of her mentor, he would be unable to tell her in person how proud he was of her.

Of course, he thought, as he sank his misery into an aquavit at Engebret, he could see which way the wind was blowing, even if Anna could not. She may have rid herself of the farmhand suitor, but it was obvious to all that Herr Bayer was in love with her. And he could give her everything she could ever want. A few months ago, Jens thought, he could have done the same.

For the first time, he wondered if he'd made a terrible mistake.

'"*Frøken Landvik may not bring the seasoned assurance of Madame Hansson to the role of Solveig, but she makes up for that with her innocence, her youth, and her exquisite rendition of Solveig's songs.*"

'And in the early edition of *Dagbladet*, the reviewer comments again on your beauty and youth and the . . .'

Anna listened to Herr Bayer no longer. She felt happy that she had managed to get through the first night, but the thought of doing it all over again the following evening was something that she could not begin to contemplate.

'Now, Anna, sadly I am only able to stay in Christiania until the morning, as I must take the ferry back to my mother's bedside as soon as possible,' said Herr Bayer, closing the newspaper.

'How is she?'

'No better, no worse,' he sighed. 'My mother has always had an unbreakable spirit and it is that alone keeping her alive. There is nothing I can do, except be with her as the end approaches. But enough of that. Tonight, Anna, I wish us to share a special dinner, during which you can tell me all that has happened since I last saw you.'

'Of course, it would be my pleasure, but I am feeling a little weary. If we are to dine together tonight, may I take a rest now?'

'Of course, my dear young lady. And congratulations again.'

Franz Bayer watched Anna leave the room and marvelled at how far she had come in the past year. And indeed, since he'd last seen her. She'd always been a bud about to burst into flower, but now she had fully blossomed, she was beautiful and under his tutelage had gained a new grace and sophistication.

Despite the fact that Anna had just pleaded exhaustion, there seemed to be a new glow about her he could not define. He hoped it had nothing to do with that violinist she'd obviously been so taken with at the soirée back in June. Last night Herr Josephson had teased him rather meanly that it was a good job he, Franz, was back in town. Herr Josephson had mentioned that his protégée had been spotted more than once taking tea with the fellow in Engebret.

Up until now, he'd been biding his time, not wishing to frighten her off. But after what Herr Josephson had said, he thought he had better make his intentions clear.

'My dear young lady, how enchanting you look tonight!'

Herr Bayer greeted Anna as she entered the dining room in her topaz evening gown. No matter how beautiful people said she looked – especially men, she thought wryly – if they saw her without the magic face powder, her freckles would be in evidence once more and they would likely consider her looks rather homely.

To repay Herr Bayer's gallantry, all Anna could think to do was to admire his jaunty new paisley cravat, hoping he wouldn't detect the insincerity in her voice.

'How was your dear family keeping when you saw them in the summer?' he asked.

'My family is well, thank you. And the wedding was beautiful.'

'I hear from Frøken Olsdatter that sadly, you and your young man have called off your betrothal.'

'Yes. Lars felt he could wait for me no longer.'

'Are you unhappy about this, Anna?'

'I think it is for the best, for both of us,' Anna replied diplomatically, taking a bite of fish. All she really wanted to do was to turn in early for the night and dream about Jens.

After coffee in the drawing room, Frøken Olsdatter brought in a decanter of brandy for Herr Bayer and, to Anna's consternation, also an ice bucket containing a bottle of champagne. It was far too late for her to consider taking alcohol and she wondered immediately if Herr Bayer was expecting other guests.

'Shut the door after you,' he called to Frøken Olsdatter and the housekeeper did as he had asked.

'Now, Anna, my dear young lady, I have something to say to you.' Herr Bayer cleared his throat. 'You must have noticed how my fondness for you has grown over the time you have lived here with me. And I hope that you appreciate the efforts I have made to guide your career.'

'Of course I do, Herr Bayer. I cannot thank you enough.'

'Let us do away with formality. Please, Anna, call me Franz. You know me well enough by now . . .'

Anna watched Herr Bayer as he lapsed into silence. For the first time since she'd known him, he seemed lost for words. Eventually, he recovered himself and continued.

'You see, Anna, I have done all this not only to nurture your talent but also because . . . because I find myself in love with you. Of course, being a gentleman, whilst you were promised to another, I could not speak out, but now you are free, well . . . I realised the depth of my feelings for you clearly this summer when we were parted. And I also know that I must leave you here alone again to return to my mother's bedside, with little idea of how long I will be gone. So, I thought it best that I express my intentions now.' He paused for a second and took a deep breath. 'Anna, would you do me the honour of marrying me?'

She looked at him in silent shock, unable to prevent her horror from painting itself on her face.

Noticing her expression immediately, he cleared his throat again. 'I understand that this proposal may have come as a surprise to you. But Anna, can't you see what we could be together? I have served you well in your career so far, and you have already reached the heights here in Christiania. But Norway is a very small country, too small to hold your talent. I have already written to several musical directors and programming committees in Denmark, Germany and Paris, telling them of your gift. And no doubt, after last night, they will hear of you for themselves. If we married, I could travel with you to Europe as you appear at the great concert halls. I could protect you, look after you . . . I have waited many years to find a talent like yours. And of course,' he added quickly, 'you have also stolen my heart.'

'I see.' Anna gulped, knowing she must respond.

'Surely you are fond of me?'

'Yes, and I am . . . grateful.'

'I believe that we form a good partnership, both on and off the stage. After all, you have lived under my roof for almost a year and know all my bad habits,' he chuckled. 'And, I hope, some of my good ones too. Therefore our marriage would not be as big a leap as it might seem to you – much in our lives would remain the same as it is now.'

Anna shuddered inwardly, knowing of all *sorts* of ways in which Herr Bayer would expect it to be different.

'You are silent, my dear Anna. I can see that I have surprised you. Whilst I have envisaged this as the natural progression for the two of us, you have perhaps not dared to think of it.'

You're certainly right about that, Anna thought. 'No,' she said out loud.

'The champagne was perhaps a little presumptuous on my part. I see now I must give you some time to consider my offer. Will you think about it, Anna?'

'Of course, Herr Bayer . . . Franz. I am honoured by your proposal,' she managed to mumble.

'I will be away for at least two weeks, probably for longer, and perhaps that will give you an opportunity to mull the idea over. I can only hope and pray that your answer will be in the affirmative. Having you stay here with me has made me realise how lonely I've been since my wife's passing.'

He looked so dreadfully sad then that Anna wanted to comfort him, just as she would wish to comfort her own father. She shook off the thought and rose to her feet, feeling there was nothing left to say. 'I will give deep consideration to what you have asked me. You will have an answer when you return. Goodnight . . . Franz.'

Anna had to force herself not to run from the drawing room, but quickened her footsteps once she was outside in the corridor. When she reached her bedroom, she closed the door and locked it with the key. Sitting down heavily on her bed, she put her head in her hands, still unable to take in what had just occurred. She racked her brain to think of any way she had unwittingly led Herr Bayer to believe she would ever marry him. She was certain she had behaved appropriately on all occasions. Never once could she remember flirting with him or 'giving him the eye', as the chorus girls of *Peer Gynt* called it.

However, Anna admitted, her parents had agreed she should live under his roof and let him feed her, clothe her and provide her with opportunities she could never have dreamt of. Not to mention the sum of money he had paid her father. Why shouldn't he assume, after all he had done for her, that his reward for his efforts lay in their permanent union?

'Oh Lord, I can hardly bear it . . .' she moaned.

The potential ramifications of Herr Bayer's proposal were huge. If she rejected his proposal, she knew it would be impossible to continue living under his roof. And then where would she go?

Anna realised then how reliant she was on him. And how many a young girl, or even an older woman such as Frøken Olsdatter perhaps, would jump at the chance to be his wife. He was rich, cultured and accepted in the highest echelons of Christiania society. He was also kind and respectful. But he must be almost three times her age.

And more to the point . . . Anna remembered the vow she had made to herself. She did not love Herr Bayer. She loved Jens Halvorsen.

27

After the performance the following evening, which felt flat and uninspired compared to the opening night, she found Jens waiting for her outside the stage door.

'What are you doing here?' she hissed. She saw the carriage waiting for her and began to hurry towards it. 'Someone might see us.'

'Have no fear, Anna, I'm not intending to compromise your reputation. I only wished to tell you myself how wonderful you were on the first night. And also, to ask you if you are quite well today?'

At this, she stopped and turned towards him. 'What do you mean?'

'As I was watching you tonight, it seemed that you were not yourself. No one else would have noticed, I promise. Your performance was excellent.'

'How could you know what I was feeling?' she asked, as tears sprang to her eyes in relief that he somehow *did*.

'Then I was right,' he said, as they reached the carriage and the driver opened the door to usher her inside. 'Can I help?'

'I . . . don't know . . . I must go home.'

'I understand, but please, we should talk – alone,' he said, lowering his voice so that the driver would not overhear. 'At least take my address.' He pressed a piece of paper into her small hand. 'Otto, my landlord, will go to the house of one of his private pupils tomorrow. I will be alone at the apartment between the hours of four and five.'

'I . . . will have to see,' she murmured, then turned from him and mounted the steps of the carriage. The driver closed the door and Anna sank onto the seat inside. She saw Jens wave, then craned her neck to watch him through the window of the carriage as he walked across the road in the direction of Engebret. As the carriage moved off, she sat back, her heart pounding. She knew perfectly well how improper it was for her to visit a man alone in his apartment, but she also knew she must speak to someone about what had occurred with Herr Bayer last night.

'I will attend the theatre at four o'clock this afternoon,' Anna told Frøken Olsdatter over breakfast the next morning. 'Herr Josephson has called a rehearsal, as he's unhappy with a scene in Act Two.'

'Will you be back for supper?'

'I would hope so, yes. I cannot imagine it taking longer than two hours.'

Perhaps it was Anna's imagination, but Frøken Olsdatter gave her the kind of look that her own mother would when she knew her daughter was lying.

'Very well. Do you wish for a carriage to collect you afterwards?'

'No, the trams will still be running and I can easily find my way home.' Anna rose and walked as calmly as she could from the breakfast table.

When she left the apartment later, she wasn't nearly as calm.

As she boarded the tram, her heart was thumping so loudly she was surprised her neighbour couldn't hear it. She disembarked at the next stop and walked swiftly towards the address Jens had given her. She tried to justify her imminent action by telling herself that this was her one friend in Christiania and the only person she could trust.

'You came,' Jens said with a smile as he opened the door to the apartment. 'Please, come in.'

'Thank you.' Anna followed him inside and along the corridor to a spacious drawing room, elegantly furnished and not dissimilar to Herr Bayer's.

'Would you like some tea? Though I'm warning you, I must make it myself because the maid left at three o'clock.'

'No, thank you. I had tea before I left, and the journey here was not far.'

'Please,' he said, gesturing towards a chair, 'will you sit down?'

'Thank you.' She did so, grateful that the chair was near the stove, for she was shivering with cold and anxiety. Jens sat down opposite her. 'This apartment seems very comfortable,' she ventured.

'If you had seen where I was living before . . .' Jens shook his head and chuckled. 'Well, let us say that I am happy to have found alternative accommodation. But let us not waste time on idle small talk. Anna, what is wrong? Can you bring yourself to speak about it?'

'Oh Lord!' Anna put a hand to her brow. 'It is . . . complicated.'

'Problems normally are.'

'The problem is that Herr Bayer has asked for my hand in marriage.'

'I see.' Jens nodded, outwardly calm, but his hands had balled into fists. 'And how have you answered him?'

'He left for Drøbak early yesterday morning; his mother is dying and he is at her bedside. I must give him an answer when he returns.'

'When will that be?'

'When his mother dies, I suppose.'

'Answer me this truthfully: how did you feel when he asked you?'

'I was horrified. And guilty too. You must understand how kind Herr Bayer has been. He has given me so much.'

'Anna, it is your talent that has given you everything you have now.'

'Yes, but he has nurtured me and given me opportunities that I could never have foreseen when I was living in Heddal.'

'Then you are equals.'

'It doesn't feel like that,' Anna persisted. 'And when I refuse him, where am I to go?'

'So you wish to refuse him?'

'Of course! It would be like marrying my own grandfather! He must be well over fifty years old. But I will have to move out of the apartment, and I will surely make an enemy.'

'I have lots of enemies, Anna,' Jens sighed. 'Granted, they are mostly of my own making. But Herr Bayer is less powerful in Christiania than either you or he believes.'

'Perhaps, but Jens, where would I go?'

There was a silence then as they both thought about what had been said. And also, what remained unsaid. It was Jens who spoke first.

'Anna, it is very hard for me to say anything about your future. Before the summer, I could have offered you everything that Herr Bayer can, and I accept that you are a woman, and that life has far more boundaries for you. However, you must remember that you are now successful in your own right – the current star in the Christiania firmament. You need Herr Bayer less than you imagine.'

'Well, I will not know how much I need him until after I have made the decision, will I?'

'No.' Jens smiled at Anna's pragmatism. 'You know how I feel about you, Anna, but even though my heart wishes to offer you everything, I have no idea what my material circumstances will be in the future. However, you must believe I would be the most miserable man in Christiania if you went ahead and married Herr Bayer. And it is not just for my own selfish reasons, but for you too, because I know you don't love him.'

Anna realised then how dreadful this must all sound to Jens, who'd confessed his love to her freely when she had yet to do the same to him. Agitated, she stood up and made to leave. 'Forgive me, Jens, I shouldn't have come. It's completely' – she searched for the word that Herr Bayer would use – 'inappropriate.'

'I admit, I find it hard to hear that another man has told you he loves you. Although most of Christiania would applaud your acceptance of his hand in marriage.'

'Yes, I'm sure.' She turned away from him and walked towards the door. 'I'm truly sorry, but I really must go.'

She opened the door, but felt his hand clutch hers and pull her back into the room.

'Please, whatever the circumstances, let's not waste this first precious moment we have ever had alone together.' He took a step closer to her and gently cupped her face in his hands. 'I love you, Anna. And I cannot say it enough. I love you.'

For the first time then, she truly believed he did. They were so close now she could feel the heat radiating from him.

'Perhaps it's also important for your decision to admit to yourself, and to me, why you *did* come here,' he said. 'Admit it, Anna: you love me, you love me . . .'

Before she had a chance to stop him, he was kissing her. And within a split second, Anna found her own lips responding, completely without her permission. She knew how wrong this was, but it was already too late, because the feeling was so glorious and so longed for that there wasn't a single reason to end it.

'Now will you tell me?' he begged her as she prepared to leave.

She turned towards him. 'Yes, Jens Halvorsen. I love you.'

An hour later, Anna used her key to open the door to Herr Bayer's apartment. Like the actress she was learning to be, she was prepared when Frøken Olsdatter waylaid her halfway to her bedroom.

'How was the rehearsal, Anna?'

'It went well, thank you.'

'What time would you like supper?'

'Perhaps I could take it on a tray in my room tonight, if that isn't too much trouble? I feel quite exhausted from the performance last night and the rehearsal today.'

'Of course. Why don't I fill you a bath?'

'That would be wonderful, thank you,' Anna replied as she walked into her room and shut the door in relief. Throwing herself onto the bed and hugging herself in ecstasy at the memory of Jens' lips upon hers, she knew that, whatever the result, she must refuse Herr Bayer's proposal.

A new whisper of gossip began to circulate around the theatre the next evening.

'I've heard he's coming.'

'No, he missed his train from Bergen.'

'Well, Herr Josephson was overheard talking to Herr Hennum and the orchestra were called in early this afternoon . . .'

Anna knew there was only one person who could confirm the rumours she'd heard, so she sent for him. Rude arrived in her dressing room a few minutes later.

'You wanted to see me, Frøken Anna?'

'Yes. Is it true? The story that's flying around the theatre tonight?'

'About Herr Grieg attending the performance?'

'Yes.'

'Well.' Rude crossed his arms around his thin body. 'That depends on who you listen to.'

Sighing, Anna put a coin in his palm and he gave her a wide grin. 'I can confirm that Herr Grieg is sitting with Herr

Hennum and Herr Josephson in the office upstairs. Whether he will attend the performance, I couldn't tell you. But as he is in the theatre, it is likely.'

'Thank you for the information, Rude,' she said as he walked towards the door.

'My pleasure, Frøken Anna. Good luck tonight.'

When 'Beginners' were called and the cast took their places in the wings, the tumultuous round of applause from the other side of the curtain confirmed that, indeed, a very important person had just arrived in the auditorium. Luckily, Anna had little time to think of the consequences, because the orchestra struck up the Prelude and the performance began.

Just before she made her first entrance, she felt a hand tugging at her arm. She turned round and saw Rude lurking beside her. He put his hands up around his mouth to whisper to her and she leant down. 'Just remember, Frøken Anna, as my mother always tells me, even the King has to take a piss.'

This sent Anna into a spasm of giggles, the hints of it still visible on her features when she walked onstage. With Jens' loving presence below in the orchestra pit, Anna relaxed and gave of her best. As the curtain fell three hours later, the entire theatre erupted into near hysteria as Grieg himself took a bow from his box. Anna smiled down at Jens as she stood on the stage accepting bouquet after bouquet.

'I love you,' he mouthed to her.

When the curtain fell, the cast were asked to wait onstage and the orchestra filed up from the pit to join them. Anna caught Jens' eye and he blew a kiss.

Eventually, a slender man, barely taller than herself, was escorted onto the stage by Herr Josephson. The cast applauded him ecstatically and as Anna studied him she realised that

Edvard Grieg was far younger than she'd imagined him. He had wavy blond hair swept back from his face and a moustache that rivalled Herr Bayer's. To Anna's complete surprise, he came straight towards her, bowed to her, then took her hand and kissed it.

'Frøken Landvik, your voice was all I could have hoped for when I was composing Solveig's laments.'

Then he turned and spoke to Henrik Klausen, the actor again playing Peer, as well as the other lead members of the cast.

'I feel I must beg an apology from all you actors and musicians for my absence so far from this theatre. There have been . . .' He paused, seeming to need to gather strength from somewhere before continuing. 'There have been circumstances that have kept me away. All I can do is to give my heartfelt thanks to both Herr Josephson and Herr Hennum for creating a production that I am proud to have been a part of. May I congratulate the orchestra for transforming my humble compositions into something magical, and the actors and singers for bringing the characters to life. I thank you all.'

Edvard Grieg's gaze fell on Anna again, as the cast and musicians began to file off the stage. He walked back to her and took her hand once more, then beckoned Ludvig Josephson and Johan Hennum to join them.

'Gentlemen, now I have seen the performance, we will speak tomorrow about some minor alterations, but I thank you for such a fine production under what I know were straitened circumstances. Herr Hennum, the orchestra was far better than I could have dreamt. You have performed a miracle. And as for this young lady,' he said, his expressive blue eyes boring into Anna's, 'whoever cast her as Solveig is a genius.'

'Thank you, Herr Grieg,' said Hennum. 'Anna is indeed a great new talent.'

Herr Grieg then leant in close to whisper in Anna's ear. 'We must talk further, my dear, for I can help your star to rise.' Then, with a smile, he released her hand and turned away to speak to Herr Josephson. Walking off the stage, Anna was again awed at the turn her life had taken. The most famous composer in Norway had publicly praised her talents here tonight. As she changed out of her costume and removed her make-up, it was difficult to believe she was the same country girl who had been singing the cows home just over a year ago.

Except, of course, she wasn't the same.

'Whatever I am now, I am,' she murmured to herself as the steady clip-clop of the horse pulling the carriage lulled her towards Herr Bayer's apartment.

Unusually, Hennum had joined the rest of the orchestra in Engebret after the night's performance.

'Herr Grieg apologises for his absence from the bar, but as you know, he is still grieving for his dead parents. But he has given me enough money to keep you all in high spirits for at least a month,' Herr Hennum declared to rowdy cheers.

All the musicians were on a high, partly fuelled by endless rounds of port and aquavit, but also by the knowledge that the meagre existence they all eked out of their salary, with little or no thanks for their efforts, had been elevated tonight by the sincere thanks and praise of the composer himself.

'Herr Halvorsen.' Hennum beckoned him over. 'Come and speak with me for a moment.'

Jens did as his conductor bid.

'I thought you might wish to know I told Herr Grieg you were a budding composer and that I'd heard some of your compositions. Simen has already told me that you spent the summer working on others.'

'Do you think that Herr Grieg could be persuaded to take a look at what I have written so far?'

'I can't guarantee it, but I do know that he is a great advocate for home-grown Norwegian talent, so it is possible. Give me what music you have, and I'll present your compositions to him tomorrow morning when he comes in to see me.'

'I will, sir, and I cannot thank you enough.'

'I have also heard from Simen that you made a difficult decision in the summer. A musician who is prepared to sacrifice all for his art deserves any assistance I can offer. Now, I must take my leave. Goodnight, Herr Halvorsen.'

Johan Hennum gave Jens a nod and walked out of the bar. Finding Simen, Jens enveloped him in a hug.

'What is this? Have you run out of women and are now turning to men?' asked his startled friend.

'Perhaps,' Jens jested. 'But I thank you, Simen. Truly, I thank you.'

At mid-morning the following day, a letter for Anna was hand-delivered to the apartment.

'Who do you think it might be from?' asked Frøken Olsdatter as Anna studied the writing.

'I have no idea,' she replied as she opened it and began to read.

A few seconds later, Anna looked up in wonder.

'It is from Herr Grieg, the composer. He wishes to visit me at the apartment this afternoon.'

'Dear Lord!' Frøken Olsdatter looked anxiously at the unpolished silver on the dresser, then at the clock on the wall. 'At what time does he wish to arrive?'

'At four.'

'What an honour! If only Herr Bayer was here to meet him too. You know what a supporter he is of Herr Grieg's music. Excuse me, Anna, but if we are to have such an illustrious guest in our house, I must prepare for him.'

'Of course,' Anna said as the housekeeper almost ran out of the room.

Anna finished her lunch, nerves beginning to gather in her stomach. As she went to change into something more acceptable to wear for tea with a famous composer, she stared at her vast new collection of clothing. Discarding various blouses for being too frumpy, too revealing, too grand, or too plain, she settled on her dusky-rose silk gown.

The doorbell rang at the appointed hour, and Frøken Olsdatter led their guest into the drawing room. Since lunchtime, flowers had been procured, cakes hastily baked; Frøken Olsdatter had been concerned that he may well arrive with an entourage, but as it was, Anna rose to greet Edvard Grieg alone.

'My dear Frøken Landvik, thank you for sparing the time

to see me at such short notice.' He reached for her hand and kissed it.

'Please, do sit down. Can I offer you some tea, or coffee?' she stuttered, unused to receiving guests by herself.

'Perhaps a glass of water?'

Frøken Olsdatter gave a half-nod and left the room.

'I'm afraid I have little time as I must return to Bergen tomorrow, and as you can imagine, I have many calls to pay here in Christiania. But I wished to see you. Frøken Landvik, you have the most exquisite voice, though I will not flatter myself that I am the first person to tell you so. Indeed, I hear that Herr Bayer has provided a guiding hand in your career.'

'He has,' she acknowledged.

'And from what I heard last night, he has done an excellent job. But his boundaries are . . . limited in terms of giving your potential the full range of opportunities it deserves. I am lucky to have the ability to personally introduce you to musical directors all over Europe. I am travelling to Copenhagen and Germany very soon and can mention your talent to those I know there. Frøken Landvik, you must understand that however much we wish it not to be so, at present Norway is a mere speck on the European cultural landscape.' He paused and smiled as he saw the look of incomprehension on Anna's face. 'What I'm trying to say, my dear, is that I wish to help you further your career outside our homeland.'

'That is most kind of you, sir, and a great honour.'

'But first, may I ask you if you are free to travel?' he asked as Frøken Olsdatter came in with a jug of water and two glasses.

'Once the production of *Peer Gynt* is finished, then yes, I have no further commitments in Norway.'

'Good, good,' he said as the housekeeper left the room. 'And you are not married or engaged to any young man presently?'

'No, sir.'

'I can imagine you have many admirers, for not only are you a possessor of great talent, but you are beautiful too. In many ways, you remind me of my dear wife, Nina. She too has the voice of a songbird. So, I will write to you from Copenhagen and see what can be done to introduce your exceptional voice to the wider world. Now, I must take my leave.'

'Thank you for coming, sir,' Anna said as he stood up.

'And may I congratulate you once more on your performance. You have inspired me. We will meet again, Frøken Landvik, I am sure of it. Goodbye.'

He kissed her hand and then glanced up at her in a way that Anna had learnt to recognise as indicating interest in her as a woman.

'Goodbye,' she said, bobbing a curtsey as he left the room.

'What do you mean, he has left Christiania?!'

'Just as I said, he has to return to Bergen.'

'Then all is lost! God only knows when he will be back.' Jens fell back into his uncomfortable chair in the orchestra pit as he gazed up mournfully at Herr Hennum.

'The good news is, I managed to have him listen to your compositions before he left. And he gave me this to pass on to you.' Herr Hennum handed Jens an envelope addressed '*To whom it may concern*.'

Jens stared at it. 'What is it?'

'It is a letter of introduction from him to the Leipzig Conservatory.'

Jens punched the air with joy. This letter was his passport to the future.

28

'I will be leaving for Leipzig when the run of *Peer Gynt* ends. Come with me, Anna, please,' Jens begged her as they sat together in the drawing room of Otto's apartment, his arms furled around her delicate frame. 'I refuse to leave you behind in Christiania in Herr Bayer's clutches. Once you refuse his proposal, I have no faith that he will behave like a gentleman.' He softly kissed her brow. 'Let us do as all young lovers in stories do and run away together. You say he has your wages in safe keeping?'

'Yes, but I am sure he will hand them to me if I ask.' Anna bit her lip and hesitated. 'Jens, it would be a grave betrayal of Herr Bayer after all he has done for me. And what would there be for me in Leipzig?'

'Why, Leipzig is the centre of the musical world in Europe! It could be a wonderful opportunity for you. Herr Grieg himself told you that the world here in Christiania is narrow and that your talent deserves a wider audience,' Jens cajoled. 'His music publisher resides there and he himself spends much of his time in the city. So there would be nothing to stop you renewing his acquaintance in future. Anna, please, think about it. I believe it is the only solution for us. Presently, I can think of no other.'

Anna looked at Jens uneasily. It had taken her a year to get used to life in Christiania. What if she couldn't do it again somewhere else? Besides, now she had grown more confident, she had begun to love being Solveig, and she would miss Frøken Olsdatter and Rude . . . But then again when she tried to imagine a life in Christiania without Jens, her heart gave a painful wrench.

'I know it's a lot to ask,' he said, reading her mind, 'and yes, you could stay here, and become the most famous soprano in Norway. Or you can aim higher, living a life of love with me and having success on a far larger scale. But of course, it will not be easy, for you have no money, and I have very little other than what my mother gave me to pay for my board and tuition in Leipzig. We would live purely on music, love and belief in our own talent,' he finished with a flourish.

'Jens, what on earth would I say to my parents? Herr Bayer will be bound to tell them what I've done. I will bring disgrace on our name. I couldn't bear for them to think . . .' Anna's voice trailed off and she put her fingers to her brow. 'Let me think about it, I must have time to think . . .'

'Of course you must,' Jens agreed gently. 'We have a month until the end of the run of *Peer Gynt*.'

'And I could not . . . I could not be with you if we remained unmarried,' Anna said, blushing furiously that she even had to mention such a thing. 'I would rot in Hell for eternity and my mother would boil herself in her cooking pot rather than face such shame.'

Jens stifled a smile at Anna's vivid imagination. 'So,

Frøken Landvik,' he said, taking her hands in his, 'are you trying to gain a *third* proposal in your streak of suitors?'

'Of course not! All I'm saying is that—'

'Anna.' He kissed her tiny hand. 'I know what you're saying and I understand. And I promise you, whether we were eloping to Leipzig or not, I would want to propose to you.'

'Really?'

'Yes, really. If we go to Leipzig, we will wed in secret before we leave, I promise. I would not wish you to compromise your morals.'

'Thank you.' Anna felt greatly relieved that at least Jens' offer was serious. That if they did 'elope' – Anna pushed down a shudder at the idea – they would at least be man and wife in the eyes of God.

'Tell me, when will Herr Bayer be back, panting for your answer?' he asked her.

'I have no idea, but' – she glanced at the clock on the wall and her hand flew to her mouth as she realised the time – 'I do know I have to leave for the theatre now. I must be there an hour and a half before the curtain rises for my face to be painted.'

'Of course. But Anna, please, you need to realise that even if I was not going to Leipzig, if you refuse Herr Bayer's proposal, I have a feeling he would not make our life easy in Christiania. Come here and kiss me before you go. I will see you later onstage, but promise me you will give me your answer soon.'

Anna arrived back at the apartment after the performance feeling completely drained. She wanted nothing more than to go straight to bed and sleep.

'Anna, how was your evening?'

Frøken Olsdatter looked at her questioningly as she brought Anna her hot milk and helped her out of her dress.

'It went well, thank you.'

'Good, I am glad for you, *kjære*. I should tell you that I received a telegram this evening from Herr Bayer. His mother passed on earlier today. He and his sister must stay for the funeral, and then he will return to Christiania on Friday.'

Only three days, thought Anna. 'I am sorry to hear his news.'

'Yes, but perhaps it is a relief that Fru Bayer is finally free from pain.'

'And I will look forward to seeing Herr Bayer on his return,' Anna lied as Frøken Olsdatter left her room. As she settled into bed, she felt her stomach constricting in nervous knots at the thought of Herr Bayer's return.

The next morning, still brooding on her predicament, Anna went in to breakfast.

'You look pale, Anna *kjære*. Did you not sleep well?' asked Frøken Olsdatter.

'I have . . . things on my mind.'

'Then you might wish to share them with me. I may be able to help.'

'There is nothing anyone can do,' she sighed.

'I see.' Frøken Olsdatter scrutinised her closely, but did not press her further. 'Will you be requiring luncheon?'

'No, I must go to . . . the theatre early today.'

'Very well, then, Anna. I shall see you at supper.'

Over the next three days, Frøken Olsdatter and the daily maid went into a frenzy of cleaning. Anna spent time practising how she would explain to Herr Bayer why she could not accept his offer of marriage.

The exact hour of his arrival was not known, but at half past three, unable to stand the tension in the apartment any longer, Anna put on her cape and told Frøken Olsdatter that she was going to take a walk in the park. The housekeeper gave her one of her looks – a mixture of disbelief and cool acceptance – which had become a regular expression recently.

As always, the clean, chilly air revitalised her. She looked out at the fjord from her favourite bench and saw the shimmering silver water in the already descending twilight.

I am where I am, she told herself, *and there is little I can do except act with gratitude and grace, as I have been brought up to do.*

As she stood up, thinking of her parents brought a tear to her eye. They had written her a brief but supportive letter consoling her on Lars cancelling their engagement and his recent abrupt departure for America. At that moment, she wished with all her heart Herr Bayer had never found her and she was safe and sound at home in Heddal and married to Lars.

'Herr Bayer will be back in time to join you for dinner,' Frøken Olsdatter said, accosting her at the door as she arrived home. 'I have filled you a bath and laid out your gown.'

'Thank you.' Anna moved past her and went to prepare for the confrontation.

'Anna, *min elskede*!' he said, greeting her intimately as she entered the dining room. He took her hand in his large one and gave it a whiskery kiss. 'Come, sit down.'

As they ate, he told her about his mother's sad passing and the details of the funeral. Anna hoped vaguely that due to his grief, maybe he'd forgotten about his proposal. However, when they went through to the drawing room to take coffee and brandy, she sensed the atmosphere change.

'So, my dear young lady, have you thought about the important question I asked you just before I left?'

Anna sipped her coffee, using the moment to gather her thoughts before she spoke. Although in truth, she had rehearsed her words a hundred times.

'Herr Bayer, I am honoured and gratified by your proposal—'

'Then I am happy!' he announced with a broad smile.

'Yes, but, having thought about it, I feel I must refuse.'

Anna watched the expression on his face alter, his eyes narrowing. 'May I ask why?'

'Because I feel I could not be what you need in a wife.'

'What on earth do you mean by that?'

'That I am not domestically oriented to run a house, or educated enough to entertain your guests or—'

'Anna.' Herr Bayer's face softened at her words and Anna realised she had stupidly used the wrong approach. 'It is typically sweet and modest of you to say such things to me, but you must realise that none of that matters. Your talent more than makes up for all the qualities you lack, and your youth and innocence is one of the reasons you endear yourself to me. Please, my dear young lady, there is no need to be humble or feel you are not worthy. I have grown very fond of you indeed. As for the cooking – why, that's what I have Frøken Olsdatter for!'

There was a silence as Anna struggled to think what other reasons she could give.

'Herr Bayer—'

'Anna, I have told you, please, call me Franz.'

'Franz, whatever you say, even though I am flattered by your proposal, I am sad to say that I cannot accept it. And that is that.'

'Is there someone else?'

She shivered involuntarily at the sudden sharp tone of his question. 'No, I . . .'

'Anna, before you continue further, you must know that even though I may have been away from Christiania for the past few weeks, I have my spies. If you are refusing my proposal for the sake of that handsome cad who plays violin in the orchestra, then I would caution you against it. Not just as a man who loves you and wishes to provide you with all you have ever dreamt of, but as your advisor and guide to a world that you are currently still too naive to understand.'

Anna said nothing, but realised her shock was written all over her features.

'So!' Herr Bayer slapped his solid thighs. 'That is it. It seems I am competing for your affections with a penniless, no-good bounder in the orchestra. I knew it,' he said as he threw back his head and laughed. 'I do apologise, but Anna, tonight you show me the true extent of your innocence.'

'Forgive me, but yes, we *are* in love!' The fact that he was laughing at her, belittling what she and Jens shared, made Anna's temper rise. 'And whether you approve or not, it is the truth,' she said, rising to her feet. 'Under the circumstances, I think it's best I leave. I wish to thank you for all you have done for me and given me. And I am sorry if my refusal has not been to your liking.'

As she began to move swiftly to the door, he caught up with her in two large strides to pull her back. 'Wait, Anna, let us not part like this. Please, I beg you, sit down and we will talk. You have always trusted me before and I would like to show you the error of your ways. I know this man; I understand who he is and the enchantment he has put you under. I do not blame you in any way. You are so innocent, and yes, you believe you are in love. Whether you now accept or reject my proposal is of no consequence. This man will break your heart and destroy you, as he has destroyed many other women before.'

'No, you don't know him . . .' Anna wrung her hands in despair, tears of frustration pouring down her cheeks.

'Now, now, try to keep calm. You are becoming hysterical. Please, let us sit down together and talk.'

Anna's energy drained from her and she allowed him to lead her back to a chair.

'My dear,' Herr Bayer began gently, 'you must be aware of the previous relationships Herr Halvorsen has conducted with other women.'

'Yes, I am.'

'Jorid Skrovset in the chorus was so heartbroken that she has refused to return to the theatre. And the great Madame Hansson herself was thrown into such a state of distress after Herr Halvorsen had his way with her that she has gone abroad to recover. Which is why you are currently playing her role in the Christiania Theatre.'

'Sir, I know for a fact from Jens that—'

'Forgive me, but you know nothing of this man, Anna,' he interrupted. 'I accept I am not your father nor, sadly at present, your intended, and therefore have little sway over your decisions. But I will tell you now, because I care for you so deeply, that Jens Halvorsen is nothing but trouble. He will crush you, Anna, as he has crushed every woman who has had the misfortune to be lured into his trap. He is a weak man, and his weakness is women and carousing. I fear for you, I really do, and have done so ever since I first heard of this . . . liaison.'

'When did you hear?' Anna whispered, not able to look at him.

'Weeks ago. And I should warn you that all at the theatre are aware of it. And yes, it was this discovery that prompted my proposal, simply because I want to save you and your talent from yourself. Know that if you go to him, he will desert you for another soon enough. And I simply cannot bear the thought of you throwing everything away for a selfish Casanova, after all we have worked for together.'

Anna remained silent as Herr Bayer poured himself another brandy.

'As you do not answer me, I will tell you what I think we should do. If you are intent on being with this man, then simply because I could not bear to watch the inevitable dramatic denouement, I agree that you should leave the apartment immediately. And then go with him to Leipzig after the run of *Peer Gynt* has come to an end.' He saw the astounded expression on Anna's face and continued. 'If you decide this is really what you wish to do, then I will give you the wages you have earned at the theatre and send you on your way. If, however, what I have said to you has some resonance in its honesty, and you are prepared to give Herr Halvorsen up and marry me after I have finished a suitable period of mourning for my mother, then please, stay here. There is no need to rush – all I need is an intention. Please, Anna, I beg you, think very carefully about your decision. For it is one that will change your life, for better or for worse.'

'If you knew all this, then why did you not say before?' she asked in a small voice. 'Surely you knew that I would refuse you?'

'Simply because I blame myself for what has happened. I was not here in Christiania to protect you from him. Now that I'm back, I can tell you that I *will* protect you. But only on the condition that you banish Jens Halvorsen from your life immediately. If you were rejecting me for a different suitor, perhaps I could accept it with grace. But in this case, I cannot, because I know he will destroy you.'

'I love him,' she said again, pointlessly.

'I know you think you do, and I understand how hard it will be for you to accept what I've demanded. But one day I hope you will come to see that I am acting in your best interests. Now, I think it is time that we both retired. I have had a gruelling few weeks and find myself very weary.' Taking her hand in his, he kissed it. 'Goodnight, Anna, sleep well.'

29

The next evening, Anna was glad to arrive at the theatre, where everything was comfortingly the same as it had always been. She had not slept a wink last night, torn between her head and her heart. A lot of what Herr Bayer had said was true, especially to the outsider. She herself had had similar thoughts about Jens, so she couldn't blame anyone else for doing the same. And of course everyone would tell her to marry Herr Bayer, not a penniless musician. It was the sensible decision.

However, none of this rational thinking solved the dilemma, because no matter which way she turned, the thought of giving up Jens Halvorsen forever was simply untenable.

And at least, she thought, as she left her dressing room to walk to the stage, she would see Jens in a few minutes, looking up at her with love and support from the orchestra pit. She'd already written him a note saying they must meet tonight after the performance and she'd summon Rude to deliver it in the first interval. When the play began, Anna tried to still her racing heart and calm herself. As she walked onstage and spoke her first lines, she surreptitiously cast her eyes down to find his.

In panic, she saw Jens wasn't there. Instead, an elderly elfin-sized man was sitting in his chair.

At the end of Act One, dizzy from fear, she came offstage and immediately summoned Rude to her dressing room.

'Hello, Frøken Anna. How are you?'

'I am well,' Anna lied. 'Do you know where Herr Halvorsen is? I saw tonight that he isn't playing.'

'Really? Well, for the first time, you've told me something I didn't already know. Shall I go and find out?'

'If you would.'

'Right, it might take me a while, so I'll see you in the next interval.'

Anna went through the second act in an agony of despair, and when Rude appeared in her dressing room as promised, she thought she might faint with tension at what he might tell her.

'The answer is that no one knows. Perhaps he's sick, Frøken Anna. But the fact is that he isn't here.'

She went through the rest of the performance in a daze. As soon as the cast had taken their last bows, Anna dressed hurriedly, then left the theatre and climbed into the carriage, directing the driver to take her to Jens' apartment. When they arrived outside his building, she stepped out, calling over her shoulder to the driver to wait for her, before running inside and up the stairs. Breathing heavily, she knocked loudly on the door until she heard the sound of footsteps approaching.

The door opened and she saw Jens. She collapsed into his arms with relief. 'Thank God, thank God. I—'

'Anna.' He drew her inside and put an arm around her shivering shoulder as he led her into the drawing room.

'Where were you? I thought that you'd gone . . . I . . .'

'Anna, please, try to calm yourself. Let me explain.' Jens guided her to the settle and sat down next to her. 'I arrived as usual at the theatre, to be told by Johan Hennum that my services in the orchestra were no longer required. They had found another flautist and violinist to replace me with immediate effect. I asked him if this arrangement was temporary and he told me that it wasn't. He paid my wages in full and sent me on my way. Anna, I swear to you, I have absolutely no idea why I was dismissed.'

'I do. Oh good Lord . . .' Anna put her head in her hands. 'For a change, Jens, this has little to do with your behaviour, and everything to do with mine. Last night, I told Herr Bayer I could not marry him. Then he told me he knew all about us! He said that I was only welcome to continue to stay with him if I'd denounce you immediately. And if I wasn't prepared to do that, then I must leave the apartment.'

'Oh Lord,' Jens sighed, understanding. 'So the next thing we know, I am asked to leave the Christiania orchestra. He probably told Hennum and Josephson I was a bad influence and distracting their new little star.'

'Forgive me, Jens. I didn't believe Herr Bayer was capable of such a thing.'

'I did, and told you so,' Jens muttered. 'Well, at least I now know the reason for my swift exit.'

'What will you do?'

'As a matter of fact, I've just been packing.'

'To go where?' Anna was horrified.

'To Leipzig, of course. One way or another, it's obvious

there is no future for me here. I decided I should leave as soon as possible.'

'I see.' Anna cast her eyes down, concentrating on not allowing herself to cry at this news.

'I was going to write to you tonight and leave the letter at the stage door.'

'You swear you were? Or are you just saying that and were simply going to disappear without saying a word?'

'Anna, *min kjære*, come here.' Jens took her in his arms and stroked her back tenderly. 'I know this has been a very difficult time for you, but I myself have only had a few hours since Hennum ended my employment. Of course I was going to tell you where I was. Why on earth wouldn't I? It was I who asked you to come with me, remember?'

'Yes, yes . . . You're right.' Anna wiped her tears away. 'I am overwrought. And so angry that you've been punished for what I've done.'

'Well, don't be. You know I had planned to go anyway, it's just happened a little sooner than I expected. Was Herr Bayer very angry with you, my love?'

'No, he wasn't angry at all. He said he didn't want me to ruin my life by being with you, and that he wished me not to see you again for my own good.'

'Which is why I was booted unceremoniously out of the pit so that you couldn't. What will you do?'

'Herr Bayer has given me a day to think about it. How *dare* he interfere in my life and yours like this!'

'We are in a state, the two of us,' he sighed. 'Well, I am leaving tomorrow – the term at the Conservatory only began two weeks ago, so I won't have missed much. And if you want to, you can join me in Leipzig when the run of *Peer Gynt* is finished.'

'Jens, after what they have done to you, I could never bring myself to return to the theatre!' Anna shuddered. 'I will come with you immediately.'

Jens looked at her in surprise. 'Are you sure that's sensible, Anna? If you walk out before the play is over, you will never again be able to work at the Christiania Theatre. Your name will be as black as mine.'

'And nor would I want to work there again,' she retorted, her eyes glittering with indignation. 'I refuse to let people, whoever they are and however important and rich, behave as if they own me.'

Jens chuckled at her fierce expression. 'Beneath that sweet exterior of yours you really are quite the firebrand, aren't you?'

'I have been brought up to know right from wrong, and I know that what they have done to you is very, very wrong.'

'Yes, it is, my love, but sadly, there's little we can do about it. Really, Anna, I caution you: however angry you are, please think carefully about coming with me tomorrow. I would hate to be the reason for the ruination of your career. And know' – he hushed her as she opened her mouth to speak – 'I do not say this because I don't wish you to come. I am simply concerned that we will board the ferry to Hamburg tomorrow, and then take the overnight train to Leipzig without even knowing where we will lay our heads once we arrive. Or whether they will even accept me at the Conservatory.'

'Of course they will accept you, Jens. You have your letter from Herr Grieg.'

'I do and yes, they probably will, but whereas I am a man and able to suffer physical deprivation, you are a young lady with certain . . . needs.'

'Who was born on a farm and had never seen an inside privy before she arrived in Christiania,' Anna countered. 'Really, Jens, I do feel you are doing your best to convince me not to accompany you.'

'Well, don't say I didn't warn you when we get there. So' – he smiled at her suddenly – 'I have done my best to dissuade you, and you have refused to accept my concerns. My conscience is clear. We shall leave together at dawn tomorrow. Come here, Anna. Let us hold each other and take strength for the adventure we are about to embark on.'

He kissed her then, and any worries she'd had about his reticence or her decision melted away. Eventually, their lips parted, and as Anna laid her head against his chest, he stroked her hair. 'Of course, there is one more thing we should discuss. We must present ourselves as married to all we meet on our travels, and at Leipzig of course. Overnight, you must become Fru Halvorsen in the eyes of the world, for no landlord would rent us a room if they knew we were not yet wed. How do you feel about that?'

'I feel that we must marry as soon as we arrive in Leipzig. I could not countenance any . . .' Anna's voice trailed off.

'Of course we shall. And don't worry, Anna, even if we must share the same bed, please believe I would always act like a gentleman. So for now' – Jens left the room then and returned a minute later with a small velvet box – 'you must wear this. It was my grandmother's wedding band. My mother gave it to me when I left, and told me to sell it if I needed the money. Shall I put it on for you?'

Anna stared at the slim gold band. This was hardly the 'wedding' she'd imagined, but she understood it would have to do for now.

'I love you, Fru Halvorsen,' he said as he put the ring gently on her finger. 'And I promise we will do it for real in Leipzig. Now, you must leave and ready yourself for tomorrow. Can you be here by six o'clock?'

'Yes, I will be here,' she replied as she walked towards the front door. 'As it's doubtful I shall sleep much tonight anyway.'

'Anna, do you have any money?'

'No.' She bit her lip. 'And I can hardly ask Herr Bayer for my wages now. It wouldn't be right. I have let him and others down so dreadfully.'

'Then we shall be as poor as beggars until we find our feet,' he said with a shrug.

'Yes. Goodnight, Jens,' she said quietly.

'Goodnight, my love.'

The apartment was silent when Anna arrived home. As she crept along the corridor, she saw Frøken Olsdatter's anxious face peep out of her room.

'I was worried, Anna,' she whispered, coming towards her. 'Thank the Lord, Herr Bayer retired early tonight, complaining of a fever. Where have you been?'

'Out,' Anna replied, turning the handle to enter her room, no longer wishing to explain herself to anyone.

'Shall we go to the kitchen? I'll make you some hot milk.'

'I . . .' Anna checked herself. This woman had been kind

to her and it would be wrong to leave without telling her. 'Thank you.' She let herself be led down the corridor and into the kitchen.

Over the hot milk, Anna told Frøken Olsdatter the whole story. And by the end of it, she was glad she had.

'Well, well,' Frøken Olsdatter murmured, 'what a heart-breaker you are, *kjære*. Gentlemen seem to be falling over themselves to woo you. So, you have decided to leave immediately and follow your violinist to Leipzig?'

'I have no choice. Herr Bayer said I must if I was not prepared to give up Jens right away. After what he asked Herr Hennum to do to Jens, I don't wish to be in Christiania a minute longer.'

'Anna, do you not think that Herr Bayer is only trying to protect you? That he has your best interests at heart?'

'But he doesn't! It's what *he* wants, not what *I* want!'

'And what about your career? Please, Anna, you are so very talented. It is a lot to sacrifice, even for love.'

'But it is necessary – I cannot stay here in Christiania without Jens,' insisted Anna. 'And I can sing anywhere in the world. Herr Grieg said himself that he would help me if I ever asked.'

'And he is an influential benefactor,' Frøken Olsdatter agreed. 'So, what will you do for money?'

'Herr Bayer said he would give me the wages I'd earned from the theatre. But I have decided I will ask him for nothing.'

'That's very honourable of you. But even those in love must eat and have a roof over their heads.' Frøken Olsdatter stood up, went to a drawer in the dresser and pulled out a tin box. Taking a key from the chain around her waist, she opened it. Inside was a bag of coins, which she handed to Anna. 'There. It is my savings. I have no current use for them and your need is greater than mine. I cannot see you leave this house to walk into an uncertain future with nothing.'

'Oh, but I can't . . .' Anna entreated.

'You can and you will,' Frøken Olsdatter said firmly. 'And one day when I hear you are singing at the Leipzig Opera House, you can invite me to come and watch you as payment.'

'Thank you, you are so very kind.' Anna was moved beyond measure at the gesture. She reached out and took Frøken Olsdatter's hand. 'You must think what I am doing is wrong.'

'Who am I to judge? Whether your decision is for the best or not, you are a brave young woman with strong principles. And I admire you for that. Perhaps when you are calmer, you can write to Herr Bayer.'

'I am frightened he may be very angry.'

'No, Anna, he won't be angry, just extremely sad. You may see him as an old man, but remember, as we get older, our hearts still function in the same way as they always have. Don't blame him for falling in love with you and yearning to keep you with him for always. Now, as you must be up with the lark tomorrow, I suggest that you go to bed and take what sleep you can.'

'I will.'

'Please, Anna, write to me from Leipzig and let me know you are safe. Herr Bayer is not the only one in this household who will miss your presence. Just try to remember that you have youth, talent and beauty. Don't waste it, will you?'

'I will do all I can not to. Thank you for everything.'

'What will you tell your parents?' Frøken Olsdatter asked suddenly.

'I don't know,' she sighed, 'I really don't. Goodbye.'

As the ferry chugged out of the fjord, bound for Hamburg and noisily belching smoke and steam from its funnels, Anna stood alone on the deck, watching her homeland disappear in the autumnal mist. And wondered if she would ever see it again.

30

Twenty-four hours later, Anna and Jens finally stepped off the train at Leipzig railway station. The sun had only just risen and as Anna was so tired she could hardly stand, Jens carried both his case and her valise. Their train from Hamburg to Leipzig had been a sleeper, but neither of them had felt they should spend their money on the comfort of a bunk. They had sat upright on the hard wooden seats all night, Jens drifting off almost immediately, his head lolling on her shoulder. As the hours had gone by, Anna had become increasingly incredulous at what she had just done.

At least it was a bright morning as they left the bustling station and walked into the central district of the city. Weary as she was, Anna's heart lifted slightly as her eyes took in the beauty of Leipzig. The wide cobbled streets were lined with impressive tall stone buildings, many of them decorated with ornate gables or carvings and boasting rows of elegant casement windows. The passers-by spoke in a clipped language that, having heard it spoken during the long train journey from Hamburg, Anna knew was German. Jens had assured her he spoke it with reasonable competence, but she could only grasp a word or two that was similar enough to Norwegian.

Eventually they found themselves in the central market square, which was flanked by the imposing red-roofed Town Hall, fronted by pillared arches and dominated by a high domed clock tower. The square was already packed with stalls and humming with activity. Jens stopped at one of the stalls where a baker was laying out an assortment of freshly baked bread. As Anna drank in the delicious smell, she realised how hungry she was.

But Jens had not stopped for food.

'*Entschuldigung Sie, bitte. Wissen Sie wo die Pension in der Elsterstraße ist?*'

Anna had no idea what the baker's gruff reply meant.

'Good, we are not far from the lodging house Herr Grieg suggested,' Jens said.

This turned out to be a modest half-timbered building situated along a narrow lane just off a road Anna saw was called Elsterstraße. It certainly had a different atmosphere to the many grand edifices they'd passed on the way, she thought warily. The district looked a little down at heel, but forcing herself to remember that this was all they could afford, she followed behind Jens as he strode up to the door and rapped the knocker loudly. After several minutes, a woman appeared, hastily tying the cord of her robe to cover her nightgown, and Anna realised it could not be later than seven in the morning.

'*Um Himmels willen, was wollen Sie denn?!*' the woman grumbled.

Jens answered her in German and all Anna could understand was 'Herr Grieg'. At the mention of his name, the woman's face relaxed and she ushered them inside.

'She says she's full, but that as it's Herr Grieg who sent us, there's a maid's room up in the attic that we could use temporarily,' Jens translated for Anna.

Up and up they climbed, the narrow wooden stairs creaking underfoot. Finally, they arrived on the top floor and the woman pushed open the door to a tiny room set under the eaves of the house. The only furniture was a narrow brass bed, and a chest of drawers with a basin and a jug atop it, but at least it looked clean.

Another conversation in German then ensued between Jens and the woman, as he gesticulated at the bed and she nodded, then left the room.

'I have said we will take it for now until I can find alternative accommodation. I have told her the bed is too narrow for us both to sleep on, so she is finding me a pallet. I will sleep on the floor.'

They both stood, looking about the room in weary silence, until the woman returned with the pallet. Jens offered some coins from his pocket.

'*Nur Goldmark, keine Kronen*,' the woman said, shaking her head.

'Take the Kronen for now, and I will change some money later today,' Jens suggested.

The woman agreed reluctantly, pocketing the coins as she issued further instructions, pointing under the bed, then left the room again.

Anna sat down gingerly. Her head was spinning with exhaustion, but more pressing than that, she needed to use the facilities. Blushing, she asked Jens if the woman had told him where they might be.

'There, I'm afraid.' He too pointed beneath the bed. 'I'll stand outside while you . . .'

With heat mounting in her cheeks, Anna agreed and once he was gone, did what she had been desperate to do for hours. Shuddering as she covered the contents of the pot with the muslin cloth provided, she allowed Jens back in.

'Better?' he grinned.

'Yes, thank you,' she replied tightly.

'Good. Now, I suggest we both get some rest.'

Anna blushed and looked away as Jens divested himself of his clothes until he stood in his cotton breeches and vest. Using his topcoat to pull over him, he lay down on the pallet. 'Don't worry, I promise not to peek,' he chuckled. 'Sleep well, Anna. We'll both feel better after it.' Then he blew her a kiss and rolled over away from her.

Anna untied the ribbons of her cloak, removed her heavy skirt and blouse, leaving her chemise and bloomers in place. She could already hear Jens' gentle snores emanating from the pallet as she crawled under the coarse woollen blanket and rested her head on the pillow.

What have I done? she thought to herself. Herr Bayer had been right all along. She was naive and headstrong and had not stopped to think through the ramifications of her actions. Now she had burnt all her bridges and had ended up in this terrible, claustrophobic room, sleeping within inches of a man she had not even married, and having to perform intimate acts with no privacy whatsoever.

'Oh Lord, forgive me for the pain I have caused to others,' she whispered to the heavens, where she imagined He must be looking down on her at this moment, writing out her ticket to the underworld. Finally, she drifted into a restless sleep.

Anna was up and fully dressed by the time Jens stirred, desperate for a cup of water and ravenously hungry.

'Bed comfortable?' he asked as he stretched and yawned.

'I will get used to it.'

'Now,' Jens said as he dressed and Anna turned away from him, 'we must change some coins to Goldmarks and find something to eat. But first, can I ask you to leave the room and I'll join you outside when I've done my business?'

Aghast at the thought that he would see what was already in the pot, Anna did as she was bid. Then, to her horror, Jens came out holding it.

'We must ask our landlady what we do with the slops,' he said as he passed her and started to descend the wooden stairs.

Anna followed behind him, her cheeks burning. A simple country girl she may have been before going to Christiania, but never had she encountered anything as unhygienic and disgusting as this. At home in Heddal, the facilities had been outdoor and basic, but far preferable. She realised that, having become accustomed to the modern bathroom in Herr Bayer's apartment, she'd never thought about how ordinary city dwellers got rid of their mess.

They found the landlady in the hall and Jens presented the pot to her as though he was handing her a tureen of stew. She nodded and pointed to the back of the house, but took it from him anyway.

'Right, all done. Let's go and find some food,' Jens said as he opened the door.

Walking along the crowded streets, Anna and Jens found a *Bierkeller* to one side of a small square and sat down at a table. Jens ordered beers, and the two of them looked up at the board on which the short menu was chalked. Anna could not read a single word.

'Well, there is bratwurst – sausages. I've heard they're very good, although a bit fattier than the ones we have at home,' Jens said, translating the menu for her. '*Knödel* – don't ask me what that is . . . *Speck*, which is bacon, I suppose . . .'

'I think I'll just have what you're having,' Anna said wearily, as the beer was delivered to the table along with a bowl of dark bread. Even though she would have preferred water, she picked up the mug and drank thirstily.

She peered out of the dingy windows to see the bustling square outside. The women for the most part wore plain dark dresses with white or grey aprons that accentuated their pale skins and chiselled Germanic features. Anna had expected to see more finery in Leipzig, as she had been told it was one of the most important cities in Europe. There was the odd carriage that clopped past, giving the occasional glimpse of a stylish feathered hat worn by wealthier women.

Their lunch arrived and Anna made short work of the potatoes and fat sausages. The beer had gone to her head and she smiled at Jens lovingly.

'How do I ask for water?'

'You say "*Ein Wasser, bitte*",' Jens replied, before his attention turned to the small street orchestra, who were playing fiddles in the centre of the square with a cap laid on the path in front of them for money. Anna watched him stretch in pleasure as he listened.

'Isn't it wonderful here? This is where our destiny lies, I am sure of it.' He reached across the table and took her hand. 'So how are you finding our adventure so far?'

'I feel unclean, Jens. When we get back, do you think it's

possible to ask the landlady if there is any place here that we can take a bath and wash our clothes?'

Jens fixed her with a hard stare. 'Anna, come now, you told me you were a country girl, used to physical hardship. Is that all you have to say about being in Leipzig?'

She thought longingly of Heddal, and the clear melted snow that was collected from outside in winter and warmed over the fire for washing. And how in the summer there were the pure, fresh streams in which to bathe. 'Forgive me. I will manage, I am sure.'

Jens picked up his second mug of beer and slugged it back. 'I should thank Herr Bayer, as he has forced me to finally walk towards my future.'

'I am glad you are so happy to be here, Jens.'

'I am indeed. Breathe the air, Anna. It even smells different. And the city is alight with creativity and music. Look at the crowd gathered around those musicians! Did you ever see such a thing in Christiania? Here, music is celebrated, not derided as a poor man's game. And now, *I* can be part of that celebration.' He drained his mug of beer and threw some coins on the table as he stood up. 'Now, I will collect my letter from Herr Grieg and go straight to the Conservatory. This is the beginning of everything I've dreamt of.'

Arriving back at their lodgings, Jens rifled through his case and collected his precious letter. Then he gave Anna a kiss and made his way to the door.

'Rest, Anna, and I will wake you with wine and good news later.'

'And will you ask if someone there might hear me sing—'

But the door had already closed behind him.

Anna sank down onto the bed. She understood now that

this 'adventure' had a completely different resonance for each of them: Jens had been running *to* something and she had been running away. And now, she thought miserably, even if it had been the wrong thing, there was absolutely nothing she could do about it.

Jens returned from the Conservatory a few hours later, even more euphoric.

'When I first arrived and asked to see the principal, Dr Schleinitz, the porter looked at me as if I was the village idiot. Then I handed him my letter, and once he had read it, he went straight to the office to fetch him! Dr Schleinitz asked me to play the violin, and then one of my compositions on the piano. And you wouldn't believe it' – at this point, Jens punched the air – 'he bowed! Yes, Anna, he actually bowed to me! We talked of Herr Grieg and he told me it would be a pleasure to teach any protégé of his. So, tomorrow I begin my studies at the Leipzig Conservatory.'

'Oh Jens! That is wonderful!' Anna did her best to sound happy.

'I also went to a tailor's shop on my way back and had to pay him double to fit me out with more appropriate clothing by tomorrow morning. I want no one to think I am a simpleton from the fjords. Isn't it wonderful?' He chuckled as he put his arms around Anna's waist and lifted her up, twirling her around. 'Now, before we go out to celebrate, we must move into our new lodgings.'

'You have already found somewhere for us?'

'Yes. It isn't a palace, but it certainly has its advantages over this. While you pack, I'll go and pay the landlady her Goldmarks, and see you downstairs.'

'I . . .' Anna was about to say she doubted she could carry

both the bags alone, but he'd already gone. A few minutes later, panting with exertion, she joined Jens with their luggage downstairs in the entrance hall.

'Right, let's be off to our new abode,' Jens proclaimed.

Anna followed him out onto the street and looked on in surprise as he merely crossed it and entered the house opposite.

'I saw the vacancy sign in the window on my way back and thought I'd go and enquire,' he added.

The house was similar to the one they'd just left, but the room was on the first floor and at least more spacious and airy than the stuffy attic. There was a big brass bed taking up most of the space, and Anna's heart somersaulted at the realisation that there was no room for a pallet on the floor.

'There's also a water closet across the landing, which means this room is more expensive, but that should please you at least. Happy, Anna?'

'Yes.' She nodded stoically.

'Good.' He handed some coins to Frau Schneider, the landlady, who Anna thought at least looked more approachable than the last one. 'There's enough for our first week's board,' he said, beaming at her magnanimously.

'*Kochen in den Zimmern ist untersagt. Abendbrot um punkt sieben Uhr. Essen Sie hier heute Abend?*'

'She's saying there's no cooking allowed in the room but that we can eat supper each evening downstairs at seven,' said Jens quietly to Anna. He turned to Frau Schneider. 'That sounds like an excellent idea. How much extra would that be?'

Again, money exchanged hands and finally the door closed behind them.

'So, Frau Halvorsen,' Jens grinned, 'how do you like our new married quarters?'

'I . . .'

Jens saw the fear on her face as she gazed at the bed. 'Anna, come here to me.'

She did so, and he held her tightly to him.

'There, there. I've already promised you that I won't touch you until you say I can. But at least we will be able to keep each other warm on cold Leipzig nights.'

'Jens, really, we must be married as soon as possible,' Anna urged. 'We must find a Lutheran church that will marry us—'

'We will, but let's not worry about it now,' he said, pulling her closer and trying to kiss her neck.

'Jens, what we are doing is a sin against God!' she said as she rebuffed his caress.

'Of course, you're right,' he sighed against her skin before letting go of her. 'Now, I fear we are both overdue a wash, and then we will go out to eat and drink. Yes?' he said, tipping her chin up so he could meet her eyes.

'Yes,' she said, smiling up at him.

31

In the next two weeks, Anna began to settle into a routine. Or at least, find things to occupy herself during the long, lonely hours when Jens was at the Conservatory.

Winter was bearing down, and their room was freezing in the mornings, so she'd often get back into bed after Jens left for the Conservatory, huddling under the warmth of the woollen blankets while waiting for the coal fire she'd kindled in the small fireplace to build up a little heat. Then she would wash and dress, and make her way outside and through the streets of Leipzig to the market to buy bread and slices of cold meat to feed herself at lunchtime.

The only hot meal they ate was that provided by Frau Schneider in the evening. More often than not, it would be some type of sausage with potatoes or soggy bread dumplings, in a nondescript sauce. Anna felt herself longing for the taste of freshly grown vegetables and the wholesome fare of her childhood.

She spent many long hours trying to compose the letters she knew she must send to Herr Bayer and her parents. With Lars' pen between her fingers, she wondered if he had sailed for America as he'd planned. And in her lowest moments, wondered if she should have gone with him after all.

Leipzig

1st October 1876

Dear Herr Bayer,

You will already know, as I am not there, that I have left to go to Leipzig. Herr Halvorsen and I are married. And happy. I wish to thank you for all you gave me. Please keep my wages from the Christiania Theatre to pay for some of it and I hope you can sell the gowns I left behind for they were very fine.

Herr Bayer, I am sorry I could not love you.

Yours,

Anna Landvik

Then she took another piece of paper and began a second letter.

Kjære Mor and Far,

I am married to Jens Halvorsen and I have moved to Leipzig. My husband is studying at the Music Conservatory here and I am keeping house for us. I am happy. I miss you all. And Norway.

Anna

Anna did not give an address, too frightened and guilty to receive their recriminations. In the afternoons, she would take a walk in the park or meander through the city streets, even though her cape was inadequate against the bitter wind, just so she could be a part of humanity. Evidence of Leipzig's musical heritage seemed to be everywhere, from various streets named after famous composers, to statues depicting their likenesses, to the very houses that Mendelssohn and Schumann themselves had once lived in.

Her favourite spot to visit was the spectacular Neues Theater, home to the Leipzig Opera Company, with its towering colonnaded entrance and enormous arched windows. She would often gaze up at it, wondering if she could ever dare hope to perform in such a place. One day, she even plucked up the courage to knock at the stage door and tried to communicate with the stage-door-keeper. But no amount of hand gestures could convey to the man that she was looking for employment as a singer.

Disheartened and feeling more and more like she didn't belong, she had found refuge in the Thomaskirche, a very grand gothic building over which a beautiful white bell tower soared. Although it was so much larger than the little church in Heddal, the smell and atmosphere reminded her of home. The day she had finally posted the letters to Herr Bayer and her parents, she had retreated there. Sitting down in a pew, she bent her head and prayed for redemption, strength and guidance.

'Dear Lord, forgive me for the terrible lies the letters contain. I think the worst one is that' – Anna swallowed hard – 'I am happy. I am not. Not at all. But I know I do not deserve sympathy or forgiveness for any of it.'

Then she had felt a gentle hand on her shoulder. '*Warum so traurig, mein Kind?*'

She looked up, startled, to see an old pastor smiling down

at her. '*Kein Deutsch, nur Norwegisch*,' she had managed to say, as Jens had taught her.

'Ah!' said the pastor. 'I know a little of the Norwegian language.'

Even though she tried her best to speak to him, his Norwegian was as limited as her German, and Anna had realised that Jens would have to speak to him about their marriage and then convince the pastor of their faith.

The highlight of her day was their supper together as she listened to Jens talk about the Conservatory: the other students who hailed from all over Europe, the rows of Blüthner practice pianos and the wonderful tutors, many of whom were also musicians in the Leipzig Gewandhaus Orchestra. Tonight it had been the Stradivarius violin he'd been allowed to play which he'd rhapsodised about.

'The difference in the quality of the sound is rather like that of a barmaid humming to a soprano singing an aria,' he enthused. 'It's all so wonderful! Not only do I get to play every day, on the piano as well as my violin, but the classes I take in Musical Composition, Harmony and Musical Analysis are teaching me so much. And in Music History, I've already studied works by Chopin and Liszt that I had never even heard of! Soon I will be playing Chopin's Scherzo No. 2 in a student concert at the Gewandhaus hall.'

'I'm so glad you're happy,' she said, trying to sound enthusiastic. 'Is there anyone you could ask if there might be a chance for me to sing?'

'Anna, I know you keep asking me,' Jens replied in between bites of his food, 'but I tell you that if you do not learn any German, it will be difficult for you to do anything in this town.'

'Surely there is someone who can just hear me? I know the Italian words to "Violetta's Aria", and I can learn the German words later.'

'Hush, my love.' Jens reached out and took her hand. 'I will try again to make some enquiries for you.'

After supper, there was always the discomfiting bedtime routine. She would change into her nightgown in the water closet, then hurry under the covers, where Jens already lay. He would wrap his arms around her and she would relax against his chest, drinking in his musky smell. He would kiss her then and she would feel her body respond to him, just as his did to her, both of them wanting more . . . But then she would pull away from him and he would sigh heavily.

'I just can't,' she'd whispered into the darkness one night. 'You know we must be married first.'

'I know, my darling. Of course we will be married eventually, but before then, surely we can—'

'No, Jens! I just . . . cannot. You know I have found a church where we can wed soon, but you must speak to the pastor to make the arrangements.'

'Anna, I simply do not have time to spare. My studies require my full attention. Besides, many at the Conservatory have new ideas. There are radicals amongst the students who believe the Church is simply there to control the people. They look to a more enlightened view, such as that of Goethe in his play *Faust*. The story deals with all aspects of the spiritual and metaphysical. I have been lent a copy to read by a friend, and this weekend I will take you to Auerbachs Keller, the bar that Goethe himself frequented and where he was inspired by a mural to write his classic.'

Anna had never heard of Goethe and his apparently illuminating work. All she knew was that she had to be married in the eyes of God before she could be in a physical union with Jens.

Christmas arrived, reminding Anna that she and Jens had been in Leipzig for three months. She had wanted to go to the *Christmette*, the midnight mass at the church, and Pastor Meyer had even given her a leaflet of traditional German hymns. She had been humming '*Stille Nacht*' to herself, excited at the prospect of singing with other people again. But Jens had insisted they should spend Christmas Eve at the home of Frederick, one of his fellow music students.

Clutching a mug of hot *Glühwein*, Anna sat silently next to Jens at the table, listening to the guttural German and hardly understanding a word of it. Jens, who was already drunk, made no attempt to translate for her. Others played instruments after dinner, but Jens never once suggested she should sing.

As they walked home through the frosty night, Anna heard the bells chime midnight, announcing the start of Christmas Day. The sound of carol singing came from the church as they passed it, and she glanced up at Jens, his face red from alcohol and the cheer of the evening. Sending up a silent prayer for her family celebrating without her in Heddal, she wished with all her heart that she were there too.

Throughout January and February, Anna thought she might go mad with boredom. Her daily routine, which had seemed bearable to begin with due to its novelty, now seemed insufferably dull. The snow had come to Leipzig and it was sometimes so cold that her fingers and toes went numb. She spent the days fetching up buckets of coal for the fire, washing clothes in the freezing scullery, or making pitiful attempts to make sense of the words in *Faust*, which Jens had told her to study to improve her German.

'I am so very stupid!' she berated herself one afternoon, slapping the book closed and bursting into tears of frustration, something she now did with alarming regularity.

Jens became ever more deeply involved with the Conservatory and its students, often arriving home after a concert at midnight smelling of beer and tobacco smoke. She would feign sleep as his arms reached out for her and tentatively caressed her body through her nightgown. She'd hear him swear under his breath at her lack of response, and as her heart beat against her chest, he'd roll over with a grunt and begin to snore. Only then could she sigh with relief and go to sleep herself.

Nowadays, she mostly ate supper alone, surveying the other residents of the lodging house from under her eyelashes. Many of them changed weekly, and Anna presumed they were travelling salesmen of some kind. However, there was one elderly gentleman who seemed to be a permanent resident like her, and took supper alone each evening. His nose was always buried in a book and he was finely dressed in an old-fashioned manner.

The gentleman became an object of fascination as she ate; Anna spent hours wondering what his story was, and why he had chosen to spend his sunset years here. Sometimes, when it was only the two of them for supper, he would nod and say '*Guten Abend*' as he walked in and '*Gute Nacht*' as he walked out. She decided he reminded her rather of Herr Bayer, with his head of thick white hair, bushy moustache and courteous airs.

'If I am even missing Herr Bayer, then I really must be miserable,' she muttered to herself one evening as she left the dining room.

A few nights later, the gentleman stood up and walked across the room with his ever-present book in his hand. '*Gute Nacht*.' He nodded to her as he approached the door to leave the room. Then in afterthought, he turned back to her.

'*Sprechen sie Deutsch?*'

'*Nein, Norwegisch*.'

'You are from Norway?' he said in surprise.

'Yes,' she replied, delighted he had answered her fluently in her native language.

'I am a Dane, you see, but my mother was from Christiania. She taught me the language when I was young.'

After the long weeks of being unable to communicate properly with anyone but Jens since she had arrived, Anna wanted to hug him. 'Then I am delighted to meet you, sir.'

She watched the man pause in thought by the door and survey her. 'You say you don't speak any German?'

'No more than a few words.'

'Then how on earth do you manage in this town?'

'To be honest, sir, I don't.'

'Your husband, he is working here in Leipzig?'

'No, he attends the Conservatory.'

'Ah, a musician! No wonder he rarely joins you in the evening for supper. May I ask what your name is?'

'I am Anna Halvorsen.'

'And I am Stefan Hougaard.' He gave her a small bow. 'And pleased to make your acquaintance. You do not work then, Fru Halvorsen?'

'No, sir, I do not. Although I hope soon to gain employment as a singer.'

'Well, in the meantime, perhaps I can assist you with the task of studying German? Or at least, give you a better grasp of the basics,' he suggested. 'We could meet here after breakfast if you wish, under the full glare of our landlady, so that your husband would not feel as though anything improper was occurring.'

'That is most kind of you, sir, and indeed, I would be very grateful for your help. But I warn you, I am a slow student and not good with my letters, even in my own language.'

'Well then, we shall just have to work hard together, won't we? So, tomorrow morning at ten?'

'Yes. I will be here.'

Anna went to bed that night feeling far more cheerful, even though Jens was yet again absent from her side, saying he was rehearsing for a concert. Simply being able to converse with another human being had been a joy and anything she could do to add a little variety to her days had to be a good thing. And if she could learn at least a little German, perhaps there would be a chance of singing in public again . . .

As the first blossoms began to appear on the trees, Anna spent her mornings downstairs, trying to teach her stubborn brain to memorise and repeat the words Herr Hougaard taught her. After the first few days, he insisted he should accompany her out on the street when she was making her daily trip to the market. He would stand a short distance away and listen carefully as she followed his instructions and bade the vendor a good morning, then requested her goods and paid for them before saying goodbye. These missions unnerved her at first, and often she would stumble over the phrases she had learnt, but slowly, her confidence began to grow.

Anna's forays into the city with Herr Hougaard began to expand as she improved over the following weeks, culminating in her ordering lunch for both of them at a restaurant, which she insisted on paying for as a thank you.

She still knew little about him, only that his wife had died some years ago, leaving him a widower. He had moved from the country to the city so that he could enjoy all the benefits of the cultural scene in Leipzig without having to care for himself domestically.

'What more do I need than a full stomach, clean sheets and clothes washed regularly, and a magnificent concert just a few minutes' walk away to stir my senses?' he had said with a broad smile.

Herr Hougaard had been surprised that Jens had not asked her to watch the many concerts he told her he performed in. He'd said they didn't have the money to spare, but Herr Hougaard said they were often free. In fact, Anna was seeing less and less of her 'husband', and just recently, there had been occasions when he hadn't come home at all. She thought one morning, as she opened the window to let in the spring air before walking downstairs for her daily lesson, that if it wasn't for Herr Hougaard, she may well have thrown herself under a tram months ago.

It was on one of their trips into the city centre at lunchtime that Anna was startled to spot Jens sitting in the window of the Thüringer Hof, one of the best restaurants in Leipzig. It was the place where the local aristocracy gathered in their fine clothes, their carriages lined up outside, with horses waiting patiently to take them home after a sumptuous lunch. Just as her life in Christiania had once been, Anna thought ruefully.

She strained to look between the carriages at Jens' dining partner. It was clearly a woman, by the bright scarlet hat with a feather in it that was bobbing as the figure talked. Inching closer, much to Herr Hougaard's amusement, she saw the woman had dark hair and what her mother would call a Roman profile, which in essence meant a big nose.

'What on earth are you staring at, Anna?' Herr Hougaard walked up behind her. 'You look like The Little Match Girl in my very own Hans Christian Andersen fairy tale. Will you wish to go and press your nose against the window, as she did?' he chuckled.

'No.' Anna tore her eyes away as Jens and the woman leant in close to talk. 'I thought it was someone I knew.'

That night, Anna forced herself to stay awake until Jens returned home, well after midnight. These days, he threw his clothes off in the water closet and slid into bed in the dark, so as not to disturb her. But of course he did. Every night.

'What are you still doing awake?' he asked her, obviously surprised to see the oil lamp still alight as he entered the room.

'I thought I'd wait up for you. I feel we hardly see each other any more.'

'I know,' Jens sighed as he collapsed into bed next to her and Anna knew he'd been drinking again. 'Sadly, this is the life of a music student at the famous Leipzig Conservatory. I barely have time in the day to eat!'

'Even at luncheon?' The words had fallen off her tongue before she could stop them.

Jens turned to her. 'What do you mean?'

'I saw you taking lunch in town today.'

'Really? Then why did you not come in and say hello?'

'Because I was hardly dressed for such a place. And you were deep in conversation with a woman.'

'Ah, yes, Baroness von Gottfried. She is a great benefactor of the Conservatory and its students. She came to a concert last week where four of us young composers were actually given the chance to perform one of our own short pieces. It's the composition I've been working on, remember?'

No, she didn't remember, but then Jens was never here to tell her anything any more.

'I see.' She swallowed hard, a wave of indignation welling up inside her as she wondered why, if he'd been premiering a new work, he hadn't invited her to watch.

'The baroness invited me for lunch to discuss possible plans for having my compositions heard on a wider scale. She has many contacts in all the great cities of Europe. Paris, Florence, Copenhagen . . .' Jens smiled dreamily and put his hands behind his head. 'Can you imagine, Anna? Having my music played in the great concert halls of the world? That would show Herr Hennum now, wouldn't it?'

'Yes, undoubtedly it would give you great pleasure.'

'What is the matter, Anna?' asked Jens, reacting to the ice in her voice. 'Come now, spit it out. You have something to say to me.'

'Yes, I do!' Anna could contain her anger no longer. 'From one week to another, I hardly see you, and yet now you tell me that you are giving concerts to which I, your betrothed, and to all the world your wife, am not even invited. You come home after midnight most evenings and, occasionally, not at all! And I sit here, waiting for you like some faithful dog, with no friends, nothing to do but chores and no prospect of continuing my own singing career! Then to crown it all, I see you at one of the best restaurants, taking lunch with another woman. There! That's what I have to say.'

Once it was clear that Anna had finished her outburst, Jens stood up from the bed. 'And now, Anna, I will tell you what I have to say: can you imagine how it is for me to lie in bed every night next to the woman I love, to be so close to her beautiful body but not be allowed to touch beyond a caress or a kiss? My God, in some ways, what small allowance you deign to make me only adds to my frustration! I lie here night after night dreaming of making love to you, to the point where I cannot rest. It is better for me and my sanity if I am not lying with you, longing for you, but instead arriving home as late and as drunk as possible so I will sink into oblivion. Yes!' Jens folded his arms defiantly. 'This . . . *life* that we are living together is neither one thing nor the other. You are my wife, but not my wife. You are withdrawn and sullen . . . and you give every impression that you would like nothing better than to go home. Anna, please remember, it was *your* decision to come here. Why do you not leave? It is obvious to all you are not happy. That *I* make you unhappy!'

'Jens, you are being very unfair indeed! You know as well as I do that I am desperate to be wed so that we can build a proper life together as husband and wife. But every time I ask you to come and meet the pastor, you say you are too weary or too busy! How dare you blame me for this situation when it is not of my making!'

'No, that part is not, you are right.' Jens' expression softened. 'But why do you think I do not wish to see the pastor yet?'

'Because you do not wish to marry me?'

'Anna' – he gave an exasperated chuckle – 'you know how desperate I am to be a real husband to you. But I don't think you realise what such an event costs. You would need a dress, attendants, a wedding feast . . . it's what any bride deserves. And what I wish you to have. But there are simply no funds for such an event. We live hand to mouth as it is.'

All the fire went out of Anna as she finally understood. 'Oh . . . but Jens, I don't need any of these things. I just want to be married to you.'

'Well, if you speak the truth, then we will marry immediately. Sadly, it won't be anything like the wedding you would have imagined as a child, though.'

'I know.' Anna swallowed hard at the thought that none of her family would be there. Not Mor and Far or Knut and Sigrid. Pastor Erslev would not preside over the ceremony and she would not wear the village wedding crown. 'But I do not care.'

Jens sat back down on the bed and kissed her tenderly. 'We will meet with your pastor and set a date.'

32

The marriage ceremony at the Thomaskirche was brief, simple and private, with Anna wearing a plain white dress she had bought with Frøken Olsdatter's money for the occasion and white flowers in her hair. Pastor Meyer smiled genially as he spoke the vows that would bind them to each other for the rest of their lives.

'*Ja, ich will*,' they each said in turn, and Jens slid his grandmother's simple gold band around her finger, his touch warm and sure. Anna closed her eyes as he kissed her chastely on the lips and, with relief, felt the Lord's forgiveness in her heart.

The small wedding party moved on to a *Bierkeller*, where Jens' musician friends played an impromptu wedding march as the newly married couple entered, and the other patrons raised their beer steins in congratulations. Over a simple meal of German wedding soup, Anna felt the reassuring touch of her husband's hand on her knee. Thanks to Herr Hougaard, she could join in the jokes and toasts with Jens' friends, and she no longer felt like a stranger in a strange world.

As they mounted the stairs to their room later that night, Jens' fingertips rested on the base of her spine, sending shivers of nervous anticipation through her.

'Look at you,' he murmured, his eyes dark with desire as he closed the door behind him, 'so tiny, so innocent, so perfect . . .' He reached for her then and pulled her into his arms, his hands travelling boldly over her body. 'I must have my wife,' he whispered into her ear, as he tipped her face up to kiss her. 'Is it any wonder I looked elsewhere for comfort?' At this, she pulled away from him.

'What do you mean?!'

'Nothing, nothing, really . . . I only mean that I want *you*.'

Before she could reply, he was kissing her, his hands caressing her back, her thighs, her breasts . . . and despite herself, it suddenly felt wonderful, natural, that her clothes and all the rest of her barriers that had separated them were finally removed so that they could become one. Carrying her to the bed, Jens stripped off his own clothes and moved to lie on top of her. Anna's own hands tentatively explored the hard muscles of his back. As he entered her, she was ready for him, knowing her body had been subconsciously practising this ever since she'd first laid eyes on him.

The process was strange to her, but as he sighed and then collapsed onto the pillow beside her, tucking her head into his shoulder, all of the horror stories she'd heard about this moment faded into oblivion. For now, he was truly hers and she was his.

For the next few weeks, Jens was home on time for supper, both of them desperate to finish their food and retire upstairs to their room. It was obvious to Anna that her husband was experienced in the art of lovemaking, and as he became less tentative with her, and she too allowed herself to relax, each night became a wonderful adventure. The loneliness of the past few months was vanquished as Anna fully understood the difference between friends and lovers. And it seemed as if their previous roles were reversed, as she constantly yearned to feel his touch on her.

'Good Lord, wife,' he said one night as he lay panting beside her, 'I'm beginning to wish I'd never introduced you to this new game. You're positively insatiable!'

And she was. Because these moments were the only part of him she fully owned. When he left her arms in the morning, and dressed to leave for the Conservatory, she saw his expression change and felt his thoughts wander away from her. She'd taken to walking with him to the Conservatory, where he'd embrace her, tell her he loved her and then disappear inside the doors to the other world that consumed him.

My enemy, Anna sometimes thought as she turned away and retraced her footsteps back home.

Herr Hougaard had noticed the new spring in her step and her ready smile as she greeted him for her lesson in the mornings.

'You seem happier now, Frau Halvorsen, and I am glad for it,' he'd said.

Spurred on by her newfound positivity, Anna's German had improved apace. She now spoke with a confidence that Herr Hougaard applauded her for. And it seemed as if each new word she grasped would lead to a flurry of others.

She resolved that she would no longer simply sit and wait for Jens to find her a singing position. She wrote a letter to Herr Grieg, telling him of her move to Leipzig, along with a request to perhaps gain a singing audition from anyone he knew in the town. Jens had enquired at the Conservatory for the address of C. F. Peters, Herr Grieg's Leipzig music publishers. Finding number 10 on Talstraße, she hand-delivered her letter to a young man who worked in the ground-floor shop, selling the sheet music. Every night afterwards, she prayed that Herr Grieg would receive her missive and reply.

One day in June, when she had managed to hold a fifteen-minute conversation in German without a single mistake, Herr Hougaard gave her a small bow.

'Frau Halvorsen, that was word-perfect. I salute you.'

'*Danke*,' Anna chuckled.

'And I must also tell you that I am soon off to take the waters in Baden-Baden as I always do in the summer months. It becomes far too hot for me here in the city and I have been feeling particularly fatigued of late. Are you and Herr Halvorsen departing for Norway when his term ends?'

'He has certainly not told me if we are.'

'I leave tomorrow morning, so I will see you again, if luck will have it, in the autumn.'

'Yes, I hope so.' Anna rose as he did, wishing that she could show her affection and gratitude to him in a less formal way than polite manners required. 'I am truly indebted to you, sir.'

'Frau Halvorsen, rest assured it has been a pleasure,' he said as he took his leave.

As Herr Hougaard left for Baden-Baden, Anna also noticed a change in Jens. He wasn't home as usual for supper and when he did arrive, he was jumpy, like a cat on hot bricks. When he made love to her, she felt a new distance.

'What is it?' she asked him one night. 'I know something is wrong.'

'Nothing,' he said sharply as he pulled out of her arms and rolled over. 'I'm just tired, that's all.'

'Jens, *min elskede*, I know you. Please tell me what it is.'

He didn't move for a while, then rolled back to face her. 'All right, I have a dilemma and I don't know what to do.'

'Then for heaven's sake, tell me what it is. Maybe I can help.'

'The problem is, you won't like it at all.'

'I see. Then you had better tell me.'

'Well, you remember the woman who you saw me having lunch with?'

'The baroness. How could I forget?' said Anna, bristling at the mention of her.

'She has asked me to go with her to Paris for the summer, where she and her husband have a château near the Palace of Versailles. She holds weekly musical soirées for the great and the good of the arts world and she wishes me to premiere my new compositions there. Of course, it is the most wonderful opportunity for my work to be heard. Baroness von Gottfried knows everyone and, as I told you, she is a great champion of young composers. She tells me that even Herr Grieg has played at one of her events.'

'Well then, of course we must go. I don't understand why this should be a dilemma for you.'

This elicited a groan from Jens. 'Anna, that is why I have not told you. The problem is, I cannot take you with me.'

'Oh. May I ask why not?'

'Because . . .' Jens sighed. 'Baroness von Gottfried doesn't know about you. I have never mentioned that I am married. To be truthful, I thought it might prejudice her good favour towards me if I did. At the time I met her, things between you and I were . . . difficult, and we were living as little more than brother and sister, or as friends. So there we are. She has no knowledge of your existence.'

'Then why do you not tell her now that I *do* exist?' Anna's voice was low and cold as she digested the underlying meaning of what her husband was saying.

'Because . . . I am frightened. Yes, Anna, your Jens is frightened of the fact that the baroness will no longer wish me to accompany her to Paris if she does know.'

'You wish for the baroness to believe you are available, so she will help you in your career?'

'Yes, Anna. Oh Lord, what an ass I am . . .'

'Yes, you are.' Anna watched dispassionately as Jens pulled the pillow over his head and buried himself beneath it like a naughty child being chastised by his mother.

'Forgive me, Anna, I truly hate myself. But at least I've given you the full facts.'

'How long does she want you to go for?'

'Just for the summer,' said Jens, emerging from underneath the pillow. 'You must understand that I am doing this all for us, to further my career and earn money so you can move from this room and one day have a proper home, as you truly deserve.'

And so you can taste the fame you believe you deserve, she thought harshly. 'Then you must go.'

'Really?' Jens looked suspicious. 'Why on earth would you let me?'

'Simply because you have put me in an untenable position.

If I forbid it, you will sulk here the entire summer and blame me for your misfortune. And despite others' persuasion to the contrary' – Anna took a deep breath – 'I trust you.'

'You do?' He looked amazed. 'Then you truly are a goddess amongst women!'

'Jens, you are my husband. What is the point of this marriage if I cannot?' she replied grimly.

'Thank you. Thank you, my darling wife.'

Jens departed a few days later, leaving Anna with enough money to see her comfortably through the next few weeks until he returned. His overwhelming gratitude for her generosity had been enough to convince her that she'd made the right decision. Every night before he left, she'd lain in bed with him, and seen him staring at her in wonder.

'I love you, Anna, I love you . . .' he'd said over and over again. And then, on the morning of his departure, he'd held her to him as if he couldn't bear to let her go.

'Promise you'll wait for me, my darling wife, whatever happens?'

'Of course, Jens. You are my husband.'

Anna got through the stifling Leipzig summer on sheer determination. With the windows thrown open to let in any breath of wind that reached the narrow street between the houses, she lay naked on the bed at night, perspiring from the heat.

She finished Goethe's *Faust* and sweated through any other book she could borrow from the town library to improve her German vocabulary. She also purchased fabric from the market and took her sewing to the park, sitting underneath a shady tree as she laboriously fashioned herself a dress out of fustian, along with a warmer cloak for the winter to come. As she measured herself for the clothes, she fretted at the fact that she was not yet twenty, but her waistline was already expanding, as other women's seemed to do once they were wed. She visited the Thomaskirche every other day, both for spiritual and physical succour, finding the cool interior of the church the only place she could escape from the heat.

She wrote regularly to Jens at the address he'd given to her before he left for Paris, but received only two brief notes in return, which said that he was well and busy meeting many of Baroness von Gottfried's important contacts. He said his composition had gone down well at the recital, and that he was working on something new in his spare time.

The château is inspiring my best work yet! How could one not feel creative in such a beautiful place as this?

As the summer dragged on interminably, Anna refused to succumb to the dark thoughts that wormed their way into her mind about Jens' rich and powerful female sponsor. He would return to her soon enough, she told herself firmly, and they could continue their married life together.

Jens had never given her an exact date for his return, but as Anna was eating breakfast one morning in early September, her landlady, Frau Schneider, asked pointedly if her husband was due back in Leipzig today, in time for the start of the new term at the Conservatory tomorrow.

'I'm sure he will be, yes,' Anna replied evenly, determined not to show her surprise. She made her way up the stairs immediately to comb her hair and change into her new dress. She stared at her reflection in the small looking glass she kept on top of the chest, and thought she looked well. There was no doubt her cheeks had filled out since Jens had left and she hoped he would approve – he, like her family, had often teased her that she was too thin.

Anna didn't leave the stuffy room for the rest of the day, nervous and excited at the thought of her husband's return.

But as dusk began to fall, so did her spirits. Surely, she thought, Jens would not miss the first day of the new term at his beloved Conservatory? Yet as midnight struck and the bells from the churches chimed in a new day, Anna removed her dress and lay down on the bed in her petticoat. She knew there would be no more trains into Leipzig station tonight.

Three days on, and Anna was frantic with worry. She walked to the Conservatory and waited until the students poured out of its doors, smoking and chatting. Recognising Frederick, the young man with whom they'd spent last Christmas Eve, she walked up to him shyly.

'Excuse me for disturbing you, Herr Frederick,' said Anna, unaware of his surname, 'but have you seen Jens at school this week?'

Frederick stared at her, taking a moment to recognise who she was. And then glanced at his friends as something passed between them. 'No, Frau Halvorsen, I'm afraid I have not.

Has anybody else?' he asked the group around him. They shook their heads, their eyes averted in embarrassment.

'I am concerned that something has happened to him in Paris, for I have not heard from him in over a month now and he was due back for the start of term.' Anna twisted the wedding ring around her finger in agitation. 'Is there anyone else here at the Conservatory who might know of his whereabouts?'

'I can ask Herr Halvorsen's tutor if he has heard anything. But I must be honest with you, Frau Halvorsen, I was under the impression that his plan was to settle in Paris. He told me he only had enough money to fund one year's tuition here. Although, of course, the school may have offered him a scholarship to stay on. Did they?' he enquired.

'I . . .' Anna felt the world spin about her and she staggered slightly. Frederick caught her arm and steadied her.

'Frau Halvorsen, you are obviously unwell.'

'No, no, I am very well indeed,' she said, pulling out of his grasp, pride squaring her chin. '*Danke*, Herr Frederick.' She nodded her thanks and walked away with her head held as high as she could manage.

'Oh my dear Lord, oh my Lord,' she muttered as she struggled home through the busy streets, still breathless and dizzy.

Collapsing onto the bed, Anna reached for the glass of water beside it and drank deeply to ease her faintness and her thirst.

'It cannot be true. It *cannot* be true. If he intends to stay in Paris, why has he not sent for me?' The bare walls of the room could not give her the answer she needed. 'He would not abandon me, no, he would not,' she convinced herself. 'He loves me, I am his wife . . .'

After a sleepless night, during which Anna thought she might go mad with the thoughts battering her mind, she staggered down to breakfast to find Frau Schneider standing in the hallway reading a letter.

'Good morning, Frau Halvorsen. I have just received very sad news. It seems your friend, Herr Hougaard, died of a heart attack two weeks ago. His family wish me to pack up his belongings and they'll send a cart to collect them.'

Anna's hand flew to her mouth. 'Oh no, please, no.' And at this point, the world went black.

She woke to find herself in Frau Schneider's private sitting room, lying on the sofa with a cool cloth on her head.

'There, there,' the older woman crooned. 'I know how fond of him you were, as was I. It must be most upsetting for you, with your husband still away. And in your condition too.'

Anna followed the woman's gaze to her stomach. 'I . . . What do you mean by my "condition"?'

'Why, your pregnancy, of course. Do you know when the baby is due? You're so very small, Frau Halvorsen, you really must take care.'

Anna felt the world spin again and thought she might vomit over Frau Schneider's velvet-covered sofa.

'Why don't you try and drink a little water?' Frau Schneider suggested, stepping towards her and proffering a glass.

Anna did so, as the woman chattered on.

'I was going to speak with you about the future when your husband returned. One of my rules here is no children. Their cries disturb the other guests.'

If Anna thought things could not get any worse, it seemed they just had.

'However, until he is back, I feel it is hardly fair to turn you out on the street. So I will be happy to have you stay here until the birth,' she said magnanimously.

'*Danke*,' Anna whispered, knowing that the woman's brief show of empathy was at an end and that she wished to get on with her morning. She stood up. 'I am well now. Thank you for your kindness and my apologies for the trouble I've caused you.' She nodded courteously to the woman before making her exit to return to her room.

For the rest of the day she lay motionless on the bed. If she stayed still with her eyes closed, perhaps the terrible things that had happened – and all that was happening *now* – would go away. But if she moved a single muscle, that would mean that she was still alive and breathing and she'd have to face reality.

'Oh Lord, please help me,' she begged.

Later, forced to rise to visit the water closet, Anna took off her dress and stood in her bloomers and chemise. Lifting the chemise, she forced her eyes downwards and acknowledged the gentle swelling of her belly. Why on earth had she never connected her growing waistline to pregnancy?

'You silly little idiot!' she wailed. 'How could you not have known? You are a naive, stupid peasant from the country, just as Herr Bayer told you!' She went to a drawer to retrieve her ink pen and paper, then sat on the bed and began to write to her husband in Paris.

'There's a letter for you this morning,' Frau Schneider said as she handed it to Anna. The child – for that was how the landlady thought of her diminutive lodger – looked up at her with hollow, sunken eyes, and for the first time, Frau Schneider saw the tiniest glimmer of hope appear in them. 'It has a French mark upon it. I am sure it must be from your husband.'

'*Danke*.'

Frau Schneider nodded, and retreated from the dining room to give the child some privacy to read it. In the past two weeks, it was Anna's ghost who had emerged from her room to look disinterestedly at whatever food Frau Schneider put in front of her, and she would take it away untouched. Frau Schneider sighed as she went to the scullery to wash the breakfast plates in the wooden barrel. She'd seen it all before. And although she felt some sympathy for Anna, she was hoping the problem would be resolved by this letter. She had learnt long ago that her residents' lives, however desperate, could not be her responsibility.

Up in her room, Anna opened the letter with trembling fingers. She had written to Jens weeks ago at the chateau, telling him of the baby. Perhaps this was finally a reply.

Paris

13th September 1877

My darling Anna,

Forgive me for taking so long to write, but I wanted to be settled here before I did so. I am living in an apartment in Paris, and taking composition lessons with Augustus Theron, a renowned professor of music. He is helping me to improve greatly. Baroness von Gottfried has been very generous to act as my benefactor and sponsor, introducing me to everyone who can help. She has even arranged a soirée in November for me to play my work to Paris society.

As I have already told you, I felt it inappropriate to tell her about us, but the truth is, Anna, that I did not wish to worry you when I left. The fact is, my money had run out and if it wasn't for the baroness's generosity, we would both be in the gutter now. I left you all I had in Leipzig, and I know you have the coins that Frøken Olsdatter gave you, so I pray you are not suffering.

Anna, I understand you must see my departure and non-return as a terrible betrayal of our love. But please believe that I DO love you. And what I have done I have done for us and our future. When my music begins to be noticed, I will be able to provide for us independently and I will come for you, my love. I swear it on the Bible you hold so dear. And on our union.

Please, I beg you, Anna, wait for me, as you promised. And try to understand what I do is for both of us. It may seem hard, but have faith in me and trust me that this is the best way.

I miss you, my love. So much.

I love you with all my heart.

Your

Jens

Anna let the letter fall to the floor and put her head in her hands, trying to collect her racing thoughts. There was no mention of the baby – had he not received her letter? And how much longer was she meant to wait for him?

This man will break your heart and destroy you . . . Herr Bayer's words echoed in her mind, eating away her resolve to trust her husband.

Somehow, Anna staggered through the next month. Having no idea when Jens would return, she watched Frøken Olsdatter's coins diminish, and decided that she must look in the city for some form of work.

For a week, she trudged the streets of Leipzig, enquiring about becoming a waitress or a pot washer, but the second any would-be employer saw her burgeoning belly, they shook their heads and sent her on her way.

'Frau Schneider, do you perhaps need any help in the kitchen or with the cleaning?' she asked her landlady one day. 'Now Herr Hougaard has gone and I wait for my husband to return, I find myself bored. I thought I might make myself useful.'

'It is not idle work we do here, but if you are sure,' the landlady replied, eying her carefully, 'then yes, I could do with some help.'

Frau Schneider started her off in the kitchen, preparing breakfast, which meant Anna had to rise at five thirty in the morning. After washing the pots, she went up to the lodgers' rooms and changed whatever bedding was necessary. The afternoons were hers, but she was back in the kitchen at five, peeling the potatoes and preparing the supper. Anna thought her situation ironic, given her lack of natural aptitude in the kitchen. It was hard endless graft, and her belly dragged painfully as she walked up and down the stairs, but at least she was so exhausted that she slept through the night.

'What have I come to?' she asked herself ruefully as she lay in bed one evening. 'The toast of Christiania, turned into a scullery maid in a few short months.' Then she prayed, as she did every night, for her husband to return to her.

'Dear Lord, please do not let my faith and love in my husband be wrong. And for all those who have doubted him to be right.'

As the chill winds of November began to blow, Anna felt a sudden pain in her stomach in the middle of the night. After fumbling to light the oil lamp beside the bed, she stood up to ease the discomfort and to her horror, saw the sheets were covered in blood. The pains clamped across her belly in regular spasms and she stifled her screams of agony. Too frightened to call out for help and incur the displeasure of Frau Schneider, Anna laboured alone through the long hours and as dawn appeared, she looked down to see a tiny infant lying motionless between her legs.

She noticed there was a piece of skin attached to its navel, which seemed to be also attached to her. She could hold her terror in no longer, and screamed with all the pain, fear and exhaustion she felt. Frau Schneider appeared at the door within seconds, took one look at the carnage on the bed and immediately ran from the room to fetch the midwife.

Anna was roused from an exhausted and feverish sleep by soft hands smoothing back her hair and placing a cloth on her forehead.

'There, there, *Liebe*, I'm going to cut the cord and clean you up,' the voice murmured gently.

'Is she dying?' Frau Schneider's familiar voice cut into Anna's consciousness. 'Really, I knew I should have asked her to go the minute I saw she was with child. This is what comes of letting my soft heart rule my head.'

'No, the young lady will be well, but sadly the babe is stillborn.'

'Well, that is most tragic, but I'm afraid I must get on.' With that, Frau Schneider left the room with a cluck of distaste.

An hour later, Anna was tidied up and sitting in clean sheets. The midwife had wrapped her baby in a shawl and handed it to Anna to say goodbye.

'It was a little girl, dear. Try not to fret. I'm sure there'll be more babes for you in the future.'

Anna looked down at her daughter's perfect features, yet already the skin had a bluish hue to it. She kissed the baby tenderly on its tiny forehead, too numb to even cry, then allowed the midwife to remove it from her arms.

33

'Now that you are stronger I wish to speak with you,' said Frau Schneider as she removed the untouched breakfast plate from Anna's lap. The child was still in bed after a week, too feeble to climb out. Frau Schneider had decided enough was enough.

Anna nodded listlessly, knowing full well what the woman would say. And hardly caring if she *did* get thrown out on the street. She didn't care about anything any longer.

'You have had no letter from your husband since early autumn.'

'No.'

'Did he say when he would return?'

'No. Only that he would.'

'And you still believe him?'

'Why would he lie to me?'

Frau Schneider gazed at Anna in despair at her naivety. 'Have you money to pay me for the past week's rent?'

'Yes.'

'And next week? And the week after that?'

'I have not looked in my tin, Frau Schneider. I will look now.' Delving under the mattress, Anna retrieved the tin.

Frau Schneider did not need to be told there were few coins left in it. She watched the child open it and saw an expression of fear pass across her blue eyes. Anna took out two coins and handed them to her landlady, then snapped the tin shut.

'*Danke*. And what about the midwife's payment? Can you give me that as well? She handed me the bill when she left. And then, of course, there is the question of your child's burial. Your babe is still lying in the town mortuary, and unless you wish her to be buried in a pauper's grave, you must arrange payment for the service and plot of earth in the churchyard.'

'How much will that cost?'

'I cannot tell you. But I think in truth, it is obvious to us both it is more than you have.'

'Yes,' Anna agreed bleakly.

'Child, I am not a bad woman, but neither am I a saint. I have become fond of you and I know you are a good, God-fearing girl who has fallen low because of a man. And I am not so completely heartless as to throw you out onto the streets after what you have suffered. But we must both be realistic about the situation. This room is the best I have to offer to guests and the amount you have earned from me doing the chores barely covers two nights of the weekly rent. And then there are your other debts . . .'

Frau Schneider looked at Anna for a reaction, but there was not a flicker in her dead eyes. She continued with a sigh. 'Therefore I suggest that you continue to help me at the boarding house, working full-time until your husband returns – if he does – and I will offer you the maid's room off the scullery at the back of the house in lieu of wages. You will be fed with the leftovers from breakfast and dinner and, on top of that, I will loan you the money you need to pay the midwife and to give your child a proper Christian burial. There, what do you say?'

Anna could say nothing. Any thoughts she might have were not within reach. She was only physically present because she had no choice, so she nodded her head automatically.

'Good. Then it is decided. Tomorrow, you will move your possessions into your new room. There is a gentleman who wishes to rent this room for a month.'

Frau Schneider walked towards the door and as her big, capable hand grasped the knob, the woman turned back with a frown.

'Are you not going to say thank you, child? Many would simply toss you out into the gutter.'

'Thank you, Frau Schneider,' Anna parroted dutifully.

The woman muttered something as she opened the door and left, and Anna knew she had not shown enough gratitude. She closed her eyes to block out reality. It was safest to stay in a place where nothing and no one could reach her.

As a bitter wind blew in the beginning of December, Anna went to the Johannis Cemetery and stood alone by the graveside of her daughter.

Solveig Anna Halvorsen.

The God she had always believed in, the love she had sacrificed everything for, and now her baby girl . . . all were gone.

In the next three months, Anna simply existed. She worked from dawn until dusk, as Frau Schneider took full advantage of the financial arrangement that had been struck when Anna was vulnerable. The landlady lounged in her private sitting room as she tasked Anna with more and more chores. At night, she lay on her pallet in the tiny room that stank of decaying food from the scullery and slops from the narrow drain in the back yard, so exhausted that she slept and dreamt of nothing.

There were no dreams left.

When she gathered up the courage to ask how long before her debt would be paid off and she could receive some wages, Frau Schneider had snarled angrily in reply.

'Ungrateful girl! I care for you by putting a roof over your head and food on the table and yet you still ask for more!'

No, it was Frau Schneider who asked for more, Anna thought that night. Nowadays, it was left to her to do everything in the lodging house and she knew she must set about finding herself another position that at least paid her some meagre wages. As she pulled off her dress and surveyed her grimy face in the looking glass, she realised she looked little better than a gutter rat: half starved, dressed in rags and smelling of filth. It would be almost impossible for an employer to offer her a position in her current state.

She thought of writing to Frøken Olsdatter, or even throwing herself on her parents' mercy. When she enquired at a pawn shop what they would pay her for the writing instrument Lars had given her, she realised it would not even cover the price of posting a letter to Norway.

Besides, what little she had left of her pride told her she

had brought all this terrible misfortune down on her own head and that she deserved no sympathy.

Christmas came and went and the freezing January days slowly drained any ounce of hope and belief that Anna had left within her. The prayers that had once been for salvation had turned to prayers that she would never wake up again.

'There is no God, it is all a lie . . . everything is a lie,' she whispered to herself before falling into an exhausted sleep.

One evening in March, she was in the kitchen chopping vegetables for the lodgers' evening meal when Frau Schneider entered, looking flustered.

'There is a gentleman here to see you, Anna.'

Anna turned to her with a look of pure relief on her face.

'No, it is not your husband. I have put the gentleman in my parlour. You will remove your apron, clean your face and come as soon as you have done so.'

With a sinking heart, Anna wondered if it was Herr Bayer coming to mock her. And didn't care if it was, she thought, walking along the corridor to Frau Schneider's sitting room. Knocking in trepidation, she was told to enter.

'Frøken Landvik! Or should I say Fru Halvorsen, as I believe we must address you now. How are you, my little songbird?'

'I . . .' Anna stared at the gentleman in utter shock, studying him as though he was an exhibit in the museum of her past life.

'Come now, child, speak to Herr Grieg,' Frau Schneider chastised her. 'She can certainly answer back when she wishes to,' she commented acidly.

'Yes, she always was a spirited girl who knew her own

mind. But then, that is the artistic temperament, madame,' Grieg retorted.

'Artistic temperament?' Frau Schneider eyed Anna with disdain. 'I thought that belonged to her absent husband.'

'This woman's husband may be a fine musician, but this young lady is the real talent in the family. Have you not heard her sing, madame? She has the most exquisite voice I've ever heard, other than that of my dear wife, Nina, of course.'

Anna listened quietly as they continued to talk about her, enjoying the slack-jawed look of shock on Frau Schneider's face.

'Well, of course, if I had known, I would have brought her into this parlour and had her sing for our lodgers as I played the piano. I myself am an amateur, but a keen one.' Frau Schneider indicated the ancient instrument sitting in a corner which Anna had never heard played since the day she'd arrived.

'I'm sure you underestimate your own abilities, dear madame.' Edvard Grieg turned his attention to Anna. 'My poor child,' he said, switching to Norwegian so that Frau Schneider couldn't eavesdrop. 'I have only recently arrived in Leipzig and received your letter. You look half starved. Forgive me, if I had known your circumstances, I would have come sooner.'

'Herr Grieg, please, do not concern yourself with me. I am well.'

'It is patently obvious you are not, and it is my pleasure to assist you in any way I can. Do you owe this wretched woman anything?'

'I do not think so, sir. I have not had wages for the past

six months and believe any debts must have been paid off long ago. But she may think otherwise.'

'My poor, poor child,' Grieg said, careful to keep his tone light under Frau Schneider's scrutiny. 'Now, I will request a glass of water, which you will fetch for me. Then you will go to your room and pack any possessions you have. Bring in the glass, then take your belongings and leave the house. I will meet you at the *Bierkeller* on the corner of Elsterstraße. In the meantime, I will handle our Frau Schneider.'

'I was just saying to Anna I have a raging thirst that will not quieten. Frau Halvorsen has offered to get me some water,' he said in German.

With Frau Schneider's nod of agreement, Anna left the room and hurried through the scullery to pack her valise as Herr Grieg had instructed her to. She filled a glass with water from a jug, and carried it to the parlour. Leaving her valise outside the door, she took the water inside.

'Thank you, my dear,' said Grieg as she handed him the glass. 'Now, I'm sure you have duties to attend to. I will see you before I leave.' Turning to Frau Schneider, he managed a slight wink at Anna, who retreated hurriedly, then picked up her valise and left the house.

Stunned by the turn of events, Anna waited by the *Bierkeller* for twenty minutes until the familiar figure of her saviour walked swiftly down the street towards her.

'Well, Fru Halvorsen, I hope that one day your absent husband will repay me for bargaining your release!'

'Oh sir! Did she make you pay for it?'

'No, it was far more trying than that. She insisted I give her a rendition of my Concerto in A Minor on that dreadful instrument of hers. She should use it for firewood to keep her lardy body warm in winter,' Grieg chuckled as he picked up Anna's valise. 'I have promised to call again to serenade her, but I can assure you I will not be fulfilling that obligation. Now, we will hail a carriage from the square to take us to Talstraße, and on the way there, you will tell me all that you have suffered at the hands of the wicked Frau Schneider. It is as if you are *Aschenputtel* and that woman your wicked stepmother, banishing you to the kitchen to be her skivvy. All that is missing is the two ugly sisters!'

Grieg offered his hand to Anna as she stepped inside the carriage. At that moment, she did indeed feel like a fairy-tale princess being rescued by her prince.

'We are going to the house of my dear friend, the music publisher Max Abraham,' Grieg said.

'Is he expecting me?'

'No, but dear madame, once he hears of your plight, he will be only too glad to offer you shelter. I have the use of a set of rooms there whenever I wish to be in Leipzig. You shall be quite comfortable until we have settled you elsewhere. I shall sleep on the grand piano if necessary.'

'Please, sir, I do not wish to cause a problem or any discomfort for you.'

'And I can assure you that you do not, dear madame. I was merely joking,' he said with a gentle smile. 'There are many spare rooms at Max's house. So now, how did you fall so far from the great heights you had attained when I last saw you?'

'Sir, I . . .'

'Actually, don't tell me!' Grieg held up his hand, then scratched his moustache. 'Let me guess! Herr Bayer's attentions were becoming unbearable. Perhaps he even proposed to you. You refused him because you were in love with our handsome but unreliable fiddle player and would-be composer. He announced he was coming to study in Leipzig and you decided to marry and follow him. Am I right?'

'Sir, please don't tease me.' Anna hung her head. 'It is obvious you know the story already. Every word you say is true.'

'Fru Halvorsen . . . may I call you Anna?'

'Of course.'

'Herr Hennum told me recently of your sudden disappearance, although I did not know the details. And it was obvious from what I'd heard in Christiania that Herr Bayer had intentions beyond your career. So the fiddle-playing husband of yours is still in Paris?'

'I believe so, yes.' Anna wondered how he knew.

'And, I'd fancy, staying in the apartment of a wealthy benefactress by the name of Baroness von Gottfried.'

'I do not know where he stays, sir. I have heard nothing from him for months. I no longer count him as my husband.'

'My dear Anna,' Grieg said, reaching out a comforting hand to hers, 'you have suffered so. Sadly, the baroness is fervent in her pursuit of musical talent. And the younger and more attractive, the better.'

'Forgive me, sir, but I hardly care to hear the details.'

'No, of course not. That was insensitive of me. But the good news is, she will soon tire of him and move on and then he will be back by your side.' He glanced at her then. 'I always said you were the spirit of my Solveig. And just like her, you wait for him to return to you.'

'No, sir.' Anna's features stiffened at his insight. 'I am not Solveig, and I will not wait for Jens to return to me. He is no longer my husband, or I his wife.'

'Anna, for now, no more of this. You are with me and you are safe. I will do all I can to help you.' He paused as the carriage drew up outside a grand and beautiful white house, four storeys high, with rows of tall, gracefully arched windows. Anna recognised it as the building of the music publisher, where she had dropped off her letter to Grieg so long ago. 'For the sake of propriety, it is better if others merely believe you fell on hard times whilst you wait for your husband to return from Paris. Do you see, Anna?' Grieg's searing blue eyes met hers for an instant as the grasp of his hand tightened on hers.

'I do, sir.'

'Please, call me Edvard. Now, we have arrived,' he said, releasing Anna's hand. 'Let us go in and announce ourselves.'

Still dazed by the events of the day, Anna was shown to the delightful airy attic rooms by the maid and was then allowed to sink into a welcome bath. After scrubbing off the grime of the past few months, she changed into a silk dress that had magically appeared on the canopied bed. Strangely, the emerald-green gown fitted her small frame perfectly.

She gazed in wonder at the beautiful view of Leipzig from the large window, the memory of being trapped in the tiny lodging house already receding as she took in the grandeur around her. She made her way downstairs as she'd been instructed, marvelling at how were it not for Herr Grieg, she would still be in Frau Schneider's grimy kitchen peeling carrots for supper.

The maid showed her into the dining room and she found herself seated at a long table between Edvard, as she must now call him, and her host, Herr Abraham. As he welcomed her into his home, Anna saw a pair of kind eyes twinkling behind his neat round glasses. Other musicians were present, and there was much laughter and good food. Even though she was starving, she was unable to eat very much – her stomach had grown unused to digesting it. Instead she sat quietly listening, pinching the skin on her forearm hard to make sure she was really here.

'This beautiful lady,' Grieg said, raising a champagne glass in her direction, 'is the most talented singer in Norway. Look at her! The very epitome of Solveig. She has already served as inspiration for some folk songs I have written this year.'

The other guests immediately requested that he play his new songs and have Anna sing them.

'Perhaps later, my friends, if Anna is not too weary. She has had a very arduous time, captured by the most evil woman in Leipzig!'

As Edvard narrated the events that had led to Anna's rescue, the guests gasping at all the right moments, she tried not to feel overwhelmed at the gruelling memories of what she had been through.

'I thought my muse had vanished into thin air! But here she was, living right under all our noses in Leipzig!' he finished with a flourish. 'To Anna!'

'Anna!'

And the table raised their crystal glasses and drank to her health.

After dinner, Edvard beckoned her towards the piano and placed some music in front of her.

'Now, Anna, in return for my heroic rescue, can you find the strength to sing? The song is titled "The First Primrose" and, as yet, no one has sung it, because it had to be you.

Come,' he said, patting the piano stool, 'sit by me and we will rehearse for a few minutes.'

'Sir . . . Edvard,' she murmured, 'I have not sung for many a long month.'

'Then your voice has been rested and will soar like a bird. Now, listen to the music.'

Anna did so, only wishing they were alone so she could at least make mistakes in private, instead of in such esteemed company. When Edvard pronounced them ready, the audience turned to them expectantly.

'Please stand, Anna, for your breath control. Can you see the words over my shoulder?'

'Yes, Edvard.'

'Then we begin.'

Anna's entire body trembled with nerves as her saviour played the opening bars. Her vocal cords had lain fallow for so long, she had no idea what would come out of her mouth when she opened it. And indeed, the first few notes were true but lacking control. Yet as the beautiful music began to fill her soul, her voice soared as it gained in memory and confidence.

As they ended the song, Anna knew it had been good enough. There was rousing applause and calls for an encore.

'Perfect, my dear Anna, as I knew it would be. Will you publish the song in your catalogue, Max?'

'Of course, but we should also hold a recital at the Gewandhaus with the other folk songs you've written, if the angelic Anna will perform them. It is obvious they were written for her voice alone.' Max Abraham gave Anna a small bow of respect.

'Then it will be arranged,' said Edvard, smiling at Anna, who did her best to stifle a yawn.

'My dear, I can see you are exhausted. I'm sure everyone will forgive you for retiring early. From what we have heard, it has been an extremely difficult time for you,' Max said, much to Anna's relief.

Edvard rose and kissed her hand. 'Goodnight, Anna.'

Anna took the three flights of stairs up to her room. And found the maid stoking the fire. A nightgown was already laid out on the big double bed.

'May I ask who these clothes belong to? They fit me so well.'

'They belong to Edvard's wife, Nina. Herr Grieg told me you had nothing with you and I was to lay out items from Frau Grieg's wardrobe,' the maid replied as she unbuttoned Anna's gown and helped her out of it.

'Thank you,' said Anna, unused to having assistance. 'You can leave me now.'

'Goodnight, Frau Halvorsen.'

When the maid had left, Anna undressed and donned the soft poplin nightgown, then slipped ecstatically between the fresh linen sheets.

For the first time in months, she sent up a prayer thanking the God she'd discarded and asking for his forgiveness for losing faith. Then she closed her eyes, too exhausted to think any more, and fell into a deep sleep.

The story of Grieg's rescue of Anna from the clutches of the wicked Frau Schneider became the talk of Leipzig and was much embellished over the ensuing weeks. And as her powerful new mentor squired her around the musical and social echelons of the city, all doors were open to them. They attended several grand dinner parties in the most beautiful houses in Leipzig, after which Anna was requested to sing for her supper, as Edvard put it. On other evenings she took part in small musical soirées with other composers and singers present.

She was always introduced by Edvard as 'the epitome of everything pure and beautiful from my home country' or 'my perfect Norwegian muse'. As Anna sang his songs about cows, flowers, fjords and mountains, she occasionally wondered if she should simply dress in her national flag so that he could wave her around in front of him. Not that she minded, of course; she was honoured he had taken such an interest in her. And compared to the life she'd had in Leipzig before, every second was a miracle.

During those few months, she met many great composers of the day, most thrillingly Pyotr Tchaikovsky, whose romantic and passionate music she adored. They all came to visit Max Abraham who ran C. F. Peters, and had developed it into one of the most revered music publishing houses in Europe.

The business was run from the same building and Anna loved to wander down to the floors below and pore over the beautifully bound books of sheet music with their distinctive light green covers, marvelling over the compositions of such luminaries as Bach and Beethoven. She was also fascinated by the mechanical printing presses in the basement, which churned out page after perfect page of sheet music at unbelievable speed.

Slowly, with the benefit of good food, rest and, most importantly, the tender care the entire household had shown her, Anna was recovering her strength and self-confidence.

Jens' terrible betrayal still seared through her, filling her with white-hot anger, but she did her best to put it – and him – from her mind. She was no longer a naive child who believed in love, but a woman whose talent could give her all she needed.

As requests for her to give recitals came in regularly from both Germany and abroad, Anna took control of her finances too, never wishing to be dependent on a man again. She saved every penny she earned, hoping that one day she could afford an apartment of her own. Edvard encouraged her, championed her and, more than that, their closeness grew.

Sometimes in the early hours, Anna would wake to the plaintive sounds of the grand piano below her at which Edvard often sat to compose late into the night.

One night in late spring, tormented by the recurring vision of her poor dead daughter lying cold and alone in the earth, she wandered down from her room and sat on the bottom stair outside the drawing room to listen to the melancholy tune Edvard was playing. Tears filled her eyes and she put her head in her hands and wept, letting the pain of her loss flow out with her tears.

'My dear girl, what is it?' Anna jumped as she felt a hand on her shoulder and saw Edvard's gentle blue eyes looking down at her.

'Forgive me. It was the beautiful music touching my soul.'

'I think it was more than that. Come.' Edvard led her into the drawing room, closing the door behind them. 'Here, sit down next to me and use this to dry your eyes.' He handed her a large silk handkerchief.

Edvard's sympathy elicited another flood of tears, which she could do nothing to hold in. Eventually, embarrassed, she looked up at him. Feeling he was owed an explanation, she took a deep breath and told him of the loss of her baby.

'You poor, dear girl. To endure that all alone must have been quite dreadful. As you may know, I too lost a child . . . Alexandra lived until she was two, and was the dearest, sweetest, most precious thing in my life. Her loss broke my heart. Like you, I lost my faith in God and life itself. And I confess, it had ramifications for my marriage. Nina was utterly inconsolable and the two of us have found it almost impossible to comfort each other since.'

'Well, at least that was one problem that I did not have at the time,' Anna said dryly and Edvard chuckled.

'My sweet Anna, you have become so very dear to me. I admire your spirit and courage more than I can tell you. We have both known genuine heartbreak and perhaps all I can tell you is that we must take solace in our music. And' – Edvard's eyes were upon her, and his hand reached for hers – 'perhaps each other.'

'Yes, Edvard,' she said, understanding exactly what he meant. 'I think we can.'

A year later, with Edvard's help, Anna was able to move out of the house in Talstraße and into her own comfortable townhouse in the Sebastian-Bach-Straße, one of the better areas of Leipzig. She went everywhere by carriage and was able to acquire the best tables at the most exclusive restaurants in the city. As her fame grew in Germany, she travelled with him to Berlin, Frankfurt and many other cities to give recitals. Apart from singing Edvard's compositions, her repertoire now included 'The Bell Song' from the newly premiered opera *Lakmé*, and 'Farewell, you native hills and fields' from her favourite Tchaikovsky opera, *The Maid of Orleans*.

There had even been a trip to Christiania for a recital at the very theatre where Anna had begun her career. She had written beforehand to her parents and to Frøken Olsdatter to invite them to the performance, enclosing enough kroner to fund the fare and making a booking for them at the Grand Hotel, where she herself was staying.

After all that had happened and how badly she felt she had let them down, Anna had waited with extreme trepidation for their replies. She need not have worried. They had all accepted the invitation and it had been a joyful reunion. Over a celebratory dinner after the recital, Frøken Olsdatter quietly informed her that Herr Bayer had recently passed away. On hearing the news, Anna expressed her condolences, but then begged her to return with her to Leipzig as her housekeeper.

Thankfully, Lise accepted the position. Anna knew that, given the circumstances, she needed someone she could trust implicitly to work for her inside her home.

As for her errant husband, Anna thought of him as little as she could. She knew the baroness had been seen in Leipzig and had heard through the gossips that there was a new young composer she was championing, but no one had heard from Jens for years. As Edvard had commented, he had disappeared like a rat into the sewers of Paris. Anna prayed he was dead. For even though the way she lived was unconventional, she was happy.

That was until Edvard arrived in Leipzig during the winter of 1883 in response to the urgent letter she had sent him.

'You understand what we must do, *kjære*? For all of us?'

'Yes, I understand,' Anna answered in tight-lipped resignation.

It was the spring of 1884 by the time he came. The maid rapped on the door of the drawing room to tell Anna there was a man waiting to see her.

'I've told him to go to the tradesmen's entrance, but he refuses to move until he's seen you. The front door's closed, but he's sitting on the doorstep.' The parlour maid pointed to a huddled figure through the large window. 'Shall I call the police, Frau Halvorsen? It's obvious he's a beggar or a thief, or worse!'

Anna heaved herself up slowly from the settle where she'd been resting and walked to the window. She saw the man sitting on the front step with his head in his hands.

Her heart plummeting into her stomach, she asked the Lord for strength once more. Only He knew how she would bear this, but under the circumstances, she had no other choice.

'Please let him in immediately. It seems that my husband is returned.'

Ally

Bergen, Norway

September 2007

"In the Hall of the Mountain King"

34

My heart was in my throat as I read of Jens' return to Anna, and I hurriedly turned the next few pages to find out what happened after his return. But Jens had chosen to skim over what must have been an agonisingly difficult few months and concentrated more on their move back to Bergen to a house called Froskehuset, close to Grieg's own Troldhaugen estate, a year later. And the subsequent premiere of his own compositions in Bergen. I skipped to the Author's Note on the final page:

> 'This book is dedicated to my wonderful wife, Anna Landvik Halvorsen, who died tragically of pneumonia earlier this year at the age of fifty. If she had not been prepared to forgive me and take me back when I appeared on her doorstep so many years after I'd left her, then I would indeed have been swallowed up by the Paris gutter. Instead, thanks to her forgiveness, we have enjoyed a happy life together with our precious son, Horst.
>
> Anna, my angel, my muse . . . you taught me all that really matters in life.
>
> I love you and miss you.
>
> Your Jens.'

I felt unsettled and confused as I closed my laptop. I found it almost impossible to believe that Anna, with her strong character and uncompromising moral principles – the very tools which helped her survive what Jens had done to her – could have forgiven him so readily and taken him back as her husband.

'I'd have kicked him out and divorced him as soon as I could,' I told the walls of the hotel room, feeling highly irritated by the conclusion to Anna's incredible story. I knew things had been different back then, but it seemed to me that Jens Halvorsen – the living embodiment of Peer Gynt himself – had got off scot-free.

I looked at my watch, seeing it was past ten o'clock at night, then stood up to use the bathroom and boil the kettle for a cup of tea.

As I closed the heavy curtains on the twinkling lights of Bergen harbour, I seriously pondered if I could have forgiven Theo for deserting me. Which I supposed he had, in the most dreadful, final way he could. And yes, I knew that I too was angry and had yet to forgive the universe. Unlike Jens and Anna, mine and Theo's story had been cut short before it had even begun, through no fault of either of us.

To stop myself becoming maudlin, I checked my emails, raiding the fruit bowl as I felt too weary to go downstairs and there was no room service after nine o'clock in the evening. I saw there were messages from Ma, Maia, and one from Tiggy, saying she was thinking of me. Peter, Theo's father, had also written, telling me he'd sourced a copy of Thom Halvorsen's book and wanting to know where to send it. I replied, asking if he could FedEx it to the hotel address, and decided that I would stay here in Bergen until it had arrived.

Tomorrow, I'd go and search out Jens and Anna's house and perhaps go back and see Erling, the friendly curator of the Grieg Museum, to hear more of their story. I liked it here in Bergen, even if, for the present, my investigation had come to a grinding halt.

The telephone by my bed jangled suddenly, making me jump.

'Hello?'

'It's Willem Caspari here. Are you okay?'

'Yes, I'm fine, thank you.'

'Good. Ally, would you like to have breakfast with me tomorrow morning? I have an idea I'd like to put to you.'

'Er . . . yes, that would be fine.'

'Excellent. Sleep well.'

The line was terminated abruptly and I replaced the receiver, feeling vaguely uncomfortable about agreeing to Willem's request. I tried to work out why, then admitted it was guilt. If I was honest with myself, there was a small flicker of something inside me that told me I was physically attracted to him. Even if my head and heart forbade it, my body was disobeying their orders and reacting of its own accord. But it was hardly a 'date'. And more to the point, from what he'd said about his partner, Jack, dying, Willem was clearly gay.

As I readied myself to go to sleep, I allowed myself a giggle; at least it was a safe crush, and probably had far more to do with his talent as a pianist than anything else. I was aware it was a powerful aphrodisiac and I forgave myself for succumbing to it.

'So, what do you think?' Willem's intense turquoise eyes bored into mine over breakfast the next morning.

'When is the recital?'

'Saturday evening. But you've played the piece before and we have the rest of the week to practise.'

'God, Willem, that was ten years ago. I'm very flattered that you've asked me, but—'

'"Sonata for Flute and Piano" is so beautiful and I've never forgotten you playing it that night at the Conservatoire in Geneva. By definition, to remember it and you ten years on means it was an outstanding performance.'

'I'm not anywhere near as gifted or successful as you,' I protested. 'I've looked you up on the internet and you are seriously big time, Willem. You played at Carnegie Hall last year! So thank you very much for asking, but no thanks.'

He eyed me and my untouched breakfast. I really did feel horribly sick. 'You're nervous, aren't you?'

'Of course I am! Can you imagine how rusty you'd be after ten years of not putting your hands on the keys?'

'Yes, but I'd also play with a new vim and vigour. Stop being a coward and at least give it a try. Why don't you at least join me in the hall after my lunchtime concert today and we can play through the piece together? I'm sure Erling won't mind, even though he might think it blasphemy to play Francis Poulenc on Grieg's hallowed turf. And the Logen Theatre, where the recital will take place on Saturday, is a lovely venue. It's the perfect way to ease you back into playing.'

'You're bullying me, Willem,' I said, now on the verge of tears. 'Why are you so keen on me doing this?'

'If someone hadn't forced me back to the keys after Jack's death, I'd probably never have played another note on the piano again, so you could say that karmically, I'm returning the favour. Please?'

'Oh, all right then. I'll come up to Troldhaugen this afternoon and give it a go,' I agreed, feeling I'd been battered into submission.

'Good.' Willem clapped his hands together in pleasure.

'You'll probably be horrified when you hear me. I did play at Theo's funeral, but that was different.'

'Then this will be a walk in the park after that. So,' he said, rising from the table, 'I'll see you at three.'

I watched Willem as he left, his slim frame belying the enormous breakfast I'd just watched him eat. He obviously lived completely on adrenaline. Back in my room ten minutes later, I opened my flute case tentatively and gazed at it as though it was an enemy to do battle with.

'What have I done?' I murmured as I took out the parts and assembled them, slowly twisting the joints together and aligning the instrument correctly. After tuning up and playing a few quick scales, I tried the sonata's first movement from memory. For an initial attempt, it didn't sound too bad, I thought as I automatically wiped off any excess moisture and cleaned under the keys before packing the flute away.

I then went out for a walk along the quay and stopped in one of the wooden clapboard shops to buy a Norwegian fisherman's jumper, as the temperature seemed to have plummeted and I only had summer clothes in my rucksack.

After heading back to the hotel to retrieve my flute, I took a taxi up into the hills, asking the driver if he knew a house on the same road as the Grieg Museum called Froskehuset. He said he didn't, but that we could both look at the names of the houses as we passed. Sure enough, we spotted it, only a few minutes' walk down the hill from the museum. Letting the taxi go, I looked up at the pretty wooden house, painted cream and traditional in design. As I walked to the gate I saw that it looked rather dilapidated, the paintwork peeling from the wood and the garden unkempt. Hovering outside, feeling like a burglar planning a raid, I wondered who lived there now, and whether I should just go and knock on the door to find out. I chose not to and continued up the hill towards the Grieg Museum.

I made for the café, feeling vaguely sick again. My appetite had deserted me since Theo had died and I knew I'd lost weight. Even though I wasn't hungry, I ordered an open tuna sandwich and forced myself to eat it.

'Hello, Ally.' Erling smiled as he came to greet me in the corner of the café. 'I hear you have an impromptu rehearsal after the recital in the concert hall this afternoon?'

'If you don't mind, Erling.'

'I never mind anyone playing beautiful music here,' he assured me. 'Have you read any more of Jens Halvorsen's biography?'

'As a matter of fact, I finished it last night. I've just been to see the house that he and Anna once lived in.'

'Ah, that's where Thom Halvorsen, the biographer and great-great-grandson, now lives, as a matter of fact. So, do you think you might be related to the Halvorsen family?'

'If I am, I can't see how. Not at present anyway.'

'Well, maybe Thom will be able to enlighten you when he returns from New York later this week. Are you watching Willem's lunchtime concert today?'

'Yes. He's extremely talented, isn't he?'

'He is indeed. As he may have told you, he had a personal

tragedy a while ago. I think it's made him more accomplished as a pianist. These events in life can kill or cure, if you know what I mean.'

'I do,' I replied with feeling.

'See you there, Ally.' Erling nodded at me and walked away.

Half an hour later, I was once again in Troldsalen, the concert hall, listening to Willem play. This time it was a lesser known piece called '*Moods*' that Grieg had written towards the end of his life, when he'd hardly been able to leave the house due to illness but had still staggered to the cabin to write. Willem played it superbly and I wondered what on earth I was doing to even consider playing with such a consummate pianist. Or more accurately, what he was doing suggesting he play with me.

After the appreciative audience had filed out at the end of the concert, Willem beckoned me down to the platform and I joined him nervously.

'I've never heard that before. It's a gorgeous piece and you played it beautifully,' I said.

'Thank you.' He gave me a curt bow, then stopped to study me. 'Ally, you're as white as a sheet! So, before you turn chicken and run out on me, let's get on with it, shall we?'

'No one can come in, can they?' I said, looking up at the doors at the back of the auditorium.

'Good God, Ally! You're starting to sound as deeply paranoid as me.'

'Sorry,' I mumbled as I took out my flute and put it together before Willem indicated we should begin. I was proud that I managed to get all the way through the whole twelve minutes without dropping a note, but I was helped hugely by

Willem's intuitive accompaniment and the incredible sweeping timbre of the Steinway piano.

Willem applauded me, the sound echoing loudly around the empty auditorium. 'Well, if that's how you play after ten years, I think I'll ask them to double the entry fee for Saturday night's recital.'

'That's very kind of you to say, but it was hardly perfect.'

'No, it wasn't, but it was a fantastic start. Now, I suggest we go through the piece together more slowly. There were a few timing issues we need to iron out.'

For the next half an hour, we practised the piece's three movements one by one. And after I'd packed up my flute and we were walking out of the auditorium together, I realised that I hadn't thought about Theo once during the past forty-five minutes.

'Going back into town?' Willem asked me.

'Yes.'

'I'll organise a taxi then.'

On the way back into central Bergen, I thanked Willem and confirmed that I would play with him on Saturday.

'Then I'm very happy,' he answered, staring distractedly out of the window. 'Bergen really is a special place, isn't it?'

'Yes, I feel that too.'

'One of the reasons I agreed to come and give the lunchtime recitals this week at Troldhaugen is because I've been asked to join the Bergen Philharmonic Orchestra as their resident pianist. I wanted to test the waters, as it would mean leaving my sanctuary in Zurich and moving to Bergen more or less full-time. And after what I told you yesterday, you know what a big thing that would be for me.'

'Did Jack live in Zurich with you?'

'Yes. Maybe it's time for a fresh start. And at least Norway is clean,' he added, his expression serious.

'It is,' I chuckled. 'And the people are very friendly. Although it must be incredibly hard to learn the language.'

'I'm lucky, I have a very quick ear. Notes and languages and the occasional maths puzzle, that's my bag. And besides, everyone here speaks English.'

'Well, I think the orchestra would be very lucky to have you.'

'Thank you.' He offered me a rare smile. 'So,' he asked as we arrived at the hotel and walked inside, 'what are you doing tonight?'

'I haven't really thought about it.'

'Join me for dinner?'

He saw my hesitation immediately. 'Sorry, you're probably tired. I'll see you tomorrow at three. Goodbye.'

Willem walked away from me abruptly and left me standing alone, feeling guilty and confused. However, I really didn't feel too well, which was very unlike me. And as I headed to my room and lay down on my bed, I thought sadly how many things were 'unlike' me just now.

35

I'd had to go shopping in Bergen to find something suitably formal and demure for the performance. And as I put on the plain black dress in readiness for the recital, I pushed away memories of donning a similar one for Theo's funeral. I applied some mascara, feeling the adrenaline starting to pump. So much so that I had to lean over the toilet and gag. Wiping my streaming eyes, I returned to the mirror to repair the mascara damage and add some lipstick. Then I picked up my flute case and coat, before taking the lift down to meet Willem in the lobby of the hotel.

Not only did I feel under the weather physically, but I'd been unsettled about Willem since his dinner invitation. In our practices together since, I'd sensed a certain *froideur* emanating from him. He had kept the conversation on a purely 'business' level, our discussions in the taxi entirely based on the music we had rehearsed.

The lift doors opened, and I saw him waiting for me in reception, looking handsome in his bow tie and immaculate black tuxedo. And I hoped I hadn't upset him with my refusal. I'd felt faint shades of the awkwardness Theo and I had experienced at the very beginning of our relationship and something told me now that Willem definitely wasn't gay . . .

'You look nice, Ally,' he said as he stood up and came towards me.

'Thanks, but I don't feel it.'

'No woman ever seems to,' he commented brusquely as we walked out of the hotel to the taxi he'd pre-booked.

Silence reigned in the car, and I was frustrated at the discomfort between us. Willem seemed distant and tense.

On arrival at the Logen Theatre, we walked inside and Willem found the organiser, who was waiting for us in the foyer.

'Come through, come through,' she said, leading us into an elegant high-ceilinged hall, the floor laid out with rows of seats and chandeliers illuminating the narrow apron balcony above. The stage was empty except for a grand piano and a music stand for myself, and the spotlights were turning on and off as the lighting engineers made their final checks.

'I'll leave you both to have a run-through,' the woman said. 'The audience will be allowed in fifteen minutes before the start, so you have thirty minutes to judge the acoustics.'

Willem thanked her then walked up the steps of the stage to the grand piano. He lifted the fallboard and ran his fingers up and down the keys. 'It's a Steinway B,' he said in relief, 'and the sound is good. So, a quick run-through?'

I took my flute out of its case and noticed that my fingers were trembling as I put it together. We played through the sonata, then I went to find the lavatory while Willem practised his solo pieces. I dry-retched yet again and as I washed my face with cold water, I mocked my ghostly reflection. I was supposedly the woman who could stomach the roughest conditions at sea without the slightest upset. And now here, on dry land, playing the flute in front of an audience for twelve minutes, I felt like a seasick novice during my first storm.

When I arrived back in the wings, I peered through the flats and saw the audience filing in. I stole a glance at Willem, who seemed to be performing some kind of ritual a few feet away from me, which involved a lot of muttering, pacing and finger exercises, and I left him be. Unfortunately, 'Sonata for Flute and Piano' was the penultimate piece of the recital, which meant I'd have to sit out of sight backstage, waiting and worrying.

'Are you okay?' Willem whispered as we heard the compere introduce him and read out the most impressive parts of his CV.

'I'm fine, thank you,' I said as a burst of applause rippled through the audience.

'I want to formally apologise for my presumptuous dinner invitation the other night. It was completely inappropriate, given the circumstances. I know where you are emotionally and from now on, I'll respect that. I hope we can be friends.'

With that, Willem walked out onto the stage and took a bow, before sitting down at the piano. He began with Chopin's fast and technically complicated Étude No. 5 in G-flat Major.

As I listened to Willem play, I pondered the endlessly intricate dance that went on between men and women. And as the final notes of the piece filled the hall, I acknowledged that part of me felt oddly deflated by Willem hoping we could be friends. Not to mention the guilt that sat at the back of my mind whenever I thought of what Theo would have made of my confusion over my attraction for Willem . . .

After what felt like a lifetime as I paced up and down the small space in the wings, I finally heard Willem introducing me and I took my cue to join him on the stage. I gave him a wide smile as a 'thank you' for his kindness and encouragement in the past few days. Then I put my flute to my lips, indicated I was ready and we began to play.

After Willem had played his final piece of the evening, I joined him back onstage and it felt very odd to be taking a bow with him. The organisers even presented me with a small posy of flowers to thank me.

'Well done, Ally, that was good. Very, very good in fact,' Willem congratulated me as we walked offstage together.

'I agree entirely.'

I turned at the familiar voice and saw Erling, the curator of the Grieg Museum, standing in the wings, flanked by two other men.

'Hello,' I greeted him with a smile. 'And thank you.'

'Ally, this is Thom Halvorsen, Jens Halvorsen's great-great-grandson and biographer. Not to mention virtuoso violinist and assistant conductor of the Bergen Philharmonic Orchestra. And may I also present David Stewart, the leader of the orchestra.'

'It's a pleasure to meet you, Ally,' said Thom, as David Stewart turned to Willem. 'Erling tells me you're doing some research on my great-great-grandparents?'

I looked up at Thom and thought I recognised him, but couldn't immediately place where from. He had the familiar colouring of the Norwegians: reddish hair, a scattering of freckles across his nose and a pair of big blue eyes.

'I am, yes.'

'Then I'd be happy to help in any way I can. Although

please forgive me if I don't make much sense tonight. I've just flown in from New York. Erling picked me up from the airport and drove me straight here to listen to Willem play.'

'Jet lag's a killer,' we both managed to say at the same time, then, after a pause, offered each other an embarrassed grin.

'It is,' I added as David Stewart turned to us.

'Unfortunately, I've got to rush off now,' he said, 'so I'll say goodbye. Thom, call me if it's good news.' He gestured his farewells and left.

'As you may know, Ally, we're trying to persuade Willem to join the philharmonic orchestra here. Any thoughts so far, Willem?'

'Yes, and some questions too, Thom.'

'Then I suggest we go across the road for a quick bite to eat and a drink. Will you two join us?' Thom asked Erling and me.

'If you have things to talk about with Willem, we wouldn't want to disturb you.' Erling spoke for both of us.

'Not at all. It will only take a simple "yes" from Willem to crack open the champagne.'

Ten minutes later, we were all sitting in a cosy candle-lit restaurant. Thom and Willem were hunched over the table, deep in conversation, so I talked to Erling opposite me.

'You were really very good tonight, Ally. Too good to neglect your talent, never mind the actual joy of playing.'

'Are you a musician too?' I asked him.

'Yes. I come from a family of them, like Thom. The cello is my instrument and I play with a small orchestra here in the city. It's a very musical town. The Bergen Philharmonic is one of the oldest orchestras in the world.'

'So,' interrupted Thom, 'we can finally order the champagne! Willem has agreed to join us.'

'No champagne for me, thank you. I never drink anything alcoholic after nine o'clock,' Willem said firmly.

'Then I think you'd better learn how to if you're moving to Norway,' Thom teased him. 'It's all that keeps us going through the long winters here.'

'Then I shall join you in honour of this occasion,' Willem said graciously, as a waiter appeared with a bottle.

'To Willem!' we all chorused, as our food arrived.

'I'm actually feeling much more awake now after a glass of champagne.' Thom smiled at me. 'So, tell me more about the connection between you and Jens and Anna Halvorsen?'

I briefly explained to him the story of Pa Salt's legacy, which had included Jens Halvorsen's biography of his wife, Anna, and the coordinates on the armillary sphere that had led me first to Oslo and now to Bergen and the Grieg Museum.

'Fascinating,' he murmured as he studied me thoughtfully. 'So perhaps we're related somehow? Although to be honest, having so recently researched my family history, I can't immediately see how.'

'Neither can I,' I reassured him, feeling suddenly uncomfortable that he might think I was some gold-digging gene-stealer. 'I've ordered your book, by the way. It's being shipped over from the States as we speak.'

'That's kind of you, Ally, but of course, I have a spare copy at home if you'd like it.'

'Thank you. Or at least I'll get you to sign mine. Since I've got you here in person, maybe you can help me with some details. Do you know what happened to the Halvorsen family in the years after Jens' biography ended?'

'More or less, yes. Sadly, it wasn't a pretty slice of human history, what with the two World Wars on their way. Norway was neutral in the First World War, but was hit pretty badly by the German occupation in the Second.'

'Really? I wasn't even aware Norway *was* occupied,' I confessed. 'History wasn't my best subject at school. In fact, I've never even thought of the effect the Second World War might have had on smaller countries outside the main protagonists. Especially not here, in this peaceful country, tucked up at the top of the world.'

'Well, we tend to learn our own country's history at school, don't we? What was yours?'

'Switzerland,' I chuckled as I looked up at him.

'Neutral,' we both chorused together.

'Well,' continued Thom, 'we were invaded here in 1940. Actually, Switzerland reminded me of Norway when I went to Lucerne for a concert a couple of years ago. And it wasn't just the snow. They both definitely feel like they have a certain disconnect from the rest of the world.'

'Yes,' I agreed. I watched Thom as he ate, still trying to work out why he seemed so familiar, and deciding I must be recognising some genetic markers I'd picked up from the photographs of his forebears. 'So the Halvorsens survived the wars?'

'It's a very sad story actually, and definitely too complex for my jet-lagged brain to tell you now. We could meet up at some point, though – perhaps tomorrow afternoon at my house? It used to be Jens and Anna's home too, and I can show you where they lived out some of the happier moments of their relationship.' Thom raised an eyebrow and I felt a vague thrill that he obviously knew their story too.

'Actually, I saw it a couple of days ago on the way up to Troldhaugen.'

'Then you'll know exactly where it is. Now, if you'll excuse me, Ally, I'm for my bed.' Thom stood up and turned his attention to Willem. 'Safe flight home to Zurich and I'm sure admin will be in touch with your contract. Call me if you think of anything further. So, Ally, two o'clock tomorrow at Froskehuset?'

'Yes. Thanks, Thom.'

'Fancy walking?' Willem asked me after we'd said goodnight to Erling, who was driving Thom home. 'The hotel's not far away.'

'I can just about manage that,' I agreed, thinking some fresh air might help my now throbbing head. We strolled through the cobbled streets and emerged at the harbour. Willem halted in front of it.

'Bergen . . . My new home! Have I made the right decision, Ally?'

'I really don't know, but it would be hard to find a more lovely place than this to live. It's difficult to imagine anything bad happening here.'

'That's what's worrying me. Am I opting out? Running away yet again from what happened to Jack? I've travelled maniacally since she died, and now I wonder if I'm coming here to hide,' he sighed as we started walking along the quay towards our hotel.

I mentally raised my eyebrows at the fact he'd called his partner 'she'.

'Or you could put a more positive twist on it and say that you were moving on, making a fresh start,' I suggested.

'I could, yes. Actually, I wanted to ask you, Ally, whether you've gone through the whole "why did I live when they died" thing?'

'Of course I have, and I still am. It was Theo who made me leave the boat we were racing shortly before he drowned. I've spent endless hours thinking how I could have saved him if I'd been there, even though I know I couldn't have.'

'Yes . . . it's a road to nowhere. I've realised that life is just a random series of events. You and I were left behind and we just have to get on with it. My psychotherapist tells me that's why I have OCD symptoms. When Jack died, I felt I had no control, so I've been overcompensating ever since. I am getting better – even that glass of champagne tonight after nine o'clock . . .' Willem shrugged. 'Baby steps, Ally, baby steps.'

'Yes. By the way, what was Jack's full name?'

'Jacqueline. After Jacqueline du Pré. Her father was a cellist.'

'When you first mentioned her, I thought "she" was a "he" . . .'

'Hah! Yup, another form of control apparently, and it works. It's protected me against any predatory female that comes my way. One mention of my partner Jack, and they back off. I may not be a rock star, but there's a number of concert pianist groupies hanging around after the performance, batting their eyes at me and asking to see my, er, instrument. One even told me her fantasy was to have me play Rachmaninoff's No. 2 to her in the nude.'

'Well, I hope you didn't feel I was one of them.'

'Of course I didn't. In fact . . .' We'd paused outside the

hotel and Willem looked out onto the calm water lapping gently against the quay. 'It was quite the opposite. And, as I said to you earlier, my dinner invitation was inappropriate. Typical me,' he sighed, suddenly morose. 'Anyway, thanks for playing tonight and I hope we can stay in touch.'

'Willem, it's me that should thank you. You've brought me back to music. Now, I have to go to bed before I curl up and fall asleep on the pavement.'

'I'm leaving first thing in the morning,' he told me as we walked into the deserted lobby. 'I have a lot to organise back home in Zurich. Thom wants me to join the orchestra as soon as possible.'

'When will you be back?'

'By November, in time to prepare for the Grieg Centenary Concert. Will you be staying on longer here?' he asked as we halted in front of the lift.

'I really don't know, Willem.'

'Well,' he said, as we stepped inside the lift and pressed the numbers of our respective floors, 'here's my card. Let me know how you get on.'

'I will.'

The lift stopped on his floor. 'Goodbye, Ally.' With a fleeting smile, he nodded at me and stepped out.

As I switched off my bedside lamp ten minutes later, I hoped Willem and I *would* keep in touch. Even if I was light years away from ever having another relationship, I liked him. And after what he'd just said, I thought he might like me too.

36

'Hi there,' Thom said with a smile as he opened the door to Froskehuset and I followed him inside. 'Come through to the drawing room. Would you like anything to drink?'

'A glass of water would be fine, thanks.'

I glanced around the sitting room as Thom went out. It was quaintly decorated in what I was coming to realise was a unique Norwegian style: homespun and very cosy. The room contained a mixture of mismatched easy chairs and a sofa with lace antimacassars laid over its back, set around an enormous iron stove, which I guessed would certainly keep the chill away at night. The one striking object in the room was the black-lacquered grand piano in the bay window, overlooking the magnificent fjord beneath us.

I went to have a closer look at the selection of framed photographs standing on a rather hideous faux-rococo bureau in the corner. There was one in particular that I was drawn to, of a little boy of about three years old – Thom I presumed – sitting on a woman's lap by the fjord in bright sunshine. They shared the same wide smiles, colouring and large, expressive eyes. As Thom came back, I could see the vestiges of the little boy in the photograph on his face.

'Sorry about the house,' Thom said. 'I only moved back in a few months ago when my mum died and I still haven't found time to change the decor. I'm more minimalist myself, more modern Scandinavian; this relic of the past isn't quite me.'

'As a matter of fact, I was just thinking to myself how much I like it. It's so . . . '

'*Real*!' we both said at the same time.

'You read my thoughts exactly,' said Thom. 'Although, as you're researching Jens and Anna, it's fitting you should see the original interior before I chuck most of it into a skip. A lot of this furniture was theirs and it's about one hundred and twenty years old now. Like everything in the house, including the plumbing. They bought the land – or should I say Anna did – in 1884, then took a year to build the house.'

'I'd never heard of either of them before I read the book,' I said apologetically.

'Well, it was Anna who was the better known of the two in Europe, but, in his day, Jens was quite a big cheese, especially in Bergen. He really came into his own once Grieg died in 1907, even though his music was highly derivative of the maestro and a lesser version of it, to be honest. I don't know how much you know about Grieg's involvement in Jens and Anna's life . . .'

'Quite a lot, having read Jens' own words. Especially what he did for Anna, recovering her from the lodging house in Leipzig.'

'Yes. Well, as you haven't had a chance to read my book yet, one thing you won't know is that it was Grieg who found Jens living with an artist's model in Montmartre. He'd been abandoned by his patron, the baroness, and was scratching a living from playing the fiddle, mostly drunk and high on opium, as many of them were in the bohemian circle in Paris back then. Apparently, Grieg gave him a severe talking-to, then paid his fare back to Leipzig, and told him in no uncertain terms to go and throw himself on Anna's mercy.'

'Who told you this?'

'My great-grandfather, Horst, who was told by Anna on her deathbed.'

'So when did Jens return?'

'In 1884, or thereabouts.'

'A few years after Grieg had rescued Anna in Leipzig? To be blunt, Thom, I felt depressed when I got to the end of the book. I couldn't understand why Anna would take Jens back after all those years of desertion. And equally, now I don't understand why Grieg would have sought out Jens in Paris. He must have known how Anna felt about him. It just doesn't make sense.'

Thom studied me as if turning something over in his mind. 'Well, that's the problem with history, as I discovered while researching my family story,' he said eventually. 'You get the facts, but it's difficult to know the actual human motivations. Remember, it was Jens who wrote the biography. We don't hear Anna's thoughts on the subject at all. The book was published after her death and was in essence a tribute to her from her husband.'

'Personally, I would definitely have reached for the meat cleaver when Jens slunk back. I thought that Lars, her original fiancé, sounded like a far more appealing option.'

'Lars Trulssen? You do know he went to America and became a poet of some renown? He married into a wealthy third-generation New York family with Norwegian roots and had a brood of children.'

'Really? Then that makes me feel much better. I felt rather sorry for him, but then, us women don't always choose the good guy, do we?'

'I don't think I'll comment on that,' Thom said with a chuckle. 'All I can say is that, to the general observer, they remained happily married for the rest of their lives. Apparently Jens was forever grateful to Grieg for saving him from the fleshpots of Paris and to Anna for forgiving him. Certainly, the two couples spent a lot of time together, being almost next-door neighbours. When Grieg died, Jens helped start a music department at the University of Bergen with Grieg's financial legacy. It's now the Grieg Academy, and it's where I studied.'

'I really know nothing of the family after 1907 when Jens' book ended, and I've never even heard any of his compositions.'

'In my opinion, there's not a lot he wrote that's worth hearing. Although when I was sorting out his many folders of sheet music that have mouldered away in boxes in the attic for years, I came across something very special. A piano concerto he wrote that, as far as I know from my research, has never been performed publicly.'

'Really?'

'With it being Grieg's centenary this year, there are various events taking place, including a major concert here in Bergen to mark the end of the year of celebration.'

'Yes, Willem mentioned it.'

'You can imagine that Norwegian music is very much on the agenda and it would be wonderful to premiere my great-great-grandfather's work. I've spoken to the Programming Committee and Andrew Litton himself – he's our revered conductor and, at present, also my conducting mentor. They've heard the piece which, in my opinion, is stunning, and it's pencilled into the programme for the concert on the seventh of December. As I could only find the piano music in the attic, I sent the piece off to be orchestrated by a very talented chap I know. But when I got home from New York yesterday, I had a message on my answerphone saying his mother had been taken ill a few weeks ago, and he hasn't even started on it yet.'

Thom paused and I could see the disappointment on his face. 'I really can't see it being ready for December. It's such a shame . . . it's far and away the best thing Jens composed, in my opinion. And of course, to premiere an original work by a Halvorsen who actually played at the first performance of *Peer Gynt* would have been perfect. Anyway, enough of my problems. What about you, Ally? Have you ever done a stint in an orchestra?'

'Goodness, no. I don't think my flute playing was ever up to that standard. I'm more of a happy amateur.'

'Having heard you last night, I'd have to disagree. Willem says you studied flute for four years at the Geneva Conservatoire. That's hardly a "happy amateur", Ally,' he chastised me.

'Maybe not, but up until a few weeks ago, I was a professional sailor.'

'Really? How come?'

Over a cup of herbal tea which Thom had found for me in a cupboard, I told him a potted history of my life and the events leading up to my arrival in Bergen. I realised I was becoming used to repeating it factually, rather than emotionally. And I didn't know whether this was a good thing, or bad.

'God, Ally! I thought my life was complicated, but yours . . . well. I don't know how you've coped in the past few weeks. I salute you, I really do.'

'I've kept myself busy delving into my past,' I said tightly, wanting to get off the subject. 'So, now that I've bored you silly with my life, do you think you can return the favour and tell me about the more modern Halvorsens? If you don't mind,' I added hastily, well aware this was Thom's family. I didn't want him to think I was making any kind of permanent claim on it. 'I mean, whatever my connection is, it must be to do with the recent past, because I'm only thirty.'

'So am I actually. I was born in June. You?'

'The thirty-first of May, so my adoptive father told me.'

'Really? Well, I'm the first of June,' Thom said.

'A day apart,' I mused. 'Anyway, carry on, I'm all ears.'

'Well' – Thom took a slug of his coffee – 'I was brought up here in Bergen by my mum, who died a year ago. Which is how I came to be living at Froskehuset.'

'I'm so sorry, Thom. As you've already heard, I know how it feels to lose a parent.'

'Thanks. It was pretty awful at the time as we were very close. Mum was a single parent and there was no dad around to support us.'

'Do you know who he was?'

'Oh yes.' Thom raised an eyebrow. 'He's the blood connection with Jens Halvorsen. Felix, my father, is his great-grandson. Although, unlike Jens, who at least did eventually come back to Anna, my father never faced up to his responsibilities.'

'Is he still alive?'

'Very much so, even though he was about twenty years older than my mother when they met. In my opinion, my father is the most musically gifted out of all the generations of Halvorsen men. And like Anna, my mother had a lovely singing voice. Basically, she went to my dad for piano lessons and he seduced her. She got pregnant by him at twenty. He refused to accept that I was his and advised her to abort me.'

'That's pretty damning. Is that what your mother told you?'

'Yes. And knowing Felix, I completely believe her,' Thom said flatly. 'She had a really rough time after I was born. Her own parents disowned her – they were a country family from the north and very old-fashioned about these things. Martha, my mother, was practically destitute. You have to remember that thirty years ago, Norway was still a relatively poor country.'

'How awful, Thom. So, what did she do?'

'Thankfully, my great-grandparents, Horst and Astrid, stepped in and offered us both a home here with them. Although I feel my mum never recovered from what my father did to her. She had terrible bouts of depression on and off for the rest of her life. And never fulfilled her potential as a singer.'

'Does Felix now recognise you as his son?'

'He was forced to when the court ordered a DNA test when I was in my teens,' Thom explained, his face grim. 'My great-grandmother had died and left the house in trust to me rather than to Felix, their grandson. Felix contested the will, saying my mum and I were money-grabbing imposters, hence the DNA test. And bingo! One hundred per cent proof that Halvorsen blood runs through my veins. Not that I ever thought it didn't. My mum would never have lied about something like that.'

'Right. Well, firstly, I'd just like to say that your past sounds every bit as dramatic as mine,' I added with a grin, which I was relieved to see Thom returned. 'Do you ever see your father?'

'Occasionally in town, but not socially, no.'

'So he lives locally?'

'Oh yes, up in the hills with his whisky bottles and an endless trail of women beating a path to his front door. Now he really is a "Peer Gynt", who never saw the error of his ways.' Thom shrugged sadly.

'Then I'm a bit confused . . .You've talked about your great-grandparents, but there seems to be a generation missing. What happened to your grandparents? Felix's mum and dad?'

'That's the story I mentioned to you last night. I never actually met either of them. They both died before I was born.'

'I'm sorry, Thom.' I was amazed to find tears springing to my eyes.

'Oh God, Ally, don't cry. Really, I'm fine and getting on with my life. You've faced far worse recently.'

'I know you are, Thom. Sorry, the story moved me, that's all,' I said, not understanding quite why it did.

'As you can imagine, it's not the kind of thing I discuss often. In fact, I'm amazed I've been able to tell you so honestly.'

'And I'm grateful to you for sharing it, Thom, really. Just one more question. Have you ever listened to your father's side of the story?'

Thom looked at me oddly. 'How could there be another side?'

'Oh, you know . . .'

'Apart from him being a useless, selfish bastard who left my mum in the lurch and pregnant, you mean?'

'Yes,' I breathed, realising I was on shaky ground. I back-tracked hastily. 'From what you've said, you're probably right, there isn't any more to it than that.'

'That's not to say I don't feel sorry for Felix sometimes,' he conceded. 'He's made an utter mess of his life and wasted his fabulous talent. Thankfully, I inherited a modicum of it and for that I'll always be grateful.'

I saw Thom check his watch and took it as a cue to leave. 'I must be going. I've taken up enough of your time as it is.'

'No, Ally, please don't go yet. Actually, I was just thinking how hungry I was. It's around breakfast time in New York. Fancy some pancakes? They're about the one thing I can make without a recipe book.'

'Thom, really, tell me if you want to kick me out.'

'I will, and I don't. But you can come and be *sous-chef* in the kitchen. Okay?'

'Okay.'

As we made the pancakes, Thom began to question me more about my life.

'From what you said earlier, it sounds like your adoptive father was very special.'

'He was, yes.'

'And all those sisters of yours . . . you can't ever have lacked for company. Being an only child sometimes got very lonely. I was desperate for siblings when I was growing up.'

'The one thing I never suffered from was loneliness. There

was always someone to play with, something to do. And I certainly learnt to share.'

'Whereas I had everything to myself and resented the fact that I was my mother's Crown Prince,' he said, flipping the pancakes onto the plates. 'I always felt a pressure from her to live up to her expectations. I was all she had.'

'Me and my sisters were only encouraged to be ourselves,' I said as we sat down at the kitchen table to eat. 'Did you feel guilty that your mother had suffered so much to bring you into the world?'

'I did. And to be brutal, when she went into her bouts of depression and told me it was all my fault that her life had gone off the tracks, I wanted to shout at her that I had never asked to be born, and that it was *her* choice.'

'Well, we are a pair, aren't we?'

He looked up at me, fork poised. 'Yes, Ally, we really are. Actually, it is nice to have someone who can understand my unusual family circumstances.'

'Me too.' I looked across the table and smiled at him. He grinned back and I felt the strongest sense of déjà vu.

'It's odd,' mused Thom a few seconds later, 'I feel like I've known you forever.'

'I know what you mean,' I agreed.

Later, Thom drove me back down into the city to my hotel.

'Are you free tomorrow morning?' he asked me.

'I have nothing planned.'

'Great. Then I'll collect you and we'll take a little boat ride around the harbour. And I'll tell you what happened to Pip and Karine, my grandparents. As I've said, it's a difficult and painful chapter in Halvorsen history. '

'Well, would you mind if we did it on dry land? My sea legs have completely disappeared since Theo died.'

'I understand. Why don't you come up to me at Froskehuset again? I'll pick you up at eleven. Goodnight, Ally.'

'Goodnight, Thom.'

I waved him off from the front of the hotel, then went up to my room. I stood by the window, looking out over the water, marvelling at the hours that Thom and I had spent talking about anything – *everything* – and how it had felt effortless and natural. I showered, then got into bed, knowing that whatever came of my investigations into the past, I was at least making new friends along the way.

And with that thought, I went straight to sleep.

37

When I woke up the next morning, the calmness I'd felt last night deserted me as I ran to the bathroom to vomit. Staggering back to the bed, I lay there with tears in my eyes, not understanding why I felt so awful. I'd always taken my health for granted, hardly suffering a single childhood illness and always being the stalwart one who helped Ma when a particularly virulent bug passed from sister to sister.

Today, I felt absolutely dreadful and pondered whether that initial bout of sickness I'd suffered on Naxos had actually been due to some form of bug in my stomach that still hadn't shifted, as I definitely hadn't felt right since. And it was getting worse . . . Surely, I thought helplessly, it was simply the tension of the past few weeks catching up with me? I needed to eat – my sugar levels were probably low – so I ordered a large continental breakfast and was determined to plough through it. *That's how you treat seasickness, Ally*, I told myself as I sat with the tray on my knee in bed and valiantly battled to eat as much as I could.

Twenty minutes later, I flushed my entire breakfast away. As I dressed shakily, knowing that Thom would be arriving in half an hour, I decided I'd ask him for the name of a good doctor as I was quite obviously ill. Just as I was thinking this, my mobile rang.

'Hello?'

'Ally?'

'Tiggy, how are you?'

'I'm . . . okay. Where are you?'

'Still in Norway.'

There was a pause before she said, 'Oh.'

'What is it, Tiggy?'

'Nothing . . . nothing at all. I just wondered if you were back at Atlantis yet.'

'No, sorry. Is everything all right?'

'Yes, it's fine, absolutely fine. I was just calling to see how you were.'

'I'm okay, and finding out lots of things about the clues Pa left me.'

'Good. Well, let me know when you're back from Norway and maybe we can meet up,' she said, with a false brightness to her voice. 'I love you, Ally.'

'I love you too.'

Taking the lift downstairs, I puzzled at how odd Tiggy had sounded. I was used to her serenity, her ability to always make everyone around her feel better by dispensing her own brand of esoteric hope. Just now, she hadn't sounded like that at all. I promised myself I would email her later.

'Hello.' Thom came towards me as I got out of the lift.

'Hi,' I said, smiling as I tried to gather my composure.

'Are you all right, Ally? You look . . . pale.'

'Yes, well, no, actually,' I said as we walked towards the hotel exit. 'I'm not feeling too well. To be honest, I haven't been for a few days. It's nothing serious, I'm sure, just a stomach bug, but I wanted to ask you if you knew of a doctor I could see.'

'Of course I do. Shall I take you there now?'

'God no, I'm not that bad, just not feeling . . . myself,' I said as he helped me into his battered Renault.

'You really do look awful, Ally,' he said as he picked up his mobile. 'Why don't I book you an appointment for later on today?'

'Okay, thanks. Sorry,' I murmured as he dialled a number on his mobile and spoke to the person at the other end of the line in Norwegian.

'Right, you're booked in for four thirty. So' – he gazed at my pale features and smiled – 'I suggest that I take you straight to Froskehuset to tuck you under a cosy eiderdown on the sofa. Then you can decide whether you would prefer to hear the story of my grandparents or for me to play my violin for you.'

'Couldn't we do both?' I smiled weakly back, wondering how on earth he could know that on this chilly autumnal day, with my queasy stomach, the thought of an eiderdown, a story and some music was exactly what I needed.

Half an hour later, snuggled up on the sofa, with the added bonus of the enormous iron stove being lit, I asked Thom to play the violin for me.

'Why don't you start with your absolutely favourite ever piece on the violin?'

'Okay.' He gave a mock sigh. 'Although looking at the state of you today, I don't want you to think it's relevant in any way.'

'I won't,' I promised, slightly puzzled by his comment.

'Okay then.'

Thom put his violin lovingly under his chin, tuned it up for a few seconds, and then the haunting strains of one of my own favourite pieces of music began to flow from his bow. I laughed out loud, understanding what he'd meant.

Thom paused in his playing and grinned. 'Told you.'

'Really, *The Dying Swan* is one of my favourite pieces too.'

'Good.'

With that, he began again, and as I lay there, cosy and comfortable, being serenaded by a naturally gifted virtuoso player, I felt honoured to have a private recital. The last poignant note died away and I put my hands together and clapped. 'That was gorgeous.'

'Thank you. So now, what would you like next?'

'Whatever you enjoy playing best.'

'Okay then. Here goes.'

For the next forty minutes, I listened to Thom playing a marvellous selection of his favourite pieces, including the first movement from Tchaikovsky's Violin Concerto in D Major and the *Devil's Trill* sonata by Tartini, and saw the way he disappeared into another world, a world I'd seen every true musician enter when they played. And I wondered again how I could have lived without music and musicians in my life for the past ten years. I'd once known that feeling too. I must have dozed off at some point, feeling so relaxed and safe and warm that I simply floated away. Until I felt a gentle hand on my shoulder.

'Sorry, so sorry,' I said, flicking my eyes open to find Thom looking down at me in concern.

'I could be seriously offended by the fact that the one

member of my audience drifted off to sleep, but I won't take it personally.'

'You mustn't, Thom, really. I promise you, it's a compliment, in an ironic sort of way. Can I use your bathroom?' I asked him, slowly getting out from under the quilt.

'Yes, it's just along the corridor to the left.'

'Thanks.'

When I returned, relieved I felt a little better than I had this morning, I found Thom in the kitchen with something bubbling on the stove.

'What are you doing?' I asked.

'Making lunch. It's past one o'clock. I let you sleep for over two hours.'

'Oh my God! No wonder you're insulted. I'm so sorry.'

'Really, Ally, from what you've told me, you've been through a lot recently.'

'Yes, I have,' I agreed, not ashamed to admit it in front of him. 'I miss Theo so much.'

'I'm sure you do. I know this sounds bizarre, but in one way I envy you.'

'How?'

'In the sense that I'm yet to feel that for a woman. I've had relationships, yes, but none of them have led anywhere. I'm yet to find "the one" that everyone talks about.'

'You will, Thom, I'm sure.'

'Maybe, but I'll be honest, I'm losing faith as I get older. It all seems too much of an effort, Ally.'

'Thom, someone will appear just as Theo did for me, and you'll just know. Now, what it is you're cooking?'

'The only other thing I can't mess up – it's pasta. À la Thom.'

'Well, I don't know what you put in it, but I'm sure my "special pasta" is far better than yours,' I teased him. 'It's my signature dish.'

'Really? I doubt it can beat mine. People flock in from the hills of Bergen simply to taste it,' he said as he drained the pasta, then poured a sauce over it and stirred. 'Kindly sit down.'

I ate tentatively, not relishing the thought of another visit to the bathroom, but found that actually, Thom's dish – a tasty mixture of cheese, herbs and ham – was going down very well indeed.

'So,' he said as he gazed at my empty bowl. 'Good?'

'Excellent. Your special pasta has revived me. I'm now ready to hear your great-great-grandfather's concerto. That is, if you're willing to play it for me?'

'Of course. Although you must remember the piano isn't my first instrument, so I won't do it justice.'

We went back into the sitting room and I settled myself back on the sofa again, upright this time, as Thom collected the music from a shelf.

'Is that the original piano score?'

'Yes,' he said, arranging it on the music rest. 'Okay, bear with me as I struggle through it, won't you?'

As Thom began to play, I closed my eyes and concentrated on the music. There was no doubt there were overtones of Grieg, but also something unique, with a gorgeous, hypnotic theme running through it, reminiscent of Rachmaninoff and perhaps a touch of Stravinsky. Thom finished with a flourish and turned to me.

'What do you think?'

'I'm humming it in my head already. It's mesmerising, Thom, really.'

'I think so too, and so do David Stewart and Andrew Litton. Tomorrow, I'm going to concentrate on trying to find someone to get on with the orchestration. I'm not sure now if anyone else can do them in time, but it's worth a shot. Honestly, I don't know how our forebears did it. It's hard enough these days with all our computerised modern aids, but to manually write each note for each instrument onto sheet music for an entire orchestra must have been a mammoth undertaking. No wonder the great composers took so long to score their symphonies and concertos. I take my hat off to Jens and his ilk, I really do.'

'You really are part of an illustrious line, aren't you?'

'Well, the big question is, Ally, are you?' Thom said slowly. 'When you left last night, I had a long think about how you could be related to the Halvorsen clan. As my father Felix was an only child, and neither grandparent had siblings either, I've only come up with one solution.'

'And what is that?'

'I'm worried you'll be offended, Ally.'

'Just hit me with it, Thom, really, I can take it,' I urged him.

'Okay, well, given my father's chequered history with women, I've wondered whether there is a possibility he had an illegitimate child. That perhaps even *he* doesn't know about.'

I stared at Thom, collating mentally what he was saying.

'I suppose it's a theory, yes. But Thom, please remember there's no proof yet that I'm any blood relation to the Halvorsens. And I feel very uncomfortable appearing out of the blue and crashing in on your family history.'

'Listen, the more Halvorsens, the merrier in my book. I'm currently the last of the line.'

'Well, there's only one way to find out. And that's to ask your father.'

'I'm sure he'll lie,' Thom said bitterly, 'as he normally does.'

'From how you describe him, I'm hoping he's nothing to do with me at all.'

'I'm really not trying to be negative, Ally. There just isn't an awful lot of positive,' Thom shrugged.

'Okay,' I said, moving the conversation on, 'let me work out the generations. So, Jens and Anna had a son named Horst.'

'They did, yes.' Thom went to his bureau and took a book from the top of it. 'This is the biography I wrote and I drew up a Halvorsen family tree. Here,' he said, handing it to me. 'It's at the back of the book before the acknowledgements.'

'Thanks.'

'Horst was a fine cellist and went away to study in Paris, rather than Leipzig,' Thom continued as I searched for the page. 'He returned to Norway and played for the Bergen Philharmonic for most of his life. He was a lovely man, and even though he was ninety-two when I was born, I still remember him being active in my early years. It was he who first put my fingers to the violin when I was three, so my mum told me. He died at the age of one hundred and one, having never suffered a day's illness in his life. Let's hope I've inherited his genes.'

'And what about his children?'

'Horst married Astrid, who was fifteen years younger than him, and they lived here at Froskehuset for most of their lives.

They had a son whom they named Jens after his grandfather, although he was always known as Pip, for some reason.'

'And what happened to him?' I asked, confused, as I studied the family tree.

'This is the story I mentioned and it's pretty harrowing, Ally. Given you're not well, are you sure you're up to it?'

'Yes,' I said firmly.

'Okay. So, Jens Junior proved himself a talented musician and set off to Leipzig to study, just like his namesake before him. But of course, it was 1936 and the world was changing . . .'

Pip

Leipzig, Germany

November 1936

38

Jens Horst Halvorsen – more commonly known as 'Pip', a nickname given when he was just a tiny seed in his mother's stomach – walked swiftly towards the grand pale-stone building that housed the Leipzig Conservatory. This morning he and his fellow students had a master class with Hermann Abendroth, the famous conductor of the Leipzig Gewandhaus Orchestra, and he was tingling with excitement. Since coming to Leipzig two and a half years ago after the narrow musical confines of his hometown of Bergen, a whole new world had opened up to him, both creatively and personally.

Instead of the beautiful – but, to Pip's ear, old-fashioned – music from the likes of Grieg, Schumann and Brahms that he had listened to with his father, Horst, since childhood, the Conservatory had introduced him to composers that were alive now. His current favourite was Rachmaninoff, whose *Rhapsody on a Theme of Paganini*, which had premiered two years ago in America, was what had first inspired Pip to write his own music. As he walked through the wide streets of Leipzig, he whistled the tune under his breath. His studies in piano and composition had fired his creative imagination and exposed him to progressive musical ideas. As well as admiring Rachmaninoff's brilliance, he had also been spellbound by Stravinsky's *The Rite of Spring*, a piece so modern and daring that even over twenty years after its Paris premiere in 1913, it still prompted his own father, an accomplished cellist himself, to pronounce it 'obscene'.

As he walked, Pip thought about the other love of his life, Karine. She was the muse that inspired him and drove him forward to improve. One day, he would dedicate a concerto to her.

They had met at a recital in the Gewandhaus concert hall on a chilly October evening over a year ago. Pip had just begun his second year at the Conservatory and Karine her first. In the foyer of the Gewandhaus, waiting to take their seats in the back row of the audience, she had dropped a woollen glove and Pip had retrieved it for her. Their eyes had met as he'd handed it back to her and they had been inseparable ever since.

Karine was an exotic mix of French and Russian parentage and had been brought up in a distinctly bohemian household in Paris. Her father was a French sculptor of some renown and her mother a successful opera singer. Her own creativity had found its *métier* in the oboe and she was one of the few women to study at the Conservatory. With her black hair as velvety as a panther's coat, and glittering dark eyes that sat above angular cheekbones, Karine's skin, even in the height of summer, always remained as pale and white as Norwegian snow. She dressed in a unique style, shunning the usual feminine adornments and preferring trousers paired with an artist's smock or a tailored jacket. Far from making her appear masculine, her clothes only enhanced her sultry beauty. Her only perceived physical imperfection – which she complained about regularly – was her nose, apparently inherited from her Jewish father. Pip wouldn't care if it was the size of Pinocchio's after a lie. To him, she was perfect, just perfect.

They had already discussed their future together: they would do their best to find jobs in orchestras in Europe, then they hoped to save enough to go to America and build a new life there. This was more Karine's dream than his, if Pip was honest. He could be happy anywhere as long as she was by his side, but he understood why she wished to go. Here in Germany, the anti-Jewish propaganda spread by the Nazi party grew apace and in other parts of the country, Jews were continually being harassed.

Luckily, the mayor of Leipzig, Carl Friedrich Goerdeler, was still a staunch opponent of the Nazi ethos. Pip assured Karine daily that nothing bad would happen to her here and that he would look after her. And when they married, he always added, she would have a Norwegian surname to replace her rather more obvious 'Rosenblum' – 'Even though you *are* a beautiful rose in bloom,' he would tease her whenever the subject arose.

But today was a glorious sunny day and the tense rumblings of the Nazi threat seemed distant and over-exaggerated. He had decided that morning, despite the chill in the air, to take the pleasant twenty-minute stroll to the Conservatory from his lodgings in Johannisgasse rather than take the tram. He reflected how the city had grown since his father's day. Although Horst Halvorsen had lived in Bergen most of his life, he'd been born here in Leipzig and the knowledge of a family connection gave Pip an extra sense of belonging.

As he neared the Conservatory, he passed the bronze

statue of Felix Mendelssohn, the music school's founder, which stood outside the Gewandhaus concert hall. He mentally tipped his cap to the great man before checking his watch and stepping up his pace as he realised he was cutting it fine.

Two of Pip's close friends, Karsten and Tobias, were already waiting for him, leaning against one of the colonnaded arches that formed the entrance to the school.

'Good morning, sleepyhead. Karine kept you up late last night, did she?' Karsten enquired with a mischievous grin.

Pip smiled amiably at his teasing. 'No, I walked here and it took longer than I thought.'

'For God's sake, hurry up you two,' interrupted Tobias. 'Do you really want to be late for Herr Abendroth?'

The three of them joined the steady stream of students now filing into the Großer Saal, a vast space with a vaulted ceiling supported by rows of pillars and an upper gallery that looked down onto the ground floor and the stage. It was used as both a lecture theatre and a concert hall. As Pip sat down, he remembered his very first piano recital here and grimaced. His fellow students and professors were a far more critical audience than any he would find in public concert houses in the future. And indeed, his performance then had been duly analysed and torn to shreds afterwards.

Now, two and a half years on, he felt almost impervious to any acid remarks about his playing; the Conservatory prided itself on producing professional musicians who were toughened up and ready to walk out of its doors to join any orchestra in the world.

'Have you seen the newspaper this morning? Our mayor has gone to Munich to meet with the Party,' whispered Tobias as they took their seats. 'No doubt to be put under further pressure to employ their anti-Semitic tactics here in Leipzig. The situation becomes more dangerous by the day.'

A rousing cheer went up as Hermann Abendroth entered the hall, but as Pip applauded, his heart beat a little faster at the news Tobias had just imparted.

That evening, he met with Karine and her best friend Elle in their usual coffee house that lay between his lodgings and theirs. The two women had been thrown together in their first term at the Conservatory, when they'd been allocated a room together. As they were both French by birth and shared a mother tongue, they had bonded immediately. Tonight Elle had brought along her young man, Bo, of whom Pip knew little other than that he was also a second-year music student. As they ordered a round of *Gose* beers, Pip was struck by the contrast of Karine's arresting dark-eyed looks against Elle's blonde, blue-eyed prettiness. *The gypsy and the rose*, he thought as their drinks arrived at the table.

'You've heard the news, I presume?' Karine lowered her voice as she spoke to him. These days, one never knew who was listening.

'Yes, I have,' he replied, seeing the tension etched on Karine's features.

'Elle and Bo are worried too. You know Elle is also Jewish, even though she doesn't look it. Lucky her,' Karine murmured before turning her attention to her friends sitting on the other side of the table.

'We think it must only be a matter of time before what is happening in Bavaria starts to happen here,' Elle said quietly.

'We must wait and see what the mayor can do whilst he is in Munich. But even if the worst happens, I'm sure they won't touch students at our school,' Pip reassured them. 'Germans have music in their hearts and souls, whatever their politics.' As he spoke, he wished that his words did not have such a hollow ring to them. He looked across the table at Bo, whose haunted eyes were sombre as he rested his arm protectively around his girlfriend's shoulder. 'How are you, Bo?' Pip asked.

'I am well enough,' he replied.

He was a man of few words who had earned his nickname because of his insistence on carrying his cello bow with him everywhere he went. Pip knew he was one of the most talented cellists at the Conservatory and great things were predicted for him.

'Where will you spend Christmas?'

'I . . .' At that moment, Bo looked over Pip's shoulder and his body jerked in shock, the colour draining from his face. Pip turned to see two SS officers in their distinctive grey uniforms sauntering through the door, pistols sheathed in leather holsters around their waists. Pip watched Bo shudder and avert his eyes. Sadly, it was hardly an uncommon sight in Leipzig these days.

The two men surveyed the occupants of the café, then sat down at a table close by.

'We are not sure of our plans yet,' Bo replied, recovering himself. He turned to Elle and whispered something to her, then a few minutes later they stood up to leave.

'They are both so frightened,' Karine sighed, as she and Pip watched the pair depart as unobtrusively as they could.

'Is Bo Jewish too?'

'He says not, but so many lie, even if they are. His concern is for the woman he loves. I think they may leave Germany soon.'

'And go where?'

'They do not know. Paris perhaps, although Elle says Bo worries that if Germany wishes to make a war, it will reach France too. My home.' Karine reached out her hand, and as Pip took it, he could feel it trembling.

'As I said, let us see what happens when Mayor Goerdeler returns,' Pip repeated. 'If necessary, Karine, we too will leave.'

The following day, Pip walked through the soft grey November mist of the Leipzig morning on his way to the Conservatory. As he approached the Gewandhaus, his legs almost buckled under him as he stared at the crowd that had gathered in front of it. Where only yesterday the glorious statue of Felix Mendelssohn, the Jewish founder of the original Conservatory, had stood proudly, there now lay nothing but a pile of rubble and dust.

'Oh dear Lord,' he muttered under his breath as he hurried past everyone, hearing the chants of abuse shouted out by a large crowd dressed in their Hitler Youth uniforms standing amidst the ruins of the statue. 'It has begun.'

When he reached the Conservatory, a mass of shocked students filled the entrance hall. He found Tobias and walked over to him. 'What has happened?'

'It was Haake, the deputy mayor, who ordered the destruction of the statue. It was all planned for when Goerdeler was in Munich. Now he will surely be forced out. And then Leipzig is lost.'

Pip searched for Karine amongst the chaos and found her staring out of one of the arched windows. She jumped as he placed a hand on her shoulder and when she turned to him he saw the tears in her eyes. She shook her head wordlessly as he took her into his arms.

All classes were cancelled that day by the principal of the Conservatory, Walther Davisson; tensions were running high in the area, and it was deemed too dangerous for the students. Karine said she was meeting Elle in a coffee shop on the corner of Wasserstraße and Pip offered to accompany her. When they arrived, Elle was sitting with Bo in a discreet alcove.

'Now that this has happened, we have no one to protect us,' said Karine as she and Pip joined them. 'We all know that Haake is an anti-Semite. Look at how he tried to enforce these horrible laws from the rest of Germany. How long before they stop Jewish doctors from practising and Aryans from consulting them here in Leipzig?'

Pip looked at the three pale faces surrounding him. 'We shouldn't panic, but wait until Goerdeler returns. The newspapers say it will be in a few days. He went from Munich to Finland on an errand for the Chamber of Commerce. I'm sure that when he hears of this, he will head back to Leipzig immediately.'

'But the mood in the city is so hateful!' Elle blurted out. 'Everyone knows how many Jews are studying at the Conservatory. What if they decide to go further and raze the whole place to the ground, like they have done with synagogues in other cities?'

'The Conservatory is a temple to music, not to a political or religious power. Please, we must all try to keep calm,' Pip reiterated. But Elle and Bo were already deep in a whispered conversation between themselves.

'That is all very easy for you to say,' Karine remarked to him in an undertone. 'You are not Jewish, and will pass for one of their own.' She studied his light blue eyes and wavy red-blond hair. 'It's different for me. Just after the statue was taken down, I passed by a group of youths on my way to the Conservatory and they screamed out "*Jüdische Hündin!*"' She dipped her eyes at the memory. Pip knew perfectly well what it meant: 'Jewish bitch'. His blood boiled, but it would not help Karine if he lost his temper.

'And what's more,' she continued, 'I cannot even speak to my parents. They are in America preparing for my father's new sculpture exhibition.'

'My love, I will keep you safe. Even if I have to take you back to Norway to do it, no harm will come to you.' He grasped her hand in his and smoothed a strand of glossy black hair from her anxious face.

'Do you promise?'

Pip kissed her forehead tenderly. 'I promise.'

To Pip's relief, things did calm down over the next few days. Goerdeler returned and promised to rebuild the Mendelssohn statue. The Conservatory opened again and Pip and Karine did their best to avert their eyes from the wreckage every time they walked past it. It seemed the music played by the students was now infused with a renewed passion and poignancy. As if they were all playing for their lives.

The Christmas break arrived but it was not long enough to allow either Pip or Karine to return home. Instead, the two of them spent a week in a small hotel, checking in as man and wife. As he had been brought up in a Lutheran household with strict views on sex before marriage, Pip had been surprised at Karine's *laissez-faire* attitude towards it when she'd suggested they sleep together only weeks after they'd met. He'd discovered that she wasn't even a virgin, as he was. Karine had found it amusing that he was so shy about the whole thing when they'd made love for the first time.

'But of course, it is a natural process for two people in love,' she had teased as she'd stood naked in front of him, arranging her long white limbs with effortless elegance, her small perfect breasts jutting upwards. 'Our bodies are made to give us pleasure. Why should we deny them?'

Over the past months, Pip had been schooled in the art of physical love and had happily drowned in what his local pastor had called the sins of the flesh. It was the first Christmas he had spent away from home, and Pip decided that being in bed with Karine was far preferable to any present he might have received at home from St Nicholas on Christmas Eve.

'I love you,' he whispered constantly in her ear as he lay next to her, whether asleep or awake. 'I love you.'

The new term began in January and Pip, knowing he had limited time left at the Conservatory, concentrated his energies on imbibing all he was taught. Throughout the freezing Leipzig winter, he hummed Rachmaninoff, Prokofiev, and Stravinsky's *Symphony of Psalms* as he trudged through the snow. And as he did so, his own tunes began to form in his head.

He'd arrive at the Conservatory, grab some blank sheet music from his satchel, and with half-frozen hands, scribble them down before they were forgotten. He'd gradually learnt that the method of composition that worked best for him was one that relied on thinking freely and letting his imagination flow, rather than that favoured by other students which involved meticulous planning of themes and writing only one carefully-arranged bar at a time.

He showed his work to his tutor, who critiqued, but encouraged him. Pip lived in a state of high excitement, knowing that this was only the beginning of his unique process. His blood pulsed with energy and pumped faster through his veins as he began to listen to his inner muse.

The city was still relatively calm as Goerdeler was standing for re-election in March. The entire Conservatory supported him, distributing pamphlets and posters urging the city to vote, and Karine seemed confident he would win.

'Even though he has so far failed to have the statue rebuilt, surely, once the people have spoken and he has been re-elected, the Reich will have no choice but to support him in the venture?' she'd said hopefully as they drank coffee with Elle after returning from a long day of canvassing.

'Yes, but we all know Haake is openly against his re-election,' Elle had countered. 'The destruction of the Mendelssohn statue fully revealed his stance on Jews.'

'Haake is just drumming up tension to feather his Nazi nest,' Karine had agreed darkly.

On the night the votes were counted, Pip, Karine, Elle and Bo joined the crowds outside the city hall. And cheered euphorically when they heard that Goerdeler had been re-elected.

Sadly, as the blossoms appeared on the trees in May and the sun finally came out, the euphoria in the city proved to be short-lived.

Pip had been working all the God-given hours in his practice room at the Conservatory. Karine sought him out with the latest news. 'Word has come from Munich – the statue won't be rebuilt,' she said breathlessly.

'That is terrible news, but please, my love, try not to worry. We have only a short time left until the end of term and then we can take stock of the situation and make a plan.'

'But Pip, what if things deteriorate more quickly than that?'

'I'm sure they won't. Now, go home and I will see you this evening.'

But Karine had been right and Goerdeler resigned a few days later. Once again, the city was thrown into chaos.

Pip was busy preparing for his formal examinations, as well as perfecting his very first opus, which was to be performed at a graduation concert just before the end of term. Staying up late into the night to complete the orchestration, he struggled to come up for air to comfort a despairing Karine.

'Elle says that she and Bo will leave Leipzig immediately at the end of term in two weeks' time and will not return. They say it is too dangerous to be here now, with the National Socialists free to demand the sanctions against Jews that other cities are enforcing.'

'Where will they go?'

'They don't know. France perhaps, but Bo is worried the

trouble will follow them there. The Reich has supporters all across Europe. I will write to my parents for advice. But if Elle leaves, so will I.'

This news grabbed Pip's full attention.

'But I thought your parents were in America?'

'They are. My father is thinking of staying there whilst the anti-Semitic storm in Europe continues.'

'And you would follow them?' Pip felt a surge of panic twist his guts.

'If my parents think it is wise, then yes, I will go.'

'But . . . what about us? What will I do without you?' he said, hearing the selfish whine in his voice.

'You could come with me.'

'Karine, you know that I do not have the money to make the journey to America. And how would I earn a living there if I don't graduate from the Conservatory and get some experience before I go?'

'*Chéri*, I do not think you understand the gravity of the situation. German-born Jews who have lived here for generations have already had their citizenship taken away. My people are not permitted to marry Aryans, or join the army, and are forbidden from flying the German flag. I've even heard talk that in some regions they are rounding up whole neighbourhoods of Jews and deporting them. If all this has already been allowed to happen, who can say how much further it may go?' She squared her chin in defiance.

'So you would sail to America alone and leave me here?'

'If it will save my life, then yes, of course. For God's sake, Pip, I know that you are involved with your opus, but I assume you would rather have me alive than dead?'

'Of course! How can you even suggest I would think otherwise?' he said, anger rising in his voice.

'Because you refuse to take this seriously. In your safe Norwegian world, there has never been danger. Whereas we Jews understand that we will always be open to persecution, just as we have been throughout history. And now is no different. We feel it, all of us. Perhaps it is simply a tribal thing, but we know when there is imminent danger.'

'I can't believe you'd go without me.'

'Pip! Please, grow up! You know I love you and I want to spend the rest of my life with you, but this . . . situation is not new to me. Even before the Reich made our persecution legal, we have always been disliked. In Paris, my father had eggs thrown at him at one of his sculpture exhibitions years ago. Anti-Semitic feelings have existed for thousands of years. You must understand this.'

'But why is it so?'

Karine gave him a small shrug. 'Because, *chéri*, history has made us a scapegoat. People always fear those who are different, and over centuries we have been forced to leave one home for the next. And wherever we arrive, we settle and become successful. We stick together, for it is what we have been taught. It is how we have survived.'

Pip lowered his eyes in embarrassment. Karine was quite right. Having spent most of his life tucked away safely in his small town at the top of the world, what Karine was telling him was akin to a fictional story of another universe. And even though he'd seen with his own eyes the rubble of the torn-down Mendelssohn statue, he had somehow justified it in his mind that it was only a random group of young men making a protest, as the fishermen sometimes did when the price of fuel for their boats rose, but the fish merchants refused to increase the price per kilo.

'You are right,' he agreed. 'Forgive me, Karine. I am a naive idiot.'

'I think it is more to do with you not *wanting* to see the truth. You do not wish for the big, wide world to disrupt your dreams and plans for the future. None of us do. But yet here we are,' she sighed. 'And the simple truth is, I no longer feel safe in Germany. So I must leave.' She stood up. 'I'm meeting Elle and Bo in Coffe Baum in half an hour to discuss the situation. I will see you later.' Karine kissed the top of Pip's head and walked away.

When she'd left, Pip looked down at the music spread across the desk in front of him. The performance of his composition was scheduled to take place in under two weeks. Whilst he berated himself for his selfishness, he couldn't help wondering now if it would ever happen.

Karine was calmer when they met again later that day.

'I have written to my parents for advice and, in the meantime, I have no choice but to wait until I receive a reply. So, I may be able to hear you play your masterpiece after all.'

Pip reached for her hand across the table. 'Can you forgive me for being selfish?'

'Of course I can. I understand the timing could not be worse.'

'I've been thinking . . .'

'About what?'

'That perhaps the best answer would be for you to come

with me to Norway for the summer. You would not have to worry for your safety there.'

'Me? Go to the land of reindeer and Christmas trees and snow?' Karine teased him.

'Really, it doesn't always snow there. I think you'll find it's rather beautiful in summer,' Pip said, immediately defensive. 'We have a small Jewish population who are treated just the same as any other Norwegian citizens. You'll be safe. And if war does break out in Europe, it will not come to Norway, and neither will the Nazis. Everyone at home says that we are far too small and irrelevant a country for them to notice us. There's also a very good orchestra in Bergen – it's one of the oldest in the world. My father is a cellist there.'

Karine's dark, liquid eyes studied him intently. 'You would take me home with you?'

'Of course! My parents have heard all about you and my intention for us to be married.'

'They know that I'm Jewish?'

'No.' Pip felt the colour rising to his cheeks and then felt angry for letting it. 'But not because I didn't *want* them to know. Simply because your religion is irrelevant. They are educated people, Karine, not peasants from the hills. Remember, my father was born in Leipzig. He studied music in Paris and is forever telling us of the Bohemian life on the streets of Montparnasse during the Belle Époque.'

It was Karine's turn to apologise. 'You're right, I'm being patronising. And perhaps' – she put an index finger to the spot between her eyes just above her nose and rubbed it as she always did when she was thinking – 'maybe that is the answer if I cannot get to America. Thank you, *chéri*. It helps me to think there is a place of sanctuary if things here get worse in future.' She leant across the table and kissed him.

As Pip climbed into his bed later that evening, he only prayed that 'the future' could wait until after the performance of his opus.

Even though they read in the newspapers of Jews being pelted with stones as they walked out of a synagogue, and many other deeply worrying incidents, Karine seemed less anxious, perhaps because she now knew there was an alternative plan. So, for the following two weeks, Pip put his head down and concentrated on his music. He dared not look beyond the moment when term ended, and waited with baited breath for Karine to receive a reply from her parents that would possibly direct her to travel to America. The thought sent shudders through him because he knew that he did not have the money to follow her until he started earning as a musician.

At lunchtime on the day of the graduation concert, at which six new short works by students would be performed, Karine sought him out.

'*Bonne chance, chéri*,' she said. 'Elle and I will be there to cheer you on tonight. Bo says he thinks that yours is the best of all the compositions.'

'That is very kind of him. And he contributes wonderfully to my opus with his cello playing in the orchestra. Now, I must attend my last rehearsal.' Pip kissed Karine on her nose and walked along the long, draughty corridor to his practice room.

At seven thirty on the dot, Pip sat in his tails in the front row of the Großer Saal, along with the five other young composers. Walther Davisson, the principal of the Conservatory, introduced them all to the audience and the first composer took to the platform. Pip was up last and he knew that he would always remember waiting for the agonising hour and a half to pass before his turn. But pass it did, and with a small prayer sent upwards, he walked up the steps, hoping he wouldn't trip as his legs were shaking so. He gave a brief bow to the audience and took his seat at the piano.

Afterwards, he couldn't remember much at all about the applause or the cheers that went up as the other composers joined him for a communal bow. All he knew was that he'd been the best he could be on the night and that was all that mattered.

Later, he was surrounded by fellow students and professors, all slapping him on the back and telling him they predicted great things for him. A newspaper journalist also asked him for an interview.

'My very own Grieg,' Karine said with a giggle after she'd managed to fight through the crowds to embrace him. '*Chéri*, your glittering career has just begun.'

Having had far too much champagne after the performance, Pip was irritated to be woken early the next morning at his lodging house by someone knocking on his door. He stumbled out of bed to open it, and found his landlady still in her nightgown, looking vexed and disapproving.

'Herr Halvorsen, there is a young lady who says she wishes to see you urgently waiting downstairs.'

'*Danke*, Frau Priewe,' he said, before closing the door and throwing on the first shirt and pair of trousers he could find.

A white-faced Karine was waiting for him outside on the doorstep. Even in an emergency, it seemed that Frau Priewe's 'no young ladies in the house' rule still stood.

'What is it? What's happened?'

'Last night, three houses in Leipzig were set on fire – Jews were living in all of them. And Bo's lodging house was one of them.'

'Oh dear Lord! Is he . . . ?'

'He's alive. He managed to escape. He climbed out of his first-floor window and then jumped. With his precious cello bow, of course.' Karine managed a sad, ironic smile. 'Pip, he and Elle are leaving Leipzig immediately. And I really feel that I must go too. Come, I need some coffee, and from the looks of things, so do you.'

The small coffee house close to the Conservatory had only just opened its doors and was deserted as they sat down at a table by the window and ordered. Pip rubbed his face to try and recover his senses. He had a serious hangover.

'Have you heard from your parents?' he asked her.

'You know that as of yesterday, I had not. And today, it's too early for the postman,' Karine replied irritably. 'It's less than two weeks since I wrote to them.'

'What are Elle and Bo going to do?'

'They will leave Germany as soon as they can, that's for sure. But neither of them has the money to travel far. Besides, none of us know where it is safe to go. As for me, my family's apartment in Paris has been rented out while my parents are in America. I have no home to go to,' she said with a shrug.

'Then . . . ?' Pip second-guessed what she was saying.

'Yes, Pip, if you are still offering it, I will come with you to Norway, at least until I hear from my parents. It is all I can do. The end of term is only a few days away and your composition has been performed, so I see no reason to delay. When I saw Elle and Bo this morning, they said that after the fires last night, the exodus of Jews from Leipzig will begin in earnest, so we must leave while we still have the chance.'

'Yes,' Pip agreed. 'Of course.'

'And . . . I have something else to ask you.'

'What is that?'

'You know that since I arrived in Leipzig, Elle has become like my sister. Her parents are dead – killed in the Great War – and she and her brother were put into an orphanage. He was adopted as a small baby and she has not seen him since. Elle was not so lucky, and it is only because her music teacher spotted her talent on the flute and viola and put her forward for a scholarship here that she even has a future.'

'So she has no home?'

'Other than the orphanage, her home is here in Leipzig, in the room she shares with me. Bo and I are the only family she has. Pip, can they come to Norway with us? Even if it's just for a few weeks. From a place of safety, they can see how the situation develops in Europe, and decide what to do. I know it's a lot to ask, but I simply cannot leave Elle behind. And as she will not leave Bo, he must come too.'

Pip looked at her desperate expression, contemplating how his parents would feel if he turned up on their doorstep and announced that he'd brought three friends home to Norway for the holidays. He knew that they would be generous and welcoming, especially as all three were musicians.

'Yes, of course they can. If this is what you think is best, my love.'

'Can we leave as soon as possible? The sooner we're gone from here, the better. *Please*? You will miss your official graduation ceremony but . . .'

Pip knew that every day that Karine stayed in Leipzig was not only dangerous, but another day closer to a reply from her parents suggesting she join them in America. 'Of course. We can all go together.'

'Thank you!' Karine threw her arms around Pip's shoulders and he saw the relief in her eyes. 'Come on, let's go and tell Elle and Bo they are to come with us.'

39

Two days later, Pip led his exhausted friends down the steamer gangplank in Bergen harbour. A brief phone call made from the principal's office at the Conservatory was all the warning his parents had received of their surprise guests. A hurried series of goodbyes and thank yous had ensued with all his friends and tutors and the principal had given him a special slap on the back, praising Pip's generosity in taking his friends back to Norway.

'I am sad not to stay until the end of term,' Pip had said as he'd shaken Walther Davisson's hand.

'I think you are sensible to leave now. Who knows? Soon it may not be so easy,' he had sighed sadly. 'God speed, my boy. Write to me when you arrive.'

Pip turned to his friends, who were staring wearily at the line of candy-coloured wooden houses on the harbour front, trying to adjust to their surroundings. Bo could hardly walk. His face was bruised from where he'd fallen to the ground after he'd jumped out of the window and Pip suspected that he'd fractured his elbow. Elle had secured his right arm to his chest with her scarf, and he had uttered not one word of complaint during the long journey, despite the barely disguised agony on his face.

Spotting Horst, his father, standing on the dock, Pip walked towards him with a broad smile. 'Far!' he said, as his father placed his arms around his son's shoulders and they embraced. 'How are you?'

'I am very well indeed, thank you. And your mother is in good health too,' said Horst, smiling warmly at all of them. 'Now, introduce me to your friends.'

Pip did so and each of them shook his father's hand gratefully.

'Welcome to Norway,' Horst said. 'We are happy to have you here with us.'

'Far,' Pip reminded him, 'remember, none of my friends can speak Norwegian.'

'Of course! My apologies. German? French?'

'French is our mother tongue,' said Karine, 'but we speak German too.'

'Then French it shall be!' Horst clapped his hands together like an excited child. 'I never get a chance to show off my excellent accent,' he said with a grin, and proceeded to chatter away to them in the language as they walked towards his car.

The conversation continued all the way up the winding road into the hills beyond the town of Bergen to Froskehuset, their home, with Pip now feeling like the odd one out, as he knew very little French. Sitting in the front passenger seat, he glanced across at his father; his receding fair hair was swept back and his features were lined by years of his constantly happy demeanour – Pip could hardly remember him without a smile on his face. Horst had grown a small goatee beard, and together with his moustache, he now reminded Pip of pictures he'd seen of French impressionist painters. As predicted, Horst had seemed delighted to meet his friends, and he'd never loved his father more for his generous welcome.

Up at the house, his mother, Astrid – looking as pretty as ever – opened the door and extended the same warm welcome, albeit in Norwegian. Her glance immediately fell on Bo, who by now was so exhausted and in pain that he was hanging onto Elle for support.

Astrid clapped a hand to her mouth. 'What happened to him?'

'He jumped out of a window when his lodging house was set on fire,' Pip explained.

'The poor darling! Horst, you and Pip take our other guests through to the drawing room. And Bo,' she said, gesturing to a chair that stood by the telephone in the hallway, 'sit down and I will take a look at your injuries.'

'My mother is a trained nurse,' Pip explained under his breath to Karine as they followed Horst and Elle along the corridor. 'No doubt at some point you will hear the story of how she fell in love with my father while caring for him after an appendix operation.'

'She looks a lot younger than him.'

'She is, by fifteen years. My father always said he got himself a child bride. She was only eighteen when she got pregnant with me. They adore each other really.'

'Pip . . .'

He felt Karine's slim, sensitive fingers on his arm. 'Yes?'

'Thank you, from all of us.'

That evening, after the doctor had been called to dress Bo's wounds and an appointment made at the hospital to check whether his elbow was fractured, Bo was helped upstairs by Elle and Astrid and put to bed in Pip's room.

'Poor boy,' said Astrid as she came back down to prepare dinner and Pip followed her into the kitchen. 'He is simply exhausted. Your father has told me a little of what is happening in Leipzig. Can you pass me the potato scraper?'

'Yes.' Pip did so.

'They are all refugees rather than three friends coming to visit Norway?'

'They are both, I suppose.'

'And how long will they be staying?'

'The truth is, Mor, I don't know.'

'They are all Jewish?'

'Karine and Elle, yes. Bo, I'm not sure about.'

'I admit, it is difficult to believe what is happening in Germany. But believe it I must. The world is a very cruel place,' Astrid sighed. 'And Karine? She is the girl you have told us so much about?'

'Yes.' Pip watched his mother continue to peel the potatoes as he waited for her to comment further.

'She seems full of life, and very bright. I'd imagine she's quite a handful on occasion,' she added.

'She does challenge me, certainly. I've learnt a lot about the world,' Pip said, a hint of defensiveness in his voice.

'Just what you need – a strong woman. What your father would have done without me, the Lord only knows,' Astrid said with a laugh. 'And I am proud of you for what you have done to help your friends. Your father and I will do what we can to support them. Although . . .'

'What, Mor?'

'Your generosity has relegated you to the sofa in the drawing room until Bo is recovered.'

After dinner on the terrace, overlooking the glorious fjord beneath them, Elle went upstairs to check on Bo, who had been taken supper on a tray earlier, then she retired to bed. Horst and Astrid announced that they too were turning in for the night and Pip heard their quiet laughter as they mounted the stairs. As he'd watched the tension slip away from his friends' faces over dinner, he had never felt prouder of his parents or more thankful to be in Norway.

'I should go up too,' said Karine. 'I'm exhausted, but it is just too magical a view to waste. See? It is almost eleven at night and there is still light here.'

'And the sun will be up long before you tomorrow. I told you it was beautiful here,' Pip said as she stood up from the table and walked across the terrace to lean over the wooden railing, which formed a barrier between the house and the endless pine trees tumbling down the hills towards the water.

'It's more than beautiful . . . it's breathtaking. And not just the scenery. Your parents' welcome, their kindness . . . I feel overcome by it.'

Pip took her in his arms as she cried quiet tears of relief on his shoulder. She looked up at him, her eyes searching his face.

'Tell me I never have to leave.'

And he did.

Horst drove Bo and Elle to the local hospital the following morning. Bo was diagnosed with a dislocated elbow and compound fracture and remained there to have an operation to reset it. Elle spent the next few days at the hospital with him, which left Pip free to show Karine the delights of Bergen.

He took her up to Troldhaugen, Grieg's house, which was only a short walk from his own and had become a museum. And he watched her delight as they visited the hut perched on the side of the fjord where the maestro had written some of his compositions.

'Will you have one of these too when you are famous?' she asked him. 'I can bring you sweetmeats and wine at lunchtime and we can make love on the floor.'

'Ah, then I may have to lock myself in. A composer must not be distracted whilst he is working,' he teased her.

'Then I may have to take a lover to while away the lonely hours,' she shot back with a wicked smile, then turned to walk away.

Laughing, Pip caught up with her and wrapped his arms around her waist from behind, halting her progress. His lips sought out the tender curve of her neck. 'Never,' he whispered. 'No one but me.'

They took the train down into the town, strolling through the narrow cobbled streets and stopping at a café for lunch so that Karine could have her first taste of aquavit.

They both giggled as her eyes watered and she pronounced it 'stronger than absinthe' before promptly asking for another. After lunch, he took her to see the Nationale

Scene Theatre, where Ibsen had once been the artistic director and where Grieg had conducted the orchestra.

'Now they play at their very own venue, the Konsert-palæet, where my father spends a large part of his life as first cellist in the orchestra,' he added.

'Do you think he could get us both employment, Pip?'

'I'm sure he could put in a good word for us, yes,' he said, not wishing to dampen Karine's enthusiasm by telling her there wasn't – and never had been – a female member of the Bergen Philharmonic Orchestra.

Another day they took the Fløibanen – the tiny funicular railway – up to the top of Fløyen Mountain, one of the seven imposing peaks that surrounded Bergen. From the viewing platform there was a spectacular vista of the city beneath them and the sparkling fjord beyond. Karine sighed in pleasure as she gazed out over the railings.

'There surely cannot be a more beautiful sight in the world,' she breathed.

Pip loved Karine's genuine enthusiasm for Bergen, given that her dreams had always hitherto focused on the far larger goal of America. She asked Pip to start teaching her some basic Norwegian, frustrated that she couldn't communicate with his mother without a translator present.

'She has been so kind to me, *chéri*, I wish to tell her how I appreciate it in her own language.'

Bo returned to the house, his right arm strapped tightly, and the evenings were spent outside on the terrace having dinner, after which an impromptu concert would ensue. Pip would seat himself at the grand piano in the drawing room, with the doors onto the terrace thrown wide open. Depending on the piece, Elle would play her viola or flute, Karine her oboe, and Horst his cello. They played everything from simple Norwegian folk songs that Horst patiently taught them, to pieces by the old masters such as Beethoven and Tchaikovsky, to more modern compositions from the likes of Bartók and Prokofiev – although Horst firmly drew the line at Stravinsky. The wonderful music sang down the hills to the fjord. Pip's life became a harmonic conjoining of all he loved and needed and he was glad that fate had brought his friends to Norway.

Only late at night as he lay there shoehorned into a makeshift bed in the room he now shared with Bo, longing for Karine's sensual, naked body beside him, did he reflect that nothing was ever completely perfect.

As a balmy August drew to a close, there were serious conversations to be had amongst the Halvorsen household about the future. The first was between Pip and Karine, late one night on the terrace after everyone else had retired. Karine had at last received a letter from her parents, who had decided to stay in America until the storm clouds of war had rumbled past. Karine's parents advised her not to travel back to Germany for the new term. Equally, they thought it unnecessary for their daughter to make the long and expensive journey to America right away, given she was safely tucked away in Norway for the present. 'They send their love and thanks to your parents,' Karine said, folding the letter back into its envelope. 'Do you think Horst and Astrid will mind if I stay on longer?'

'Not at all. I think my father is a little in love with you. Or at least, with your oboe playing,' Pip said with a smile.

'But if I am to stay on here, we cannot continue to impose on your parents' hospitality. And I miss you, *chéri*,' Karine whispered as she snuggled into him and delicately nipped his ear with her teeth. Her lips searched for his and they kissed, before Pip broke away as a door opened upstairs.

'We are under my parents' roof, and you must understand that—'

'Of course I understand, *chéri*. But perhaps we could find our own place together here. I long to be with you . . .' Karine reached for his hand and put it to her breast.

'And I with you, my love,' Pip said, gently manoeuvring his hand away lest anyone caught them unawares. 'But even though my parents can accept many things that others in Norway would not, any suggestion of sharing the same bed whilst we are unmarried – whether under their roof or ours – would not be acceptable. And disrespectful of all they have done for us.'

'I know, but what can we do? This is agony for me.' Karine rolled her eyes. 'You know how I need that part of our relationship.'

'As do I.' Pip sometimes felt as though he was the female and she the male with regard to their physical union. 'But unless you are prepared to convert from your faith in order to marry me, then this is the way it is in Norway.'

'I must become a Christian?'

'More accurately, you would have to become a Lutheran.'

'*Mon Dieu!* That is a high price to pay for making love. In America, I am sure there are no such rules.'

'Maybe, but we're not in America, Karine. We live in a small town in Norway. And however much I love you, to blatantly live with you under the noses of my parents is something I just could not do. Do you see?'

'Yes, I do, I do, but to convert . . . well, it would be a betrayal of my people. Yet my mother was a gentile before she converted to marry my father, so genetically, I am only half-Jewish. I must ask my parents for their opinion. They have left the telephone number at my father's gallery for emergencies and I feel that this is one. And if they agree, can we marry soon?'

'I'm not completely sure of the rules, Karine, but I think the pastor would need to see your baptism papers.'

'As you know, I have none. Can you get it done here?'

'You would do that? Be baptised a Lutheran?'

'A few drops of water and a cross on my forehead does not make me a Christian in my heart, Pip.'

'No, but . . .' Pip felt she was rather missing the point. 'Apart from us being able to make love, are you sure you wish to marry me?'

'Forgive me, Pip,' Karine said, smiling. 'My need to answer the practical side of things has overruled the romantic part of our conversation. Of *course* I wish to marry you! So I will do what is necessary to make it happen.'

'You would really convert for me?' Pip was overwhelmed and touched. He knew only too well what her heritage meant to her.

'If my parents agree, then yes. *Chéri*, I must be sensible.

And I am sure any god – whether yours or mine – will forgive me, given the circumstances.'

'Even if I'm beginning to think you only want me for my body,' Pip teased her.

'Probably,' she agreed equably. 'I will ask your father tomorrow if I may make a call to America.'

Pip watched as Karine left the room and thought how she constantly blindsided him with her mercurial temperament and quixotic train of thought. He wondered if he would ever truly understand her complexity. At least if they were able to marry, he'd never find himself bored in the future.

Karine's parents returned their daughter's call the following evening.

'They have agreed,' she said sombrely. 'And not just so that I can marry you. They feel I would be safer taking your surname, just in case . . .'

'Then I am very happy, my love,' he said, sweeping Karine into his arms and putting his lips to hers.

'So.' Karine pulled away from him eventually, the expression in her eyes lighter. 'How soon can it be arranged?'

'As soon as you meet the pastor and he agrees to baptise you.'

'Tomorrow?' she said as her hand travelled towards his groin.

'Be serious,' he chastised her, groaning at her touch then reluctantly removing her hand. 'Are you happy to stay here in Norway for now?'

'There are worse places to make a life, and for the present, we must take one day at a time until we know what will happen. You know I love it here, apart from your horrible language, of course.'

'Then I must try to find immediate work as a musician to support us. Either in the orchestra here, or perhaps in Oslo?'

'Perhaps I too can find work.'

'Maybe you can, when you have at least learnt more than the words for "please" and "thank you" in our "horrible" language,' he teased her.

'Okay, okay! I am trying.'

'Yes.' Pip kissed her on the nose. 'I know you are.'

Astrid cooked a celebration dinner for the six of them when Pip and Karine announced that they wished to marry.

'Will you and Karine settle here in Bergen?' she asked.

'For now, yes. If you can help us find musical employment, Far,' said Pip.

'I can certainly make enquiries,' replied Horst, at which point Astrid stood up and clasped her future daughter-in-law in her arms.

'Now, that is enough about practicalities. This is a special evening. Congratulations, *kjære*, and I welcome you to the Halvorsen family. I am especially happy as I believed that we would lose Pip and his talents to Europe or America. And you have brought our son home.'

Pip translated his mother's words and saw tears in her eyes, and in those of his wife-to-be.

'Congratulations,' Bo said suddenly, toasting them. 'Elle and I hope to follow your lead soon.'

Astrid, who knew the pastor of the local church well, went to talk to him. Whatever she said to him of Karine's Jewish heritage, she kept to herself, but the pastor agreed to baptise her immediately. The Halvorsen household attended the short service, and later back at the house, Horst drew Pip aside.

'It is a good thing that Karine has done today, in more ways than one. I have a friend in the orchestra who has just returned from playing in a concert in Munich. The Nazi campaign against the Jews is growing apace.'

'But surely it will never touch us here?'

'One would think not, but when a madman has caught the attention of so many, and not just in Germany,' Horst added, 'who knows where it will all end?'

Soon afterwards, Bo and Elle announced that for now, they too were staying in Bergen. Bo's plaster had been removed, but his elbow was still too stiff to play the cello.

'Both of us are praying it will recover quickly. He is so very talented,' Elle confided to Karine in their shared bedroom that night. 'All his dreams depend on it. For now, he has found himself work at a chart maker's shop in the harbour. There is a small apartment above it which we have been offered. We have pretended we are already married and I will clean for the chart maker's wife.'

'You can both speak enough Norwegian to do this?' Karine asked her friend jealously.

'Bo is a fast learner. I just work hard. Besides, the chart maker is German, which as you know is a language we both speak quite well.'

'And will you marry for real?'

'We long to, yes, but we must save the money. So for now,

we must live a lie. Bo says the truth belongs in a heart, not on paper.'

'And I agree.' Karine reached her hand across to Elle. 'Promise we will remain close when you move into the town?'

'Of course. You are my sister in all but name, Karine. I love you and cannot thank you and Pip enough for what you have done for us.'

'And will we too soon have our own roof over our heads?' Karine asked Pip the following morning, after telling him Elle and Bo's news.

'If the interview tomorrow goes as I hope, then eventually yes,' Pip agreed. Horst had secured him an audition with Harald Heide, the conductor of the Bergen Philharmonic Orchestra.

'It will, *chéri*,' Karine reassured him with a kiss, 'it will.'

Pip was almost more nervous when he arrived at the Konsert-palæet than he had been when he'd auditioned for a place at the Conservatory. Perhaps, he thought wryly, it was because this time his performance had consequences in the real world, whereas back then he'd been a carefree youth with no responsibilities except to himself. He made himself known to the woman in the ticket booth, who led him down a corridor and into a spacious practice room, containing a piano and stacks of music stands. He was soon joined by a tall, broad-shouldered man with merry eyes and thick dark-blond hair, who introduced himself as Harald Heide.

'Your father has certainly praised your talents on more than one occasion, Herr Halvorsen. He's clearly delighted to have you back home in Norway,' he said, shaking Pip warmly by the hand. 'I understand that you play both the piano and the violin?'

'That's correct, sir, although piano was my main instrument when I studied in Leipzig. I hope to become a composer one day.'

'Come then, we will begin.' Herr Heide gestured to Pip that he should take a seat at the piano, while he himself sat down on a narrow bench that stood against one wall of the room. 'Whenever you're ready, Herr Halvorsen.'

Pip's hands trembled slightly as he raised them over the keyboard, but as he launched into the slow series of bell-like tolls that opened the first movement of Rachmaninoff's *Piano Concerto No. 2 in C Minor*, his nerves left him. The stormy passion of the music filled him as he closed his eyes, mentally hearing the accompanying parts of the string and woodwind sections as his fingers danced through the rapid progression of arpeggios that followed. He was halfway through the lyrical slow section in E flat major when Herr Heide stopped him.

'I think I have heard enough. That was really quite marvellous. If you play the violin even half as well, I can see no reason not to offer you work, Herr Halvorsen. Now, let us go to my office and we will talk further.'

Pip returned home an hour later, walking on air, and immediately broke the news to Karine and his family that he was now officially employed by the Bergen Philharmonic Orchestra.

'I will only be a "swing", covering piano and violin when the regulars are unavailable or unwell, but Herr Heide tells me the current pianist is old now and often unable to perform. He may retire soon.'

'Franz Wolf is like a creaking gate and has arthritis in his fingers. You will have many chances to play. Well done, my boy!' Horst slapped him on the back. 'We will play together just as Jens, my father, and I used to.'

'Did you also tell him that you are a composer?' Karine pressed him.

'Yes, but Rome wasn't built in a day, and for now I am just grateful I can support you as a husband should once we are married.'

'And perhaps one day I can join you in the orchestra too,' Karine said with a pout. 'I don't think I'm going to make a very good *Hausfrau*.'

Pip translated what Karine had said to his mother and she smiled. 'Don't worry. Whilst you and your father are making music, I will teach Karine all she needs to know about looking after a home.'

'Two Halvorsens once more in an orchestra, a son about to be married and, I'm sure, many grandchildren to love in the future.' Horst's eyes twinkled with happiness.

Pip saw Karine raise her dark eyebrows at him. She had often said she was not the maternal type and was far too selfish to have babies. He didn't take her seriously; it was her way to try to shock by saying the unthinkable. And he loved her for it.

Karine and Pip were married the day before Christmas Eve. A fresh fall of snow lay in a pristine blanket over the city, and the twinkling lights that bedecked the streets of central Bergen added a fairy-tale atmosphere to the proceedings as the two of them rode in a horse-drawn carriage to the Grand Hotel Terminus. After the reception party that Horst had insisted on paying for, the newly-weds finally said goodnight to their guests and made their way upstairs. As they entered their hotel room, which had been given to them as a wedding present by Elle and Bo, they fell into each other's arms with a hunger that only six months of abstinence could produce. As they kissed, Pip released the buttons of Karine's cream lace gown, and as it slid from her shoulders and arms, his fingertips followed its path downwards, trailing across her elegant collarbones before moving to brush her dusky pink nipples. She moaned and grabbed a handful of his hair, releasing his mouth from hers, and guided his head towards her breast. She gasped in pleasure as his lips closed around her nipple and she simultaneously pushed the dress down over her hips so that it finally fell to the floor. Then Pip lifted her in his arms and carried her to the bed, his breathing rapid and shallow, driven mad by desire. As he stood beside the bed and clumsily began to divest himself of his clothes, Karine knelt up on the mattress and stopped him.

'No – it is my turn now,' she said huskily. She deftly unbuttoned first his shirt, then his trousers. A few seconds later she drew him down on top of her and they lost themselves in each other.

Afterwards they lay together sated, listening to the clock in the old town square as it struck midnight.

'That was definitely worth converting for,' Karine announced, propping herself up on her elbow and smiling into Pip's eyes as she stroked his face with the back of her fingers. 'And if I hadn't said it before, I say it now, as your wife of a few hours – and I want you never to forget it: I love you, *chéri*, and I cannot remember ever being happier than I am tonight.'

'Nor can I,' he whispered, taking her hand from his cheek and pressing it to his lips. 'Here's to always.'

'Always.'

40

1938

As the snow and rain fell incessantly on Bergen during January, February and March, and the brief hours of daylight fell swiftly into darkness, Pip spent several hours each day at rehearsals with the Bergen Philharmonic. At first he was only called on to perform in the evening concerts once a week at most, but as poor Franz, the old pianist, began to take more time off due to his worsening arthritis, Pip gradually became a regular fixture in the orchestra.

Meanwhile, his spare time was consumed with composing his first concerto. He showed no one the results of his efforts. Not even Karine. When it was finished, he would dedicate it to her. In the afternoons after rehearsals, Pip would often stay on in the concert hall. There, surrounded by the ghostly atmosphere of an auditorium without an orchestra or audience, he would work on his composition at the piano in the pit.

For her part, Karine was kept busy by Astrid, who she had come to love dearly. Her Norwegian slowly began to improve and she did her best to learn the art of homemaking under her mother-in-law's good-natured guidance.

As often as Elle's work would allow, Karine would meet her friend in the tiny apartment above the chart maker's shop on the harbour front and the two of them would discuss their hopes and plans for the future.

'I can't help feeling jealous that you have your own home,' Karine confessed over coffee one morning. 'Pip and I are now married, yet we still live under his parents' roof and sleep in his childhood bedroom. It is not the most seductive location for romance. We must always take care to be quiet, but I long for the freedom to make love with abandon.'

Elle was used to her best friend's bold statements. 'Your time will come, I am sure,' she smiled. 'You are lucky to have the support of Pip's parents. For us, it is still difficult. Bo's elbow is far better than it was, but it has not yet recovered sufficiently to allow him to audition for the orchestra here, or anywhere else for that matter. He is devastated that he cannot pursue his passion at present. As I am, too, for that matter.'

Karine knew exactly how that felt – having been confined to a domestic environment since arriving in Bergen, her own musical ability had been limited to the casual evening performances at Froskehuset. But she also acknowledged that her problems paled into insignificance compared to the challenges that faced Elle and Bo.

'I'm sorry, Elle, I'm being selfish.'

'My sister, you are not. Music is our lifeblood and it is hard to live without it. At least something good has come of Bo's inability to play. He enjoys his work with the chart maker and has thrown himself into learning about methods of navigation. For the time being, he is content, and so am I.'

'Then I am glad,' said Karine. 'And happy we are still

living in the same town and can see each other as often as we want. I don't know what I'd do without you.'

'Or I without you.'

In early May, Pip announced to Karine that he had saved enough money to be able to rent a tiny house on Teatergaten, in the heart of the town, only a stone's throw away from the theatre and the concert hall.

When he told her, Karine burst into tears. 'It is very good timing, *chéri*. Because apart from anything else, I should tell you that I am . . . *mon Dieu!* I am pregnant.'

'But that's the most wonderful news!' Pip exclaimed, rushing to his wife's side and enveloping her in an ecstatic embrace. 'Try not to look so horrified,' he teased, as he tipped her quivering chin up so that he could meet her gaze. 'You, with all your naturalistic beliefs, should be the first to admit that a child is simply the result of two beating hearts in love.'

'I know all that, but I am sick as a dog every morning. And what if I don't like the child? What if I turn out to be a terrible mother to it? What if—'

'Hush now. You are simply frightened. As all new mothers-to-be are.'

'No! The women I know have always revelled in their pregnant state. They have sat there like broody mares patting their burgeoning stomachs and enjoying the attention. And all *I* see is an alien inside me, taking away my flat stomach and sucking dry my energy!'

With that, Karine collapsed against him in a further fit of noisy sobbing.

Pip suppressed a smile, took a deep breath and did all he could to console her.

Later that evening, they told Horst and Astrid they were to be grandparents. And that he and Karine would be moving into a home of their own.

A general round of congratulations ensued, although Horst did not hand Karine a glass when the bottle of aquavit was produced.

'You see?' she complained as she climbed into bed next to him. 'All my pleasures are now in the past.'

Pip chuckled as he pulled her into his arms and his hand reached under her nightgown to caress the tiny bump. It was, he thought, like the first sighting of a half-moon in a starry sky. He and she had made it together. And it was a miracle.

'It is only another six months, Karine. And I promise that on the night of the birth, I will bring an entire bottle of aquavit to your bedside and you can drink the lot.'

In early June, they moved into their new house on Teatergaten. Although tiny, it was pretty as a picture with its duck-egg-blue clapboard exterior and a wooden terrace leading from the kitchen. Over the summer, while Pip was at work, Karine, with Astrid and Elle's help, worked hard to decorate the interior and placed pots of petunias and lavender on the terrace. In spite of their meagre budget, it gradually became a haven of homely tranquillity.

On the night of his twenty-second birthday in October, Pip came home from the theatre after an evening performance to find Karine, Elle and Bo standing in the sitting room.

'Happy birthday, *chéri*,' said Karine, her eyes dancing with excitement as the three of them moved aside to reveal an upright piano that was placed behind them in the corner of the room. 'I know it's not a Steinway, but at least it's a start.'

'But how . . . ?' Pip asked her in astonishment. 'We haven't the money for such a thing.'

'That is for me to worry about and for you to enjoy. A composer must have his own instrument available at all times in order to pursue his muse,' she said. 'Bo tried it and says it has a good tone. Come, Pip, and let us hear you play.'

'Of course.'

Pip went to the piano and ran his fingers over the fall-board that protected the keys, admiring the simple inlaid marquetry that decorated the golden wood on the panel above it. There was no maker's mark, but the instrument was well constructed and in excellent condition, and had obviously been lovingly polished. He lifted the fallboard to reveal the gleaming keys and then searched around for something to sit on.

Elle stepped forward hastily. 'And this is a gift from us,' she said, producing an upholstered stool from its hiding place behind a chair and placing it in front of the piano. 'Bo carved the wood himself and I sewed the seating pad.'

Pip glanced at the finely turned pine legs and the intricate needlepoint pattern on the cushion. He felt overwhelmed. 'I . . . don't know what to say,' he said as he sat down. 'Except thank you, both of you.'

'It is nothing compared to what you and your family have done for us, Pip,' said Bo quietly. 'Happy birthday.'

Pip lifted his fingers to the keyboard and began to play the first few bars of Tchaikovsky's *Capriccio in G Flat*. Bo was right, the instrument did indeed have a beautiful tone, and he thought excitedly how he could now work on his concerto at any time of the day or night.

As Karine grew larger, her due date only a few weeks away, Pip sat at his beloved piano, scribbling frantically and experimenting with chords and harmonic variations, knowing that once the baby arrived, the peace of the household would soon be disturbed irrevocably.

Felix Mendelssohn Edvard Halvorsen – his first name given after Karine's father – arrived into the world happy and healthy on 15th November 1938. And just as Pip had suspected, after all Karine's fears, she took to motherhood like a duck to water. Whilst Pip was glad to see her so fulfilled and content, he had to admit that he sometimes felt excluded from the close-knit mother-and-baby bond. All his wife's attention was focused on their precious son and Pip both adored and resented the change of focus in equal measure. The thing he found hardest to cope with was that in the past, Karine had always encouraged him to work on his composition; but these days, it seemed that every time he sat down at the piano, she shushed him. 'Pip! The baby is sleeping and you will wake him up.'

However, there was one particular reason that made him glad that Karine *was* in a maternal cocoon – it meant that she did not care to glance at the newspapers, which every week seemed to reveal escalating tensions in Europe. After the annexation of Austria by Germany back in March, there had been a glimmer of hope at the end of September that war might be averted: France, Germany, Britain and Italy had signed the Munich Agreement, which conceded the Sudetenland area of Czechoslovakia to Germany, in return for a pledge from Hitler that Germany would make no further territorial demands. The British prime minister, Neville Chamberlain, had even announced in a speech that the agreement would lead to 'peace for our time'. With all his heart, Pip prayed that Mr Chamberlain was right. But as the autumn wore on, the talk in the orchestra pit and on the streets of Bergen was increasingly gloomy – few believed that the Munich Agreement would hold.

At least the Christmas festivities provided a welcome hiatus. They spent Christmas Day at Horst and Astrid's house with Elle and Bo. On New Year's Eve, Karine and Pip held a small party in their own home and as the midnight bells rang in the new year of 1939, Pip took his wife into his arms and kissed her tenderly.

'My love, all I am I owe to you. I can never thank you enough for what you have been to me. And given me,' he whispered. 'Here's to all three of us.'

On New Year's Day, Karine – who had been persuaded to leave Felix in the tender care of his grandparents – together with Pip, Bo and Elle, boarded the Hurtigruten ship in Bergen harbour and they set sail up the magnificent western coast of

Norway. Karine even forgot her maternal pangs as she gazed at the countless stunning sights they passed. The Seven Sisters waterfall, suspended on the edge of the Geirangerfjord, was her favourite.

'It is truly breathtaking, *chéri*,' she said as she stood on deck with Pip, muffled in layers of wool against the sub-zero temperatures. They both stared in awe at the incredible natural ice sculptures that had formed when the tumbling streams had frozen solid in mid-flow at the onset of winter.

The Hurtigruten sailed on and up the coast, darting in and out of the fjords and stopping at all manner of tiny ports with food supplies and mail deliveries, providing a lifeline for the residents of the isolated communities dotted along the coast.

As they sailed towards the northernmost point of their voyage, Mehamn, high on Norway's Arctic coast, Pip explained the phenomenon of the aurora borealis to his companions.

'The Northern Lights are like the Lord's very own heavenly light show,' he said, trying to summon the beauty of the spectacle into words and knowing he was failing.

'You have seen it?' asked Karine.

'Yes, but only once, when the conditions were right and the lights appeared as far south as Bergen. I've never taken this trip before.'

'How is it formed?' asked Elle, as she stared up at the clear, starry sky above them.

'I am sure there's a technical explanation,' Pip conceded, 'but I am not the person to provide it.'

'And maybe there is no need for one, anyway,' said Bo.

The passage up from Tromsø was choppy and both the women took to their cabins as the ship approached the North Cape headland. The captain announced that this was the best vantage point from which to see the Northern Lights, but knowing how sick Karine was, Pip had no choice but to leave Bo alone on deck staring up to the heavens and go below to care for her.

'I told you I hated the water,' Karine groaned as she crouched over the bag that had been thoughtfully provided for those suffering from seasickness.

Dawn broke over more tranquil waters as they left the North Cape and sailed south back towards Bergen. Bo greeted Pip in the dining room, his features flooded with excitement.

'My friend, I saw them! I saw the miracle! And its majesty was enough to convince the most fervent non-believer in a higher power. The colours . . . green, yellow, blue . . . the entire sky was lit with radiance! I . . .' Bo choked on his words, then recovered himself. His eyes glistening with unshed tears, he reached out his arms to Pip and clasped him in a hug. 'Thank you,' he said. 'Thank you.'

Back in Bergen, so as not to disturb baby Felix, Pip retreated to the deserted concert hall, or to his parents' house to use the piano there. He found his brain was foggy, due to the endless broken nights when Felix would scream incessantly from a bout of colic to which he was particularly prone. Even though Karine would get up to attend to the baby and leave her husband to sleep, knowing how much work he had to do, the high-pitched noise of Felix's cries reverberated around the paper-thin walls of the little house so that rest was impossible for either of them.

'Perhaps I should simply slip some aquavit into his bottle and have done with it,' said an exhausted Karine over breakfast after a particularly bad night. 'That baby is killing me,' she sighed. 'I am so sorry for the disturbance, *chéri*. I cannot seem to quieten him. I am simply a bad mother.'

Pip put his arms round her and smoothed away her tears with his fingers. 'Of course you're not, my love. He will grow out of it, I promise.'

As the summer approached, both parents despaired of ever having a full night's sleep again. Then on the first night of silence, they both woke automatically at two o'clock, the hour when the caterwauling would normally begin.

'Do you think he's all right? Why isn't he crying? *Mon Dieu!* What if he's dead?!' said Karine, flying out of the bed to run to the cradle wedged into a corner of the tiny room. 'No, no, he is breathing and doesn't seem to have a fever,' she whispered, standing over Felix and putting her hand to his forehead.

'Then what is he doing?' Pip asked.

A smile began to form on Karine's lips. 'He is sleeping, *chéri*. Just sleeping.'

As peace was restored to the household, Pip went back to work on his music. After much thought, he had decided to call it *The Hero Concerto*. The story he'd read of the priestess who flouted the rules of the temple by allowing her young admirer to make love to her, then, when he drowned, throwing herself into the sea after him, suited Karine's dramatic and independent nature well. Besides, Karine *was* his 'Hero', and Pip knew that if he ever lost her, he would do the same.

One afternoon in August, he put down the pencil he used to write on the sheet music and stretched his arms above him in relief. The last orchestration was now complete. His composition was finished.

The following Sunday, he and Karine took baby Felix up by train to visit his parents at Froskehuset. After lunch, he handed out the sheet music containing the parts for cello, violin and oboe and asked Karine and Horst to study them. After a quick rehearsal – they were both experienced sight-readers – Pip sat down at the piano and the little orchestra began to play.

Twenty minutes later, Pip rested his hands in his lap and turned to see his mother wiping tears from her eyes.

'My son wrote that . . .' she whispered, glancing up at her husband. 'I think he has inherited your own father's gift, Horst.'

'Yes, indeed,' said Horst, also visibly moved. He clapped a hand on Pip's shoulder. 'It's truly inspired, my boy. It must be played to Harald Heide as soon as possible. I am convinced he will wish to premiere it here in Bergen.'

'Of course, it's all down to me for buying you the piano,' said Karine airily as they sat on the train on the way home. 'And now, when you become rich, you can replace the pearl necklace I sold to buy it.' She reached over to kiss his cheek as she saw the shocked expression on his face. 'Do not fret, my love. You have done Felix and me proud and we love you.'

Pip plucked up the courage to seek out Harald Heide at the concert hall before the first evening performance of the week. Finding him backstage, he explained that he had written a concerto and wished to gain Harald's opinion on it.

'No time like the present. Why don't you play it for me now?' Harald suggested.

'Er . . . very well, sir.' Nervously, Pip sat down, put his fingers to the keys and played the entire concerto through from memory. Harald did not stop him, and when Pip had finished, he applauded him loudly.

'Well, well, it's very, very good indeed, Herr Halvorsen. The recurring theme is delightfully original and hypnotic. I'm already humming it. Glancing through these pages, I can see that some of the orchestration will need work, but I can give you some help with those. I wonder,' he said as he handed the sheets of music back to Pip, 'whether we have another young Grieg in our midst. There was a definite strain of his work within the structure, but perhaps I also heard Rachmaninoff and Stravinsky in there as well.'

'I am hoping you heard a bit of me too, sir,' Pip replied bravely.

'Indeed I did, indeed I did. Well done, young man. I think we might look towards adding it to the programme in early spring, which would give you time to work on the orchestration.'

After the concert, Pip took the liberty of waking up his sleeping wife. 'Can you believe it, *kjære*?! It's happening! By this time next year, I may be a professional composer!'

'That is the most wonderful thing I have ever heard. Not that I doubted it for a second. You will have influence,' she said with a giggle. 'I will be the wife of the famous Pip Halvorsen.'

'Of course, I will be "Jens Halvorsen",' he corrected her. 'Taking the proper name of my grandfather before me.'

'Who I'm sure would be very proud of you, *chéri*. As I am.'

They toasted the news with a glass of aquavit each and then completed the celebration with a silent bout of lovemaking, so as not to disturb Felix, who lay peacefully asleep in his cot at the bottom of their bed.

Why is it that happiness is always short-lived? Pip asked himself miserably as he read in the newspaper on 4th September that, following the German invasion of Poland on 1st September, France and Britain had declared war on Germany. As Pip left the house and walked the short distance to the concert hall for a rehearsal, he could feel the pall of gloom which hung over the town's residents.

'But Norway managed to remain neutral in the last war, so why not in this one? We are a nation of pacifists and should have nothing to fear,' said Samuel, one of Pip's fellow musicians, as the orchestra tuned up their instruments in the pit. All of them were agog at the news and buzzing with nervous tension.

'Ah, but remember that Vidkun Quisling, who leads the fascist party here in Norway, is doing his best to drum up support for Hitler's cause,' replied Horst sombrely as he rosined his cello bow. 'He has already presented many lectures on what he calls "the Jewish problem". And should he come to power, God forbid, there can be little doubt that he would take the side of the Germans.'

After the concert, Pip drew his father to one side. 'Far, do you really think that we will become involved in this war?'

'I'm afraid it is possible.' Horst shrugged sadly. 'And even if our nation resists the call to bear arms for either side, I have my doubts that the German regime will leave us be.'

That night, Pip did his best to console Karine, whose eyes burnt once more with the fear he had seen in Leipzig.

'Please, calm yourself,' he said to her as she paced up and down in the kitchen, holding a wriggling Felix protectively to her breast, as if the Nazis would suddenly burst through the front door and wrest her son from her arms. 'Remember that you are now a baptised Lutheran and your name is Halvorsen. Even if the Nazis invade here, which is very unlikely, no one is to know that you're Jewish by birth.'

'Oh Pip! Please, stop being so naive! They would only need to take one look at me to see the truth. And then a little investigation would reveal it. You do not understand their thoroughness – they will stop at nothing to root us out! And what about our son? He has Jewish blood! Perhaps they will take him too!'

'I cannot see any way they can discover it. And besides, we have to believe they will not come here,' Pip said, pushing his father's earlier comments determinedly to the back of his mind. 'I've been told by several people that there is a constant trickle of Jews coming from Europe via Sweden to Norway to *escape* the Nazi threat. They see it as a safe haven. Why can't you?'

'Because they may be wrong, Pip . . . they may be wrong.'

She sighed suddenly, and collapsed into a chair. 'Will I always be forced to feel fear?'

'I swear, Karine, I will do everything I can to protect you and Felix. Whatever it takes, my love.'

She looked up at him, her dark eyes haunted and disbelieving. 'I know that is your wish, *chéri*, and I thank you for it, but sadly even you may not be able to save me this time.'

Just as had happened after the Mendelssohn statue in Leipzig had been reduced to rubble, Pip felt the atmosphere of tension calming in the following month, as everyone in Norway began to accept the situation and react to it accordingly. King Haakon and their prime minister, Johan Nygaardsvold, did all they could to reassure their citizens that Germany was not interested in their tiny corner of the world. There was no need to panic, they reiterated, although the army and navy had been mobilised and various precautions were already being put in place in case the worst did happen.

At the same time, Pip, guided by the experienced and nurturing hands of Harald, spent hours perfecting his orchestration. Just before Christmas, Harald gave him the wonderful news that *The Hero Concerto* was to be included in the Spring Programme. This engendered further rounds of aquavit when he arrived home after the concert that evening.

'And my first performance will be dedicated to you, my love.'

'And I will be there to hear you give birth to your masterpiece. You were there when I gave birth to mine,' she said as she threw herself drunkenly into his arms. And then they made love with noisy abandon, unimpeded by their son, who was staying overnight at his grandparents'.

41

On a rainy March morning in 1940, Pip sat across the breakfast table from his wife, and saw a frown deepen on her brow as she read the letter from her parents.

'What is it, my love?' he asked her.

Her eyes met his. 'My parents say that we should leave for America immediately. They are convinced that Herr Hitler's plan is for world domination. That he will not be sated until he has control of Europe and then beyond. See, they have sent as many dollars as they could to help us with the cost of the voyage.' She waved some thin notes at him. 'If we sold the piano, we could easily find the rest of the money. They say France and even Norway are no longer safe from invasion.'

Pip, only weeks away from his premiere, scheduled for a special Sunday concert at the Nationale Scene theatre on 14th April, met her gaze steadily. 'Forgive me, but how can your parents, who are thousands of miles away, know more about the situation in Europe than we do?'

'Because they have an overview, a neutrality that we here cannot have. We are "in" it, and perhaps we are all deluding ourselves here in Norway, because it is all we can do for comfort. Pip, truly, I think it is time for us to leave,' she urged him.

'My darling, you know as well as I do that the future for all three of us rests on the success of the premiere of my concerto. How on earth can I walk away from that now?'

'To keep your wife and child safe, perhaps?'

'Karine, please don't say that! I have done all I can to protect you and will continue to do so. If we wish to make our future in America, I must have a reputation that goes before me. If I don't have it, I will arrive as simply another would-be composer from a country most Americans have never heard of. I doubt I'll walk into the New York Philharmonic or any other orchestra as a tea boy, let alone as someone to be taken seriously.'

Pip saw the sudden anger flash in Karine's eyes. 'Are you sure it is the money you wish for? Or is this more for your own ego?'

'Please, stop patronising me,' he said coldly as he rose from the table. 'I am your husband, and the father of our son. And it is up to me to make the decisions in this house. I have a meeting with Harald in twenty minutes. We'll talk about this later.'

Pip left the house, seething with resentment and thinking that sometimes Karine pushed him too far. As well as reading every newspaper he could lay his hands on, his ear was constantly to the ground, carefully monitoring the chatter on the streets and in the orchestra pit. There were two Jewish musicians amongst their ranks and neither of them seemed to think there was a reason to panic. And no one had so far suggested that Herr Hitler had imminent plans to invade Norway. Surely, he thought as he walked through the streets of the town, Karine's parents were scaremongering? Given the premiere was in three weeks' time, it would be total madness for them to leave now.

And for once, Pip thought, a surge of irritation rising inside him at the undermining of his opinions, Karine would listen to her husband.

'Then so be it.' Karine shrugged dismissively as Pip told her that evening that his plan was for the family to remain in Bergen until after the premiere. 'If you believe that your wife and son are safe here, I have no choice but to trust you.'

'I do believe you are safe. For now anyway. In the future, we can take a view as necessary.' Pip watched her as she rose from her chair after listening tensely to his strong rebuttal of her parents' thoughts and her own instincts. 'Of course, I cannot stop you leaving if that is what you wish to do,' he added with a weary shrug.

'As you have pointed out, you are my husband and I must bow to your opinion and judgement. Of course, Felix and I will stay here with you. It is our place.' She turned away from him and continued towards the door. Then she paused and turned back. 'I just pray that you are right, Pip. For God help us all if you are not.'

Five days before Pip's concerto was due to be premiered, the German war machine attacked Norway. The country, whose merchant fleet was fully occupied helping Britain to provide a blockade in the Channel to protect it from invasion, was taken completely unawares. The Norwegians, with their skeletal navy, did their best to defend the ports of Oslo, Bergen and Trondheim, even managing to destroy a German warship in Oslofjord carrying arms and supplies. But the bombardment from sea, sky and land was incessant and unstoppable.

As Bergen was beleaguered, Pip, Karine and Felix retreated up into the hills to the sanctuary of Froskehuset and sat there in terrified silence, listening to the buzz of the Luftwaffe overhead and the sound of gunfire in the town below them.

Pip could not raise his eyes to meet Karine's gaze; he knew exactly what it would contain. They got into bed that evening, both of them silent, and lay there like two strangers with Felix asleep between them. Eventually, unable to bear it any longer, Pip searched for her hand.

'Karine,' he said into the darkness, 'how can you ever forgive me?'

There was a lengthy pause before she answered. 'Because I must. You are my husband and I love you.'

'I swear that, even now this has happened, we are safe. Everyone says the citizens of Norway have nothing to fear. The Nazis only invaded us in order to protect the passage of their iron ore supplies from Sweden. It is not about you and me.'

'No, Pip.' Karine gave an exhausted sigh. 'But it is always about *us*.'

Over the next two days, the residents of Bergen were assured by their German occupiers that they had nothing to fear and that life would go on as normal. Swastikas hung from City

Hall, and soldiers in Nazi uniforms filled the streets. The town centre had been badly damaged during the battle for Bergen, and all future concerts were cancelled.

Pip was in despair. He had risked his wife's and his son's life for a premiere that now would never take place. He took himself outside and walked up and into the forest. He slumped onto a fallen tree and put his head in his hands. For the first time in his adult life, he wept with shame and horror.

Bo and Elle came to visit them that evening up at Froksehuset and the six of them discussed the situation.

'I hear our brave King has left Oslo,' said Elle to Karine. 'He's hiding somewhere up in the north. And Bo and I are leaving too.'

'When? How?' asked Karine.

'Bo has a fisherman friend who works out of the harbour. He has said he will take us and any others who wish it across to Scotland. Will you join us?'

Karine threw a furtive glance at Pip, who was deep in conversation with his father. 'I doubt my husband will want to come. Are Felix and I in danger here? Elle, please tell me. What does Bo think?'

'None of us knows, Karine. Even if we reach Great Britain, the Germans may invade there too. This war is like a plague that spreads everywhere. At least here, you are married to a Norwegian, and are now a Lutheran yourself. Have you told anyone here of your original religion and heritage?'

'No! Well, apart from my parents-in-law, of course.'

'Then perhaps it is best you stay here with your husband. You have his name, and the history of his famous Bergen family to protect you. It is not the same for Bo and me. We have nothing to hide behind. We are only grateful to Pip and his family for giving us sanctuary and leading us out of danger. If we had stayed in Germany, then . . .' Elle shuddered. 'I have heard stories of camps for Jews, of whole families disappearing from their homes in the dead of night.'

Karine had heard them too. 'When will you leave?'

'I will not tell you. It is best that you don't know, in case things here get worse. Please say nothing to Pip, or his parents.'

'Will it be soon?'

'Yes. And Karine,' Elle said, grabbing her friend's hand, 'we must say our goodbyes now. And I can only hope and pray that one day we will meet again.'

They embraced then, their eyes glistening with tears, and took each other's hand in a show of silent solidarity.

'I will always be here for you, my friend,' Karine whispered. 'Write to me when you reach Scotland.'

'I will, I promise. Remember that despite his misjudgement, your husband is a good man. How could anyone except those of our race have foreseen this? Forgive him, Karine. He cannot understand what it is like to always live in fear.'

'I will try,' Karine agreed.

'Good.' With a small smile, Elle stood up from the sofa and gestured to Bo that she was ready to leave.

As Karine watched them go, she knew with a certainty that came from her soul that she would never set eyes on either of them again.

Two days later, Karine and Pip braved the journey down the hillside and made their way home. They saw smoke was still billowing from the burnt-out houses along the harbour side that had been destroyed in the shelling and fires.

The chart maker's shop was one of them.

Both of them stood and gazed at the smouldering heap in horror.

'Were they in there?' Pip choked out the words.

'I don't know,' Karine replied, remembering her promise to Elle. 'Maybe.'

'Oh dear Lord.' Pip fell to his knees and started to weep, but as he did so Karine spotted a platoon of German soldiers marching down the road.

'Stand up!' she hissed. '*Now!*'

Pip did as he was told, and both of them nodded deferentially at the soldiers as they passed by, hoping they would be seen as simply a young Norwegian couple in love.

On the morning of what should have been the premiere of *The Hero Concerto*, Pip woke to find that Karine had already left the bedroom. Seeing Felix was still happily asleep in his little bed at the bottom of theirs, he went downstairs to find his wife. Walking into the kitchen, he found a note propped up on the table.

Gone to find bread and milk. Back soon. x

Pip went to the front door and wandered anxiously into the street to look for her, wondering what on earth had possessed her to leave the house alone. He could hear the odd pop of gunfire in the distance – there were still pockets of the Norwegian army putting up a fight to the bitter end, although no one was under any illusions as to who the victors were.

Not seeing a soul in the deserted street whom he could ask about his wife's whereabouts, Pip went back inside the house and went to rouse his son. Felix, who was now seventeen months old, climbed out of bed, then toddled down the stairs holding his father's hand. There was another sudden loud burst of gunfire.

'Bang bang!' Felix said with a grin. 'Where Mama? Hungry!'

'She'll be back soon, let's go and see what we can find you to eat in the kitchen.'

Pip understood immediately why Karine had gone out as he opened the food cupboard to find it was bare, then noticed the two empty milk bottles standing by the sink. Pip resorted to a scrap of bread left over from supper last night to keep Felix quiet until she returned. He sat the boy on his lap and read him a story, trying to concentrate on something other than his own fear.

Two hours later, there was still no sign of Karine. In desperation, Pip knocked on his neighbour's door. The woman comforted him with the fact that there were already food shortages, and that she herself had queued for over an hour yesterday to buy bread.

'I'm sure she'll be back very soon; she may have had to travel further than usual to find some provisions.'

Pip went back home and decided he could stand it no longer. After dressing Felix, he left the house, holding his little son firmly by the hand. Billows of acrid smoke from the Luftwaffe's bombing raid still hung across the bay, and the occasional sound of gunfire continued. The streets were mostly deserted, even though it was past eleven o'clock. He saw that their usual bakery had its shutters closed, as did the greengrocer and fishmonger further along Teatergaten. He heard the heavy footfall of a patrol, and as he turned the corner, saw them marching towards him.

'Soldier!' Felix pointed to them, oblivious to any danger they represented.

'Yes, soldier,' Pip said, racking his brains for where Karine might have headed to. Then he thought of the small parade of shops on Vaskerelven, just past the theatre. Karine would often ask him to go there on the way to or from work if there was anything they needed.

As he approached the theatre, he looked up and saw that the front of it was completely blown away. He choked in horror at the sight. His immediate thought was that although he had the original piano music up at Froskehuset, the rest of his orchestration had been kept under lock and key in the theatre's main office.

'My God, they're almost certainly all gone,' he muttered, distraught.

Averting his gaze so as not to show his distress and fear to his son, Pip marched past the remains of the theatre, determined not to allow himself to dwell on what had been inside.

'Far? Why people sleep?' Felix pointed to the square a few yards away, and it was then that Pip saw the bodies – maybe ten or twelve – which looked as though they had been thrown to the ground like discarded rag dolls. He could see that two of them were dressed in Norwegian army uniform, and the rest were obviously civilians – men and women and a young boy too. There must have been a skirmish earlier and innocents had got caught in the crossfire.

Pip tried to pull his son away, but Felix stayed rooted to the spot, pointing at one of the bodies.

'Far, we wake Mor up now?'

Ally

Bergen, Norway

September 2007

"Åse's Death"

42

Tears were stinging my eyes as Thom, who had paced up and down while telling me his tale, finally collapsed into a chair.

'God, Thom, I simply don't know what to say. How utterly awful,' I whispered eventually.

'Yes. Dreadful. It's so hard to believe it was only two generations ago. And that it happened right here, in what you have so far thought of as our safe haven at the top of the world.'

'How on earth could Pip have coped after Karine died? He must have felt completely responsible for her death.'

'Ally, I . . . He didn't. Cope, that is.'

'What do you mean?'

'Pip brought Felix up to stay here with his grandparents after he'd found Karine shot dead in the square. He told Horst and Astrid he was going out for a walk, that he needed some time to think. When he didn't return by nightfall, Horst went out to look for him. And found him dead in the woods just above the house. He'd taken his father's hunting gun from the shed and killed himself.'

I was rendered speechless, shock and horror coursing through me. 'Oh my God, poor, poor Felix.'

'Oh, he was all right,' Thom said abruptly. 'He was too young to understand what had happened and Horst and Astrid took him in, of course.'

'But still, losing both his parents in a day . . .' I read Thom's expression and decided to shut up.

'Sorry, Ally,' Thom conceded, having heard the hardness in his own voice. 'Actually, what I think is even worse was that, having never been told the truth about how his father died, some bright spark in the Bergen Philharmonic decided to impart the news one day, thinking Felix already knew.'

'Ouch,' I shuddered.

'He was twenty-two and had just joined the orchestra. I've often wondered if that's what made him go off the rails, lose focus and start drinking . . .' Thom's voice trailed off.

'Perhaps,' I answered gently, wanting to reply that yes, I was sure the revelation was enough to destabilise anyone, but refraining from it.

Thom jumped up suddenly as he glanced at his watch. 'Time to go, Ally, or we'll miss your doctor's appointment.'

Leaving the house, we jumped into the car and Thom drove fast down the hill towards central Bergen. Arriving at the surgery, he swung the car up in front of the entrance. 'You go in and I'll follow you when I've parked.'

'Really, there's no need, Thom.'

'I'll come in anyway. Not everyone speaks English or French in Norway, you know. Good luck.' He smiled at me and headed off to the car park.

I was called in immediately, and even though the female doctor's English wasn't perfect, it was good enough to understand what I was trying to tell her. She asked me various questions, then gave me a thorough pelvic examination.

As I sat up afterwards, she said she wanted to do some blood tests and take a sample of urine.

'What do you think the problem is?' I asked nervously.

'When was your last menstrual period, Miss . . . D'Aplièse?'

'I . . .' The truth was, I couldn't remember. 'I'm not sure.'

'Is there a chance you could be pregnant?'

'I . . . don't know,' I replied, unable to compute the enormity of her question.

'Well, we will take the tests for blood just to rule out anything else. But your uterus is definitely enlarged and therefore your sickness is probably due to the first few weeks of pregnancy. I'd say you are currently about two and a half months along.'

'But I've lost weight,' I said. 'It can't be that.'

'Some women do, due to the sickness. The good news is that the nausea tends to calm down after the first trimester. You should be feeling better very soon.'

'Right. Er, thank you.' I stood up, feeling suddenly breathless and faint as she gave me a sample pot to take to the bathroom and directed me to the phlebotomy nurse. Leaving her consulting room, I found the nearest loo, did what I needed to and then sat there, sweating and shaking, desperately trying to recall the last time I'd bled.

'Oh my God,' I said to the echoing walls. It had been just before I'd joined Theo and his crew on the boat to train for the Cyclades race in June . . .

As I staggered out of the bathroom to go and give some blood, I thought darkly about how many times I'd heard a woman say she hadn't realised that she might be pregnant. And I'd always laughed at them, wondering how any woman could miss a monthly bleed without it entering their mind.

Now *I* was that woman. Because with everything else that had happened in the last few weeks, I just hadn't noticed the lack of it.

But how? I thought as I found the nurse who'd be taking my blood and rolled up my sleeve so she could tighten the elastic strap above my elbow. I'd always been so careful, taking the Pill like clockwork. But then I thought of that night on Naxos when I'd been so ill in front of Theo and he'd looked after me so tenderly. Was it possible that it had in some way affected the contraceptive effect of the Pill? Or had I simply forgotten to take it one day in the turmoil after Pa's death . . . ?

Walking back to reception, I handed in my urine sample and was told the results would be back tomorrow afternoon, and that I should call the surgery to get them.

'Thank you,' I said to the receptionist and turned to see Thom at my shoulder.

'Okay, Ally?'

'I think so, yes.'

'Good.'

I followed Thom back to the car and sat in silence as he drove me to my hotel.

'Are you sure you're all right? What did the doctor say?'

'Oh, that I was . . . run down, stressed. She's doing some tests,' I replied casually, not prepared to divulge the details of what had been a potentially life-changing fifteen minutes until I'd come to terms with it myself.

'Well, I have an orchestra call at the Grieg Hall tomorrow morning, but why don't I pop along to your hotel and see how you are afterwards at about noon?'

'Yes, that would be great. Thank you for everything, Thom.'

'That's okay. And I'm sorry if my story earlier distressed you. Call me if you need anything, won't you?' he said as I got out of the car and saw the look of concern on his face.

'Of course I will. Bye.'

As I watched the car disappear back up the quayside, I hovered outside the entrance to the hotel. I needed to know for certain, and the pharmacy I'd spotted as Thom and I had driven here would be about to close. I ran the few hundred metres up the hill, arriving breathless just as they were about to shut the doors. I bought what I needed, and walked at a far more sedate pace back to the hotel.

In the bathroom, I followed the instructions and waited the two minutes they told me it would take.

Daring to glance at the plastic stick, I saw that even after a few seconds the line was turning undeniably blue.

That evening, I ran through a gamut of emotions. Overwhelming relief that I wasn't really sick, only pregnant, followed by the dual fears that not only was something happening to my body over which I had no control, but that I would have to cope alone when it arrived. And then eventually, and totally unexpectedly, a slow-building joy began to bubble away inside me.

I was having Theo's child. Part of him lived on . . . and was currently inside me, growing and getting stronger each day. There was something so miraculous about this thought that, despite the fear, I cried tears of joy at the way life really did seem to find the means by which to replenish itself.

Once over the initial shock, I stood up and paced the room, no longer feeling lethargic and sick and scared, but infused with a new energy. This was happening, whether I liked it or not, and now I had to think about what I would do. What kind of a home could I give my child? And where? I knew that money was luckily not an issue. And I certainly wouldn't lack for help if I wanted it, what with Ma in Geneva and Celia in London. Not to mention the five doting aunts that my sisters would become. It wouldn't be a conventional upbringing, but I swore to myself that I would do my best to be both mother and father to mine and Theo's baby.

Much later, when I settled down to try and sleep, it suddenly occurred to me that not for one second since I'd known for certain had it crossed my mind not to have it.

'Hi, Ally,' Thom said as he kissed me on both cheeks in the hotel lobby the following day. 'You look better today. I was worried about you last night.'

'I am feeling better . . . I think,' I added, giving him a wry smile. And deciding that, in fact, I was desperate to share my news with someone. 'Actually, it looks like I'm pregnant and that's why I've been feeling so dreadful.'

'I . . . Oh wow, that's wonderful . . . isn't it?' he said, trying to gauge my thoughts.

'Yes, I really think it is, Thom. Even if it's a big shock. And unexpected, and there's no father, but, I feel so . . . happy!'

'Then I'm happy for you too.'

I knew Thom was still looking at me to make sure I wasn't simply being brave. 'Really, I'm okay with it. In fact, I'm better than okay.'

'Good. Then congratulations are in order.'

'Thank you.'

'Have you told anyone else yet?' he asked me.

'No. You're the first.'

'Then I'm honoured indeed,' he said as we wandered out of the hotel towards his car. 'Although, I am wondering whether what I had planned for you this afternoon is now suitable, given your delicate . . . condition.'

'What was it?'

'I was thinking we might pay a visit to Felix to see what he's got to say for himself. But as it's bound to be upsetting, perhaps we should leave it for now.'

'No, really, I'm absolutely fine. I'm sure the fear of feeling so rotten made me even sicker. Now I know the reason for it, I can start to plan. So yes, let's go and see him.'

'As I said yesterday, the chances are that even if he does know of your existence, he'll deny it. I was living right under his nose and he still refused to accept that I was his son.'

'Thom?' I asked him once we were seated in the car.

'Yes?'

'You seem more certain than I am that I have a family connection to you and the Halvorsens.'

'Maybe I am,' he agreed as he started the engine. 'Fact one: you told me your father gave each of you girls a clue to your pasts, to where your stories began. And in your case it was my great-great-grandfather's book. Fact two: you are or have been a musician, and it's been proved scientifically that talent can be passed down in the genes. Fact three: have you looked in the mirror lately?'

'Why?'

'Ally, look at us!'

'Okay.' We put our heads together and peered into the rear-view mirror.

'Yes,' I concluded, 'we are alike. But to be honest, it was one of the first things I thought when I came to Norway: that I looked like everybody else here.'

'I agree that you have the Norwegian colouring. But see? We even have similar dimples.' Thom marked his with his fingers, and I followed his lead, marking mine too.

I reached over the gearstick and gave him a hug. 'Well, even if we find out we're not related, I think I've found my new best friend. Sorry if that sounded like a line from a Disney film, but I'm feeling like I'm in a movie just now, one way or the other,' I said, laughing at the absurdity of it all.

'So,' he said as we pulled away from the kerb, 'tell me again that you're really up to this? That you're ready to visit the troll on the hillside, who might or might not be your biological father.'

'I am, yes. Is that what you call him? A troll?'

'That's kind compared to what I have called him in the past, let alone the adjectives my mother used.'

'Don't you think we should warn him we're coming?' I asked as we set off along the harbour.

'If he knows we are, he'll almost certainly be "out", so no.'

'Well, at least tell me a little more about him before we get there.'

'Apart from the fact that he's a useless waster who's let both his life and talent go to shit?'

'Thom, come on now. From what you told me yesterday, Felix had a dreadful time as a child. He lost both his parents in the most horrific way.'

'Okay, okay, Ally, I'm sorry. It's just years of learnt resentment, which admittedly was fuelled by my mother. In a nutshell, it was Horst who taught my father to play the piano. And apparently, so legend has it, he was playing concertos by ear at the age of seven, and had composed his own by twelve. Orchestrations and all,' Thom added as he drove. 'He won a scholarship to study in Paris at seventeen, and having then won the Chopin competition in Warsaw, was accepted into the orchestra here immediately. He was the youngest pianist the Philharmonic has ever employed. My mother told me that things went downhill from there. He had no work ethic, turned up late for rehearsals, often hungover, and by the evening he was drunk. Everyone put up with it because he was so talented, until they couldn't anymore.'

'A little like his great-grandfather, Jens,' I mused.

'Exactly. Anyway, eventually they threw him out of the orchestra for pitching up late, or not at all, once too often. Horst and Astrid also washed their hands of him and had no choice but to turn him out of Froskehuset. I think it was a case of what therapists these days call "tough love". Although Horst did give him the use of the cabin he and Astrid had built years ago when they wanted to spend time hunting up in the woods. It was extremely basic to say the least. He mostly lived off the women he charmed and, so my mother said, ricocheted from one to another. Even now, since he added electricity and running water, it really is little better than a glorified hut.'

'He's sounding more like Peer Gynt with every sentence you utter. How did he manage with no job?'

'He was forced to earn some money to fund his alcohol consumption by giving private piano lessons. That's how he met my mother. And sadly, not a lot has changed in the past thirty years since then. He's still a drunk, broke, an ageing lothario and completely unreliable.'

'What a waste of his talent,' I sighed.

'Yes, tragic. So there we are. The potted story of my father's life.'

'But what does he do up here all day now?' I asked as we climbed higher and higher into the hills.

'I couldn't really tell you, other than that he still takes the odd pupil, then promptly spends the money he earns from it on whisky. Felix is getting old, although that's not to say that he's lost his charm. Ally, I know it sounds inappropriate given why we're going to see him, but I'm worried he might hit on you.'

'I'm sure I can cope, Thom,' I said with a grim smile.

'I'm sure you can. I just feel . . . protective of you. And I'm starting to wonder why I'm even putting you through this. Maybe I should go and see him alone and explain the background first?'

I could feel the tension emanating from Thom and sought to ease it. 'At present, your father is absolutely nothing to me. He's a stranger. We're . . . *you're* taking a wild guess at what might or might not be. And if it is or it isn't, it won't be painful for me, I promise.'

'I hope not, Ally, I really do,' he said, slowing the car down and parking it close against a pine-tree-clad slope. 'We're here.'

As I followed Thom up the rough overgrown steps that apparently led to some form of habitation, I understood that this was a far more painful event for him than it was for me. Whatever lay at the top of the steps, I'd still had a father who had loved and cherished me all the way through my childhood. And I certainly wasn't looking for or needing another.

At the crest of the hill, the steps began to lead downwards and I saw a small wooden cabin nestled in a clearing amongst the trees. It reminded me of the witch's house in the story of Hansel and Gretel.

Standing in front of the door, Thom squeezed my hand. 'Ready?'

'Ready,' I said.

I watched him hesitate before he knocked. Then we waited for a response. 'I know he's in, because I saw his moped at the bottom of the hill,' Thom muttered as he knocked again. 'Sadly, he can't even afford a car these days and besides, he's been stopped so many times by the police in the past, he seems to think a bike's a more invisible mode of transport. God, he's so stupid!'

Eventually, we heard the sound of footsteps inside and a voice said something in Norwegian as the front door opened. Thom translated for me. 'He's expecting a pupil and thinks we're them.'

A figure appeared and I stared into the bright blue eyes of Thom's father. If I'd been expecting a raddled old man with a bulbous whisky nose and a body that had been broken after years of alcohol abuse, then I'd been wrong. The man standing on the doorstep was barefooted and wearing a pair of jeans with a large rip at the knee and a T-shirt that looked as if he'd slept in it for days. I'd already worked out that he must be in his late sixties, yet he only had a smattering of grey in his hair, and few telltale lines of age on his face. If I'd seen him on the street, I would have thought him at least a decade younger than he was.

'Hello, Felix, how are you?' said Thom.

He blinked at us in obvious surprise. 'I'm fine. What are you doing here?'

'We came for a visit. Long time, no see, et cetera. This is Ally.'

'New girlfriend, hey?' His eyes alighted on me and I felt him appraise me physically. 'Pretty.'

'No, Felix, she's not my girlfriend. Can we come in?'

'I . . . the housekeeper hasn't been in recently, so it's a mess, but yes, please do.'

I'd understood none of the preceding conversation of course, as they'd spoken in Norwegian.

'Does he speak English?' I whispered as I followed Thom inside. 'Or French?'

'Probably, I'll ask him.' Thom explained my linguistic disability and Felix nodded, instantly switching to French.

'*Enchanté*, mademoiselle. You live in France?' he asked as he led us through to a large but chaotically untidy sitting room, littered with teetering piles of tattered books and newspapers, used coffee cups, and random pieces of clothing discarded carelessly on various pieces of furniture.

'No, Geneva,' I explained.

'Switzerland . . . I went there once for a piano competition. It's a very . . . organised country. You are Swiss?' he asked as he indicated that we should sit down.

'Yes,' I answered, surreptitiously pushing an old sweater and a squashed trilby hat to one side to make room for me and Thom on the battered leather sofa.

'Well, that's a shame, for I was hoping we could discuss Paris, where I misspent my youth,' he said with a hoarse chuckle.

'I'm sorry to disappoint you. Although I do know the city quite well.'

'Not as well as I do, mademoiselle, I assure you. But that is another story.' Felix winked, and I didn't know whether to shudder or giggle.

'I'm sure,' I responded demurely.

'Could we speak in English, please?' said Thom abruptly. 'Then we can all understand.'

'So what brings you here?' asked Felix, switching languages as he'd been asked to.

'In a nutshell, Ally is searching for answers,' said Thom.

'To what?'

'Her true heritage.'

'What do you mean by that?'

'Ally was adopted as a baby, and her adoptive father died a few weeks ago and passed on some information that would help her find her biological family. If she wanted to,' Thom added. 'She was given the biography of Jens and Anna Halvorsen, written by your great-grandfather, as one of the clues. So I thought you might be able to help her.'

I saw Felix's eyes flicker over me again. He cleared his throat, before reaching for a pouch of tobacco and some papers and rolling a cigarette. 'How exactly do you think I can help?'

'Well, Ally and I have discovered that we're both the same age. And . . .' – I watched Thom having an inner struggle with himself before he continued – 'I wondered if there was any woman you'd known . . . as a girlfriend, perhaps . . . that . . . well, had a baby girl around the same time as Mum had me?'

At this, Felix let out a bark of laughter and lit up his cigarette.

'Felix, it's not a laughing matter, please.'

I reached for Thom's hand and squeezed it, trying to keep him calm.

'Sorry, I know it isn't.' Felix recovered himself. 'And Ally, is that short for Alison?'

'Alcyone, actually.'

'One of The Seven Sisters of the Pleiades,' he remarked.

'Correct. I was named after her.'

'Were you indeed?' he reverted to French suddenly and I wasn't sure if it was a deliberate ploy to irritate Thom or not. 'Well, Alcyone, sadly I know of no further offspring of mine. But if you wish me to call all my former girlfriends and ask if they, unbeknown to me, begat a baby girl thirty years ago, then I'd be happy to do so.'

'What did he say?' Thom whispered to me.

'Nothing important. So Felix,' I continued in fast French, 'don't blame Thom for asking difficult questions. I always thought that this was a wild goose chase. Your son is a very good person and he was only trying help me. I know your relationship has been difficult in the past, but you should be proud of him. Now, we won't take up any more of your time.' I stood up, feeling I'd had enough of his patronising manner. 'Come on, Thom,' I said, reverting to English again.

Thom stood up too and I saw the pain in his eyes. 'God, Felix, you really are a piece of work,' he commented.

'What have I done?' Felix protested with a shrug.

'I knew it was a waste of time,' Thom muttered angrily as we walked quickly to the door to let ourselves out then started to make our way back up the steps.

I felt a hand on my shoulder. It was Felix.

'Forgive me, Ally, it was a shock. Where are you staying?'

'At the Havnekontoret hotel,' I said tersely.

'Okay. Bye then.'

I ignored him and hurried to catch up with Thom.

'I'm sorry, Ally, it was a stupid idea,' he said as he unlocked the car door and climbed inside.

'No, it wasn't,' I comforted him. 'Thank you for trying. Now, why don't we go back to your house and I'll make you a calming cup of coffee?'

'Okay,' he said, as he reversed and we drove off at a pace, the small engine of the Renault roaring like an enraged lion at the unnecessary force of Thom's foot on the pedal.

Back at Froskehuset, Thom disappeared for a while, clearly wanting to be alone. I understood now how deep the pain of the past went for him. Felix's rejection had left an ugly festering scar which, having met Felix, I doubted could ever be healed. I sat on the sofa, passing the time by looking through the old handwritten sheet music of the piano concerto that Jens Halvorsen had written, which was placed in an untidy stack on the table in front of me. And as I idly scanned the first page, I noticed some numbers written in small lettering in the bottom right-hand corner. My brain did its best to fumble back to my schoolgirl lessons, and I took out a pen and translated the numbers in the back page of my diary.

'Well, of course!' I said out loud with a whoop of triumph. *This might cheer Thom up*, I thought.

'Okay?' I said when Thom eventually reappeared.

'Yup.' He sat down next to me.

'I'm so sorry you're upset, Thom.'

'And I'm sorry I introduced you to him. Why did I expect him to be any different? Nothing and nobody changes, Ally, and that's the truth.'

'Perhaps you're right, but listen, Thom,' I interrupted him, 'sorry to change the subject but I think I've just discovered something very exciting.'

'What is it?'

'Well, I suppose you just assumed that this concerto was the work of your great-great-grandfather, Jens?'

'Yes. Why wouldn't I?'

'Well, what if it wasn't?'

'Ally, his name is on the front page of the original sheet music.' Thom looked at me in confusion and pointed to it. 'It's sitting there in front of you. It says it was written by him.'

'What if the piano concerto you found wasn't by your great-great-grandfather Jens, but actually by your grandfather, Jens Halvorsen Jnr, more commonly known as Pip? What if this was *The Hero Concerto*, dedicated to Karine, which was never played? And that for reasons you explained yesterday, perhaps Horst put it away in the attic, because he couldn't even bear to hear it again after what had happened to his son and daughter-in-law?'

My thoughts hung in the air and I waited for Thom to catch them.

'Carry on, Ally. I'm listening.'

'I know you said that the concerto sounded Norwegian, and yes, it has influences certainly. And I'm no music historian, so don't quote me, but the music you played me yesterday just didn't fit with what was coming out of the early twentieth century. I heard strains of Rachmaninoff and, more importantly, Stravinsky in there too. And *he* wasn't composing his seminal works until the 1920s and 30s, well after the first Jens Halvorsen died.'

There was another pause, and I watched Thom as he thought about what I'd said.

'You're right, Ally. I suppose I just assumed it was the first Jens' work. Old sheets of music are just old to me, whether they've been around for eighty or ninety or a hundred years. I found so much sheet music up there in the attic that was definitely by the first Jens Halvorsen, I just presumed the concerto was by him too. And it doesn't call itself *The Hero Concerto*, does it? You know, the more I think about it, the more I have a feeling you might be right,' Thom agreed.

'You told me that the whole official orchestral score was almost certainly blown away when the theatre was bombed. This,' I said, pointing to the sheets, 'was probably Pip's original piano music, written before he'd even decided on a name for it.'

'My great-great-grandfather's works up to this one were far more romantic and derivative. This has fire, passion . . . It's different from anything else I've heard that he wrote. My God, Ally.' Thom gave a weak smile. 'We started with your mystery and it now looks as if we're dealing with mine.'

'As a matter of fact, there's irrefutable proof,' I pronounced and even I could hear a smugness to my tone.

'Is there?'

'Yes, look.' I pointed out the small letters inked at the bottom right-hand corner of the page.

'MCMXXXIX.' I read the letters out loud.

'So?'

'Did you do Latin at school?' I asked him.

'No.'

'Well, I did, and those letters stand for numbers.'

'Yes, even I know that much. But what do these represent?'

'The year 1939.'

Thom was silent as he digested what it meant. 'So, this *was* my grandfather's composition.'

'From the date on it, it must have been, yes.'

'I . . . don't know what to say.'

'No, neither do I. Especially after what you told me yesterday.'

We both sat in silence for a while.

'My God, Ally, it really is the most incredible find,' Thom said, finally recovering his powers of speech. 'I mean, not just because of the emotional connotations, but also the fact that it was originally due to be premiered by the Bergen Philharmonic almost seventy years ago. And because of everything I've told you, it never saw the light of day again.'

'And Pip had dedicated it to Karine . . . his "hero" . . .' I bit my lip as tears sprang to my eyes. The resonance in my own life wasn't lost on me.

I thought how they'd both been young too, just beginning their lives, when fate had cruelly intervened. And I thought then how lucky I was to live in a better time, to still be alive, and, with luck, have the privilege of caring for the child that was living inside me.

'Yes.' Thom had read my expression, and gave me a spontaneous hug. 'Whatever we discover we are to each other, Ally, I swear, I'll always be there for you. Promise.'

'Thanks, Thom.'

'Now, I'm going to take you home and then pop into the

Grieg Hall to find David Stewart, the leader of the orchestra. I have to tell him the story of *The Hero Concerto*. And he has to help me find someone who can orchestrate it in time for the Grieg Centenary Concert. It has to be played that night. Simple as that.'

'Yes,' I agreed, 'it does.'

There was a message waiting for me at reception when I walked into the hotel after Thom had dropped me off. I opened it in the lift, and to my surprise, I saw it was from Felix.

'*Call me*,' it said. He'd left a mobile phone number.

I would not call, of course, after his appalling behaviour earlier today. I took a shower and got into bed, mulling over the events of the day, and thought again how my heart went out to Thom.

Thom, who'd known from the very start of his life that he had a father who knew of his existence and yet had rejected him. And I remembered nights as a teenager, when I had railed against Ma's or Pa Salt's authority and wished for my real parents, who I'd been sure would understand me far better.

As I fell into sleep, I realised more than ever that my childhood had been blessed.

43

Before I did anything else the next morning, I called the doctor to get the results of my urine sample. As I knew it would be, the test was positive and the doctor sweetly congratulated me.

'When you arrive home in Geneva, Miss D'Aplièse, you must make arrangements for maternity services,' she added.

'I will. And thank you very much.'

I lay back on my bed, drinking weak tea, as I couldn't stand the smell of coffee. Even though I still felt as sick as a dog, now I knew it was natural, it didn't worry me. I made a mental note to order a pregnancy book online. I hadn't got a clue about anything to do with having a baby, but then did any woman until it happened to her?

I'd always been rather ambivalent about motherhood, with no strong feelings for or against. It had been one of those things that may or may not happen to me in the future. Theo and I had talked about it, of course, giggling as we came up with ridiculous names for our imaginary offspring. And discussing how the goat barn on 'Somewhere' would have to be large enough to house our sun-kissed brood as they enjoyed a childhood straight out of a Gerald Durrell novel.

Sadly, that idyll was not to be for us. And at some point in the near future, I must decide where I wanted to have the baby. And where 'home' actually was.

The telephone by my bed rang and I picked it up. Reception told me I had a call from a Mr Halvorsen. Presuming it would be Thom, I told the woman to put it through.

'*Bonjour, Ally. Ça va?*'

To my horror, it was Felix.

'I am well, yes,' I replied abruptly. 'You?'

'As well as my old bones will allow, yes. Are you busy?'

'Why?'

There was a pause on the line before he replied. 'I'd like to talk to you.'

'What about?'

'I don't want to discuss it over the telephone, so let me know when you're free to see me.'

I could hear from the timbre of his voice that whatever it was, it was serious.

'In an hour or so? Here?'

'Fine.'

'Okay. See you then.'

I was sitting in reception waiting for him when he arrived, holding a scuffed motorcycle helmet in one hand. As I stood up to greet him, I wondered if the light was unkind, or whether he really had aged overnight. Today, he looked like the old man he was.

'*Bonjour*, mademoiselle,' he said as he forced a smile. 'Thank you for sparing the time to see me. Is there somewhere we can go to talk?'

'I think there's a residents' lounge. Will that do?'

'Fine.'

I led him through the lobby and into the empty lounge. He sat down, gazed at me for a while and then gave a weak smile. 'Is it too early for a drink?'

'I don't know, Felix, it's up to you.'

'Coffee then.'

I went off to find a waitress to bring coffee and a water for me, thinking how deflated Felix looked this morning, as if the energy that drove him on had disintegrated and he was left crumpled and empty. We made small talk until the waitress delivered our drinks then left, and I knew whatever it was had to be said undisturbed and in private. I looked at Felix expectantly as he took a sip of his coffee, noticing that his hands shook as he held the cup.

'Ally, first of all, I want to talk to you about Thom. You're obviously close to him.'

'Yes, but I should point out that we haven't known each other for longer than a few days. It's quite extraordinary. There's a real bond between us already.'

Felix's eyes narrowed for a moment. 'There must be. I thought you two had known each other for years from the way you behaved together yesterday. Anyway, moving on, I suppose he's told you the story of how I refused to accept I was his father?'

'He has, yes.'

'Would you believe me if I said that, up until I took that DNA test, I sincerely thought he wasn't mine?'

'If you say so, I must.'

'I do, Ally.' Felix nodded vehemently. 'Thom's mother, Martha, was a student of mine. Yes, we had a brief affair, but perhaps Thom was never told that at the same time, she had a steady long-term boyfriend. In fact, she was engaged to him when we met and their wedding was already planned.'

'I see.'

'Without wanting to sound arrogant,' Felix continued, 'Martha took one look at me and that was that. She fell head over heels in love, to the point of obsession. And of course for me, the whole thing had meant nothing. Putting it bluntly, it was sex and that was an end to it. I'd never wanted anything more from her, or any other woman for that matter. To be truthful, Ally, I've never been the marrying kind, and certainly not father material. Perhaps these days you'd use the expression "commitment-phobe", but I always made it clear to my girlfriends how it was. I grew up in the age of free love, the Swinging Sixties, when everyone was suddenly freed from the old rules. And for better or worse, that attitude never left me. It's just who I am,' he shrugged.

'Okay,' I said, 'so when Thom's mother told you she was pregnant, what did you say to her?'

'That if she wanted the baby, which I believed at the time was bound to be her fiancé's child, given we had only slept together on a couple of occasions, then she should tell him and marry him as soon as possible. She informed me that she'd broken off the engagement the night before, because she'd realised she didn't love him. Apparently, she loved *me*.' Felix put a hand to his forehead and dragged it down over his eyes. 'I'm ashamed to say that I laughed in her face, told her she was crazy. Apart from the fact that there was no proof the baby was mine, the idea of us settling down together and playing happy families was absurd. I lived hand to mouth in a freezing cabin . . . What on earth could I have offered a woman and a child, even if I'd wanted to? So, I sent her away, believing that if she knew any future with me was a dead end, she'd have no choice but to go running back to her fiancé. But of course, she didn't. Instead, shortly after the birth, she ran to Horst and Astrid – my grandparents – who by that time were ninety-three and seventy-eight, and told them what a bastard I'd been to her. If my relationship with them had been rocky before, that finished it for good. My grandfather and I barely spoke again before he died, even though I'd worshipped him as I grew up. Horst was a wonderful man, really, Ally. When I was younger I thought of him as my hero.' Felix looked up at me miserably. 'Do you think I'm a bastard, Ally? Like Thom does?'

'I'm not here to pass judgement on you. I'm here to listen to what you have to say,' I said cautiously.

'Okay, so Martha disappeared after I'd told her I wanted nothing to do with the baby, though she did write to me and tell me she was continuing with the pregnancy, and was staying with a friend of hers up in the north near her family until she'd decided what to do. She continued to tell me she loved me in the endless letters she wrote to me. I didn't reply, hoping that my silence would encourage her to move on. She was young, and very attractive, and I was sure she'd have no problem finding someone else to give her what she needed. Then I . . . got a letter with a photograph enclosed just after the birth. I . . .'

Felix paused and I watched him gaze at me oddly, then he continued. 'I didn't hear from her for the next few months, until one day I saw her pushing a pram in town here in Bergen. Being the coward I am' – he grimaced – 'I hid from her, but then asked a friend of mine if he knew where she was living. And it was he who told me my grandparents had taken her in because she'd had nowhere else to go. The friend she'd been staying with had kicked her out apparently. Thom may have told you that she suffered from bouts of depression, and I can only imagine that she suffered postnatally.'

'How did you feel about her living with your grandparents?' I asked him.

'Bloody furious! I felt they'd been manipulated to take in a woman who claimed to have my child, but what could I do? She'd managed to convince them completely. They'd already written me off years before as an immoral waster, so my behaviour was just par for the course in their eyes. Jesus Christ, Ally, I was so angry. Angry for years. Yes, I'd made a mistake by getting a woman pregnant, but they never wanted to hear my side of the story, not once. Martha had made them believe that I was a shit and that was that. Listen, I'm going to get a drink. Want something?'

'No, thank you.'

I watched him stand and leave the lounge in search of the bar by reception. And I tried to remember Pa Salt's words about the other side of a story. Everything Felix had said so far made sense. And even if he was an irresponsible drunkard, I didn't think he was a liar. If anything, he was far too blunt and open. If the story was true, then I could see his point of view completely.

Felix arrived back with a large whisky in his hand.

'*Skål!*' he said as he took a big slug.

'Have you ever tried to tell Thom any of this?'

'Of course not.' He laughed out loud. 'From the day he was born, he was told what a rotter I was. And besides, he grew up incredibly defensive of his mother, and understandably so,' he added. 'Although as the years went by I did feel sorry for him, whether he was or wasn't mine. I knew from local gossip that Martha was sliding in and out of depression. At least the fact that Thom lived with my grandparents for the first few formative years of his life must have given him some essential stability. Martha really was a bit of a flake; she had a childlike quality to her, always believing that everything would be just as she wanted it.'

'So, you left the situation as it was until you found out Thom had inherited your family house?'

'Yes. Horst had died when Thom was eight, but my grandmother, who was considerably younger than him, died when Thom was eighteen. When the solicitor told me I'd been left Horst's cello and a small financial bequest, and that everything else had gone to Thom, I really felt I had to do something.'

'How did you feel when you found out you *were* Thom's father?'

'Absolutely astonished,' Felix admitted as he took another gulp of his whisky. 'But that's nature for you, isn't it?' he chuckled. 'Playing its little tricks. I know me contesting the will made Thom hate me even more. But given what I've just told you, I'm sure you can understand why I was convinced Thom was a cuckoo sitting in my hereditary nest.'

'Were you happy when you knew Thom was yours?' I asked him, feeling vaguely like a therapist analysing a client. Theo would have loved this, I thought.

'To be honest, I can't remember what I felt,' Felix admitted. 'I got very drunk for a few weeks after the test came back positive. Martha, of course, wrote me a vitriolic letter of triumph, which I threw on the fire.' He gave a deep sigh. 'What a mess, what a bloody mess.'

Both of us sat there silently for a while, me digesting what he'd told me. I felt a pervading sense of sadness for lives that had gone so wrong.

'Thom tells me you were a very talented pianist and composer,' I ventured.

'"Were"? I'll have you know I still am!' Felix smiled genuinely for the first time.

'Then it's a shame you don't use your talent.'

'And how do you know I don't, mademoiselle? That instrument sitting in my cabin is my lover, my torturer and my sanity. I may have been too drunk and unreliable for anyone to employ me professionally, but that doesn't mean to say I've stopped playing for myself. What do you think I do in that godforsaken cabin all day? I play, play for me. Perhaps one day I'll let you listen,' he said with a grin.

'And Thom too?'

'I doubt he'd want to, and I suppose I can't blame him. He's been the victim in this situation. Caught between a bitter, depressed mother and a father who never took responsibility for him. He has every right to despise me.'

'Felix, surely you should tell him what you've just told me?'

'Ally, I promise you, I'd only have to say one negative word about his precious mother, and he'd be out of the door. Besides, it would be cruel to destroy Thom's lifelong belief that she was the innocent party and remove her pedestal, especially now she's dead. What does it matter?' he sighed. 'What's done is done.'

I liked Felix more then, because what he'd just said showed that he cared about them. Even if it was obvious he hadn't done much to endear himself to his son.

'So, can I ask you why you've just told me all this? Is it because you want *me* to tell Thom?'

Felix stared at me for a few seconds, then picked up his whisky glass and drained it. 'No.'

'Then is it to tell me that Thom was right? That I'm another illegitimate child of yours? By another conquest?' I joked, even as the look in his eyes told me he had more to say.

'It's not as simple as that, Ally. Shit! Excuse me.' Once again, he stood up and almost ran to the bar, returning a few minutes later with another huge whisky. 'Sorry, it goes without saying I'm an alcoholic. And for the record, I play far better when I'm drunk.'

'Felix, what is it you want to tell me?' I urged him, worrying that he'd lose his train of thought as the whisky soaked into his bloodstream.

'The thing is . . . I saw it yesterday when you and Thom sat side by side on my sofa, like two damned peas in a pod. And I put two and two together. I've been up all night thinking whether it was right or wrong to tell you. Contrary to everyone's opinion of me, I do have some moral and emotional codes. And the last thing I want to do is cause any further damage than I already have.'

'Felix, please just *tell* me,' I repeated.

'Okay, okay, but as I said, this is guesswork for me too. Right . . .'

I watched him as he felt for something in his pocket and drew out an old envelope. He put it down on the table in front of me.

'Ally, when Martha wrote to me to tell me she'd given birth, she enclosed a photograph.'

'Yes, you said. Of Thom.'

'Yes, of Thom. But she was also cradling another baby in her arms. A baby girl. Martha had twins. Do you want to see the letter and the photograph?'

'Oh my God,' I muttered and gripped the side of the sofa as my surroundings suddenly span around me. I put my head between my legs and felt Felix come to sit beside me and pat my back.

'Here, Ally, take some whisky. It always helps for shock.'

'No.' I flapped the glass away, the smell making me nauseous. 'I can't, I'm pregnant.'

'Jesus!' I heard Felix exclaim. 'What have I done?'

'Just pass me my water. I'm feeling a bit better now.'

He did so and I took a few gulps, feeling the faintness passing.

'Sorry about that, I'm really okay now.' I eyed the envelope sitting on the table and reached for it. With hands that shook as much as Felix's, I opened it and out slid a piece of notepaper and an old black-and-white photograph of the pretty woman I knew was Thom's mother from the framed photographs at Froskehuset. She was cradling two swaddled babies.

'Can I read the letter?'

'It's in Norwegian. I'll have to read it to you.'

'Yes. Please do.'

'Okay, firstly it gives the address, which is St Olav's Hospital in Trondheim. The date is 2nd June 1977. Right, here we go.' Felix cleared his throat. '"My darling Felix, I thought I should let you know that I have given birth to twins. One boy and one girl. The girl came first, just before midnight on 31st May, our son appearing a few hours later in the early hours of 1st June. I'm very tired because of the long labour and I may be in here for another week or so but I'm recovering well. I enclose a photograph of your babies, and if you want to see them now they're here, or me, then please, come and visit. I love you. Martha." There. That's what the letter said.'

Felix's voice was husky and I thought he might be close to tears.

'The thirty-first of May . . . my birthday.'

'Really?'

'Really.' I looked at Felix blankly, then back down again at the babies in the photograph. They were indistinguishable in their blankets and I had no idea which one I might be.

'I can only assume that, given Martha had no home or husband, she decided she'd have to put one of you up for adoption immediately,' said Felix.

'But surely, when you saw her in Bergen when she'd returned after the birth, you must have wondered where the other baby' – I gulped hard – 'where *I* was?'

'Ally,' Felix said, tentatively putting a hand on mine, 'I'm afraid I assumed that the other twin had died. She never mentioned your continued existence to me ever again – or, as far as I know, to my grandparents or to Thom. I thought that maybe it was simply too painful a memory, so she had chosen to wipe it from her mind. Besides, I hardly spoke to her after that, and if I did, it was only words of anger and bitterness.'

'This letter . . .' I frowned in confusion. 'It's as if Martha believed you two would be together?'

'Perhaps she thought that me seeing the photograph of what were apparently my offspring would prompt an emotional response. That since they'd entered the world, I'd have no choice but to take my responsibilities seriously.'

'Did you reply to her?'

'No, Ally, forgive me, but I didn't.'

My head felt as if it were about to burst with the information I'd just been given, my heart equally full of conflicting emotions. When I hadn't known that Felix was almost certainly my genetic father, I'd been able to rationalise what he'd told me about the past. But now, I didn't know how I felt about him.

'It might not be me. There's no solid proof at all that it is,' I muttered desperately.

'True, but looking at the two of you together, along with your birth date and year and the fact your adoptive father sent you in search of a Halvorsen, I'd be pretty surprised if it wasn't,' Felix said mildly. 'It's very easy to find out for sure these days, as I know to my cost. A DNA test will confirm it immediately. I'd be glad to help you do that if you wanted to, Ally.'

I laid my head against the back of the sofa and breathed in deeply as I closed my eyes, knowing I didn't need to confirm it. Everything fitted, as Felix had just said. And besides all the reasons he'd just cited, there was the fact that the moment I'd set eyes on Thom, I'd felt as though I'd known him all my life, that he was familiar somehow. We *were* like two peas in a pod. So many times in the past few days we'd voiced the same thought simultaneously and laughed about it. The idea that I had found my twin brother made me feel dizzy with happiness, but at the same time I had to deal with the fact that my birth mother had had to choose which baby she would give away. And that she had chosen me.

'I know what you're thinking, Ally, and I'm sorry.' Felix cut into my thoughts. 'If it's any help at all, when Martha first told me she was pregnant, she said she was convinced it was a boy and that was what she wanted. I'm sure it was a case of gender making the decision for her. Nothing more.'

'Thanks, but just now it doesn't make it feel any better.'

'No, I'm sure. What can I say?' he sighed.

'Nothing. Not yet, anyway. But thanks for sharing this with me. Would you mind if I kept the letter and the photograph for a bit? I promise to return them.'

'Of course.'

'Excuse me, but I want to go for a walk. Alone,' I added pointedly as I stood up. 'I need some fresh air.'

'I understand. And again, forgive me for telling you. I certainly wouldn't have if I'd known you were pregnant. It must make it worse.'

'As a matter of fact, Felix, it makes it much better. Thanks for being so honest with me.'

I walked out of the lounge, then out of the hotel's front entrance into the biting, salty air. I began to walk briskly along the quay, heading in the direction of the sea. Ships were docked, loading and unloading their cargos, and eventually I reached a bollard and sat down on its hard, cold surface. The day was breezy and as my hair flew around my face, I secured it with the hairband that I always kept around my wrist.

So now I knew. A woman called Martha had conceived me in Bergen with a man called Felix, given birth to me and promptly given me away. My rational mind told me that the latter was simply the inevitable result of my investigation into my true parentage, but still, the pain of my mother choosing me out of the two of us burnt through me.

Would I have preferred to have been the child she'd kept and to have swapped places with Thom?

I just didn't know . . .

But what I *did* know was that from the day I was born, there'd been a parallel universe running alongside my own that could easily have been *my* destiny. And now the two had collided and I was veering left and right through both of them at the same time.

'Martha. My mother.' I said the words out loud, and wondered if, given her Christian name, I'd have called her 'Ma' too? I smiled at the irony as I looked up at a couple of passing seagulls gliding on the wind. Then I thought of the life that was growing inside *me*, a life I'd never expected to exist . . .

Even after only twenty-four hours of knowing, and having never properly considered the idea of motherhood before that, the protective instinct that welled inside me was as deep as any love I'd ever felt.

'How could you have given me away?!' I screamed to the water. 'How could you?!' I asked again with a sob in my voice. I let the tears flow freely down my cheeks, and the rough wind dried them as they fell.

I'd never know why she did. Never hear her side of the story. Never know how much she had suffered as she'd handed me over and said goodbye to me for the last time. And had probably hugged Thom twice as tightly, because she'd still had him to cherish.

As my stream of consciousness ran wild, I stood up and began to pace briskly again, my thoughts crashing together as the waves in the harbour, confused at being unable to flow naturally, mirrored my despair.

It hurt. It really bloody hurt.

What did I come on this journey to find? I asked myself. *Pain?*

Ally, you're veering towards the self-indulgent, I told myself firmly. *What about Thom? You've found your twin brother.*

Yes. What about Thom?

And as I began to calm down and think about the positives, I realised that – just like Maia who'd gone in search of her past – I'd found love too, albeit in a very different way to her. Only last night I'd gone to bed feeling sympathy for Thom and his difficult childhood. I also confessed to myself that I'd worried up to now about how close I'd felt to him. And, being unable to categorise what he was to me, had held back from admitting I felt love for him. But I did. And now that I knew he was my twin brother, it meant all those feelings were natural and acceptable.

When I'd come here to Norway, I'd lost the two people that mattered most to me in the world. And as I took the long walk back along the quayside to the hotel, I knew that the pain of discovery was more than made up for by finding Thom.

Arriving back at the hotel completely exhausted, I went up to my room, told reception to block my phone, and fell into a deep, dreamless sleep.

It was dark when I woke up. I looked at my watch and saw it was just after eight in the evening and that I'd slept for several hours. Throwing off the duvet, I went to wash my face with cold water, and as I did, I remembered what I'd been told by Felix. But before I started to dissect it any further, I realised I was starving, so I threw on a pair of jeans and my hoody and went downstairs to get something to eat in the restaurant.

As I walked through the lobby, to my surprise, I saw

Thom sitting on one of the sofas. He jumped up as soon as he saw me, an expression of concern on his face.

'Ally, are you all right? I tried to call your room, but your phone was blocked.'

'Yes . . . Why are you here? We weren't meant to meet today, were we?'

'No, but around lunchtime, I opened the front door to a hysterical Felix. My God, Ally, he was actually crying, so I took him inside, fed him some whisky and asked him what on earth was wrong. He told me that he'd said something to you he shouldn't have, but that he hadn't known beforehand you were pregnant. He was frantic about your state of mind. Said you'd taken yourself off for a walk along the harbour.'

'Well, as you can see I haven't thrown myself in. Thom, would it be all right if we carried on this conversation in the restaurant? I'm absolutely ravenous.'

'Of course. That's a good sign, anyway,' Thom said with genuine relief as we found a table and sat down. 'Then he told me the whole sorry story.'

I peered at him over the top of the menu card that I'd grabbed. 'And?'

'Like you, I was obviously very shocked, but Felix was so upset that I actually found myself comforting him. And feeling sorry for him for the first time in my life.'

I called the waitress over, asked her to bring some bread immediately and ordered a steak and chips. 'Want anything?' I asked Thom.

'Why not? I'll have the same as you. And a beer, please,' he called after the waitress.

'So when you said your father told you the "whole" story,

did that include the truth about your mother when Felix first met her?'

'Yes, although whether I believe him or not is another matter.'

'As a complete bystander to all of this up until a few days ago, I think I did believe him. Not that it excuses him for what he did . . . or should I say, *didn't* do,' I added hurriedly, not wanting Thom to think I was taking sides and defending Felix. 'But maybe it does go some way to explaining his behaviour. He felt out-manipulated by everyone.'

'I'm afraid I'm not at the stage yet where I can trust him, or begin to forgive him, but at least today I saw some remorse. Anyway, enough of how I may or may not feel. How about you? You're the one who's had the shock. I'm so, so sorry, Ally. I feel I should apologise for being the child my mother kept.'

'Don't be silly, Thom. We'll never know the true reasons why she did what she did, and even if it is pretty awful for me to think about it just now, what's done is done. For my own peace of mind, I'd like to see if the hospital where Martha gave birth to us has a record, and perhaps some details of my subsequent adoption. And if you don't mind, for us both to take a DNA test.'

'Of course. But really, Ally, I don't think there's much doubt, is there?'

'No,' I said as the bread arrived and I tore off a piece, then crammed it greedily into my mouth.

'Well, at least your appetite seems to have recovered, despite the trauma. Ally, this may be an inappropriate moment to start thinking about the positives, when you're still having to deal with the shock of the negatives, but I've just realised I'm going to be an uncle. That makes me very happy.'

'It's never too soon to start looking at the upside, Thom,' I agreed. 'Before I came to Norway, I felt so lost, so alone. And now it seems as if I've found myself a whole new family. Albeit that my real dad is a drunken reprobate.'

Thom reached his hand out to me across the table and I took it shyly. 'Hello, twin sister.'

'Hello, twin brother.'

We held hands for some considerable time after that, both of us, I knew, brimming with emotion. We were two halves of a whole. It was as simple as that.

'It's odd—' we both said at the same time and giggled.

'You first, Ally. You are the eldest after all.'

'Goodness, that's a strange thought. I've always played second fiddle to Maia in my family. And rest assured I shall be taking full advantage of my newfound position of superiority,' I teased him.

'I don't doubt it for a second,' Thom said. 'Now, we were both saying that something was odd . . .'

'Yes, but I've forgotten now which thing it was specifically, as there are so many things that are odd just now,' I said as our supper arrived.

'You're telling me!' He poured his beer and raised it to my glass of water. 'Well, here's to us, reunited after thirty years. You know what?'

'What?'

'I'm no longer an only child.'

'True,' I said. 'You know what else?'

'What?'

'The Six Sisters now have a brother.'

44

Thom suggested over supper that I should move with immediate effect in to Froskehuset.

'There's nothing more miserable than staying in a hotel and technically, Ally, half of this house should probably be yours anyway,' he added as he carried my rucksack up the steps to the front door later that evening.

'By the way,' I asked him, 'what does "*Froskehuset*"' actually mean?'

'"The Frog House". Apparently Horst told Felix that he used to keep a replica of the frog that Grieg carried with him on the music rest of the piano. I've no idea what happened to it, but perhaps it had something to do with the naming of the house.'

'Well, I think that clinches it.' I smiled as Thom dumped my rucksack in the hall and I reached into a side pocket to pull out my own little frog. 'Look, this is the other clue Pa Salt left me. I saw dozens of similar ones in the Grieg Museum.'

Thom took it and studied it. Then he smiled at me. 'He was directing you here, Ally. To your real home.'

Thom and I organised a genetic test and Felix insisted on providing samples of saliva and a hair follicle. Within a week, it was duly confirmed that I was indeed Thom's twin and Felix my newfound father.

'Obviously because we're different sexes, we're not identical,' I said, as we studied the data in the results letter. 'We both have our own separate DNA profile.'

'Obviously. I'm far prettier than you are, big sis.'

'Thanks.'

'Anytime. So, shall we call our errant father and tell him the happy news?'

'Why not?' I agreed.

Felix duly appeared that evening with a bottle of champagne, and whisky for himself. And the three of us toasted to sharing the same gene pool. I could see Thom was still very reticent with his father, but trying hard because of me. I also noticed how Felix was attempting to make amends. And at least, I thought, as I sipped a thimbleful of champagne with my father and my brother, it was a start.

Felix got up to take his leave, swaying as he walked to the door.

'Are you sure you're safe to drive that thing up the hill?' I asked him as he donned his helmet.

'I've been doing it for nigh on forty years, Ally, and I haven't fallen off yet,' Felix grunted. 'But thanks for asking. Long time since anyone cared enough to do so. Goodnight, and thanks. Don't be a stranger, will you?' he called as he stumbled off into the night.

Closing the door behind him, I sighed, knowing I mustn't show the pity I felt for Felix in front of Thom.

But as usual, my twin had read my mind.

'It's okay,' he said as I came back into the room and went towards the stove to warm my cold hands.

'What's "okay"?'

'That you feel sorry for Felix. As a matter of fact, despite myself, so do I. I'm not ready to forgive him for what he did to my mum, but actually seeing his mother lying dead in the street, and then having his father take his own life a few hours later . . .' Thom shuddered. 'Even if he can't remember the details, it couldn't be much worse, could it? And who knows what scars it left on him.'

'Yes, who knows?' I agreed.

'Anyway, enough of Felix, Ally.' Thom breathed out, then stared at me. 'I have something else that I'd like to share with you.'

'Really? You look so serious, I'm wondering if you're about to tell me I have another brother or sister.'

'That's for Felix to say, and who knows?' he joked. 'But this is something more . . .' – Thom struggled to find the right word – 'fundamental.'

'I can't imagine how much more fundamental it can get than finding out that I'm actually a Halvorsen by birth.'

'Ally, unwittingly, you've just hit the nail on the head. Now, I want to show you something.' He stood up and walked across the room to the small bureau which stood in the corner, took a key from a vase on top of it and unlocked it. He opened a drawer and retrieved a file, then came back to sit on the sofa next to me. I said nothing, just waited for him to collect his thoughts, whatever they were.

'Okay, do you remember how irritated you were after you'd read Jens Halvorsen's biography about him and Anna? How you couldn't believe that Anna had just taken Jens back without a murmur after deserting her in Leipzig for all those years?'

'Of course I do. And I still don't understand it. Jens says himself in the book that he thought she'd given up on love and on him. And she's described as such a feisty character, I find it impossible to believe she'd just accept him back the way she did.'

'Exactly.' Thom stared at me again.

'Spit it out then,' I encouraged him.

'What if she had to?'

'Had to what?'

'Accept him back?'

'You mean for the sake of form? Because in those days a woman couldn't be divorced without a scandal?'

'Yes, but not exactly. You're certainly on the right lines as far as the morality of the era went.'

'Thom,' I said, 'it's past eleven o'clock at night and I'm not really up for a game of Twenty Questions. Just tell me what it is you're getting at.'

'Okay, Ally, but before I do, I seriously have to swear you to total secrecy. And that includes Felix, our father. I haven't told another living soul about this.'

'Thom, you're beginning to sound as if you've found the golden fleece buried under Froskehuset. Please, just get on with it.'

'Sorry, it's just that it's seriously inflammatory. Right, the thing is, when I was researching Jens and Anna Halvorsen's relationship with Grieg for my book, I followed in their footsteps and went to Leipzig. And this is what I found.'

Thom took an envelope from the file, pulled out a sheet of paper inside it and handed it to me. 'Take a look at it.'

Scanning it, I saw it was the birth certificate of an Edvard Horst Halvorsen. 'Our great-grandfather. So what?'

'I'm sure you can't remember off the top of your head, but in Jens' biography, he describes how he returns to Leipzig in April 1884.'

'No, I can't remember, to be honest.'

'Well, here's the photocopied page from the book.' He handed it to me. 'I've highlighted the relevant passage. But, according to the birth certificate, Horst was born on 30th August 1884. So technically, Anna gave birth to a live child after a four-month pregnancy. Even a century on, that's still impossible.'

I examined the date on the birth certificate and saw he was right. 'Well, perhaps Jens simply forgot the exact month he'd returned to Leipzig? After all, he was writing it in retrospect, many years after the fact.'

'That's what I thought too. Initially, anyway.'

'Are you trying to say that the baby Anna carried – in other words Horst – couldn't have been Jens' child?'

'Yes. I am.' Thom's shoulders sagged suddenly, whether in relief or desperation or fear, I didn't know. Maybe it was a mixture of all three.

'Okay, I'm with you up to now. So what else did you discover after that to confirm your theory?'

'This.'

Thom handed me another sheet of paper from the file. I could see it was a photocopy of an old letter written in

Norwegian. Before I could complain I couldn't read it, he handed me another sheet of paper. 'It's translated into English.'

'Thank you.' I read through the contents, which were dated March 1883.

'It's a love letter.'

'It is, yes. And there are many more where that came from.'

'Thom,' I said, looking up at him, 'who is this letter from? Who is the "Little Frog", as he signs himself?' And before he could answer, I suddenly knew. 'Oh my God,' I muttered. 'You don't need to tell me. You said there were more?'

'Dozens more. He was a very prolific correspondent. He wrote almost twenty thousand letters to various people over his lifetime. And I've checked the handwriting against those at the Bergen museum. It's definitely him.'

'So,' I said, swallowing hard, 'where did you find these?'

'They've sat here in this room right under everyone's noses. And have done for the past one hundred and ten years.'

'Where?' I scanned the sitting room.

'I found the hiding place completely by accident. A pen rolled under the grand piano over there, and as I knelt down to pick it up, I hit my head on the underside. I looked up and noticed there was a narrow wooden lip of maybe one inch deep that had been added to the frame. Look, I'll show you.'

We both went down on our hands and knees under the piano to see what he meant. And there, placed in the centre under the string section, was a wide but shallow plywood tray tacked roughly to the base. Reaching up, Thom grabbed the bottom of it and slid it out of the narrow wooden brackets.

'See?' he said as we crawled out from under the piano and he placed the tray on the table. 'Dozens of them.'

I carefully picked up letter after letter, examining them in wonder. The ink on the yellowing vellum was so faded as to be almost illegible – even if I'd been able to read Norwegian – but I could make out that the dates ranged from 1879 to 1884 and that they were all signed by a '*Liten Frosk*'.

'And even though he was always known as "Horst", you might have noticed that on his birth certificate our great-grandfather was originally christened "Edvard",' Thom continued.

'I . . . don't know what to say,' I said, staring down at the beautiful script on one of the pages in front of me. 'These letters from Edvard Grieg to Anna are surely gold dust. Have you shown them to an historian?'

'As I said earlier, Ally, I've shown them to no one.'

'But why on earth didn't you include them in your book? These are absolute proof there was a relationship between Grieg and Anna Halvorsen.'

'Actually, it proves more than that. Having read each and every one of them, it tells the reader that without doubt, they were lovers. For at least four years.'

'Wow. Well, if that's true, I'm sure you'd have sold millions of copies of a book that included such a steamy revelation about one the most famous composers in the world. I don't understand why you didn't, Thom.'

'Ally,' he said with a frown, 'surely you can guess why not? Haven't you put two and two together yet?'

'Don't patronise me, Thom,' I retorted irritably. 'I'm trying to see the big picture, but give me time. So, these letters confirm that Anna and Grieg were lovers. And I presume you think that it was Grieg who fathered Anna's baby?'

'I have to believe there's a very good chance he did, yes. You remember I told you it was Grieg himself who went to search Jens out in the gutters of Paris? That was in late 1883, when he had been separated from Nina, his wife, for most of the year and was based in Germany. Then in the spring of 1884, just as Jens appears on Anna's doorstep, Grieg is reunited with Nina in Copenhagen. And Edvard Horst Halvorsen is born in the August.'

'Edvard Horst Halvorsen, Grieg's son,' I murmured, trying to take in the enormity of such a possibility.

'As you said yourself after you'd read the story, why on earth would Grieg go to Paris and seek Jens out six years after the fact? And why would Anna be prepared to take him back? Unless some kind of deal had been struck between herself and Grieg for the sake of propriety. We have to remember that, at the time, Grieg was one of the most famous men in Europe. Even though it was acceptable for him to be seen escorting talented muses such as Anna about town, he couldn't have risked anything so grubby as to be outed as the father of an illegitimate child. And don't forget that Grieg was separated from Nina at the time and there's documentary evidence from archive programmes that he and Anna travelled through Germany together giving recitals. There may well have been gossip about their relationship, but her husband's arrival back on the scene would have put paid to any speculation when a baby arrived a few months later. Anna and Jens moved to Bergen within the year and the baby was presented in Norway as theirs.'

'And Anna would have accepted that was what she must do? Live a lie?'

'You must remember that Anna was famous at the time as well. Any whisper of scandal around her would have ended her singing career too. She realised Grieg would never divorce Nina. And if nothing else, we both know Anna was a pragmatic and sensible young woman. It's my bet that they cooked this up between the two of them.'

'But if you're right, and Jens came back to find Anna already four or five months pregnant, why did he stay?'

'Probably because he knew that if he didn't, he would have died in poverty on the streets of Paris very soon after. And Grieg almost certainly promised to do all he could to help Jens make a name for himself in Norway as a composer. Don't you see, Ally? It suited them all.'

'And then within the space of a year, the two couples were living virtually next door to each other right here. Goodness, Thom, do you suppose Nina ever suspected what had happened?'

'I honestly couldn't say. There's no doubt she adored Edvard and he adored her, but being married to such a celebrity came with a price, as I think it always does. Perhaps she was content that her husband had returned to her. And of course, there was Horst. Living so close meant Grieg could have seen his possible son as often as he wanted without giving cause for suspicion. Remember he and Nina had no living children of their own. In one of his many letters written to a composer friend, Grieg says he doted on baby Horst.'

'So Jens just had to put up with the situation.'

'Yes. Personally, I think he was well and truly punished for deserting Anna. He lived forever under the musical shadow of

Grieg, almost certainly bringing up his illegitimate child as his own.'

'So why did he write a biography of the two of them, if he and Anna had such a secret to keep?'

'You probably know that Anna died in the same year as Grieg. This was when Jens' compositions really began to take off. I should think the book was little more than a bid to cash in on the fame Jens felt he'd never achieved up to that point. It was a bestseller in its day and probably earned him a decent amount of money.'

'He should have been more careful with his dates,' I observed.

'Who was to know, Ally? Unless they went to Leipzig in search of Horst's original birth certificate like I did.'

'Yes, over one hundred and twenty years later. Thom, all of this is pure speculation.'

'Have a look at these,' he said, pulling three photographs out of his file. 'There's Horst as a young man, and there are his two possible fathers. Now which one do you think he resembles?'

I looked down at them and saw there was little doubt. 'But Anna was blue-eyed and fair, just as Grieg was. Horst may well have taken his looks from his mother.'

'True,' Thom agreed. 'All this is fuelled by the only tools we have available to us when we're researching the past: documentary evidence, and a large helping of supposition.'

I'd only been half listening to Thom as it suddenly began to dawn on me what it meant.

'So if you're right, then Horst, Felix and you and I . . .'

'Yes. As I said at the start, Ally, strictly speaking, you may not be a Halvorsen after all.'

'Seriously, Thom, it's almost too much to take in. If we wanted to, could we prove it one way or another?'

'Absolutely. Grieg's brother, John, had children, and their descendants are living today. We could present the evidence and ask if they'd agree to a DNA test. I've thought about contacting them a hundred times, but then I think that, for the uproar it would cause and the possible damage to Grieg's pristine reputation, what would be the point? This all happened over one hundred and twenty years ago, and personally, I would like to get publicity for my music for the *right* reasons, not because I'm cashing in on some historical scandal. So I've made the decision to let the past rest in the past. Which is why I didn't put what I'd discovered in the book. You must make your decision too, Ally, and I can't blame you if you wanted to find out for sure, even if I'd prefer to let it rest.'

'Goodness, Thom. I've spent thirty years very content not to know anything at all about where I came from. So I really think that for now, one new gene pool is enough,' I said with a smile. 'What about Felix? You said you haven't told him?'

'No, because I couldn't trust him not to get drunk and start announcing he's the great-grandson of Grieg, and putting us all in the shit.'

'I agree. Wow,' I sighed, 'what a story.'

'Yes. And now I've got that off my chest, do you fancy a cup of tea?'

When it arrived a few days later, I showed Thom my original birth certificate. I'd written to the hospital and to the local registry of births and deaths in Trondheim, not only because

I wanted to see the evidence, but also to discover any details I could about how Pa Salt had found me.

'See?' I said. 'I was originally named "Felicia", presumably after Felix.'

'I rather like it. Very pretty and girly,' Thom teased me.

'Sorry, but girly is something that I am not. Ally suits me much better,' I countered.

I showed him another document that had arrived with the certificate, saying I'd been adopted on the third of August 1977. It had an official-looking stamp at the bottom, but no further details.

'All of the adoption agencies I contacted have written back to me, telling me there were no records in their possession of any official adoption, and that they therefore concluded that it had been undertaken privately. Which means that Pa Salt must have met Martha at some point,' I mused as I put the most recent letter back into the file.

'Just a thought, Ally,' Thom said suddenly, 'but you've told me how Pa Salt adopted the six girls, all named after the Pleiades stars. What if it was *him* that chose *you*? What if it was *me* who was left behind?'

I thought about this and realised Thom had a point. And it immediately lessened the pain. I stood up and went over to him as he sat at the piano and put my arms round his neck, kissing the top of his head. 'Thank you for that.'

'That's okay.'

I looked at the music sitting on the rest, with pencilled notes scrawled across it. 'What are you doing with that?'

'Oh, just looking at what the chap David Stewart recommended to tackle the orchestration of *The Hero Concerto* has done so far.'

'And how are they coming along?'

'From what I've just seen, I'm not impressed, to be honest. It's highly doubtful it's going to be ready to be premiered at the Grieg Centenary Concert in December. We're almost at the end of September and the finished music has to be with the printers by the end of next month to give the orchestra time to rehearse with it. Having got the go-ahead from David to include it in the concert programme, I'll be devastated if it doesn't make it, but these' – he shrugged – 'they just don't feel right at all. And they're certainly not up to scratch to show the leader.'

'I wish I could do something to help,' I said. Then a thought jumped into my mind, although I wasn't sure whether I should voice it.

'What it is?' Thom asked. I was learning it was impossible to keep anything private from my newfound twin.

'If I tell you, promise me that you won't dismiss it out of hand?'

'Okay, I won't. So go on.'

'Felix – I mean, our father – could do it. He is Pip's son after all. I'm sure he'd have a feel for his own father's music.'

'What?! Ally, are you completely insane? I know you're trying to have us all play happy families, but really this is a step too far. Felix is a drunkard and a waster, who's never seen anything through in his life. I'd hardly give our grandfather's precious concerto to him to destroy. Or even worse, get halfway through and give up. If we have any chance of premiering this at the concert, that is definitely not the route to take.'

'You do know that Felix still plays for hours every day? Just for his own amusement? And you yourself have told me endlessly that he was a genius, composing and orchestrating his own work as a teenager,' I persisted.

'Enough, Ally. The subject is closed.'

'Okay.' I shrugged as I walked from the room. I felt frustrated and upset. It was the first disagreement Thom and I had had so far.

Later that afternoon, Thom left the house for an orchestra call. I knew that he kept Pip Halvorsen's original sheet music in the bureau in the sitting room. Completely unsure if I was doing the right thing or not, I unlocked the bureau and extracted the pile of paper. Then I put it into a carrier bag, picked up the keys to the car I'd recently rented, and left the house.

'What do you think, Felix?'

I'd explained the story behind *The Hero Concerto* and how we were desperate to get it orchestrated. I'd just listened to him play the concerto from beginning to end. And even though he'd not set eyes on it before, he'd performed it without a single mistake. And with a technical proficiency and a flair that marked out a seriously gifted pianist.

'I think it's wonderful, really. My God, my old dad was talented.'

Felix was visibly moved and instinctively, I went to him and squeezed his shoulder. 'Yes, he was, wasn't he?'

'Tragedy that I can't remember him at all. I was little more than a baby when he died, you see.'

'I know. And it was a tragedy that this piece never got its premiere. Wouldn't it be wonderful if it did?'

'Yes, yes, with the right orchestration . . . for example, here in the first four bars, an oboe, joined by a viola there' – he pointed to the score – 'but with the timpani coming in almost immediately as a surprise, like this.' He illustrated the beat with two pencils. 'That'll shock those who think they're listening to another Grieg pastiche.' He grinned mischievously and I saw the light in his eyes as he reached for some blank sheet music and filled it in with the arrangement he'd just described. 'Tell Thom that would be a master stroke. And then,' Felix said as he started to play again, 'the violins arrive, still accompanied by the timpani to give that undercurrent of danger.'

Again he quickly filled in some bars on the sheet music. Then he stopped suddenly and looked up at me. 'Sorry, I'm getting carried away. Thanks for showing this to me, though.'

'Felix, how long do you think it would take you to fully orchestrate this?'

'Two months, perhaps? Maybe it *is* because my father wrote it originally, but I can already hear exactly how it should be.'

'How about three weeks?'

He stared at me, rolled his eyes and chuckled. 'I assume you're joking?'

'No, I'm not. I'll have to get a photocopy of the piano music done for you, but if you could orchestrate this and present it to Thom as brilliantly as you've just done for me, I doubt he or the leader of the Bergen Philharmonic Orchestra would be able to say no.'

Felix sat in silence for a while as he thought about it. 'So, you're challenging me? Is this to prove to Thom that I can do it?'

'Apart from the fact that this is currently on the programme for the Grieg Centenary Concert in December, yes. Because from what I've just heard, you're utterly brilliant. And if you don't mind me saying so, the time limit will mean you absolutely have to focus.'

'That was a mixed bag of compliments and insults, young lady,' Felix snorted. 'I'll choose to take the compliments, because of course, you're right. I'm far better working to a deadline and there's been a distinct lack of them around here in the past few years.'

'So you'll have a go?'

'If I take this on, I'll do much better than just having a go, I can assure you. I'll start tonight.'

'Well, I'm afraid I'll have to take the original piano music with me. I don't want Thom to find out what we're doing.'

'Oh, don't worry about that, it's in my head already.' Felix gathered the music together, collated it into a neat pile and handed it to me. 'Drop me off a copy tomorrow, but from then on, I don't want to have you constantly turning up here checking up on me while I'm working. So, I'll see you three weeks from today.'

'But—'

'No buts,' Felix said as he followed me to the door.

'Okay, I'll drop the music off tomorrow. Bye, Felix.'

'And Ally?'

'Yes?'

'Thanks for giving me the chance.'

45

During the following three weeks, I did a lot of pacing around the house. I knew that to orchestrate a symphony well would normally take months of arduous work. But even if Felix managed to complete the first five minutes, I hoped it would be enough to convince Thom of what I'd heard myself. If he'd done nothing, then nothing was lost and Thom would never know.

Everyone deserves a second chance, I thought to myself as I heard the front door open and Thom arrive home from playing the opera *Carmen* with the orchestra. The concert season had begun and as he collapsed onto the sofa, grey with fatigue, I handed him a chilled beer from the fridge.

'Thanks, Ally. I could get used to this,' he said as he opened the beer. 'And as a matter of fact, I've been thinking about things over the past few days.'

'Oh yes?'

'Have you decided yet where you're going to have Thumbelina?'

This was a pet name for the baby, which had originated from Thom asking me what size he or she currently was, and me – with my brand-new pregnancy book as a guide – using my thumb to describe it.

'No, I haven't.'

'Well, how about staying here at Froskehuset with me? You keep saying how you're itching to refurbish it, and I certainly don't have time to do it. Given that nesting instinct thing you read about in the pregnancy book the other day, how about channelling it practically and setting to work? In return for bed and board, which is mounting up given the current size of your dual appetites,' he teased me. 'And, of course, official ownership of half of it?'

'Thom, really, this is yours! I'd never dream of taking half of it from you.'

'Well, how about if you invested some cash, if you have any, in updating this place? I'd call it a fair swap. See? I'm not being quite as generous as you thought.'

'I could certainly ask Georg Hoffman, Pa's lawyer. I'm sure he'd see it as a good investment. It's not going to take much cash to update this, although I was thinking that awful eyesore of a stove needs to be ripped out and replaced with a modern fire, and maybe some underfloor heating for the rest of the house. Oh, and then the boiler needs replacing and all the bathrooms re-plumbing, because I'm fed up of having a dribble of warm water when I take a shower, and—'

'There we go,' Thom chuckled. 'I'd reckon on at least one million kroner to do the job properly. The house is worth about four million, so I'd be paying you a little extra as my interior designer. We'd have to agree that if one of us needed to sell it in the future, then the other one would have the right to buy their share, but Ally, I think it's important that you feel you and the baby have a home of your own.'

'I've done all right without one up to now.'

'You've never had a child up to now. And as one who grew up in a home that my mother constantly reminded me wasn't ours, I'd like my niece or nephew not to have that worry. Perhaps I could offer my services as a father figure and mentor until another one arrives on the scene. Which I'm sure he will one day,' he added.

'But Thom, if I stayed here . . .'

'Yes?'

'I'd have to learn Norwegian! And it's impossible.'

'Well, you and the baby can learn together,' he said with a smile.

'But what happens when one, or both of us, do find someone else?'

'As I said, we can sell it, or buy the other one's share. Besides, don't forget it does have four bedrooms. And as I refuse to allow you to be with a man I don't approve of, there's no reason why we couldn't live in a commune here together. Anyway, personally I don't think we should worry too much about what *might* happen. Isn't that one of your own favourite lines?'

'It used to be, but . . . I have to plan for our future now.'

'Of course you do. Motherhood is changing you already.'

And as I settled into bed that night, I thought how Thom was right. I wasn't just thinking of me anymore, but what was best for my little one. There was no doubt I was happy here, secure and peaceful in this country I was beginning to love. And the fact I had been denied my true heritage made it somehow more important that my child be allowed to embrace theirs. We would do it together.

The next morning, I told Thom that, in principle, I thought it was a wonderful idea and that I'd love to stay and have the baby here.

'I'll also see if I can get Theo's Sunseeker yacht sailed over here. Even if I can't ever pluck up the courage to get back aboard myself, maybe you'd like to take your niece or nephew around the fjords of Norway for me in the summers.'

'Great idea,' agreed Thom. 'Although for the baby's sake, Ally, if not yours, you are going to have to get back on the water at some point.'

'I know, but it's not for now,' I said brusquely. 'The only thing that worries me is what I would do after I've played interior designer and given birth.' I put the pancakes he loved on the table for breakfast.

'See? You're doing it again, Ally, projecting into the future.'

'Shut up, Thom. You're looking at a woman who's worked all her life, had a challenge every day.'

'And you don't think that moving to a new country and having a baby is enough of one?'

'Of course it is, for now. But even though I'll be a mother, I'll have to do something else too.'

'I could probably throw you a bone,' Thom said casually.

'What do you mean?'

'There's always a place in the orchestra for a flautist as talented as you. As a matter of fact, I was going to suggest something to you.'

'Oh, and what was that?'

'You already know about the Grieg Centenary Concert, the one which is meant to include *The Hero Concerto*, but probably won't now. The first half includes the *Peer Gynt*

Suite and I was thinking how very apt it would be to have a real-life Halvorsen play the opening bars of 'Morning Mood'. In fact, I've already mentioned it to David Stewart, and he thinks it's a wonderful idea. What do you think?'

'You've already spoken to him?'

'Ally, of course I have. It was a no-brainer and—'

'Even if I'm rubbish, my name will get me the gig,' I finished for him.

'Now you're just being deliberately obtuse! He heard you play with Willem at the Logen Theatre, remember? What I'm trying to say is that you never know where that night may lead. So I really wouldn't worry too much about finding a job if you do decide to put down permanent roots here.'

My eyes narrowed as I glared at him. 'You've got it all worked out, haven't you?'

'Yes, I have. Just like you would have done too.'

Exactly three weeks to the day after I had taken the concerto to Felix, I knocked on his front door with trepidation. There was no answer for a while and I began to suspect that even though it was almost noon, Felix was still sleeping off a hangover.

And when he arrived at the door, bleary-eyed and in a T-shirt and a pair of boxer shorts, my heart sank.

'Hi, Ally. Come in.'

'Thanks.'

The living room smelt of stale alcohol and tobacco, and my tension grew as I saw the empty whisky bottles lined up like skittles on the coffee table.

'Sorry about the mess. Sit down,' he said, gathering up a tatty blanket and pillow from the sofa. 'I'm afraid I've slept where I've fallen for the past few weeks.'

'Oh.'

'Drink?'

'No thanks. You do know why I'm here, don't you?'

'Vaguely,' he said, running a hand through his thinning hair. 'Something to do with the concerto?'

'That's right, yes. Well?' I said briskly, now desperate to know if he'd risen to the challenge.

'Yes . . . Now, where did I put it?'

There were piles of sheet music stacked all over the place, many other sheets crumpled into balls which had been there on my last visit and were now collecting dust and cobwebs where they'd been thrown. I watched miserably as he hunted through bookshelves, overflowing drawers and behind the sofa where I sat.

'I know I put it somewhere for safekeeping . . .' he muttered as he bent down to look beneath the piano. 'Aha!' he said in triumph as he opened the top of the gorgeous Blüthner grand piano and secured it with the wooden rod. 'Here it is.' He reached inside and took out a mammoth pile of sheet music. Bringing it over to me, he dumped it on my knees, which nearly collapsed under the weight of it. 'All done.'

I saw the first sheets were the original piano part, held in a clear plastic file. The next section was for the flute, the next for the viola and then the timpani, just as he'd described. I turned over file after file of immaculately written music, and by the time I'd got to the brass section, I'd forgotten how many instruments he'd done the orchestration for. I looked up at him in sheer unadulterated amazement and watched him smile back at me smugly.

'If you'd known me for longer, my newfound dearest daughter, you might have known that I always rise to a musical challenge. Especially one as important as this.'

'But . . .' My eyes fell on the whisky bottles on the table in front of me.

'And as I vividly remember telling you, I work better drunk. Sad but true. Anyway, it's all there, ready for you to take to my beloved son and get a verdict. Personally, I think my father and I have produced a work of genius.'

'Well, I'm not qualified to judge the quality, but certainly the amount you've done in the time you've had is a miracle.'

'Night and day, darling, night and day. So, off you go.'

'Really?'

'Yes, I want to go back to sleep. I haven't had much since I last saw you.'

'Okay,' I said as I stood up clutching the enormous bundle to my chest.

'Let me know the verdict, won't you?'

'Of course I will.'

'Oh, and tell Thom from me that the only part I'm not convinced about is the horns coming in with the oboe in the third bar of the second movement. It might be a little too much. Goodbye, Ally.'

With that, the door was closed firmly behind me.

'What is that?' Thom asked as he arrived home after an orchestra call that afternoon and noticed the piles of sheet music placed neatly on the coffee table in the sitting room.

'Oh, just the completed orchestration for *The Hero Concerto*,' I said casually. 'Cup of coffee?'

'Please,' he answered, then did a comical double-take as he realised what it was he was looking at.

I walked calmly to the kitchen, poured the coffee and returned to the sitting room to find Thom already leafing through the pages, just as I'd done.

'How? When? *Who?*'

'Felix. In the past three weeks.'

'You're kidding me!'

'No, I'm not.' I wanted to punch the air in triumph at his astonished expression.

'Well, of course,' he said, clearing his throat so his voice came down an octave, 'I don't know what the quality's like, but . . .'

I watched as he hummed the oboe part, and the violas, then turned to the timpani and began to chuckle. 'Brilliant! I like that a lot.'

'Are you angry?'

'I'll tell you later.' He looked at me then and I saw the exhilaration and true respect in his eyes. 'But at first glance, Felix has done an incredible job. Forget the coffee, I'm calling David Stewart to catch him before he leaves. I'll take it down to him now. I'm sure he'll be as astounded as we are.'

As I helped him gather the music together, and waved him out of the door, wishing him good luck, I felt exhilarated.

'Pip,' I whispered as I looked up at the stars from the front door. 'Your "Hero" is finally going to get her premiere.'

As the autumn ticked by and plans for the performance of the concerto – complete with Felix's inspired orchestration – gathered momentum, I was kept busy with plans of my own. I'd contacted Georg Hoffman and explained the situation. He'd agreed that it sounded like a sensible idea to put a roof that I partly owned over my and my baby's heads. I'd added my meagre savings and Theo's small bequest to the pot and then I'd started on the renovation of Froskehuset. A vision had already taken shape in my mind of a beautiful Scandinavian retreat, with reclaimed pale pine floors and walls, furniture from young Norwegian designers and the latest in energy-saving technology.

I'd been struggling with the fact that technically, both Thom and I should do the right thing by Felix and, at the very least, hand him a third ownership of the house when we changed the deeds to include me on them. When I'd tackled Felix on the subject of his share of Froskehuset he'd grinned at me. 'No thanks, my darling. It's kind of you to offer, but I'm quite happy here in my cabin and we both know exactly where the money would go anyway.'

Also, last week, Edition Peters – known as C. F. Peters when it was Grieg's publishing house all those years ago in Leipzig – had already enquired about *The Hero Concerto* and a recording was planned with the Bergen Philharmonic for the new year. As the legal heir to the performing and publishing rights of his father's work, plus his own work on the orchestration, there was every chance Felix stood to earn a lot of money if the concerto was as big a success as Andrew Litton believed it would be.

With my conscience salved, and whether it was the nesting instinct or not, I felt full of optimism and energy as I interviewed local tradesmen and builders, consulted with the planning authorities, and pored over endless magazines and websites. I thought how my sisters would laugh at me, Ally, being interested in interior design. And pondered how hormones were responsible for so many of our human actions.

As I leafed through a book of fabric samples, I realised guiltily that I hadn't called Ma nearly as often as I should have while I'd been in Bergen. Or Celia for that matter. And now that I'd just passed the supposed 'danger time' of three months, both of them deserved to know the news.

I dialled Ma in Geneva first.

'Hello?'

'Ma, it's me, Ally.'

'*Chérie!* How lovely to hear from you.'

I smiled in relief as I heard the warmth and complete lack of reproach in her voice.

'How are you?' she asked.

'Well, that's quite a question as it happens,' I said with a rueful laugh. And then, punctuated by her expressions of surprise and wonderment, I told her all about Thom and Felix and how Pa Salt's clues had led me to them both.

'So I hope you'll understand, Ma, why I've decided to stay on in Bergen for a while longer,' I said finally. 'And there's one more thing I haven't told you that complicates matters slightly. I'm pregnant with Theo's child.'

There was a momentary silence from the other end of the line, then a delighted intake of breath. 'But that's the most wonderful news, Ally! I mean, after all you've . . . been through. When's the baby due?'

'On the fourteenth of March.' I thought it too much information to tell her that, after the scan had confirmed an exact date, I'd worked out that the baby had been conceived on or around the day of Pa's death.

'Oh, Ally, I couldn't be happier for you, *chérie*. Are you happy too?' she asked me.

'Very,' I reassured her.

'As your sisters will be too. They will be aunties and we will have a new baby visiting Atlantis. Have you told them yet?'

'I haven't, no. I wanted to tell you first. I have been in contact with Maia, Star and Tiggy in the last couple of weeks, but I can't seem to get hold of Electra at all. She hasn't answered my texts or emails and when I phoned her agent in Los Angeles and left a message, nobody returned my call. Is everything OK with her?'

'I'm sure she's just very busy – you know how hectic her work schedule is.' Ma's reply came after what I thought was a tiny pause. 'As far as I know, she's fine.'

'Well, that's a relief. But also, when I called Star in London, I asked to speak to CeCe, and Star just said she wasn't there. I've heard nothing from either of them since.'

'I see,' said Ma noncommittally.

'So do you have any idea what that's all about?'

'I'm afraid not. But again, I'm sure there's nothing for you to worry about.'

'You will let me know if you hear from them, won't you?'

'Of course, *chérie*. Now, tell me more about your plans for when the baby arrives.'

After I'd eventually put down the phone to Ma, having also invited her and any of my sisters she could round up to the Grieg Centenary Concert in December, I dialled Celia's number. Like Ma, she sounded delighted to hear from me.

I'd already decided that I wanted to tell Celia in person about the baby, knowing what an emotional moment it would be for her. There was also the unresolved matter of Theo's ashes.

'Celia, I'm afraid I haven't got long to talk now, but I wondered if you'd mind if I flew over to see you in the next few days?'

'Ally, you don't need to ask. You're welcome here any time. I'd adore to see you.'

'Perhaps we could go to Lymington, to . . .' I couldn't help the catch in my voice as I said the words.

'Yes, it's time,' she answered quietly. 'We'll do it together, as he would have wanted.'

Two days later my flight landed at Heathrow, where Celia was waiting for me in the arrivals hall. As we drove out of the airport in her ancient Mini, she glanced across at me.

'Ally, I hope you don't mind, but we're going straight to Lymington rather than Chelsea. I don't know if I ever mentioned to you that I still have a cottage there. It's only small, but it's where Theo and I used to camp out in the school holidays so that we could sail together. It seemed . . . fitting somehow that we should stay there.'

I reached across and squeezed her hand as it clutched the steering wheel tightly.

'Celia, it sounds perfect.'

And it was. The little bow-fronted cottage was nestled right in the heart of Lymington's Georgian town centre, surrounded by cobbled streets and quaint pastel-coloured buildings. We dumped our bags in the narrow entrance hall and I followed Celia into the cosy beamed sitting room. Then she took my hands in hers.

'Ally, before I show you to your room, I just want to warn you, this cottage only has two bedrooms, one is mine, the other . . . well, it's where Theo used to sleep and obviously it still contains . . . a lot of memories.'

'That's okay, Celia,' I assured her, as always touched by her kindness and consideration towards me.

'Perhaps you'd like to take your bag upstairs? I'll light the fire and get started on supper. I brought some bits and pieces with me so I could rustle something up for us. Unless you'd prefer to eat out?'

'I'm more than happy to stay in, thanks, Celia. I'll be straight back down to help you.'

'The room's the first door on the left at the top of the stairs,' she called to me.

I picked up my rucksack and climbed the stairs. At the top, I saw a low wooden door, roughly stencilled with the words 'THEO'S CABIN'. I pushed it open and saw a narrow bed beneath the sash window, with a worn toffee-coloured teddy bear wearing a miniature fisherman's sweater propped up against the pillows. The uneven walls were scattered with pictures of yachts, and above the painted chest of drawers hung an old-fashioned red and white striped lifebelt. Tears pricked my eyes as I registered the similarity to my own childhood room at Atlantis.

'My soulmate,' I whispered, suddenly feeling Theo's essence all around me.

Then I sat down on the bed, picking up the teddy bear and clutching it to my chest, as the tears spilled down my cheeks at the full realisation that Theo would never see his own child.

That evening, Celia and I chatted companionably as she dished up the chicken casserole. A fire was crackling in the grate of the sitting room and we settled ourselves on the faded squashy sofa to eat.

'This place is so homely, Celia, I can understand why you love it here.'

'I was lucky enough to inherit it from my parents. They were sailors too and it was the perfect place to bring Theo when he was growing up. Peter never really took to sailing, and anyway, he was nearly always abroad on business in those days, so Theo and I spent a great deal of time here one way and another.'

'Talking of Peter, have you heard from him recently?' I enquired gently.

'Strangely enough, I have. In fact, I'd go as far as saying we've become quite chummy in the past few weeks. He's been calling me regularly and there's even talk of him coming over to stay with me in Chelsea at Christmas. As we both seem to be at a loose end.' A faint blush rose on Celia's delicate cheekbones. 'I know it may sound trite, but it's as though Theo's death has somehow washed some of the bitterness between us away.'

'It doesn't sound trite at all. I know he hurt you terribly, Celia, but I really got the feeling that he's seen the mistakes he made and how they hurt you.'

'Well, no one is perfect, Ally. And maybe I've grown up too and seen some of the things I got wrong. I certainly know that when Theo was born, he was my world for years. I pushed Peter away, and as you've probably realised, he isn't good at being ignored.' She smiled.

'No, I can imagine. I'm happy that you're back on speaking terms, at least.'

'I did actually tell him that you and I were coming down to spread Theo's ashes at sunrise tomorrow morning, but I haven't heard back from him. Typical Peter,' Celia sighed. 'He never was any good at communicating on the things that really mattered.

'Anyway, that's quite enough about me,' Celia said. 'I want to hear all about what you've been doing in Norway. You already mentioned in the car that you'd been following up the clues your father left you. If you feel up to it, I'd love you to tell me the whole story.'

Over the following hour, I recounted the details of my strange quest to discover my roots. As in my conversation with Ma, the only detail I omitted was the possible genetic link to Edvard Grieg. Like Thom, I felt it was a revelation best kept to myself. Without solid evidence, it meant nothing and was therefore irrelevant.

'Well, I'm astounded, I must say!' Celia exclaimed when I'd finished and we'd both set aside our supper trays. 'You've found yourself a new twin brother, and a father as well. It's quite an extraordinary turn of events. How do you feel about it?'

'I'm thrilled actually. Thom is so . . . like me,' I said with a smile. 'And I hope I'm not being insensitive when I say that, although I lost my mentor in Pa Salt and my soulmate in

Theo, I seem to have found another man who I connect with, but in a completely different way.'

'Ally, dear, I think it's just marvellous! What a journey you've been on these past few weeks.'

'Actually, Celia, the journey isn't quite over yet. There's something else I have to tell you.' I looked into her eyes, noting the quizzical expression in them, and took a deep breath. 'You're going to be a grandmother.'

The look of puzzlement turned to one of momentary incomprehension as my words sank in. Then her mouth broke into an ecstatic smile and she reached across the sofa to clasp me in the tightest of hugs.

'Ally, I can barely dare to believe it. Are you sure?'

'Quite sure. The pregnancy was confirmed by a doctor in Bergen. And a week ago, I went for my first scan.' I rose from the sofa to retrieve my handbag, fumbling around in it until I found what I was looking for. I drew out the grainy black-and-white image and handed it to her. 'I know it doesn't look like much, but Celia, this is your grandchild.'

She took the scan and studied it, her fingers tracing the blurred outline of the tiny life growing inside me.

'Ally . . .' Her voice was choked with emotion as she finally spoke. 'It's . . . the most beautiful thing I've ever seen.'

After we'd laughed and cried and hugged each other a dozen times more, we settled back on the sofa, both of us slightly dazed.

'At least now I can contemplate our . . . task tomorrow with some hope in my heart,' said Celia. 'Talking of that, because we must, I've a sailing dinghy that I keep at the marina. It seems to me that the obvious thing to do is for both of us to sail out at dawn and . . . lay him to rest on the sea.'

'I'm s-so sorry,' I stammered, 'but I just can't. After Theo died, I swore I would never take to the water again. I hope you understand.'

'I do, dear, but please, think about it. As you said yourself, one can't simply block out the past. I think you already know that Theo would have hated to think that he'd separated you from your passion.'

And in that moment I knew that however difficult it might be, I owed it to Theo, and to our child, to get back onto a boat.

'Celia,' I said eventually, 'you're right. It's exactly what we should do.'

I woke to my mobile alarm before sunrise the next morning, feeling momentarily disoriented before I felt the texture of something bristly against my cheek. Switching on the bedside light, I saw Theo's old teddy lying on the pillow beside me. I reached out to grasp it and buried my nose in its rough fur, as if I could somehow breathe in his very spirit. I got out of bed and dressed quickly in leggings and a thick jersey before making my way downstairs, where Celia was already waiting. No words were needed as I glanced at the innocuous blue urn she was holding.

The streets of Lymington were deserted as the two of us left the cottage and walked down to the marina in the milky half-light that preceded the dawn. As we stopped on the wooden jetty where Celia's dinghy was berthed, the only other sign of activity nearby was a neighbouring fishing boat. The two crew members nodded to us briefly, before continuing their task of mending their nets in preparation for the day's catch.

'You know, Theo would have loved this. The eternal rhythm of the tides and the sea, continuing as it has since the beginning of time.'

'Yes, he would have loved it, wouldn't he?'

We both turned at the familiar voice and saw Peter walking towards us. I watched Celia's stunned expression and then the way her face lit up as Peter opened his arms to her and she walked into them. I stood where I was, letting them have their moment together, but then they walked towards me and Peter hugged me too.

'Okay,' said Peter, his voice cracking, 'we'd better get on with it.'

As Celia clambered aboard, Peter whispered in my ear, 'I just hope I don't disgrace myself in front of you both by throwing up my breakfast at this very solemn moment. I'm not good on the water, Ally.'

'And at the moment,' I breathed, 'nor am I. Come on,' I said, holding out my hand to him, 'we'll do this together.'

We climbed aboard and I steadied Peter and sat him down as I nervously found my own sea legs.

'Ready to go, Ally?'

'Yes,' I reassured Celia as I raised the sails and cast off the lines.

The first golden-pink rays of sunlight were reaching out to touch the coastline, sparkling on the crests of the lazy waves as we sailed out into the Solent. Celia took the helm while I moved about the deck, adjusting the sails. The crisp breeze propelled the dinghy through the water and gently lifted my hair off my face, and although I'd been dreading being back on the sea, I felt oddly at peace. Images of Theo flashed through my mind, but for the first time since he'd left me, my thoughts of him filled me with joy as much as with sadness.

As we reached a spot a few hundred metres offshore with a magnificent view of Lymington harbour, we reefed the sails and Celia ducked below, emerging a few seconds later with the blue urn cradled in her hands. We walked towards Peter, looking green in the stern of the boat, and helped him to standing between us.

'You take it, Peter,' said Celia, as the morning sun in all its glory finally broke free over the horizon.

'Ready?' he said.

I nodded, and we all clasped our hands around the urn, so outwardly insignificant but imbued with so many dreams, hopes and memories. As Peter lifted the lid and threw the contents into the breeze, we watched the fine mist of ash drift down to join the foaming sea beneath us. I squeezed my eyes shut and a single tear trickled down my cheek.

'Goodbye, my darling,' I whispered, as my hand moved instinctively to caress the curve of my stomach. 'Just know that our love lives on.'

46

7th December 2007

As usual, I was awake early, nudged by a gentle fluttering from inside me. I checked the time and saw it was just past five, and only hoped that this was not the shape of things to come, that the baby had not already established its sleep pattern in my womb. It was still dark outside as I peeked blearily through the curtains, to see a thick layer of frost covering the window. After using the bathroom, I climbed back into bed to try and drift back into sleep. Today would be a long day, I knew. The Grieg Hall would be full to its capacity of 1,500 people for the Centenary Concert tonight. And amongst the audience would be my friends and family. Star and Ma were flying over to Bergen this afternoon to attend the concert and I was tingling in anticipation of seeing them.

In an odd sort of way, I felt my pregnancy and the baby inside me were communal: even though I was the mother and guardian, its arrival on earth in three months' time would provide a link between a group of previously disparate human beings.

There was the link with my newfound past – Felix, my

blood father, and Thom, my twin – then the five aunts, all of whom would no doubt dote on him or her. Electra, who had finally sent me a congratulatory email in response to mine, had already FedExed a box of hideously expensive designer baby clothes. I'd had moving emails from most of my sisters, and of course Ma, who I knew in her quiet, understated way would be desperate to take a newborn in her arms and relive the precious memories of when we had all arrived into her care. Then there was Theo's side of the family: Celia and Peter, who were part of my most recent present, and who were also coming tonight. And who I knew were going to be a very welcome part of my and my baby's future.

'The circle of life . . .' I muttered to myself, thinking how, certainly for me, in the midst of dreadful loss, there had been new life, new hope. And just as Tiggy had said about the beautiful rose blooming for its time, then other buds on the same plant beginning to flower as the petals dropped from the old one, I too had learnt the miracle of nature. And even though I had lost the two most important people in my life in the space of a few months, I had been replenished with love that I knew could only grow stronger, and I felt blessed by it.

And tonight, after the performance, the different strands of my story would meet for the first time over a dinner.

Which brought my thoughts back to Felix . . .

The programme tonight was very straightforward: it would open with the *Peer Gynt* Suite, and, in fact, with *me* on the flute, Jens Halvorsen's great-great-granddaughter playing those iconic first bars, just as he had over a hundred and thirty-one years ago at the premiere. Or, as Thom and I had mulled over in private, perhaps even the composer's great-

great-granddaughter. Whichever way it was, neither of us would be playing fraudulently. Thom would be close by, playing first violin – Jens' second instrument – and Halvorsen history would complete a full circle.

Much had been made of our family link in the Norwegian media, the interest heightened by the fact that the second half of the programme would be the premiere of Jens Halvorsen Junior's recently unearthed piano concerto, orchestrated by the composer's son, Felix, who would be leading the orchestra on the piano.

Andrew Litton, the hallowed conductor of the Bergen Philharmonic, had been ecstatic to discover the lost work and amazed by Felix's inspired orchestration – let alone the length of time it had taken to complete them. Yet when Thom had asked David Stewart whether his father might be permitted to actually play the concerto himself on the night, the leader of the orchestra had refused point-blank.

Thom had returned home after the conversation and shaken his head at me. 'He said he knows Felix of old, and the premiere of this work and the night itself are just too important to put at risk. And I have to say, I agree, Ally. However wonderful your idea was to reunite what is' – he pointed to my bump – 'in essence five generations of Halvorsens musically, Felix is the weakest link. What if he goes on a bender the night before and simply doesn't turn up? You know as well as I do that the success of this concerto depends on the pianist. If he was just clashing the cymbals at the back, that would be different, but Felix would be taking centre stage. And the powers that be at the Philharmonic don't want to risk the ignominy of our dear papa not turning up. As I told you, he was sacked all those years ago because he'd proven himself so unreliable.'

I'd understood. But I was not prepared to give up on Felix.

So I'd been to see him in what Thom and I had named his 'pit' and asked him whether, if I went into battle for him, he could give me his firm promise – on his soon-to-be-born grandchild's life – that he would attend all the rehearsals and show up on the night.

Felix had stared at me that morning through his bleary, alcohol-infused eyes and shrugged. 'Of course I will. Not that I need any rehearsal. I could play it in my sleep with a couple of bottles inside me, Ally, my darling.'

'You know that isn't how it works,' I'd remonstrated with him. 'And if that's going to be your attitude, then . . .' At that point, I'd turned away and headed towards the front door.

'Okay, okay.'

'Okay what?' I'd asked him.

'I promise I'll behave.'

'Really?'

'Yes.'

'Because I've told you to?'

'No. I'm pledging myself to this because it is my father's concerto and I want to do him proud. And also, because I know that no one can play it better than I can.'

I'd then gone to see David Stewart myself, and when he'd yet again refused to countenance Felix playing, I'd resorted – I was ashamed to admit – to a dose of blackmail. 'Felix is, after all, Pip's son and therefore arguably the legal owner of the rights to the concerto,' I'd said, eyes lowered to stop me from blushing. 'My father's having serious doubts about it being performed. He's concerned that if he can't play the music the way his father would have wanted it, then perhaps it's best not to include it in the concert at all.'

I was banking on the fact that the orchestra desperately wanted to give the first performance of the most exciting home-grown composition since Grieg's own to the world. And thank God, my instincts had been right. David had finally buckled and agreed.

'However, we'll have Willem rehearse with the orchestra too. Then at least if your father lets us down, the entire evening won't be a disaster. And I won't even announce he's playing to the press beforehand. Deal?'

'Deal,' I'd said as we'd shaken on it and I'd walked out, head held high, mentally celebrating my coup de grâce.

Even though Felix *had* been true to his word, and had arrived on time to rehearsals over the past week, we all knew there'd be no guarantee he'd turn up when it mattered. After all, he'd done it before.

Felix hadn't officially been announced as the pianist, and Thom told me he'd discovered that there had been two different sets of programmes printed – one with Felix's name on it, the other with Willem's.

I felt rather guilty about this, as it couldn't be very satisfactory for Willem's ego to know he was – to coin a musical phrase – playing second fiddle to an ageing, unreliable drunk. Simply because his surname was Halvorsen. However, he was playing Grieg's Piano Concerto in A Minor during the first half, which was at least some consolation.

One evening last week, I'd gone to watch Thom playing in the orchestra, and Willem had featured on the piano, performing Lizst's Piano Concerto No. 1. As I'd watched his slim, talented fingers fly across the keyboard, nostrils flaring, shiny dark hair flopping over his brow, I'd felt a familiar lurch in my stomach that had nothing to do with the baby tucked away inside me. And I'd told myself that at least my instinctive physical reaction to him meant that I might in time recover from the loss of Theo, even if it was not for now. And that I shouldn't feel guilty about it. I was thirty years of age and had a lifetime to live. And I was sure Theo would not want me to walk through it like a nun.

Ironically, Thom and Willem had become close, initially bonded by working together, but with a personal friendship developing alongside the professional. Thom had asked Willem over to the house next week and I hadn't decided yet whether I'd prefer to be in or out.

Finally surrendering to the fact that I was not going to get any more sleep this morning, I switched on my laptop to check my emails. I saw there was one from Maia and I opened it.

> **Darling Ally, I just wanted to say that my thoughts are with you today. I wish I could be there too, but it's a very long way from Brazil to Norway. We have taken to the hills as even for me, the weather in Rio is too scorching. We are staying at the fazenda and I can't tell you how beautiful it is here. It needs a lot of renovation, but we're discussing plans to turn it into a centre for kids from the favelas, so they can come up here and have freedom and space to run about in the glorious nature. Anyway, enough of me. I hope you and the baby are doing well and I can't wait to meet my new niece or nephew. I'm so proud of you, little sis. Maia xx**

I smiled at the email, glad to hear that she sounded happy, then went to take a shower before donning my tracksuit bottoms, one of the few remaining pieces of clothing I had that would fit around my expanding middle. I refused to waste money on maternity clothes, and spent most of my days in one of Thom's roomy jumpers. I'd bought a stretchy black dress to wear for my appearance on the stage tonight, and Thom had sweetly commented how lovely I looked in it, but I suspected he was just being kind.

After making my way down the stairs, I went into the makeshift kitchen, which had been temporarily relocated to the sitting room as the house renovations continued, and comprised a sideboard with a kettle and a microwave on top of it. The kitchen was currently stripped back to its bare bones, but at least, I thought, most of the hard work was now done. We had a new boiler and the contractors were about to install the underfloor heating, but the work was taking *twice* the time I'd expected and I was panicking that the house wouldn't be finished before the baby made its appearance. The nesting instinct drove me on and, quite understandably, drove the builders mad.

'Morning,' said Thom, appearing behind me, his hair standing upright from sleep as it always did. 'Well, today's the day,' he sighed. 'How are you feeling?'

'Nervous, excited, and wondering—'

'Whether Felix will turn up,' we chorused together.

'Coffee?' I offered as the kettle boiled.

'Thanks. What time does your gang arrive?' he asked as he wandered distractedly over to the new floor-length glass windows that opened onto the terrace and allowed a full, glorious view of the fir trees and fjord below.

'Oh, all at different times today. I've told Ma and Star to pop round to the artist's entrance before the show to say hello.' Butterflies roamed around my already bilious stomach at the thought. 'It's so ridiculous, isn't it? I'm far more worried about a handful of my friends and family there watching than I am about what any critic might say.'

'Of course you are, it's natural. At least you get your solo out of the way right at the start, then we just have to sweat until Felix has played the very last note of *The Hero Concerto*.'

'I've never performed in front of an audience of this size,' I complained. 'And certainly not a paying one.'

'You'll do fine,' he said, although as I handed him his coffee, I could sense his nervousness too. It was a big day for both of us. We felt that, between us, we had conceived a new musical entity that was about to be brought into the world. And tonight, we would be proud parents at its birth.

'Are you going to call Felix to check he's remembered?' Thom asked.

'No.' I'd already decided that I wouldn't. 'This has to be up to him, and him alone.'

'Yes,' he sighed, 'it does. Right, I'm off to shower. Can you be ready to leave in twenty minutes?'

'Yes.'

'God, I hope he shows up.'

It was then that I realised that despite any protests to the contrary, Felix's appearance tonight meant even more to Thom than it did to me.

'He'll be there, I know he will.'

However, as I took my place in the orchestra for the rehearsal two hours later, and saw the empty piano stool, my confidence waned. At a quarter past ten, when Andrew Litton said we could wait no longer to begin, I nursed my mobile tensely between my hot palms.

No, I would not call him.

Willem had been called to take Felix's place at the piano and Thom flashed a desolate look at me as Andrew Litton raised his baton to begin.

'How could you? You shit!' I swore under my breath, before I saw Felix running through the auditorium towards the stage, breathless and pale.

'I doubt a person here will believe me,' he said as he climbed the steps. 'But my moped broke down halfway down the hill, and I had to hitch myself a lift the rest of the way. I've brought the kind lady who rescued me from the roadside with me to prove it. Hanne,' he called out, 'am I telling the truth?'

One hundred and one pairs of eyes followed Felix's pointing finger to the back of the auditorium, where a nervous middle-aged woman stood, obviously embarrassed.

'Hanne, tell them.'

'Yes, his moped broke down and I gave him a lift.'

'Thank you. There will be a ticket waiting for you at the box office for tonight's performance.' Felix turned to the orchestra and bowed theatrically. 'Forgive me for holding you all up, but sometimes, things are not as they seem.'

After the rehearsal, I saw Felix leaning by the artist's entrance smoking a cigarette and caught up with him.

'Hi, Ally. Sorry about that. A genuine reason, for a change.'

'Yes. Do you want to go for a drink?'

'No thanks, darling. I'm on my best behaviour for tonight, remember?'

'I do. It's pretty amazing, isn't it? Four, or even five generations of Halvorsens up there tonight.'

'Or Griegs, as the case may be,' he said with a shrug.

'I . . . You know about that?'

'Of course I do. Anna told Horst on her deathbed, and where the letters were hidden. And then he told me just before I went off to Paris to study. I've read all of them. Pretty steamy stuff, eh?'

I was stunned at his casual revelation. 'You've never thought to say anything? To use it?'

'Some secrets really should be kept secrets, don't you think, my darling? And you of all people should know that it's not where you come from genetically, but who you *become*. Good luck tonight.' With that, Felix offered me a wave and disappeared out of the stage door.

At six thirty, Star texted me to say that she and Ma were here. I collected Thom from the musician's green room and we walked along the corridor, me feeling decidedly nervous about introducing my twin brother to my sibling.

'Ma,' I said, quickening my footsteps as I saw her, looking effortlessly chic as always in a Chanel bouclé jacket and navy skirt.

'Ally, it's so wonderful to see you, *chérie*.' Ma folded me in her arms and I smelt the familiar aroma of her perfume, which indicated safety and security.

'Hello, Star, it's so wonderful to see you too.' I hugged her, then turned to my twin brother, who was staring slack-jawed at my sister. 'And this is Thom, my newest sibling,' I said as Star looked up at him and smiled shyly.

'Hello, Thom,' she responded and I nudged him to reply.

'Yes, hello. It's, um, wonderful to meet you, Star. And you, er, Ma . . . I mean, Marina.'

I frowned at Thom, who was being very peculiar. Thom was normally effusive in his greetings and I felt a little cross that he hadn't been just now.

'And we are pleased to meet you, Thom,' Marina answered. 'Thank you for taking care of Ally for me.'

'We take care of each other, don't we, sis?' he said, still staring at Star.

Just then, a call came over the tannoy for the orchestra to gather onstage.

'Right, we have to go, I'm afraid, but we'll see you afterwards in the foyer,' I said. 'God, I'm nervous,' I sighed as I kissed them both goodbye.

'You will be wonderful, *chérie*, I know you will,' Ma comforted me.

'Thanks.' With a wave, I walked back down the corridor with Thom. 'Cat got your tongue?' I asked him.

'Goodness, your sister's pretty, isn't she?' was all he could say as I followed him onto the stage for our pre-show pep talk with Andrew Litton.

'I'm worried,' I whispered to Thom as we filed back onto the stage at exactly seven twenty-seven that evening to a round of tumultuous applause. 'He still seems sober. And he told me he plays far better drunk.'

Thom chuckled as he saw my frown of genuine anxiety. 'I actually feel sorry for Felix. The poor man can't win! And remember, he has the whole of the first half, plus the interval to remedy the situation. Now,' he whispered, 'stop worrying about him and enjoy this wonderful moment of Halvorsen – or Grieg – history. Love you, sis,' he added with a grin as we parted to take our places in the orchestra.

I sat down in my seat amongst the woodwind section, knowing that within three minutes I would rise to play the first four bars of 'Morning Mood'. And that, as Felix had said to me earlier, it didn't matter who had originally conceived me. Only that I'd been given the gift of life and it was up to me to make it – and myself – the best it could be.

As the lights dimmed and a hush descended, I thought of all those who loved me, somewhere out in the darkness of the auditorium, willing me on.

And I thought of Pa Salt, who had told me I'd find my greatest strength at my weakest moment. And Theo, who had taught me what it was to truly love another person. Neither of them were physically present, but I knew they would be so proud of me as they watched over me from the stars.

And then I smiled at the thought of the new life inside me, that I was yet to know.

I put the flute to my lips and began to play for all of them.

Star

7th December 2007

"The Hero Concerto"

The lights dimmed in the auditorium and I watched my sister rise from her seat on the stage. I could see the contours of the new life inside her clearly defined beneath the black dress. Ally closed her eyes for a moment as if in prayer. When she finally lifted the flute to her lips, a hand reached for mine and squeezed it gently. And I knew Ma was feeling the resonance too.

As the beautiful, familiar melody, which had been part of my and my sisters' childhood at Atlantis, floated out across the hall, I felt some of the tension of the past few weeks flow out of me with the swell of the music. As I listened, I knew that Ally was playing for all those she had loved and lost, but I understood too that just as the sun comes up after a long dark night, there was new light in her life now. And as the orchestra joined her and the beautiful music reached a crescendo, celebrating the dawning of a new day, I felt the same.

Yet, in my *own* rebirth, others had suffered, and that was the part I had yet to rationalise. I'd only understood recently that there were many different kinds of love.

At the interval, Ma and I went to the bar, and Peter and Celia Falys-Kings, who introduced themselves as Theo's parents, joined us for a glass of champagne. As I watched the way Peter's arm rested protectively on Celia's waist, they looked like a young couple in love.

'*Santé*,' said Ma, as she chinked her glass against mine. 'Isn't this the most wonderful evening?'

'Yes, it is,' I replied.

'Ally played so beautifully. I wish your other sisters could have been here to see her. And your father, of course.'

I watched Ma's brow furrow in sudden concern and wondered what secrets she kept. And how heavily they weighed on her. As did mine.

'CeCe couldn't make it then?' she asked me tentatively.

'No.'

'Have you seen her recently?'

'I'm not at the apartment very often these days, Ma.'

She didn't press me further on the subject. She knew not to.

A hand brushed my shoulder and I jumped. I've always been very sensitive to touch. Peter broke the pregnant pause, although I was used to those. 'Hi, everyone.' He turned to Ma. 'So, you're the "mom" who cared for Ally during her childhood?'

'Yes,' she replied.

'You did a wonderful job,' he said.

'That's down to her, not me,' Ma replied modestly. 'All of my girls make me very proud.'

'And you're one of Ally's famous sisters?' Peter turned his gimlet eyes on me.

'Yes.'

'What's your name?'

'Star.'

'And which number are you?'

'Three.'

'Interesting.' He looked at me again. 'I was number three as well. Never listened to and never heard. Yes?'

I didn't reply.

'Bet a lot goes on inside that head of yours, right?' he continued. 'It sure did in mine.'

Even if he was right, I wouldn't tell him. So I shrugged silently instead.

'Ally is a very special human being. We both learnt a lot from her,' said Celia, giving me a warm smile as she changed the subject. I could tell she thought my silences meant I was struggling with Peter, but I wasn't. It was other people who found them difficult.

'Yes, indeed. And now we're to be grandparents. What a gift your sister has given us, Star,' said Peter. 'And this time, I'm going to be there for the little one. Life is just too damned short, isn't it?'

The two-minute bell rang, and everyone around me drained their glasses, however full they were. We all filed back into the auditorium to take our seats. Ally had already filled me in by email on her discoveries in Norway. I studied Felix Halvorsen closely as he walked onto the stage, and decided that the genetic link to him had had little impact on Ally's physical characteristics. I also noticed his rolling gait as he walked towards the piano and wondered if he was drunk. I sent up a small prayer that he wasn't. I knew from what Ally had said earlier how much this evening meant to her and her newfound brother, Thom. I'd liked him immediately when I'd met him earlier.

As Felix lifted his fingers to the keys and then paused, I

felt every member of the audience holding their breath with me. The tension was only broken as his fingers descended onto them and the opening bars of *The Hero Concerto* were played in public for the first time. According to the programme, just over sixty-eight years after they had been written. For the following half an hour, each one of us was treated to a performance of rarity and beauty, created by a perfect alchemy between composer and interpreter: father and son.

And as my heart took flight and soared upwards with the beautiful music, I saw a glimpse of the future. 'Music is love in search of a voice.' I quoted Tolstoy under my breath. Now, I had to find *my* voice. And also the courage to speak out with it.

The applause was deservedly tumultuous, the audience on their feet, stamping and cheering. Felix took bow after bow, beckoning his son and his daughter out of the orchestra to join him, then quietening the audience and dedicating his performance to his late father, and his children.

In this gesture, I saw living proof that it was possible to move on. And to make a change that others would eventually accept, however difficult.

As the audience began to rise from their seats, Ma touched my shoulder, saying something to me.

I nodded at her blankly, not taking in her words, and murmured that I'd see her in the foyer. And then I sat there. Alone. Thinking. As I did so, I was vaguely aware of the rest of the audience walking up the aisle past me. And then, out of the corner of my eye, I saw a familiar figure.

As my heart began to pound, my body stood up of its own volition and I ran through the empty auditorium to the crowd milling around the back exits. I searched desperately for another glimpse, begging that unmistakable profile to reappear to me amongst the milieu.

Pushing my way through the foyer, my legs carried me out into the freezing December air. I stood in the street, hoping for another sighting just to make sure, but I knew the figure had disappeared.

Acknowledgements

So many people helped me with the research for *The Storm Sister*.

My friends at Cappelen Damm, my fantastic publishing house, were instrumental in introducing me to the people I needed to speak to. So the first (and biggest) thank you goes to Knut Gørvell, Jorid Mathiassen, Pip Hallen and Marianne Nielsen.

In Oslo: Erik Edvardsen at the Ibsen Museum, Lars Roede at the Oslo Museum, Else Rosenqvist and Kari-Anne Pedersen at the Norsk Folkemuseum. Also, Bjørg Larsen Rygh at Cappelen Damm (whose dissertation on drains and plumbing in Christiania in 1876 went above and beyond the call of duty!). Hilde Stoklasa, from the Oslo Cruise Network, and a special thank-you to the staff at the Grand Hotel in Oslo, who fed and watered me at all times of the day and night as I wrote the first draft.

In Bergen: John Rullestad, who introduced me to Erling Dahl, the ex-director of the Edvard Grieg Museum at Troldhaugen, and Sigurd Sandmo, the current director. Henning Målsnes at

The Bergen Philharmonic Orchestra, and Mette Omvik, who gave me some great detail on Den Nationale Scene theatre in Bergen. The renowned Norwegian composer Knut Vaage, who explained the mechanics of composition and orchestration. My thanks also go to the staff at the Hotel Havnekontoret in Bergen, who looked after me during my stay there.

In Leipzig: Barbara Wiermann at the University of Music and Theatre 'Felix Mendelssohn Bartholdy', and my lovely friend Caroline Schatke from Edition Peters in Leipzig, whose father, Horst, brought us together under the most coincidental and poignant of circumstances.

I am not very nautical by nature so on all matters maritime I was helped extensively by David Beverley, and in Greece by Jovana Nikic and Kostas Gkekas from Sail in Greek Waters. For their assistance with my research for the Fastnet Race, I'd like to thank the staff at both the Royal London Yacht Club and the Royal Ocean Racing Club in Cowes. Also, Lisa and Manfred Rietzler, who took me out on their Sunseeker for the day and showed me what it could do.

I would also like to thank my fantastic PA, Olivia, and my hard-working editorial and research team of Susan Moss and Ella Micheler. All of whom have had to work very flexible hours as we juggle with not only the Seven Sisters series, but also the rewriting and editing of my backlist books.

My thirty international publishers from around the world – particularly Catherine Richards and Jeremy Trevathan at Pan Macmillan UK, Claudia Negele and Georg Reuchlein at Random House Germany, Annalisa Lottini and Donatella

Minuto at Giunti Editore in Italy, and Peter Borland and Judith Curr at Atria in the USA. They have all been so supportive and have embraced the challenges – and excitement – of a seven-book series.

My incredible family, who are so very patient as I currently spend my life permanently attached to a manuscript and a pen. Without Stephen (who also doubles as my agent), Harry, Bella, Leonora and Kit, this writing journey would mean very little. My mother Janet, my sister Georgia, and Jacquelyn Heslop, and a very special mention to 'Flo', my faithful writing companion, who we lost in February and still miss dreadfully. Also, Rita Kalagate, João de Deus and all my incredible friends at the Casa de Dom Inácio, in Abadiânia, Brazil.

And lastly, to YOU, the readers, whose love and support as I travel to the four corners of the earth and hear *your* stories, inspire and humble me. And make me realise that nothing I could ever write can compete with the amazing and endlessly complex journey of being alive.

Lucinda Riley
June 2015

Bibliography

The Storm Sister is a work of fiction set against an historical background. The sources I've used to research the time period and detail of my characters' lives are listed below:

Munya Andrews, *The Seven Sisters of the Pleiades* (North Melbourne, Victoria: Spinifex Press, 2004)

Finn Benestad (ed.), *Edvard Grieg: Letters to Colleagues and Friends* (trans. William H. Halverson (Columbus, Ohio: Peer Gynt Press, 2000)

Finn Benestad (ed.) and William H. Halverson (ed. and trans.), *Edvard Grieg: Diaries, Articles, Speeches* (Columbus, Ohio: Peer Gynt Press, 2001)

Erling Dahl Jr., *My Grieg: A Personal Introduction to Edvard Grieg's Life and Music* (Bergen: Vigmostad & Bjoerke, 2007)

Robert Ferguson, *Henrik Ibsen: A New Biography* (London: Faber & Faber, 2010)

M. C. Gillington, *A Day with Edvard Grieg* (London: Hodder & Stoughton, 1886)

Robert Graves, *The Greek Myths* (London: Penguin, 2011)

Robert Graves, *The White Goddess* (New York: Farrar, Straus and Giroux, 2013)

Henrik Ibsen, *Peer Gynt* (Harmondsworth: Penguin Classics, 1970)

David Monrad-Johansen, *Edvard Grieg*, trans. Madge Robertson (New York: Princeton University Press, 1938)

Oslo Jewish Museum, *What Happened in Norway? Shoah and the Norwegian Jews* (2013)

Rudolf Rasmussen, *Rulle: De andre. Minner og meninger om livet på scene og podium* (Oslo: Classica Antikvariat, 1936)

Author's Note

The Seven Sisters series is based on the legends of the Seven Sisters of the Pleiades star cluster, and is a huge project: seven books, six of them about each of the sisters Pa Salt has adopted from around the world and brought back to Atlantis – his fairytale home, nestling in a private peninsula on the shores of Lake Geneva.

So many of my readers have written to me with questions about the series, and possible answers to the unanswered mysteries the first book in the series poses, that I decided I should include a Q&A section at the end of each book.

For me, the series is simply one huge story, which I'm chopping into seven parts, though each book is 'stand alone' and the story of each one of my very unique sisters can be read in any order, as each book begins at the same moment in time. But underlying each story is a hidden plot running throughout like a delicate thread, the full story of which will form the basis to the seventh book.

The research for both the allegorical and historical elements of the plot has been a serious challenge and I hope the following Q&A explains a little of the background to the series and my amazing Ally's story. Yet, despite the 'technical' side of writing the plot and getting the fine detail right, as always, *The Storm Sister* is completely holistically written and I have simply followed my characters' lead. It's an often moving and surprising journey for me as I'm writing, as I hope it has been for you, the reader.

Please go to www.thesevensistersseries.com, where you can read more about the mythology and astronomy of the Seven Sisters constellation, together with more information on Grieg and his masterful *Peer Gynt* Suite, the Leipzig Music Conservatory, the Fastnet Race and one of the oldest orchestras in the world, the Bergen Philharmonic.

Finally, thank you so much for taking the time to read Ally's story – I know it is long, but I can only end it when the characters tell me that their story is over – for now . . .

Lucinda

Q&A

What made you choose Norway and Grieg's music for *Peer Gynt* as the backdrop for *The Storm Sister*?

I was only five when my father arrived back from his travels in Norway, bringing with him a long-playing record of Grieg's *Peer Gynt* Suite. It really did become the background music to my own childhood, as he eulogised about the beauty of the country, especially the magnificent fjords. He told me that if I ever got the chance in the future, I had to go and see them for myself. Ironically, just after my father died, Norway was the first country that invited me to visit on a book tour. I remember sitting on the plane, my eyes brimming with tears, as I flew to what he had called the top of the world. I felt – just like Ally – that I too was following my late father's words. I have visited Norway numerous times since my initial journey there and, like my father before me, I fell in love. So there was little question of where the second book in the Seven Sisters series would be set.

What kind of challenges did you face in writing the second instalment of a seven-book series? How was it different from writing the first book, *The Seven Sisters*?

It was only when I set to work on Ally's story that I actually realised the challenge I'd set myself in writing such a vast, complex series. Apart from writing Maia and Ally's modern-day story, plus the huge amount of research on the historical sections of each book, I've had to make sure that the timeline fits accurately with the movements of the previous sister's book. For example, if Ally has had a conversation with any of her sisters at 'Atlantis', each location and the exact words spoken have to be double-checked for timing and accuracy.

Never mind keeping tabs on the detail of the underlying 'hidden' plot that runs through the books . . . or the allegorical Greek references and anagrams that form the backdrop to the series. It's a little like playing with a Rubik's Cube – one line fits, but then another falls out of place. This series has stretched me cerebrally as well as creatively. I want each novel to be able to stand alone as well, so I've had to come up with interesting premises to explain to new readers the main plot line of Pa Salt adopting all the girls, without being too repetitive for those who have read the previous sisters' stories.

How did you approach the task of researching the historical events and iconic cultural figures from Norway that are featured in *The Storm Sister*?

The Storm Sister is based on real historic figures and iconic Norwegian figures such as Edvard Grieg and Henrik Ibsen, although my portrayal of these characters' personalities in the book is down to my imagination, rather than actual fact. My fictional characters – in this case, Anna and Jens – are woven into the factual truth of real-life events.

A lot of Ally's fictional quest to discover her past was

based on my own Norwegian journey as I searched to uncover the story of *Peer Gynt* and Grieg. Some of those I met on my research trip appear as themselves in the book and I thank them for allowing me to use their real names in the story.

Erik Edvardsen at the Ibsen Museum was my first port of call. It was he who told me that Ibsen had asked Grieg to write the incidental music for his poem, and showed me the photographs from the original production of *Peer Gynt*. Then he told me about Solveig's 'ghost voice', whose real identity is still unknown to this day. This gave me the key to the 'past' story. The whole historical perspective on Norwegian life in the 1870s came from Lars Roede at the Oslo Museum.

As always when describing real people, I try my best to do them justice, especially with someone as meaningful to Norway and the wider world as Edvard Grieg. I went twice to Bergen, where I had the great pleasure of spending time with Professor Erling Dahl, the world's foremost expert on Grieg, and recipient of the Grieg Prize. He showed me around the Edvard Grieg Museum – Grieg's former home – in Troldhaugen, and I was actually allowed to sit at Grieg's grand piano! In Bergen, I read as much as I could about Grieg and his contemporaries, and I pored over the details of the original production of *Peer Gynt*. Luckily, he was a prolific diarist and correspondent and there's nothing better than reading the words that historical figures have actually written. It's the best insight you can get. And I always have to remember I'm a storyteller first, not an historian.

I also met Henning Målsnes at The Bergen Philharmonic Orchestra, who explained the way an orchestra is managed on a day-to-day level, as well as the Orchestra's wartime history. And the renowned Norwegian composer Knut Vaage explained to me the process of orchestral composition with an historical perspective.

Now that you are on the second instalment of the series, has your overall plan for the ending changed or do you still have a clear end in sight?
The ending has been planned from the start. The secrets that will eventually come to light are all in my head. This hidden plot line runs through the series, and I have to ensure this is subtle and consistent through all the books. Only my husband knows the plot of the last book, though recently he said he's forgotten it already . . . !

We not only see Norway, but we are also taken to the musical city of Leipzig in Germany. Did you travel there for research too?
Yes. It's a beautiful city, on its way to being restored to its former glory. Germany is one of my favourite countries, and I have travelled there often to meet my readers. And of course, Grieg studied there for three years and Edition Peters, his music publisher – run at the time by a close friend called Max Abrahams – is still based there. I often find I have strange coincidental experiences when I'm writing. Caroline Schatke, an old friend, contacted me to say she had just moved from Cambridge University to work for a company in Leipzig called Edition Peters, and that she was currently sitting in the very building I was actually writing about at the time. This company has been the publisher of Grieg's music since it was written over a hundred years ago.

You touch upon the horrors of World War II in this book, as you have done in previous books. Why do you feel it is such an important subject to explore in your writing?
The Second World War happened less than eighty years ago. Most people today have relatives who were affected by it in some way. It is a dreadful rupture in our world history, and affects any novel set in any country between 1938 and 1945. I researched the history of Leipzig and the plight of its Jewish population, and I felt that the destruction of the statue of Felix Mendelssohn marked a pivotal moment, a 'point of no return' for the city. Learning about what happened in Norway was also eye-opening, as it is a theatre of war that often isn't taught in history classes.

Have you always had an interest in classical music? And how has this shaped your descriptions in the novel?
I trained as a ballet dancer from the age of three to sixteen, so I have grown up with classical music all my life. Grieg's *Peer Gynt* Suite has always been one of my favourites – both 'Morning Mood' and 'In the Hall of the Mountain King' are such iconic pieces of music. Everyone would recognise both if they heard them; they have become so ingrained in popular culture, having been used (and abused) in so many television programmes and commercials, films, and even at theme parks.

What's your best memory of Norway? Did you discover anything that made you change your initial plan for the book?
I absolutely loved travelling up to Trondheim and seeing the fjords and the snow-capped mountains beneath me from the aeroplane. My aim is to take a Hurtigruten cruise through them one day when I have time. But most of all, it was the

people I met there. They were so warm and welcoming and it is always a pleasure to go back.

How does Ally match up to her mythological counterpart? What aspects of her did you modernise?

In Greek mythology, Alcyone, the second sister, was known as 'the Leader' and her star is one of the brightest in the cluster. During the 'Halcyon days', when the world was filled with joy, prosperity and tranquillity, her Greek namesake watched over the Mediterranean Sea, making it calm and safe for sailors. To reflect this for a modern audience, I made Ally a brave, strong woman who knows her mind and is a natural leader. She loves the sea and makes her mark as a sailor, but she also falls deeply in love with Theo Falys-Kings – which is an anagram of Asterope's Greek mythological lover, the King of Thessaly. The 'Evil Eye' necklace that Theo buys for Ally is a symbol of her being a protector of sailors. And it is when she is forced to separate from her love that her story leads to tragedy, just as in the Greek myth.

In this book, we find out a little bit more about the mysterious Pa Salt. Has it been a challenge to keep the ending a secret, and what have you made of your fans' speculations on #WhoIsPaSalt?

I enjoy reading the different theories that readers come up with, and sometimes have a quiet giggle at them. I'm thrilled that my readers have been so captivated by the series and have been speculating so much on social media. Of course, nobody knows the truth except me (and my husband if he can ever remember it), and it hasn't been a challenge at all to keep it a secret – it's been great fun.

At the end of *The Storm Sister*, we catch a glimpse into the perspective of Star, the third sister. Can you give us a hint as to what her journey will contain?
Star is a fascinating, enigmatic character, and I'm enjoying delving further into her perspective. I am still writing her story, and it's set in England. It's been a change to explore my own country's history and its various landscapes. And it's meant I have been able to write from home, as I always have to live for a while in the country I'm writing about. Star's story will take us from the wilds of Cumbria and the raw beauty of the Lake District to the excesses and social whirl of Edwardian London.

What would you like readers to take away from *The Storm Sister*?
I would like my readers to be inspired by Ally's strength and positivity. Ally goes through so much in *The Storm Sister*. I can't tell you how much I cried writing the Fastnet Race scenes and especially Theo's memorial service. Ally is an incredibly determined woman, and despite the amount of grief she endures, she manages to find a new source of creativity, a new home and a new family in which she can raise her and Theo's child. Just as Pa Salt's last words to her predicted, 'In moments of weakness, you will find your greatest strength,' I hope this is true for all of us.

Please see www.thesevensistersseries.com for more background to the series and the historical and mythological references used in each book.

In the Ibsen Café,
Grand Hotel, Oslo

Sitting at Edvard
Grieg's piano at his
home in Bergen,
Troldhaugen

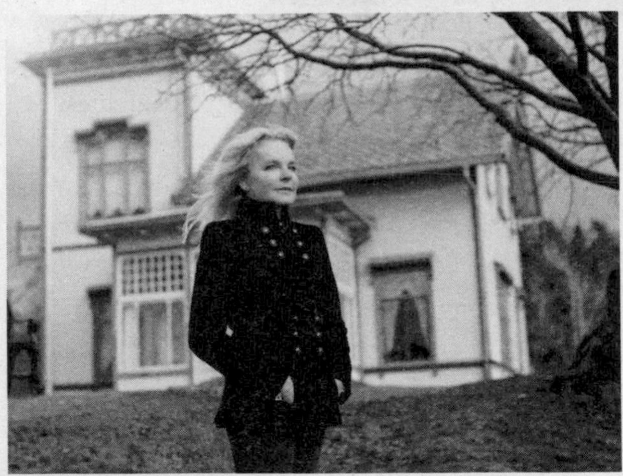

Outside Troldhaugen
now a museum

The Storm Sister

To discover the inspiration behind the series, including Greek mythology, the Pleiades star cluster and armillary spheres, please see Lucinda's website:

www.lucindariley.com

Also on the website is information on the real events, places and people featured in this book – Grieg's Peer Gynt suite, Henrik Ibsen, the Leipzig Conservatory in Germany, the Bergen Philharmonic Orchestra and the Fastnet Race.

Read on for an extract of

The

Shadow Sister

the third book in the spellbinding
Seven Sisters series

1

I will always remember exactly where I was and what I was doing when I heard that my father had died . . .

With my pen still suspended above the sheet of paper, I looked up at the July sun – or, at least, the small ray of it that had managed to trickle between the window and the red-brick wall a few yards in front of me. All of the windows in our tiny apartment looked onto its blandness and, despite today's beautiful weather, it was dark inside. So very different from my childhood home, Atlantis, on the shores of Lake Geneva.

I realised I had been seated exactly where I was now when CeCe had come into our miserable little sitting room to tell me that Pa Salt was dead.

I put down the pen and went to pour myself a glass of water from the tap. It was clammy and airless in the sticky heat and I drank thirstily as I contemplated the fact that I didn't *need* to do this – to put myself through the pain of remembering. It was Tiggy, my younger sister, who, when I'd seen her at Atlantis just after Pa died, had suggested the idea.

'Darling Star,' she'd said, when some of us sisters had gone out onto the lake to sail, simply trying to distract ourselves from our grief, 'I know you find it hard to *speak* about how you feel. I also know you're full of pain. Why don't you write your thoughts down?'

On the plane home from Atlantis two weeks ago, I'd thought about what Tiggy had said. And this morning, that's what I had endeavoured to do.

I stared at the brick wall, thinking wryly that it was a perfect metaphor for my life just now, which at least made me smile. And the smile carried me back to the scarred wooden table that our shady landlord must have picked up for nothing in a junk shop. I sat back down and again picked up the elegant ink pen Pa Salt had given me for my twenty-first birthday.

'I will not start with Pa's death,' I said out loud. 'I will start when we arrived here in London—'

The crash of the front door closing startled me and I knew it was my sister, CeCe. Everything she did was loud. It seemed beyond her to put a cup of coffee down without banging it onto the surface and slopping its contents everywhere. She had also never grasped the concept of an 'indoor voice' and shouted her words to the point where, when we were small, Ma was once worried enough to get her hearing tested. Of course, there was nothing wrong with it. In fact, it was the opposite – CeCe's hearing was overdeveloped. There was nothing wrong with me when a year later Ma took me to a speech therapist, concerned at my lack of chatter.

'She has words there, she just prefers not to use them,' the therapist had explained. 'She will when she's ready.'

At home, in an attempt to communicate with me, Ma had taught me the basics of French sign language.

'So whenever you want or need something,' she'd said to

me, 'you can use it to tell me how you feel. And this is how I feel about you right now.' She'd pointed at herself, crossed her palms over her heart, then pointed at me. 'I – love – you.'

CeCe had learnt it quickly too, and the two of us had adopted and expanded what had begun as a means of communication with Ma to form our own private language – a mixture of signs and made-up words – using it when people were around and we needed to talk. We'd both enjoyed the baffled looks on our sisters' faces as I'd sign a sly comment across the breakfast table and we'd both dissolve into helpless giggles.

Looking back, I could see that CeCe and I became the antithesis of each other as we were growing up: the less I spoke, the louder and more often she talked for me. And the more she did, the less I needed to. Our personalities had simply become exaggerated. It hadn't seemed to matter when we were children, squashed into the middle of our six-sister family – we'd had each other to turn to.

The problem was, it mattered now . . .

'Guess what? I've found it!' CeCe burst into the sitting room. 'And in a few weeks' time we can move in. The developer's still got some finishing off to do, but it'll be incredible when it's done. God, it's hot in here. I can't wait to leave this place.'

CeCe went to the kitchen and I heard the whoosh of the tap being turned on full blast, knowing that the water had most likely spattered all over the worktops I had painstakingly wiped down earlier.

'Want some water, Sia?'

'No thanks.' Although CeCe only used it when we were alone, I mentally chided myself for being irritated by the pet name she had coined for me when we were little. It came from a book Pa Salt had given me for Christmas, *The Story of Anastasia*, about a young girl who lived in the woods in Russia and discovered she was a princess.

'She looks like you, Star,' five-year-old CeCe had said as we'd stared at the pictures in the storybook. 'Perhaps *you're* a princess too – you're pretty enough to be one, with your golden hair and blue eyes. So, I will call you "Sia". And it goes perfectly with "Cee"! Cee and Sia – the twins!' She'd clapped her hands in delight.

It was only later, when I'd learnt the *real* history of the Russian royal family, that I understood what had happened to Anastasia Romanova and her siblings. It hadn't been a fairy tale at all.

And nor was I a child any longer, but a grown woman of twenty-seven.

'I just know you're going to love the apartment.' CeCe reappeared in the sitting room and flopped onto the scuffed leather sofa. 'I've booked an appointment for us to see it tomorrow morning. It's a shedload of money, but I can afford it now, especially as the agent told me the City is in turmoil. The usual suspects aren't queuing up to buy right now, so we agreed a knockdown price. It's time we got ourselves a proper home.'

It's time I got myself a proper life, I thought.

'You're *buying* it?' I said.

'Yes. Or at least, I will if you like it.'

I was so astonished, I didn't know what to say.

'You all right, Sia? You look tired. Didn't you sleep well last night?'

'No.' Despite my best efforts, tears came to my eyes as I thought of the long, sleepless hours bleeding towards dawn, when I'd mourned my beloved father, still unable to believe he was gone.

'You're still in shock, that's the problem. It only happened a couple of weeks ago, after all. You will feel better, I swear, especially when you've seen our new apartment tomorrow. It's this crap place that's depressing you. It sure as hell depresses me,' she added. 'Have you emailed the guy about the cookery course yet?'

'Yes.'

'And when does it start?'

'Next week.'

'Good. That gives us time to start choosing some furniture for our new home.' CeCe came over to me and gave me a spontaneous hug. 'I can't wait to show it to you.'

'Isn't it incredible?'

CeCe opened her arms wide to embrace the cavernous space, her voice echoing off the walls as she walked to the expanse of glass frontage and slid open one of the panels.

'And look, this balcony is for you,' she said, as she beckoned me to follow her. We stepped outside. 'Balcony' was too humble a word to describe what we were standing on. It was more like a long and beautiful terrace suspended in the air above the River Thames. 'You can fill it with all your herbs and those flowers you liked fiddling around with at Atlantis,' CeCe added as she walked to the railing and surveyed the grey water far below us. 'Isn't it spectacular?'

I nodded, but she was already on her way back inside so I drifted after her.

'The kitchen is still to be fitted, but as soon as I've signed, you can have free rein to choose which cooker you'd like, which fridge, and so on. Now that you're going to be a professional,' she said with a wink.

'Hardly, CeCe. I'm only doing a short course.'

'But you're so talented, I'm sure you'll get a job somewhere when they see what you can do. Anyway, I think it's perfect for both of us, don't you? I can use that end for my studio.' She pointed to an area sandwiched between the far wall and a spiral staircase. 'The light is just fantastic. And you get your big kitchen and the outdoor space, too. It's the nearest thing to Atlantis I could find in the centre of London.'

'Yes. It's lovely, thank you.'

I could see how excited she was about her find and, admittedly, the apartment *was* impressive. I didn't want to burst her bubble by telling her the truth: that living in what amounted to a vast, characterless glass box overlooking a murky river could not have been further from Atlantis if it tried.

As CeCe and the agent talked about the blonde-wood floors that were going to be laid, I shook my head at my negative thoughts. I knew that I was being desperately spoilt. After all, compared to the streets of Delhi, or the shanty towns I'd seen on the outskirts of Phnom Penh, a brand-new apartment in the city of London was not exactly a hardship.

But the point was that I would have actually *preferred* a tiny, basic hut – which would at least have its foundations planted firmly in the ground – with a front door that led directly to a patch of earth outside.

I tuned in vaguely to CeCe's chatter about a remote control that opened and closed the window blinds and another for the invisible surround-sound speakers. Behind the agent's back, she signed 'wide boy' to me and rolled her eyes. I managed a small smile in return, feeling desperately claustrophobic because I couldn't open the door and just *run* . . . Cities stifled me; I found the noise, the smells and the hordes of people overwhelming. But at least the apartment was open and airy . . .

'Sia?'

'Sorry, Cee, what did you say?'

'Shall we go upstairs and see our bedroom?'

We walked up the spiral staircase into the room CeCe said we would share, despite there being a spare room. And I felt a shudder run through me even as I looked at the views, which *were* spectacular from up here. We then inspected the incredible en-suite bathroom, and I knew that CeCe had done her absolute best to find something lovely that suited us both.

But the truth was, we weren't married. We were *sisters*.

Afterwards, CeCe insisted on dragging me to a furniture shop on the King's Road, then we took the bus back across the river, over Albert Bridge.

'This bridge is named after Queen Victoria's husband,' I told her out of habit. 'And there's a memorial to him in Kensington—'

CeCe curtailed me by making the sign for 'show-off' in my face. 'Honestly, Star, don't tell me you're still lugging a guidebook around?'

'Yes,' I admitted, making our sign for 'nerd'. I loved history.

We got off the bus near our apartment and CeCe turned to me. 'Let's get supper down the road. We should celebrate.'

'We haven't got the money.' *Or at least*, I thought, *I certainly haven't.*

'My treat,' CeCe reassured me.

We went to a local pub and CeCe ordered a bottle of beer for her and a small glass of wine for me. Neither of us drank much – CeCe in particular couldn't handle her alcohol, something she'd learnt the hard way after a particularly raucous teenage party. As she stood at the bar, I mused on the mysterious appearance of the funds that CeCe had suddenly come into the day after all of us sisters had been handed envelopes from Pa Salt by Georg Hoffman, Pa's lawyer. CeCe had gone to see him in Geneva. She had begged Georg to let me come into the meeting with her, but he'd refused point-blank.

'Sadly, I have to follow my client's instructions. Your father insisted that any meetings I might have with his daughters be conducted individually.'

So I'd waited in reception while she went in to see him. When she'd emerged, I could see that she was tense and excited.

'Sorry, Sia, but I had to sign some stupid privacy clause. Probably another of Pa's little games. All I can tell you is that it's good news.'

As far as I was aware, it was the only secret that CeCe had ever kept from me in our entire relationship, and I still had no idea where all this money had come from. Georg Hoffman had explained to us that Pa's will made it clear that we would continue to receive only our very basic allowances. But also, that we were free to go to him for extra money if necessary. So perhaps we simply needed to ask, just as CeCe presumably had.

'Cheers!' CeCe clinked her beer bottle against my glass. 'Here's to our new life in London.'

'And here's to Pa Salt,' I said, raising my glass.

'Yes,' she agreed. 'You really loved him, didn't you?'

'Didn't *you*?'

'Of course I did, lots. He was . . . special.'

I watched CeCe as our food arrived and she ate hungrily, thinking that, even though we were both his daughters, his death felt like my sorrow alone, rather than ours.

'Do you think we should buy the apartment?'

'CeCe, it's your decision. I'm not paying, so it's not for me to comment.'

'Don't be silly, you know what's mine is yours, and vice versa. Besides, if you ever decide to open that envelope he left for you, there's no telling what you might find out,' she encouraged.

She'd been on at me ever since we'd been given the envelopes. She had torn hers open almost immediately afterwards, expecting me to do the same.

'Come on, Sia, aren't you going to open it?' she'd pressed me.

But I just couldn't . . . because whatever lay inside it would mean accepting that Pa had gone. And I wasn't prepared to let him go yet.

After we'd eaten, CeCe paid the bill and we went back to the apartment, where she telephoned her bank to have the deposit on the flat transferred. Then she settled herself in front of her laptop, complaining about the inconstant broadband.

'Come and help me choose some sofas,' she called from the sitting room as I filled our yellowing tub with lukewarm water.

'I'm just having a bath,' I replied, locking the door.

I lay in the water and lowered my head so that my ears and hair were submerged. I listened to the gloopy sounds – *womb sounds*, I thought – and decided that I had to get away before I went completely mad. None of this was CeCe's fault and I certainly didn't want to take it out on her. I loved her. She had been there for me every day of my life, but . . .

Twenty minutes later, having made a resolution, I wandered into the sitting room.

'Nice bath?'

'Yes. CeCe . . .'

'Come and look at the sofas I've found.' She beckoned me towards her. I did as she asked and stared unseeingly at the different hues of cream.

'Which one do you think?'

'Whichever you like. Interior design is your thing, not mine.'

'How about that one?' CeCe pointed to the screen. 'Obviously we'll have to go and sit on it, because it can't just be a thing of beauty. It's got to be comfy as well.' She scribbled down the name and address of the stockist. 'Perhaps we can do that tomorrow?'

I took a deep breath. 'CeCe, would you mind if I went back to Atlantis for a couple of days?'

'If that's what you want, Sia, of course. I'll check out flights for us.'

'Actually, I was thinking I'd go alone. I mean . . .' I swallowed, steeling myself not to lose my impetus. 'You're very busy here now with the apartment and everything, and I know you have all sorts of art projects you're eager to get going on.'

'Yes, but a couple of days out won't hurt. And if it's what you need to do, I understand.'

'Really,' I said firmly, 'I think I'd prefer to go by myself.'

'Why?' CeCe turned to me, her almond-shaped eyes wide with surprise.

'Just because . . . I . . . would. That is, I want to sit in the garden I helped Pa Salt make and open my letter.'

'I see. Sure, fine,' she said with a shrug.

I sensed a layer of frost descending, but I would not give in to her this time. 'I'm going to bed. I have a really bad headache,' I said.

'I'll get you some painkillers. Do you want me to look up flights?'

'I've already taken some, and yes, that would be great, thanks. Night.' I leant forward and kissed my sister on the top of her shiny dark head, her curly hair shorn into a boyish crop as always. Then I walked into the tiny broom cupboard of a twin room that we shared.

The bed was hard and narrow and the mattress thin. Though both of us had had the luxury of a privileged upbringing, we had spent the past six years travelling round the world and sleeping in dumps, neither of us prepared to ask Pa Salt for money even when we'd been really broke. CeCe in particular had always been too proud, which was why I was so surprised that she now seemed to be spending money like water, when it could only have come from *him*.

Perhaps I'd ask Ma if she knew anything more, but I was aware that discretion was her middle name when it came to spreading gossip amongst us sisters.

'Atlantis,' I murmured. *Freedom* . . .

And that night, I fell asleep almost immediately.